The
BOOK
of
ILE-RIEN

The
ELEMENT of FIRE

and

The DEATH
of the
NECROMANCER

The
BOOK
of
ILE-RIEN

Martha Wells

tor publishing group
new york

THE BOOK OF ILE-RIEN

The Element of Fire copyright © 1993 by Martha Wells
The Death of the Necromancer copyright © 1998 by Martha Wells

A Tordotcom Book
Published by Tom Doherty Associates / Tor Publishing Group
120 Broadway
New York, NY 10271

www.tor.com

Tor® is a registered trademark of Macmillan Publishing Group, LLC.

ISBN 978-1-250-87313-2 (paperback)
ISBN 978-1-250-32667-6 (ebook)

Our books may be purchased in bulk for promotional, educational, or business use. Please contact your local bookseller or the Macmillan Corporate and Premium Sales Department at 1-800-221-7945, extension 5442, or by email at MacmillanSpecialMarkets@macmillan.com.

First Edition: 2024

Printed in the United States of America

0 9 8 7 6 5 4 3 2 1

Author's Note

The Element of Fire was my first novel, written around 1990, when I was twenty-six. It was published in hardcover in 1993 and paperback in 1994, by Tor Books. It was a finalist for the 1993 Compton Crook/Stephen Tall Award and a runner-up for the 1994 Crawford Award. *The Death of the Necromancer* was my third novel, and a finalist for the Nebula Award in 1998.

The world of Ile-Rien is also the setting for the Fall of Ile-Rien trilogy (*The Wizard Hunters, The Ships of Air,* and *The Gate of Gods,* published by HarperCollins). Kade Carrion also appears in the short story "The Potter's Daughter" in the anthology *Elemental,* edited by Steve Savile and Alethea Kontis, published in 2006 by Tor Books. Nicholas Valiarde and Reynard Morane appear in the short story "Night at the Opera," which is set before the events in *The Death of the Necromancer.* It can be found in *Between Worlds: The Collected Ile-Rien and Cineth Stories* and in *PodCastle* episode #400.

This is a new edition of *The Element of Fire* and *The Death of the Necromancer,* and both were revised in 2022.

The
ELEMENT of
FIRE

And New Philosophy calls all in doubt,
The Element of fire is quite put out;
The Sun is lost, and th'earth, and no man's wit
Can well direct him where to looke for it.

—John Donne, "An Anatomie of the World"

CHAPTER ONE

THE GRAPPLING HOOK skittered across the rain-slick stone of the ledge before dropping to catch in the grillwork below the third-story window. Berham leaned back on the rope to test it. "That's it, Captain Sir. Tight as may be," the servant whispered.

"Well done," Thomas Boniface told him. He stepped back from the wall and looked down the alley. "Now where in hell is Dr. Braun?"

"He's coming," Gideon Townsend, Thomas's lieutenant, said as he made his way toward them out of the heavy shadows. Reaching them, he glanced up at the full moon, stark white against the backdrop of wind-driven rain clouds, and muttered, "Not the best night for this work." The three men stood in the muddy alley, the dark brocades and soft wools of their doublets and breeches blending into the grimy stones and shadow, moonlight catching only the pale lace at the wrists or shirt collars of Thomas and his lieutenant, the glint of an earring, or the cold metal sheen on rapiers and wheellock pistol barrels. It was a cool night and they were surrounded by failed counting houses and the crumbling elegance of the decaying once-wealthy homes of the River Quarter.

Thomas personally couldn't think of a good time to forcibly invade a foreign sorcerer's house. "The point of it is to go and be killed where you're told," he said. "Is everyone in position?"

"Martin and Castero are up on the tannery roof, watching the street and the other alley. I put Gaspard and two others at the back of the house and left the servants to watch the horses. The rest are across the street, waiting for the signal," Gideon answered, his blue eyes deceptively guileless. "We're all quite ready to go and be killed where we're told."

"Good," Thomas said. He knew Gideon was still young enough to see this as a challenge, to care nothing for the political reality that sent them on a mission as deadly as this with so little support. Glancing down the alley again, he saw Dr. Braun was finally coming, creeping along the wall and uncomfortably holding his velvet-trimmed scholar's robes out of the stinking mud. "Well?" Thomas asked as the sorcerer came within earshot. "What have you done?"

"I've countered the wards on the doors and windows, but the inside . . . This person Grandier is either very strong or very subtle. I can't divine what protections he's used." The young sorcerer looked up at him, his watery eyes blinking fitfully. His long sandy hair and drooping mustache made him look like a sad-faced spaniel.

"You can't give us any hint of what we're to find in there?" Thomas said, thinking, *This would have been better done if I hadn't been saddled with a sorcerer who has obviously escaped from a market-day farce.*

Braun's expression was both distressed and obstinate. "He is too strong, or . . . he might have the help of some creature of the Fay."

"God protect us," Berham muttered, and uneasily studied the cloudy darkness above. The others ignored him. Berham was short, rotund, and had been wounded three times manning barricades in the last Bisran War. He claimed that the only reason he had left the army was that servants' wages were better. Despite the little man's vocal posturing, Thomas was not worried about his courage.

"What are you saying?" Gideon asked Dr. Braun. "You mean we could fall down dead or burst into flame the moment we cross the threshold?"

"The uninitiated so often have ill-conceived ideas about these matters, like the fools who believe sorcerers change their shapes or fly like the Fay. It would be exceedingly dangerous to create heat or cold out of nothing—"

"Yes, but—"

"That's enough," Thomas interrupted. He took the rope and tested it again with his own weight. The first floor of the house would be given over to stables, storage for coaches or wagons, and servants' quarters. The second would hold salons and other rooms for entertaining guests, and the third and fourth would be the owner's private quarters. That would be where the sorcerer would keep his laboratory, and very likely his prisoner. Thomas only hoped the information from the King's Watch was correct and that the Bisran bastard Grandier wasn't here. He told Gideon, "You follow me. Unless, of course, you'd like to go first?"

His lieutenant swept off his feathered hat and bowed extravagantly. "Oh, not at all, Sir, after you."

"So kind, Sir." The brickwork was rough and Thomas found footholds easily. He reached the window and pulled himself up on the rusted grating, balancing cautiously. He felt the rope jerk and tighten as Gideon started to climb.

The window was set with small panes of leaded glass and divided into four tall panels. Thomas drew a thin dagger from the sheath in his boot and slipped the point between the wooden frames of the lower half. Working the dagger gently, he eased the inside catch up. The panels opened inward with only a faint creak. Moonlight touched the polished surface of a table set directly in front of the window, but the darkness of the deeper interior of the room was impenetrable. It was silent, but it was a peculiar waiting silence that he disliked.

Then the window ledge cracked loudly under his boots and he took a hasty step forward onto the table, thinking, *Now we'll know, at any rate.* Dust rose from the heavy draperies as he brushed against them, but the room remained quiet.

"Was that wise?" Gideon asked softly from below the windowsill.

"Possibly not. Don't come up yet." Thomas slipped the dagger back into his boot sheath and drew his rapier. If something came at him out of that darkness, he preferred to keep it at as great a distance as possible. "Tell Berham to hand up a light."

There was some soft cursing below as a dark lantern, its front covered by a metal slide to keep the light dimmed, was lit and passed upward. Thomas waited impatiently, feeling the darkness press in on him like a solid wall. He would have preferred the presence of another sorcerer besides Braun, the rest of the Queen's Guard, and a conscripted city troop to quell any possibility of riot when the restive River Quarter neighborhood discovered it had a violent foreign sorcerer in its midst. But orders were orders, and if the Queen's guards or their captain were killed while entering Grandier's house secretly, then at least civil unrest was prevented. An inspired intrigue, Thomas had to admit, even if he was the one it was meant to eliminate.

As he reached down to take the shuttered lamp from Gideon, something moved in the corner of his eye. Thomas dropped the lamp onto the table and studied the darkness, trying to decide if the hesitant motion was actually there or in his imagination.

The flicker of light escaping from the edges of the lamp's iron cover touched the room with moving shadows. With the toe of his boot Thomas knocked the lantern slide up.

The wan candlelight was reflected from a dozen points around the unoccupied room, from lacquered cabinets, the gilt leather of a chair, the metallic threads in brocaded satin hangings.

Then the wooden cherub supporting the right-hand corner of the table Thomas stood on turned its head.

He took an involuntary step backward.

"Captain, what is it?" Gideon's whisper was harsh.

Thomas didn't answer. He looked around the room as the faces in the floral carving over the chimneypiece shifted their blank white eyes, their tiny mouths working silently. The bronze snake twined around the supporting pole of a candlestand stirred sluggishly. In the woolen carpet the interwoven pattern of vines writhed.

Keeping hold of the rope, Gideon chinned himself on the window ledge to see in. He cursed softly.

"Worse than I thought," Thomas agreed, not looking away from the hideously animate room. Unblinking eyes of marbleized wood stared sightlessly, limbs and mouths moved without sound. *Can they see? Or hear?* he wondered grimly. *Most likely they can.* He doubted they were here only to frighten intruders, however effective they might be at it.

"We should burn this house to the ground," Gideon whispered.

"We want to get Dubell out alive, not scrape his ashes out of the wreckage."

"How?"

Good question, Thomas thought. The vines in the carpet were lifting themselves above the surface of the floor like the tentacles of a sea beast. They were as thick around as a man's wrist and looked strong, and metallic glints that had been gilt threads in the weaving were growing into knife-edged thorns. It was only going to get more difficult. Thomas caught up the lantern and stepped down into a chair with arms shaped into gilded lampreys. They struggled viciously but were unable to turn their heads back far enough to reach him. From there he stepped down to the hardwood floor and backed toward the doorway.

Gideon made a move to climb into the window but the viselike tentacles were reaching up above waist-height and groping along the edge of the table. Thomas said, "No, stay back."

At the sound of his voice the vines whipped around and stretched out for him, growing prodigiously longer in a sudden bound. Thomas threw himself at the door.

The latch was weak and snapped as his weight struck it. He stumbled through and caught himself, just as something thudded into the dark paneled wall in front of him. He dropped the lantern and dove sideways, scrambling for cover between two brocaded chairs and the fireplace.

Embedded in the wall, still quivering, was a short metal arrow; if he had come through the doorway cautiously it would have struck his chest. The lion heads on the iron firedogs snapped ineffectually at him as he pushed himself farther behind the chairs, thinking, *Where the hell is he?* The sputtering candle sent shadows chasing across crowded furniture and everything moved. Then in the far corner he saw the life-sized statue of an archer. Naked to the waist and balancing a candleholder on his head, he was drawing a second arrow out of the bronze quiver at his side and putting it to his short bow.

Rolling onto his back to make himself a smaller target, Thomas dropped the rapier and drew one of his wheellocks. He'd loaded both pistols down in the alley, and now as he wound up the mainspring, an arrow thudded into the overstuffed chair seat. The other chair began to edge sideways using the clawed feet at the ends of its splayed legs; without thinking Thomas muttered, "Stop that." He set the spring, braced the pistol on his forearm, and fired.

The plaster statue shattered in the deafening impact. The shot scarred the wall behind it and filled the room with the stink of gunpowder.

Thomas got to his feet, tucked away the empty pistol, and picked up his rapier. *Now the whole damned house knows I'm here.* He hadn't planned to do this alone either, but the vines filling up the first room and curling round the doorway into this one committed him to it.

Avoiding the animate furniture, he went to the door in the opposite wall and tried the handle. It was unlocked, and he eased it open carefully. The room within was dark, but the archway beyond revealed a chamber lit by a dozen or so red glass candelabra.

Thomas pulled the door closed behind him and moved forward. The dim light revealed stealthy movement in the carvings on the fireplace mantel and along the bordered paneling. In the more brightly lit chamber beyond the arch, he could see an open door looking out onto the main stairwell.

He stopped just before the fall of light from the next room would have revealed his presence. There was something . . . Then he heard the creak of leather and a harsh rasp of breath. It came from just beyond his range of sight, past the left side of the arch. They knew Grandier had hired men to guard the house; it was the only way the King's Watch had been able to trace the sorcerer, since there was no one in the city who could identify him. The man in the next room must have heard the shot; possibly he was waiting for the protective spells to dispose of any intruders. Thomas had planned on something to distract the sorcerer's human watchdogs, to send them down to the lower part of the house, if Gideon would just get on with it . . .

From somewhere below there was a muffled thump, and the floorboards trembled under his feet. Thomas smiled to himself; shouts and running footsteps sounded from the stairs as the hired swords hastened for the front door. In theory, he wasn't disobeying the King's orders to keep the raid on Grandier's house secret. Placed correctly, a small charge of gunpowder could blow a wooden door to pieces while making little noise, and the houses to either side of Grandier's were empty anyway.

The waiting guard did not take the bait with the others, but went forward to stand at the doorway into the stairwell, his rapier drawn. He was big, with greasy blond hair tied back from his face, and dressed in a dun-colored doublet. Thomas had already decided to kill him and had started forward when the man turned and saw him.

The hired sword's shout was muffled by the clatter of his comrades on the stairs and he rushed forward without waiting for help. Thomas parried two wild blows, then beat his opponent's sword aside and lunged for the kill. The man jerked away and took the point between the ribs instead of under the breastbone, dropping his weapon and staggering back. Cursing his own sloppiness, Thomas leapt after him, grappling with him and trying to drive his main gauche up under the man's chin. In another moment Thomas eased the limp body to the floor. Blood pooled on the rug and on his boots, but hopefully the others were occupied below and there was no one left to follow his trail.

He glanced quickly around the room and noted it was free of the sorcerous animation. There was a closed door on the opposite wall, and it bore examining before he ventured out onto the main stairs.

As Thomas was reaching for the handle, he felt a sharp stab of unease. He stepped back, his hand tightening on his sword-hilt, baffled by his own reaction. It was only a door, as the others had been. He reached out slowly and felt his heart pound faster with anxiety as his hand neared the knob.

Either I've lost my senses, he thought, *or this door is warded.* Testing it with his own reactions, he found the ward began about a foot from the door and stretched out to completely cover the surface. It was a warning, with a relatively mild effect, more than likely meant to keep the hired swords and servants away from this portion of the house. It could also explain why the dead man hadn't left his post to investigate the pistol shot or to follow his comrades to the front entrance. He had been guarding something of crucial importance.

Thomas stepped back and kicked the center panel, sending the door crashing open. Beyond was a staircase leading upward, softly lit by candlelight glowing down from the floor above.

Bracing himself, Thomas stepped through the ward and onto the first step, and had to steady himself against the wall as the effect faded. He shook his head and started up the stairs.

The banister was carved with roses that swayed under a sorcerous breeze only they could sense. Thomas climbed slowly, looking for the next trap. When he stopped at the first landing, he could see that the top of the stairs opened into a long gallery, lit by dozens of candles in mirror-backed sconces. Red draperies framed mythological paintings and classical landscapes. At the far end was a door, guarded on either side by a man-sized statuary niche. One niche held an angel with flowing locks, wings, and a beatific smile. The other niche was empty.

Thomas climbed almost to the head of the stairs, looking up at the archway that formed the entrance to the room. Something suspiciously like plaster dust drifted down from the carved bunting.

A tactical error, Thomas thought. Whatever perched up there wasn't decorative. He took a quiet step back down the stairs, drawing his empty pistol. The air felt warm; beneath his doublet, sweat was sticking the thin fabric of his shirt to his ribs. From the powder flask on his belt he measured out a double charge and poured it into the barrel. He pushed the bullet and wadding down with the short ramrod, thinking that it would be quite ironic if the pistol exploded and ended the matter here.

Thomas wound and set the spring, carefully aimed the pistol at the top of the archway, and fired. The fifty-caliber ball tore through the light ornamental wood and into the body of the plaster statue that clung to the molding above the arch. Thomas shielded his face as splintered wood and fragments of plaster rained down. A sculpted head, an arm, and pieces of a foot thudded to the floor.

He climbed the last few steps and stopped at the front of the gallery, which was now wreathed in the heavy white smoke of the pistol's discharge. This next trap wasn't bothering to conceal itself.

Ponderously the angel statue turned its head toward him and stepped out of its niche in the far wall. Thomas shoved the empty pistol back into his sash and drew the second loaded one, circling away from the angel. It was slow, its feet striking the polished floor heavily, plaster wings flapping stiffly.

It stalked him like a stiff cat as he backed away. He wanted to save the pistol for whatever was behind the next door, so he was reluctant to fire.

Then his boot knocked against something that seized his ankle. He fell heavily and dropped the wheellock. It spun across the polished floor and somehow managed not to go off. Rolling over, he saw that the hand and arm of the broken statue had tripped him and was still holding onto his ankle. He drew his main gauche and smashed at it with the hilt. The hand shattered and fell away, but the angel was almost on top of him.

With a desperate scramble backward, he caught the base of a tall bronze candlestand and pulled it down. The heavy holder in the top struck the statue in the temple and knocked loose a chunk of plaster. It reared back and Thomas got to his feet, keeping hold of the candlestand. As it lurched toward him again he swung the stand. A large piece of the wing cracked and fell away as the blow connected. The creature staggered, suddenly unbalanced.

Past the stumbling statue he saw movement on the stairs. There were dark writhing shapes climbing the steps, dragging themselves upward on the banisters. He backed away, realizing it was the vines that had sprung out of the carpet in the first room. *Are they filling the entire house?* The situation was horrible enough, it hardly needed that. And he had known he couldn't get out the way he had gotten in, but he had hoped to have the front door as an option. Now that way was blocked. Thomas dropped the candlestand and turned to the other door.

He pulled it open and one quick glance told him the room seemed unoccupied by statues. He slammed the door closed as the angel lumbered awkwardly toward him, and braced against it as he shoved the bolt home. He stepped back as the thing battered against the other side.

Moonlight from high undraped windows revealed shelf-lined walls stacked with leatherbound books, most chained to the shelves. It was a large room, crowded with the paraphernalia of both library and alchemical laboratory, quiet except for the erratic tick of several lantern docks. There was a writing desk untidily crammed with paper, and workbenches cluttered with flasks and long-necked bottles of colored glass. It smelled of tallow from cheap candles, the musty odor of books, and an acrid scent from residue left in the containers or staining floors and tabletops. He drew his rapier again and moved around the overladen tables, inherent caution making him avoid the stained patches left by alchemical accidents on the floor. He knew he would have to come back to this house at some point: the desks and cabinets crammed with scribbled papers would undoubtedly hold some of Grandier's secrets, but now he hadn't time to sort the vital information from the trash.

Thomas circled the rotting bulk of a printing press and a cabinet overflowing with ink-stained type, and stopped. At the far end of the room, hidden by stacked furniture and shadows, was a man seated in a plain chair. He faced the wall and seemed to be lost in thought. Dressed in a black cope and a baggy scholar's cap, he had an angular face and was lean in profile, and his hair and beard were gray. He didn't seem to be breathing.

Then Thomas saw the shimmer of reflected moonlight from the window and realized the man was encased in an immense glass ball. Wondering at it, he took a step forward. The enigmatic figure didn't move. He went closer and lifted a hand to touch the glass prison, but thought better of it.

As if the gesture was somehow perceptible to the man inside, he turned his head slowly toward Thomas. For a moment his expression was vacant, eyes fixed on nothing. Then the blue eyes focused and the mouth smiled, and he said, "Captain Thomas Boniface. We haven't formally met, but I have heard of you."

Thomas had not known Galen Dubell closely, the fifteen years ago when the old sorcerer had been at court, but he had seen the portraits. "Dr. Dubell, I presume." Thomas circled the glass prison. "I hope you have some idea of how I'm to get you out of there."

There was another heavy crash against the door. The statue, the animate vines, or something else was battering its way in.

"The power in this bauble is directed inward, toward me. You should be able to break it from the outside," Dubell said, his composure undisturbed by the pounding from the door.

It would be dangerous for the old sorcerer but Thomas couldn't see any other way. At least the heavy wool of his scholar's robe would provide some protection. "Cover your head."

Using the hilt of his rapier, Thomas struck the glass sphere. Lines of white fire radiated out along the cracks. The material was considerably stronger than it looked, and cracked like eggshell rather than glass. He hit it twice more, then it started to shatter. A few of the larger shards broke loose, but none fell near the old man.

Galen Dubell stood carefully and shook the smaller fragments out of his robes. "That is a welcome relief, Captain." He looked exhausted and bedraggled as he stepped free of his prison, glass crackling under his boots.

Thomas had already sheathed his rapier and was overturning one of the cabinets beneath the window. He stepped atop it and twisted the window's catch. Cool night air entered the stuffy room as he pushed it open. An ornamental sill just below formed a narrow slanted ledge. Leaning out, he could see the edge of the roof above. They would have to climb the rough brickwork.

He pulled his head back in and said, "I'm afraid we'll have to take the footpad's way out, Doctor." He just hoped the old man could make it, and speedily; the battering at the door was growing louder.

Dubell scrambled up the cabinet easily enough. As if he'd read Thomas's thought, he said, "It's quite all right, Captain. I prefer the risk to more of Urbain Grandier's hospitality." He might have the easier time of it; he was almost a head taller than Thomas.

As Dubell pulled himself carefully out onto the narrow sill, the door gave way.

The sorcerer used the scrollwork around the window casement as a ladder, drawing himself up toward the roof. Thomas swung out onto the sill after him and stood, holding onto the window frame. Broken fragments of brick sprinkled down as Dubell grasped the edge of the roof above.

Thomas boosted him from below and Dubell scrambled over the edge. Digging fingertips into the soft stone, Thomas started to pull himself upward. Dubell had barely been able to grasp the ledge from here; Thomas knew he would have to stand on top of the cornice before he could reach safety.

There was a crash just inside. Straining to reach the edge of the roof, Thomas bit his lip as something gave way beneath his left boot. Fingers wedged between the soft brick, he groped for another hold and felt the mortar under his hand crumble.

From above, Galen Dubell caught his arm in an iron grip and supported him as he found another foothold. For a man who must do little with his hands besides write or do scholarly experiments, Dubell was surprisingly strong. The man's gentle demeanor made it easy to think of him as nothing more than an aged university don and to forget that he was also a wizard.

Thomas scrambled over the edge, his muscles trembling with the strain. "I thank you, Doctor," he said, sitting up, "but there are those at court who won't appreciate it."

"I won't tell them about it, then." Breathless with exertion, Dubell looked around, the damp breeze tearing at his gray hair and his cap. "Are those your companions?"

There was a shout. The two men he had stationed atop the tannery were waving from the edge of the next roof.

"Stay there!" Thomas shouted back. "We'll come to you."

Slowly they made their way up the crest of the pitched roof to the edge where the others were throwing down some planks to bridge the gap. The slate tiles were cracked and broken, slipping under their feet. They had just crossed the makeshift bridge to the tannery when Thomas turned to say something to Dubell; in the next instant he was lying flat on the rough planks with the others as the timber frame of the building was shaken by a muffled explosion. Then they all retreated hastily across the tannery roof, choking on acrid smoke, as flames rose from the Bisran sorcerer's house.

———

"So much for keeping this quiet," Thomas remarked to Gideon. The two men sat their nervous horses, watching from a few lengths down the street as Grandier's house burned. There was a crash as the façade collapsed inward, sending up a fireworks display of sparks and an intense wave of heat. The neighborhood had turned out to throw buckets of water and mud on the surrounding roofs and mill about in confusion and panicked excitement. The real fear had subsided when the residents realized the fire was confining itself to the sorcerer's home, and that only a few stray sparks had lit on the surrounding structures.

Three of the hired swords had been taken alive, though Thomas doubted they would know much, if anything, about Grandier's intentions. His own men had obeyed their orders and come no farther than the front hall, so they had been able to escape the fire. There had been one casualty.

Gaspard, one of the men who had been posted in the court behind the house, had been hit by a splintered piece of flaming wood as he tried to escape from the explosion. His back and shoulder had been badly burned and he had only escaped worse by rolling in the muddy street. Dubell had insisted on treating the injury immediately, and Thomas was only too glad to permit it. Now Gaspard sat on a stone bench in the shelter of a hostler's stall, his shirt and doublet cut away so Dubell could treat the blistering wound. Berham was handing the sorcerer supplies from Dr. Braun's medical box and Dr. Braun himself was hovering at Dubell's elbow. Thomas suspected that Berham was providing more practical assistance than Braun.

"The fire is hardly our fault."

Gideon shrugged. "Blame Grandier for it."

"Yes, he's a cunning bastard."

Gideon glanced at him, frowning. "How do you mean?"

Thomas didn't answer. Dubell had finished tying the bandage and Martin helped Gaspard stand. As Castero led their horses forward, Thomas nudged his mare close enough to be heard over the shouting and the roar of the fire. "Gaspard, I want you to ride with Martin."

"Sir, I do not need to be carried." The younger man's face was flushed and sickly.

"That was not a request, Sir." Thomas was in no mood for a debate. "You can ride behind him or you can hang head down over his saddlebow; the choice is yours."

Gaspard looked less combative as he contemplated that thought, and let an exasperated Martin pull him unresisting to the horses.

Berham was packing the medical box under Braun's direction while Dubell stared at the fire. Thomas had been considering the question of why Grandier had not killed Galen Dubell. The answer could simply be that Grandier might have wanted to extract information from the old scholar, and his plan had gone awry when the King's Watch located the house. But somehow he didn't think it was going to be simple. *The fire should have started when I broke the glass ball. Yes, it served the purpose of destroying Grandier's papers, but why not kill all the birds with one stone? Unless he wanted us to rescue Dubell.* But why? To announce his presence? To show them how powerful and frightening he was? To make them distrust Dubell?

As Berham took the medical box away to pack on his horse, Thomas waved Dr. Braun over and leaned down to ask him, "Is it possible for Grandier to . . . tamper with another sorcerer, to put a geas on him?"

Braun looked shocked. "A geas can be laid on an untrained mind, yes, but not on a sorcerer like Dr. Dubell."

"Are you very sure about that?"

"Of course." After a moment, under Thomas's close scrutiny, Braun coughed and said, "Well, I am quite sure. I had to put gasçoign powder in my eyes to see the wards around the house, and a geas, or any kind of spell, would be visible on Dr. Dubell."

"Very well." That was as good as they were going to get without taking the old scholar to Lodun to be examined by the sorcerer-philosophers there, and there was no time for that.

Dubell came toward them. "An unfortunate fire," he said wearily. "There was much to learn there."

"I thought you said it was dangerous to create fire out of nothing?" Thomas asked Braun, exercising a little of his frustration on the most annoying target.

"It is," Braun protested, flustered.

Dubell smiled. "It depends on one's appreciation of danger."

"So much does," Thomas agreed. "They'll have some questions for you at the palace."

"Of course. I only hope my small knowledge can aid you."

"We'll find Grandier," Gideon said, coming up beside them.

Dubell's eyes were troubled. "If he continues his mischief on such a grand scale, he will be hard to miss. He'll also be a fool, of course, but he may not see it that way."

"Oh, I hardly think he's a fool," Thomas said. Castero and Berham had gotten Gaspard mounted up behind Martin, and they began to turn their horses away from the crowded street. As the others went down the alley, Thomas took one last look at the burning house. So far Grandier had shown an odd combination of ruthlessness and restraint, and he was not sure which he found more daunting. The sorcerer had snatched Galen Dubell out of his home in Lodun, indiscriminately slaughtering the servants who had witnessed it. For no practical reason, since Lodun University was full of wizards and scholars of magic who had been able to divine Grandier's identity within hours of examining the scene. Yet the fire that could have been so devastating stuck to Grandier's house like pitch and refused to spread to the ready tinder of the other old buildings. As much as he might wish to, Thomas couldn't see it as a gesture of defiance. He only wondered where, in what corner of the crowded city, the word had passed to watch for a sorcerous blaze in the night, and what to do then.

CHAPTER TWO

"Does the mask fit?" Anton Baraselli looked up at the young woman who sat on the balcony railing, her feet swinging under her tattered red skirt.

Gray eyes stared back at him from the pale features of the distorted half mask. "It fits. Do I have the part?"

Baraselli sat at his table on a balcony overhanging the main room of the Mummer's Mask tavern, where his acting troupe made its home. He was middle-aged, his dark hair wispy on his nearly bald head, but the newness of his clothes reflected his troupe's recent prosperity. He could barely hear the woman's deep voice over the shouted conversation, drunken arguments, and the competing strains of mandolin and viola that rose up from the rowdy crowd on the tavern's main floor below. The wealthier patrons were drinking in the small private rooms off the second-floor gallery, the shutters propped open so the music could reach them clearly.

"Well, you've no troupe to recommend you," Baraselli said, leaning back. He didn't want to pay her as much as she might ask. His last Columbine had run off to be married, leaving without a backward glance yesterday morning.

Baraselli had come to Ile-Rien from conquered Adera years ago when all forms of the Aderassi theater were despised and confined to back alleys and peasant festivals. Now the war with Bisra was over and Ile-Rien's capital was more cosmopolitan and free with its money. Vienne was a jewel of a city in a rich setting, standing on temperate plains roughly in the center of the country, with rolling hills and olive groves on the warmer coast to the southwest, rich forested midlands, and black-soiled farmland in the terraced valleys of the high country to the north. Baraselli had liked it, and now that Commedia and other foreign theatricals were popular he liked it a great deal more.

The woman took the mask off and tossed it onto the table. Her hair was dirty blond and her narrow face with its long nose and direct eyes was plain, too plain to ever play the unmasked heroines. Her faded red dress was old and well worn, better than a country woman's but no false finery either. Whatever the rumormongers thought, professional bawds made terrible actresses.

She looked toward him with a grin. Smoke from the candles and clay pipes below reached up to touch the tavern's high-beamed ceiling and spread out like a cloud behind her. It was an interesting theatrical effect, but there was something about the image that Baraselli found faintly disquieting. She said, "I'm not here to make my fortune. I'll take what you paid the last one."

She had good teeth, too. "All right, you're our Columbine. But on sufferance, mind. We've got an important engagement, a very important engagement. It happens when you attract the crowds and praise we have. If you don't give a fine performance, you're out. If you do, well, it's one silver per fortnight and a fair share of whatever they throw onto the stage."

"That's well, I agree."

"Anton! Look out the window." Garin, still wearing the gray beard from his Pantalone costume, came pounding up the stairs.

Baraselli had no time for games, with the accounts still to do tonight. "What? I'm busy."

Garin pushed past him and threw open the window shutters.

"Damn it, you'll let the night air and the bogles in, you fool." Baraselli stood abruptly, jarring the table and slopping wine onto the stained floor.

"But look at this." Garin pointed. The Mummer's Mask stood in a huddle of taverns and old houses on the side of a low hill commanding a good view of the River Quarter. Lying before them were the narrow overhung streets of the older and poorer area, which eventually led into the vast plazas and pillared promenades surrounded by the garden courts of the wealthy. Farther to the west and standing high above the slate and wooden roofs were the domes of churches, the fantastic and fanciful statues ornamenting the gables of the fortified Great Houses, the spires of the stone-filigree palaces on the artificial islands on the river's upper reaches, all transformed into anonymous shapes of alternating black and silver as clouds drifted past the moon. But now, against the stark shadowy forms of the crowded structures of the River Quarter, they could see the bright glow of fire, a harsh splash of color in the darkness.

"Down near Cross Street, I think," Garin said, frowning.

More of the troupe had drifted up the stairs in his wake, curious. "Lord save it doesn't spread," one of them whispered.

"Another bad omen," Baraselli muttered. One of the clowns had died of fever last month. Clowns were traditionally good luck in Adera, if not in Ile-Rien, and having one of them die unexpectedly had shaken the other performers. *Gods and spirits, no more omens before this of all performances,* Baraselli prayed.

"Maybe it's a good omen," the new Columbine said, selecting an apple out of the bowl on the table and watching the worried actors with oblique amusement. "Some people think fire is."

Dark smoke streamed into the night sky.

———

They rode through St. Anne's Gate and into the cobbled court between the high walls of the Mews and the Cisternan Guard Barracks. The façades of the two buildings were almost identical, though time and weather had scarred the dressed stone in different ways. Each was entered by three great archways that faced one another across the length of the court. Now torches threw reflections up onto the mist-slick stone as grooms and stablehands hurried to take the horses or curious Cisternans wandered out to see what the excitement was.

Thomas dismounted and handed the reins to one of the grooms. He took off a glove to rub the horse's nape, then let the man lead her away. This was Cisternan Guard territory, but it was also the closest entrance to the palace, and he wanted Galen Dubell within a warded structure before Grandier made another attempt on him.

The palace wards repelled fay, sendings, and any other form of magical attack. They were fitted together like the pieces of a puzzlebox, or a stained glass window, and drifted constantly, moving past each other, folding over each other, wandering at will over their domain. They would prevent the sorcerous abduction that Grandier had used to snatch Galen Dubell from his home in Lodun, and the palace's other defenses were more than adequate to hold off hired swords.

As Thomas crossed the court toward the two sorcerers, the Cisternan Commander Vivan joined him. The Cisternans were the regular guard for the palace, their ranks drawn from the families of the wealthy merchant classes or the gentlemen landowners. Vivan had held the post of commander for the past five years, and even though the Cisternans were ultimately under the King's authority, Vivan had no particular political ax to grind, and Thomas found him easy to deal with. The Commander said, "A midnight expedition? How exciting."

"I would have preferred to stay here and help you guard the stables, but duty called," Thomas told him.

Vivan snorted. The old king, Fulstan, had made the Cisternans his body-guard out of dislike for the Albonate Knights, who had held the post tradi-tionally. When Fulstan's son Roland had taken the throne, his mistrust of anything belonging to his father had led him to demote the Cisternans and return to the Albons. Going from the King's Own to the King's Old had been a great loss of prestige for them and the Queen's Own had never let them for-get it. Another sore point was that their ceremonial tabards were dark green trimmed with gold, making them good targets and appropriate decor during midwinter festivals.

Gideon reined in near them and dismounted, asking, "Captain, what orders?"

"Send these gentlemen back to the Guard House." As the lieutenant came closer and Thomas could lower his voice, he added, "Go to Lucas. Tell him what happened and then wait to see if the Dowager Queen has questions for you. I'll see him after this meeting." He wanted to double his share of the guard placements and put a watch on Dubell.

"Yes, Captain." Gideon nodded.

Vivan was eyeing Galen Dubell with grudging curiosity as he and Braun dismounted. He asked, "What were you doing, kidnapping scholars out of the Philosopher's Cross?"

"Exactly," Thomas said as he went to join the sorcerers. "I could never keep anything from you."

Thomas led Dubell out of the wet chill of the courtyard and through the in-ner gate at its far end, passing under the spikes of an old portcullis. Dr. Braun trailed behind them. In the wall beyond, a heavy ironbound door guarded by two alert Cisternans led into the corridor that ran inside the protective inner siege walls. The corridor was raw stone, lit by oil lamps and undecorated ex-cept for scribbled writings by present and long-dead occupants. Dubell shook his head. "I lived here for many years and there are still parts of this place I have never seen. I am quite lost, Captain."

"We're in the siege wall opposite the south curtain wall. The Summer Res-idence and the Adamantine Way are behind us at the opposite end of the cor-ridor, and we're going toward the King's Bastion." This siege wall divided the newer section of the palace with its open garden courts, domed Summer Res-idence, and the terraces and windowed façades of the Gallery Wing from the jumbled collection of ancient blocky bastions, towers, and walls on the west side.

A steep stairway led up into the King's Bastion, which loomed above the Old Courts and the Mews. As they climbed, the surroundings began to show rapid signs of improvement, the rough stone softened by hangings and over-laid by carved paneling. The ancient cracked tiles had been recently scrubbed and polished, reflecting the light from hall lanterns of stamped metal and glass as soft pools of gold. They passed Cisternan guards posted on each landing, and began to hear the bastion's hum of activity, never still at any time of night. At the fourth level, Thomas led them out of the older stairwell and across the land-ing to the carved-oak Queen's Staircase. They were in the heart of the bastion now, and the men posted here were Queen's guards.

Dubell paused on the landing, looking up at the wide staircase with its dark wood carved into flowing bands and banisters set with fragments of mirror glass. Then he shook his head as if at his own folly and said, "It has been a long time."

Dubell had been led this way on the day of his exile ten years ago, to see the Dowager Queen and to hear his sentence, which so easily could have been death. Thomas acknowledged the guards' salute, and thought it fortunate all around that Ravenna had been lenient with Galen Dubell.

The top of the staircase opened into a vestibule, the first room in the Dowa-ger Queen's State Apartments. The King's State Apartments were on the oppo-site side of the bastion, and the young Queen Falaise lived in another suite on the floor just below. They passed the young pages waiting in the vestibule and went in to the Guard Chamber, a long richly paneled room lit by glass-drop chandeliers. Gideon was already there and several Queen's guards surrounded him, demanding to know how the night's work had gone. They called greetings as Thomas entered, and he went forward to ask Gideon, "Did you see Lucas?"

"Yes, and he spoke to Ravenna," Gideon reported, keeping his voice low. "But the Bisran ambassador came in and demanded to see her. They're in the Privy Council Chamber now."

That was an irritation they didn't need. "Damn. What does he want at this time of night?"

"Who knows?" Gideon shrugged. The ambassador was a diplomat, not a sol-dier, and the young lieutenant didn't think him a matter of much importance.

Thomas considered a moment. Something to do with Grandier? If it was, then there went all hope of keeping the River Quarter incident quiet.

"Queen Falaise has been asking for me." Gideon looked uncomfortable. "Will you need me anymore tonight?"

Thomas eyed him a moment, but said, "No, you can go on."

As Gideon left, Thomas saw Dubell was taking his leave of Dr. Braun, who had apparently decided not to brave an interview with the Dowager Queen. The other guards were watching the sorcerers curiously, which at least meant that news of their adventure hadn't flown too far ahead of them. There were also two young Albonate squires waiting self-consciously in the corner. *So Renier is already here,* Thomas thought. Whether that was good or bad depended on what mood the King had been in when he had sent him. He said, "We'll wait in here, Doctor," as Dubell turned back toward him, and they went into the anteroom.

Tapestried hangings with a Garden of Paradise theme matched the carpet and table covers, cloaking the large, high-ceilinged room in rich shades of green. Renier stood before the immense marble hearth, abstractedly watching a manservant build up the fire. He was Preceptor of the palace's chapter of Albonate Knights, which was a military order founded for the protection of the King's person, and the only order of knighthood in Ile-Rien that still meant more than a courtesy title. They were members of some of the highest families in Ile-Rien, brought into the Order as boys, living in monastic discipline until they were knighted by the King. Renier would probably have made a better country bishop than a preceptor, but in his tenure he had kept the Order's tendency toward religious fanaticism under tight control. He had broad shoulders and was muscled like a bear, and still rode to tourney on King's Ascension Day, easily managing the weight of the heavy ceremonial mail. Over his court doublet and lace-trimmed collar, he wore the bedraggled coat of sackcloth and poorly cured leather all Albon knights bore in honor of St. Albon, who had done some wandering in the wilderness before his sainthood.

Renier looked up at their entrance, saw Dubell, and smiled. "Success."

Thomas watched the Preceptor greet Dubell, and wondered just how much Renier had known of tonight's expedition.

The door opened again and Lord Aviler stood there, eyeing them thoughtfully. He was dark-haired, dressed in the bloodred state robes of the Ministry, and his handsome sallow face was carefully controlled. He nodded to Renier and Galen Dubell, then his gaze shifted to Thomas. He said, "The River Quarter is on fire."

Thomas smiled slightly to himself and went to lean casually against the mantelpiece. "Only a small portion of it." Aviler had followed so quickly behind them that he knew the man must have been lying in wait.

"A stupid mistake." Aviler moved farther into the room, his folded hands covered by the hang of his sleeves. Thomas wondered if the pose was intentionally copied from the High Minister's late father, or if it was only habit. Aviler had recently inherited the post of High Minister of the body of nobles and merchant and artisan guilds who formally advised, or were supposed to advise, the King, and had a great deal of theoretical power. But the Dowager Queen Ravenna actively opposed him, Queen Falaise ignored him except on social occasions, and no one had been able to do anything with Roland one way or the other since he had taken the throne at the end of Ravenna's regency last year. Aviler was statesman enough to resent this and just inexperienced enough to occasionally reveal his feelings.

"Really, my lord, what do you want me to say?" Thomas raised his brows inquiringly. "That the mission was in danger of being found out so I set the city on fire to confuse the issue?"

Before Aviler could reply, Galen Dubell said quietly, "It was unavoidable."

"Dr. Dubell." Aviler acknowledged him stiffly. "It's a pity you couldn't have returned sooner and avoided this consternation."

"That was my intention, my lord, but my plans went somewhat astray when my household was murdered and I was abducted." Dubell said it with such grace that Aviler was actually caught off guard.

"So Galen Dubell is a diplomat as well as a scholar," Renier said softly to Thomas as Aviler recovered his composure. "He was something of a recluse when I knew him, but I suppose years of academic infighting at Lodun will give anyone eyes in the back of his head. It's good he's returned."

Thomas wasn't about to admit he missed Dr. Surete, who had held the post of Court Sorcerer since he could remember and had died suddenly last month of pleurisy. Surete had been seventy years old, had called every man under the age of sixty "boy," and had been the terror of the court for his ability to use sardonic invective like a bludgeon.

Thomas said, "Let's hope Dubell's not anxious to get back to Lodun soon. We're going to need his help." Dr. Surete's assistant, Milam, had been killed in an accident before Surete himself had died, and since then there had been nothing but argument over who would receive the appointment while lesser talents like Dr. Braun vied for attention.

Renier looked at him thoughtfully. "Lose anyone?"

Thomas's expression betrayed nothing. "Does it matter?"

Renier said softly, "Forgive him, Thomas. He's a boy and he was angry."

"I thought you'd given up on the priesthood," Thomas answered, thinking, *If His Majesty Roland wants me to die in the line of duty, it's his business, but he could have chosen a better time. If he doesn't see that Grandier is a danger to the state* ... At Renier's look he added, "It isn't my place to condemn him or forgive him. But tell me, did Denzil suggest the plan to Roland, or was it someone else?"

Renier stiffened visibly. "I know of no plan."

The double doors into the Privy Council Chamber beyond the anteroom opened and the Bisran ambassador stepped out, his expression grim. He was an older man, with the pale olive skin and hawklike profile of the Bisran aristocracy. Ile-Rien and its capital and court were alien to him, and his disapproval was evident. The excessive formality of the Bisran Court made it stagnant and stultified, while in Ile-Rien landlaw had traditionally permitted high officers and even personal servants to address kings and queens as "my lord" or "my lady," and to forgo obeisance almost entirely. The ambassador's dark plain clothing and simple white collar also marked him as a member of their sect that regarded any kind of ornamentation as a work of Hell; the opulence of the palace must seem a personal insult.

The ambassador's hard eyes swept the room, pausing on Galen Dubell's scholar's cope and narrowing in dismayed disgust. Turning to the High Minister, he said, "Another sorcerer for the King's menagerie, Lord Aviler?" In Bisra, the magical as well as most of the philosophical arts were condemned, though the theurgic magic their priest-magicians practiced had been a deadly barrier against outside attack during the war. Sorcery that was not performed under the auspices of the Bisran Church was outlawed, and punishable by death.

Aviler hesitated, his diplomatic smile turning thin with annoyance, unable to find the right words to defend Dubell's honor without insulting the ambassador.

Before the silence could last long enough to give the Bisran a victory, Thomas interposed, "Perhaps that's a subject you should discuss with the King himself?"

The ambassador flicked a resentful glance at him and received only an ingenuous smile in response. As a matter of policy, Roland did not receive the Bisran ambassador, who was not very pleased with this arrangement, since it required him to address his demands to the considerably less malleable Dowager Queen. *But why is he here in the middle of the night?* It could be just obstinate determination to get a hearing no matter who he inconvenienced, but Thomas doubted it. To compound the Bisran's discomfort, he added, "But I'm sure my lady Ravenna dealt with you to her best ability."

The ambassador said, "Her Majesty was most . . . civil," and favored him with the same cold scrutiny he had employed on Dubell. The Bisran Court did not allow favorites to wield political power, so the ambassador tended to discount Thomas's position and influence, and cordially hated him as well. It probably didn't help either that the shape and tilt of Thomas's black eyes gave his face a naturally cynical slant, and that with his dark hair and beard this effect made him resemble certain popular portraits of the Prince of Hell. If the ambassador had noticed the evidence Thomas's climb on a wet and dirty building had left on his clothing, no doubt he attributed it to some adventure in debauchery.

Turning stiffly back to Aviler, the ambassador said, "Another matter. I wanted to make certain you understood that if Ile-Rien offers shelter to the devil's son Grandier, the cost may be more than you are prepared to pay."

Aviler bowed, his reserved manner masking a certain wariness. "I assure you, my lord Ambassador, Ile-Rien has no intention of offering shelter to a criminal sorcerer who has caused your land such pain."

Besides, Grandier hasn't asked for shelter, Thomas thought. *Unfortunately.* And since the Bisran sorcerer had announced his arrival in Ile-Rien by abducting a prominent Lodun scholar of Galen Dubell's reputation, it hardly seemed possible that he would.

But it was likely that the ambassador was only using Grandier's presence in the city as an excuse for a confrontation with Ravenna, and if he was being prodded by the Bisran War College to take a more aggressive stance with the Dowager Queen, it could only mean trouble. Bisra was miles of dry flat plains, and only tribute from its conquered states kept its coffers full. The Bisran Church exercised rigid controls on a populace that was land-poor and half-starved in the country and hovered at the brink of mob violence in the crowded cities. Ile-Rien had its uprisings and city mobs as well, but usually over taxes, and they were scattered outbreaks that could be negotiated and settled within a few days. Bisra seemed to teeter always on the edge of chaos, and with Ile-Rien's rich land and its Church's policy of tolerance toward the pagan Old Faith as a constant irritant, war had been inevitable and frequent.

And now Urbain Grandier's depredations had made them even more desperate.

Thomas watched critically as the ambassador nodded with bare courtesy to Lord Aviler and strode to the anteroom door, the page stationed there barely managing to swing it open in time.

As the door closed Aviler shook his head and said softly to Galen Dubell, "My apologies, Doctor. To a Bisran, any man in a scholar's gown is half demon."

Dubell's expression was closed and enigmatic. "And a sorcerer, of course, is all demon."

From the Privy Council Chamber two Queen's guards entered and stepped to either side of the doors as the Dowager Queen came into the room. Everyone bowed and she acknowledged them with a nod and a slight smile. "Gentlemen. Forgive the delay." Her graying red hair was tucked up into a lace cap and she wore a dark informal morning gown. She was over fifty now, and the years hadn't diminished her beauty, but transformed and refined it. Only the faint laugh lines around her mouth and the shadow of strain at the corners of her eyes betrayed her age. She took a seat in the brocaded canopy chair beside the hearth, her attendant gentlewoman settling on a cushioned stool behind her. "Dr. Galen Dubell, I'm glad to find you in good health. Perhaps you can help us in explaining this matter."

"Yes, my lady. You saw my letters concerning Urbain Grandier?" Dubell said, stepping forward.

"Yes. Dr. Surete brought them to me when he requested your return to court. His unfortunate death delayed the matter just long enough, it seems. When the messages came from Lodun telling of your disappearance I had already sent an order lifting the ban and requesting your return." As she spoke she was already unfolding a square of half-completed black-work embroidery and looking for the needle that marked her place. Ravenna always had to have something to do with her hands. It was a habit that disconcerted all but the most resolute of petitioners and foreign ambassadors, but Thomas noted it didn't seem to faze Dubell.

The old sorcerer bowed to her. "I am honored, my lady."

Ravenna gestured that away. "Tell me more about this Grandier. He has an odd name for a Bisran."

Watching the Dowager guardedly, Aviler said, "We have some knowledge about his early life. Urbain Grandier was a Bisran sorcerer and scholar, though it is believed his father was from Ile-Rien, possibly a visiting priest, or even a noble, journeying there during one of the temporary treaties in force in the year of Grandier's birth. This would explain his surname, which is certainly not Bisran. Stubbornly, he refused to take another name, and this probably contributed to the suspicion with which he was regarded there."

She frowned at her embroidery. "His original offense was some outrage concerning nuns, and the Bisran Church removed his sanction to perform sorcery? And then he was arrested by the Inquisition?"

"Yes, my lady. After his escape from the Inquisition, Grandier brought on a plague and apparently made subtle changes in the weather over the Kiseran plain, some of their richest farmland, and destroyed most of their last year's harvest. The Bisran theurgic sorcerers are said to be near exhaustion with holding off magical attacks on Church officials and the War College."

Ravenna smiled tightly without looking up from her embroidery. She hated Bisra even more than she had hated her dead husband, the old king Fulstan. "One might point out that it is nothing more than they deserve."

"One might," Aviler agreed. "But the point is that Grandier has suddenly chosen to come to Ile-Rien."

Thomas shook his head, briefly amused. Aviler's relationship with the Dowager Queen was an acrimonious one.

For her part Ravenna merely studied the High Minister a moment. Her fine long-fingered hands had paused on the embroidery, the gold needle catching the firelight. That might mean anything; Thomas had known her to order an execution, explain to the culprit why it had to be done, and deny the family's fervent pleas for mercy, all without missing a stitch. Then she drew the strand of thread up tight and said, "Tell me about the events at the convent, Lord Aviler." She nodded to her gentlewoman. "Lady Anne knows she has permission to leave the room should she hear anything that causes her to fear for her modesty."

As Lady Anne bit her lip and looked studiously at the floor, Aviler frowned and said, "The original incident took place at a convent in a town called Lindre, in the northern part of Bisra. Grandier was accused of corrupting the nuns, causing them to blaspheme against their own Church, to attack each other, to perform rituals that—"

"According to the Inquisitors General of Bisra," Galen Dubell interrupted gently, "he caused them to corrupt themselves." He had moved toward the hearth and was staring into the fire, an expression in his eyes that Thomas couldn't interpret. "They found evidence of human blood used in rituals, symbols and books banned for centuries, the darkest magic . . . There was even some evidence of an agreement with a Lord of Hell."

As the others watched Dubell in silence, Thomas said, "In Bisra they still burn hedgepriests for putting curses on cows. Why do you feel you can trust the Inquisition's reports?"

"True, Captain." Dubell turned back to them. "The Inquisitors were, of course, lying. They manufactured the evidence, or most of it. Scholars who are not even sorcerers may have items in their possession that an evil mind can misinterpret. And Urbain Grandier was a scholar. He studied the stars, as well as the body and its ills and humors. He was also very outspoken in his opinions, and involved in the printing of inflammatory pamphlets. It was for this that he came under the Inquisition's scrutiny. The incident of some hysterical nuns at the Lindre Convent was used against him and he was given the usual sentence of torture and imprisonment."

Dubell's voice had an enthralling quality. It might have been facilitated by the growing warmth in the room or the fatigue that was catching up with Thomas, but he seemed to be painting a particularly vivid picture of the man Grandier had been.

After a moment Dubell shook his head. "It turned him, you might say. He escaped eventually, and began to commit many of the crimes of which they had accused him, but on a larger scale. The plague, for instance. It caused pockets of a poisonous humor to form beneath the skin, which burst when the victim was in death agony and spread the disease to anyone who stood nearby. It caused so much chaos entire cities were disrupted; the sick went untended . . . Only a man well versed in healing-sorcery could have devised something so terrible, and only a man driven mad with the lust for revenge could have brought himself to implement it." In the firelight, Dubell's face was a mask of pain. Then he sighed. "When I heard that a man calling himself Grandier had become established in Vienne and was believed to be a sorcerer, I thought it best to bring the matter to Dr. Surete's attention. I only wish I'd acted sooner."

Renier had gone to the round table in the center of the room and was looking through the faded parchment and leather maps stacked there. He pulled one out and found Lindre, then thoughtfully tapped the red cross that marked the town. "You knew Grandier very well?"

"No. His excesses and the motivation for them were much discussed at Lodun, where there is great interest in the natural, as well as the magical, arts." Dubell smiled. "And the printing of an occasional pamphlet."

"We know," Aviler said dryly. He paced a few steps, his face severe and only half-visible in the candlelight. Aviler's late father had made his fortune in trading voyages to the East before he had settled down to take over the Ministry, and the stigma of those origins made Aviler the Younger careful to preserve the proper aristocratic disdain toward the occasional political commentary from Lodun. But the High Minister dropped the subject and only asked, "Why does Grandier come here now?"

Dubell spread his hands. "I don't know. But whatever his reason, he must be stopped and driven away."

Ravenna nodded. "Excesses in Bisra are all well and good, but he cannot be allowed to commit them here. I agree, Doctor. But why did he seek you out? Some special grudge?"

Dubell looked thoughtful. "It has been ten years since Dr. Surete and I last tended to the palace wards. With Surete dead and Grandier rumored to be in the city, I thought it best that I should see to them again. The warding stones that hold the etheric structure of spells in formation around the newer sections of the palace must be examined individually, though in the Old Courts where the wards are tied to the structures themselves such attention is not necessary. But now I realize the situation is even more urgent than I thought. If Grandier meant to keep me from examining the wards after Dr. Surete's death, then he must have some way to circumvent them."

Aviler looked up, frowning. "How is that possible?"

"The wards are not unlimited or infallible. The sorcerers who constructed them directed them to react to certain situations in certain ways. But their creators could not, and did not, think of every situation. If a fay knew where the gaps were that their movement occasionally creates, it could pass through them unharmed." Galen Dubell smiled. "Dr. Surete knew the most about the wards. He could tell you their names."

"I see," Aviler muttered.

"Do you? Good." Ravenna finished part of the pattern and spread the square of needlework out on her lap. "Dr. Dubell, when can you begin this examination of the wards?"

"Immediately," Dubell told her. "It will take several days, as some portions may only be performed during certain hours of the night."

"Good, but we must continue the search for Grandier."

Thomas said, "The King's Watch found that house; they'll find him." The King's Watch was a euphemism for the network of spies set up by the late Aviler the Elder to keep an eye on discontented nobles living in the city and the foreign cults that had begun to appear then. It was they who had been able to find Grandier's River Quarter house when the Lodun sorcerers had named him as Galen Dubell's abductor.

Ravenna nodded, her attention still on her needlework. "Very well. That is enough for now. Dr. Dubell must rest before he begins his work and I know you gentlemen have much to attend to."

As they made to leave, Ravenna added, "Stay a moment, Captain."

Thomas waited, and when the doors had closed behind the last of the others, she asked, "It was difficult?"

"Fairly," he admitted.

Ravenna lifted a brow. "That's hardly an answer."

He watched her a moment thoughtfully. That Roland had sent him on a mission designed to cause his death probably rankled her more than it did him. "Is that why you wanted me to stay, to indulge my sense of self-pity?"

"Oh, don't start. Roland could send you to the edge of the earth and I would not care." She smiled, but her expression became bitter as she smoothed a section of the embroidery. "Master Conadine was sent for today from the Granges to help deal with Grandier. He should be here within the week. It was the worst stupidity not to wait for him and to send you with only Dr. Braun."

"If I'd had the choice, I might have gone anyway," Thomas admitted. "If we had waited any longer Grandier could have killed Dubell."

"And taken a handful of men, and only Dr. Braun?" Her lips thinned. "Never mind. Roland did it to aggravate me, and we know who encouraged him to it, don't we?" Ravenna tested the sharpness of her needle with a finger, then selected another out of the case Lady Anne held ready for her. "And what other mischief has Denzil been up to lately?"

Thomas took a seat on a stool near her chair, feeling his weariness as a tight pain across his shoulders. The episode with Grandier had worried Ravenna more than she had revealed to Aviler or the others, but he let her change the subject. He said, "He visited a banker on the Riverside Way yesterday, but that was about a gambling debt. If he's planning something now, he's taking more care with it."

"Perhaps." Ravenna carefully threaded the needle. "Someday he will miscalculate."

Thomas shrugged. "Roland can always pardon him." Denzil was Duke of Alsene, Roland's older cousin on his father's side, and acknowledged favorite. There were men who had more respect for the finer feelings of their dogs than Denzil had for Roland, but the young King still clung to him. It was undoubtedly Denzil who had talked Roland into sending a small contingent of the Queen's Guard to beard Grandier in his lair, knowing Thomas would be bound to lead them, and knowing that it would infuriate Ravenna. Thomas reminded himself there was nothing to be done about it tonight. But he was looking forward to the moment when the news reached Denzil that he had gone into Grandier's house and brought Galen Dubell out alive without losing a single man. "What did the Bisran ambassador want?"

"To accuse us of harboring Grandier." She made a gesture of exasperation, willing to be led away from the subject of her son's favorite. "And also to present a new list of their heretics sheltering in Ile-Rien, so they could be arrested and returned to Bisra to burn for their crimes. That the Bisran Inquisition has no authority within our borders is immaterial, apparently. I wish I knew why the ambassador is so certain that Grandier is here with our blessings." She coughed, and Lady Anne hastily produced a lace-edged cloth for her.

Watching her accusingly, Thomas said, "You're not feeling well." She had caught a lung flux last winter when they had gone to Bannot-on-the-Shore to quell a minor upheaval among the March Barons. Her vitality made it difficult to remember that she was not a young woman anymore, and Thomas still regretted allowing her to ride with the Guard instead of going in an enclosed carriage, even if it had let her surprise the barons in the middle of their secret conference. The disease had weakened her lungs despite the best efforts of apothecaries and sorcerer-healers, and she wasn't up to any more midnight rides over ice fields, whatever she might think. "You didn't have to see Dubell tonight, or the ambassador."

"It is very damp out, and you are not my nursemaid." She tucked the cloth into her sleeve, unperturbed. "I wanted to get this over with as quickly as possible. And if the palace wards are weakening . . ." After a moment, Ravenna shook her head. "And what do you think of Dr. Dubell?"

Thomas knew she wasn't asking about the man's abilities as a sorcerer. "He's no fool. He handles himself very well."

"Lord Aviler—the old Lord Aviler, not that young puppy of a High Minister—had great faith in Dubell. Despite his past disgrace." She sighed. "But I've kept you long enough."

Thomas stood up, took her hand, and kissed it. She said, "Oh, and I'd almost forgotten." She rummaged in her sewing case, and pulled out a ribbon-tied packet of letters to hand to him.

"What is it?"

"An annoyance for you to deal with."

He accepted the packet with an expression of distaste. "And I was afraid I might have to sleep tonight."

"Oh, it isn't urgent. At least not to me." She smiled. "Enjoy."

Stepping out into the Guard Room, Thomas turned the packet over curiously. Ravenna never forgot anything; it must be something she didn't want to discuss. Before he could untie the bound letters, he saw that Galen Dubell was waiting for him. "A moment, Captain?" he asked.

"Yes?"

"Forgive me if the question is intrusive, but Lord Aviler does not care for you?" The High Minister had already gone, though Renier was still in the Guard Chamber, speaking quietly to the two Albonate squires.

"Lord Aviler is like that." Dubell's expression held nothing but mild curiosity. After a moment, Thomas found himself saying, "He doesn't approve of favorites. He's studied enough history to know what damage I could do if I were inclined to it."

"I see." Dubell smiled. "Does Queen Falaise still have her entourage of poets?"

Falaise had been a princess of Umberwald when Ravenna had chosen her to marry Roland a year ago. At eighteen she was four years younger than the King, and if Ravenna's motive in choosing her for a daughter-in-law had been to pick someone she could teach and influence, she had made one of her few mistakes. Falaise might have been the quiet studious girl that the ambassadors had described when she was a third daughter with few prospects, but once here and safely wed to Roland she had taken to palace life like a beggar child let loose in a bakery. "Yes, she does. City gossip reaches you all the way out in Lodun?"

"City gossip is a treasured commodity. The servants bring it in with the milk every morning. The general opinion, I gathered, was one of relief that she had chosen to turn her attentions to harmless poets, considering what else she could have done."

Thomas agreed, "She could have had guardsmen."

"Or sorcerers." Dubell's expression turned serious. "I owe you a great debt, Captain."

Thomas looked at him sharply. "I think you've already repaid that debt." Without Dubell's assistance, Gaspard would have died.

Dubell gestured that away. "Nevertheless, if I can help you in any way, do not hesitate to call on me."

As Dubell turned to follow the servants waiting to take him to his rooms, Renier intercepted Thomas. "There's something I have to show you." He looked worried.

Thomas was weary and didn't want to see anything right now that meant more potential trouble. Resigned, he followed Renier to a quieter corner of the Guard Room. "What is it?"

"A letter. It arrived today in a packet of dispatches from Portier. The courier's a trusted man who swears he never let the packet out of his sight." The big man unfolded a square of paper. "This is a translation I had a priest do."

Thomas took the paper, frowning. "What language was it in?"

"Old Church Script."

Thomas read the first scribbled sentence aloud, "'O Best Beloved'?" He looked up, puzzled. "To whom was it sent?"

"Roland. But the priest said that's the proper way to begin an old riddle-song, which is what this is."

> *Where the music is not heard,*
> *There was a light not seen,*
> *There are barren hills home to multitudes,*
> *And dry lakes where fish are caught above a*
> *city's towers. Catch the incantation, solve the song.*

"The answer is a simple one: the Fay," Renier said.

There was only one person acquainted with Roland whose feelings would naturally express themselves in poetic forms of the past. "You know who this is from," Thomas said. This was grim news.

"The country folk are calling her Kade Carrion now." Renier shrugged, uneasy. "I suppose we're lucky; she could have sent something that exploded or told the secrets of whomever picked it up."

Roland's older sister, the bastard princess who had never forgiven anything. Thomas tapped the rolled paper against his palm. "An odd coincidence, with Galen Dubell here. Ravenna decides to pardon the man who first told the bane of our lives that she was a witch, and the witch herself starts meddling again." She had chosen her moment well. *We have more than enough to deal with from Grandier, and Kade is too dangerous to ignore.*

Renier's brow furrowed in consternation. "She's been quiet for almost six months. Why now?"

Across the room, a musician had taken a seat at the spinet and now played the opening verse of a popular new ballad, about a man who fell in love with a fayre queen and was taken away by her. *He couldn't have chosen an air more inappropriate to the moment,* Thomas thought. He said, "One hundred and ninety-seven days. I keep count. She might be in league with Grandier." Though Grandier had killed to protect himself, and Kade was rather like a cat—if the mouse was dead it was no good playing with it anymore. *But people change.*

Renier shook his head regretfully. "There's not much else we can do. The sentry positions have already been doubled and tripled for Grandier's sake." His eyes flicked up to meet Thomas's. "Dubell is going to tend the wards."

Thomas had been thinking along those lines himself. "Yes, he is, isn't he?"

"We've nothing to go on."

Thomas handed him back the letter. "Watch him anyway."

CHAPTER THREE

At the first creak of the door, Thomas was up on one elbow and drawing the main gauche from the belt hung over the bedpost. Then he recognized the man entering the room and shoved the long dagger back into its sheath. "Damn you, Phaistus."

The young servant shrugged and knelt beside the hearth to scrape the ashes out, muttering to the unresponsive andirons, "Well, he's in a mood."

Thomas struggled out of bed. Despite the high ceiling and the natural tendency for drafts, the room was almost too warm; daylight shining through the high windows reflected dazzlingly off the whitewashed plaster of the walls. His scabbarded rapier leaned against a red brocaded chair and his other three civilian dueling swords hung on the wall, along with the heavier, broad-bladed weapons used for cavalry combat. He ran a distracted hand through his hair, working the tangles out, and said, "What's the hour?"

"Nearly midday, Sir. Ephraim's outside. He said you wanted him. And Master Lucas brought that Gambin fellow in."

"Good." Thomas stretched and grimaced. A few hours of sleep had done little besides give his bruised muscles time to stiffen. While Phaistus banged things on the hearth, he found his trousers and top boots on the floor underneath the bed's rumbled white counterpoint and started to dress. "Clean that pistol."

The servant stood, wiping his hands on his shirttail and glancing over the draw table where Thomas had left his wheellock and reloading gear. "Where's the other one?"

Thomas grabbed up a pewter jug and threw it at Phaistus, who ducked, grinned, and went on with what he was doing. Phaistus had come to the Guard House as a kitchen boy, silent and terrified, but had grown out of it before his voice changed. "I obviously don't beat you enough." Thomas went to the table and pushed back his sleeves to splash water on his face from the bowl there.

Unfazed, the boy asked, "Going to kill Gambin, Sir?"

"It's a thought." Deciding he could wait to trim his beard, Thomas picked up the scabbarded rapier and went into the small anteroom.

Ephraim was waiting for him. He was a little old man, the pockets of his faded brown doublet and breeches stuffed with sheaves of paper, the ballads he sold on the street. His stockings were mud-stained and one of his shoes had a large hole in the toe. He grinned and pulled his battered hat off. "You wanted to see me, Captain?"

"Someone sent a packet of letters to the Dowager Queen through Gambin. I want you and your people to find out who hired him."

Ephraim rubbed his grizzled chin. The best of the civilian spies Thomas employed, Ephraim was discreet enough for the occasional official mission as well as for Thomas's own needs. "That could be difficult, Sir. That Gambin lad hires out to so many there's no telling whose business he's on today, and he mightn't have a reason to go back to the fellow, you know."

"Gambin's here now. I'll make sure he does."

Ephraim nodded. "Ahh. That's a different matter. The usual wages?"

"A bonus if you find out by tomorrow."

"Oh, I can't make any promises." Ephraim looked flattered. "But we'll do our poor best."

Thomas left him and went down the staircase toward the clash of steel and loud talk from the large hall on the lower floor. The old, rambling house stood just inside the Prince's Gate, where it was dwarfed by the bulk of the King's Bastion and the Albon Tower. For seventy years the house had been the headquarters of the Queen's Guard and the property of whoever held the commission of captain. The carved knobs topping the stairway's balusters were gashed and chipped from practice bouts up and down the steps, and the walls still bore the faint scars of powder burns from more serious skirmishes.

The Queen's Guard were all scions of province nobility or second sons of landed families, with few expectations of large inheritances. The requirement for membership was a term of service with a crown troop, preferably cavalry, and an appointment from the Queen. In general, the Queen's Own were unruly and hard drinking, and carried on jealous and obsessive rivalries with both the Cisternans and the Albon Order. They were also the most effective elite force in a country where, until a few years ago, private armies had abounded; commanding them had been Thomas's only ambition for a long time.

As he reached the second-floor landing, Dr. Lambe was just coming out of the archway that led into the other wing. Dressed in a stained smock, the apothecary was followed by a young boy weighed down with various satchels and bags of medical paraphernalia. Thomas asked Lambe, "Did you see Gaspard?"

"I did, Captain, and I'm not sure I believe it." Lambe adjusted the cap on his balding head. Apothecaries prepared the herbal remedies used by sorcerer-healers, and many, like Lambe, also made good physicians, even without any sorcerous skill. Healers learned in magic were in short supply everywhere but in Lodun, where the university drew them by the dozens.

"What do you mean?"

"The burns are scarred over already." He shrugged. "I knew Galen Dubell had a reputation for healing-sorcery, but what did the man do?"

"Whatever it was, he did it quickly. He used some things Braun had."

"Dr. Braun's not so bad." Lambe caught Thomas's expression and added, "He's not a steady sort, I'll give you that, Sir, but he has the makings of a fine practitioner in him. But this work of Dr. Dubell's . . . It would be an honor to hand the man bandages."

Thoughtfully, Thomas watched Lambe go, then turned into the small second-floor council room where Lucas waited for him.

The dingy walls were hung with old maps and a few tattered remnants of flags, some of which were trophies from the last war, while others were more recent acquisitions from the Cisternan Guard, who would undoubtedly give a great deal to learn where they were. In the glass-fronted bookpress were classical treatises on warfare, manuals of drilling, musketry, fencing, and tactics, *The Compleat Body of the Art Military* and *Directions For Musters*. Lucas Castil, the First Lieutenant of the Queen's Guard, was leaning back in a chair, nursing a tankard, his boots propped up on the heavy plank table beside a wine bottle and another tankard.

Gambin was standing in the corner in an attitude that suggested he wanted to be as far away from Lucas as possible, and his long face was sullen. Gambin was a spy as well, but without Ephraim's sense of professional integrity. He worked most often for the lesser lords of the court, and this was the first time Thomas had considered him anything more than a minor irritant. He was dressed in a red-and-gold-slashed doublet, the peacock finery of a court hanger-on that was particularly hateful to the eyes after a hard night and little sleep. Gambin said, "I've business elsewhere, Captain, if you don't mind." The bravado in his voice was unconvincing.

Lucas raised an eyebrow. Thomas glanced at the lieutenant as he set his rapier down. Ignoring Gambin, he poured wine into the other tankard, tasted it, and winced in disgust. He said to Lucas, "Adijan '22? Are you mad?"

Lucas shrugged. "It wakes me up."

"It wakes the dead." Thomas dropped into a chair and looked at the spy. He waited until Gambin's pale eyes shifted away from his, then said, "Someone gave you a package."

"They do. I'm handy for that," Gambin muttered.

"This was for the Dowager Queen."

The spy licked his lips. "Was it?"

"Was it?" Lucas echoed.

"It was," Thomas said. He drew the rapier from the fine black leather of the scabbard and out of the corner of his eye saw Gambin shift nervously. The hilt was unadorned beyond the inherent elegance in the shapes of the half-shell guard and the blunt points of the quillons, and the metal was worn smooth from use. Thomas ran a finger down the flat of the narrow blade, apparently giving all his attention to the shallow dents and scratches it had collected. "Who gave it to you?"

"I'm not saying I had any package."

Lucas pulled the packet of letters out of his rumpled doublet and dropped it on the table. Last night, after discovering that it was Gambin who had delivered the packet to one of Ravenna's gentlewomen, Thomas had given it to Lucas along with instructions to bring in the spy.

Thomas held the rapier up and sighted along the blade. Despite last night's misadventures, it was still unbent. "Where'd this package come from, then?"

Gambin laughed nervously. "There's no proof I had anything to do with that."

Thomas looked up at him. "A queen's word is not good enough?" he asked softly. "That's dangerously close to treason."

"I . . . That's . . ."

"Who gave it to you?"

Gambin made the mistake of changing defensive tactics. "I can't tell you that."

"'Can't'? Surely not 'can't,'" Lucas pointed out. "Perhaps you mean 'shouldn't'? There is a distinct difference."

"I meant I don't know who it was; he had his man give it to me," Gambin protested.

"That's a pity." Thomas laid the rapier gently back on the table and stood up. "You're no use to us, then, are you?"

"So I'll be on my way, then."

"Yes, do that."

Gambin hesitated, started to speak, then made a sudden dash for the door. Thomas caught him as Gambin faltered in the doorway at the sight of a group of guards dicing in the next room. He slung the spy around and slammed him face-first onto the table.

Lucas deftly rescued the wine bottle and moved it out of the way.

Gambin yelped, the cry escalating into a scream as Thomas twisted his arm upward at an unnatural angle. He said, "Keep yelling. There's no one to hear you who gives a damn. Now I suggest you consider an answer."

"Look here, I . . . I'll find out who it is for you. I swear, he . . . I've got friends that can find him." Gambin's voice rose in desperation.

"I think you're lying. Doesn't it seem like he's lying?" Thomas asked Lucas.

Lucas shrugged. "Well, he is handy that way."

"No, no, it's the truth," Gambin panted. "I'll find him."

"Are you sure?" Thomas put a little more of his weight on the man's abused arm bone.

Gambin shrieked. "Yes, yes! I swear it!"

Thomas let him go and stepped back. Gambin fell to the floor, gasping. He staggered to his feet, clutching his arm, and stumbled for the door. Thomas stood his chair upright and recovered his tankard from the floor. He gestured at the wine bottle Lucas was holding protectively. "Are you keeping that all for yourself?"

Lucas passed it to him as he took his own seat. "I thought it woke the dead."

"It does. That's what bad years are for." He poured the tankard full and took a long drink. He resented wasting the time on Gambin, and wanted to get back to the problem of Grandier. The three prisoners they had taken last night had known nothing. The man who had hired them had worn a hood and a mask, which was a common practice for nobles and the wealthy slumming in low taverns, and they had not been able to decide if he was a Bisran. Which might mean Grandier spoke without an accent, that the man who had done the hiring had not been the sorcerer but another confederate, or that the hirelings were too witless to have known him for Bisran if he had been wearing a Bisran cornet officer's tabard. *We know nothing about Grandier,* Thomas thought in disgust, *except rumor and common knowledge.* "I suppose Gideon relieved you at dawn."

"Yes, and he was disgustingly cheery about it." Lucas sighed. "I can't recall being that energetic as a youth. Who's following Gambin?"

"Ephraim, the one that pretends to be a ballad-seller."

"Oh, hiring out, are we?"

"Had to. All the regulars from the King's Watch are still looking for Grandier."

"Grandier's a bad business." Lucas picked up the packet of letters and glanced through it. "So you're having an affair with the Countess of Mayence?"

"A long, torrid affair. I get very effusive about it in the one dated last month." Thomas didn't mind his lieutenant's raillery. Lucas was perhaps the first man Thomas had learned to trust entirely, when with the rest of the Queen's Guard they had been employed as couriers and intelligence-gatherers during the last Bisran War. Since they were both dark enough to pass for Aderassi, the two of them had once spent six days disguised as mercenaries from that small country in a Bisran cavalry encampment on the wrong side of a wide and rising river. The Bisran commander had staged executions of captured officers of the Ile-Rien army as after-dinner entertainment, and the bounty he had offered for Queen's Guardsmen was enough to support a well-to-do merchant family for a year.

"Yes, I particularly enjoyed that one." Lucas spread the letter out on the table to examine the signature. "It's a good forgery. I'd think there were some truth to it if I didn't know you were too proper a gentleman to stand in line with the good countess's grooms and lackeys. I expect it's a lucky thing the Dowager thinks so, too."

"It's hardly luck. If Ravenna had asked me if I'd actually slept with the countess, I would've had to tell her I honestly couldn't remember. Most of the court ladies are starting to look alike to me." Thomas and Ravenna had not been lovers for more than a year, since her health had first begun to fail, and she knew that he had had other women since then. It hadn't changed anything between them; their relationship had passed that point long ago. The only woman she would have objected to was Falaise. Not too many years ago palace coups had ignited as quickly as fires in a dry summer; Ravenna could not afford to have the man who commanded her guard become attached to a daughter-queen who in many ways was still an unknown quantity, and who one day might like to rid herself of a dominating mother-in-law.

But even though the letters had failed in their purpose, they were an annoyance at a time when Ravenna needed him free to help her, and not constantly guarding his own back. Thomas tapped the packet. "This was done by someone who doesn't know Ravenna."

Lucas nodded. "Someone who doesn't realize how little she appreciates people who trouble with her personal"—he paused and his mouth quirked—"matters."

Thomas strongly suspected his friend had been about to say "affairs." He let it pass and said, "It's more the sort of thing that would work with Roland. I wonder if our anonymous schemer plans to try it." If some disgruntled courtier also tried to drive a wedge between Roland and his cousin Denzil in this manner, Thomas wished him luck, but it was far more likely this asinine trick was the brainchild of one of the Duke of Alsene's cronies. Inspired by a few casually dropped hints by Denzil himself, of course.

Lucas looked thoughtful. "I wonder if it's been tried already."

Thomas shook his head. "I'd think the screams would have been audible even over on this end of the court. But there's no way to be certain."

"Surely Renier, the ideal of perfect knighthood, would know."

Thomas snorted. As the ideal of perfect knighthood, Renier was not without flaws. He was a skilled swordsman but tended to depend too much on his weight and size, using his greater strength to bowl over smaller opponents. This technique had some merit: there were many men who unwisely dueled with the Preceptor of the Albon Knights only to end with his footprints down their backs. Renier had knocked Thomas down once in a friendly duel, and when the Preceptor had stepped in close to follow up, Thomas had retaliated by slamming him in the groin with the hilt of his main gauche. Renier didn't seem to hold it against Thomas, and his good humor never seemed to suffer. But Renier had a misguided perception of loyalty, and while he was not a bad influence on the young King, he was not a good one either. He often went out of his way to repeat to Roland what everyone else in his hearing said, without regard for Roland's sensibilities or the safety of those whose careless words were later used against them. Thomas said, "The ideal of perfect knighthood thinks it's his duty to tell Roland every word I say to him, and God knows what His Majesty would make of the question."

"Well, whatever you think." Lucas got to his feet slowly. He was only a few years older than his captain, but he moved like a much older man when he was tired. *The reflexes go,* Thomas thought, looking at the rapier lying on the table. *And that's that.*

Lucas said, "I'm off to a well-deserved rest. Oh, there's that entertainment at court tonight. Will you need me?"

"No, Gideon and I will take it. I've doubled the duty list for it, what with all our other little troubles." The acting troupes brought to court by the Master of Revels didn't ordinarily present much of a problem. Before they reached the palace they were examined for foreign spies or suspected anarchists, and the actors seldom turned mad and attacked anyone. "What sort of play is it?"

"An Aderassi Commedia."

Thomas winced. "Well, it could've been a pastoral." He drained the tankard.

"Oh, there's this. I'd forgotten." Lucas picked up a leather dispatch case from a pile along the wall and tossed it onto the table. It was stuffed with papers.

Thomas looked at it without enthusiasm. "What's that?"

"The King's Watch sent it over. It's some writings and copies of documents from Grandier's heresy trial in Bisra."

"You're joking." Sitting up, Thomas pulled out the papers and thumbed through the pages of faded script. "How did they get it?"

"A Viscondin monk who was traveling in Bisra attended the trial. He asked one of the officiating priests if he could copy the documents, and they allowed it. None of it was considered secret, or important, apparently. The King's Watch said it wouldn't be of any use, but they know how you are about these things so they sent it along."

As Lucas left, Thomas spread out the papers. The Viscondin Order was one of the few brotherhoods that could still cross the border to Bisra freely. The Church of Ile-Rien and the Church of Bisra had declared ecclesiastical war on each other when the bishops of Ile-Rien decided against purging the country-side of the pagan Old Faith. The Bisran Inquisition had started its persecution of sorcerers at about the same time, and the Church of Ile-Rien's objections to it had caused Bisra to outlaw most of the independent religious orders.

The Viscondin monk had copied the court documents in the original Bis-ran. Thomas could read Low Bisran, but not the elaborate High Script used for their official documents. He doubted the monk had been able to either, and the King's Watch had probably not bothered. He sorted the unreadable documents aside to send to the palace clerks for translation.

It was clear even from the monk's crabbed notes on the evidence that Grandier had been a victim. The nuns' testimony had been confused and contradictory, and the details of how Grandier had enchanted them were vague at best; if they had brought such charges in Ile-Rien a magistrate would have had them all hauled off to gaol for false witness and wasting the time of a law court. According to the monk, one nun had even tried to recant her testimony but the judges had refused to hear her.

Grandier had been tortured with fire, the choking-pear, and the other devices the Inquisition used to obtain confessions of heresy. Despite this the

sorcerer had refused to confess, and had been sentenced to the question ordinary and extraordinary. He had been subjected to both strappado, having
been hoisted by his bound arms and dropped to a stone floor, and squassation,
during which the executioner had attached heavy weights to the victim's feet,
then hoisted and dropped him to within a few inches of the floor until limbs
had been dislocated. *The scars would be visible on his face, his hands. Even if he's
healed himself, he can't conceal that kind of injury. It would be a miracle if he
could straighten his back or walk without limping,* Thomas thought.

Grandier disappeared from his cell a few weeks after his torture. A month
later the priest who had brought the original complaint died insane. Within
another month the bishop who headed the Inquisitorial Committee followed
him. The witch-pricker, who had probably falsified the demon marks he had
reported finding on Grandier's body during torture, died later in "terrible de-
lirium," as the monk described it. The account ended there, before the plague
and the other horrific disasters now attributed to the outlaw sorcerer.

If he wasn't working dark magic before the trial, Thomas thought, *he is now.*

———

The afternoon at the Mummer's Mask passed slowly as the tavernkeepers recovered from the night before and the acting troupe prepared for the night to
come. Baraselli and his assistants sat at a big round table on the tavern's main
floor arguing over which characters they would use tonight, while the actors
lounged nearby feigning disinterest. Shafts of sunlight from the cracked windows glittered off the dust in the air and the various paraphernalia of the stage
that had been hauled out for inspection.

Silvetta, the actress who played one of the heroines, said, "What did you say
your name was?"

There was a moment of hesitation before the woman who had been hired
for the Columbine mask answered, "It's Kade." She sat on top of a wine-
stained table, her legs folded beneath her skirt in a position that most women
of better breeding would have found difficult if not impossible. The playing
cards she shuffled were a tattered pack belonging to the tavern.

"Really? Don't tell Baraselli." Silvetta shuddered, rolling her eyes in a gesture better suited for the stage. "Bad luck, ill omens, that's all he talks about.
But they don't give children that name here anymore, do they? Except in the
country. Are you from the country?"

"Yes."

"When did you learn Commedia?"

"I traveled around with one for a while and learned the Columbine mask. That was after I got out of the convent," Kade told her.

Silvetta leaned forward. "Why were you in a convent?"

"My wicked stepmother sent me there."

"Oh, you're telling me a tale." Personal questions out of the way, she said, "Do my fortune again."

Kade's brows quirked. "I doubt it's changed any in the past hour."

"You can't tell; it might have."

"You can tell," Kade said, but began to lay out the cards for the fortune anyway.

Corrine, the other heroine, appeared out of a back room carrying two dresses visible only as tumbled confections of sparkled fabric and lace. "What do you think, this blue or that blue?"

Both women paused to give the matter serious consideration. "That one," Silvetta said finally.

"I think so," Kade agreed.

"What are you wearing?" Corrine asked her.

Kade suspected she was anxious to make sure she wasn't going to be out-shone by the woman playing her maid. With a shrug of one shoulder, Kade indicated the loose red gown she wore over a low-necked smock. "This."

"You can't wear that," Silvetta objected.

"I'm playing a maid." She laughed. "What else should I wear?"

The free fortune-telling had won Silvetta over completely. She said, "At least let me curl your hair."

Kade ran a hand through fine limp hair that the dusty sunlight was tempo-rarily transforming into spun gold. Ordinarily she considered it the color of wheat suffering from rotting blight. "With an iron?"

"Of course, you goose, what else?"

"I hate that."

Corrine draped the gowns over a chair and said, "The thing to do is to attract attention to yourself. There's plenty of men there—gentlemen, lords, wealthy men—on the lookout for mistresses. Of course, it's not often you can get something permanent, you understand, but it's worth a go."

"Really?" Kade asked, her tone a shade too ingenuous, but not so much so that the other two women suspected subtle mockery.

"Much better than an actor," Silvetta said, and jerked her head in the direction of the tavern entrance. The actor who played the Arlequin stood there talking to one of the tavernkeeps, having just come in from the street. He was darkly handsome, clean-shaven after the current fashion in Adera, and didn't look at all like the other actors who played clowns.

After a moment, Kade said, "How well do you know him?"

Silvetta answered, "He's new. Baraselli hired him last month when the other Arlequin died."

Kade glanced at her. "Was he an old man?"

"Oh, no, all our clowns are young. He died of a fever. It was very bad luck."

The Arlequin had looked in their direction, and seemed to be staring at Kade. Corrine, who apparently had only one thought in her head, grinned and said, "He likes you."

But Kade, who could read wolfish contempt in those dark eyes, snorted. "Hardly," she said, and by sleight of hand managed to insinuate the card for future wealth into Silvetta's fortune.

———

Thomas spent the afternoon checking on the progress of the inquiries he had set in motion last night, but the King's Watch had made little headway so far. He had wanted to sound out Galen Dubell on the subject of his onetime student Kade Carrion, but last night hadn't seemed the right moment after the sorcerer's rescue from three harrowing days as Urbain Grandier's prisoner.

Galen Dubell had moved into the late Dr. Surete's old rooms, and Thomas found him there when the afternoon sun was glowing through the windows and filling the high-ceilinged room with light. The old Court Sorcerer had needed this room when his eyes had started to fail; the multipaned windows in the west wall took full advantage of the daylight. Gold-trimmed bookshelves covered the other walls and a globe still shielded by its protective leather cover stood in the corner. The rest of the furniture was buried under piles of more books and a fine layer of dust.

When the servant led Thomas into the room, Dubell looked up from his writing desk and smiled. "Captain." He was wearing a battered pair of gold-rimmed reading spectacles and open books were spread out on one side of the partners desk Dr. Surete had once shared with his assistant, Milam.

Thomas said, "I wanted to thank you for what you did for my man last night. He would have died if you hadn't healed him."

Dubell smiled. "You are welcome, but I don't think that is the only thing you came to speak about. Please be direct."

Well, well. Thomas leaned on a bookshelf and tipped his plumed hat back, finding himself more amused than discomfited. Directness was not something one encountered often at court. "We've had a message from an old acquaintance of yours. His Majesty Roland's half sister, Kade."

"So that's it." Dubell took off his spectacles and tapped them thoughtfully against the carved arm of his chair. For the first time he looked like a young man who had gradually grown old rather than the model of an aged wizard-scholar who had sprung fully formed out of the fertile ground at Lodun University. "Indeed, I know Kade."

"She was your apprentice."

"Not quite. I was the first to show her the uses for the talent she already had. A mistake I have already paid for. Ten years is a long time to be banished from the city of one's birth." He shook his head, dismissing the thought. "But you have had a message from her?"

"Yes. It seems to suggest she's about to pay a visit."

"In person? That is odd. She usually sends tricks disguised as gifts, doesn't she?"

"If you can call them that." Kade's tricks ranged from the dangerous to the ridiculous. The goblet that no adulterer could drink from had provided some embarrassing and humorous moments for the entire court. A gift of a necklet that, once clasped, contracted and cut the wearer's head off had been considerably less entertaining. The ancient knight who had arrived last midwinter with his beheading game had been one of the most frightening but the least substantive. Of course, Renier had fallen for it like a sack of rocks off a wall. It had taken the Preceptor of the Albon Knights off on a two-month quest that was notable for its pointlessness and not much else. Presumably the fay sorceress had watched from a distance, laughing her own head off. When violent, Kade was about as subtle as a thrown hammer; when devious, she still preferred to sign her name. As an enemy Thomas would have preferred Kade over Urbain Grandier; she, at least, was a known danger. "Could she be coming to see you?" he asked.

Dubell got to his feet and went toward one of the windows that looked out on the Rose Court five stories below. Thomas followed him.

The stone paths below formed gray rivers among islands of small red and white fall roses. On one of those shaded rivers were a gallant and a court lady, standing close together in conversation. There was something furtive in the turn of the woman's head that spoke of an assignation. They couldn't know they were being watched by the Captain of the Queen's Guard and the man who would probably be made Court Sorcerer sometime in the next few months, but in the palace someone was always watching.

After a moment Dubell said, "Kade could have seen me more easily at Lodun. Why should she wait until now?"

"I can't answer that, Doctor. She's only half human and I don't understand why she does anything." No one had been able to answer the question "why" when Kade's mother appeared at court twenty-five years ago to captivate the old king Fulstan. No one had known she was Moire, a great queen in her own right from one of the multitude of fayre kingdoms that hid under ancient barrows, deceptively deep lakes, or the disappearing islands that lay off the southern coast. She had held Fulstan's attention constantly, day and night, for one year before departing and leaving behind her a baby daughter like a forgotten piece of baggage and a man who was far worse a king than he had ever been before.

Dubell had a way of seeming to pick up on someone else's train of thought. He said, "I remember her mother. I was a young man then. The King's Company was performing *The Fortunate Lands* and suddenly she was there, dressed in black and her jewels like stars. The Queen of Air and Darkness." He picked up a book from the window ledge and absently added it to a stack on a nearby chair. "A wiser man might have seen a potential danger in Kade. The fay who appear the most human are often more changeable and vindictive than their monstrous brethren. But I saw only an isolated child with the first stirrings of real power and the wit and the will to use it. I admit I have never felt guilty, Captain. I gave her only an elementary tutoring in the craft. If I hadn't, she would have found someone else. I'm sorry for what she has done with the knowledge since then, but I assume no responsibility for it." He looked back at Thomas seriously. "I suspect that may be *lèse-majesté*."

Thomas shrugged. "Perhaps, but it's a mild form of it." *Compared to most of what goes on here.* "And we do need your help." He was sure Dubell realized that until another court sorcerer could arrive he had them over a barrel, and Thomas was curious to see if the man would come out and admit it.

Dubell shook his head. "I took a vow of fealty when I first came here years ago. Whatever differences of opinion have arisen since then can have no bearing on it."

He stood there watching the garden below, his stooped shoulders revealing his bone-weary exhaustion. Galen Dubell spoke so freely it made suspicion difficult, even for someone in whom suspicion was a deeply ingrained habit. *And how many times does a man have to swear undying loyalty before you have to give him the benefit of the doubt?* Thomas thought. *At least until events prove otherwise.*

The couple in the court below had moved somewhere out of sight. Dubell asked, "Has anything been heard of Grandier?"

"No, not so far. He's not going to be so easy to find again. You haven't re-membered anything else you heard that might hint of his plans?" Thomas asked without much hope. They had gone over all this exhaustively last night on the way back to the palace.

"No, I saw and heard very little of anyone." Dubell spread his hands. "A thing to be glad of, since I expect that is why they allowed me to live."

Thomas let out his breath, frustrated. "I don't know. This is a very complex game he's playing."

Dubell nodded. "So it is," he agreed. "So it is."

———

With winter on the way, the days were growing shorter, but as night dropped over the city on this particular day, Thomas felt he had done a great deal and gotten absolutely no results for any of it. As he leaned on the balustrade of the Queen's loggia and repeated to his young lieutenant Gideon the last message from the King's Watch commander, he was even more convinced of it.

One of the roofed terrace's walls was open to the night and to a view of the park and the river canal where it ran for a time within the towering bulk of the palace's outer curtain wall. Paintings on oiled silk hung from the edge of the roof, rippling slightly in the sharp coolness of the evening breeze.

"They've lost Grandier's trail completely," Thomas told Gideon. Both were dressed in dark brocades for court, with lace at collars and cuffs and over-lapping their top boots. Thomas wore Ravenna's signature color of red in the ribbons on his sleeves and his sword knot. "Which isn't surprising at this point. He was here secretly long enough to establish that house; he could have bolt-holes all over the city by now."

"That's not very encouraging," Gideon said with a rueful expression. One of his duties was the command of the group of Queen's guards that formed Queen Falaise's escort, and he had been attending to her most of the day in-stead of participating in the more exciting search for Grandier.

"That's an understatement." Thomas watched the breeze ripple the surface of the canal. Gideon had been Falaise's lover for the past month, and he wondered if the younger man realized that he knew it. Thomas hoped it didn't become awkward. *I've known him since he was a boy,* he thought. *I'd hate to have to kill him.* Muted music and laughter drifted up the graceful staircase to the loggia. The open doors in the archway below led into the entrance hall of the Grand Gallery where the night's entertainment for the court was being staged. Thomas said, "Grandier's playing with us. I think he wanted us to find him the first time, and the question of why isn't an easy one." He shook his head. "I'll have to talk to the King's Watch commander again tonight."

"Yes. Well, there's one other thing." Gideon lowered his voice. "My lady Falaise wants to see you. I know what you've said about that, Captain, and I have put her off, but . . ."

"I'll take care of it." *You'd think the woman didn't have any sense of self-preservation,* he thought. Thomas was trying to avoid giving Queen Falaise an opportunity to make him any offers he would be honor-bound to tell her mother-in-law Ravenna about. "Who is she with at the moment?"

"Aristofan, he calls himself." Gideon grinned. "His real name is Semuel Porter."

"Which one is he?"

"The pimply one."

Thomas sighed. "They're all pimply, Gideon."

"The pimply one with the red hair." He hesitated. "Braun's coming this way."

Thomas glanced around. Dr. Braun, dressed for court in a black velvet scholar's gown, was gesturing erratically at them from the landing below the loggia. "He seems to have something on his mind," Thomas said.

Gideon looked down at the young sorcerer with thinly veiled contempt. "He nearly got Gaspard killed fumbling around with the wards at that wizard-house."

"Then perhaps it will offset all the times that Gaspard has nearly gotten himself killed," Thomas said, his voice dry. "Go on back to Falaise. See if you can tactfully encourage her to show up for court."

"Sir." Gideon saluted and headed for the stairway leading to the upper levels, and Thomas went down to meet Dr. Braun.

"I have something I need to discuss with you," Braun said hurriedly as Thomas reached him.

Dr. Braun was worried, and his normal hangdog expression had given way to a look of frightened intelligence. Thomas found himself asking seriously, "What is it?"

"Captain!" The voice hailed him from the arched entrance to the Grand Gallery.

Hell, it's Denzil, Thomas thought. He told Braun, "If it can't wait, tell me quickly."

Braun hesitated, his nervous eyes on the approaching Denzil. "It can wait," he said. "I'll come to the Grand Gallery later."

"Are you certain?"

"Yes." Braun began to sidle uneasily away.

"Very well."

Braun nodded and all but bolted out of the entrance hall.

Thomas went to join Denzil.

The Duke of Alsene's father had been a wastrel and little better than a bor-der bandit who managed to lose most of the family properties by the time of his death. Denzil had inherited the Duchy of Alsene at age eight, surrounded by a large family of grasping and impoverished noble relatives. Seven years later when he had come to court and captured Roland's favor, all those prop-erties had been restored, and he had been made generous gifts of land, court offices, and the incomes that came with them. Now he had his own cadre of debauched and worthless young nobles, and he encouraged them to plot and spread rumors and otherwise annoy Ravenna, even though two of his foolish friends had gone too far, and died for it on the Traitor's Block outside the city. Ravenna was continually balked by his influence over Roland, and if Denzil's family had deliberately trained him for the part he played now, they couldn't have done better.

"I've heard some unpleasant rumors about the crown's intentions toward my manor at Bel Garde, Captain," Denzil said, adjusting the set of his gloves and deliberately not looking at Thomas. The King's cousin was the mirror of the perfect courtier. His blond hair was curled to perfection, his beard perfectly trimmed, his handsome features unscarred by the ravages of battle, work, or time, his amber doublet trimmed with aglets and his gold-embroidered breeches the height of fashion. That might be part of the attraction Denzil had for Roland; the King had always been an awkward boy. "Perhaps you can put me right on it."

"I would be happy to put you right, my lord," Thomas said easily.

The Duke's eyes lifted to meet his, cold blue and opaque, and very much at

odds with the pettiness he was affecting. After a moment he smiled ingenu-
ously. "I've heard that a cavalry officer thinks my manor there is some sort of
threat."

That was enough to tell Thomas that Denzil already knew all and was only
trying to bait him. Bel Garde was built around a fortified tower overlooking the
city. In the last century it had withstood a two-year siege and it would make an
ideal staging area for an attack on the city wall. That Denzil should be owner
of such a valuable and potentially dangerous property was a sore point with
the older nobility and particularly Ravenna. Thomas silently damned whoever
had let slip their plans to Denzil and said, "It isn't a manor, Sir. It's a fortress,
and in violation of the edict against private fortifications." The edict helped
discourage rebellious nobles, but Roland had managed to avoid the issue of
Denzil's property at Bel Garde for the past year. He had finally given in to Lord
General Villon's diplomatic prodding, but the difficulty had lain in keeping it
from Denzil until they could get a signed warrant from Roland.

"Who has said this?"

"Lord General Villon, the commander of the siege engine cavalry."

Denzil snorted. "He's a fool."

Thomas lifted his brows. "It is possible he was misled by the moat and the
crenellated walls."

Denzil fingered one of the tawny stones set into the cup hilt of his rapier,
apparently trying to decide if the mockery was worth taking issue with or not.
Thomas knew the gesture for an empty one, perhaps put on for the benefit of
a group of courtiers now crossing the foyer to the gallery behind them: Denzil
was a superb duelist, but Thomas couldn't challenge him because of his loyalty
oaths to the royal family. Denzil could initiate a challenge himself, but despite
provocation, he seemed to be saving it for a time when Thomas was badly
wounded or on his deathbed. Denzil finally said, "And so he will destroy it?"

"Only fill in the moat and tear down the walls. The estate itself will be better
for it in the long run. I'm told by those who should know that it presents a
golden opportunity to extend the park and put in formal gardens."

Denzil's expression suggested this was the equivalent of eating one's children. He said, "Surely this plot did not originate with the King."

"This edict has been posted in the Council Chamber for two years and a
great many lords have already submitted to it. I would hardly call it a plot, Sir."

Denzil gestured that logic away. "You would not call it so, Sir," he said stiffly.
"I would like to know why you are my enemy, Sir, and despise me so."

It was one of Denzil's best tactics with Roland; he could turn any mild criticism into a personal attack on himself. Thomas said, "I suppose if I ever gave you any thought, I might despise you, Sir, but I can't imagine circumstances in which I would be compelled to give you any notice at all."

The expression of artificial indignation in Denzil's eyes hardened to real anger, and for a moment Thomas was hopeful. But Denzil was only foolish about things that endangered other people's lives, not his own, and the moment passed.

"We will see, Sir," Denzil said softly.

Thomas waited until the Duke had vanished through the main doors of the Grand Gallery before starting down the steps after him. Denzil couldn't have gotten wind of the plans for Bel Garde any time before this afternoon, at the earliest, or he would have confronted Roland about it when he saw him this morning. Wager then that Denzil had approached Thomas impulsively. Wager then also that he would approach Roland sometime tonight, instead of waiting for a private audience, in the hopes of provoking Ravenna into an unflattering and public argument with the King.

Walking through the oversized double doors of the archway was like walking into a wall of sound. The combination of the music from the musicians' galleries above the raised dais and the babble of conversation echoed off the high sculpted contours of the ceiling and shivered the rock-crystal chandeliers. The room was so immense that what Thomas knew to be a large crowd appeared sparse. Visiting nobles, courtiers, ministers, and wealthy merchants invited out of courtesy or political necessity milled in large groups around the bases of the marble-sheathed columns, the orange trees potted in silver tubs, or the fountains running with wine.

Thomas made his way through the crowds toward the dais, occasionally greeting an acquaintance. In the center of the room, the play had just started on a raised plank stage with wooden classical columns and a painted backdrop of an Aderassi marketplace. A gaudily dressed Pantalone with a pointed beard and a mask with a long hooked nose was in loud mock argument with a Pulchinella with a rounded back, protruding stomach, and a high peaked cap. Some of the crowd were even paying attention to it.

Cisternan guards were stationed at all the entrances to the gallery, though they were armed only with swords. The Queen's Guard and the Albonate Knights were permitted to carry firearms in the royal presence at court, but no one else.

The polished-stone dais supported the three chairs of state for Ravenna, Falaise, and Roland. Roland was surrounded by his servants and a few courtiers who had been called up to speak to him. An Albon knight stood guard at his back. Next to him Falaise's chair was empty.

Ravenna was firmly established on the opposite side of the dais from her son. Four guards were gathered near her and a lady-in-waiting sat on a stool at her side.

Thomas swept off his hat and bowed to Roland, who was hidden behind his wall of servants and hangers-on, to Falaise's empty chair as a matter of form, and to Ravenna, who smiled down at him. As he climbed the dais, the guard nearest her caught his signal and stepped out of earshot. Thomas kneeled beside Ravenna's brocaded chair and said, "There's news."

Ravenna put her sewing down. "Elaine dear, come and stand in front of me, there's a good girl. Here, wind this thread back on the spindle." The young woman's full skirt, puffed sleeves, and wide plumed hat effectively shielded them from curious eyes.

"Denzil knows about the plans for Bel Garde. It's likely he'll confront Roland about it tonight. You know what will happen," Thomas told Ravenna.

Ravenna's face set. "Villon's been working on Roland for the past two months. He said he'd give the order." She shoved her sewing into her satchel and started to stand.

Thomas said, "Don't."

She stopped, looking down at him, her hands white-knuckled on the arms of her chair.

"Roland won't listen to you. Or worse, he'll do the opposite."

She grimaced. "He will do what I—"

He regarded her steadily. "Face it, Ravenna; it's a fact."

She sat back down with a thump. "Damn Denzil to hell. Damn you to hell. Hand me that fan, Elaine. Oh, don't cringe so, child; I'm not angry with you, am I?" She fanned herself rapidly, the delicate silk construction somehow holding up under the pressure of her grip. "I want you to kill Denzil, Thomas."

Thomas nodded. "Fine. Is now soon enough? I believe I can hit him from here if Elaine would step out of the line of fire."

"No, no. I'll get him eventually. I'll think of something. You'll think of something; it's your duty."

"My duty is protecting you and Falaise," he reminded her.

Ravenna snorted in disdain. "Damn Falaise to hell. What I mind most is that Denzil's making a fool of the boy. Treating him like a puppy to be petted or kicked as the mood takes him. God, I hate that."

Thomas didn't answer.

She twisted the fan between her fingers, then extended it with a snap. "Well?" she asked softly.

Thomas turned over a couple of options, then said, "Send the order tonight. Tell them to start a breach in Bel Garde's curtain wall."

She hesitated.

He continued, "There was a mistake. You thought Roland had signed the warrant, or was about to sign it. You sent the order yesterday."

"Ah." She bit her lip thoughtfully and the fan's motion slowed. "I will order them to stop work immediately when I realize what an unfortunate mistake has been made. I will be properly apologetic. I will repair it with my own funds."

Thomas waited, watching her as she thought it over. A breach in a supporting section of the curtain wall would be difficult to repair, especially with gentle mismanagement, and could be made to buy them at least six months. It would also keep General Villon, who was away with his troop at the moment, from being compromised.

"It will do," Ravenna said. "Elaine, find me that lap desk, please."

As the girl brought the flat wooden box with the ink bottle and pen set, Thomas noticed the crowd around Roland had cleared and one of the stewards was presenting Dr. Galen Dubell to the King. As Dubell bowed deeply, Roland said, "Come up here, Sir, and tell me how things are at Lodun."

Roland had wanted to go to Lodun or the smaller university farther off in Duncanny, but Ravenna had needed him here during her regency, and before that, Fulstan had refused to even let the boy make a progress there to see the place. *It couldn't have hurt,* Thomas thought as Ravenna's pen scratched across the parchment. *He'd have tired of it in a few months, but it would have made him happy. God knows, they might even have been able to teach him something.* Roland resembled his father, with his curling brown hair and blue eyes, but his features were a good deal more delicate. The King's servants would never have let him out of his rooms looking anything other than immaculate, but he still managed to look incongruous in his cloth-of-gold slashed doublet, and the lace of his falling band was beginning to turn.

Galen Dubell climbed the dais and took a seat on the stool a servant whisked into place for him. Roland asked a question and the sorcerer's answer made him laugh. Thomas looked over the crowd for Denzil and spotted him in deep conversation with a man he didn't recognize. Denzil's companion had dark hair and sharp features, and though he was dressed in the heavy brocades of court finery, he was obviously ill at ease. That might not be due to the lofty company: most of the city's monied class was here, bringing with them all the rivalries and old scores that wanted settling. But something about the way he was standing, the way he turned his head, made Thomas think he was observing the crowd and the room with particular care.

If this was some new advisor of Denzil's, he hadn't been in the last report. And if the spies paid to watch Denzil were taking bribes to leave out certain details, then there were going to be a few new heads adorning the spikes on the Prince's Gate come morning. But in that case, surely the man wouldn't casually wander into a court function. *He might be only an acquaintance,* Thomas thought. But Denzil seemed to draw all of his acquaintances into his plots eventually.

Then Denzil broke off the conversation and started toward the dais. "Here it comes," Thomas said quietly to Ravenna.

When the Duke of Alsene bowed in the Dowager Queen's direction she smiled sweetly back at him and nodded graciously.

The steward caught Roland's attention unobtrusively and stepped aside as Denzil bowed.

Roland said, "Welcome, cousin." He looked pitifully glad to see the older man.

With just the right amount of theater Denzil said, "Your Majesty, my home is in danger."

Caught by surprise, Roland said, "You told me your home was here."

Thomas winced. Roland's reply had the distinctive sound of a lovers' quarrel rather than a sovereign dressing down a lord, and the courtiers near the dais were growing quiet to listen.

Denzil recovered smoothly. "It is, Your Majesty. I was speaking of my old home at Bel Garde."

"General Villon has spoken to me about it. It's in violation of my edict because the walls are greater than twelve feet in height." Roland shifted uncomfortably. "They will be careful of the surrounding land, and it will improve the view."

Denzil's expression remained stern. "Your Majesty, it is my ancestral home. Its walls have defended our family for generations, and are a symbol of my allegiance to your crown."

Roland's brow furrowed. "I will give you another manor in compensation. There is an estate at Terrebonne that—"

"My cousin, it is Bel Garde that concerns me." The carefully calculated interruption, the appeal in his expression were all part of the deliberate assertion of his personality over the younger man's.

Thomas could see Roland waver. The King said, "You are a trusted councilor."

Denzil bowed again. "There is none more loyal than I, my cousin, and I need Bel Garde to defend that loyalty."

Then Galen Dubell, forgotten at the King's side, said something to Roland. The King looked down at him, startled.

Denzil caught a hint of something that worried him. Almost too sharply he said, "What was that, Sir?"

Frowning in thought, Roland said, "It is an interesting point. Why do you need the fortress, Sir, when you are under my protection?"

There was a tension in Roland's voice that quieted the rest of the conversations around the dais and stopped Ravenna's pen. Denzil hesitated, staring at the young King. Then he made a gracious bow. "I need it . . . to present it to you, Sire."

There was a moment's silence as the surrounding courtiers digested that, then a polite murmur of congratulations and applause. "Oh, how delightful!" Ravenna exclaimed loudly.

"I accept it, Sir," Roland said happily. "I'll have my best architect put in magnificent gardens, and then I will return it to you."

There was more applause. Ravenna folded the half-written order and handed it to Thomas. "I shall like Bel Garde a great deal with a new formal park."

Thomas allowed himself a slight smile, and dropped the paper into a nearby brazier. "You'll like it even better with your troops all over it."

CHAPTER FOUR

Behind the wooden backdrop of the stage, in the small actors' area curtained off from the glories of the gallery by dusty velvet drapes and a canopy, confusion reigned.

Ignoring the outcries and exclamations from the actors and clowns rushing around in the lamp-lit gloom and musty heat behind her, Kade had enlarged a hole in one of the dark blue curtains to see out to the rear of the gallery. The back wall was mostly paned glass, its windows looking out onto the terraces and a wide expanse of garden designed to provide a harmonious view.

She remembered that garden, though she could see little of it now through the glare of candlelight on window glass and the darkness beyond. She could have pointed to the stand of sycamore trees, or the hill with its classical ruins carefully constructed to look aged and abandoned. She had expected to remember the palace, but she had not expected its sights, textures, and scents to press in on her in such an overpowering way. The walls were stained with powerful auras of old battles, old anger, love, pain. They hummed with the revenants of the emotions and magics of long-dead sorcerers. She had left her own marks here, somewhere. She was not pleased at the idea of coming upon one of them suddenly.

Here Kade had learned her first real sorcery from Galen Dubell. He had taught her High Magic, with its slow painstaking formulas that used alchemy and the powers of the astral bodies to understand and compel the forces that governed the universe. Galen had been an excellent teacher, his instruction touching on everything from the simplest healing charms to the architectures of the Great Spells that eventually took on lives of their own. When he was banished for that teaching, Kade had been sent to the Monelite Convent, where she had learned about herbal poisons and the Low Magic of witchcraft from the village women. Later she had learned what she could of fay magic from her mother, but her human blood kept her from shape-changing and practicing many of the other skills that came so easily to the Fay. It had been Galen's teaching that had enabled her to survive. Human sorcery was painstaking and slow, but powerful, using numbers, symbols, carved stones, music, and other tools to explain the unexplainable, to control and direct the astral forces the Fay only toyed with.

I shouldn't have come back, Kade thought. Somewhere between here and the Mummer's Mask, her courage had fled, leaving her to pick up the pieces of her plan alone. Not that it was a good plan to begin with. She felt an overwhelming desire to discard it and stay with Baraselli's acting troupe for a few weeks. The gods of the wood knew the actors could use the help. Only one thing stopped her.

I might be able to stand feeling like a coward, but I can't live with feeling like this much of a fool. And it would be foolish to turn back when she had come this far. But the more she thought about it, the more the idea of returning to Knockma or Fayre with nothing solved and facing the same old difficulties seemed worse than continuing on this course.

It had become apparent to her that she needed to go home, to the palace at the heart of Ile-Rien, to face her past. To face her half brother Roland, to see if it was really him she hated or the memories and the father he represented. And perhaps to face Ravenna as well, to show the Dowager Queen what that once-unlovely changeling fay child had become. *To get her approval?* Kade asked herself suddenly. *I bloody well hope not.* She bit her lip, fingering the frayed edge of the curtain. *So it's either stay with Baraselli's troupe forever, or go on with what I came to do, what I said I had to do,* she thought. A group of women passed in front of the windows, the light glittering on their satin gowns, gems, and starched lace collars, their motions hampered by layers of underskirts, hip rolls, and fashionable puffed sleeves. *Perhaps I'll wait and see how the play does before I decide.*

She turned back to the troupe's frantic clamor as Garin hopped through the curtained stage doorway. He was immediately attacked by three other actors and their helpers, who began to tear off his Pantalone costume and wrestle him into the Brighella outfit. Kade picked the wig and cap off the floor and handed it to them, trying not to get her fingers torn off by their frantic grasping.

Baraselli peered through a gap in the backdrop. "Terrible," he moaned. "It isn't going well at all."

"Damn it, man, I've done my best," Garin snapped, his voice muffled because Uoshe was forcing a new shirt over his head. "If it isn't good enough, then you get out there."

Unlike other theatricals, Commedia had no playbook for the actors to learn.

The plot was determined by the characters, and the actors learned only the standard lines for one role and supplemented them with whatever jokes or local gossip came to mind. Garin was doing the unfamiliar Brighella role more ad lib than usual and using the standard lines only when he could remember them; it was confusing everyone else terribly.

Garin had taken the extra role because the worst had happened. The Master of Revels and the Cisternan guards who examined entertainers for the court had refused to allow the clown who played Brighella entrance into the palace. The clown had a cousin who was on a list of participants in an ill-fated Aderassi independence revolt. The officials had been terrifyingly polite about the whole thing, and Baraselli, suspecting them all to be magicians of the blackest kind for knowing about it in the first place, had not dared to speak even a word of protest.

In the prisonlike barrenness of the questioning rooms of the St. Anne's Gate Guard House, the troupe had been kept waiting for hours. Partly, Kade knew, to give those who had reason to be nervous a chance to betray themselves, but mostly to allow the clerks to look through the rolls of "undesirable" names that the King's Watch endlessly compiled.

"And what's your name, darling?" the Cisternan guard had asked Kade when it came her turn.

Kade knew the robed academician in the corner of the whitewashed questioning room was a sorcerer, using spells to search out hostile magic. As the guard asked her the question, Kade felt the sorcerer's spell settle over her like a cold mist, invisible and intangible to anyone not trained in magic. It met the masking spell she had prepared and set around herself hours earlier, then slid across and away without friction. The sorcerer's second and third spells did the same. He stopped there, just as her masking spell was beginning to fray on the edges. He might have cast five or six spells and caught her out; Kade, being Kade, had taken that risk. If the sorcerer had detected either her magic or that she was fay, she would have thought of something else.

In answer to the guard's question, she had said, "Katherine of Merewatch. They call me Kade." Merewatch was a hamlet near the place she made her home much of the time, and so it was factual enough not to set off the truth spell that blanketed the whole room. It was a complex spell, older than she was, as intricate and detailed as the inside of a Portier clockwork toy. It had the combination of ruthless logic and artistry about it that marked it as old Dr. Surete's work. Despite great temptation, she decided not to tamper with it.

The guard stared at her a moment. She had a minor qualm, wondering if they had really burned the only portrait of her, as Roland had claimed they had so long ago. But the man only said, "You ought to change that, you know. Could make trouble for you."

"But it's what my mum calls me."

"Your lookout, then. And how's your mum's family called?"

"She didn't have one that I knew of. In Merewatch they called her Maira." Also true; the deep northern brogue of the Merewatch inhabitants rendered Moire as Maira. Kade sensed a faint tremor in Surete's truth spell, but her statement was on that very narrow line of truth and falsehood, and it didn't betray her.

Neither questions nor spells had shown anything odd about the actor who played Arlequin, and that puzzled Kade.

She had suspected him of something, of what she wasn't completely sure, but she knew the palace's protections to be good ones. She had gotten through them with a substantial helping of fayre luck and the willingness to take a risk, and she knew that having been born inside the wards had let her pass them and any other traps Surete might have laid. It didn't seem possible that an ordinary human sorcerer could accomplish it.

Perhaps he's just an ass, she thought, watching the Arlequin now in the backstage confusion. He was sitting on a props box, watching the others with a grin, cool and unaffected by the frantic activity.

Kade lifted her leather Columbine mask and wiped the sweat off her face. She knew she should be going onstage again soon, but with all the Brighella confusion, she couldn't tell if they were getting close to her part or not. Possibly overwhelmed with relief at sighting the end of the play, the others might skip her last entrance entirely.

Kade moved to where she could glimpse the front of the Grand Gallery through a gap where the curtain met the stage's edge. There was a good view of the dais from here.

If seeing the palace again affected her, it was even more of a shock to see its inhabitants. *Roland has changed—for the worse,* she thought. *Worse still, Ravenna hasn't changed at all.* Despite the new gray in her red hair, the Dowager Queen was still delicate, still lovely, and still ruthlessly self-assured. And every woman at court was still hiding behind a fan while following Thomas Boniface with her eyes. That Kade had joined in this pastime enthusiastically as a child somehow did not make it any better. She had to admit, at least in the privacy of her own thoughts, that while he was a touchy and arrogant bastard, he was still well worth looking at.

She remembered deep-set dark eyes, and a remarkably ironic smile. He had long been known as one of the jewels of the court, even when blond gallants were more often in fashion. She watched him leave the dais and cross the crowded gallery until he was out of her view. He must be nearing forty now, but the years hadn't changed him much and there was only a little gray in that dark hair. *Don't be an even bigger fool than you already are,* Kade told herself. He and Ravenna had been made for each other.

Baraselli had given off moaning and now raced around trying to collect the props for the finish. He rushed up to Kade and thrust a gold candelabrum at her. "Quick, hold this."

An instant later she realized it was gold paint over iron and dropped the thing with a curse. It clanged on the tiled floor.

"What is it?" Baraselli cried out, with the same hysterical urgency he would've shown if she had fallen to the floor in a dead faint.

"I sprained a finger," she growled at him, tucking her smarting hands under her armpits.

"A sprain? Oh God, it could've been your foot!" He grabbed up the candelabrum and fled toward the stage with it.

Fayre luck, hell, Kade thought. She could hear Silvetta shouting at one of the heroes and vaguely remembered she should be onstage for that.

She headed for the curtain. If she hadn't stood there like a dolt and held the thing . . . The intensity of her magic could be affected for a short time.

———

When Queen Falaise entered with Aristofan, or Semuel Porter, on her arm, and Lieutenant Gideon and the rest of her escort trailing her, Thomas had decided it would be more politic at the moment to leave the dais and take a turn through the crowd. He also wanted to find Dr. Dubell, and caught up with him as the sorcerer was leaving the gallery.

They stood in one of the gracefully arched doorways at the opposite end of the room, just far enough away from the milling groups of guests to be able to hear each other.

"You may have made an enemy," Thomas told him.

"Possibly, but I certainly didn't intend to provoke all that." Dubell looked back toward the dais, frowning a little.

Thomas leaned against the curve of the archway and regarded him thought-fully. "What did you say to Roland?"

"Well, he asked me what I taught at Lodun besides sorcery, and I told him it was debate and logic, and we spoke a bit about how orators use it. Then Lord Denzil started his speech. Finally I couldn't contain myself. I said, 'It's an in-valid argument.' His Majesty said, 'What is?' and I said, 'He seems to be claim-ing that he needs the fortress to protect you, but under landlaw of course you're his protector.' The King quite liked that idea, I think." Dubell shook his head, ruefully amused. "It's almost the right phase of the moon to start the crucial work on the palace wards, and I'd hate to be distracted. At Lodun we're all very experienced in how to give each other the cold shoulder at dinner, but I've been away from court so long I'm out of practice dealing with quarrels of this kind."

"The thing to do would be to bring it to my attention, at least in your case," Thomas said.

"Would it?" Dubell met his eyes seriously.

"It would."

"Then I will remember to do that." Dubell inclined his head. "Good night, Captain."

Dubell left, and Thomas turned back into the gallery. He had never offered either support or protection to anyone at court lightly, and he wasn't really certain what had prompted him to do it for Galen Dubell. Except perhaps that the old man had survived decades of court intrigues and still seemed to have retained both his optimism and his honesty, and Thomas didn't want to see that change. He looked back toward the dais where Denzil now sat at Roland's feet, making his King laugh at something, all ill feeling apparently forgotten.

Apparently.

Thomas turned away from the dais and looked around for Dr. Braun, but if the young sorcerer was here he was lost in the crowd.

The Commedia was almost over. Thomas hadn't paid much attention to it, except to notice that it was a little better than the farces performed almost nonstop for market-day crowds. This troupe had apparently altered its perfor-mance to accommodate a more sophisticated audience. He stopped near the stage beside a group of outland nobility to watch two of the clowns performing the climactic sword duel. Instead of uncoordinated acrobatics that would have bored most of their audience, with its connoisseur's appreciation of dueling, they did it in exaggeratedly slow motion, allowing them to perform intricate moves that would otherwise have been beyond them.

Thomas had also noticed the masked actress who played Columbine. She was standing within about twenty feet of him on the opposite end of the stage from the other actors and was the apparent instigator of the duel for some reason that he assumed would make sense if he had seen the entire thing. With tousled blond hair and a red dress that would have been more appropriate on a disreputable wood nymph, she was hardly as glamorous as the two demure heroines, but she had her tattered skirts kilted for the acrobatics and undoubtedly had the most attractive knees.

Oddly, the actor playing the Arlequin stood behind her in the shadow of a painted scenery column, not quite off the stage but not on it enough to be part of the action. There was something in the man's stance that kept Thomas's attention. The Arlequin seemed to be focused on the actress a few feet in front of him, and not on the mock duel. His half mask was dark and trimmed with coarse false hair, with deep scarring wrinkles around its pinhole eyes and snub nose. His brown baggy clothes were patched and torn, and there was a bedraggled rabbit tail on the top of his cap. Then the Arlequin took a half step forward and the air around his bare feet seemed to blur. The shadows near the column pooled around him like tar.

Thomas swore, turned, and brushed past the spectators, headed toward the Cisternan guard stationed at the nearest archway. He grabbed the guard's pike and said, "Get Galen Dubell; get him now."

The guard stared. "Sir . . . ?"

"He should be on his way to the North Bastion. Tell him we're under attack. And give me that."

This settled the Cisternan's hesitation at taking orders from another officer. He surrendered the pike and slipped back out of the archway.

"What is it?" The Cisternan Commander Vivan hurried over from his post.

Thomas said curtly, "The actor playing the Arlequin is in the process of transforming into something. Get ready to contain it or we're all going to be dead."

Vivan looked toward the stage, startled, then headed toward the next Cisternan guardpost at a run.

Thomas took the pike and started toward the Arlequin, ignoring the curious stares. His pistols weren't loaded and there wasn't time to do it. He came up behind the Arlequin at an angle, out of its line of vision. Through the breaks in the scenery he saw more Cisternans edging up behind the stage. A murmur of unease grew as the crowd saw the guards moving and began to sense something wrong.

The change was so quick it was moments before the panic started. Suddenly the Arlequin's exposed flesh turned mottled and patchy and the actor's leather mask and rough costume seemed to enlarge and meld with its face and body. Then it was twice the size of the man it had been and its legs were taking on the demon-shape of a goat's hindquarters.

A woman in the crowd screamed, and up on the stage the Columbine actress whirled and saw the Arlequin just as the creature rocked forward to leap at her. Not close enough yet to do anything else, Thomas threw the pike.

The weapon struck the Arlequin's arm, staggering it. Wailing, it jerked the pike out and tossed it away, scattering yellowed bits of flesh.

The crowd and the actors fled in panic and the Cisternans had to fight their way through the rush.

Trying to push past the panicked spectators himself, Thomas saw the Arlequin strike one of the actors who hadn't fled quickly enough, slamming him through the wooden backdrop. It pushed a column aside, knocked another actress down, then charged the woman playing Columbine. Incredibly, she waited until it was almost on her, then ducked out of the way and leapt off the stage. Its own momentum carried the Arlequin to the end of the platform before it could stop itself and turn.

Thomas broke free of the crowd and picked up the fallen pike. The Cisternan guards circled the stage, pikes leveled at the snarling creature. Thomas moved to join them, noting that some of his own men were running up to help. He hoped Gideon was getting Ravenna and Falaise out of the gallery, but he couldn't spare a look over his shoulder.

A shot went off from somewhere behind them, then another, echoing thunderously against the marble facings, but the Arlequin didn't react. Thomas knew there were some creatures of Fayre immune to gunfire and silently damned Galen Dubell for not being here. The Arlequin darted at one of the Cisternans, testing them. It seemed reluctant to face the pikes again. Thomas shouted, "Steady, we can hold it!"

He glanced sideways and saw the masked Columbine actress, a little to the side and behind him, watching the Arlequin.

Everyone else with any sense had long since fled. "Get out of here!" he yelled at her.

She glanced at him and obligingly backed up a few steps. *Madwoman,* Thomas thought.

Abruptly the Arlequin rushed forward with sudden and blinding speed. It slammed into two Cisternans, knocked both men aside with a force that must have broken their necks, then changed course and lunged toward Thomas.

It caught the top of his pike before he could brace the butt against the floor. He let go and dove out of the way. The Arlequin overshot and crashed into a brandywine fountain in an explosion of plaster and brass pipes. Dripping with brandywine, it struggled out of the debris and turned to come at him again as he rolled to his feet. A guard threw another pike at the creature and caught it a glancing blow as Thomas drew his rapier. The Arlequin pounced forward and was almost on top of Thomas when he shoved the sword into its chest.

The creature's forward motion against the rapier sent Thomas falling backward. His back struck the hard floor, momentarily knocking the breath out of him. Then the Arlequin straddled him, falling forward on top of him. Its smell was foul, like rancid milk. Desperately he twisted the hilt and pushed, the creature's own weight helping to drive the rapier through cartilage and muscle. He felt the vibration through the hilt as the blade snapped, then the Arlequin shrieked and leapt away from him.

Thomas scrambled back and shoved to his feet. One of the Cisternans tossed him a sword, but the Arlequin leapt backward onto the stage. At least the thing was slowing down—and still dripping brandywine. Thomas glanced around and spotted one of his men. "Martin, go get a torch."

The Arlequin paced around on the creaking wood of the stage, snarling at them. As Thomas glanced back he saw that the actress who had been struck down in the first attack was on her hands and knees, trying to crawl toward the edge of the stage. Before he could move to distract the Arlequin, it whirled and saw her. She screamed and the Arlequin grabbed up a painted column and hurled it at her.

Suddenly Columbine was on the stage and shoving the other woman out of the way. The wooden missile hit her in the back and knocked her off the stage, sending her crashing to the floor in a heap of splintered wood.

Damn it, Thomas thought. *Damn brave madwoman.* He looked around as Martin ran up with the lit torch, a makeshift affair of a chair leg, a torn piece of someone's underskirt, and lamp oil. Thomas took it and moved forward slowly. The Arlequin shifted away, wary, ready to charge again.

Thomas's first thought was to lure it away from the wooden stage, knowing the stone and marble facings in the rest of the room would give them time to put the fire out. But he suspected the Arlequin's instinct would be to take as many people with it as possible; when it was racing around like a monstrous torch, it would have plenty of opportunity.

In the pile of shattered wood, the Columbine actress stirred. She pushed herself up, shaking her head dizzily as her actor's mask fell away. Thomas was thinking, *She must have a head as hard as a brick* . . . Then she looked up and saw the Arlequin just as it turned and saw her.

Instead of rushing her, it gave that wailing cry again. Thomas took the moment of distraction to run forward and hurl the torch.

He saw the actress struggle to her knees, her hands a flurry of motion. Thinking it over later, he thought she had scraped up a handful of splinters, spat on them, and tossed them at the Arlequin. They flew farther than their weight allowed, blown by some invisible wind to scatter around the creature's feet.

The torch struck the brandy-soaked fur on the Arlequin's chest, which caught fire as if it had been dipped in pitch. The Arlequin wailed and battered at the air around it, as if fighting an invisible wall. Something trapped it, holding it contained, a hardening of the air that the heat of the flames shivered against.

The Arlequin dissolved into a cloud of thick black smoke. Its wails ceased and it curled up like a roll of paper kindling. Thomas saw Dubell arrive through the arched doorway leading from the long hall, and realized the fight had lasted only a short time.

Actors and guests who had scattered around the room behind columns or furniture began to emerge from hiding.

The guards began to search around for wounded and dead. Thomas walked slowly over to where the Columbine actress still sat in a pile of scrap wood. She watched the monster burn with a grin of undisguised triumph.

He already knew who she must be, but it still took him what seemed moments to put together the direct gray eyes and the long straight nose with a forgotten portrait in an upstairs hall, and with the wildness of the magic she had just performed.

Kade looked up at him, met his gaze, then winked.

CHAPTER FIVE

Thomas said, "May I congratulate you on a spectacular entrance?"

Kade looked up at him from the floor. After a moment, her lips twisted ruefully. "It was one of my best."

Dubell moved to Thomas's side. He looked at what was left of the Arlequin, at the destruction in the gallery, and down at Kade. "Was this your doing?" His voice was incredulous.

For a moment her expression was that of a small child caught stealing an apple. "No." As she got to her feet, Thomas saw there were wood chips in her hair from the broken column the Arlequin had thrown at her. She seemed defensive. "It followed me here."

Thomas moved a few paces away. The Cisternans and his own men were scattered, collecting the wounded and the dead. There were still courtiers milling around toward the end of the room. Now would be a terrible time for a pitched battle.

Dubell met Kade's eyes a long moment, then he said thoughtfully, "Did it really?"

"Well, in a way it did." She began to pull the splinters out of her hair. "But it joined the troupe before I did, and I think it killed one of the clowns to get a place. I would have stopped it sooner but I'd touched some iron, and it took a bit to wear off."

Renier and a group of Albon knights burst in through the archway and started toward them. The hide-and-sackcloth coats they wore over the lace and velvets of court finery made them look like ancient barbarians arriving to loot a city. Thomas went forward quickly to stop Renier. "Let Dubell handle her," he said in a low voice.

Renier signaled his knights to halt. "Who is she?"

"Kade Carrion."

Renier stared. "My God, we've got to—"

"No," Thomas said pointedly. "If he can get us out of this without a blood-bath, we've got to let him try."

Renier considered, then nodded tensely. "Very well." He signaled the other knights to move back.

Thomas nodded, thankful that while Renier wasn't a particularly brilliant statesman, he wasn't a bloodthirsty idiot either.

"Did she cause all this?" Renier asked, frowning around at the chaos in the gallery.

Thomas glanced back at Kade and Galen Dubell. She watched them, wary and a little angry. Her brows were darker than the pale blond of her hair, so the effect was that when she was looking at you, you knew it. He thought about her leaping to push the other actress out of danger and said slowly, "I don't think so."

Then Kade's eyes focused past them and her expression changed. Thomas followed her gaze and swore. Roland stood in the archway the knights had come through. Thomas said, "Renier . . ."

"What?" Renier looked around and gasped. "Damn that boy." He sheathed his sword and strode toward Roland, deliberately placing himself between the King and the sorceress.

Thomas turned back toward Kade, aware that the other guards in the room had held off on his order. He would have to decide what he minded more, dying or behaving this stupidly.

Galen Dubell watched Kade thoughtfully. With gentle firmness he said, "Kade, don't."

She looked up at the older man, her gaze losing some of its intensity. "I didn't come here to kill anyone—even him."

Renier, as Preceptor of the Albonate Knights and the only man in Ile-Rien allowed to touch the King without his permission, seized Roland's arm and hustled him out of sight. Dubell watched as they disappeared, then turned a worried eye on Kade. "Then why did you come here?"

She smiled. "For an audience with my dear brother, of course."

And that, Thomas thought, *is not going to help matters at all.*

———

The gallery smelled of ash and sour wine. Many of the chandeliers and lamps had gone out, throwing the upper half of the huge chamber into shadow. The court had been dispersed, and Ravenna, Roland, and Falaise had retired to a nearby solar with watchful guards. A breeze, created by an open door or window somewhere up one of the long galleries, swept gently through the huge chamber, lifting the heat and the stench.

"How long had he been with the troupe?" Thomas asked Baraselli.

The Aderassi actor-manager moaned and would have sunk to his knees again but for the two Queen's guards who were struggling to hold him up. The Master of Revels hovered worriedly nearby; it was on his responsibility the troupe had passed the final check at the gate.

"No one's done anything to you, and no one will, if you just answer the question." Thomas kept his voice mild, despite his growing irritation. It was easier to question recalcitrant anarchists under torture than someone who was so busy collapsing that he could hardly stay coherent enough to speak.

"Only a month. Only a month. I didn't know!"

Dubell had moved quietly up behind the actor-manager. His lips moved soundlessly for a moment, then he looked up at Thomas and nodded. Baraselli was telling the truth.

"Who recommended him?" Thomas nodded to the guards, who cautiously released their hold of the man and stepped back.

Baraselli swayed on his feet, but stayed upright. "It was his first mask, he told me. He'd learned it from an old actor he lived near. He did it well, and he came to us just after Derani died."

"Who was Derani?"

"He played the Arlequin until he died of fever."

Dubell asked, "What were the symptoms?"

Baraselli whipped around, staring at the tall sorcerer in fear, but something in Dubell's expression and mild demeanor calmed him. He said, "He . . . His skin was hot to the touch, and his wife said he couldn't keep anything down, not even water, and he had blood in his, pardon, piss, and . . . We paid to have the apothecary in to him, but he just died."

There was something familiar about that. And convenient, for the Arlequin. Thomas asked, "When was this?"

"Last month. Well, a month and a fortnight ago."

Thomas shook his head, pressing his lips together. There was a pattern here, a deadly one. He looked up at Dubell. "About a month and a fortnight ago Dr. Surete's assistant, Milam, fell down a stairway in the North Bastion and broke his neck. A week after that Surete himself died of pleurisy. It came on suddenly, and by the time anyone realized how serious it was, he was dead."

Dubell's brows drew together as he considered it. He said, "It's the easiest of dark magics to bring sickness, and the hardest to detect. It's simplicity itself to send a bookish and uncoordinated young scholar down a staircase. If one has the stomach for that sort of thing, of course." He nodded at Baraselli. "He's telling the truth, and I doubt he can reasonably be held responsible for Kade's actions. What will be done with him?"

Even without the confirmation of Dubell's truth spell, Thomas was inclined to believe Baraselli. He had observed enough people under stress to read the sincerity in those hysterics. He told the Master of Revels, "Give him his money and tell him to take the others and go away."

Baraselli sobbed and tried to fall to his knees in thanks. The Master of Revels gestured sharply to the Cisternans waiting nearby, who intercepted the actor-manager in mid-grovel and hauled him away.

"It's either a hell of a coincidence, or a hell of a plot," Thomas said quietly to Dubell. He knew which he favored.

Dubell sighed. "There are no coincidences."

Thomas watched him thoughtfully. "I would have thought it difficult for a wizard to hex another wizard, especially someone like Dr. Surete. He was the Court Sorcerer for two decades."

"If a sorcerer is in fear for his life, he might test every object he is about to touch with a sprinkle of gasçoign powder or some other preparation that reveals the presence of magic." Dubell made an absent gesture. "But Surete and Milam were not in fear for their lives. The spell could have come to them on anything—a forged letter purporting to be from a friend, an apple sold to them by a street vendor. . . ."

As Dubell stood lost in thought, Thomas watched their other guest. Kade Carrion paced around the remains of the stage that the servants were dismantling. As she walked around the painted panels scattered on the floor and the stacks of singed planks, he had two distinct impressions of her. The first was that she was only a young girl with a tangled mop of hair and a tattered red dress, not oblivious to the consternation she was causing but not particularly worried by it either. The other was that here was a creature ephemeral yet solid and real, who walked with the night and the wild hunt. *Dubell is the only one who really knows her,* Thomas thought. *And even he isn't certain what her game is now.*

If she hated her brother and the rest of the royal family as much as she claimed, she wasn't without motive. Their father, Fulstan, hadn't been much use as a king: he had neither Ravenna's head for finance and diplomacy nor the ability to listen intelligently to advisors who did. The fayre queen Moire had drained him of what vitality and strength of character he possessed, leaving him bitter and old before his time. He had taken out his anger at Moire's abrupt departure on anyone in his reach, especially on Moire's daughter. No one directly in his power had mourned his death.

Urbain Grandier, however, had no motive, at least not one that Thomas knew.

Kade might be in league with the Bisran sorcerer, but discovering what she knew wasn't going to be easy.

Dubell was looking toward the center of the stage platform, where what was left of the Arlequin had burned down into a heap of some foul-smelling dark powder. "Be careful not to step in that black powder," he called to the servants who were warily clearing away the debris. Then Dubell turned and saw Kade, whose curiosity had already led her ankle-deep into the black powder. She lifted her head, surreptitiously rubbed a stained bare foot against her calf and looked the other way. Dubell shook his head irritably.

The Albon knights had by now arrived in force. There were about forty of them in the gallery, guarding the arched doorways and the terrace windows, pacing the musicians' balconies, and watching Kade. The rest of their number were patrolling the palace with most of Thomas's men and the Cisternans.

Behind the dais, Renier emerged from the wide oak door inset with panels of stained glass. It was the gallery entrance to the solar where the royal family had retired to fight things out. He walked up to Thomas and said softly, "Roland wanted to put her under arrest, but Ravenna has talked him out of it. Apparently she's in favor of giving the sorceress the audience she wants, and trying to settle it quietly."

Thomas thought wearily, *Yes, Renier, tell me all about how the anointed King still can't win an argument with his mother.* He said, "Really."

Renier either did not recognize the sarcasm or ignored it out of habit. "My guess is they'll give her the audience."

Thomas eyed him. "Very likely. I suppose, in the long run, it is better than going to war with her in the middle of the palace, killing everyone who stumbles into the way."

As Galen Dubell turned back to them, Renier asked, "Dr. Dubell, could you tell what that creature was?"

Dubell nodded, gesturing back toward the ruin of the stage. "It wasn't fay. It was a construction of wood and animal bone, animated by a very powerful spell, called a golem. I'm not sure, but I imagine it was designed to resist anything the weight and size of a pistol ball. It's a relatively new technique which I believe will come in quite handy on the battlefield once it's perfected. Doesn't help at all for cannonballs, though. The combination of the weight and size—" Dubell recollected himself and shook his head. "But that is neither here nor there."

"How did it get past the wards?" Thomas asked, looking at the heap of black powder.

Dubell met his eyes frankly. "I've done some work with the wards, nothing that should weaken them. They shouldn't have let this creature pass through. I believe something has affected the ward structure, making the gaps their continual movement creates larger, making those gaps appear in locations predictable to someone. It would take an intimate knowledge of the construction of the wards, at least as great a knowledge as Dr. Surete had, but it would be possible. And, perhaps more disturbing, the spell that caused the golem to shape-change from the appearance of a man to that of the creature we saw here would have to be actuated by someone close at hand."

Slowly, Thomas said, "You mean the sorcerer was here, in the gallery."

"Or an assistant, who carried in the charm designed to trigger the golem. I have looked for Grandier's power-signature, but the ether in this room is free of it." Dubell nodded to himself. "Yes, I believe it was only an assistant who was here tonight."

"What a chance to take," Renier said sourly. "There was a witchman who tried to cause trouble last year. Surete said there was a disturbance in the wards, and had some of us come with him while he tracked it to the source. We found the witchman hiding in an empty house in the Philosopher's Cross, sitting on the floor and crying like a baby. Surete said he must have tried to do a sending against someone in the palace, but the wards stopped it and followed his magic back to him and took his mind away. We knew that he tried something because he had more witch-poisons and hair amulets on him than you can imagine, but it didn't help him at all."

Dubell's attention had gone back to Kade; his expression was worried. *As well it might be,* Thomas thought. Had the golem been activated by a confederate of Grandier's or by Kade herself? He nodded to Kade, who was still wandering the stage. "Did she tell you why she wanted an audience with Roland?"

"No." Dubell was silent a moment. "Her abilities here, in the mortal world, are not as great as when she is in Fayre, and it is difficult to fatally wound her with anything other than a weapon of iron. But . . . it appeared the creature was attacking her?"

"Yes," Thomas admitted. It had certainly meant to kill her.

"I hope so, for all our sakes."

The door to the solar opened and one of the stewards emerged, harried and somewhat the worse for wear. He hesitated, then approached Thomas and Renier. He said, "His Majesty will see the sorceress now."

Thomas said, "Good. Go and tell her."

The steward blanched visibly.

Thomas relented. "Very well, I'll tell her."

As Thomas approached, Kade looked up, a strange creature not at all like the child he barely remembered, or the fifteen-year-old girl in the portrait. He said, "His Majesty will see you now."

She lifted her brows. "Will he? And I thought he would be so glad to see me he'd have run out into my arms long before this." There was a bitterness underneath the light irony in her voice.

"You were mistaken."

"I suppose." She shrugged, abandoning repartee with a disconcerting abruptness.

Thomas turned and walked back toward the solar's door without looking to see if she followed.

After a moment she caught up with him. "This isn't turning out right at all," she muttered.

He glanced down at her. "Oh? Who did you plan for the Arlequin to kill?"

She snorted. "You don't really believe that. And I don't know who sent it so you won't find out from me." Her mouth quirked. "Oh, was I supposed to pale and let something slip at that point? I'm sorry, I was thinking of something else."

Thomas didn't slam the door of the solar open with any more force than necessary, and bowed her in with elaborate courtesy.

The old solar wasn't used much, and the three huge windows covering the farther wall had already been shuttered by painted panels in preparation for winter. The scene on the panels was a lurid traditional hunting landscape, subtly at odds with the other paintings on the oak-sheathed walls, the hangings of brocaded satin and striped silk, and the delicately carved furniture. Thomas remembered that this room was one of those that had been redecorated after the death of Roland's father; the painted panels reflected the old king's taste, and had probably been left unaltered by mistake. He thought Ravenna might have chosen the room for that rather than its convenience to the gallery.

Roland was slumped in his chair in a sulk, Denzil seated beside him. Falaise's face was still a little reddened under the powder, as if she had been weeping from anger. She had chestnut hair and blue eyes, and her natural prettiness had been transformed by her coiffure and costume into fashionable beauty. She wore a blue gown trimmed with gold ribbons and seed pearls, and against the somber colors of the rest of the room she looked like an orchid thrown into a dirty alley. Ravenna was the only one who appeared calm. Her hands were busy on her embroidery and she didn't look up at their arrival.

There was a stiff silence in the room and the dregs of a bitter argument lay heavy in the air.

Thomas realized it was his duty to announce Kade, the steward having apparently seized the opportunity to escape. Sensing that calling her "the evil fay sorceress" would probably please her no end, he said, "The Princess Katherine Fontainon," then moved to take his place at Ravenna's side.

Kade's fair skin made her helpless against a sudden blush.

Ravenna looked up and said, "How lovely to see you again, dear child."

Kade curtsied in what had to be an intentionally graceless fashion. "I'm sure it's just as lovely for you as it is for me, Stepmother."

"I'm not your stepmother, dear," Ravenna reminded her calmly. "Your mother did not bother with the travesty of marriage with your father, and it would hardly have served the purpose if she had, because he was already my husband at the time. You know this, but it seems to please you to hear me repeat it."

In a whisper plainly audible to the rest of the room, Denzil said to Roland, "Cousin, this is all too dull."

Ravenna snapped, "Roland, send him away. This is private."

Roland glared. "I could ask you to send your paramour away too, Mother."

In the ensuing moment of silence, Kade snorted in amusement.

Thomas glanced briefly heavenward. Denzil looked at Roland in irritation as the implication in the unfortunate phrasing of the King's retort sunk in.

Realizing what he had said and reddening faintly, Roland continued defiantly, "This is a family matter and he is the only one of my family who is truly fond of me."

"What a sad thought," Kade added helpfully. "Sad, but true."

Roland stared at her, meeting her eyes for the first time since she had entered the room. "What do you want here?"

Kade ignored the question. She looked to Ravenna, who had gone back to her embroidery. After a moment the Dowager Queen said, "And how is your dear mother, child?" as if her prepared greeting had never been interrupted.

Ravenna's expression was as polite as a judge passing sentence; Kade looked ironic and amused. "She's in Hell," she said.

Ravenna's brows lifted. "Wistful thinking, certainly."

"Oh no, she really is," Kade assured her. "We saw her go. She lost a wager."

"My condolences," Ravenna said dryly, as the rest of the room digested that. Kade had just reminded them all of her strangeness, and Ravenna had taken the point. "Now tell us why you've come here in this unseemly fashion, as an actress of all things, bringing an enemy with you and disturbing our peace."

"What are you more worried about, that I brought you a battle or that I was with an acting troupe? Never mind." Kade shrugged, playing with the frayed threads on the edge of her sleeve. "I have quite a few enemies; I can't help it if they follow me about. As to why I'm here . . ." She paced a few steps, not looking at them, hands clasped behind her back and the dingy lace of her petticoats swirling around her feet. "I just wanted to see my family, and my dear younger brother."

The slight emphasis on the word "younger" made Roland sit up and flush.

Kade looked from Ravenna to Roland, her gray eyes passing over the quietly watching Falaise.

This isn't turning out right at all, she had said outside, Thomas remembered.

Ravenna just watched her, until Kade said, "I want to make an agreement with you."

"Was it agreement you wanted when you sent my court those cursed gifts?" Roland demanded. "How many of us have you tried to kill?"

"Then there's the death of King Fulstan," Denzil added helpfully, before Kade could answer. "His illness was very sudden, was it not?"

"I see no point in resurrecting either the dead, or the rumors of years past." The gaze Ravenna turned on Roland's cousin should have transformed him into stone. He only nodded politely at her. "Kade, what agreement are you—"

Unable to contain himself, Roland interrupted, "Why would we want to deal with you, sister?" Contempt twisted his voice. "You've threatened us, ridiculed us—"

"Threatened? Oh, what a king you are, Roland." Kade clasped her hands dramatically and said mockingly in falsetto, "Oh, help, my sister is threatening me!" She looked down at her brother, lip curled in disgust. "If I wanted to kill you, you would be dead."

Roland was on his feet. "You think so?" he said. "When you cursed the name of our family—"

"You mewling idiot, so did you!" Kade shouted, her sarcasm abruptly giving way to rage.

"You're lying; I never did. It was you who—"

"Silence, both of you," Ravenna said, but something in her tone told Thomas she had rather enjoyed the argument.

Brother and sister stared at each other a long moment. Kade's hands were at her sides, curling into fists, uncurling.

Damn it, he's too close to her, Thomas thought. The Albon knight nearest Roland had eased forward, ready to snatch him out of his sister's reach.

Then Roland turned away from her and threw himself down in his chair. Kade turned her back on him and walked stiffly to the other side of the room, her hands shaking.

Into the silence Ravenna said, "You haven't said what agreement you want to make, dear."

In a voice almost a whisper, Kade said, "You make me wish I never . . ." She stopped, shook her head. "Landlaw and courtlaw, Stepmother. Landlaw favors the first-blooded child of the female line. That's Roland. But courtlaw favors the first-blooded child of the male ruler. That's me." Kade stopped to watch them a moment, their silence, their concentration.

She shrugged. "Roland's little ass is planted firmly on the throne. That gives him the advantage. And you base your power on landlaw, Stepmother. You founded your regency on the rights it gave you. You keep your guard by its traditions." She met Thomas's eyes a moment. He returned her gaze imperturbably. She went on, "But there are still those who think I should have been the heir."

Without looking up from her embroidery, Ravenna said, "Do you want to be Queen, dear? When you were fifteen you said you didn't. You spat on the throne and said it was a foul thing and you wouldn't have it as a gift. And yes, there are still those who would put you on it, or at least long enough to secure the succession for a more manageable candidate."

Kade shrugged. "It's caused you no more trouble than it has me."

"Then what is your solution, dear?"

"I'll sign an agreement formally giving up my claim on the throne and any Fontainon family properties. Have your counselors draw it up." She gestured eloquently at the King. "And I'll even stop 'threatening' Roland."

Ravenna frowned. "And what do you want in return?"

Kade was deliberately silent until Ravenna looked up at her. "The freedom of my old home," she said softly.

"That's impossible," Roland said, his voice low and harsh.

"Oh, it's hardly that," Kade told him.

Ravenna still looked thoughtful. "And what has brought this change of heart about?"

"I have my own reasons." Kade smiled thinly. "You don't have anything I want enough to make me tell you what they are."

"But why, dear?" Ravenna seemed genuinely curious.

"Because I want it."

Ravenna lifted her brows. "That isn't much of a reason."

Kade made her a half bow. "It's always been enough for you."

Have to give her that one, Thomas thought. *Good shot.*

Ravenna's hands paused on the fabric and she stared at Kade. Her voice hardened. "You don't know enough to judge me, Katherine."

Kade tilted her head. "Don't I? You've always thought yourself fit to judge me. It's only fair."

"You are young, you know nothing, and life is not fair."

"I know enough, and life is what you make it."

There was a pause.

Ravenna said quietly, "If you are to stay here, there are proprieties that must be observed. . . ."

"No conditions. I haven't made any." Kade smiled. "It's only fair."

The whole idea was so unlikely it took Thomas a few moments to realize that Ravenna was seriously considering it. In a low voice, he said to her, "It isn't worth it, my lady. It's too dangerous."

"Very likely," Kade agreed, idly twisting a lock of her pale hair.

Thomas knelt beside Ravenna's chair so he could see her face. "Don't do it."

Ravenna looked at him, then regarded Kade for a long moment. Her opaque blue eyes betrayed no emotion. She said, "I accept your proposition, dear."

"No," Roland said, his voice unsteady. "I forbid it."

Ravenna turned a basilisk gaze on her son. He trembled, whether from anger or fear it was difficult to tell, but said, "I won't have her here."

For a long heartbeat the outcome was in doubt. Thomas realized he was holding his breath. The room was silent in suspense, as if they observed someone poised on the brink of a chasm. Even Denzil had lost his expression of detached amusement and watched the struggle in fascination.

Then Roland's nerve broke. He pounded his fist on the chair arm and shouted, "I don't want her here! Damn you, can't you listen to me?"

It was a retreat. A shadow crossed Denzil's face that might almost have been disappointment. Ravenna started to speak but Kade interrupted her. "Oh, come now, Roland." She smiled. "You have more to worry about than me."

He glared at her uncertainly. "What do you mean?"

She said, "The palace wards are still in place. I felt them when I came in." She frowned thoughtfully and laid a hand flat on the marble veneer of the fireplace. She curled her fingers, drawing something out of the stone that was gray and wriggled.

It came out with a shower of stone chips, but without leaving a hole in the mantel. Kade held it between thumb and forefinger like a boy with a rat, a spidery, boneless thing that struggled frantically. It was hard for the eyes to fix on it. "This is a frid. It's harmless. It lives in stone and eats crumbs spilled on the floor. But it shouldn't be here."

She dropped it. It hit the hardwood floor with a splat, hopped once to reach the hearthstone, and disappeared beneath the pitted gray rock like a duck diving under water.

"I'd say the wards aren't proof against the Fay anymore. You have a problem, Stepmother." Kade bowed to the room in general and was out the door before anyone could react.

Roland leapt up and moved to stand over Ravenna's chair. "You have overreached yourself this time, Mother," he said. The protest convinced no one. His face was red with thwarted anger, but he had lost his chance to defy her.

"Have I? What would you have done, Roland?" she asked, as if not terribly concerned with his answer.

"Arrested her!"

"And if she didn't want to go with the guards? Power is relative, my lord." Ravenna let heat creep into her voice. "I thought I'd taught you that if nothing else. Tell me you understand."

She looked up at him, waiting. Roland stared at her.

Lounging back in his chair, Denzil said, smiling, "Really, cousin, it's beneath your notice."

Roland turned to him. After a moment he nodded. "Perhaps you're right." He looked back to Ravenna, lips twisted with contempt. "Do what you like, Mother; it doesn't concern me."

Then Roland stalked toward the door, his page scrambling to open it for him and his knights smoothly surrounding him.

Denzil stood and bowed to Ravenna with an ironic smile. "Congratulations, my lady. Very well played."

Ravenna watched him, her eyes opaque. "How old are you, Denzil?"

"I am twenty-six, my lady."

"And do you intend to be twenty-seven?"

Denzil's smile widened. "I depend upon it, my lady." He bowed again and followed Roland's departing retainers.

"What a good idea," Ravenna said to the room at large. "Why doesn't everyone go?"

When Ravenna phrased an order as a question it was a good indication that her temper had reached the boiling point. Falaise started to speak, reconsidered, and stood up to let Gideon conduct her out. Ravenna's guards and attendants all moved hurriedly to wait for her outside.

Thomas had started for the door when Ravenna said, "Stay here, Captain."

Unwillingly he stopped, his back to her, waiting until the others filed out before turning around.

Ravenna shoved her sewing aside and rested her face in her hands. The flicker of light from the hearth played about the red highlights in her hair and the metallic threads in the embroidery of her gown. Without moving, she said, "Don't look at me like that."

He folded his arms. "I am not looking at you in any particular way."

"The hell you're not." She lifted her head and rubbed her temples. "If she had been my daughter I'd have married her off to the God-King of Parscia. Civil war would have been the least of his worries."

Thomas gave up pretense and let her see how angry he was. He leaned on one of the flimsy rosewood tables that looked so out of place next to the blood-splashed hunting scenes that dominated the room and said, "Civil war may be the least of your worries now that you've let her in here. Before this she was taking out her revenge in small pieces, which was a damn sight better than what she could've chosen to do. Now she wants something more."

Ravenna sat back. "She may well get it, whatever it is," she said seriously. "Did you see the way she dealt with me? And I think there was a moment when Roland actually forgot Denzil was in the room. She makes a fine enemy."

"She could be a deadly enemy. She's grown now and she doesn't want a child's revenge anymore," Thomas told her. Ravenna was single-minded and ruthless in a way that would have been devastating had it not been for the lack of any sadism. She had been born to be an absolute ruler as some men were born to paint or write music. She wanted to bring Kade back into the fold, to direct the sorceress's powers and talents to her own ends. He didn't think Ravenna understood the bitterness of wounds that had never healed.

"A child's revenge," Ravenna said, looking into the fire. "I wish I had a child's revenge. Fulstan wore away at them, both of them. When I discovered all he had done . . . And I didn't realize it until he'd made my son a coward."

Fulstan's treatment of Roland and Kade had been at its worst when Kade was fourteen and Roland twelve, at the time when Ravenna was away on the borders during the last Bisran War. Thomas had been a lieutenant then, traveling with Ravenna and the rest of the Guard. There had been no one at the palace with the courage to inform the Queen that while she was managing supply lines and browbeating her generals into cooperation, Fulstan was destroying Ile-Rien's future through its heir. Thomas had long wondered if Fulstan hadn't known exactly what he was doing. If he wasn't striking back at Ravenna in the only way open to him. God knew she had been indifferent to anything else he'd ever done.

At this time it had also been an open secret that Thomas was Ravenna's lover. Most of his conversations with the late king had been limited to details of the execution Fulstan planned for Thomas on the day Ravenna died, or grew tired of him. *He did have a gift for words. Perhaps he would have been happier as a poet than a king.*

Ravenna was saying, "Had my children been bastards I think all of us would be the happier for it."

Thomas let his breath out, suddenly weary. "Very eloquent. Now what are you going to do about it?"

She stood up and flung her sewing to the floor. "Sixteen years ago when I approved your appointment into my guard, I knew I was making a mistake!" she shouted.

"Probably," Thomas agreed. "And I suppose that bit of misdirection, while admirable, though not quite up to your usual standards, is the only answer I'm going to get."

She stared at him, then shook her head, her expression turning wry. "If I had an answer, I wouldn't need misdirection." After a moment of thought, she asked, "Can we trust Galen Dubell?"

And that was that, even if he stood there and argued until he fell down dead of old age. Thomas rubbed the bridge of his nose. It wasn't the first time Ravenna had given him a headache. He said, "I think so. I don't think he knew she was coming here." Thomas shrugged. "But he's genuinely fond of the girl, and there are people who are going to mistake that for collusion. It would be against your best interests to be one of them."

"Yes, we need him. Braun and his little apprentices are no good for serious work like this. The sorcerers we sent for from the Granges and Lodun haven't even reached the city yet. That's suspicious in itself. I'll tell Renier to send more messengers." Ravenna paused, her back to him, her slender form silhouetted against the light of the fire. "I want you to watch her, Thomas."

"I gathered that," he said dryly. "I've already arranged for it."

There was a discreet tap on the door, and Ravenna irritably called, "Enter."

It was the steward who had made his escape from the solar earlier. He said nervously, "My lord High Minister Aviler is requesting an audience, my lady."

"Oh, he is? Well, I'm in the mood for him, as a matter of fact. Tell him he may enter, and don't think I didn't notice when you disappeared earlier, Saisan. Let's not make a habit of that, hmm?"

The steward bowed. "No, my lady."

As he withdrew, Thomas said, "Fond as I am of Aviler, I have some things to attend to."

"Thomas?" she said quietly.

"Yes?" He stopped halfway to the door.

"You're the only man I know who doesn't hate, dislike, or fear me, and it is a blessed relief simply to speak to you; did you know that?"

Because the High Minister was already coming through the door behind him, Thomas swept off his hat in his best formal court bow and said, "My lady, it is my very great pleasure."

———

On his way back to the Guard House, Thomas took the immense circular stairwell that led up from what had been the main hall of the Old Palace two centuries earlier and now linked the wing that held the Grand Gallery with the older defensive bastions. The gray age-old stone of the banisters and the central supporting column were carved into flowing ribbons and bands that ended in the heads of gryphons, lions, and unrecognizable animals from the artisan's imagination. The lamplit twilight of the stairwell was cool, and echoed faintly with the humming activity of the rest of the palace.

Thomas wondered what Kade Carrion was doing now.

The first time she had used her power against the court had been on a Saints' Day ten years ago. It was held on Midsummer Eve because combining the Church's holy days with the Old Faith's festivals made it easier for the priests to get a respectable turnout for the services, especially in the country where most of the population still considered themselves pagan. Outside, the city streets had been packed with costumed entertainers, traveling merchants, and celebrating crowds, while in the High Cathedral the bishop was saying the Saints' Day Mass before the royal court. At the culmination of the service, pandemonium had erupted. Objects levitated and smashed into walls. Candlelamps, altar vessels, and stained glass windows shattered. It had been a display of raw uncontrolled sorcerous power.

Dr. Surete had been Court Sorcerer then, and he had immediately sensed the cause of the disturbance. It was Kade.

Galen Dubell, who had been at court working with Surete, admitted that for most of the past two years he had been secretly teaching Kade the rudiments of sorcery. This in itself was not a crime. But Kade was the illegitimate daughter of the king. She was older than Roland and courtlaw gave her a claim on the throne. She was also half fay, and elements at court and in the Ministry had been advising Ravenna that Kade was dangerous almost since the girl's birth. The next day Ravenna had banished Dubell to Lodun and sent Kade out of the city to the Monelite Convent, perhaps knowing she would not long remain there. Many had wondered at the time why Ravenna had shown the daughter of her husband's mistress that much mercy, when no one in Ile-Rien except the disgraced Galen Dubell would have objected to Kade's execution. But they knew that Ravenna did everything for her own reasons, and asking for an explanation when none was offered was useless.

In the solar, Ravenna had unintentionally said "my children" and Thomas didn't think she was including the two stillborn girls buried in the High Cathedral's crypt. Ravenna had wanted Kade to be the canny, beautiful daughter she had never had, and in some ways she still wanted that. But that was exactly what that brave, daft, strange-eyed sorceress would never be.

There was a clatter as Martin appeared on the landing above and called, "Captain?"

"What is it?" Martin had been sent with the other Queen's guards to see that the palace was secure after the Arlequin's disturbance. Thomas suspected the expression of relief on the young man's face indicated that he was about to pass a thorny problem on to someone else.

"Trouble, Sir," Martin said as Thomas reached him. He led the way off the landing to a short pillared hall. "We just found him. It's Dr. Braun."

On one side of the hall an oaken door stood open. Thomas followed Martin into a small room furnished as a salon. It had been used as a waiting room for foreign ambassadors when the Old Hall had been an audience chamber.

Braun lay crumpled on an eastern carpet whose rich color was distorted by his blood. He lay as if he had been sitting on the stool at the high writing desk when he had slumped to the side and fallen to the floor.

Two more Queen's guards waited there, Castero and Baserat. Both were looking at the corpse as if trying to decide what to do with it. Thomas went past them and knelt beside the body. The carpet was soaked with blood and squished unpleasantly underfoot. Carefully he lifted the young man's head and saw that his throat had been cut. The edges of the wound were straight, not ragged. It had been done smoothly, with a very sharp knife. The body was cold and beginning to stiffen. "Who found him?" he asked.

"I did," Martin said. "We came past this room earlier on the first quick search and missed him. You can't see the body from the door since the secretaire is in the way. When we were working our way back just now doing it thoroughly, I walked all the way in and saw him."

"He's cold, so he must have been here before that, Sir," Baserat added.

"Yes, and he must have been killed here," Thomas agreed. The carpet was evidence enough of that. Braun had been leaving from the gallery, going back to the King's Bastion, and must have stepped into the little room to speak to someone. Someone who had come up behind him at some point during the course of the conversation and skillfully slit his throat.

"What is this?"

Thomas looked up to see High Minister Aviler standing in the doorway, watching them suspiciously. It wasn't surprising that the High Minister's audience with Ravenna had been a short one; in her current mood it would have been succinct. Thomas answered, "At first glance it appears to be a dead man."

"I realize that." Aviler stepped into the room, his long state robes brushing the floor, keeping a wary eye on the other guards. *As he well might,* Thomas thought, if this were really the murder in progress the man obviously half hoped it was. Martin and the others, who were probably still uncertain whether they had neglected their duty and didn't appreciate Aviler's presence as a witness to it, were no doubt helping this impression by their obvious attitudes of belligerence and guilt.

The High Minister came to the edge of the blood-soaked carpet and stopped, frowning, as it became apparent the death was some hours old. "Braun," he said in surprise, recognizing the young sorcerer. "Who did it?"

"That's a good question." *Why? is another good question,* Thomas thought, though he could guess at least part of the answer. *Poor bastard. He said it wasn't important . . .*

CHAPTER SIX

THE AIR SMELLED like rain. Kade sat on the ledge of the fourth story of the North Bastion, leaning on a stone porpoise and watching the sky. The clouds were gray and heavy, though sunlight broke through in occasional patches. Across the maze of paved courts and formal gardens below were the high walls and steeply pitched roof of the Gallery Wing, more modern and airy in its design than the blocky bastion at her back. It was a cool day, and a damp breeze tore at her hair.

She could feel the wards. They stretched from the bottom of the outer walls to a point high above the palace, forming an invisible, constantly shifting dome. Years ago Galen Dubell had shown her how to use gasçoign powder made from hart's horn and crab's eyes to see the corona of light that marked their presence, and to use ash or flakes of charcoal to track their movements. Bad weather tended to push them closer to the earth; perhaps that was why they seemed to be intruding into her thoughts today.

The frid must have slipped in through one of the naturally occurring gaps between the individual wards. If it had blundered directly into one, the harmless powerless creature would have been eaten in an instant. If the motion of the wards was slowing, then the frid—and the golem for that matter—might simply have been lucky enough to slip through. The new sorcerer Braun might have been as incompetent at tending the wards since Dr. Surete's death as he had been at defending himself from whoever killed him. Galen Dubell had only been back a day: not much time to make up lost ground with as complex an etheric structure as the wards.

However it had gotten in, Kade was fairly sure the golem had been sent for her. She had enemies enough among the courts of Fayre, without even considering those among the mortal sorcerers. There were many fay who wanted Moire's strongholds, especially Knockma, and Kade was determined not to give them up.

Someone moving through the garden below reminded her that she was being followed, but the passerby did not glance up. Kade had dodged the men who were watching her, though they probably knew she was somewhere in this bastion. It didn't matter; all she needed was a few moments' privacy.

Seeing Roland and Ravenna again had stirred a whole nest of unpleasant memories. *He stood there and said I cursed the name of our father, as if nothing had ever happened. As if I hadn't held him while he prayed to the Church's God for our father to die,* she thought. Roland was only two years younger than she; he couldn't fail to remember.

Fulstan had always been a frightening presence in their lives, but during Ravenna's long absences from court in the last years of the Bisran War, he had been at his worst. Kade's memories of those times were particularly vivid. The day Fulstan had beaten to death one of Roland's servants, a boy no older than the ten-year-old prince. *Gods, how can Roland forget that? Those little bones breaking* . . . In sheer terror Roland had sent away his other young servants, and even his pages, sons of high nobility meant to grow up with him and become his companions and advisors. Fulstan had permitted this, because it had left Roland alone.

Except for me, Kade thought. Looking back, she could see that they should have spoken to someone, that Roland could have sent a letter to Ravenna . . . As the daughter of the king's supernatural and despised leman, Kade had had fewer options, but neither she nor Roland had been able to believe that a world existed where help was available.

Landlaw expected even a sovereign to be responsible for his behavior, even if courtlaw did not, but Fulstan had been careful. He had made the Cisternans his personal guard instead of the Albon Order, thereby ridding himself of the interfering presence of an Albon preceptor. He had never done anything to Roland that would leave an outward sign. He had surrounded himself with sycophants and cronies, and he had been a terror to the palace women.

For a long time he had been wary of Kade, perhaps half hoping, half fearing that her mother, Moire, would return to claim her. He had treated his daughter with contempt, reviled her, held her up to the court as an object of ridicule, but he had never touched her. Until that day of her fifteenth summer, when he had pinned her in a corner of her room and told her that as she grew older her looks were almost passable . . .

The next day had been Midsummer Eve and the Saints' Day episode in the cathedral. She had been banished to the convent, and six months later Fulstan was dead.

Kade cursed softly to herself, coming back out of the past to the cloudy day and the breeze lifting her hair. *It's no good to think about it; it's over. If Roland hates you for leaving him, that's his decision. You were a prisoner escaping a cell, and you took the first chance you had.* At least that was what Galen Dubell had told her, two years ago at Lodun.

From the open window a few paces along the ledge to her left came the sound of a door squeaking open, then a moment later the muted thump of something heavy being shifted. *That's Galen,* Kade thought, easing herself up the wall to stand on the ledge. The servants never moved anything.

She stepped around the elaborately figured window casement and onto the wooden sill. Galen Dubell was in a corner of his room, piling stacks of books atop a stout wooden chest. He finished and straightened his back with a sigh, turned, and saw her. "Kade."

His expression was disturbingly neutral. She wondered at his lack of re-action. Even though she had never fallen off anything high enough to hurt herself, he hated to see her walk on ledges. She said, "I wrote and told you that I was coming back. Didn't you get the letter?"

"No, I never received it," he said slowly. "I would have tried to dissuade you."

"You told me I should face my anger and that would help me get rid of it. I take it this wasn't exactly what you meant." Kade spoke with a sinking heart. And she had thought her decision to return to the palace to confront her past was sensible and wise.

"Perhaps I didn't know what I meant." He almost smiled. "Perhaps I've be-come too used to dealing with old men who would rather talk than act. But if this is the way you must do it, then I wish you luck."

"But you don't want me to involve you," she said, and thought, *How calmly that came out.* The wooden window frame was rough against her hand and she realized she was gripping it very tightly.

He held her gaze gravely. "That might be for the best."

It was not what she had wanted to hear. She had wanted him to look exas-perated and say, *That wasn't what I meant at all, you little fool; now stop feeling sorry for yourself and come down out of that window.*

"Something is going to happen here, Kade," he was saying. "I don't know what it is yet, but I have to be free to deal with it."

And not be banished again because of me. She said, "I know. It's someone called Grandier."

He frowned. "What do you know about him?"

"He tried to kill you." Kade shrugged.

"He failed."

She shook her head, trying to put the anger away. "The lesser fay won't even speak his name. They're more afraid of him than they are of me. The ones from the higher courts say they've never heard of him, but it's pretense. They wouldn't tell me the truth anyway."

"He's in the city, perhaps closer than anyone realizes. Dr. Braun was killed last night. I'm certain Grandier had something to do with it, and that means he must have someone inside the wall already." Galen let out his breath, his face weary. "I could use your help, but I dare not take it. Do you understand?"

"Yes, well, I suppose I do." She managed not to say it with too poor grace.

He watched her carefully. "And you must give me your word that you won't harm anyone here, no matter what provocation."

Kade couldn't look at him anymore. Her voice was more bitter than she intended. "You know I can't promise that." She slipped out of the window and began to make her way down the ledge to an unused balcony. Behind her, he called with a trace of his old exasperation, "Be careful, damn it."

The guards spotted her again when she had reached the ground floor and was coming out of the entrance into the Rose Court. Kade picked up her skirt and bolted down one of the stone-paved paths between the rosebushes. As she reached the wall of the court, she heard heavy bodies crashing into the thorny and not-so-delicate hedges. The wall was rough and pitted and she scaled it easily.

Reaching the top, she crouched amid the tangled vines and took a quick glance around. As she had seen from above, the area between the bastion and the high walls of the Gallery Wing was a honeycomb of intersecting gardens and courts, some old and familiar and others that were recent additions. She ran lightly along the wall, jumped to a narrower intersecting wall, and ran along its length. She heard a yelp and a crash as the vines on the first wall gave way on someone. As she spun around to look, her lace underskirt caught on a lionhead spout on the wall's rain gutter, throwing her off-balance and forcing her to jump down.

She landed heavily in a pile of raked leaves. She was in a long and irregularly shaped garden, with a clipped lawn and overflowing flower borders, most of it rambling out of sight behind the wall and sheltering hedges.

Kade got to her feet and strolled toward the mossy fountain just around the curve of the wall, prepared to be mildly amused when they caught up with her.

In the fountain, water spouted from pitchers in the hands of stone nymphs.

Kade wriggled her toes in the cool grass. The garden widened out from this point on, becoming larger and more grand than she had first supposed. In the wide area of lawn were yew bushes shaped into a scaled-down battlement with towers half circling a large round mosaic of a massive sundial. Distracted, it was moments before her eyes focused on the man and the woman seated on a bench beneath a honeysuckle arbor only a few yards from her; the play of the fountain had covered their voices. It was Queen Falaise and Denzil.

Falaise saw Kade at almost the same moment. She stood, jerking her hand free of Denzil's grasp, and hurried toward her. Kade, who was more used to catching people unawares than being caught, stood there and stared.

The Queen stopped a few feet from her, said uncertainly, "My lady Katherine . . . ah, Kade?" She wore a dress of rose and pearl and clutched a small book in a white-knuckled grasp. Like most aristocratic women would have been, she was out of breath from the exertion of walking quickly across the garden. Falaise hadn't been crying, but there was something stricken in her blue eyes that amounted to the same thing.

Kade felt herself look stupid. She said, "Yes?" hoping to provoke an explanation.

A little desperately, Falaise said, "We had an appointment."

Kade realized that the Queen was not seeing her as a sorceress or as her husband's dangerous sister, but only as another woman. "Yes, an appointment," she repeated helpfully, nodding.

Denzil reached them and caught Falaise's arm again. The Queen flinched and dropped her book, which barely missed the fountain. Kade stooped immediately to rescue it from the damp ground.

Denzil said, "Another appointment, my lady?" His smile was confident and amused. A brief glow of sunlight breaking through the cloudy sky touched his blond hair, the powder blue of his doublet, the gems ornamenting his sword. He and Falaise made a beautiful couple.

Falaise hesitated. "Yes, I . . ."

"I was late." Kade brushed dirt off the little book's sheepskin binding.

"Yes, she was," Falaise agreed instantly. She stepped away from Denzil, the movement stiff and awkward.

He chuckled and bowed slightly to make the point that he was allowing her to escape. "Then I'll leave you to your appointment."

His arrogance was too obvious for Kade to leave well enough alone. "Do that," she said.

Amused and ironic, he met her eyes and bowed. "My lady."

They watched him cross the garden toward the gate behind the hedges. Kade didn't know Denzil very well. He had been presented to court shortly before she had left. He had attached himself to Roland shortly thereafter.

There was nothing she hated more than people who didn't take her seriously.

Falaise sat down on the edge of the fountain, heedless of what the moss would do to her silk damask skirts.

This near to the Queen, Kade was suddenly conscious that the climb on the bastion's ledge and her fall into the leaves hadn't done her dress any good. But her grubbiness was bound to aggravate Ravenna, and she resolved to let her clothing degenerate as far as modesty allowed. "Where are your guards?" she asked Falaise.

Falaise shook her head slightly. "This is my private garden. When I give audiences here they wait beside the gate. I bribed my ladies to go down to the grotto."

"Why didn't you call them back?"

"That wouldn't do any good." Her face was bleak.

Falaise had the calm of someone who has been miserable for a long time and expected to go on being miserable. Kade shifted uneasily. "It's difficult for someone to make advances when there are a lot of men standing around looking at him as if they want to kill him. They're Queen's guards; even Roland can't order them away when they're protecting you."

Falaise looked away wearily, the wind playing with her curls and ribbons. "It isn't that sort of advances."

"It doesn't matter what sort of advances. It always worked for Ravenna's ladies when—" *When my father* . . . "—when they needed it," she finished, but Falaise didn't notice the lapse.

"He wouldn't let me call them."

Kade snorted. "Do it anyway."

"It's easy for you to say." Falaise gestured helplessly, the puffed sleeves of her gown almost hiding the movement.

Kade watched her a moment, then sat on the fountain rim beside her. "Not always."

But Falaise opened the book on her lap and turned the pages distractedly. By craning her neck Kade could see it was written instead of printed, and by a hand not as fine as a professional clerk's. Poetry, she guessed, and it would hardly be from Roland. Falaise slammed the book closed and said abruptly, "What do I call you, Katherine or Kade?"

"Kade."

"Kade. Did you ever turn yourself into a bird?" Her expression was wistful.

Kade lifted her brows. "I thought about it, but I decided I wanted to live." It came to her that Falaise wasn't really much of a coward. Denzil must have browbeaten her thoroughly. Possibly most men in authority over her had browbeaten her thoroughly. "Human sorcerers can't shape-change, not if they ever want to turn back into themselves. Most fay can, but I never had to badly enough to make the experiment. "

"That's a shame." Falaise fingered the book again. "It would be wonderful to just turn into something and fly away."

They sat in the quiet a moment, with not even birds to interrupt the fountain's bubbling. Then Kade remembered something and asked her, "What did you mean when you said Denzil wasn't making that sort of—"

A man came running around one of the yew hedges toward them. He threw himself at Falaise's feet so enthusiastically Kade had to scramble out of the way to avoid being tumbled into the fountain.

More graceful, Falaise kept her balance and said in exasperation, "Aristofan, please—"

The young man kneeling at her feet was handsome with russet hair and eager brown eyes. He was dressed for court in blue and gray and had lost his feathered hat in his run across the lawn. "It was him, wasn't it? That was why you didn't want me to come to you today. You must tell me what he wants from you."

Kade looked down at herself to make sure she hadn't inadvertently faded from sight.

"No, I can't, I told you." Falaise spoke firmly, but then she stroked his hair. "Really, it's all right."

"Don't mind me," Kade said. "I'll just stand over here, shall I?"

Aristofan clasped the Queen's hand ardently. "Don't you trust me? I'd do anything for you."

Falaise smiled fondly. "Sometimes I almost think you would."

One of the men following Kade appeared at the top of the wall, spotted her, and waved back to his companions. "Well," Kade said, "I have to leave before they decide I'm holding you prisoner and roll in a couple of cannon."

"Please." Falaise looked up at her. "You won't say anything?"

"I don't know anything." Kade started away, then stopped and looked back. "If you're going to tell someone, tell Ravenna."

Falaise looked down at Aristofan's head, her expression drawn and troubled.

To avoid Falaise's guards, Kade left the garden by going over the wall behind the battlement hedge. She was still not quite ready to be followed again, and she rejoined the path that led away from the Queen's garden only when she was out of sight of the gates. The path wandered past walled herb gardens then abruptly opened out to the paved area below the terraces of the Gallery Wing. The smooth stone of the Gallery Wing's walls was butter colored and would glow like gold in the full sunlight. She climbed the steps and walked along the terrace, looked at the view of the rolling lawn, the trees, and the artificial temple ruins, and wondered about Galen Dubell.

I'm not going to sit like a lump while he fights this Bisran bastard Grandier single-handed. Does he honestly expect me to do that? No, he couldn't, she decided. It was incredible. If she were going to behave in that ridiculous fashion to one of the few friends she had, then she might as well have stayed in the convent and saved years of trouble. *Galen isn't an idiot. Grandier trapped him once; he might do it again. He knows he needs help; he just can't ask for it.*

She stopped, drew a toe meditatively over a pattern in the paving stone. She was tired of being followed.

Kade closed her eyes and pulled glamour out of the damp air and the dew on the grass, wove it with the afternoon sunlight filtered through the clouds, and drew it over herself like a concealing blanket. If anyone saw her she would appear as another courtier, a servant, whatever they expected to see.

She would help Dubell, and she had an inkling of how to go about it.

———

"Well, that's been a waste of time," Thomas told Lucas.

They had just finished questioning the last of Dr. Braun's apprentices and servants and had elicited nothing but a tearful confession from the sixty-year-old chamberlain about a few pennies' worth of misappropriated household funds.

During the questioning, Lucas had been entertaining himself by flipping a small boot dagger from hand to hand, and now he sent it into the table with a thud. "So, who killed the poor bastard? The chamberlain?"

The room was damp and too warm, despite the open window. Thomas stood up from the table piled with papers and moved restlessly to the room's little balcony, unbuttoning the top of his doublet. From here he could look down onto the hall where servants wandered, off-duty guards gathered, and the main life of the Queen's Guard House was concentrated. He leaned against the rough pillar in the corner of the balcony and said, "He's too short. Braun was sitting at a clerk's writing desk and the stool was a foot or so taller than an ordinary chair. Whoever cut the good doctor's throat was at least my height. The way that old man's back is bent he'd never have been able to reach him."

On the stone-paved floor of the hall below, some of the men had discarded their doublets to practice swordplay on wooden targets and one another. Constant work was required to keep in top form for the real duels, which usually lasted no more than a few moments, depending on the relative skill of the opponents, and often ended with a death or a crippling. All used their regular dueling swords rather than the blunt-tipped weapons often employed for practice, and it was only due to the skill of the combatants that so little blood was being shed. There were not as many men off duty as usual; all the guardposts and duty shifts had been doubled since last night.

All this morning Thomas had noted a tension on the wind that hadn't been there yesterday. Everyone knew the danger of dark and deserted places, but the palace had always been safe ground from any but human opponents. Two Cisternan guards had been sent back to their families in boxes today, the first casualties in a new and uncertain war. The rest of the court had also finally bothered to notice the danger, and today there were complaints, mild hysteria, and loud questions about why someone wasn't doing something.

"If you're going to be clever about it, we won't be able to arrest anyone," Lucas pointed out.

The pillar Thomas leaned against still bore the nine-year-old bullet hole that had signaled the end of his predecessor's career. He picked at the splintered area thoughtfully and said, "We're looking for a throat-slitter who takes an unprepared man from behind but who still scruples at robbery." Braun had been wearing a respectable amount of court jewelry, including a diamond-studded presentation medal from Lodun and several gemstones given to him by past wealthy patrons. All had been left on the body. "That eliminates most of the servants but certainly throws suspicion on every member of the nobility in the palace. And Grandier."

Lucas tipped his chair back against the yellowed plaster wall. "Always Grandier. What did Braun have that Grandier would want to kill him for?"

"Information." And thinking of information, Thomas wished the clerks would hurry with the translation of the documents chronicling Grandier's trial in Bisra. They knew so little about the man, and he wanted to take advantage of every resource, no matter how sparse it might be.

Lucas nodded. "You think Braun saw something someone preferred he didn't . . ."

"Or remembered something. He tried to talk to me last night but we were interrupted by Denzil."

"Coincidence?" Lucas lifted his brows in speculation.

Thomas glanced back at him. "Which coincidence? Braun wanting to tell me something or Denzil interrupting at the opportune moment?"

"We're not going to get anywhere if you keep inventing new questions." Lucas glanced briefly toward the window, which opened onto the narrow alley between the house and the stone wall of the old armory. "Half the palace is saying that it was the sorceress."

"Not a bad suggestion, except she was already in the gallery performing bad Commedia in front of everyone who matters in the city when I saw Braun alive. The body was long cold by the time she left." Thomas shook his head. She was also too short. "Today she lost her guards in the Queen's garden. One of them reported it an hour ago."

"What was she doing there?"

"Talking to the Queen, apparently."

"Odd." Lucas frowned, looking puzzled at the idea that anyone might want to talk to Falaise. Possibly because they were all so used to discounting her influence, it was hard to remember that she had any power in her own right at all. "What's going to come of that, do you think?"

"Not much." Thomas smiled. "They can't banish Falaise."

Lucas was silent a moment, watching Thomas. "Your great friend High Minister Aviler is implying it was a Queen's guard."

Thomas's lips twisted in annoyance. "What a helpful suggestion. How in hell did he come up with it?"

Lucas shrugged uneasily. "The usual way. There was some loud muttering about Braun, some of the men blaming him for his incompetence when you were trying to get Galen Dubell out of Grandier's house. Braun was never half the help old Dr. Surete was."

"So one of them takes it on himself to remove the irritant? It's unlikely." But Gideon had said something about Braun last night. And Lucas clearly believed it was a possibility, though he wouldn't say it outright.

Thomas was struck by an unpleasant image. Braun, unable to find Thomas in the crowded gallery, stopping a faceless Queen's guard on a deserted stair. Asking him to take a message to his captain, stepping into a quiet parlor to use the writing desk . . . But Thomas had always seen Braun as a pitiable figure, and the young sorcerer had been coldly eliminated in a way that didn't agree with the theory of a guard murdering him in sudden anger. Then again, Braun was a sorcerer and would surely have had some means of defending himself; he would almost have to be taken from behind . . .

The door creaked as a servant opened it to usher in Ephraim, the ragged ballad-seller and professional spy.

"Good news?" Thomas asked as the old man grinned and bowed to both of them.

Ephraim pulled off his cloth cap and began to knead it conversationally. "In a manner of speaking, Sir. It's quite a tale. The Gambin lad's dead, you see."

If he had his throat slit around the same time as Braun did, I'm going to retire, Thomas thought, and kept the surprise off his face. "What happened?"

"From the beginning it was that a couple of my own boys followed Gambin to see if he would lead us to the fellow who hired him, and he led them a merry way, Sir, but he ended up back at the palace quarter and entered Lord Lestrac's house." Ephraim hesitated. Not from trepidation, but more as if he were still trying to sort things out in his own mind. "After a bit he came out, and the boys followed Gambin on a wandering way back to his home ground, and waited outside his house, as they hadn't any instructions to do otherwise. Before dawn this morning a young woman arrives, and she goes in and starts to yell for help. The boys figured they should go in and see what the matter was, and as Gambin didn't know either of them they could say they were passersby. Well, they didn't have to say much at all, because Gambin was dead, you see, without a mark on him.

"When I got there I sent for a lady who lives down in the Philosopher's Cross and knows a bit about these things, and in her opinion it had the look of a wicked sending about it, though I never heard of Gambin to trouble with sorcerers before. She said it was most likely in something he was given, some token, that was enspelled to murder the lad whenever the master was finished and didn't want the likes of anyone asking questions. It cost extra for her to search for the token, and I thought you'd want your own people to do that, so I locked up the house and came on here."

"You've done your best," Thomas told him, preoccupied. This was another piece in the puzzle. And it was a damn good thing he had set Ephraim on this job; without him, it might have been days before news of Gambin's death reached Thomas, and the evidence of sorcery in the killing might have been gone by then. "Tell them to get you a drink, and the Paymaster has your fee."

Ephraim's bow was unpolished but sincere. "Oh, that's very good of you, Captain."

When the spy had left, Lucas grimaced. "Well, well. Lord Lestrac is our nameless letter-forger, and Gambin is silenced the same way you think Dr. Surete and Milam were. Another connection to Grandier?"

"Maybe." The attempt with the letters was the sort of unsubtle ineffective trick Denzil's friends were famous for in their attempts to please him, and of which the Duke unconcernedly let them suffer the consequences. "It almost seems as if there are two different players, or factions, at work. Grandier with his sorcery, and then someone else plaguing us with little distractions. Gambin was hired by the second person, and when he was compromised, Grandier killed him."

"If they're working together. They might not be." Lucas worked his dagger out of the table, frowning at it. "There's no way to tell."

Thomas bit his lip thoughtfully, considering his options. He said, "I want you to send men to search Gambin's house and pick up the body; I'll want an opinion on it from Dubell."

"How lovely for him," Lucas said dryly, getting to his feet. "You know, if I'm not mistaken, Lestrac is also a friend of Denzil's. I think the good Duke of Alsene maintains that house for him."

"He does. And it was searched by the King's Watch about two days ago. They didn't discover anything." Lestrac's house was one of a group of manses for royal dependents that were built up against the outside of the palace's west wall. Lestrac was a landless dissipated young nobleman, useful occasionally as a tool for Denzil but not much else. He had never been implicated in one of Denzil's plots deeply enough to send him to the traitors' graves outside the city, but he assisted Roland's cousin in the spreading of rumors and lies. Thinking it over, Thomas shook his head. "Even if we did connect a friend of Denzil's to Grandier, it won't prove anything to Roland. To convince him we'd have to catch Denzil standing over the royal bed with a drawn sword, and even then I'm not sure he'd believe it."

"Lestrac was supposed to have dabbled in black magic in his wilder days, and bargained with demons, like Grandier. The letters might have been his own idea, and he could have killed Gambin himself," Lucas pointed out.

Thomas wasn't convinced. "I heard he dabbled, but I never heard he dabbled all that successfully. Finding the token should settle it. Have them be especially careful of anything valuable on Gambin's body. If I were Grandier, I would have put the spell on the payment that was given him." He paused. "I'll see Lestrac myself."

Lucas frowned. "Will you take Dubell with you?"

Thomas shook his head. "He's still a target for Grandier and I'm not sure I want to risk him. He may be the only protection the palace has."

Lucas eyed him, not happily. "So you go to Lestrac's house where Grandier is hiding and he kills you because Galen Dubell is safe back here. Does that make sense?"

Thomas had to concede the point. "It's not a perfect plan, I'll admit. I'll take one of Braun's apprentices. They aren't completely useless."

"Or take me."

Kade Carrion sat in the window, perfectly composed, the ragged hem of her dress tucked under her feet. How she had gotten there without either one of them hearing her was incredible; from her attitude she might have been there for the past hour.

"What are you doing here?" Lucas asked, so startled he dropped a hand to his sword.

Her look said she suspected his sanity. "Listening. Next you'll ask me how much I heard, to which I'll very likely reply 'enough.' Can't we dispense with all that?"

Lucas looked at his captain and raised an eyebrow inquiringly. Thomas shook his head minutely, and asked Kade, "Take you where?"

She made an impatient gesture. "To what's-his-name's house where you think Grandier is."

Thomas leaned back against the pillar and folded his arms. "Why do you want to go?"

She rolled her eyes in exasperation. "I'm offering to help."

"And in such a touching and spontaneous way. If I refuse your help?"

She appeared to seriously consider the question. "I might follow anyway. I'm good at that. Or not. I might do a lot of things; the day is young."

This was ominous. "And I'm expected to trust you?"

Apparently outraged, she sat up straight against the window casement and said, "I gave my word."

"No, you did not." Thomas was fairly certain he would have recalled that.

"I did."

"When?"

He saw her hesitate, then she gave in and grinned. She said, "So I didn't. Come on, you know you want me to go. I'm lucky."

"Lucky for whom?" Lucas muttered.

"This isn't a game," Thomas said, wary. She had her own brand of charm, that was certain. And Thomas realized that even against his will he was tempted by that charm. *Because she's different, or because she's dangerous?* he asked himself, irritated. *Stop being ridiculous and concentrate.* "You've said you want to help, but you haven't told me why. And you haven't been terribly helpful in the past."

"The past is the past." Kade tilted her head to one side, watching him with those very direct eyes. "Grandier would have killed Galen Dubell, who is my oldest friend." She finished lightly, "I can't have that, can I?"

Trusting her was a decided risk, but if Grandier was in that house, or had been there and left more traps, Kade would be their best hope. And so far Thomas had come across nothing to suggest that she was the Bisran sorcerer's ally. *And this is certainly one way to find her out if she is.* He said, "Very well."

CHAPTER SEVEN

T HE HOUSES THAT clustered against the palace's west wall presented blank stone façades to the public, most of their life and wealth turned inward. The clouds had closed up overhead and a light rain had started, settling the dust and washing away the habitual stench of the street, preparing to turn it into a river of mud. Street vendors who sold ribbons, trinkets, foodstuffs, and amulets to protect against night-dwelling fay were gathered in damp clumps around the pillars of the promenade that faced the line of houses. Coaches splashed by, trying to reach their destinations before the storm started in earnest; few of the wealthier residents were abroad at this hour, and most had retreated into the rich shops farther under the sheltering roof of the promenade. The street was mostly unobserved, for which Thomas was glad. He hated an audience for this sort of work.

Lestrac's house was four stories topped by a steeply pitched red tile roof, set between the towering residence of a ship owner and the winter home of a minor noble.

Rain dripping off his hat, Thomas stepped back to look up at the barred windows while Castero banged on the door. Another Queen's guard tried the double carriage doors while the others spread out in front of the house and attempted to look innocuous. There was no back alley and no other exit. He had brought twenty men, which was overkill if this was Lestrac's own plot. If Grandier himself was in there despite the earlier search by the King's Watch, the entire troop might not be enough.

There was no answer at the door. Thomas started to tell Castero to break it in when he glanced down and found Kade Carrion at his elbow. The water that was beading on his dark cloak was dripping from her hair and her dingy red dress. She had appeared so suddenly it was possible that she had simply risen out of the mud. She had been investigating the street on her own, wandering about in a random fashion and poking around doorways. "There's someone in there," she said positively.

Thomas eyed her. "Is it warded?"

She stared at the door, brows drawn down in concentration. "No. It should be."

"Open it," Thomas told Castero.

The guard drew his pistol and used the heavy butt to pound the lock. The wood around it cracked and Castero used his shoulder. As he struck the door it swung backward and came off its hinges.

Kade slipped past Thomas almost before the door gave way. As she ducked inside Castero jumped back and muttered, "Pardon me."

If it's a trap, she's determined to spring it first. Thomas signaled Baserat and another two guards to stand watch outside and followed her, drawing his rapier.

Inside was a high-ceilinged area with a stone staircase curving up the wall to the second-floor entrance. The floor was stone paved, and a black coach with polished brass fittings stood in front of the carriage doors. Light came in through high narrow windows in the outside wall. There was stabling beneath the stairs, and Thomas nodded for one of his men to investigate it.

Kade was halfway up the steps. Thomas called to her, "Give us a moment, please." She threw her arms up in exasperation, but stopped, tapping her foot impatiently.

The guard flushed a couple of frightened grooms out of the stalls where they had been attempting to hide. From the number of horses stabled there, Lestrac was indeed home and entertaining.

Thomas put two more men to watch the servants and to keep any fugitives from escaping behind them, then headed toward the stairs, the others following him. Kade was off again as soon as he started up. Behind him, Castero whispered, "Captain, should we let her go first? I mean, she is a woman."

"Presumably she knows that," Thomas told him.

At the top of the steps, just before the wooden doors, Kade stopped them with an outflung arm. After a moment of intense study of the dirty stone of the landing, she tore a scrap of cloth from her skirt hem, licked it, and stooped to rub it over some invisible spot on the flagstones. Something came away bright blue, and Kade flicked the cloth over the edge of the landing.

"A ward, but it wasn't working anymore. It was old," she admitted, and stepped up to push the door open.

It was the first room of a suite of salons, the dying embers in the hearth revealing landscape paintings, papered walls, heavy oak cabinets, and brocaded chairs. Sprawled around on the fine furnishings and all drunk into unconsciousness were three young men Thomas recognized as sprigs of nobility, and two women whose elaborate and revealing costumes proclaimed them upper-class bawds. A bottle had broken on the floor and wine had seeped into the carpet. From the smell, they had been lacing the stuff with syrup of poppies. Some of the candles were still lit, their holders half buried under bizarre shapes of dripped wax.

"We've interrupted a party," Thomas told Castero, who grinned, and tipped one of the unconscious young men off a couch.

"A dull one," Kade said, looking around with a puzzled expression.

Thomas considered her a moment, suddenly recalling that she was a member of the royal family and had spent some of her youth in a convent, then decided to let it go. If he had known Lestrac was going to be hosting an orgy, he would have reconsidered allowing Kade to accompany them into the upstairs rooms, but he was damned if he was going to say anything about it now.

"A livelier brood in here, Captain," a guard called from ahead, and Thomas followed him into the next room.

There were five of them in a central parlor, and they had leapt up from a card table, overturning their chairs, fumbling clumsily for swords. They were all drunk, though not quite to the advanced stage of their companions in the other room. "What is this?" one of them demanded muzzily. Thomas thought he might be the second son of the Count of Belennier, though he wasn't certain. He ignored the question and nodded to the guard who was covering them with a pistol, who immediately said, "Drop your swords, gentlemen."

While they disarmed, Thomas quietly told Castero, "Leave a few men down here to watch this lot, and take the others on ahead to search the rest of the house. Lestrac is the one I want."

"What about me?" Kade whispered, standing at his elbow again.

"You go with him," Thomas snapped.

"Why?"

"You're here to spring sorcerous traps, not to stand about and be entertained by me."

"Oh. My mistake." She didn't sound particularly chastened, but she followed Castero and the others.

Turning back to the group held at bay, Thomas suddenly recognized what he had thought at first to be a completely unfamiliar face. It was the dark-haired stranger he had seen with Denzil at the disastrous court last night. There was nothing unusual about him; he had the same pale bedraggled look as the others, the early lines on his face that came from too much drinking. But there was something about his eyes . . . Guarding a queen of stubborn and definite opinions in the crowded courts had made Thomas preternaturally sensitive, and people who were hiding something usually betrayed it in some way, either in look or gesture or simply by the way they stood. This man was hiding something.

The object under scrutiny seemed to realize he was being watched, and swayed a little against the table. Thomas smiled to himself. *He's also not as drunk as he's pretending.* "Where's Lestrac?" Thomas asked the group in general.

"He's about somewhere," answered the second son of the Count of Belennier, who seemed to have elected himself the spokesman. "You'll pay for this, forcing your way into a gentleman's house—"

"I'll discuss that with the gentleman in question."

"Well, he's about somewhere." The young man stared around blearily, as if expecting Lestrac to suddenly appear.

"How long have you been here?"

"Oh, all day." Recalling he was outraged, he protested, "And you've no right to question us, if it's Lestrac you're after."

And he's about somewhere. That would be all Thomas could get out of them until he actually produced Lestrac, but the chances were they hadn't been here yesterday when Gambin had visited the house. At least, if Lestrac had any sense at all they wouldn't have been here.

"Don't let them talk to each other," Thomas told the guard with the pistol, and moved on after the others.

They went from one well-appointed room to another and up the central staircase to the third floor, the guards spreading out to search more thoroughly as Kade flitted before them checking for magical traps.

After a short while, it became apparent that the only inhabitants were those they had already discovered and that Lord Lestrac was nowhere to be found. Thomas and Castero met back in a central parlor on the second floor.

"He must be on the run, Captain." The young guard absently kicked a chair.

"Unfortunately." Thomas looked around, one eyebrow lifted in an ironic appraisal of the empty room. It seemed clear. Lestrac had used Gambin in a minor plot against Thomas. When it failed to have the expected result, Lestrac had panicked, used magic to dispose of Gambin, and fled. "How very neat and tidy." The other guests had been herded into the next salon under guard. A few had families influential enough that they would have to be released, but Thomas hated to do it before he knew where Lestrac had gone. Each one was a potential accomplice.

Kade wandered into the room from the stairwell. She looked around, apparently in a state of deep consternation. "It's here. I don't know what, but it's here. And it's not." She moved around, touching things, stooping to look under the furniture.

Anything to be an annoyance, Thomas thought. But the longer he was in the house the more suspicious it seemed to him. There was more here than appeared, or something out of place, and he wasn't willing to leave until he found what it was.

Kade straightened suddenly. Her examination of the parlor had led her to the far wall. "How many rooms on this floor?"

Castero stared at her. "Nine."

"Eleven upstairs." Thomas saw what she was getting at, and suddenly realized what was wrong about the place. It was the position of the stairwell in relation to the second floor. He went to stand beside Kade and ran a hand across the paneled wall. "Look at the way the top of this meets the ceiling. It's a false wall. There must be a moving panel or—"

Kade said, "No, not a panel." She placed a palm on the center of the wall and leaned in, whispering to it. Thomas stepped back as the shape of a door slowly formed out of the dark wood, as if a sculptor were molding it out of clay. Grinning with triumph, Kade stepped back as it solidified.

As she reached for the handle, Thomas caught a handful of her tattered smock and hauled her out of the way. He stepped to one side of the door, motioning for Castero to take the other. Castero stepped hastily into position, winding his pistol. At Thomas's elbow, Kade silently bounced with excitement.

Thomas twisted the handle and flung the door open.

It was a banqueting room with a long table and sideboards, lit by a dripping candelabrum and chandeliers. A man was seated at the end of the table, slumped over forward.

Thomas advanced cautiously toward him. There was a half-empty wine bottle on the table, two more on the floor beneath it.

Thomas used a handful of the man's unkempt blond hair to pull him upright. It was Lestrac. The lean, dissipated features were slack and sickly red. His eyes didn't focus, and the pupils were so wide they seemed to cover most of the white. His breath was quick and panting, as if he were running for his life. *It's poison,* Thomas realized. *Belladonna or henbane, something that the Aderassi criminal guilds are always using to put each other out of the way.* Holding the young lord up, he could feel his burning skin. "Who did this to you, Lestrac? Was it Grandier?"

The dying eyes seemed finally to focus. "No, no, not him. . . ." Lestrac shuddered weakly, the effort of speaking almost too much.

"But you know him. Was he here?"

"No, he's . . . He told me he'd teach . . . power. I should have known."

"Where is he now?"

"It was Dontane, on Grandier's orders," Lestrac said suddenly, his voice growing stronger. He made a convulsive movement and caught the front of Thomas's doublet. "Captain Boniface, you've got to get that bastard Dontane."

Lestrac started to slide out of the chair and Thomas caught him and shoved him back. The nobleman's head lolled and his eyes were wide open and staring, though he still breathed. Thomas let him go and stepped back. That was it, Lestrac would stay like this, impossible to wake, until he died in a few hours. *But they've made a mistake, perhaps their first,* Thomas thought. Someone, perhaps Lestrac himself when he hired Gambin, had acted out of turn, revealing that Grandier had the help of others who could come and go inside the palace. *And if Denzil isn't involved somehow . . .* He told Castero, "Send someone for the men from the gate watch. We're going to tear this place apart."

As Castero left, Kade did a quick circuit of the room, checking the walls for more concealed doors. Watching her, Thomas knew that at least to some extent she was enjoying herself, and that she certainly didn't give a damn for the fact that Lestrac had all but expired a few moments ago. He didn't know why that should bother him, since he didn't care either and knew that if even half of what he suspected were true, Lestrac would have been executed anyway. And to some extent he was also enjoying himself. Perhaps her reaction annoyed him because it was so much in tune with his own.

Kade had drifted back to the table and now took the wine bottle and emptied the last of its contents onto the polished surface. She stirred the pool twice with a finger and stared into it intently.

Unwilling to ask, Thomas stepped up behind her to see what she was doing.

Without looking up, she reached out and grabbed his wrist. Before he could pull away, he saw a shadow come over the wine pool and something move within it. It was a man. At first the image was shifting and muddy, but abruptly it cleared, revealing the face of the man in the other room, the man who had been with Denzil at court last night.

Kade said quietly, "I thought so. He was in here, and they fought, or at least argued. Violent emotions always make the strongest impressions."

She let Thomas go and he stepped back, and the pool became only spilled wine again. He hadn't realized until then how the sounds of his men searching the next room and the occasional drunken protests of Lestrac's friends had temporarily faded as the picture appeared in the pool. "Is he a sorcerer? Did he conceal the door?"

"Maybe. But that one might have done it, too." She nodded toward Lestrac's still form. "You said he knew some of the art, and it wasn't a very powerful illusion, though it was tricky."

Thomas nodded to himself. "He brought Dontane in here, Dontane killed him, then walked out through the unconcealed door on this side. He stayed with the others to make sure Lestrac didn't come staggering out gasping accusations. He must have known how long it would take to die from the stuff. Any later and we would have missed him."

Kade looked thoughtful, then turned for the door, remarking pointedly, "Well, I'm certainly glad I bothered to come."

After considering Lestrac's slumped body a moment more, Thomas followed her.

Later, Thomas had the guards carry Lestrac out past the group gathered in the parlor. Leaning on the billiard table, which was extravagantly covered in green velvet and lit by candleholders mounted on its raised sides, he watched the nobles react with varied degrees of befuddled shock. Including Dontane, whose reaction was perfectly in keeping with the rest.

"When do we carry out this lot, Captain?" Castero asked.

"Now. Take them to the Cisternan Guard House for the present." He touched one of the silver bells fitted above the billiard table's goal. "All except Dontane."

Dontane looked up, but if he was startled he concealed it well. As Castero and the other guards herded Lestrac's guests out, Thomas waited patiently. When they were gone, that left Dontane, three watchful guards at the door, and Kade, who sat on top of a sideboard swinging her feet. As Thomas looked at her and started to speak, she announced, "I've been a help, and shown quite a bit of restraint, and I think I should be allowed to stay and watch."

It was harder than Thomas would've thought to conceal his smile. He said, "Well put."

Watching them with contempt, Dontane said, "I assume there is some reason for my being singled out." He swayed slightly and steadied himself on a chair.

"You assume correctly." Thomas watched him a moment more, wondering how long the playacting would last. "How long have you known Lord Lestrac?"

"Not long. But I am a friend of the Duke of Alsene."

"That puts you in the minority, then, because no one else here is." It would have been foolish to deny the connection; Dontane must realize he would've been seen at court last night. *And why attend court at all, except to activate the golem so it could attack a certain sorceress.* Thomas folded his arms, deciding on a more direct attack. "I know you poisoned Lestrac."

Dontane drew himself up. "That is an insult, and I will challenge you for it." He stiffened resentfully as one of the guards at the door chuckled.

The man was certainly presenting a good performance of a foolish young noble. Thomas said, "You were in that room with Lestrac. Were you discussing a spy named Gambin, perhaps?"

"I don't know what you're talking about."

"He's lying," Kade interrupted.

"Yes, thank you, I know," Thomas told her patiently.

"I suppose I should be flattered that you find it necessary to have your pet witch here to deal with me," Dontane sneered. But he had lost a little of his pretense of drunken nonchalance. Thomas thought Kade's presence was making the man uneasy. *As well it might.*

"'Pet witch.' I like that," Kade said, apparently addressing the blue faience vase sitting next to her on the sideboard. "I'm going to put a curse on him."

"If you can't be quiet you'll have to leave, pet," Thomas said.

Kade turned a look of narrow-eyed reproach on him, then regarded Dontane with so much sly malice it had to be artificial.

Thomas studied him, then asked, "Are you a sorcerer?"

Dontane's expression was calm. "I am not."

"Then are you a dabbler in magic, like Lestrac?" He hadn't forgotten the young lord's last words: *He told me he'd teach power.* If one had a taste of power, enough to hide a door by illusion, or to witch a useless spy dead, the temptation to learn more at the hands of a master like Grandier might be overwhelming.

"No, I am not," Dontane said, looking away in disgust.

Had he hesitated, deciding how to answer? "Is he a sorcerer?" Thomas asked Kade.

She dug a moment in the pocket of her smock, and when she drew her hand out her fingers were covered with a dark powdery substance. She touched her forefinger carefully to the corner of each eye, then looked up at Dontane.

Dontane smiled, scornfully. "Well, witch?"

She held his gaze a moment, then said, "I think he knew what I was doing."

Dontane snorted derision and looked away. Watching him carefully, Thomas asked, "And what was that?"

"Putting gasçoign powder in my eyes. If he had been using a spell, or if there had been a spell on him, I would see it. It doesn't prove he isn't a sorcerer."

Dontane smiled. "Alchemical powders are hardly a secret."

"Maybe," Thomas agreed. He had heard of gasçoign powder as well, but that explanation for Kade's actions hadn't immediately leapt to mind. If Dontane wasn't trained in the craft of sorcery, he had at least been much around those who were. "Where's Grandier keeping himself these days?"

"Who? I don't know the name." It was said admirably, with just the right amount of confusion.

Thomas smiled. "Then you must have been under a bushel. Everyone else knows it." After Dr. Braun's murder, rumor had spread out of control in court circles and Urbain Grandier's name had been prominent, though without any real detail.

Dontane's expression froze and for a moment he looked dangerous, and not at all like the drunken puppies that Castero had herded out.

Dangerous, Thomas thought, *but weak, like Lestrac, Someone's useful tool.* He said, "You will be glad to know that I am extending the hospitality of the palace to you."

"You'll regret this." Dontane gathered up the remains of his façade, and spoke with drunken arrogance.

"I'm sure one of us will," Thomas agreed.

———

It was evening by the time they returned to the palace. The rain had stopped but the clouds still obscured the stars and the waning moon. Thomas had seen the prisoners settled in the Cisternan Barracks, with Dontane in one of the cells specially warded against the use of sorcery. Then he set off through the corridor within the outer wall toward the King's Bastion. He wanted to find

Lucas and hear what they had found at Gambin's house, though he suspected it wouldn't be much. The answers he needed would have to be pried out of Dontane. It was pure luck they had managed to catch him at all.

Pure luck, and Kade, who had disappeared again after they passed through the Prince's Gate, taking her confused motives with her. She couldn't be here simply to cause trouble. Thomas might have eventually realized Lestrac's hidden room was there without her help, but he would never have gotten into it in time to question the dying man.

He climbed the rough-cut stone staircase that angled up into the King's Bastion. The tapestry-concealed entrance on the third floor gave onto a long central mirror-lined gallery, which was unusually crowded and noisy for this time of night.

Thomas made his way past a group of loudly talking courtiers and saw the cause of the excitement.

Denzil was dueling with Aristofan, Queen Falaise's poet-companion. They had stripped to their shirts and were stalking each other up and down the length of the candlelit room. The young poet was intent but breathing hard, and was obviously having the more difficult time. Denzil, his blond hair tied back, was moving with easy grace and confidence. It was the social event of the night, the women watching from behind fluttering fans, the men commenting on the performance and quietly placing wagers.

Thomas joined Lucas, who was watching from the sidelines with the old Count of Duncanny and a few other bystanders. "How did it start?" Thomas asked him.

Lucas shrugged. "The boy accused Denzil of insulting the Queen in some way and Denzil challenged him. It's all very mysterious. Neither will say exactly what the insult was."

Arms folded and eyes critical, the old count said, "I don't think they know."

Most duels were sparked by boredom. Courtiers and city-dwelling nobles with little to do except drink, gamble, and argue fought over everything from their wives' honor to the score of card games. This one had a certain impromptu look; there were no seconds and they were fighting in the flickering inadequate light of the long gallery.

Face shining with exertion, Aristofan was quick to take advantage of the openings in Denzil's guard, but his blade never seemed to connect. After a few moments, Thomas recognized Denzil's technique, which was one he had often used himself for training inexperienced swordsmen. Denzil was completely controlling the fight by maintaining a constant distance between himself and the young poet. Denzil was the taller man, and with his longer reach and better control, Aristofan hadn't even a chance of wounding him.

The Duke of Alsene was using a special dueling sword with a black metal cup hilt that matched his main gauche. Thomas noticed Aristofan was using a businesslike dueling rapier. "Where did he get that sword?" He looked at Lucas.

Lucas shifted uncomfortably. "You should have seen the one I took away from him. The boy was going to try to defend himself with a piece of jewelry."

Thomas snorted. "Getting sentimental in our old age, are we?"

"Won't help," the count said quietly.

Thomas sensed movement near him and looked down to find Kade Carrion at his elbow again, watching the fight with a faint look of contempt. He was beginning to wonder if the woman was intentionally following him. As if aware her presence had been noted, she asked, "What's this about?"

Several nearby watchers looked around at the shabby figure of the sorceress in surprise, having not realized she was there until that moment. Thomas said, "Possibly the Queen's honor, possibly nothing. Public opinion is divided at the moment."

She glanced up at him suspiciously. "Oh."

Denzil was continuing to play with Aristofan, turning the duel into a cat-and-mouse game Thomas began to find repellent. *He should end it. Bastard.*

Kade asked suddenly, "Are the rumors about Denzil and Roland true?"

Thomas automatically glanced around to see if any of Denzil's tale-bearing friends were within earshot. Roland had a morbid fear of idle talk, and what the gossips would make of Kade's innocent question would reach his ears in no time. Her presence had cleared the immediate vicinity of everyone except himself, Lucas, and the Count of Duncanny, who was a staunch supporter of Ravenna's faction, and Thomas didn't see any real reason not to answer her question. "If they are, it isn't because of any affection or desire on Denzil's part, at least." He had always seen Roland and Denzil's attachment as a strange sort of parasitic relationship on both sides, and he found himself searching for a way to explain it. "And I don't think it matters. Denzil's real control over Roland is the friendship they had when they were boys. If Roland had other favorites, or even if he managed to notice Falaise's existence for once, it would mean taking his attention away from Denzil, which Denzil can't allow. Roland must know how easy it is for a king to attract admirers; Denzil doesn't want him to discover how easy it would be to use a rival against him."

Denzil was apparently finding the fight as it was boring. He stepped back, tossing away his main gauche and drawing a second one from his sash. The hilt on the long dagger was overelaborate and the blade looked oddly heavy.

A moment later this was explained as Denzil pressed a hidden catch on the weapon's hilt. Two metal rods popped out of the central blade and snapped into positions at acute angles to it. Their movement revealed that the center blade had a serrated edge.

The Count of Duncanny shook his head in disgust and walked away.

Kade squinted, frowning. "What is that?"

"It's for breaking blades," Thomas explained.

"I thought that's what quillons were for."

Thomas said dryly, "Obviously we were all mistaken."

Aristofan shifted his stance and adjusted his grip on his rapier. The weapon was obviously heavier than what he was used to, but it still wouldn't hold up against the main gauche's serrated edge. Aristofan and Denzil circled each other.

"You're about to lose a blade," Thomas told Lucas.

"I've been doing this twenty years and I never needed anything like that," Lucas said, exasperated. "This isn't a duel; it's a murder. That young idiot ought to give over."

"It would look bad. People would talk." Thomas's voice was heavy with irony.

Lucas made an impatient gesture. "He'd be alive to hear them. He's only a poet; why should he care what people say?"

"Everyone does," Kade said.

Thomas looked down at her and saw the tension in the way she was standing, the intent look in her gray eyes, and realized what she was about to do. He decided to let her.

Aristofan attempted a desperate parry and Denzil trapped the boy's sword in his elaborate main gauche and snapped the blade. The Duke's first slash opened a long cut on Aristofan's cheek; his second never landed.

Kade slammed into Denzil from the side. He staggered and twisted away from her, landing heavily. Before she could leap on him, Thomas caught up with her from behind and pulled her out of the way. Denzil leapt to his feet, threw down his sword, and started toward her.

Thomas shoved him backward and said, "Temper, my lord. Take them one at a time."

They were treated to a good view of Denzil with the veneer of civility stripped away. "How dare that bitch interfere with me!" he shouted.

Aristofan had fallen to the floor and was pressing his arm to his face, trying to staunch the blood flow. A couple of watching servants ran forward to help him.

"I'll do more than interfere with you, posturing monkey," Kade sneered at the infuriated Denzil. "Why don't you take on someone with a chance against you?"

"There's a thought," Thomas remarked pleasantly.

Denzil focused on him and his expression changed. He smiled and gestured back toward the fallen poet. "Is that the problem, Captain? Am I usurping your duty?"

They regarded each other for a moment, long enough to realize the entire chamber had fallen silent. Thomas turned and saw Roland standing in the doorway at the far end of the room, his attendants grouped around him. After a moment of angry contemplation, the King strode forward and shouted, "What is this?"

"What do you think it is?" Kade asked him with withering contempt.

Roland turned a slightly darker shade of red, embarrassment added to anger, and said, "You will all stop this immediately."

There was some shuffling among the spectators as they tried to look as if they were obeying. The main figures in the drama simply stood there and stared at him.

Roland looked at Denzil and started to speak, then abruptly wheeled and stormed out of the room. Denzil recovered his sword and went after him without even a glare for anyone else.

———

As Thomas expected, Lucas and the others had found nothing incriminating at Gambin's house that had any bearing on Urbain Grandier. They had brought the body and its effects back to the palace and Galen Dubell had promised to examine them.

Thomas had gone out to the portico that extended off the third floor to take a shortcut across to the main part of the building when Kade caught up with him.

She asked loudly, "Why did you stop me?"

He turned to face her. The threatened afternoon storm had never produced more than a light rain, but the evening breeze was damp and strong, rocking the lamps hanging from the columns and tearing at her hair. He asked, "Why did you let me?"

He watched her mentally back up to begin again. She demanded, "What did Denzil mean by 'usurping your duty'?"

She could hear it from anyone, and was perfectly capable of badgering him about it. He said, "Queen Falaise had a lover, a young stupid man like Aristofan, nearly helpless with a sword. He became too arrogant, she sent him away, and he insulted her in front of important witnesses. I killed him."

Kade turned that over for a moment. Her eyes narrowed. "You wanted to stop the duel."

"Yes." In spite of everything, he was surprised. For someone who leapt to conclusions as often as she did, her leaps were fairly accurate.

She stared at him. "You bastard, if you want to kill Denzil, have the guts to do it yourself; don't use me for it."

It was foolish to be angry with her, but Thomas found himself saying tightly, "If you don't want to be used, then don't open yourself to it by behaving stupidly and leaving other people to pick up the pieces. You can't play the spoiled witless child all your life."

"Well, it's better than what you're playing at, isn't it?"

"I wouldn't know, having never been so lacking in initiative that I had to act like a raving idiot to get what I wanted."

As Kade drew breath to answer, there was a crash beneath their feet as a glass-paned door was flung violently open on the balcony of the floor below. Both of them flinched.

"My lord—" Denzil's voice said.

"Don't call me that, not while we're alone." It was Roland.

Thomas remembered that this terrace was directly above the balcony of one of Roland's private solars. He and Kade regarded each other in silence. They could hardly object to each other's eavesdropping, Thomas supposed, having just come to the mutual conclusion that they were both too despicable to live in polite company anyway.

Denzil asked, "Are you all right?"

"You ask me that?"

The voices below had grown softer. Thomas took a silent step forward to the railing to hear more clearly. After a heartbeat, Kade joined him.

"What? Were you worried?" Denzil's voice had a laugh in it. "That was barely worth the effort."

"You take too many chances. But you should have left that boy alone. He's nothing." Roland was oblivious to the fact that Aristofan was perhaps a year or two older than himself.

"He insulted me. And you should thank me for ridding you of him. He's your wife's lover."

"He's nothing. All the married women in the city have lovers. My mother has lovers. God knows my father had worse habits—"

"Don't. If your honor means nothing to you, it means something to me."

And how is Roland's honor affected by an insult to Denzil? Thomas wondered. Where was Dr. Dubell to ask the pertinent question?

"Sometimes I think you're the only one."

Denzil did not dispute this. "I'm sorry I upset you. That bitch of a sorceress—"

"Is my sister."

At his side Thomas sensed Kade stiffen.

"And where was she when you needed her?"

"She ran away. I loved her and she left me behind without a second thought."

Kade shivered once, a slight movement with all the intensity of a restrained convulsion. Thomas found himself unwillingly sympathetic. Roland had been the Crown Prince; his exiled sister could hardly have taken him with her, as if they were farm children escaping a harsh master. And the choice to stay with him in the city had been taken from her by Ravenna's command.

Kade drew back as if to leave. Impulsively, Thomas put a hand on top of hers on the railing and she froze. At that moment an army probably couldn't have kept her on that balcony by force, but that gentle touch seemed enough to hold her there.

"Who stayed with you?" Denzil asked.

"You did. I'd have died without someone."

"Then it's a good thing she wasn't all you had." There was silence, then a creak as one of the men below opened the door.

Thomas released Kade's hand, and she vanished back through the archway.

CHAPTER EIGHT

K ADE FOUND HERSELF in need of company. Falaise was the only person
she could think of who might possibly be willing to put up with her, and
Kade was in such a mood that she was willing to put up with moping,
which was probably what Falaise was doing at the moment.

The Queen's apartments were on the fifth level of the King's Bastion, but
when Kade came up the stairs to where she could see the doorway of the first
antechamber, it looked like a disturbed anthill. Gentlewomen and maidservants were running in and out, and Queen's guards were stalking around outside the door. *That doesn't look promising,* Kade thought. She didn't particularly
want to start another sensation, so she crept back down the stairs and out of
sight.

The next stairwell gave onto the cathedral-like entrance of an old gallery,
and she stopped in front of the oaken doors carved with willows and birds
of paradise. This was the hall where the royal portraits were kept, "where the
family was interred," as some long-ago courtier had referred to it.

After a moment of hesitation, Kade went inside.

It was cold with the chill of marble, fine wood laid over stone, and gilded
frames, and it felt barren as rooms that have never been lived in feel. The hall
lanterns illuminated ancestors, distant relations, and the notables of this or
other ages, which Kade passed by without more than a cursory glance. There
was only one set of portraits here anyone ever came to see. They were the
Greancos, the portraits of the royal family.

Other painters had done royal portraits that were scattered about the palace
or presented to favored nobles, but Greanco had been a seventh son of a seventh son, with half his mind in the Otherworld. Having a portrait done by him
was to take a chance at having one's soul revealed. Fortunately for Greanco,
this held a fascination for Ravenna and her family that had kept him at court
longer than anyone else would have put up with him.

Knowing the effect and having felt it before didn't help; shivers ran up Kade's
back as she stood beneath those canvas eyes. She had to fight the conviction

that there were people watching her who disappeared when she turned to face them.

She stopped before the portraits of the old kings: Ravenna's father and grandfather. Their hard eyes stared down at her. Both men had been beleaguered warrior kings, and the primary impressions the portraits gave were those of guile and strength. Undoubtedly they would have found Ravenna a proper daughter; her strong features were echoed in theirs. But what would they think of Roland, Kade wondered. Or herself, for that matter? *Probably not much,* she decided. Why Ravenna's father had chosen to settle the ruling right on Fulstan and not on her was a mystery. Perhaps he had not entirely trusted her, or perhaps he mistook independence for willfulness. Kade had heard that Fulstan had always put on a good show for his father-in-law. It hadn't mattered in the end, and Ravenna had had the kingdom in reality, if not in name. *We all make mistakes,* she told the portrait silently, as she moved on. *But some of us have to live with them.*

There were solemn representations of other relatives, and courtiers she should have known, generals or statesmen who had walked these rooms when she was a child and had since died. But like the children she had played with until her father found reasons to send their families away, she only dimly remembered their faces and couldn't quite recall their names.

Then she circled a pillar and found herself facing the portrait of Fulstan in his prime. Surprisingly, Kade could look at it without emotion; Greanco had painted an empty slate, a weak vessel that had not yet been subjected to the stresses that would deform it. He had faithfully depicted the handsome features, the full brown hair, and the wide-set blue eyes but had managed to give the impression that the beauty was transitory, and not something that grew out of character, that would last through age. The later portrait that revealed the older bitter man was said to hang in Ravenna's bedchamber, there only because the Dowager had reportedly said that she couldn't think of a better place for him than nailed up there on the wall, watching.

After the Arlequin's attack, Denzil had brought up the subject of Fulstan's suspiciously quick illness and death, and Kade had felt an odd mingling of triumph and guilt. She had been almost certain for years that she had caused Fulstan's death with that same unskilled power that had smashed the cathedral's windows, that she had wished him dead all the way from the Monelite Convent. But she was a little afraid of those thoughts, too. She wanted to think her sorcery had some control, that it wasn't as wild as her fay magic. But study was the only cure for lack of control; she should be studying in the quiet peace of Knockma instead of stirring up trouble here.

The next portrait was of Roland as a child. The better-known and inferior portrait by Avisjon hung in a more prominent location downstairs. Despite the trappings of royal tunic and mantle, the scepter and the Hand of Justice, Greanco had captured Roland's frightened eyes all too well.

She wandered down the wall a little and unexpectedly encountered her own portrait.

I should have known, she thought, staring. Ravenna wouldn't have let Roland burn the rags Greanco used to wipe his brushes, let alone one of his paintings.

When it had first been painted so long ago, Kade had been upset that her awkwardness and anxiety had been so well revealed. Now she saw what had really been there. It was pain.

So that's what it was like, she thought. *It seems I might have forgotten.*

Kade now understood why Ravenna had the portrait put away after it was complete. It was also a reproach. How it had found its way up here she couldn't imagine.

She stepped back to where she could see both her own and Roland's portraits and thought, *Did I run away?* At the time it had seemed a glorious escape. *What would have happened if I'd stayed? Nothing or everything.* She couldn't remember being angry at Roland when she left for the convent. She felt like a contributor to that expression on Roland's young face that Greanco had captured so well, and she didn't like the feeling. *I should leave, tonight, now,* she thought wearily. *This isn't turning out the way I imagined and I'm just in the way. Now that they've seen me again they probably won't even be afraid of me anymore.*

Kade remembered that hot Midsummer Eve's day when the power had come flowing out of her as if she were a bottle shattered from pressure within. She hadn't had any grudge against the cathedral itself; in fact, she rather regretted the destruction of those stained glass windows. She had done simple magics under Galen Dubell's tutelage, but that had been the first time the ability had risen in her with such strength, the first time she could focus it at will. It had been marvelous. But it was the first and only time. She would not reach that peak so easily again. The only road to that kind of power was the one of hard study, and she had dedicated the years since to mastering her abilities, though it had never been easy. And perhaps she had let the more painstaking magics of sorcery take second place to the easy power of fayre.

She turned to go, but she had missed the paintings on the other side of the gallery and now one caught her eye. It was an informal portrait of a younger Ravenna with an elite group of her Queen's Guard and the officers. She sat in the center, dressed in a mantua of black velvet and flame silk, a rose of diamonds on her breast. A younger Thomas Boniface leaned on the chair at her side and slightly behind her, with the rest of the guards grouped around, all handsome and all with a pronounced air of danger.

Kade didn't remember seeing it before. It must have been done after she had left, to commemorate the recently victorious Bisran War, when Ravenna had brought the years of fighting to an end. It was odd that it wasn't somewhere downstairs, but Kade supposed that it had been scandalous for an independent queen with a useless husband to have her portrait done with a group of young men. But then that was Ravenna down to the bone, and Greanco had conveyed that, too. During that war, Ravenna had traveled extensively around the disputed borders with her guard and one or two maidservants. Knowing Ravenna, she had probably chaperoned the maidservants more than they had chaperoned her. A few bishops had spoken out against her, but the rest of the country thought the Church poked into other people's morals too much as it was; landlaw barely took notice of adultery, and queens had traditionally taken lovers among their personal bodyguard.

It was the tacit rules of landlaw that allowed Ravenna to keep command of the Queen's Guard when she should have passed it on to Falaise as the younger woman was crowned. Under landlaw, a personal bodyguard could not be inherited or given away without the liege's permission. If there was something Ravenna was good at, it was manipulating laws and circumstances to her own ends.

I should learn to do that, Kade thought, bitterly amused at herself. But fayre had few laws, or at least few that made sense. Like the court, the denizens of the Kingdoms of Fay fought, plotted, and stabbed one another in the back to excess, but they were soulless creatures and their passions were short-lived and shallow. The outcomes of their games didn't really matter to them, and there was nothing like the solid trust that was reflected in this portrait . . .

You are getting sentimental, you idiot.

The next portrait was of Thomas Boniface, also in informal dress. Even for a Greanco it was dark and elusive. Though Thomas was more than ten years the elder, he and Denzil had much the same presence in person: arrogant and sensual and well aware of their own worth, both wolves in lapdogs' clothing.

The portrait suggested that in the captain's case the arrogance might be tempered by irony.

Tradition dictated that the Captain of the Queen's Guard as well as the Preceptor of the Albonate Knights renounce all familial connections so their whole loyalty would be to the crown. Nepotism and interfering relations could be permitted with other nobles who served in the palace, but these positions were seen as too important. Renier had been duke of something, Kade remembered, when he handed the whole thing over to a younger brother and took his post for Roland. Thomas would have been Viscount Boniface.

Both court offices came with a huge amount of wealth and some land, but gave up the right to leave that wealth to any heir other than the next man appointed to the position. If the Albonate preceptors lived to retire they were usually created a duke and awarded estates and income. It was assumed the same thing would be done for the Captains of the Queen's Guard, but in recent history all of them had died at duty.

Kade realized abruptly that Thomas Boniface probably expected the same to happen to him. If he outlived Ravenna his position at court would not be a good one. Roland and Denzil were both against him, and Falaise seemed helpless to protect anyone including herself. That was what the portrait conveyed, Kade knew suddenly. It was the face of a man who took service with the crown accepting the possibility of eventual betrayal and a violent death, but not one who enjoyed having to kill people whose main crime seemed to be stupidity.

Kade turned away and started resolutely for the stairs, telling herself, *I don't know why I care; I don't even like him anymore anyway.*

Then the nagging restlessness that had plagued her coalesced into dread, and she stopped in the doorway. Her heart was fluttering. She took a deep breath, her hand pressed to her chest, and tried to think what it could be.

Something's gone wrong; something's happening. She forced herself to move forward, to start down the stairs. *I've got to get to Galen.*

"What kind of a man is Grandier?" Thomas asked.

Kneeling on the floor beside the wall niche, Galen Dubell paused to give the question serious consideration. "He is driven," he said finally, looking up at Thomas seriously. "And in pain. The worst sort of opponent to face."

They were in one of the deep cellars of the Old Palace, the rough stone walls glistening faintly in the flickering light of the candlelamp. Stone pillars as wide as draft carts stretched up into darkness to meet the arched ceiling somewhere overhead. The dirty straw-dusted floor was littered with broken or empty barrels, boxes, and odd pieces of ironwork. Battered and forgotten siege engines, lowered through traps in the ceiling sometime in the dim past, looked like the metal skeletons of beached sea monsters in the half-light. Wandering at the edges of the light were Baserat, Treville, and Martin: the three Queen's guards Thomas had assigned to watch Dubell when the old man's work took him into deserted corners of the palace. They were fighting both boredom and nerves and trying to look unaffected.

In an effort to discover what was wrong with the wards, Dubell was examining the warding stones buried in various locations around the palace. He was also planning on moving the keystone. He could remove it with Thomas and the guards present, but he would have to convey it to its new resting place alone. Thomas wasn't happy about Dubell moving about the undercellars of the palace unguarded, but the keystone was kept safe by being hidden away among the hundreds of other warding stones. Dubell was the only one who would know its exact location.

After carefully examining the dull-colored egg-shaped warding stone, Dubell replaced it in its wall niche and sealed it up with clay, handing the bucket back to the unwilling servant boy who had been drafted for the task.

"Driven by what?" Thomas asked, though he wasn't sure why he was pursuing the subject. Though if it provided no insight into Grandier, it might reveal something about the way Dubell thought.

"By his convictions." Dubell climbed to his feet awkwardly and they started toward the pillars in the center of the cavernous room, the boy trailing behind.

The cellar was damp, but the air was neither too hot nor too cold, and not at all stale, as if the airshafts within the thick walls of the Old Palace overhead might have openings somewhere in the cellar's ceiling.

Thomas had followed Dubell down here to ask him what he had found out about Gambin's death, but Dubell hadn't been able to discover what the spy had been killed with or how it had been done. Now that Thomas was down here, he might as well wait until Dubell was finished; the old sorcerer might be helpful during Dontane's questioning. Thomas said, "I don't understand why his convictions would lead him against us. This isn't Bisra. If a sorcerer steals or kills his neighbor, he's hanged just like anyone else, but not for practicing magic."

Dubell gestured with his trowel. "That, of course, is the difficult point. Why is he here at all? In Lodun we believe he has never been across our borders before, even though his father was from Ile-Rien. He has certainly never been accused of a crime, justly or unjustly, by our crown or magistrates. Which leads me unfortunately to believe that his grudge against this land or this city is ideological, in which case there is little that can be done to deter him."

Thomas shook his head. "I can't agree with that. There's a member of the city Philosophers' Academy who has invented some kind of clockwork that can add figures when she turns the knobs on the outside. The Inquisitors General in Bisra heard about it and have declared her a devil's servant, and if she ever crosses their border they'll kill her. If Grandier considers himself such a scholar, why isn't he still over the border giving hell to the Bisran crown?"

"It would certainly seem more sensible of him. Unless"—Dubell paused as the idea occurred to him—"he has been offered money by someone to persecute us."

"That's been considered." In Bisra, mobs surrounded the churches where the Inquisition held court, accusing one another of witchcraft and seeing demons under every bush. If it came out that the Bisran crown had employed a man who had escaped the death sentence for black magic, there would be riots it would take them weeks to put down. Thomas kicked a pillar thoughtfully. He would have to consider ways to let the appropriate rumors slip across the border. "Grandier might do it, if they offered him something he wanted badly enough."

Dubell shook his head, brow furrowed. "If I were him, I think my quarrel against them would run too deeply."

"There are several possibilities as to who could have hired him." Thomas had no wish to discuss the possibilities of who were nearer at hand than Bisra; not with Galen Dubell, at any rate. "And you have never heard of this man Dontane?"

"Not in connection with Urbain Grandier. Not at all, in fact. The poison that the poor fellow Lestrac was given tends to cause hallucinations and delusions before the sleep that soon turns to death. He might have accused the man falsely."

Thomas didn't think it had been a delusion. Lestrac had been too certain, too angry in his betrayal. "Kade seemed sure that he was the one in the room with Lestrac. She made his likeness form in a pool of wine."

"That is not entirely a tried-and-true method. Kade is"—Dubell hesitated—"quite brilliant in a peculiar way. But she also tends to let her imagination get the best of her."

Thomas, who also thought of Dubell as brilliant in a peculiar way, didn't comment.

Dubell stopped at one of the huge pillars and pointed to a square section near the base that had been carved out and refilled with clay. "This is where the keystone is buried. I've already prepared the new location for it, and it will only take me a short time to convey it there. Not long enough to cause any degeneration in the wards."

Frowning, Thomas knelt to look at the clay seal more closely. "This is recent. Have you looked at it before?"

"No." Dubell stooped anxiously, and started to pry out the clay. "Perhaps Dr. Surete . . . God, if it's been this all along . . ."

The explosion was like a cannon going off directly over their heads. The stone pillars trembled with the shock of it, releasing a rain of dust and rock chips from above. Thomas stood, then staggered as the floor slipped suddenly under his feet. Deafened by the noise, he waited for thousands of tons of stone to come crashing down on top of them.

The walls shuddered back into stillness.

Thomas and the other guards stared at each other in blank shock. "What . . . ?" whispered Baserat.

Dubell had rocked back on his heels with the concussion but kept digging away at the clay seal. It broke under the pressure and he shoved his hand back into the niche. "It's empty," he said, and began to curse Grandier.

Thomas hauled Dubell to his feet. "Come on," he said and led him and the three guards at a run toward the stairs. *It might have been the city armories,* he thought. The two long stone buildings housed stores of gunpowder and stood on the opposite side of the inner wall from the Gallery Wing. But even if both had gone up at once . . . No, there was no accidental cause for an explosion like that; the palace was under attack, from outside or from within. He tried to remember who had been on duty in the building overhead, and where Ravenna was likely to be.

They reached the staircase at the far end of the shadowy darkness. Thomas took the lamp from the guard who had had the presence of mind to bring it and held it up. The narrow stairs spiraled upward, unblocked as far as the light reached.

Thomas said, "Load your pistols."

Dubell took the lamp and moved to peer uneasily up into the stairwell as the guards loaded their weapons with the swiftness of long practice. By the time Thomas closed the cover over the priming pan of his second wheellock and tucked it back into his sash, he had calmed himself enough to think clearly. If the few of them were going to do any good, there could be no mistakes.

He started up the stairs, the others following behind him. The four-story climb might have stretched to infinity.

They had reached the second flight when there was a yell from behind and Thomas turned back. Treville slumped on the stairs, clutching his side. The figure standing over him was nightmarish; it looked like a man, but its skin was gray and foul, its clothes in brown tatters, its hair a torn greasy mop. It seemed as though they froze there, staring at the apparition, for moments, but it must have been only half a heartbeat because the creature never had another chance to move. On the stairs below, Baserat struck upward at the same time that Martin fell on it from above, almost succeeding in impaling himself on the other guard's sword.

Dubell flattened himself back against the wall so Thomas could get past. The two guards stood back from the creature now, looking down in shock. Thomas had to put a hand on Martin's shoulder to move him out of the way before he could see it.

Its narrow features twisted in death, it looked like a man who had been held prisoner in a dark place for a very long time and starved. The wound in its chest where the point of Baserat's rapier had emerged was bloody but also burned, as if the metal blade had been red-hot.

Dubell edged down past them and helped Treville sit up. Thomas picked up the weapon the creature had used. It was a bronze short sword, with a narrow blade and wickedly sharp edges. Not much protection against a steel weapon, but it did its job well enough on human flesh.

"It was up above us, perched there, Captain," Baserat said, his voice a little unsteady.

"What is it?" Thomas asked Dubell.

"Fay, but I don't recognize what sort." He finished staunching Treville's wound and looked up at them. "With the keystone removed from the matrix for more than a few hours, the wards would begin drifting away from the outer walls of the newer sections of the palace. The creatures must have been waiting for a large enough opening."

Thomas felt everyone's gaze on him. He had known it must be an attack, but he had assumed the enemy was human. Ignoring the cold dread creeping up his spine, he looked down at Treville. "Can you walk?"

"Out of here I could run." The man grinned weakly.

"Good." Thomas looked at the others. "Let's go, gentlemen."

Dubell helped Treville to his feet, then reached back to collar the servant boy and pull him farther up the stairs. "Here, boy, carry the lamp, and don't fall behind."

The boy took the lamp in a shaking hand and whispered, "Yes, Sir."

The air in the stairwell was growing warmer. It might mean the entrance above them was blocked, or the building overhead had caught fire, or collapsed entirely. *It might have been Kade. It might have been her plan all along,* Thomas realized. He had no idea why that thought made him so angry. She had never promised him anything.

The final turn brought Thomas to face the wooden doorway at the top of the stairs, which still stood open as they had left it earlier. The darkened corridor was blocked by the collapse of its wood-and-plaster ceiling. Dim lamplight shone down from the resulting gap in the passage above.

Thomas climbed the debris and took a cautious look through the opening in the ceiling. Above them was a passageway, its floor and one wall wood while the rest was the original stone. The source of the light was hidden around a corner farther up the way. He thought about the layout of the Old Palace and decided they were near the lower kitchens and storerooms. There were many ways leading out into the rest of the structure from here; some would have to be unblocked.

"All right," he said to the others, "this is our way."

It took some moments to get Treville up into the passage, his wound making their efforts to help difficult and painful for him. Just as Thomas gave Dubell a hand up, Baserat signaled them hastily for silence. "Hear that?" he whispered.

In another moment they all did. There were people farther down the passageway. For an instant Thomas found it a relief that they were not the only survivors of some immense disaster, then the faint sound turned into a tumult as shouts and a woman's scream echoed down to them.

"Save your pistols," Thomas told them. The unspoken thought was on all their faces. *Because we don't know what we'll find upstairs . . .*

Thomas ran down the passage and burst through an archway into a large low-ceilinged storeroom. A group of men and women dressed as servants was trapped in a corner, half surrounded by a dozen or so of the sickly emaciated fay. The servants fought the creatures off with torches and makeshift clubs and whatever else they had been able to find. The fay rushed their new attackers as they entered the room. The first leapt at them, waving its sword over its head, and was disemboweled by Thomas's rapier. A bronze sword swung at him from the side and he swept it away and punctured the owner's chest.

One fay kicked over a lamp, sending the room into near darkness. *Obviously the creatures can see in the dark,* Thomas thought, parrying another thrust. *Pity we can't.*

Dubell shouted something and clapped his hands. Immediately a small bright ball of pure light appeared over his head and hovered there, flooding the room with a stark white illumination.

From behind, something grabbed Thomas's arm and swung him around. The strength was astonishing for a creature so apparently delicate. He slammed the rapier's heavy hilt into its face and it fell away from him with a shriek.

As he turned, Thomas saw that three more fay had come at them from the door to the passageway. *Hell, they must have been following us up the stairs.* One had attacked the wounded Treville from behind, and he was now sprawled bleeding on the floor. Martin leapt over his wounded friend to knock the creature away from him; as it staggered back he drove his rapier through it.

Nearby another fay grappled with Dubell, trying to plunge its sword toward his face, but he managed to hold it off. Then Dubell shifted his weight and shoved the creature up against the wall. Thomas stepped up behind Dubell, said, "Pardon me, Doctor," and finished it off.

All the other fay in the room were down. The spell light above Dubell's head died away as the servants relit their lamps, and the strange unwavering white light was replaced by the familiar flickering yellow.

"Captain," someone gasped at his side, and Thomas turned and saw Berham. The servant had armed himself with a crude but effective iron club. "Captain, there's fighting in the hall by the round stair. We could hear the shots. That's where we were making for."

"Good." As an afterthought, Thomas asked, "Do you know what's happened?"

"No, Sir, I couldn't say that." Berham's story was like their own. He had been visiting nearby when the explosion had occurred. As a veteran of the last war, his instincts had taken over and he had gathered survivors, armed both men and women with what was available, and set off to join the organized resistance.

Martin came up to them as Berham finished, saying bitterly, "Dr. Dubell said Treville's gone, Sir. The bastards go for the wounded like wolves."

"Aye," Berham said softly, looking back toward the bodies of his companions who had not survived the ambush. "I noticed that."

"Take his sword and give it to Dr. Dubell. Let Berham use the pistols. We'll come back for the bodies when we've secured the palace," Thomas told him, and thought, *I sound like a bloody idiot of an optimist.*

But it was what the other two men wanted to hear. As they moved to obey, Thomas went to where Dubell still knelt beside Treville. Dubell looked up at Thomas and said, "I'm sorry."

"It wasn't your fault," Thomas said automatically.

Dubell's face was drawn. "The fay are attacking in force. This is no raid. It's another damned war, Captain."

Another damned war, Thomas thought. *But the Bisran army fought us for two decades and they never got as close as this.*

As they returned to the others, Baserat was leaning over the fay that Thomas had disemboweled, poking the entrails experimentally with the tip of his sword. "See, it looks human to me."

"You're right. I wish I had my glasses." Dubell peered down at the creature, then said, "As I thought. The Unseelie Court, or the Host, as they are more commonly called. On their nightly rampages they seize human captives whom they will use to attack their fellows." He paused as Martin came up and handed him Treville's rapier. Dubell looked at the weapon as if he wasn't sure what it was, then said, "Yes, of course."

"What makes men turn into that?" Thomas nudged the corpse with the toe of his boot. It was hard to believe it, though he knew Dubell must be right.

"Prolonged exposure to the influence of the Host. Their captives become like them. Iron becomes poison to them. They gain some powers of the Fay, but they lose their souls in the process."

The room had grown silent as the others listened, watching them with bruised faces and apprehensive eyes.

Something bumped his elbow and Thomas looked down to see the servant boy who had somehow managed to survive so far, peering interestedly down at the fay's corpse.

"Berham," Thomas said. "Keep this one with your lot."

"Yes, Sir," Berham said, gesturing sharply. "Come away from there, boy, before you get in the way."

There would be far too many people wandering about without Berhams to organize them. Unarmed retainers and servants, children who could not fend for or protect themselves, sheltered women who might not think to pick up a weapon. "We have to get moving," Thomas muttered.

Kade was on the stairs in the King's Bastion when the explosion shook the Old Palace. She held onto the balustrade as the walls trembled in sympathy with the adjoining building. A stiff breeze poured up the stairwell; the stink it carried made her wince. The shaking stopped and the beams supporting the stairs gave an uneasy creak before deciding to hold. Kade started down again, stumbling occasionally because her legs were trembling for some reason. The inexplicable wind had ceased with the reverberations of the explosion, but it had left the air smelling of mud, stale water, and death.

It can't be the wards, Kade told herself uneasily. *It can't be.*

She found the bottom of the stairway blocked by a panic-stricken crowd of palacefolk and servants and she had to go back up a flight to work her way around by back passages. She could smell smoke now, from fires that had caught when candles and lamps were knocked over.

When she reached the long gallery that connected the bastion to the Old Palace, it was badly lit and in chaos.

Albon knights milled around the doors and Renier was shouting orders. Over the noise, someone yelled, "If you don't send them to help us fight the fire, they won't have anywhere to retreat!"

Kade ducked into the crowd, slipping past a mailed arm before it could stop her. She emerged onto the wide balcony of the great spiral staircase that led down into the main hall of the Old Palace.

It was a pitched battle.

The main hall was on two levels and the wide sweep of steps leading down to the lower portion was where the battle line had been drawn. Furniture, boxes, and other debris had been piled up at the top of the steps as cover for the defenders. Queen's guards and a few Albon knights and Cisternans defended the barricades along with disheveled courtiers, retainers, and servants who had either taken up weapons or crouched back behind the defenders and reloaded pistols. The lower half of the hall was walled away by a palpable unnatural darkness. Missiles flew out of that darkness, bronze-tipped bolts of a deadly effectiveness demonstrated by the number of corpses sprawled on the floor.

Kade started down the staircase, one hand on its wide banister. The zoomorphs carved on the stair's central column leered out of the shadows as they were briefly illuminated by torches, adding to the nightmare quality of the scene. Refugees struggled past her, palacefolk and wounded guards.

As she fought her way closer, she began to see past the curtain of shadow in a way the others defending the barricade below could not. There was movement in that darkness, mangled faces, shifting forms, distorted or partly human. *The wards must be gone, at least over the Old Palace and the Gallery Wing; that's how this mess got in,* Kade thought, and forced herself to keep moving down the stairs toward that chaotic darkness stretched across the hall. *But what drove them here?* It was the Unseelie Court, the rulers of the dark fay and the other creatures who fed on blood and terror, who rode the night in the form of the Host, preying on humans and destroying every living thing in their path. They traveled the sky on dark windy nights accompanied, the church priests claimed, by the souls of the dead and wreaking havoc wherever they went.

At the bottom of the stair, Kade started toward the barricade, dodging running forms, ignoring startled glances of recognition. As she reached the hastily erected wall of broken furniture and tried to peer through it, she heard, "If it isn't the Queen of Air and Darkness."

The voice was sibilant and soft and came to her clearly over the noise. She looked down slowly and saw the face through a gap in the barricade. It was Evadne, one of the princes of the Unseelie Court. His narrow features might have been called handsome by someone less picky about character, even if his skin was powder blue. But though his expression was that of a wistful fay child, his eyes were gloating and entirely adult. Kade said, "Your eyesight is as bad as your sense of humor." She had never truly accepted her mother's title, which Evadne must know.

He grinned up at her, revealing pointed teeth. "Why don't you join us, my sister? What has the Seelie Court ever given you that you should risk your life to side with them and battle us?"

Kade ignored the growing knot of coldness in her stomach and laughed at him. The Seelie Court was the highest court of the Otherworld. Titania and Oberon ruled it, but spent little time in governing the fay who swore allegiance to them, and occupied most of their days in fetes, rades, contests, or other unreal pastimes of Fayre. The fay loosely attached to the Seelie Court loved daylight and music but were often dangerous to humans, either through acts of mischief or simple lack of concern over human frailties.

The Queen of Air and Darkness was not truly a member of either court, and Kade did not like to think about what would happen to the balances of power in the Otherworld, which she only vaguely understood herself, if this were to change. Evadne must be very confident to risk making that offer. She said, "The Seelie Court has given me nothing, which is far better than the trouble you've given me. What makes you think I'd throw my fortune in with either of you?"

His features drew into a pinched sneer. "The Host grows in power by the moment. The mortals' pitiful protections are scattered and you can't stop us. I'll destroy you myself."

"Promises, promises. Who's your master? Is it Urbain Grandier?"

The eyes hardened. "We have no master."

"I'll tell him you said that when I meet him."

Evadne stepped back, fading away into a darkness even Kade's sight couldn't penetrate. "I expect," he whispered, "that you will. . . ."

Kade dropped to the floor and used the hem of her dress to wipe a clear spot. Evadne had given her an idea. *Those were powerful wards; they couldn't simply dissolve.* They must be about somewhere. If she could find one . . .

"Hey, come away from there." She looked up to see a man in a Cisternan officer's colors, who started back when he recognized her.

Kade said, "I need chalk, wax, and some burnt coal." At his expression she shouted furiously, "Do you want help or not?"

An unblocked corridor outside the storerooms led Thomas and the others into the main hall.

Wounded and refugees were climbing the huge spiral stair up into the King's Bastion and a thick white pall of smoke from pistols and muskets hung in the air. Out of the confusion, Thomas spotted the Cisternan Commander Vivan. He stepped forward and caught the other man's arm. "What did we lose?"

Vivan ran a hand through his dark hair and didn't seem to notice when it came away bloody. He said, "They're in the Gallery Wing, and probably all of the east side."

Thomas kept the shock off his face. "What about the King's Bastion?"

"Secure. Everything inside the inner wall is secure. They didn't come through there."

"The wards," said Galen Dubell, who was suddenly standing beside them. "They have drifted away from the newer structures of the palace, but the foundations in the older sections act as keystones themselves and are holding the wards in place there."

Thomas nodded. "Good, it'll give us breathing room." What he wanted to do most was slam Vivan up against a wall and demand to know where Ravenna and Falaise were, but there was no time, and no sense in it. He knew Lucas and Gideon were on duty and for now he would just have to trust that they had gotten both queens to safety. He said to Vivan, "You're trying to push them back so you can close the siege doors at the top of the stairs?"

"Yes. If we fall back now, they'll push forward and we'll all go, but the sorceress said—"

Thomas stared. "Who?"

"The sorceress said if we gave her some time she could keep them back long enough to let us retreat."

"Where is she?"

"At the barricade." As Thomas started away, Vivan called after him, "Thomas! They're throwing elf-shot."

That explained the ominously still forms that bore no visible wounds.

Thomas spotted Kade's tattered form crouching near the center of the barricade between two Cisternan guards firing muskets. He began to make his way over to her.

She had drawn some kind of design on the floor and was dripping wax from a lighted candle onto it. She was muttering continuously at it and Thomas thought she was saying a spell until he was close enough and realized she was cursing.

He crouched beside her and said, "How much longer?"

She tossed her head to get the hair out of her face and said, "Hours, days, weeks, how should I know?"

A bronze crossbow bolt shot through the barricade and clattered off the stone floor between them. They both hunched their shoulders instinctively and Kade said, "Close," in a conversational tone. She tossed her hair back again.

Thomas reached over and tucked her hair into the back of her smock for her.

She muttered, "Thank you," without looking at him, a slow flush spreading up her cheeks.

He said again, "How much longer?"

"Not long. I'm almost done. Listen, what I'm doing is calling a ward." She stopped, grimacing as the barricade shuddered under another onslaught. "Impatient bastards."

"Calling a ward?" he prompted.

"Yes. Its name is Ableon-Indis and it's supposed to be over the St. Anne's Gate but it's lying across the top of the King's Bastion now. I don't know why."

"Someone's taken the keystone," Thomas told her.

"Damn. That would be the reason, then. The newer wards float away from their places without the keystone in the etheric structure, but the King's Bastion has the strongest warding spells in the old parts of the palace. It's drawing the drifting wards over to it. Not that it's helping much." Her expression was grim. "Anyway, when I finish this the ward should fall toward us here. If I'm lucky it will come to ground right here along the barricade. When we leave, the Host will surge forward, run into it, and get an unpleasant surprise. But Ableon-Indis will start moving upward again almost immediately. What I'm doing here isn't as strong as the warding spells still drawing it to the King's Bastion."

Thomas nodded. "So we'll have only a few moments at best?"

"Yes."

"It'll be enough."

She looked up quickly and grinned.

Berham made it over to them and knelt beside the barricade. "Albons are holding the doors in the bastion, Sir," he reported.

"Which officers are up there?"

"Just Sir Renier that I could see, Sir. They said if I came in they wouldn't let me go back because the idea was to get everyone out, you see."

"All right." Thomas looked around and saw Martin nearby. He waved him over and said, "Find Commander Vivan and spread word that when I give the order to fall back everyone's to stop firing immediately and head for the stairs. We'll have our retreat covered but not for long." As Martin hurried off he told Berham, "You tell the reloaders to make sure they get the wounded out of here before we have to move."

"Yes, Captain," Berham said, pushing to his feet. "By God, this might work."

As Berham made his way back to the reloaders, Thomas saw a disturbance on the other side of the hall. Soot poured out of the great hearth in a dusty cloud. Thomas stood and started toward it. There was something coming down the chimney.

Closer, he could see that the head emerging from under the stone mantel was like a horse's in size and shape. But its eyes were glazed over and white and it looked as though its coat had been removed with a dull knife. It had teeth like a lion. Thomas drew his pistol, but before he could wind the mainspring, the creature plunged out of the fireplace and fell on a group of men and women who had been reloading muskets. It swung its great horse's head from side to side, its teeth tearing as they scrambled to get away.

Reaching it, Thomas drew his rapier and slashed at its side. As it turned toward him with a scream of rage, he drove the point through its neck. It teetered, then fell toward him, dragging him down as it slumped onto the floor.

A second creature emerged from the fireplace. Thomas dropped the rapier and wound the pistol's spring, then braced it on his forearm and fired.

The ball hit the creature in its broad chest along with three other shots fired from different areas of the hall and a fourth ball that all but shattered the wooden mantel of the hearth. The creature dropped like a stone.

Galen Dubell appeared at Thomas's side, pointed at the fireplace, and gestured. The creature's body caught fire as if it had been dipped in pitch and flames shot up the chimney. "That should hold them for a while," Dubell said with satisfaction.

Thomas shoved himself upright and went to put a foot on the fay-horse's neck to work his rapier free. He asked, "Can you help Kade?"

"No, anything I could do might only counteract the effect she is attempting to create and then we would be dead." Dubell smiled grimly. "But I can harry the enemy and perhaps give her more time."

As the sorcerer strode off Thomas looked after him, a little nonplused. *Disasters agree with you,* he thought.

As others ran up to carry the wounded, more fay charged the barricade and Thomas joined the defenders.

Nightmare images flung themselves out of the darkness and were driven back by pistol balls or pikes wielded over the barricade. There were hideous animal-shapes with distorted bodies and wicked intelligent eyes, creatures with oddly human faces and bodies that were formed into startling shapes, and other things that vanished so quickly the mind discounted what the eyes saw. Their shrieking and keening mixed with the blasts of muskets and pistols was deafening.

Thomas had lost track of time when Vivan grabbed his arm and said, "She's ready."

Thomas looked around. The wounded had vanished up the stairway and Commander Vivan had already sent the last few reloaders running after them. Thomas said, "Pass the word: When I give the order, stop firing and fall back into the bastion." He stepped back where he could see Kade and waited for the word to pass down the line.

When the guards at each end signaled ready, Thomas looked at Kade. She nodded, and he yelled, "Fall back!"

Discipline held remarkably, even among the Albon knights, who didn't think themselves obliged to listen to anyone.

The shrieking din from their attackers rose in a crescendo. Thomas moved with the others to the foot of the stairs and looked back for Kade, not seeing her among the crowd.

She was still crouched beside the barricade. Thomas saw what she had been waiting for. The Host surged up toward the barricade and met a wall of hostile air. Some dissolved into myriad colors that shrieked toward the ceiling and away like fleeing ghosts. Some popped like soap bubbles and disappeared while others fell backward, marked by horrible wounds.

Kade smiled tightly to herself, leapt to her feet, and ran.

Thomas waited for her to reach the stairway before starting up. She was a little ahead of him halfway up the second tier when she was thrown back against the banister as if something had struck her.

The Host started to pour over the barricade. Thomas reached Kade and lifted her up. She was unconscious but still breathing and weighed practically nothing.

The third tier passed in a blur with the fay on the stairs below. Then the Albon knights were closing the siege doors behind him, foot-thick oak panels sheathed with iron. They slammed them to and shoved the heavy locking-bolts home. The foyer was crowded with wounded guards and refugees, and the light was dim and smoky.

Kade let him know she was awake and wanted to be put down with a sharp elbow in his ribs. He set her on her feet and she staggered slightly. "What happened to you?" he demanded, his breath coming hard from the rapid climb.

"I don't know. Ow." She felt the side of her head gingerly. "Where's Galen?"

The old sorcerer was already on the other side of the gallery, helping with the wounded. As Kade turned away to go to him Thomas said, "Wait."

She paused, wary, and he asked, "Did you know this was going to happen?"

"No." Her voice was scornful. "That is the Unseelie Court, the Dark Host, the enemy of light. I wouldn't have anything to do with them. They were the ones who tricked my mother into accepting a wager she couldn't possibly win.

I wasn't much fond of her, but no one deserves— And they would just as soon do the same to me."

He had to be sure. "You didn't mention you knew how to manipulate the wards."

"I wouldn't have been able to call that ward down if the keystone had still been in its place. Removing it destroyed the etheric structure that held the wards in their courses." She winced and touched her head again, then continued more calmly. "Galen taught me how to track wards in a puddle of ash, and the way I called Ableon-Indis to me was only a variation on the spells used to temporarily hold a ward in one place, which every apprentice knows. Ask him if you don't believe me."

There was a muffled thump from the other side of the siege doors, then an echoing roar, as some thwarted creature expressed its displeasure. If Kade had not bothered to aid the defenders, they would have been on the other side of those doors now. Thomas thought, *She didn't have to do it, and it certainly wouldn't serve her purpose if she meant us any harm.* He said, "It won't be necessary to ask him."

Kade hesitated, as if she was just as inexperienced at accepting trust as he was at giving it. Then she turned without a word and slipped into the crowd. Renier pushed past the other Albons clustering near the siege doors to reach Thomas and said, "The doors are holding."

Thomas asked, "What started it?" It had occurred to him that he still didn't know exactly what had exploded or where, except that it was somewhere in the Old Palace or the Gallery Wing.

The big knight looked like he had been run over by a wagon. The final touch was a perfect black eye. He said, "I only know we've lost half the Cisternan Guard and anyone who was posted past the main hall of the Old Palace. Including one of your lieutenants. I saw him going that way just before it happened."

Gideon would be with Falaise in the King's Bastion. "Lucas Castil?"

"Yes, that's him."

"God damn." Thomas leaned back against the wall and used the full sleeve of his shirt to wipe the sweat off his forehead. He could still smell the fayhorse's acrid blood. "Where's Ravenna?"

"She's here in the bastion; I've seen her. Roland was in the Gallery Wing when it happened. We got him out barely in time." Renier hesitated, then said, "I have to talk to you in private."

Thomas looked up at him. With Kade on the other side of the gallery, there was no one to eavesdrop except for their own men, who were standing or lying about in various positions of pain or exhaustion, but Renier's expression was deadly serious.

As they moved off a little, Thomas asked, "How did you get that eye?" Considering everyone else's wounds, it was oddly minor.

"The King was a trifle upset at certain developments," Renier answered with a noticeable lack of expression.

"Well, he's a great comfort to all of us," Thomas snapped. *We've given our lives for an idiot child.* And Lucas was dead.

Renier didn't seem to notice the comment. He seemed almost dazed. "Thomas, I'm not sure about this, but . . ."

Renier hesitated such a long moment Thomas had to take a better hold on what was left of his patience. "Go on," he said in a level tone.

"A knight stationed on the Prince's Gate Tower reported to me a short while ago. He said they could see fires and fighting in the streets. It's not just the palace quarter; it's the city."

CHAPTER NINE

RENIER SPREAD THE gilt-edged map on the table and indicated a spot with one calloused finger. "The Cisternan Barracks were overwhelmed in the first few moments." He cast a worried glance at Commander Vivan, who was slumped in a chair by the fire.

"They came through St. Anne's Gate, then?" Thomas asked.

"No. Mind, the reports we have come from grooms and stablehands who were able to seal off the Mews to keep the creatures out of the Old Courts, but they said the attack seemed to come from the inner gate into the palace, not the outer gate. As to how that was managed . . ." Renier shook his head.

They were in the Queen's Guard House, in one of the small rooms adjacent to the practice hall. The walls were hung with leather and parchment maps and the door was open to the hum of talk from the hall. They knew the human—or once-human—members of the Host had been used as cannon fodder in the initial attack, and that the fay had come after, but Thomas felt they still did not have an accurate picture of how the invasion had taken place. He said, "We still don't know what that explosion was."

"It wasn't the city armories. You can see them from the top of the inner wall. But that's what everyone thought. The off-duty Queen's guards were heading that way to repel what they thought was an attack through St. Anne's Gate when they were stopped at the Old Hall. My men were right behind them."

Thomas saw Gideon drawing breath to make a comment, and cleared his throat. Their eyes met and the younger man subsided with disgruntled reluctance. Most of the guards felt that the main body of the Albon Knights should have followed them down into the Old Hall, instead of staying in the relative safety at the top of the stairs. Thomas was willing to concede that someone had to hold the siege doors; whether the task had required almost the entire Albon troop was another matter. But it had been an act of disorganization rather than cowardice, and he wanted to keep the trouble among the two troops to a minimum. Looking back to Renier, Thomas said, "In the cellars it sounded as if the explosion was almost directly overhead; it must have been somewhere in the Gallery Wing."

"But there's nothing there to explode, not with that sort of force, not unless they brought it with them," Renier protested.

"Maybe they did." Vivan's voice startled them.

Only an accident of history had placed the Queen's Guard House in the area protected by the ancient wards of the inner walls. They had lost far too many men as it was, but the Cisternan Guard, and their families living within the barracks and adjacent to it, had been nearly destroyed.

After a moment, Renier cleared his throat. "We should hear from the commanders of the city levies by morning."

Thomas shook his head. There were over six thousand city volunteers, half musketeers and half pikemen, organized into regiments based on their neighborhoods. Both the crown and the Ministry had the right to call them out, but in the chaos of this night that would be impossible. "The city levies won't be able to form; they'll be too busy defending their own homes and it will be suicide to go out into the streets tonight."

Renier regarded the map again. "The Host has never attacked in force before. It has harried travelers, solitary farmsteads, but never . . . Well, the gate garrisons will be trapped inside until daylight, at least. The Host can't attack when the sun's out."

Thomas had been told by Kade that the main body of the Host was composed of powerful quarrelsome spirits from the Unseelie Court, who could agree on nothing but revelry and fighting the Seelie Court, their opposites in Fayre. In their wake would be fay predators: hags, bogles, spriggans, things that haunted lonely places or preyed on travelers. Thomas said, "They can't attack in the kind of organized force they used on us in the Old Palace, but there's a mob of dark fay following them like scavengers after an army. They aren't organized, but they can stand the daylight and they will attack at any opportunity."

Renier pursed his lips in disapproval. "You heard that from Kade Carrion, I assume. I'd prefer another source for that intelligence."

Thomas controlled an inexplicable surge of irritation, and without too much acid in his voice asked, "Who else did you have in mind to question?"

Frowning, Renier shook his head. "Still . . . There's no help for it, I suppose. Does she know if Grandier is aiding them?"

"No, but he must be involved somehow." Thomas considered a moment. "The Host was depending on surprise, and they had help. Someone knew to go down into that cellar and take the keystone, and whoever it was is probably still here with us." Dontane might have known who that traitor was, but he must have died with the other prisoners and the guards in the Cisternan Guard House.

Renier looked up. "Perhaps the man who killed Dr. Braun got the location of the keystone out of him before he died."

Thomas managed not to roll his eyes. "Braun was killed instantly; he wasn't tortured for information."

"If we could get the keystone back—"

"It could be hidden anywhere." Thomas shook his head, frustrated. "We can't count on that."

"Well, we can't beat our heads about it now." Renier leaned over the map. "The corridors in the outer walls have been sealed. The rooftops and the open areas of the Old Courts are protected by the wards, and the ironshod siege doors are keeping them from coming through the King's Bastion to us. The only thing we can do now is wait it out."

If Renier wanted to "wait it out" with a traitor in their camp it was his business. But Thomas had no reason to argue the point while he still had a few more preparations to make.

Lord General Villon and the siege engine cavalry were posted at the Granges, a royal fortress about fifty-five miles to the south. It was the mobile force closest to the city, except for Denzil's small private garrison still in residence at Bel Garde. The fay might be able to take the city, but they couldn't hold it. They couldn't close the iron-hinged gates, use the cannon mounted on the walls, or the stockpiles of arms. Villon had proven troops and a populace that would rise to aid him as soon as they saw his flags.

Renier rolled up his map and went back out into the hall. Thomas caught Gideon's arm and said softly, "If anyone's going to offer to hold Renier's sword while he falls on it, it's going to be me; is that clear, Sir?"

Gideon smiled reluctantly. "Yes, Sir, it's clear."

As the others left, Thomas hesitated a moment over Vivan, but he had no idea what to say to him.

He walked out through the hall, where things were beginning to calm down as the night wore on without attack. The refugees in the house were mainly palace servants and retainers who didn't mind bedding down on a clear space of floor as long as there was a roof overhead and plenty of iron lying about. They were stretched out on blankets along the walls or huddled in groups telling one another their horror stories from the last few hours. Children played on the second-floor balconies with nerveless unconcern, but no one apparently felt secure enough to put out any of the lanterns, despite the number of people trying to sleep. The only real disturbance was an old man kneeling in the far corner praying at the top of his lungs, while a nervous young girl anxiously pleaded with him to stop.

Queen's guards and the few remaining Cisternans prowled the house like caged cats, checking their weapons over and over again and alert for anything. The refugees of higher class were crowded in the Albon Tower and the Gate Bastion, with the King's Bastion being kept as a buffer area between the fay in the Old Palace and the fortified court. Thomas had preferred this arrangement, knowing that if he had to have a large group of civilians under his protection in a battle, it was better to have ones who were trained to take orders without question. Ravenna and Falaise and their entourages were safely ensconced on an upper floor.

In the entrance hall he found Phaistus, standing before the partly open doors and looking tentatively up at the cloudy night sky. "What are you doing?" Thomas asked him.

Phaistus jumped, then shifted the heavy coil of rope tucked under his arm. "Berham wanted this in the tower, Captain."

His reluctance was understandable. On the open roads of the country, the Host traditionally attacked from above, swooping down on men like hawks on mice. Except that hawks were unquestionably kinder in dispatching their mice quickly than the Host would be with human captives. The wards still clinging to this side of the palace were supposed to protect them while outside, but the wards had failed before.

"Well, come on, then." Thomas hauled him out into the open court.

The night air was chill, the court lit only by light seeping through cracks in shutters and closed doors. The Albon Tower high above them was only a dim shape in the darkness, clouds streaming swiftly across the moon. Phaistus hurried along in Thomas's shadow, casting worried glances at the sky.

The first level of the tower had become an infirmary, and the sick familiar odor of cauterization hit Thomas as soon as he went in.

The wounded lay on pallets along the walls of the high-ceilinged hall. There were women and children among them, far too many. They had been hacked

up by the bronze blades of the human servants of the Host, burned in the sporadic fires that had broken out from overturned lamps, or bitten and clawed by
the fay. There were no victims of elf-shot. If someone was hit by one of those
tiny harmless-looking stones he fell down and never moved or spoke again, no
better than breathing dead, and was lucky if starvation or thirst killed him before the stone found his heart. Anyone struck by elf-shot had been left behind,
or smothered by Dr. Lambe or one of the other apothecaries.

Fires had been lit in the two great hearths, and dozens of lamps and candles
added their stains to the smoke-blackened rafters. The furniture had been
pushed aside to make way for more pallets, and Thomas had to climb over a
couple of tables to reach the other end of the room. It brought back less-than-
pleasant memories of the Bisran War, of border villages overrun and taken
before the inhabitants could scatter into the forest, and of the aftermath of
battle.

Dr. Lambe stood near the long draw table where bags of instruments and
jars of medicinal herbs were laid out. He looked exhausted and considerably
the worse for wear. He looked up at Thomas's approach and said, "Captain,
when can we leave?"

"As soon as it's daylight. The Host won't be able to form then." Thomas
made himself sound sure despite his own doubts.

Lambe didn't look reassured. "And how sure are we of that?"

"I have it on fairly good authority." He had to admit, "What might be wandering the streets is another matter, but they won't be after just anyone."

Lambe glanced upward. The King was on one of the upper floors, guarded
heavily. "You're right about that."

The palace was a trap, and they couldn't afford to be caught in it. Ravenna
and Roland would have to be gotten to safety. *Whether Ravenna likes it or not,*
Thomas thought. His first choice was to get them out of the city and to Villon
at the Granges—and they would have to be together. Roland would be swept
under by the chaos and lose his throne to the first opportunist with a troop.
Ravenna could ride the storm.

Galen Dubell crossed the room toward them. Like Dr. Lambe, the hem and
sleeves of his robe were stained with dried blood. "What sort of protections are
we employing for the evacuation?" he asked.

Before Thomas could answer, an Albon knight stepped up to them and said,
"His Majesty requires an audience, Captain Boniface."

Thomas looked at him, but the knight's face betrayed nothing. After a moment he said, "Very well," and turned to Dubell. "Doctor, could you send a message to my lady Ravenna and let her know I'll be unable to attend her for a short time?"

Startled, Dubell looked from Dr. Lambe's stricken expression to the other Albon knights who had suddenly appeared in the room. He said, "Yes, of course."

Thomas followed the knight to the bottom of the narrow stairwell that led up into the tower, where there were two more Albons waiting for them. He took in their appearance without comment and they started up the stair.

It was a long way up to the fifth level of the tower, the many lamps that illuminated the stone steps making the air smoky and close. There were knights standing guard at each level.

On the landing there were two more Albons at the wide oaken door. The knight who had come after Thomas smiled and said, "His Majesty has requested that you disarm before coming in to him."

Thomas met his eyes. As a member of the Queen's Guard and an appointed officer he had the right to go armed in the royal presence, and he also knew what any sort of protest to that effect would mean to Roland, and what would happen if they searched him inside and found a concealed weapon.

In silence he handed over both pistols, his main gauche, boot dagger, and unbuckled the rapier from his baldric.

One of the knights opened the door and they went inside.

The room was far too warm and too crowded. The gold threads in the red tapestries caught the candlelight and cast it back. There were more Albon knights, all showing signs of the past battle. Some of Roland's younger courtiers were playing cards at a table in a corner, and somewhere out of sight a musician played a soprano recorder. Renier wasn't present. Roland was seated in a tapestry-draped armchair, Denzil at his side.

As Thomas bowed, Roland said, "Kneel, Sir."

Even though he was hearing the latch of a trap snap shut, it was second nature to make it look like an easy gesture.

Denzil smiled lazily and said something inaudible to Roland that made the young King giggle and redden with embarrassment. Thomas realized Roland was not drunk yet, but he was definitely well on the way, and he would have bet anything it was Denzil's doing.

Roland fiddled with a torn piece of lace on his cuff, his eyes large and dark. "What is my mother doing now?"

"She's resting, Your Majesty." Thomas kept his expression even and his voice level. The room had quieted, and the courtiers watched with a fascinated intensity that combined sly amusement at someone else's misfortune and fear for their own necks.

"And my Queen? My cousin has said she refuses to attend me here."

Thomas wondered if Falaise knew she had refused to attend Roland. Probably not. "She isn't well, Your Majesty, and your mother required her to stay in her rooms." This was a lie, but he wasn't going to throw the young Queen to the wolves to save his own skin. *If the matter doesn't become academic in the next few moments.*

Roland said, "Oh." Even at this time, he realized Falaise was not likely to ignore a direct order from Ravenna. But Denzil nudged him with an elbow, causing the knight standing guard behind their chairs to tighten his grip on his sword-hilt. Thus prompted, Roland said, "And my sister?"

"She's in the Guard House, Your Majesty."

Denzil idly twisted one of his rings. His hands were trembling slightly, probably from excitement. He said, "She was seen smearing blood on the lintels and cornerposts of the Guard House. Now why was she doing that, we wonder?"

How the hell should I know? "I don't know, Your Majesty." Thomas directed his answer to Roland, just to see Denzil's expression tighten with anger. It was hardly likely to be anything detrimental; even Kade wouldn't put a curse on a house and then settle down in it for the night. And she obviously hadn't made a secret of what she had done. It sounded more like a feast-day practice one of the foreign cults in the city performed.

Roland absently rubbed the carved arm of the chair, thinking over his next move. Denzil leaned toward him familiarly, watching Thomas out of the corner of his eye, and whispered something. Roland giggled and looked guilty.

Thomas allowed himself to look just slightly bored. Denzil's attempts to prey on his nerves were having more effect on the Albon who was standing behind him and could hear what he was saying.

Finally Roland said, "Perhaps you told her to do it."

"Why would I do that, Your Majesty?" Thomas had always known that if he had to die to please a royal ego, he wanted it to be as scandalous, messy, and politically inconvenient for as many persons as possible. Disappearing into the depths of the Albon Tower was not a scenario he preferred.

Roland didn't answer immediately. He bit his lower lip and looked at his cousin.

Denzil stood and strolled around the room, behind Thomas and out of his sight. He said, "We don't know what part she had in this attack."

Thomas kept his eyes on Roland. "She was almost killed in the retreat from the main hall." Defending her this way could be dangerous for both of them, but he wasn't sure what Denzil was after.

Roland looked surprised. "She was?"

Standing too near him, Denzil brushed Thomas's hair aside to reveal the pearl drop in his right ear. "That's a gift from the Dowager Queen, is it not?"

The door opened and a knight bowed his way in. "Pardon, Your Majesty."

Denzil stepped away from Thomas. Roland shifted in his chair nervously. "What is it?"

"The Queen . . . The Dowager Queen has sent a messenger requesting Captain Boniface's immediate presence."

All eyes in the room went to Roland as most of those present realized the implications of this. Thomas thought, *Don't provoke her, boy, not now.* Ravenna was exhausted and angry and sitting on top of the best-organized force left in the palace with an armory at her back. But if Roland pushed her into a civil war just because he could, then he didn't deserve to be King, let alone to live.

Roland stared at the knight. Denzil started to speak but abruptly Roland waved him to silence and said, "Fine, then, go on. I'm tired."

Thomas stood, bowed, and left the room. He collected his weapons in complete silence from the knights on the landing, then went down the stairs. Martin was pacing restlessly near the outside door.

Reaching him, Thomas said, "Tell her you saw me outside and I'll be there in a few moments."

Martin said, "Yes, Sir," and bolted back across the court. Thomas went the other way, along the tower's wall, until he came to a place in deep shadow but with a good view of the door.

He pulled his cloak around him and stood with folded arms, watching the cloud-strewn sky. The cool wind lifted the hair off the back of his neck, and he thought for a few moments about treason and murder.

But he had learned more from Denzil than Denzil had from him. *He thought he had me. He was sure of it.* He had tried to provoke Thomas to fight. He wanted Ravenna and Roland at each other's throats; he wanted the palace in chaos.

Denzil was confident. He had expected the attack.

He took the keystone, or he ordered it done, Thomas thought. *Never mind how he knew where it was; I'll work that out later. He may have killed Braun himself. And I don't have a shred of proof against him.*

There was only one thing Denzil could want in return for treason of such a magnitude.

The young Duke of Alsene had so much already from Roland. Would he abandon a secure existence on a chancy bid for the throne, based on such infirm ground as the help of a foreign sorcerer? *But is Denzil's existence secure?* Thomas asked himself. *Or more importantly, does he think his existence is secure?* Roland was still Ravenna's son, and Fulstan's. He could have Denzil killed on a whim, at any time. And he was still a young man; he could become as changeable in later life as his father had.

As a patch of moonlight illuminated the court, a swift smooth shadow crossed it. Something large enough to be flying above the wards yet throw a man-sized shadow on the pearl-gray paving stones.

Thomas leaned back against the wall, his dark clothing blending into the rough stonework. A reminder from the Host.

As it passed out of sight and the clouds crept back over the moon, the Albon knight he had suspected was following him stepped quietly out into the court from the door of the tower.

Thomas waited until the man gave up and disappeared back inside, then he started back to the Guard House.

Denzil was in league with Grandier, and regardless of the consequences, he was going to have to die.

———

In the Guard House, Kade sat on the floor near the stairs. She turned over another card from the deck she had found, winced, swept the scattered cards together, and reshuffled them. Something was happening in the Albon Tower, something interesting, and no one would tell her about it. *Who can I pry it out of?* she wondered, looking speculatively around the quiet hall and laying out the cards again.

No one seemed to find her presence objectionable. The refugees had brought her everything from amulets to prayer books to touch for luck, and she had collected several apples, an egg, a few ribbons, and a battered daisy as propitiatory gifts. The guards were all nobles and so less superstitious, but treated her as a sort of mascot, which was better behavior than she had had from any-one connected with the crown in a long time. They knew who had been on the wrong side of the bastion's siege doors with them, and were acting accordingly.

Falaise had sent her a pair of boots. The woman who had brought them had said they were a boy-page's boots, made for a masque last month and brought along accidentally in the trunk the Queen's ladies had hastily packed before leaving the King's Bastion, but the Queen had "thought they would suit best." *She meant they looked big enough,* Kade thought. Falaise and her ladies had small perfect feet, not ugly long-toed things better suited for walking on tree branches. But the boots were soft, blue-stamped leather with gold stitching, and she liked them immensely.

She rubbed the bruised lump on her head thoughtfully. That is, no one objected to her presence openly. She still didn't know what she had been hit with in the retreat to the King's Bastion. An object that small of wood or stone would have certainly startled her, but not knocked her reeling and half conscious against the banister. No, the object had been cold iron, and no fay had cast it at her.

And Thomas Boniface had carried her up the stairs.

That had triggered a memory, a tactile child's memory. She had been six or seven, playing on the warm dusty stones of a palace court with servants' children, and suddenly found herself among a forest of sharp hooves and tall equine legs, horses snorting and dancing around her. For a moment she had found it wonderful. But just as fear had time to set in, a strong arm had caught her around the waist and lifted her out of danger with a muttered "And what do you think you're doing?" She had been deposited on the side of the court with the other children, out of harm's way, and left with a memory of a deep voice and a masculine scent combined with the musky sweat of horses.

Her father had heard about it somehow. He heard about everything some-how. He had called her a whore. When she had told Galen about it, he had slammed things around his small study and muttered to himself for an hour, but he was not quite worldly enough to realize what was bothering her and explain it away. It wasn't until weeks later when a scrubwoman had explained to her what a whore was that she understood she couldn't possibly be one. *A whore,* she thought, old stale anger rising again. At that age. *It's a wonder that I'm not mad as a wool-dyer.* It was a wonder she wasn't as helplessly at sea in the world as Roland was.

"Excuse me, my lady?"

She looked up to see a nervous dark-haired gentlewoman on the stairs above, looking down at her hesitantly. Kade thought her one of Falaise's ladies, but she wasn't the one who had come before. Then the woman said, "My lady, the lady Ravenna would like to speak to you in her chamber."

"Oh," Kade said. She collected the cards and stood up.

She followed the woman up the lamplit stairs to the third floor. The rooms Ravenna and Falaise had taken were in a single suite. There was a group of Queen's guards and two Cisternans standing in the anteroom having a low-voiced, intense, and agitated conversation Kade was sure would have been quite interesting, but the gentlewoman opened the inner door to Ravenna's chamber for her, curtseyed, and fled.

Ravenna sat alone near the shuttered window, head turned to look down at the empty hearth. A few carved chests stood open, and richly embroidered robes and rugs were tumbled about and piled in the chairs. Kade fought a surge of anxiety that suddenly welled up in her gut; she was not a child anymore.

"I wanted to know your intentions." Ravenna turned to look at her, finally. "Why you are still here."

Kade looked down and noticed her feet again. She said, "Why shouldn't I be here?"

"'Why shouldn't I be?'" Ravenna mocked. "Your wit astonishes me. Of course, everything I've built with my life and my blood is tumbling down around my ears; why shouldn't you stay and watch?"

"If you already know then why are you asking?" Kade said it quietly, and looked up to deliberately meet Ravenna's eyes. *That was good. I did that well.*

"Oh, never mind." It was Ravenna who looked away. "I suppose if you actually had some sort of motive, you would give me an answer."

Kade sighed, then realized the old Queen's sharp eyes were on her again and felt a chill that didn't come from the air. Ravenna had set a trap for that telltale expression of relief. "Well," Ravenna said slowly. "Do you still want the throne?"

"No! I just said that; I didn't mean it." *I should have known that would come back to haunt me.* "Can't you just leave me out of your idiot power struggles?" But it was easy to talk about the throne. Ravenna couldn't understand how little it meant to her.

Ravenna's mouth hardened. "No, I cannot. I'm old, and frightened. I get angry when I'm frightened and your brother does not know when to stop pressing me. Or rather, he lets Denzil tell him that it is all some sort of game, and that his mother will forgive him anything, because she wants him on the throne. Well, I'm having second thoughts about that."

Kade folded her arms. "Don't bother having first thoughts about me, because I won't do it."

Ravenna's hard gaze came back to her again, cynical and doubting. Kade said, "I'm serious. It's hard enough being a queen in Fayre, but this is . . . real."

"I wish Roland knew that. I tried to teach him to rule, but he doesn't understand. Our people aren't serf-slaves, like Bisran peasants. They'll riot in the cities and rebel over the vine-growers' excise in the country. The balances of power that must be maintained among the nobles of this city alone . . ." She tapped her fingers on the chair arm and shook her head. "I push Roland, to test him, to make him strong, but he backs away. Then he lets Denzil goad him into pushing me too far."

Kade studied her curiously. Even in the soft candlelight Ravenna was all glinting sharp edges—her sharp profile, her jewels, her eyes. She wondered if her brother understood that someday his mother would be gone, and there would be nothing to cushion him from the battleground of the court. "If not Roland, and not me, then who?"

Ravenna seemed to ignore the question. She said, "I planned it so carefully. I let the Ministry and the guilds gain power. The nobles"—she invested the word with considerable contempt—"clung to each other in salons all over the city, alternately whining and shouting about it, but they couldn't stop me. I reduced the walls of their private strongholds, took away their private armies, so if the flower of nobility wanted to rebel against Roland they'd have a damned hard time doing it. And Aviler has some concept of how a state should function; he would have been able to keep Roland from making too bloody a fool of himself. I made an enemy of Aviler, even though his father was one of my closest friends, because if I had ever shown him favor Roland would never have listened to him. Of course, Roland never listened to him anyway. And now we don't know where Aviler is, or if he's alive." She stopped and looked away. "If not you, then no one."

Kade anchored her gaze on the floor. *She is already speaking of Roland in the past tense.*

After a long moment of silence Ravenna said, "I'm rather an all-or-nothing sort of person when it comes to violence. Roland doesn't understand that."

There was a returning quality of strength and calculation in her tone that made Kade look up.

Ravenna watched her carefully again. "Thomas is rather an all-or-nothing sort of person when it comes to loyalty. I don't think anyone at court understands that, excepting myself and the Guardsmen. You could come to understand it."

Kade stared at her, feeling completely transparent under that gaze. A slow flush of heat reddened her cheeks.

Ravenna said, "Are you sure you won't reconsider my offer? The benefits are considerable."

Kade grated out, "Listen, you dried-up old bitch—"

Ravenna smiled.

Kade took a deep breath to give herself enough air to get the words out. "If you want my help in pulling your fat out of the fire, then you can damn well keep your offers and your speculations to yourself, because I don't want to hear them and I won't, do you understand?"

"Quite well, thank you, dear." Ravenna nodded pleasantly.

Kade stalked out the door and slammed it behind her.

The anteroom was empty. *Why do I stay here?* Kade raged at herself. *I meant to cut off all these old ties, say what I wanted to say, and forget about all of it. To get some peace at last. But I've done nothing but get into stupid arguments with Roland and make Ravenna think she can put me under her thumb again. How dare she even imply . . . Imply what?*

She paced a tight circle in the anteroom, remembering Ravenna's smile at her angry response. *Did I just make a mistake?*

The door to the hall opened and Thomas walked in. Kade jumped guiltily.

"Did you put blood on the lintels and the cornerposts of this house?" he asked her, keeping his voice low.

She held her hand out, to show him the fresh cut across the skin of her palm, and thought, *He has such dark eyes, like velvet.* She was starting to blush again, for no accountable reason. To distract herself, she asked, "What happened while you were gone?"

He regarded her for a moment. "What is it for?"

God, can no one answer a direct question? She folded her arms and looked at the floor. "To keep fay out. To let them know I'm in here, and that I'm not receiving visitors."

"Will it work?"

She shook her head. "Not that well. The ones it will keep out wouldn't be that difficult to deal with anyway. But it's something."

"Why did you choose here, and not one of the other buildings?"

Not wanting to answer, she began to tap one foot in growing irritation. He waited. Finally she lifted her chin and said, "I like it here. There, are you happy?"

He said, "Delighted," and went into Ravenna's room.

Well, I handled that brilliantly, Kade thought. A soft noise made her glance back and she saw Falaise standing in the doorway to her room. She was wearing a pale blue, heavily embroidered mantua and her hair hung like a chestnut curtain. She looked like a startled fawn. "What is it?" Kade asked her, temporarily distracted.

Falaise made a noise like a strangled gasp and vanished back into her room.

Kade followed her. Inside was the tumbled splendor of a parlor attached to a small bedchamber, three ladies-in-waiting looking up at them in surprise. Falaise stopped in the middle of the room and shrieked, "Out! I want to be alone!" It wasn't the full-throated bellow Ravenna was capable of but it worked well enough. As the gentlewomen scurried for the door, Kade stayed where she was, correctly surmising that the order had not been directed at her.

As soon as the door closed behind the last woman, Falaise seized a wineglass from the table and dashed its contents onto the polished floorboards. As Kade stared, the Queen shoved a chair away from the wall that adjoined the Dowager Queen's quarters and crawled under a table, placing the glass to the wall and her ear on the glass.

"What are you doing?" Kade asked, baffled.

"There's a weak board here. I can hear through to Ravenna's room."

"Brilliant!" Kade climbed onto the table and pressed her ear to the wall, but couldn't hear anything but muffled voices. "What are they saying?"

"Shhh."

Short of dragging Falaise out from under the table by the ankles and taking her place, which would cause them to miss some of the conversation, there was nothing to do but wait. Kade paced, tangled her fingers in her hair, and tried to contain herself.

Finally, as doors slammed out in the anteroom, Falaise crawled out from under the table and sat back on the floor with a sigh.

Kade bounced with excitement. "Well?"

Falaise scrubbed wine out of her ear with the sleeve of her mantua. "It was a terrific fight."

"About what?"

"He has a plan for leaving the palace because we're going to be attacked by the fay again. He said they're just waiting, they have a traitor inside helping them, and that when they can come through cracks in the walls, we can't hope to keep them out forever."

There was nothing wrong with that assessment. "He's right."

Falaise sat back on the floor, hugging her knees, looking up at her quizzically. "Are the wards working?" The question was anxious, but not panicky.

Kade decided to tell her the truth. "They're working up above us. But most of them aren't touching the ground anymore. It's only the siege doors and the gates keeping the Host out."

"I see." The Queen bit her lip.

"But what did they fight about?" Kade demanded.

"We're going to be leaving in the morning. But Ravenna doesn't like some part of the plan, and it made her very angry. She yelled and threw things, and said she didn't intend to die alone."

Kade frowned. "Really?"

"Yes, and he told her she was too mean to die at all, alone or in company, and if she thought he was fool enough to fall for these mock hysterics then she should think again and she was going anyway if he had to tie her to a horse." Falaise shook her head, an irritated kitten. "Something happened in the Albon Tower, something to do with Roland and Denzil. But she already seemed to know what it was, and they didn't discuss any details."

"Hell, that's not much." *Maybe I can find out more downstairs.* As Kade reached for the door Falaise said, "If you find out anything else, will you come and tell me?"

Kade shrugged one shoulder. "All right."

"Thank you."

Leaving the room, Kade wondered if Falaise had heard her own conversation with Ravenna, and if it mattered. *It might. She is full of surprises.*

———

Thomas crossed the hall and went into the map room. The fire burned low behind the grate and Vivan was gone; he was unsure if that was a good sign or not. He stood for a moment contemplating a faded parchment map of the city on the table. He needed to go back up to Ravenna, but he didn't trust his temper quite yet.

He knew she would agree to his plan. She wouldn't let emotion get in the way of necessity for too long, and it was only his part in it that disturbed her.

And whatever she did, he didn't intend to give in to her this time.

"Captain! Captain, look!" someone shouted from outside the room. Stepping toward the door, he saw Gideon surrounded by a noisy group of guards and conducting another man across the hall in an apparently friendly headlock.

Thomas started forward as Gideon released his captive with an affectionate shake, and felt an idiot grin spreading over his face as he saw who it was.

Lucas and a younger guard named Gerard, whom they had also given up for dead, staggered into the room under the enthusiastic greetings of their comrades.

Lucas grinned back at him. "What are you gaping at?"

"Why aren't you dead?" Thomas caught the older man in an embrace. "And where the hell have you been?"

Lucas dropped onto a bench at the table. "I've been banging on a bloody gate, trying to get the idiot on the other side to let us in. Before that we were crawling through the streets on our bellies. Look, God bless that man for a saint!"

Anticipating the request, Phaistus was bringing in an armful of wine bottles and tankards.

As the wine was passed around, Lucas said, "It's a wonderful story; do you want to hear the version where I climbed the St. Anne's Gate in a hail of fay arrows with my sword in my teeth and a fainting Gerard slung over one shoulder?"

"You lying bastard!" Gerard objected, slamming down the tankard that someone had just handed him, spraying everyone around him with the contents.

"We got out the Postern Gate, actually," Lucas admitted more soberly. "It's a ruin, no sign of anyone. We couldn't come along the outside wall; there's a lot of somethings-or-others congregated along it that we didn't want too close a look at. We had to go several streets over to get around and back to the Prince's Gate. There's a very large hole in the park side of the Gallery Wing. I couldn't get very close but it looked as though something erupted out of the floor in the Grand Gallery."

Thomas knew Lucas well enough to recognize the fear in his gaze. That fear was masked by bluff, as it was in most men, and the louder the bluff the greater the fear. It was very loud in that room right now. "Out of the floor?" he asked. "Are you certain?"

"Yes. Don't ask me what it was; I've no idea. If we hadn't been in the portico and halfway outside already when it happened, we'd be dead." Lucas turned his tankard around thoughtfully. "As it was we lost Arians, Brandon, and Le-sard." He looked up. "That I know of."

Thomas told him. "Twenty-six altogether, not counting you two."

"That many." Lucas looked away.

"What's it like in the city?" Gideon asked softly.

"It was hard to tell. We saw some houses broken into and burned out, but others locked up tight. No one's out on the streets anymore that we could see. There was ten or so palacefolk that crept out with us, but they decided to chance it in the city. We thought we'd try to make it back here so we could die with our friends like gentlemen." He looked around at everyone. "So? How have you lot been keeping busy?"

CHAPTER TEN

THOMAS AWOKE KNOWING what it felt like to be a corpse—stiff and cold. The fire had burned down to coals, emitting nothing but a dim red glow. Any heat produced was lost in the frigid air. He eased out of the chair and pulled wood out of the stacked pile beside the hearth. His hands were numb.

The kindling he dumped on the coals caught and he started to add the logs. After a timeless wait the heavier wood started to burn and he began to feel alive, and only two or three times his age.

Sitting on the floor in front of the fire and still shivering, he heard the timber frame of the house creak in protest against the onslaught of a harsh wind. It was an oddly sudden cold spell for this time of year.

They should be due for two to three more months of fall rain before winter set in. It never got this cold until after midwinter.

He climbed to his feet and found his cloak on the floor across the room and bundled up in it, then went out into the hall. Only two lanterns were lit there now, and it was as cold as a saint's bed. An old house with this many restless bodies crowded into it could never be entirely silent, but all the sounds—footsteps of patrolling guards creaking the boards on an upper story, the fitful stirring of sleepers on the hall floor, a child's frustrated crying—were oddly muted. Shadowy forms wrapped in blankets stumbled around the dark cavern of the hall's huge fireplace, building up a fire in the hearth that had been scraped clean and unused since last winter. Once they got the blaze going, warmth from the chimney would help heat the upper floors, though not nearly enough for comfort.

Thomas started upstairs, buttoning up the sleeves of his doublet.

There was a small window looking out into the court from the second-floor landing. Ice was starting to form on it already. Clouds still streamed across the sky, allowing the shrinking moon to briefly illuminate the court one moment, leaving it in pitch darkness the next. He could hear the wind howling, and the front wall protesting faintly in response.

He didn't hear Kade's footsteps but was somehow unsurprised when he noticed her standing beside him.

She said, "Grandier had to work on this for days."

He looked down at her but there wasn't quite enough light to see her expression. She looked like a fanciful drawing with her hair flying in all directions and a torn piece of petticoat dragging the ground. She wore a blanket over her shoulders and the night muted the red of her dress, making her look very human and solid. He asked, "How did he do it?"

"A shift in the wind one day, gather clouds from over the sea the next. Very slow work, and very subtle. Oh, it might have made it a little cooler than it should have been, or there was less rain or more rain. But who would notice?"

The slender moon peeping through a gap in the swift-moving darkness above revealed clouds like monoliths, black streaming giants crossing the sky.

Thomas watched the clouds. This was obviously meant to be the last nail in their coffin, trapping them within the city, forestalling aid. "Can you do anything?"

She shrugged. "The spells to do this were set and done months ago, when the forces were favorable. Now the planets aren't in the right houses for influencing the weather, and they won't begin to favor atmospheric magic for another month, at least. His timing of its arrival is excellent, and there's no saying how long it will last. Galen might know of something to try, but I don't. I'm only the Queen of Air and Darkness by inheritance, and I don't have a degree in philosophy from Lodun."

They stood there quiet for a time. The wind's fury made the timber and stone wall of the house seem flimsy, as if they were separated from a vicious animal by only a thin layer of decorative fence. Thomas found himself watching Kade. He was no longer certain what to think about her, and that disturbed him far more than it should, considering everything else there was to worry about. *I always try to understand my enemies,* he thought, *but it's time to admit that the one thing she is not is an enemy.* Finally, he asked, "What does it mean to be the Queen of Air and Darkness?"

Her brow furrowed, she said, "I don't have a kingdom, except for the castles my mother kept. Some of them are in little pockets of the Otherworld, some are in this world, but protected by spells. But in a way . . . From knowing Titania, Oberon, the other rulers of Fayre, I have the sense that what I am somehow defines what they are. I might exist to balance them, the way they exist to balance the Unseelie Court. But it isn't good and evil, either. I'm not particularly evil most of the time, and they aren't particularly good hardly any of the time, at least not by human standards." She shivered, and the moonlight brought silver to her hair. "The Unseelie Court doesn't approve of balance, and they're always scheming to upset things. My mother, Moire, accepted a wager from them, that she could steal all the grain from Oberon's stables without missing a single seed. She got past the fay guarding the stables by changing herself into a beautiful white mare, and she made all the grain vanish—except for one flax seed. The Unseelie Court had suborned a flower sprite that lived in the stable, and it hid the seed in the bell of a flower, so Moire couldn't find it. So she lost the wager, and they sent her to Hell. They seemed to think I should be grateful for it. She wasn't a nice person and we didn't exactly live in a state of joy together, but she was my mother." After a moment she seemed to shake off the recollection and pulled her blanket more closely around her. "The weather will be worse tomorrow. Grandier wouldn't have spared us the snow."

Thomas hadn't missed the hurried change of subject. He wondered why she had told him so much. He asked, "Spared us?"

Kade looked up at him.

"When did it become 'us'?"

She turned from the window and started to walk away, but stopped after a few steps. "Do you remember me?" she asked.

Because of the intimacy of standing here in the shadows watching death come out of the north, or just that he was becoming used to her way of speaking, he knew what she meant. He said, "Not the way you looked, not really. Not very well." He had been away with Ravenna most of the time that Kade had lived in the palace. He recalled occasional glimpses of a gawky youth, that was all.

"I remember you."

He didn't reply. The silence stretched, and Kade faded back into the shadows.

Thomas turned away from the window and went down the stairs and back to the map room. The weather was one more thing to worry about, one more factor to take into account. At least a freeze would put off the possibility of a plague brewing up among the unburied dead in the east quarter of the palace, and the rest of the city.

As he neared the open door of the map room, he saw an outline of a long cloak or robe silhouetted by the edge of the firelight. Someone was there. Thomas stopped in the doorway, feeling an inexplicable chill that had nothing to do with the cold.

But a flare-up from the fire showed him it was only Galen Dubell warming his hands near the hearth, his stooped shoulders shivering faintly underneath his heavy robe.

Stepping into the room, Thomas said, "You're awake early, Doctor."

Dubell looked up and smiled. "It's a trifle cold for my old bones." He shook his head. "I'll begin work on countermeasures against this weather as soon as it's light. You realize it is not natural."

"Kade told me." Thomas lit the candlelamps with a twig from the fire, and began to go through the maps stacked on the table, looking for the one of the city walls and the solid paths through the water meadows. Under the maps, he found the pile of translated Bisran court documents instead. They had been sent over the night of the attack, and he had never had the chance to look at them.

Dubell took the armchair near the hearth that Commander Vivan had occupied some hours ago. "I must admit, Kade is not the same girl I once tutored," he said.

Thomas sat down on the bench and began idly paging through the trial documents. He said, "I would hope not." The list of questions and answers was much the same as the monk's account had been. Grandier had refused to name accomplices, which must have cost him a great deal. Thomas also thought the Inquisition showed an unhealthy degree of interest in sexual relations with demons.

After a long silence Dubell said, "I find myself wondering at her motives."

Thomas looked up. Dubell's expression was vaguely troubled. "I don't think it's as complicated as it seems. She has unfinished business with Roland and Ravenna." Thomas had been younger than Kade was now when he had had the devastating and final confrontation with his father, when he had left to pursue the commission of captain that would allow him to legally and permanently disown his entire family. The urge to try to settle old arguments and angers had been strong, and his attempts along those lines had turned out just as badly as Kade's seemed destined to.

"Perhaps you're right." But Dubell didn't seem convinced.

Thomas turned over the last page of the trial transcript and glanced over the next closely written document. A note at the top described it as a Bisran priest's description of Grandier's confession during his questioning.

Thomas skipped through most of a page of unconvincing preamble as to why this disclosure wasn't violating the sanctity of confession. The rest of it read:

... and he confessed to me quite freely. He had not dealt with the darkness, or at least the Evil One as we recognize it. He had been approached by the aspects of the Fay, who had offered him powers beyond the reach of mortal sorcery in exchange for mortal souls, which they must annually tithe to Hell to preserve their soulless immortality. He had refused these offers, but our ill treatment (I but repeat his words) had caused him to reconsider. They had offered him swift travel and flight, but what he would bargain for was the terrible ability to alter his physical form, that no wizard of human blood had been able to accomplish. This would cause great pain to him, and once done he would never be able to resume his own shape, nor any other shape that he would assume and abandon, and it required that he could not assume a shape in an image worn by a living man, he must destroy its original before he could assume it ...

... before he could assume it. Thomas found himself wiping his hands off on his trouser legs. It had the ring of truth about it as nothing else in the Bisran documents had. It was far too realistic for a Bisran priest, who had been trained to find evil influence in every lung fever and to hate magic like a mortal enemy, to fabricate. *This is true; this is what he told them after they drove him mad with torture and accusations. And if you were Grandier, which shape would you choose ... ?* He looked up at Galen Dubell.

The sorcerer was sitting absolutely still and watching him with an expression of thoughtful speculation. He was no longer shivering from the cold. "What are you reading, Captain, that has apparently been so revealing?"

"Nothing in particular. A dispatch from Portier." Thomas's rapier stood against the wall near the hearth perhaps four steps away. He started to stand.

"I don't think so."

The gentle contradiction held no menace, but Thomas stopped. He had betrayed himself somehow, but Dubell had always shown a talent for guessing at others' thoughts. *I can't let him kill me now. If he burns these papers and walks out of here no one will ever know until it's far too late. It may already be too late.*

The old sorcerer said, "Perhaps the time for the masquerade is over anyway. But I think I've been found out."

"It's a priest's report of Grandier's ... of your confession during your trial." Thomas slid the document across the table, but the sorcerer didn't take the bait and reach for it. Thomas kept expecting the mask to drop but it didn't. It was still Dubell's face, Dubell's eyes. Dubell's look of regret.

"Indeed," Urbain Grandier said softly. "I didn't expect to have anyone take it seriously. Not in Bisra, at least. They all believed I was hand in glove with the Prince of Hell. As to how the incriminating document followed me here, I suppose I can credit the Church's league of brotherly spies."

The fire popped loudly in the silence. Thomas felt the extreme danger that lay in carrying on this conversation but was unable to stop. Knowing and believing were two different things. If a weapon had been in reach, there was a good chance he would have hesitated with it, and that would have been fatal. *And he looked up at me over Treville's dead body and said, "I'm sorry."* He said, "Did you do it when you kidnapped him from Lodun?"

Grandier looked mildly surprised. "Oh, no. It was long before that. I kidnapped myself, you see."

It would have had to be that way. Dr. Surete's death, and Milam's. *It was simplicity itself, he told us, if one had the stomach for it.* Grandier watched him with a dead man's eyes. Thomas said, "Why haven't you let the Host in yet? That's part of your bargain, isn't it? Your payment to them."

"The Unseelie Court did me a great service," Grandier agreed. "I owe them much. The first shape I took was that of the man who served as the secular judge at that farce the Inquisition deemed my trial. He was so cold, so forbidding even to his own family that aping his manner presented no challenge. He was powerful, and I took my revenge as I liked. I lived as him for nearly half a year, before I tired of it. Then it was a young servant in his house, for I needed to move about without drawing attention to myself. . . ." Grandier gestured the memory away, his expression wry in the firelight. "But my plans do not always coincide with those of my associates, a fact they fail to understand."

A log shifted in the fire and Grandier reflexively glanced toward it. Thomas rolled backward off the bench, grabbed his sword from where it stood against the wall, and whipped off the scabbard. Grandier leapt out of the chair, his hand moving as if he were gathering something out of the air to toss it. Thomas saw the sorcerer's quick motion and scrambled sideways, coming to his feet as a blue blaze of light struck the wall where he had been. It splashed on the bricks, sizzling and smoking like acid. Thomas threw himself at Grandier with a suicidal lack of caution. But Grandier dodged backward with surprising agility and the tip of the rapier only slashed a yard-long hole in the hanging fold of his sleeve.

They both saw Kade standing in the doorway at the same time.

Thomas's first thought was that faced with the situation the only reasonable conclusion she could come to was that he was attacking Galen Dubell. But it was Grandier she stared at.

Her expression had a kind of growing incredulous fury, a combination of wounded pride at being fooled and all-too-human betrayal. The sorcerer regarded her, and his gaze held all of Dubell's intelligence and wit and the gentle humor he employed on those who pleased him. He said, "No, it wasn't your fault."

The fury flared and ignited and she took a step toward him. But Grandier's hand came out of his robes and he tossed something at her. It wasn't a deadly flash of sorcerous light. It was a handful of iron filings.

Iron wouldn't harm Kade as much as it did other fay, but it would interfere with her ability to do magic. Even as Thomas started forward Kade leapt back to avoid the filings. Grandier pushed past her and out the door. As he crossed the threshold, the candles and the fire extinguished with a hiss as if all had been doused with water. It plunged the room into shadow.

Thomas banged into the heavy table that had somehow moved into his way, shoved it aside, and ran out into the hall.

Grandier was halfway to the outside door, Kade running after him. The few lamps that were lit extinguished as the sorcerer passed them. Thomas shouted for the guards in the hall to follow him, but in the confusion and darkness he couldn't tell if any heard.

Thomas caught up with Kade in the entry hall and together they slammed out the door and into the frozen mud and cold of the court. The clouds had opened up again and the moonlight was stark white, the wind a tearing force, and Grandier was nowhere to be seen.

Kade spun around, trying to look in every direction at once. Thomas did a quick circuit of the court, but found nothing.

"Damn it, where is he?" he muttered. Grandier, loose in the confusion of the palace . . .

As he reached Kade's side again, she looked up and said, "Oh, no."

Thomas followed her gaze. A shadow had appeared and now grew on the moon's narrow face, becoming larger and larger. It was a blot of greater darkness dropping toward them out of the night.

She said, "He's opened the wards."

Without having to discuss it they both went for the nearest shelter, the lee side of the well house. They were too far from the Guard House, from the entrance of any building. The winged fay plunged toward the ground, then seemed to hover above the courtyard, as insubstantial as a shadow.

The well house's door was on the far side, Thomas knew. They could edge around to it if they were lucky, if the fay beast was half blind.

Thomas started to slide along the wall and Kade grabbed his arm and whispered, "Don't move." He hesitated, thinking, *Does she know what she's doing?* Then he noticed the quality of the light change as the moon's sparkle on the ground around them became almost palpable, and remembered Kade's ability to eavesdrop without being seen, and that one of her fay powers was supposed to be illusion.

The creature that touched ground lightly in the courtyard was a living shadow, the moonlight seeming to bend away from it. In the jumble of dark shapes that composed it, Thomas could see only a snakelike motion and the pointed delicate razor-outline of a claw held at an unlikely angle.

Kade whispered, "Moonlight, shadow, moonlight, shadow . . ."

Thomas thought, *Thank God we're downwind.* Then he saw Grandier, walking toward the bizarre thing. A moment later sorcerer and creature were aloft, soaring upward at an incredible speed.

Kade slid down the wall to sit in the mud.

The illusion around them dissipated into tiny sparkling droplets of light that fell to the ground like beads of dew and disappeared. Fayre glamour, Thomas realized. He said, "Very good," and gave Kade a hand up.

Kade swayed a bit as she stood, not bothering to brush the mud and dirt off her dress. She shook her head in frustration and ran a hand through her hair. "He let the wards move back into place, after he was past them. Why did he do that?"

Thomas assumed it was a rhetorical question. At least, he had no idea how to answer. The door to the Guard House swung open and torchlight poured into the court. There were shouts from the direction of the Albon Tower. The timing was too good. He wondered if Grandier had cast another spell besides the one to extinguish the candles, a spell to create confusion and keep everyone else inside.

Then Kade demanded, "What did he do with Galen?"

She was looking up at him, those clear gray eyes angry and beginning to be afraid. Not having read the priest's document, she would not have understood that part of the conversation. He said, "Galen's dead."

———

"Mother, this seems like cowardice," Roland said. He stood huddled in a heavy fur cloak, attended by Renier and two servants, all dressed for hard riding in frigid weather. The other knights charged with guarding him paced about warily, a short distance away. It was barely dawn, and the sky was a solid gray roof, low and threatening. A half hour ago the wind had died and the snow had begun to fall.

Ravenna pulled her hood up over her tightly braided hair and adjusted her gloves. "No, dear, it seems like survival." She turned to Elaine, who stood quietly at her elbow. "Wrap your scarf more carefully, child; this cold could ruin your skin."

Thomas folded his arms and tried not to show his frustration; it was just like Roland to balk at the eleventh hour. Staying in the palace, at Grandier's mercy, was impossible.

They stood in the court below the Albon Tower, an island of relative calm amid the bustle of preparations for the evacuation. Under his cloak Renier wore a gold-embossed gorget and back- and breastplates as many of the Albon knights did. Thomas and most of the other guards preferred the heavy leather buff coats that offered almost as much protection as the awkward armor pieces and allowed more freedom of movement. In the dim morning light servants ran past, coaches and wagons were being loaded, horses saddled or harnessed, all in apprehensive haste. Nothing had been said about last night's confrontation in the Albon Tower, and nothing would be said, unless Roland was an utter fool. *Which is not entirely out of the realm of possibility,* Thomas thought.

"I'm not deserting my court," Roland muttered stubbornly.

"Roland," Ravenna said with a sigh. "You are the court, the crown, and the throne. This place has only symbolic value; you can rule just as well from Portier or the Granges. But only if you're alive."

Roland looked away, a little mollified. "I dislike having them say we ran, that's all." He hesitated a long moment, and Thomas silently contemplated the gray sky and braced himself to let Ravenna handle the next objection. But Roland said, "Is it really true about Dr. Dubell?"

Panic and rumor had spread through the crowded halls, and Thomas had spent most of the night trying to quell it. Ravenna's eyes went hard and she said, "Yes, it is true." The news had not sat easily with her; she had hated the thought that she could be deceived along with everyone else.

Roland bit his lip, not meeting her eyes, then nodded. "I see." He turned abruptly and went back toward the tower, the snow crunching under his boots, his servants and knights trailing him. Renier shook his head and followed.

Ravenna smiled ruefully. "A pretty speech I gave about symbolic value, don't you think? One might imagine I believed it." She eyed Thomas with mild annoyance. "I'm still angry with you. I didn't enjoy being coerced into this, but you've got your way, and I suppose that's the height of male ambition."

"That's amusing coming from you," Thomas said without rancor. They had been through this all last night, when he had finally persuaded her to accept his plan for the retreat.

"Perhaps." She watched him a moment, a flicker of something other than cool control in her eyes. "For all your faults, I trust you'll come out of this alive." She started across the court without waiting for a reply.

Though he needed to be elsewhere now, Thomas found himself pausing to watch her. Occasionally he was surprised anew by the idea that someone so frail could also be so strong.

"Captain."

He looked up. Denzil stood only a few steps away, dressed in heavy brocades and a fur-trimmed cloak, snow collecting in his hair. Ravenna and Roland's presence in this section of the court had for the moment cleared it, and the servants loading wagons near the Guard House were making enough noise to cover their voices. Though, undoubtedly, eyes watched them from most of the surrounding windows. Thomas said, "Are you sure you don't want to save this performance until you have a better audience?"

Denzil acknowledged that with a smile, but said, "At times your impatience with Roland is ill concealed. From your manner one would be tempted to think you despise your King."

"I don't despise him, I pity him. He actually loves you."

"Of course he does." Denzil's smile widened, and for the first time Thomas felt he was being allowed to see the man's real face, the truth behind the sham he put on for Roland, for the court. The petulance, the pretense of shallow vanity, were gone, replaced by intelligence and an amused contempt for those the mask had fooled. "And it was well done, wasn't it?"

"It furthers your purpose."

"Whatever that is." Denzil paced a few steps. "I can say anything I want to him, do anything I want to him, cause him to do whatever I want"—he looked up, his blue eyes mocking—"I can tell you about it with perfect impunity. And I have made him love me for it."

Thomas looked away, seeing and not seeing the wounded being helped into a wagon near the door of the tower. He felt stupidly, irrationally angry for Roland's sake. *Why? You'd think I'd know better than to give a damn about the feelings of a boy-king who spits on me.* He was as blockheaded as Renier, who actually believed in his oath of knighthood. But he said, "And what a conquest it was. A boy whose father taught him to take abuse. Undoubtedly he believes he deserves you."

"Perhaps he does. Weakness is its own reward."

Denzil was just as maimed as Roland, but in his own way, with his hate turned outward instead of festering within. *But Denzil's intelligent enough to see it. Probably he does see it. And probably revels in it.* Thomas said slowly, "You are a piece of work."

"Yes, but it's my own work," Denzil answered easily, sounding pleased. "And I've gotten nearly everything I've ever wanted."

And now you're getting a reaction from me, something else you've always wanted. Thomas put a little bored doubt in his voice and said, "Have you?"

"Nearly everything. I wanted you, once, before I realized how much it would have harmed my cause with Roland."

Still watching the wagons, and inwardly a little amused, Thomas said dryly, "How flattering."

"My pride demanded it, because I could sense how you hated me."

A flurry of wind tore through the court, scattering snow around their boots.

Thomas searched for the words that would deal the deepest wound, and then said, "I know. I found your motives transparent." He looked back at Denzil, and was rewarded by the ill-concealed anger in those cold blue eyes.

"Words," the Duke said softly. "Ravenna is growing old, Thomas. Take care that when she falls, you don't fall with her."

"You take care. When I fall, I'm taking you with me," Thomas said, and walked away.

———

The Prince's Gate yard, the buffer area between the smaller inner gate and the towering bulk of the outer gate, was closed in by a wall and the south side of the Gate Bastion. Queen's guards and Albon knights manned the walls, last night's tensions forgotten among this morning's fears.

Thomas's horse danced sideways in the churned mud and snow, glad to be out of the stables, and he reined her in. Fifty of the Queen's guards, with Vivan and most of the surviving Cisternans, sat their horses with him, waiting for the lookouts on the walls to give the clear signal. Snowflakes caught like crystal in their hat brims, hair, and the fur of their cloaks. Renier waved from the top of the wall, then the main gate swung open and they rode out.

Many of the wealthy houses along the row had been caught by surprise. The doors and windows had been smashed through, revealing dark empty openings, snow blowing freely in. They would prove perfect daytime lurking places for the fay. A few houses across the way were still tightly shuttered and bore no outward sign of invasion, but nothing stirred as they rode out into the street.

There were a few bodies half buried in the snow. Their horses, battlefield trained to ignore such things, would have walked right over the first had Thomas not guided them around. The Unseelie Court could not appear while the sun was visible, even when it was dimmed by the gray snow clouds. They would not be faced with the power that had driven them out of the Old Palace unless the clouds grew considerably darker, blocking out most of the light. But the dark fay that followed the Host were not so hindered. There would be things that flew, that traveled beneath the snow, that would leap down at them from the rooftops and the broken windows of the houses around them. So Kade Carrion had told them.

Thomas wondered where Kade was, if she was watching or if she was back in Fayre. After Grandier's escape they had gone into the kitchens attached to the Guard House to talk. The servants had fired the ovens and it was almost warm. It was not deserted either; men and women were packing supplies for the journey. Along the side where the stores were kept, among barrels of apples, flour, and barley and shelves stacked with rounds of yellow and white cheeses covered with wax, they had stopped. Kade sat on an apple barrel, fixed her eyes on the rubies in his cloak pin, and said, "How do you know he's dead?"

He had brought the copy of Grandier's confession, and handed it to her.

She read it through twice, her eyes bleak. He said quietly, "He wanted us to be completely dependent on one sorcerer, and he chose Galen Dubell. He killed Dr. Surete and Milam after Surete had convinced Ravenna to let Dubell return. He told me how himself, after the golem attacked you in the Grand Gallery. He said it would have been simplicity itself to give either the Court Sorcerer or his assistant an enspelled object, especially if it seemed to come from a friend. So they died, like Dubell himself, his household at Lodun, that clown in your acting troupe, a spy called Gambin, and Lord Lestrac, who knew too much of their plan and was prone to dangerous mistakes. Maybe there were others. We'll probably never know.

"I thought Denzil was Grandier's agent in the palace. That he'd taken the keystone. But Denzil didn't know where it was kept—only Dr. Braun and Dubell knew that. The night Braun was killed he must have thought of something or found something that he believed important, and he was afraid to tell me with Denzil so nearby. He was on his way back to the King's Bastion. Dubell was coming along the same way toward the gallery. They met, and Braun must have decided to tell Dubell what he had meant to tell me. They went into that salon and . . . Braun idolized the man and had no reason to be suspicious. He would never have thought twice about turning his back on him. Neither would I, for that matter, and I don't do that lightly. Grandier played his part very well."

Kade turned the paper over, and studied the blank back of it.

Thomas said, "You told him you were going to get into the palace with an acting troupe, didn't you?"

She nodded. "He said he never received the letter."

"But he did. You were right when you said the golem was after you. All Grandier had to do was find out which troupe was likely to get the invitation to court and plant the golem among them. You were the one who knew Galen Dubell the best; you were the one most likely to expose an imposter.

"I think it was Denzil who brought him here. Lestrac and Dontane were the contacts between them, so Denzil wouldn't know that Grandier had taken Dubell's place. That way Grandier could talk Roland out of leaving Bel Garde its walls, and we'd think of Dubell as his own man and no friend to Denzil. Denzil's antagonism would be real, and no one would suspect the link between them. It was the only way for him. Grandier was scarred and maimed by torture, and it would've been impossible to go unnoticed with his own appearance. He used this to move around undetected in Bisra and have his revenge on the priests in the Inquisition, to cause the plague and the crop failure."

For the first time Kade met his eyes. "Why did he let the wards close again? He could have held them apart and let the Host down on us. He could have done that at any time."

"I don't know. I don't know why the man does anything," Thomas confessed. He remembered the burning house in the River Quarter, and how the magical fire had considerately failed to spread to the other buildings on the crowded street. He had noted it at the time, the equal portions of viciousness and restraint, and he understood it no more now than he had then. "Why he would help Denzil of all people . . . I don't think it was malice against Galen Dubell. It was just that he was perfect for Grandier's purposes. He was trusted, well-known, but he'd been a recluse for ten years. He was living alone at Lodun, without family—"

She interrupted, "He stopped taking students last year. He said he was working on a treatise on . . ." She stopped, and buried her face in her hands.

He stepped close and pulled her hands down. She wasn't crying. He might have expected grief and rage, but this wounded silence was pain itself. "I'm going to need your help."

Kade seemed to realize he was holding her hands and pulled free. Standing up, she moved away a few steps. Not turning to look at him, she said, "I'm leaving. That's what I was going to tell Galen when I heard you call him Grandier."

"Why?"

She looked back at him. This time there were tears streaking her face, but her expression was that familiar one of exasperation. "There is nothing for me here, especially now."

But he had still told her what the plan was, how he had intended for Dubell to cover the escape to Bel Garde, the closest defensible position that could be reached before nightfall. She had listened without comment. Before leaving he had said, "There's a difference between running away from your fears and walking away from your past. For your own sake, make sure you know which is which."

And that was a damn pompous thing to say to her, he thought now.

The first of the six wagons carrying the wounded who had survived the night left the shelter of the gate and trundled down the frozen mud of the street. They were guarded by about half the surviving Cisternans and a large party of servants and retainers—men, women, and children. Thomas would rather have kept the Cisternans together, but he knew they would obey his orders whereas there was no guarantee of that with Albon knights. Vivan and the other few remaining Cisternans would come with his group.

It was a relief to be outside, to be moving. Inside the walls, it seemed everything was held together by threads that were beginning to unravel.

Thomas looked back at his men grouped around the gate. Baserat was checking the set of his pistols in the holsters on the saddlebow. Thomas also had two long wheellock pistols in saddle holsters and was wearing a rapier with a wide cavalry blade. A dueling rapier was slung over his shoulder.

One large armed party, mounted with only one wagon for supplies, left the gate and headed down the street in the opposite direction. It was the Count of Duncanny, who had chosen to lead away his family, retainers, and some of the other nobility and palacefolk who could not be counted on to keep up in a hard ride. They had some Albons with them, and Thomas could only guess what their chances might be.

The count did not turn around as they rode away, but he lifted one hand to them in farewell.

Thomas noted the similarity to a funeral procession.

The men on the palace wall had vanished. He hoped the fay, and Grandier, didn't guess the significance of that for another few moments, at least.

The last wagon passed out of the shadow of the Prince's Gate and Thomas nodded a signal to a guard waiting there.

Thomas spurred his horse and they were off. The crash of two coaches barreling through the gate signaled the eruption of the quiet street into pandemonium.

Surrounding the coaches were Lucas and about twenty Queen's guards, the other Cisternans, and a few volunteer Albon knights. Behind them rode the rest of the Queen's Guard and the Albon troop.

Grandier would anticipate their escape. He knew they would have to move now, before the snow choked the streets. Thomas hoped he hadn't anticipated any further.

The promenades and tall houses of the palace quarter flashed by. Out of the corner of his eye, Thomas saw a horse stumble and go down. He couldn't tell who its rider was.

The attack came. A large dark-winged creature struck the top of the first coach, leaping away immediately as its claws encountered the iron nails embedded in the roof. But the coach swayed under the weight and fell sideways, two of its wheels crushed beneath it. The driver tumbled free and the horses screamed, staggering and fighting their harness. The second coach shuddered to a halt beyond it as more fay leapt off rooftops and sprang up out of the mud and snow in the street.

Thomas wheeled his horse, leading the escort group of Queen's guards and Cisternans to surround the two coaches. They fetched up against the dressed stone wall of a fortified town house.

Thomas looked back toward the second company. If Renier didn't follow his instructions . . . No, the Albon troop and the rest of his men had split off with the wagons as the fay had attacked the coaches. They were heading up the Avenue of Flowers, riding pell-mell for the gate out of the city. But even as he saw them go, an illusion of a confused roiling mass of horsemen settled in their place.

She's here, she's done it. A moment later he saw Kade leap off the back of the coach that Berham had driven and disappear into the illusion she had created. He had intended for Dubell to cover the retreat of the second troop with illusion, the plan he had fortunately not had time to reveal to the old sorcerer. Kade could do it with fayre glamour, which neither the fay nor Grandier would be immune to. Until this moment he had not thought she would.

The coaches had been empty but for their drivers. Ravenna, Roland, and Falaise were on horseback in the midst of the Albon troop, the wagons carrying the supplies and the wounded, and the rest of the Queen's Guard. Ravenna had ridden under conditions almost as desperate during the war, it was one of the few things Roland did well on his own, and Gideon was under orders to keep Falaise on her mount if he had to tie her there. If Grandier was watching, Thomas knew his own presence with the coaches would add verisimilitude to the deception.

Then the fay were on them and there was no more time for worry about the others. Thomas emptied both pistols at the flying creature that had struck the first coach as it stooped on them again, then used the heavy cavalry rapier to slash down at the fay that clustered about his horse. A gunpowder blast erupted somewhere nearby, with the shriek of wounded men and horses—the barrel of a too hastily loaded wheellock exploding.

The horses were trained to kick in battle and their ironshod hooves kept the fay back at first. Then Thomas saw Baserat go down and an instant later something struck the side of his own horse, knocking it sprawling. He managed to fall clear and the horse tore itself free, staggered up, and bolted. As Thomas struggled to get to his feet, a fay leapt on him from behind and slammed him to the ground. He twisted and shoved an elbow back into it, expecting a bronze blade in his vitals, then the hilt of the rapier that was still slung across his back touched the thing's head. He heard the creature's flesh sizzle and it yelped as it leapt away.

Thomas stood and cleared a path through the creatures with his cavalry blade and put his back to the wall of the house. Blood was slicking his sword-hilt—his own possibly, though he couldn't remember being wounded. He saw the second coach collapse and the misshapen dark fay swarming over it, and grimly anticipated their disappointment at its empty interior. He wished Kade had not come with them after all. He hoped she was controlling the illusion from a distance, or had gotten herself away by now.

Above the screams and shouts of men, horses, and fay, he heard the crash of a door slamming open from farther down the side of the house. He thought to work his way down there in case someone had found a way inside where they could retreat, but one of the humanlike servants of the Host came at him, swinging its sword wildly. He stepped forward and neatly speared its throat with the rapier's point, then something struck him in the leg just above his right knee. For a moment he felt only the slight pain of a bee sting. Then the ground was rushing up at him, then nothing.

CHAPTER ELEVEN

As KADE TRIED to reach the partial shelter of the wall of the house, a clawed hand caught her hair and the back of her cloak, hauling her around. It was a bogle, a short, squat, ugly thing with muddy gray skin and harsh yellow eyes, and it was grinning at her. She pulled a handful of glamour out of the cold air and flung it into its eyes, giving it an all too temporary blindness, and it fled away shrieking. *Damn things,* she thought, dodging one of the coaches and its plunging horses. *Why anyone allows them to exist is beyond me.* If she ever got back to Fayre she would consider dedicating the rest of her life to removing its inhabitants from the face of the earth.

Kade fetched up against the wall of the house, just as the carriage doors slammed open and men poured out. Private troops . . . No, there were sprigs of white and red tucked into some of their hatbands, the colors of city service. A trained band.

She could feel the iron mixed into the mortar of the wall behind her as a distant heat. The proximity of so much iron made her wary, but she hadn't felt any real emotion she could identify since early this morning.

She hadn't been able to leave. The idea of returning to Knockma and being alone with her thoughts was difficult enough to face, and the lump that had been in her throat for hours seemed to be keeping her from any decisive action.

Men came to the aid of the small group formed into a defensive knot between the two wrecked coaches and the house, and the fay began to disperse. The bulk of the house was probably what had saved many of the guards. The flighted fay large enough to carry off humans had not been able to reach them. A thick haze of white smoke from pistols and muskets hung over the street now, but Kade could see that the glamour that formed her illusion was beginning to dissipate. The reflective quality of ice and snow had produced glamour in abundance. A trick on Grandier, that his foul weather produced material for her illusions.

Kade slipped inside the door with the others as the house troops withdrew. In the large stone-floored room within were half a dozen coaches, stabling for many horses, and the confusion of wounded and dying men.

She made her way across the chamber. Nearly to the bottom of the stairs into the main house, she saw a dead man on the floor in Cisternan colors. She recognized him as their commander, Vivan, who had helped her in the palace hall battle. She hesitated, but there was nothing to be done, and in another moment the crowd pushed her on.

She couldn't see any of the Queen's guards, or Thomas, anywhere. With nothing else to do, she decided to look for them.

She headed up the stairs and into the maze of rooms on the second floor. From outside, faced with only the one uncompromising gray wall, she hadn't realized the house was so large. The beautifully appointed rooms were crowded with refugees from the surrounding neighborhood, mostly shopkeepers and clerks or members of the wealthier artisan classes whose homes hadn't withstood the attacks. They were making an awful noise, yelling, screaming, complaining, children crying, though as far as Kade could tell the house had never been penetrated by fay. Surely they were only stirred up by the battle outside. Surely they hadn't been like this since last night.

She fought her way through crowded rooms until she saw a young servant bustling by, carrying an armload of rolled linen bandages. She caught his arm. "Whose house is this?"

He didn't even look at her oddly. It probably wasn't the most witless question he had answered today. "Lord Aviler's house, the High Minister."

Kade let him go. She remembered Aviler a little from the night of the Commedia, but mostly from the conversation between Thomas and Lucas she had eavesdropped on. His position in all this was obscure, at best. *And why do I care?*

She found another stairway and went up. The third floor would hold audience chambers and more private entertaining rooms and salons. It was unguarded, since custom and fear of irritating their patrons kept any of the refugees from venturing up there.

It was mercifully quiet. Then she heard voices raised in argument, and in a sudden silence one familiar voice. *It can't be . . .* She followed the sound to a carved double door that let her into a large state dining room with a long polished table and candelabra hung with colored glass drops. A group of battered Queen's guards and the lieutenant Gideon faced Denzil and a group of Albon knights while tall, sallow Lord Aviler looked on. But seated nearby was Falaise.

Kade stood stock-still, trying to disbelieve her eyes. The Queen was sitting in an armchair, her head down and her hands knotted in her lap. She looked like a prisoner.

Kade started down the room toward them before they saw her. Denzil noticed her first, and Gideon stopped shouting to follow his gaze. She thought, *If Denzil smiles at me there will be trouble.* But the Duke's expression of angry contempt didn't change.

Kade focused on Falaise. "What are you doing here?"

The Queen looked up, her eyes locked on Kade's with desperate intensity. She was dressed for hard riding, in a man's breeches under a plain hunting habit, with a cloak wrapped around her. "We were attacked, and I was separated from my guards. Lord Denzil found me and brought me here." Falaise's voice held suppressed terror.

"He abducted her and brought her here," Gideon corrected Falaise, watching Aviler. "She would be safely out the city gates by now if—"

"If you had been competent to get her out the gates—" Denzil interrupted.

"Sorceress," Aviler said. His voice, used to addressing the loud and argumentative city assemblies, overrode theirs.

Kade looked at him. His expression was watchful and carefully wary. A part of her not concerned with death and the present had time to observe: *I must look more than half mad.*

Aviler said, "Lord Denzil told me you had left the city."

She said, "Ask him why he didn't take her after Roland and the others. Ask him why he didn't take advantage of the escape we bought for them." *And when did it become "we"?* she asked herself.

Aviler's gaze went from Kade to Denzil. "He has already explained himself."

Gideon swore in exasperation. "You're in this with him, aren't you?" One of the other guards put a cautioning hand on his shoulder.

Denzil said, "We were separated from the main troop, and the Queen had to be gotten to safety." His expression reflected angry concern, and Kade thought, *He's acting. He's doing it very well, but he's acting. Does Aviler know that?* She couldn't tell. Aviler seemed to be mainly worried over what she was going to do. *I'm not the danger here, you idiot.*

To Falaise, she said, "Do you want to be here?"

As the Queen started to answer, Denzil interrupted smoothly, "Of course she doesn't. She would rather be with her king."

Aviler spared an unreadable glance for him, but kept his attention on Kade. He said, "The Queen must choose for herself whom she wishes to accompany. I offered to let her go with her guards, but—"

"My lady, please," Gideon begged Falaise, going to his knees beside her chair. "For your honor and your safety, you know we'll protect you."

Kade looked down at the Queen. "Or come with me."

Falaise's frightened eyes went to Denzil. She was afraid to accept help from another woman, Kade realized. With that thought came a cold fury, but it was a fury wrapped in cotton wool, like the rest of her reality. Falaise turned back to her and shook her head helplessly. Kade walked out of the room.

She went out into the maze of salons, seeing weary servants and retainers and battered soldiers, but no one she recognized. She could have asked for directions, she supposed, but she was not in the mood for questions. Then she saw Berham disappearing into one of the doorways carrying an armload of firewood. She hurried to catch up with him.

It was the antechamber to a suite. Inside were Queen's guards she recognized and two men in Cisternan colors. Several were wounded, and all looked up at her in surprise. Berham stopped as he saw her. He said, "Oh, I'm glad to see you. We thought you'd gone off."

"Where's Thomas?" The words were out before she realized it. It crossed her mind that this was the first time she had called him anything but "you bastard."

Berham eyed her, then he opened the next door and stepped back to let her go in.

She stopped in the doorway.

It was a bedchamber, cold and musty despite a new fire in the hearth. Thomas lay unconscious on the bed, still wearing the doublet and blood-stained buff coat from the battle. It took her moments to recognize him. She had never thought to see him so still, so bloodless under the tan of his skin. A thin elderly man in a velvet doctor's cope sat next to him on the bed. Lucas stood over him. He was hatless, and looked as if he had been caught too near a pistol blast; his face and the side of his doublet were flecked with powder burns. Martin stood at the foot of the bed, leaning on the bedpost, and the sleeves of his white shirt were blood-soaked. The young servant Phaistus was backed into a corner, trying to stay out of the way.

Kade took a step into the room, Berham brushing past behind her.

She asked, "What is it?" Her voice was unsteady and she hated herself for it.

The doctor glanced back at her, but said nothing.

Lucas said, "Answer her."

The lieutenant's tone was even and reasonable but the doctor looked up at him and blanched. He said hastily, "I can't find a wound serious enough to cause this. It has to be elf-shot. There's nothing to be done."

Sensation returned and hit Kade with the force of a hammer. She stumbled and steadied herself against the wall. "Get him out of here," she said.

Martin consulted Lucas with a quick glance. He saw something in the other man's expression that constituted agreement, and caught the doctor by the thick collar of his cope and slung him toward the door.

The doctor had a highly developed sense of self-preservation. He scrambled to his feet and darted out without a threat or protest.

Kade went to sit on the bed. She touched Thomas's face. His skin was hot but his sweat was freezing. Distractedly she noticed that the striped wool of the bedclothes was faded, but the plumes topping the canopy were still pure white and the headboard had a design of twining laurel leaves. It spoke well for Aviler. She knew Denzil would have been too petty to provide his enemy a decent place in which to die.

She found the elf-shot by finding the hole it had burnt through his trouser leg. Elf-shot never appeared to leave a mark, and the tiny fragment was lodged just under the skin of his lower thigh. It must have glanced off the heavy leather of his boot top and entered his flesh at an angle. It was why he was still alive. The stone had not had time to work its way further into his body on its eventual track toward his heart.

She said, "I need a silver knife. It doesn't have to be pure, but it should have as little base metal as possible."

Martin said, "That's an alchemy tool. Where would—"

"Or a piece of family plate," Lucas interrupted. "Berham."

"No sooner said." Berham dropped the wood and hurried for the door. He was limping, Kade noticed. *It's not too bad; he's walking. Worry about him later.*

"Have you done this before?" Lucas asked her.

He didn't ask her if she thought she could do it, and she was so grateful she answered honestly. "No, but I've seen it done." Or at least attempted. Other doctors or sorcerer-healers had tried to cut out a fragment of elf-shot on the rare occasions when it was close enough to the surface of the skin to find, but most made the mistake of using iron rather than silver. And elf-shot didn't lose its power once it was embedded in a human body; if a sorcerer did manage to remove it, he was just as likely to have it seek his own heart instead. The fay who cast the shot sometimes removed it for reasons of their own, but those instances were few and far between.

Victims of elf-shot were usually killed to keep them from suffering further, if they didn't die immediately. It was a perfect opportunity for Denzil, or High Minister Aviler. And Thomas Boniface was a disliked favorite whose patron and troop were out of the city by now, if they lived. *The doctor might talk. Maybe we should have killed him.* It was too late for that now. *And why do I care?*

Because from the moment you set foot in the palace, he did not treat you as a child, a fool, or worse, a court lady. He treated you as exactly what you are, whatever that is, and he knew what Galen's death did to you.

She paced the room with rabid impatience until Berham returned. He shut the door hastily behind him and brought a small delicate paring knife out of his doublet. "Will this do?"

Kade took it from him and felt the nearly pure silver resonate through her. "Perfect," she said. "Now all of you get the hell out of the way."

If she had spared enough notice, she would have been surprised to see that they did just that.

She passed the knife through a candle quickly, and that would have to do. It was a little too dull but Thomas would be in no position to notice.

She sat down on the bed and gently probed for the fragment. It wasn't there anymore. It had worked its way deeper already. She cursed, fighting a foolish surge of panic, and thought, *Why can't anything ever be easy?* She knew where it had to be. It hadn't had time to move more than an inch or so down into the muscle. She saw her hand was trembling, and she was glad Thomas was deeply unconscious because he would otherwise have surely said something infuriating at this point. *Now,* she thought, and carefully inserted the knife.

A little blood welled up, and after a long heartbeat she felt the knife vibrate as the elf-shot adhered to it. *Hah, it worked.* Gently she withdrew the blade. As soon as the tiny fragment was free she closed her fist around it to keep it from flying at someone, stood, and started toward the fireplace. Then she felt it pushing at the skin of her palm.

She froze, staring at her closed hands. If she let it go, God knew who it would head for. *But I'm fay,* she thought against the rising dread. *It can't hurt me.*

There's no such thing as half human, Galen Dubell had told her once long ago, and she had typically ignored his words. *One drop of red blood is enough.* She whispered a fay charm of warding danger, and felt the elf-shot press at her hand, pushing through the skin. Fighting panic, she hoped the planet of influence was close enough and shouted the Lodun formula for the destruction of dangerous objects.

The sorcery worked where the fay magic had not. She felt the fragment catch fire and hastily scraped it off her hands onto the hearthstone. It burned bright blue for an instant, then disappeared.

She sank down and sat on the floor. All those years that elf-shot could have put her out of their misery and the Unseelie Court had never thought to make the experiment, to test to see if she had the same immunity to it as the other fay did.

Idiots, she thought. Her palm burned like hell.

She turned back to the bed and saw Thomas move his head on the pillow. Feverishly, but he had moved.

She had forgotten anyone else was still in the room, and was startled to find Lucas standing next to her. He took her hand and turned it over. "God damn," he muttered when he saw the burn. "Hey, Ber—"

Berham appeared with a handful of snow scraped from a window ledge. He slapped it into her palm.

She snatched her hand away, then realized the cold had cut the intensity of the pain nearly in half. She watched Thomas while Berham fussily bandaged the burn, and was rewarded by seeing him move twice more.

———

Much later, Kade sat on a stool by the fire and looked at the deep red mark on her hand. It didn't seem inclined to blister, so she supposed it couldn't be too bad. Unlike pure fay magic, the craft of mortal sorcery was a messy business and she was used to hurting herself occasionally. *Messy, but more certain,* she thought.

She had helped the other wounded as best she could, but without the philtres and salves that were so necessary to healing-sorcery, or the ingredients with which to mix them, there wasn't much she could do. She could have made a healing stone, but that only worked for disease, not torn flesh. A well-stocked apothecary box would have saved lives tonight. The charms to give strength and to hold the soul to the body had little efficacy without the herbal preparations that soothed the wounds. The effort had left her cold and dreadfully tired, and she would have traded all her fay ancestry for half of Galen Dubell's skill at healing-sorcery. And she knew that if she had devoted all her attention to study, she would have had that skill by now.

Kade was worried about the wound in Thomas's leg. The spell she had used to knit the flesh together had seemed to work, but the wound was deep and there was no telling how the elf-shot had affected it. By the firelight, his hair and beard were inky black against his fever-pale skin. She resisted the urge to get up and walk over to the bed again. *You thought the world ended when you found out Galen was dead, but when you heard that fool of a doctor say elf-shot . . .*

She took a deep breath and faced herself. It was idiocy to deny it. How could she not know? But looking back, she couldn't see when it had happened. She was not sure how her childhood passion figured into it, or when her carefully preserved distant appreciation of him had been intensified by intimacy. She was even less certain when the thought *I want this man for a friend* had become *I want this man.*

Simply because she had never felt it before didn't mean she couldn't recognize it, even though it wasn't very much like the poets and books had described it. Some had implied that the depth of the emotion would hurt; they had not said it would be like the blunt end of a poleax in the pit of the stomach.

She had wondered if being fay would make her unable to love; it had certainly made her unable to feel even the slightest fondness for any of her relations. She had thought she loved Roland once, but then had decided that if she really had, she would not have been able to leave him. She had thought herself as cold as her mother Moire and the rest of the fay, who put on a great show of grand passion but who, underneath their shallow surfaces, had hearts as empty as broken wine barrels. To find that she was capable of love, that it was happening now and under less than ideal circumstances, was more than a shock. It was horrific. And worse, like every other bubbleheaded court lady, she had fallen in love with the Captain of the Queen's Guard. When she was a youth at court, someone had proclaimed undying passion for him every other week. Trying to guess who he was going to show interest in and who he was going to brush off had been a game with Ravenna's gentlewomen. Kade felt herself a fool, and she had seen too much bloodshed and horror in the last few days to seek the comfort of childishly wishing herself dead.

She would have to think about what to do at some point. *Not right now,* she told herself. *Just not right now.*

———

Thomas turned his head toward the light. It resolved into a glowing orange fire in an unfamiliar hearth. The room was dark, except for one candle that he could see as a dim glow through the curtain at the foot of the bed. He felt the sweat-drenched heat of a receding fever, and everything ached. Except the wound in his thigh that felt like a hot coal had been buried beneath the skin.

He sat up on one elbow and parted the bloody and burned (*Burned?* he wondered) fabric to examine what looked like an especially clean sword thrust. It was closed over with a new pink scab, a sign of sorcerous healing.

Then he saw Kade sitting on a footstool by the fire, where she had blended into the light and its reflection on the polished stone hearth, a creature of amber, rose, and old gold. One could never tire of looking at her, he decided. There was always something new to see, an effect made even more interesting because she produced it unintentionally and entirely without artifice. They stared at one another for a time, until Kade blinked and shook herself.

"Where are we?" he asked her.

"Lord Aviler's town house. You've been near dead most of the day, because you were hit by elf-shot."

It took a moment for the words to sink in. He said, "I couldn't have been."

"Very well, argue about it as if you weren't unconscious when it happened."

Thomas looked at the wound again. "Did you cut it out?"

"Obviously."

"It couldn't have been easy." It was supposed to be impossible.

"I have had a hard day," she admitted with dignity, lifting a handful of sweat-soaked hair away from her forehead.

He saw the bandage wrapped around her hand and asked, "What happened there?"

"Nothing." After a moment of hesitation, she said, "Denzil's here, with Falaise."

It took a moment for the words to sink in. Thomas closed his eyes. "No."

"Yes. He got her away from Gideon and the others when they were attacked. They followed him here, but she's too terrified of Denzil to take their help, and Aviler stands about like a great idiot, saying the Queen must decide who escorts her."

Thomas fell back on the bed and contemplated the underside of the tester for a moment. "You realize that a short while ago I was as good as dead and this was all someone else's problem."

"You're welcome. I think I know why Denzil's here."

He sat up again, taking a deep breath to steady himself as dizziness threatened. "I'd appreciate it if you'd tell me."

"Aviler. If he's in this plot with Denzil and Grandier, that's one thing, but if he's not . . . he isn't just going to stand there and watch."

The High Minister. A man who would support Roland despite personal differences, knowing he could increase the political power of the Ministry and the guilds and it would never occur to the young King to stop him. A man with no patience for royal favorites. A man with nothing but suspicion for royal favorites. "You're right." With the help of the bedpost, Thomas hauled himself up and stood carefully, wincing at the tight pain of the wound. Limping around on it wasn't going to do it any good, but he hardly had a choice.

Kade was fiddling with her hair again. She said, "Falaise knows something."

Thomas looked down at her. She was obviously reluctant. "Why do you think so?"

"She's afraid of Denzil."

"She should be." He limped to the foot of the bed and found his dueling rapier and main gauche. He drew the sword to check the blade and saw it was nicked and dented but still unbent.

"I know that," Kade said with asperity. "But *she* doesn't know that, not unless she knows more than she should."

Thomas hesitated, thinking it through. "How much do you think she knows?"

"She won't tell me. She doesn't think I can protect her. But I think she'll tell you."

"She may have tried to already, and I thought she was after something else. I should have listened to her, but the woman never gave any sign she could think before." If they somehow escaped the current situation, that might save Falaise's neck. He could say she had confided to him early suspicions of Denzil but had been unable to give him anything definite. That would keep Roland or some ambitious courtier from charging her with treason along with Denzil. *If we get out of this. Damned optimist.* Then he realized the full implication of what Kade had said and looked down at her in surprise. "Doesn't think you could protect her? That's ridiculous. You're not a supporter of Ravenna, Roland, or Denzil; you're the only one who could protect her with impunity."

Kade considered that. "Maybe she just can't trust anyone anymore."

Slipping his baldric over his head, Thomas thought, *That's an idea we could all have sympathy with.*

The door opened and Lucas entered, then stopped abruptly as he saw Thomas. "You're alive," he said, smiling. "And I thought I was about to be promoted."

"Careful, I might take you up on that." Thomas gritted his teeth as he put his weight on his bad leg.

"Oh, I'd have to decline under these circumstances."

"Typical of you. How many are we?"

"Eighteen. Not as bad as I thought it would be for a moment there, but bad. Commander Vivan's dead, and Baserat . . ."

As he listed the familiar names, Thomas shook his head. He would have to deal with it later. Worse that he didn't know if their sacrifice had accomplished anything, if Ravenna and Roland had been able to get out of the city. Lucas finished with, "—and hard as it is to believe, Denzil's here with—"

"I know. I'm about to go and give him the good news about my premature survival. Do you know where Falaise is?"

"Yes, Martin found where they're keeping her. Gideon and some of the others are hanging about outside her rooms, making sure no one makes off with her."

The Queen was ensconced in a suite in the opposite wing. Bloody and ragged, Thomas and Kade drew considerable attention passing through the house. Thomas limped, and resisted the urge to steady himself on the walls. They finally arrived at a suite guarded by five weary, battered men with the badges of city service, who were in turn being watched by Gideon and six other Queen's guards.

Gideon was pacing, and when Thomas and the others entered the anteroom where the guards were gathered, he looked like he was in agony. Stiffly he began, "Sir, I—"

Thomas said, "Shut up," and walked past him into the next room.

The city guards watched with great interest and made no attempt to stop him, but inside were several of Denzil's contingent of Albon knights, given to him by Roland and sworn to his personal service. Thomas said, "Gentlemen, really."

The knights were well aware that denying a Queen's Guard lieutenant the right to see the Queen was irregular enough, but denying it to the Queen's Guard Captain was practically equivalent to abduction. One of the older knights looked uneasy. "We have our orders—" he began.

Falaise threw open the door and stood there, her eyes wide. She was still dressed for riding and her hair was coming down. She said, "Captain, thank God you're all right."

"I think your orders have just been countermanded." Thomas smiled.

Falaise tapped the knight who was blocking the door on the shoulder, saying in an irritated tone, "Get out of the way."

Thomas thought that if Kade were ever foolish enough to get herself into a similar situation, she would have probably punched the man in the kidney. The knights reluctantly moved aside.

Then from the anteroom Denzil pushed his way in through the city guards, Lord Aviler behind him. The High Minister looked mildly surprised to see them. Denzil stopped when he saw Thomas, and his eyes narrowed dangerously.

Yes, Thomas thought, *how awful that it all doesn't go your way.* He said, "I was looking for the Queen. It seems the King has temporarily misplaced her." He wondered if Denzil would challenge him now.

The air in the room was brittle enough to break.

"She is under my protection," Denzil said.

"Yes, I've heard all about that, but it isn't necessary anymore."

"I have men here—"

"You have twenty armed men sworn to your service, my lord," Aviler interrupted. "And you, Captain, have about an equal number of Guardsmen in any condition to fight. I have a hundred city troops in service to the Ministry, and I suggest we leave them all to their duty of keeping this house secure."

"A very diplomatic suggestion." Thomas inclined his head.

Abruptly Falaise said, "I . . . thank you for your help, Lord Denzil, but I do not . . . require it any longer."

Denzil stared down at her a long frozen moment. "As you wish, Madame." He turned away and left the anteroom. Aviler bowed sardonically and followed him.

Thomas followed Falaise into the room and closed the door behind him. It was a perfect setting for her, with light sarsenet hangings and mirror-glass set in the paneling. There was no maid in evidence. He wondered briefly if Falaise had sent her female attendants away, or if she had even been offered any. *Was Denzil on his way here just now because he heard I was, or because he knew Falaise was alone? And was that why Aviler was trailing after him?* He leaned on the back of a tapestry-covered armchair to take the weight off his leg and said, "My lady, I think there are some things we need to discuss."

"Yes." Falaise sat down on the daybed and looked up at him anxiously. "About Denzil."

Kade had vanished somewhere along the way, though Thomas suspected she was nearby and within earshot. He wasn't worried about that. She already suspected most of what Falaise was about to tell him. "How much do you know about the Duke of Alsene's plans?"

"Nothing, not really. He . . ." Falaise looked away nervously. "Denzil suggested that if my husband were to have to leave the throne, I might consider marrying him."

Landlaw again. The oldest traditions held that by being the King's wife, Falaise took on part of the mystique of the crown, if not its authority. If Roland died without leaving children, and one of the possible heirs married Falaise, it would go far to strengthen his claim in the minds of a great many people. There were a considerable number of families with enough royal blood to pursue the throne, and many technically closer to it than Denzil's. But none of them had tried to suborn Falaise . . . *It implies he's fairly sure she's soon to become a widow.* "That's treason."

Her expression was earnest. "I know."

Thomas closed his eyes and rubbed the bridge of his nose. "What did you tell him?"

"I didn't answer him." She made a helpless gesture. "I tried to put him off. I was afraid if I said no he would tell Roland lies about me, but if I said yes, even if I didn't mean it, he might go through with what he planned. I didn't know who to go to."

Yes, you did. You just couldn't get me to listen to you. Thomas noticed she had refrained from pointing that error out to him, but it would have been against Falaise's lifelong training to tell a man in authority that he had made a mistake. No, she would try to delicately manage him, which would make it all the more difficult to get the truth out of her. Yet that tactic had worked well with Denzil. She must have made a good job of stringing him along, if she had kept it up for several days without the young Duke losing his patience. Thomas could easily imagine Falaise swooning, gracefully weeping, and doing everything a woman about to give in did except actually give in. He looked up. "And he didn't give you any hint of how he was going to accomplish this?"

"No. If he had, would that make things any better?"

"Probably not."

Falaise was knotting the ribbons on the sleeve of her coat. "It is very bad, isn't it?"

"Yes. If we ever get the evidence against him to bring a formal charge of treason, then he can take you to the gallows with him. You could bring the charge yourself, but I doubt Roland would take your word over Denzil's. There are plenty of others who know Denzil and probably would take your word before his, but their opinions won't count." Thomas shook his head wearily. "We'll just have to make sure it won't come to that."

She nodded. "How?"

It was just one more reason for Denzil to die a hero's death at the earliest opportunity. It might not stop Grandier now, but it would clear up a number of miscellaneous side issues and relieve the feelings of several people, among them Kade, Ravenna, Falaise, and himself. But it didn't make it any easier. They were not under Roland's nervous eye anymore, but with the knights and High Minister Aviler as biased witnesses, it was still a difficult problem. "The less you know now, the better," he told her.

"Wait." She hesitated. "I wanted to tell you that my patronage is yours, whatever happens. I know that Roland is against you, but if the Duke of Alsene is gone he would be so much easier to deal with, and if things get back to the way they were . . . When Ravenna isn't here anymore, when I'm patron of the Queen's Guard, I want you to stay as captain." Her eyes lifted to meet his for the first time. "My patronage, and my very sincere . . . regard."

Oh, fine, Thomas thought in annoyance. In the language of the court, her meaning was clear. Regard equaled favor, and favor meant access to her bed in return for his support. He kept his expression neutral. "I'll remember that, my lady."

———

Listening in the anteroom, Kade knocked her head ungently against the wall and thought, *And that is the tale of my life.* She slipped out, unnoticed.

———

When Thomas went out into the anteroom, Lucas was telling Gideon, "—and when he heard about it he went absolutely mad, and you're lucky if you're not—"

They both looked up when he shut the door. Thomas said to Gideon, "When this is over we're going to have a talk, but until then we won't refer to it. Now stay here and make sure no one walks off with her."

The young lieutenant winced. "Yes, Sir."

Thomas went out, Martin and Lucas following him. A man wearing a steward's chain approached them, somewhat warily. "Lord Aviler would like to see you, Captain."

Lucas raised an eyebrow and casually adjusted one of the pistols in his sash, but Thomas shook his head. He followed the man through a small gallery hung with family portraits and to a door at the far end, the others trailing along. As Aviler's man knocked on the door, Lucas dropped into one of the armchairs and Martin leaned on the wall. The steward eyed them nervously, but didn't voice any objections.

Inside was a study warmed by a fire in a pink marble hearth and lit by gray late-afternoon light from two windows in the far wall. The floor was covered with bright eastern carpets probably brought back from the trading voyages Aviler the Elder had made his fortune on. Through chance or careful planning, they managed not to clash with the striped red silk covering the walls. The High Minister stood with his back to the fire as Thomas stepped in. He motioned for the steward to withdraw, then said, "Lord Denzil's preparing to leave. I thought you might be interested."

Thomas limped to one of the windows. The snow had stopped and the view gave onto the street below where they had fought that morning. The wrecked coaches were still there, though the city troop must have brought in the bodies. The carriage doors below were just opening. Night would fall in an hour or so; it was a nearly suicidal time to be venturing out.

Aviler said, "For a house under siege, there's a great number of people coming and going. I know what you're planning."

Thomas watched Denzil emerge on horseback with his men grouped behind him. They began to pick their way down the snow-choked street. He turned back to the Aviler. "Do you?"

"You're going to take the good Duke of Alsene down. If I hadn't been there, your lieutenant would have killed him in my dining room." Aviler crossed to a long draw table piled with books and papers and sat on one corner, watching him. "I don't mind what you do to each other, and he did put the Queen in unpardonable danger by keeping her from leaving the city." He leaned forward. "But don't do it here."

Thomas watched him thoughtfully. "I don't have that choice anymore, it seems. And he's done more than put the Queen in danger."

"I can hardly believe anything you tell me at this point."

Thomas started for the door. "Then I won't tell you. But if you think he's going to join Roland, you're laughably wrong. Send someone to follow him and you'll find he's taking the street back to the palace. Then ask yourself why."

He went out. Lucas looked up as he shut the door behind him and said, "Well?"

Thomas told him, "We're getting the Queen out of here tomorrow, whatever it takes."

The court rode into Bel Garde in the late afternoon, and now in the gateyard Ravenna sat her horse amid the turmoil of servants, courtiers, Albons, Cisternans, and her own men, watching as Renier ordered guard placements. The late Dr. Braun's apprentices already stood before the closed outer gates, working with books, incense burners, and other odd tools to temporarily ward those fragile barriers of metal and wood against the fay. They had been attacked again passing through the city gates, and several parties had been scattered or killed, but the fay had not followed them out. Satisfied with the arrangements being made here, Ravenna let her guards urge her farther into the fortress.

Once through the inner gate and the portcullis, Bel Garde's celebrated interior court with its fountains and miniature gardens was visible, though smothered now under a heavy blanket of snow. The stonework on the newer bastion looming over them was as ornate as gilded filigree, with curves, curls, and the faces of classical luck sprites worked into the carving. A gem of a fortress, someone had called this place. *Yes,* Ravenna thought, *but because a sword is jeweled does not mean the blade is no longer deadly.* "Find Lieutenant Gideon and tell him to bring Falaise to me at once," she told the nearest guard.

As he rode off she looked down to see Elaine trotting beside her horse and tugging urgently on her riding skirt. "My lady, if you don't come out of this wind you'll get your sickness again."

Ravenna leaned down to remonstrate with her and found herself coughing helplessly into her sleeve.

Acknowledging physical weakness was not something she did gracefully. Once she could speak again, she cursed Elaine, the guards who came to help her down, and, rather unjustly, her horse, who stood rock steady with well-trained patience throughout the whole episode.

They led her through a wide door into a large, beautifully appointed entry hall. It was too cold to remove her cloak, but Ravenna had to admit the relief from the wind was welcome. She gestured Elaine away impatiently and paced, knotting her fingers together, noting the servants who worked to build up the fire were her own and not those of the fortress. "I want this place searched top to bottom."

"Yes, my lady."

The guard she had sent after Falaise came through the door, letting in a blast of cold air. His eyes were worried and Ravenna tensed. "My lady," he said, "Lieutenant Gideon and the other men who rode escort to the Queen aren't anywhere to be found."

Ravenna stopped, staring at the carved paneling in front of her. "And Falaise?"

"Not with the Albons or His Majesty's party."

Ravenna nodded grimly to herself. "Denzil."

———

Later, Thomas sat in front of the fireplace in the parlor of the suite they had commandeered for a headquarters. Gideon and most of the others were guarding Falaise, and Lucas had led an expeditionary force consisting of himself, Martin, and the two Cisternans down into the kitchens after food. Berham and Phaistus were sitting at a table across the room making bullets, the older man holding the leather-wrapped bullet mold and the younger carefully pouring hot lead from the small crucible.

The most badly wounded guard had died a short while ago. With men Thomas had led and fought beside for years dying and in constant danger, it was foolish to grieve over the death of someone he had in actuality never really known, but he found his thoughts turning to Galen Dubell.

He had never been so completely taken in by anyone, Thomas decided, and that was what disturbed him the most. He had first come to court younger than Roland was now, and had made his way through all the traps and pitfalls alone. Never allowing himself to trust anyone, he had escaped machinations that had ruined others and had learned how to deceive with the best of them. Perhaps he had believed Grandier because the old sorcerer had never asked for anything.

Thomas wondered how Dubell had felt when he had realized the trusted friend or servant that Grandier must have pretended to be had been watching, learning, gathering information for an impersonation that would kill its victim. If the old man had even been allowed to realize that, if he hadn't died in complete ignorance of what was happening to him.

Kade wandered into the room with the air of someone waiting for a public coach and settled into the other chair, and he was glad of the distraction. Thomas had not asked her why she hadn't left the city. They had all assumed she had the means to do so, though they had never had any proof of it.

It had occurred to him that he was taking her for granted, like taking gunpowder for granted when one carried pistols much of the time.

And now she was staring at him. He said, "Yes?"

She said, "What do you think Roland will do when he finds out about Denzil and Falaise?"

He had the feeling this wasn't really what was on her mind, but he wasn't willing to pursue that suspicion. He said, "I don't know." At the moment he was too tired to care about a possible outburst from Roland, though he supposed later he would have to manage it. Interesting to think how it was possible to grow out of the need for power, and to desire freedom from the constant wrangling of those who still wanted it. "Roland, Denzil, and Falaise make an interesting triangle. It's a pity I can't confuse the issue any further by pursuing Falaise." The young Queen was beautiful, but so were most of the other women at court. She was also the kind of woman for whom men would continually ruin themselves, and he was past that stage. Did Denzil want Falaise, or was that the only way he knew to approach her? Falaise had evidently not wanted him. Thomas doubted she wanted anybody. Her offer to him had held no warmth. She offered her body because she thought it was part of the process of sealing the agreement.

Was I like that? Thomas wondered. *Was that what I thought when Ravenna first approached me, all those years ago?*

Kade interrupted his thoughts. "Why not?"

He had time to notice that he had spoken to her in the offhand way he might speak to a friend, without any regard for propriety or anything else. He also suspected he had just opened the way for her to ruthlessly question him about whatever subject occurred to her, but it was too late to stop at this point. "If I were going to raise a child, I'd have started before now."

Kade greeted this with another long moment of enigmatic silence, then she said, "Oh." She looked into the fire for a little while, then chuckled to herself.

He glanced at her suspiciously. "What?"

"Nothing." Another pause, then she asked, "How did Denzil get such a hold on Roland? That he can threaten the Queen, of all people, with her too afraid to ask for help?"

Thomas watched the fire for a moment, remembering. "Right before your father died, Roland tried to kill himself by cutting his wrists, but he bungled it. Denzil found him, bandaged him up, concocted a story to explain it. He also kept him from attempting it again."

Kade bit her lip, thinking, then shook her head. "But that almost seems like Denzil must care for him, and I may be odd, but I can't imagine that."

"You can care for someone and hate them at the same time. And Denzil was nothing without Roland's support then. He needed a live prince to attach himself to." He glanced over at her. "Don't look like that. Roland didn't have to fall into Denzil's clutches. Look at you. You haven't got a Denzil hanging about somewhere in Fayre, have you?"

"Of course not." She shuddered theatrically. "And I was not looking guilty, I was looking thoughtful."

Thomas hadn't said the word "guilty," but he didn't intend to point that out. If she could fall into such an obvious trap then she must be considerably distracted.

A log rolled to the edge of the hearth, and he stood, somewhat awkwardly, supporting himself on the arm of the chair, to push it back in with the poker.

Kade winced. "I'm sorry about that."

He dropped back into the chair. "About saving my life? There's a cheery sentiment."

She refused to be diverted. "What if it never heals?"

She was just as well aware as he was about what it would do to his speed in a fight. "Well, I'm getting old for a duelist. It probably won't make any difference in the long run."

"Don't say that; I have enough to worry about." Kade slumped further down in her chair. "How are we going to get rid of Denzil?"

Thomas wondered how she could sit like that without breaking her back. He answered, "I'm going to kill him, if I ever get the chance. But I'd like to do it without dooming Falaise, myself, or anyone else."

"I could do it. Roland hates me anyway, and he can't come after me where I live."

He snorted. "I'm hardly likely to ask you to do a thing like that."

"It's nothing I haven't done before."

The somewhat airy way she said this caused him to doubt that she was as indifferent as she pretended, but he answered, "I don't care if you go about murdering people every afternoon. You'd make me look a fool or a worse scoundrel than Denzil, and I'd think of some horrific way to retaliate."

She shrugged and rubbed the arm of the chair distractedly. "It shouldn't matter, even if I am related to him. I wished my father dead."

Thomas frowned. "What makes you say that?"

Her eyes on the fire, Kade said slowly, "I wished it, very hard, with everything I had, which I was beginning to realize might be quite a bit. And he died."

"He didn't just fall over dead," Thomas told her, exasperated.

"Yes, he did." She held her ground, stubborn.

"No, he did not. Were you there?"

Kade waved a hand. "No, of course not, but I know what happened because I caused it."

This was ridiculous. "I don't know why I bother to listen to you argue in circles."

Kade made another frustrated gesture. "Because you can't come up with anything better than 'No, he did not.' How do you know? My magic was wild then, I didn't know what I was doing, I could have caused any amount of harm."

Thomas considered her for a long moment. He said finally, "Does it matter, as long as he's dead?"

"No, I suppose not." She sank even further in her chair and stared at the fire.

Thomas glanced back at the two servants. Berham was deep into a story of one of the last battles of the Bisran War, and Phaistus was so engrossed in it he was getting hot lead all over the table. He turned back to the fire. "Fulstan was poisoned."

Her expression went blank. It was hard to tell if she was astonished or not. He said, "Ravenna did it. I got the poison for her. It was foxglove, as I recall."

Kade stood up and walked around the room in a circle. After a few moments she wandered back to the fire and sat down again as if she had just arrived.

Thomas added, "Believe it or not, Ravenna never quite realized what Fulstan was doing to you or to Roland. She's very single-minded. He knew he should be wary of her, but she couldn't touch him under court- or landlaw, and I suppose he thought his position was safe. After your little outburst in the cathedral, she began to wonder why you'd become such a terror. I discovered some of the details for her so she sent you out of the city to the convent. You'd been gone a week when Roland botched his attempt to bleed to death, and when she heard about that she made the decision." He shrugged. It all seemed a very long time ago. "There wasn't any dancing in the streets, but most of the mourning was insincere."

She was silent for a long time, and Thomas listened to the fire crackle and Berham's voice in the background. Finally Kade said quietly, "I never thought anybody wanted to kill him but me. Even Roland thought it was something he did, like not riding well enough or playing games badly."

Thomas leaned forward and added another log to the fire. "Well, it was time you knew."

———

It was much later and most of the house was asleep when Kade made her way up to the highest attic and eased up the sash of a window there, mindful of the nails in it. It was cold, bitterly cold, with a patina of frost glittering over every surface and clouds hiding the stars. It was very dark and the moon was in its waning; in the Old Faith, it was the dark time, the death of light magic. The reigning time of the Host. The gray-black rooftops spread around her like an angular unmoving sea. She could just see the palace from here as an odd collection of shapes, some recognizable as towers, another as the dome of the Summer Residence. The faint glow of witch-light flickered over the walls.

She climbed out onto the slate-shingled roof of the gable just below and sat in front of the window, to keep anything from trying to enter the house behind her back. She shivered and hugged her knees, though she had augmented her clothing with a man's shirt Berham had found for her and Thomas's battered buff coat.

I did not kill my father. Her emotions were as tangled as a jumbled collection of beaded necklaces. She wished she could untangle the strands and run them through her fingers one by one. Disappointment, that she could understand. It was not an odd emotion for someone who had believed a lie was the truth, particularly as it was a lie she had told herself. Confusion, anger, remembered fear, all these were explicable, if hopelessly intertwined. It was the strange sensation of release, the sense of freedom that she couldn't understand, that made her face hot and her hands numb with the strength of it. As if something tightly coiled inside her chest had relaxed a trifle. It seemed to make other things possible as well. It seemed to imply that it might be possible to forget, eventually. *Time to stop dreaming like a child,* she told herself with an irritated toss of her head. Time to think and plan.

She closed her eyes and whispered, "Boliver, come here now; I need to talk to you." A gust of wind carried the words away.

Nothing happened. *I hate it when he makes me do this.* "As Queen of Air and Darkness, and on my sovereignty of Knockma, I call Boliver Fay."

For a long breathless moment there was no answer, then out of the cloud-covered sky a star fell. It plunged toward her and landed lightly at her feet, then resolved with a flash of light into Boliver, who said, "It's not bloody easy getting here, you know." He was about Kade's height, wizened and red-bearded, and his vivid blue eyes were worried. He wore a high-peaked hat and a somewhat tattered velvet doublet.

"No, I don't know. That's why I called you. How is Knockma?"

"Not so good. There are members of the Host drawn up on the border to Fayre, though not a sign of them on the mortal side, so far. They didn't like you much to begin with, and now with you taking the human part in this war—"

"Is everyone all right?" Kade had worried about her household. Some of them were human, and none terribly good at defending themselves.

Boliver was offended. "You know I wouldn't let anything happen to our lot. But why are you doin' this? Have you gone witless? You didn't make up with your brother by chance?"

"No, of course not." Kade doubted she ever would. Roland wouldn't welcome such an overture, and she wasn't certain she wanted to make it anymore. There was too much history between them, and they might only remind one another of things better forgotten. The news that he had tried to take his own life had been an unpleasant surprise, and her thoughts shied away from it. She looked out over the dark dead city again. "I've got a reason for it."

"'A reason,' she says. Oh, joy." Boliver rolled his eyes.

She rubbed her forehead. "I'll hold Knockma for us, don't worry."

"I'm not worried." He let his knees knock and his teeth chatter convincingly. "I'm petrified. I've no wish to vanish down Evadne's gullet. Or watch me bosom companions do likewise."

"Neither do I." She shifted impatiently. "I need your help."

He snorted. "As if I had a choice."

"Well you don't, so be quiet and listen. I need you to fly over the palace and tell me what you can see."

"Fly over the palace? What have I done to deserve it? With all those boglie-woglies everywhere?"

"Yes. I'd do it if I could, but I can't, and that's all there is to it!" Boliver was her oldest friend in Fayre, and she didn't want to risk him, but there was no other way to learn what she needed to know. If there was one thing Kade regretted, it was her lack of the fay abilities to shape-change and to fly.

"Yes, yes. I know. You've got your head set on defeating the Unseelie Court and their minions one-handed, I suppose, and there's no dissuading you. Well, wish me luck."

She stood as he vanished into starlight and streaked away toward the shadowy bulk of the palace towers. "Luck," she whispered.

CHAPTER TWELVE

THOMAS WOKE BEFORE dawn, the wound in his leg stiff and sore. Despite the fire, the room was frosty and he sat on the bed and struggled into his doublet. He stood and limped around until he could walk without obviously hobbling, then tried to do a fencer's full extension. He got halfway down and needed the help of the bedpost to get back up.

Phaistus was sleeping in front of the doorway, rolled up in a rug and snoring. He hadn't stirred when Thomas was bumping around the room and didn't wake when he stepped over him and opened the door.

The anteroom was lit only by two candles on the mantel, their soft light making the blue wallpaper dissolve into shadow and hiding the disarray of the fine furnishings. Kade sat on the floor with the contents of an ebony trinket cabinet spread out around her. It was probably the silver-gilt curiosities and mother-of-pearl boxes that had attracted her attention, but it was the seashells, the baby's skull, and the ostrich egg that had undoubtedly kept it.

She looked up at him. "Are you going back to the palace today?"

It was too early for this. He dropped into an armchair. "Wouldn't that be an extraordinarily foolish thing to do?"

"I don't know. I don't think about things that way." She held up a seashell with her bandaged hand, passed the other hand in front of it, and the shell disappeared. "I suppose it would depend on why you were going. And who went with you." She pulled the shell out of her right ear. "Do you want to find the keystone?"

Thomas watched her. She was giving the shell the sort of concentration usually reserved for a deep philosophical problem. He was certain Denzil had returned to the palace yesterday, and he meant to discover why. He had thought the keystone was a lost cause. "Would that do any good?"

She kept her gaze on the shell. "The wards themselves are still there, drifting over the older parts of the palace, and the other wardstones are still in place. If we replace the keystone, it will pull the wards back down into their original courses, and the Host will have to leave or be trapped inside."

Thomas knew Grandier must have taken the stone, probably soon after he had arrived at the palace, but that still didn't leave them a clue of where to look for it. "He could have hidden the keystone anywhere inside the palace. Or more likely, he handed it to Dontane, that night at court when he was there, to hide somewhere in the city. It would be like looking for one certain rock in a quarry."

"But it's a very special sort of rock. If I could get to one of the plain ward-stones, and take a chip from it," Kade said slowly, "I might be able to use it in a spell, to find the keystone."

Thomas frowned. "How?"

"Years and years ago when all the stones were placed in the warding spell, they became one. Even when the keystone has been removed, and the matrix isn't there anymore, the stones remember. It's like using a lock of hair to find a person." She rubbed a thumb over the shell in her hand, vexed. "I should have thought of this before we left the palace yesterday."

"There aren't warding stones in the Old Courts. It would have been just as dangerous to go into the other part of the palace then as it is now," he said. *And you had other things to think about.* "If you came with me, you could do this spell while we were in the palace, and discover if the keystone is still there?"

Kade considered this a moment, her gaze moving over the collection of curiosities on the floor. "No. Am I a fool for being honest?"

"No. Am I a fool for expecting you to be honest?" Even as he said it he realized it was true. He had been prepared to believe her answer, even if it had served her purpose.

Kade didn't look up at him. "So, whatever are we going to do?" She closed her hand, and opened it again. The shell had vanished.

"Don't play coy; it ill becomes you."

She pulled the shell out of her ear again and for the first time faced him directly. "All right, will you say I can come with you, or do we have to have a loud fight about it and attract the attention and speculation of the entire house?"

Thomas sighed, leaning back to look up at the ceiling. "I don't know, I could do with a loud fight. Gets the blood moving." He had seriously considered asking her to come already. She could escape any danger far more readily than he could, and with her help his chances of accomplishing something increased to the point of the almost possible.

Kade made the shell vanish again, stood to lean on his chair arm, and apparently found it in his ear.

This time he saw it come out of her sleeve. "Get away from me," he told her cordially.

Kade smiled. "I'm going with you, aren't I?"

He said, "Yes. We'll both be fools together."

———

Falaise did not complain when told she had another long ride ahead of her. She seemed just as anxious to go as they were to send her on her way.

The Queen's presence had assured them the loan of some of Aviler's horses, and the servants readied them in the large roofed court that held the house's stables. The large chamber was warmed somewhat by the presence of the animals and was probably one of the more comfortable areas of the house. This did not entirely account for the number of city guardsmen who had ostensibly shown up to see them off, probably on Aviler's orders.

Thomas was sending all the guards who had survived the flight from the palace, even the most badly wounded. Aviler would probably interpret this as the basest form of distrust, but at the moment the last thing Thomas cared about was the High Minister's opinion of him.

He drew Lucas aside while Gideon was helping Falaise to mount and said, "I'm not going with you. I'm going back to the palace."

He hadn't thought this would be well received and he wasn't mistaken. Lucas stared at him incredulously. "Why?"

They keep asking me that, Thomas thought. *Do I seem bored, that I have to invent these things to keep myself busy?* "Why do you think? That's where Denzil went. He must realize that we'll get the Queen out of here, and with her gone he's not likely to come back."

Lucas was unconvinced. "What if he isn't there?"

"If he is, it's the best chance I'm likely to have at him. If he's not, I can at least have a look at what's happening there before I go on to Bel Garde." He didn't know if Aviler had sent someone to follow Denzil or not; probably not, and he didn't want to give his own plan away by asking. It seemed unlikely that Aviler was in the plot with Denzil, but it had seemed unlikely that Galen Dubell was anything other than what he had appeared.

Lucas grimaced in dismay. "Send someone else, Thomas. Or I'll go."

"No, it's a fool's mission. I'm not Roland, to send someone off to die on an idiot whim." Thomas glanced around. The argument, though low voiced, was attracting the attention of the city guards who were loitering in the stable. And of Lord Aviler himself, who watched from the narrow second-floor balcony where an arched door led into the rest of the house.

Lucas noticed and made a concentrated effort to appear calm. "You're going alone?" he asked.

Thomas found himself curiously reluctant, as if he were admitting to something. "No, Kade is coming with me."

Lucas winced.

"She's a sorceress, and she can get me back in without a fight."

"I know, I know." Lucas hesitated. He looked toward the other men who were saddling the horses, or waiting half nervously and half impatiently for them to get on with it. "She could do it by herself. You don't need to go with her."

Thomas shook his head. "She's not invincible, she only thinks she is."

"So do you." Lucas looked back at him, saying deliberately, "In your condition, you'd probably slow her down."

"Then it's no loss to anyone if I don't come back."

Thomas had spoken with more heat than he had intended, but Lucas seemed to realize that line of argument was not going to get him anywhere. He said, "I'll wait for you here."

"I need you to go with Falaise."

"Gideon can do that. He's not a fool; he'll get her there."

They were both silent a moment. Thomas didn't want to force the issue, not here, not now, and not with an audience. He said, "All right, then, but keep a couple of the men with you. And don't wait too long. If it takes more than a day, we'll have to hole up somewhere for the night, and this place may not be safe much longer. If something starts to happen, get out and ride like hell for the gates."

Lucas nodded distractedly, then without looking at him said, "You know that girl's half in love with you."

"Falaise will keep." Thomas spared a glance at the Queen, who sat her horse with a kind of delicate ease, a few ringlets escaping from her hood. "If anything, it will make things easier in the long run—"

"I'm not talking about Falaise." He hesitated. "You didn't see her when she thought you were dying. I did."

There was only one other "her" he could mean. Thomas said slowly, "Well, she's the excitable type."

"It was more than just that."

"You're mad," Thomas told him, but couldn't help thinking about a woman who chuckled wickedly to herself at odd moments and offered to kill people for him.

"I'm only telling you to watch yourself, that's all," Lucas said, his expression serious. "She's not exactly an ordinary woman."

"I realize that," Thomas said. *Believe me, I realize that.*

Lucas persisted, "You think you do, but I've known you a long time and you've got a blind eye when it comes to this type of woman."

Thomas said, "Now I know you've gone mad," and turned and went back toward the others. Gideon was holding the bridle of Falaise's horse and looked up as he approached. Thomas said, "Do you think you can get her back to Roland without losing her somewhere along the way?"

The younger man's eyes lit up at the chance to redeem himself. "I'll get her there safely if I die for it."

"Don't die until she's out of the city."

Falaise leaned down and said, "Captain, remember what I said."

"I will, my lady," he answered, thinking, *Let's all survive the day at least before we start plotting again.*

Kade was waiting beside the sorrel gelding Thomas had chosen for their outing. He had managed to get his buff coat back from her, and she was wearing instead a thick wool doublet that Berham had scavenged for her over about a dozen other layers of assorted clothing. She asked, "What was all that about?"

He checked the girth, then swung up into the saddle. "None of your concern."

"I'll wager it was."

He looked down at her. "Would you like to be left behind?"

"Not particularly," she answered brightly, dropping the matter with an insight that shouldn't have surprised him. She held up a hand and after a moment he leaned down and helped her climb up behind him. Two grooms opened the carriage doors, allowing in a wave of frigid air, and she said, "What a nice day this is, except for the prospects of being killed and freezing to death and all that."

Thomas, feeling the light pressure of her weight at his back, tried to avoid thinking about what Lucas had said.

He guided the horse out onto the street and waited until Gideon, Falaise, and the others had started on their way to the city gates, then turned back toward the palace. The sky was gray, almost the same color as the dingy snow piled deep, and the wind played roughly over the tops of the houses. He was reluctant to take the direct route they had used to escape, but the first side street he picked was blocked halfway down by rubble and a pile of collapsed scaffolding, some noble's building project that had not withstood the shock of the attack, let alone the test of time.

They backtracked, then cut through an alley to the next street. It was slow going, the horse picking its way through the knee-deep drifts with some difficulty. The town houses towering up on either side gradually gave way to the more dilapidated structures of the trading classes. The shingled roofs became wood instead of slate, the brick facades showed signs of wear, and ramshackle balconies overhung the street. It was hard to tell how much damage had been done here; the windows were tightly shuttered as if for night, and there was no sign of life. Thomas kept an eye on the tops of the buildings, and spotted the fay before it saw them only because he noted the unevenness in the spacing of the ornamental gargoyles atop the roof of an aging church. Kade said, "Wait," and he reined in, the horse sidling uneasily. The quality of the light around them changed as Kade covered them with illusion. They moved slowly on beneath the waiting presence, unnoticed.

They had ridden a short distance down the deserted street when Kade said suddenly, "I wonder why they did it."

He had no idea what she meant. "Who did it?"

"The Unseelie Court." He felt her shrug. "The Bisran document said they wanted souls to trade to Hell for their immortality, but that's nonsense. Not even the Host trades with Hell. Besides, you can't just send someone there; they have to go on their own. So what did Grandier give them?"

Once Thomas had known who Grandier was, the plot had started to peel away like the layers of an onion, but there was still much they didn't know. Grandier's motivation for helping Denzil for one; Thomas refused to believe Grandier was acting simply out of madness. "Maybe it isn't what he gave them, but what he's promised them. What would they want?"

"The only thing that stands against them is the Seelie Court. And iron wielded by humans."

Thomas asked, "Destroying us isn't going to do anything to the Seelie Court, is it?"

He felt her shrug. "No, they don't care about anyone."

"So . . . They can't destroy our ability to make iron. No matter how badly they ravage the countryside, they can't get every blacksmith." He paused as an errant gust of freezing wind whipped down into the street, momentarily making breathing difficult, then continued, "Bisra will invade long before they can get around to that, and they'll have another iron-wielding army to deal with."

Kade sounded thoughtful. "Will the Bisrans come here?"

"No, they'll strike at Lodun. It's closer to their border, and they have to eliminate the sorcerers there before they advance any farther. If they move fast, if our crown troops are still trying to retake this city, they just might succeed." Lodun had been a small town before the founding of the university. It had since outgrown its confining and protective walls and depended on the strength of the border garrisons for its defense against possible attack from their longtime enemy. With the capital in chaos and unable to send provisions or fresh troops, those garrisons could be swept away. "There are some powerful sorcerers there, but without troops to back them they can't hold off a large assault. The Bisrans would have to cross a countryside where there would be a peasant in every bush with a matchlock; but of course that wouldn't do more than delay them. They would finish us, then tear through Adera and Umberwald." It would be a long bloody war.

"Human sorcerers," Kade said suddenly.

"What?"

"I was wrong. The enemies of the Unseelie Court are the Seelie Court, iron, and human sorcerers."

"Which Lodun is well supplied with. Grandier could have told them that he would destroy Lodun. And he will. Bisra will do it for him." It was a neat bit of reasoning, but it didn't explain Denzil's position. Could he possibly be bargaining to be a puppet princeling under Bisra's domination? There wouldn't be anything left worth ruling; the Bisran Church would condemn as a heretic everyone from Lodun, sorcerer-philosophers to the peasants who kept a sprig of rowan over their doorways. "Right now Grandier has us over a barrel. We're on the defensive, forced to react to whatever he chooses to do. If Bisra invaded again, we would have to forget an attempt to retake this city and use the troops to fortify Lodun and the border."

"But Grandier must hate Bisra, hate it worse than anything," Kade protested.

Thomas reined in. "There's something coming down the street."

Kade leaned around him. "I can't see it."

"It was near the ground."

The horse reared suddenly, and it took Thomas all his strength to wrestle it down. Kade slipped off and staggered in a high drift, and Thomas dismounted. He held onto the reins and tried to soothe the horse as the animal whinnied and jerked its head. Behind him Kade murmured a curse. He looked down and saw white mist rising out of the snow. It was no more than a foot or so above the ground, but turning thick and solid with alarming speed.

The horse made a violent convulsive movement that nearly yanked Thomas off his feet; he let go of the reins to avoid being knocked down. The horse bolted awkwardly away, leaving a trail of blood in the snow. It was only able to make a short distance up the street before it staggered and collapsed, felled by whatever was rising out of the ground.

The nearest building, a three-story stone structure that seemed to lean slightly under the weight of the snow, had a staircase running up its side to the roof. Though it looked casually put together and was slippery with ice, it seemed a safe haven at the moment. Kade had already retired to a step above the rising mist, and Thomas quickly climbed after her.

"It's a boneless," Kade said. She dug in the pockets in her smock and muttered to herself. Above her rough gloves, her wrists were dotted with blood where she had touched the ground to catch herself when she had stumbled. "This may be a problem. It doesn't have eyes to fool, and I don't have a spell that can hold it back, the way it oozes around obstacles."

Thomas said, "Go farther up."

They climbed to the second floor and Thomas stopped to see what the creature would do. The mist had taken on a kind of half solidity, becoming a white undulating form. On the step above him, Kade shifted impatiently.

It reached the stairway and hesitated. A white translucent tendril touched the bottom step, then it flowed onto it and began to climb after them. "I didn't know it could do that," Kade said, obviously taking the thing's action as a personal affront. Thomas gave her a push to get her started and they climbed up to the third floor.

The houses were so close together that the street might have been lined with one continuous structure. The garrets of one hung over the next roof, and the overhanging balconies were awkwardly shoved together. There was a slippery step down to a projection of ice-covered roof, then a brief scramble over the wooden rail to the next house's balcony. Kade climbed like a monkey.

They went that way down the street, balcony to balcony, taking to the icy roofs only when it was absolutely necessary. They were more exposed to the wind up here and the cold was intense. Thomas kept up a good pace, trying to ignore the aching wound in his leg.

They reached the end of the street, which opened into a square with the far side formed by the palace wall and the Postern Gate.

It was deadly quiet. Before the attack, this area had been a small market-place, crowded with street vendors, musicians, pickpockets, and noisy opportunists proselytizing new cults. Now it looked as if it had been run over by a cavalry charge. The ramshackle stalls that had grown like spiderwebs between the pillars of the large countinghouse were smashed, and the statues atop the public fountain were broken off, their naked copper pipes leaking trails of ice.

The last house had partially collapsed, and the nearest stairway to the street level was blocked by wooden debris.

As Thomas wrested the heavy wooden boards aside, Kade said suddenly, "What are you going to do afterward?"

"After what?"

"After this is over."

He stopped and stared at her. She held onto the wooden railing and shivered with cold, and had put the question with the same puzzled intensity she had shown during their speculation over the Host's motives. He said, "Don't you think that question is a bit premature?"

"Would you accept Falaise's offer?" she persisted.

There was a smudge of dirt on her nose, which he decided not to mention to her. He said, "Do you have to know everything?"

"I wasn't asking about everything."

He turned back to clearing the stair. "I might have to accept it." It wasn't a decision he wanted to make at the moment.

"Only if you wanted things to go back to the way they were before."

Only if he wanted to hold onto that power he had sentimentally wished to be rid of last night. "Why would I want to change it?"

It wasn't a question but she answered it anyway. "Because there are things you don't like about it, like killing people who get tricked by Denzil or get in the way of someone powerful—"

"Do you mind?" he interrupted her. He shoved the last board aside and they climbed down to ground level.

The Postern was smaller than the huge edifices of Prince's and St. Anne's. It had no gate tower and was much narrower. One of the great doors stood open, the other lay in the plaza. Thomas hoped whatever had rammed into that yard-thick wood now dearly regretted it. "Lucas was right," he said. "The way that door's been flung, something broke out, not in."

They paused in the rubble-strewn shadow of the last house and Kade considered a moment, frowning. "They'll expect us through the Prince's Gate, since it was safe before."

"They'll be watching all the gates."

"They might not. They're not very quick thinkers, most of them, and they might not remember things like that. And Denzil didn't have too many knights with him."

"He may not have any knights with him now. He can't afford witnesses," Thomas said dryly.

They skirted the square, staying close to the buildings, finally reaching the shadow of the wall and slipping through the gate.

To the right of the snow-covered yard there was a high wall, part of the inner defenses designed to trap intruders, and to the left, the three-storied Gate House with gaping holes in its dressed stone wall. Directly ahead was the icy canal, which came in under the north wall and went out under the east, where it was covered over by stone for a mile or so before rejoining the main river that cut through the city. The drawbridge that had allowed access to the rest of the palace compound was a ruined heap, but the siege wall beyond it still stood, blocking the view of the park. Thomas stopped beside a hole in the Gate House wall and took a cautious look inside. "I want to see what's around the Gallery Wing before we rush over there. If I can get up to the second story here, I can see over that wall."

Kade followed him through the gap, saying, "Why do you think Denzil's in the Gallery Wing?"

"I don't know where he is, but that's where the Host seemed to hit the hardest, and that's where the explosion was. I'd like to see just what in hell they wanted there."

Light came down through the torn roof, and the shattered beams had buried many of the defenders. Only the cold kept the atmosphere from resembling a charnel house, and a dull patina of ice hid most of the unpleasant details. The interior staircase had come free of the wall and hung at a crazy angle, but a pile of smashed beams and rubble allowed Thomas to climb to a window on what had been the second floor.

"They might have any reason for doing that," Kade said.

Thomas winced as beams shifted underfoot. "Yes, well, I'd like to know what it was."

"It might have to do with the way they arrived here. However that was."

Something about the way she said it made Thomas wonder for a moment if she had some suspicion she wasn't ready to explain. He considered pressing her about it, but he reached the window and found the shutters jammed shut. He had to brace himself and batter the hinges off with his sword-hilt.

He pried the shutter away. On the other side of the canal, the park stretched out, an ice field marked by the occasional snow-covered tree. Beyond the park, the Gallery Wing stood, the inner wall and the bastions to the other side looming like monoliths, contrasting dramatically with its graceful outlines. Nearer to the Gate House was the dome of the Summer Residence, which doubled as an observatory for astrologically inclined nobles and scholars. A wall sprouted out of the circular building and met the side of the Old Palace, sheltering the Gallery Wing and the gardens from the public areas on the other side. There was a servants' passage in that wall, and in the thick outer wall of the Old Palace. They could make their way out the opposite side of the Gate House and along the curtain wall, cross the canal where the unused mill bridged it, then enter the Summer Residence and take the passages into the Gallery Wing.

He climbed awkwardly down again, trying to avoid putting weight on his weak leg. Kade, who had been prowling about the place on her own, met him with a worried expression. She said, "The stupid dark fay have used most of the glamour around here. If it's like that all through the inside, I won't be able to hide us from them."

Thomas considered that. He had come too far to go back at this point. "If you want to stay here and wait for me, or start back—"

"Do I look like a coward?" she asked, with an exasperated expression.

"No, you don't look like a coward."

For some reason this seemed to disconcert her considerably, and Thomas reminded himself again to be careful. She tapped one foot impatiently, then said, "Well, all right, then. Let's go."

CHAPTER THIRTEEN

KADE FOUND HER warding stone along the passage into the Old Palace. It was cold and silent in the narrow little hall, and only the soft glow of a lamp they had appropriated from the Summer Residence held back the darkness. Thomas waited while Kade dug through the clay seal near the bottom of the wall to pull out the rounded water-smoothed stone.

He used his dagger to chip a piece off for her, and when he handed the stone back, she said, "That's odd. It's tingling, as if it's still part of the warding spell."

She was staring at the stone in perplexity, so he said, "Maybe it's something to do with the wards over the Old Courts?"

"Maybe. It's very odd." But she replaced the stone in its niche and they moved on.

When they reached the Gallery Wing, the narrow passage opened into a small bare room with a curtained doorway in the far wall. Thomas pushed it open a slit, seeing that they had come out about where he had thought they should. On the right wall was the wide sweep of stairs leading back into the lesser galleries, which would eventually lead to the Grand Gallery with its terrace giving onto the park. To the left was the arched entrance to the Old Palace and the main hall. This area at least was empty, bare of any intrusion except a fall of blown snow across the parquet floor.

They hadn't seen any fay, though twice in their trek across the palace, Kade had steered them around places where she seemed to sense some presence. Most of the creatures who could stand daylight were out hunting the streets. As for the others, and the main body of the Host, they might be hidden anywhere. It had been a cold trail marked by the dead, and the amount of damage was worse than Thomas had suspected. Now he waited until Kade put out the lamp, then he pushed the curtain aside and went cautiously to look into the entrance of the nearest gallery. At his side, Kade said, baffled, "What is this?"

Light fell through narrow windows high in the opposite wall to illuminate a formal gallery with a vaulted ceiling and delicately sculpted columns with blue and gold inlay. The floor was littered with refuse and debris, most of it looted from other portions of the palace. There were pallets made of tattered blankets, tapestry work pulled from walls, and the heavy damask of curtain material. Gold and silver plate, dented candleholders, and ornaments prized off statues formed glittering heaps. Thomas picked his way through it, thoughtful and wary of anything that might be lurking under one of those piles. Besides the loot, there were more prosaic items such as a scatter of gunflints, green glass shards from a shattered wine bottle, and more of the trash left by military camps. With the toe of his boot, he turned over an empty wooden powder flask and said, "It's a troops' billet."

Kade's nose wrinkled in disgust. "Troops? Denzil's troops?"

"Very likely. Bel Garde is a private estate, and he has the right to maintain a force to garrison it, even if it is within sight of the city." *But where are they now?* Thomas wondered. Plain to see why he had to have them. *You can't take a throne without a private force whose loyalty you can trust, but why aren't they here?* Jewelry stolen from the bodies of the slain had been left casually about. He picked up a pearl clasp and saw it still held strands of long dark hair from where it had been torn from its owner's head. He tossed it back onto the floor in disgust and looked around, entertaining the idea of torching the place. Broken furniture would provide plenty of kindling. But it would reveal their presence, and when the troopers returned they would only move to the next gallery.

He glanced back at Kade and saw she stood on the edge of the encampment, frowning uneasily. "What is it?"

"There's a great lot of iron in here." She retreated to a marble bench along the wall and began to scrape the bottoms of her boots off on it.

Thomas knelt and brushed gloved fingers across the layer of dust and filth covering the warm butter color of the inlaid wood floor; he found small particles that glinted dully in the light. "Iron filings. They're everywhere." So these men did not quite trust their fay allies. He had wondered if they would find evidence of the human servants of the Host that had led the attack, but they wouldn't be here in the presence of all this iron. They might have been only shock troops, to be expended in the battle. If the siege lasted much longer, the Host would certainly be able to replenish their supplies, when starvation began to drive more people out into the streets.

He dusted his hands off and went back to where Kade waited at the edge of the camp.

"If they stayed here last night"—she swiped at her boot one last time, brushing the last of the dust off—"where are they now?"

"If we knew that, we'd be a damn sight better off." Thomas considered, weighing the danger against what else they might discover. "We have to go farther in."

She gave a half shrug. "Very well. But I think it's going to get worse."

They followed a lesser-used path toward the center of the Gallery Wing, through a connected row of state dining rooms and smaller pillared halls, and it was there they found most of the dead. Many had died running, caught alone by some creature of the Host with the walls shaking from the explosion and lamps going out in the foul wind that followed. There were small groups of Cisternan guards and sometimes servants and courtiers who must have tried to band together to escape. Worst of all, they came upon a small room with the remains of a smashed barricade across the door, where a group had held out for a time.

Hours, at least, Thomas thought, leaning against the remains of the doorframe and feeling a rage as cold as the ice outside. *Judging by the condition of the room.* He recognized some of the men, and one of the women. She was Lady Anne Fhaolain, one of Ravenna's gentlewomen, and she clutched a fireplace poker in a delicate hand that had never held anything more dangerous than a sewing needle. He would have to tell Ravenna that Anne had died bravely, swinging a weapon. He would also have to convince himself that if he had been here the result would have been the same, only there would be one more body in the cold little room.

He turned away to find Kade standing behind him. She trembled in impotent fury. She said softly, "There's nothing that can make up for this. Not if I hunt him all the way to Hell itself."

Somehow he hadn't expected that it would make her as angry as it did him. He said, "You take this all very personally."

After a moment, Kade shook herself all over, like a cat coming out of the rain. "I take everything personally."

There was more evidence of the presence of the fay. Not far from the sad little room, they found a silken web stretched across the width of an arched doorway. Kade examined it cautiously, then detached it from the doorframe. It drifted gently to the floor, all in one piece like a fine section of lacework. So far they hadn't found any answers to their questions. The day was getting on and Thomas's bad leg ached from walking, and he knew they didn't have much

time left here before the danger became extreme. They would have to settle for
seeing the Gallery Wing and then making their way out.

They reached the foyer of the Grand Gallery, where there was a heavy foul
smell, reminiscent of bats in a deserted cathedral. Thomas whispered to Kade,
"They could be in the walls all through here."

She nodded. "Spriggans. They're asleep. I hope." She flitted past him into
the archway. He saw her pause there, and as he came up beside her he saw why.

Light from the steps that gave onto the loggia illuminated the foyer, and the
arched entrances provided a panoramic view of the Grand Gallery. The floor
had been blown up from below and the back wall of windows onto the terraces had been smashed outward. This had to be the source of the explosion
the night of the attack. *This was the center of it, then,* Thomas thought, and
beside him Kade said grimly, "They did a job of work in here."

The orange trees between the pillars were frozen but still green; the cold had
caught them so by surprise. Thomas sensed there was something alive here
and looked up from the blasted ruin of the floor to the shadowy stillness of the
vaults above. But nothing moved in the silence.

In the center of the room, the foundation stones had been pushed up from
underneath by some powerful force and scattered on the bare twisted earth
visible beneath. But not scattered randomly. Thomas took a few steps into the
room, wondering at it, then climbed the dais so he could get a better view. As
he had thought, the broken area of the floor was in the shape of a large circle,
with an outline too perfect to be accidental. The shattered stones formed concentric circles within it. It couldn't be anything but a fayre ring.

Peasants found them occasionally in the deep country, circles of trampled
grass, stones, or strange growth, and avoided them like the dangerous infes-
tations that they were. Stories about humans who blundered or ventured into
them were not pleasant; usually they were found on the edges of the rings as
dried, withered husks, as if they had aged a hundred years in a moment. Any
attempts to recover the bodies caused them to dissolve into dust.

If they were all like this, Thomas couldn't imagine someone foolish enough
to wander into one accidentally. It felt dangerous, and it was as unmistakable
as a sharp drop off a cliff.

Kade stood regarding the ring for a long moment, and now she followed
Thomas up onto the dais. She said, "Fancy that." She sounded more satisfied
than anything else, as if the sight confirmed some hypothesis of her own.

Looking down at her, Thomas felt the beginning of a new suspicion. He said, "They used that thing to get in somehow, didn't they?"

Still distracted, she nodded. "They came through it. With the wards confused and floating away, and no spells guarding it, it was the easiest way. I mean, not too easy, with the stones on top of it like that, but all of them together could do it."

"Through it?"

"Yes." She glanced at him a little warily, then explained, "It's a doorway."

"A doorway to where?"

"To Fayre, maybe. To lots of places."

He looked back at the ring, its tumbled stones a silent presence in the shadowy room. Kade grabbed his elbow. "Listen."

After a heartbeat, he heard it, too. Voices, echoing down through the long galleries locked in cold silence.

Thomas hurried back to the archway, trying to pinpoint the direction. Tracking sound echoing off so much stone and marble wasn't easy. The men might be in any one of the several galleries and long halls that led up to the Grand Gallery. Neither he nor Kade had spoken in louder than a whisper, and it was doubtful that whoever was coming this way had heard them.

He motioned for Kade to follow and they crossed the spriggan-haunted foyer. Thomas chose a smaller hall used for diplomatic processions, where the sound had for a moment seemed louder. They went down it, keeping to the partial shelter of its supporting pillars. The voices had ceased.

"I don't think this was it," Kade whispered.

"No, it must be another—"

They both heard the footsteps at the same time.

Kade looked around frantically. "There's not enough glamour in here."

Thomas searched hastily along the wall and found the unobtrusive servants' door that was designed to blend into the paneling. He went to it, sliding his hand down the crack that marked it until his fingers touched the catch. He pulled it open. Inside was a cramped stair leading up into the wall. Climbing it, they came to a landing with a damask-curtained doorway and another broader stair leading down and away from the hall. Thomas pulled the curtain back and saw that the door led to a small musicians' balcony, one of many spaced around the gallery.

He put his hat aside and crouched down, crawling out to look down through the balusters. Kade followed him.

Denzil and Dontane walked into the gallery from an archway below. *So the bastard's alive,* Thomas thought, brows lifted. Dontane had been imprisoned in the Cisternan Guard House during the attack, and Thomas assumed he had been killed with the others. The two men were arguing animatedly; they were trailed by three men armed as common troopers. The Albon knights who had accompanied Denzil at Aviler's house were probably dead; they would not have betrayed Roland, and it must have been obvious at this point that the young Duke's game was more serious than a petty attempt to disgrace the Queen's Guard.

Denzil was dressed for battle, and Dontane still wore black court brocades. He made quick, nervous gestures when he spoke, but it seemed to be more from intensity and anger than anything else.

The echoes were a hindrance. The two men spoke more quietly after the first shouting that had revealed their presence, and Thomas couldn't make out what they were saying. He heard Denzil mention Bel Garde, and he thought he heard Roland's name, but the rest was inaudible.

He edged back and sat up on one elbow, pulling a pistol out of his sash and winding its mainspring. The faint click it made was disguised by the two men's voices.

Kade glanced back at him, raising her eyebrows inquiringly.

He motioned for her to go back through the doorway and she crawled backward out of the way.

The range was not the best; with a pistol, closer was better. Thomas steadied the weapon on his arm and squeezed the trigger. Both men reacted to the sound of the blast; Denzil staggered. Thomas scrambled back out the door, shoving the empty pistol back into his sash. There would be no confusion about where the shot had come from; the white smoke hanging over the little balcony would reveal his presence like a flag.

Kade was already on the landing, and he followed her down the wider stair. It came out through another servants' door in the foyer, and he heard running footsteps and a man shouting. Drowning it out was a low humming sound that seemed to come from everywhere.

Looking around, Kade gasped, "Damn, but that woke them up."

A gray-skinned spriggan with a face like a melted wax mask dropped out of nowhere to land within arm's length of them; Thomas ran it through with his rapier almost before he realized it was there. It reeled away shrieking and more of the creatures appeared in the doorways, racing toward them down the halls. Something troll-like, squat, and hairy blocked a doorway, snarling at them.

If they could just get outside and out of the things' sight, Thomas knew Kade could hide them with illusion. He thought of the broken expanse of windows in the Grand Gallery. This idea must have occurred to Kade because she was already dragging him in that direction.

They ran under the archway and toward the broken windows that led out to the terrace and the park. Skirting the torn section of floor where the ring lay, they were almost there when a clawed demon-horse leapt up the terrace steps. Thomas swore, spun around, and drew his last loaded pistol.

The howling pack of spriggans rushed toward them in leaps and bounds; Thomas fired into the group. They scurried and scattered as the ball tore through them.

Something shoved him from the side and he stumbled, then felt his bad leg give way. Unable to catch himself, he fell over the edge of the broken floor . . .

. . . and felt a rush of warm air as he landed in soft verdant grass. He gasped and pushed himself up. He was in a wide-open field under a sky of an odd crystalline blue. Nearby, Kade rolled to her feet and shook out her hair, dislodging only a small amount of the greenery caught in it. Around them was a ring of stone menhirs, each nearly ten feet in height and weathered by great age. It was warm and the grass was the deep green of spring, touched with splashes of red from poppies.

Thomas stood up, stumbled a little, and looked around. About a hundred yards away the craggy face of a cliff towered above them, dotted with grassy clumps and hung with a thick growth of ivy. In the distance he could see that the ground rose gently up in a gradually increasing grade, as if they were in a deep bowl-shaped valley. "Where in hell are we?"

"Knockma," Kade said. She looked defensive.

He stared down at her. "Fayre?"

"No. Well, yes. In a way." At his expression she burst out, "If you don't trust me I really can't think why, because I haven't done anything deceptive for days."

But Thomas had looked up at the sky, and barely heard her. The deep blue was there, and far above floated drifts of puffy whiteness that were clouds, but there was a barrier that seemed to hang at about the level of the cliff top. It seemed solid and yet malleable, and was transparent, allowing the sunlight in but gently muting it. He felt a soft breeze, stirring the grass with a faint rushing sound, and the barrier shimmered with it as if it were made of the most delicate glass or . . . He managed to tear his eyes away and turned to Kade. "Is this . . . the bottom of a lake?"

She bit her lip. "Yes."

He was getting over the shock, and starting to realize exactly how angry he was. "You knew all along how the Host got into the palace."

Kade paced around in a circle, not looking at him. "I knew about the ring. It was how my mother got there in the first place years ago, but Galen and Surete and the others added a spell to the wards that blocked it. The ring could have faded away; sometimes they do." Though he hadn't had a chance to reply, she threw her arms up in exasperation and continued, "All right, and I sent Boliver to fly over the palace last night and he said they must be using the old ring because there weren't any new ones. I didn't say anything because I wasn't sure." She stopped and shook herself. "No, that's not true either. I don't know why I didn't tell you."

He held his temper. "You could have mentioned what you were about to do."

"There wasn't time."

"There was time when we were standing there staring at the ring before we heard Denzil and Dontane." He looked around for his rapier and found it buried in the high grass a few feet away. It and his pistols had come through the ring intact, and he wasn't sure whether to be surprised by that or not. He slipped the blade back into the scabbard and said, "Damn it, woman, I trusted you. I told you something I swore I'd take to my grave unsaid. I let you watch while I shot the goddamn King's buggering cousin. You know enough to get me drawn and quartered a dozen times over!" He was shouting at her now. "You could have bothered to mention that you not only had a quick method of escape from the palace, but that it involved taking me into Fayre, which I think you realize is not a place where I wanted to go!"

Kade shouted back, "I had to think about it, and by the time I did there wasn't time anymore! And this is not exactly Oberon's Court. I mean, I live here and it's not the most dangerous place on the map for humans, and you could credit me with some sense." Her smaller lungs gave out and she sat down hard on the grass. After a deep breath, she continued in a normal tone, "And I'm not used to trusting people either and I find it very frightening, and sometimes I don't know what to think about you."

What she had said about trust being frightening had hit home with more force than she could have realized. More calmly, he said, "Neither do I."

Neither spoke for a few moments. Kade sat in the grass and looked tired.

Thomas felt he could hardly argue with her for saving their lives, even if it had involved frightening him half to death. He said finally, "So you live here?"

"Actually, over there." She pointed.

He looked behind them and then up, and thought, foolishly, *No, you haven't seen everything.* More than half the length of the lake away, a small round island was suspended in the crystal surface of the illusory water. On top of the island, stretching high overhead, was a castle. It was ancient, its stones tinted green by moss, its three towers capped with round turrets in a style decades out of date, stairways curving up them like twining vines. What was amazing was that its reflection in the water that was not water was not a reflection.

A second castle grew downward from the island that was the base of the one on the lake's surface, like a stalactite growing from the roof of a cave. It was a mirror image of the castle above, and the sharply pointed top of its tallest, or lowest, turret was gently brushed by a willow tree.

"It's nice, isn't it?" Kade said softly, standing at his side now.

Thomas felt he had to agree. "Did you make it?"

"No, it's been here forever. It's a Great Spell, like the palace wards, only more complicated and much older. The people from Merewatch, the village up on the shore, can fish in the lake and row boats on it, and drown in it if someone down here doesn't happen to be watching. But if you know it's a spell, you can walk into it without getting wet." She dragged a foot through the grass thoughtfully, then said, "I'm sorry I brought you here without saying anything first. It was rude."

He looked down at her, admitting, "I overreacted. I didn't know there would be places like this. I thought it was all blood and bogles, like the city is now."

"I hate bogles." She pointed back to the ring marked by the stone menhirs. "That's the Knockma Ring. I think it was here before the lake. With it I can make a ring anywhere there isn't iron or wards or something to prevent it. It's the only ring I know of that can do that, and both the Seelie and the Unseelie Courts want it. I can send us back to the street outside Aviler's house, to see if Lucas and the others have left yet." She hesitated. "Now that Denzil's dead . . ."

Thomas shook his head. "I don't know if he's dead. I'm sure I hit him, but he might be only wounded."

Kade frowned. "That would be very inconvenient."

"To say the least." Thomas couldn't get his mind off the castle. "When you're inside, are you upside down?"

"No, that would be silly. It's bad enough as it is, with the stairs all funny in some places. In the middle, between the castle on top and the one below, you have to climb a ladder for a bit and no one likes it."

They stood in silence for a time, until Thomas saw something oddly like a large red dog leaping over the grass toward them. "A friend of yours?" he asked.

Kade said with a sigh, "I suppose so. That's Boliver."

By the time Boliver arrived, he had managed to become a wizened little man about Kade's height with red hair and an odd peaked hat, and the bluest eyes Thomas had ever seen.

When he had reached them, Kade asked, "How did you know I was back?"

"How could I help but know? They must have heard the yelling in the next century." He jerked his head back toward the castle. "The others are watching with a spyglass from the wind tower, and it fell to me to come out and ask just what was doing." He eyed Thomas speculatively.

Kade shaded her eyes and peered at the castle. "Don't they have anything better to do?" She shook her head in annoyance and turned back to Boliver. "Have the Host tried an attack yet?"

He said, "No, but I been to the village and they say they've seen a hag in the pond and there's been odd things setting the dogs to barking and the sheep to running."

Kade winced in genuine pain. "It's what I thought." She nodded to herself, resigned. "The Host will come here soon."

Thomas hated to see her so torn and desperate. "Look, you've done enough. Send me back to Aviler's house and stay here."

She shook her head. "No, that's what they want. If I let them chase me about, then they'll know they can make me do anything they please."

Thomas understood that only too well. It was a damnable trap, one he had been caught in most of his life. He watched her, knowing there was nothing he could do to help her, that his own involvement had made her decision all the more difficult.

She paced and tugged on her hair. "This place is very strong. It can hold itself against them without me for a time. The village . . . Damn it, the village." She stopped and told Boliver, "Go up and tell them there's going to be a battle; tell them to run."

"Very well, I will." The fay hesitated then and, with what had to be uncanny and devastating perception, said, "So, here's your reason. Well, he's got my heartfelt sympathy."

Thomas lifted a brow at Kade, though it was a struggle to keep his expression neutral. The look Kade directed at Boliver should have dissolved him into charred coal on the spot. She said quietly, "You're dead."

Boliver shifted uneasily, as though realizing he might have overstepped himself. He said, "I'll just go and have a word with the village, shall I?"

"Yes, why don't you do that."

"Have to be quick, you know. Wouldn't want to be caught by the Host."

"It wouldn't be nearly as terrible as some things I've just thought of."

"Ah. I see. Well, I'll be going now." Boliver whirled around rapidly, becoming a ball of heatless flames. He shot toward the lake surface above like a firework.

"Do me one favor," Thomas said.

"What?" She was blushing furiously and attempting to ignore the fact.

"Don't kill Boliver."

Kade sighed, managing a rueful smile. "I wasn't going to. I just wanted to think about it for a bit." She dug in the pocket of her smock and produced the chip taken from the wardstone. "I can do this now."

She started toward the castle, and, still half unwilling, he followed her.

As they reached the base of the hilly garden, the castle had begun to look almost ordinary, as if it were perfectly normal to hang upside down from an island suspended in glass with its top turret brushed by a tree. If he had ever thought about it at all, Thomas would have expected a place like this to be eerily perfect, without blemish, as if it were carved out of marble, all imperfections smoothed away. This fayre castle had cracked stones where heavy climbing vines had silently invaded, moss growing around its windows, and was crumbling around the edge of its parapet.

Below the lowermost turret, a stone stair curved up the hillside garden to meet one of the windows, and Thomas followed Kade up to the top. The garden itself was a little overgrown, as if it was only tended when someone had the time. The grass was tall, flowers hung out of their beds, and heavy rosebushes had all but taken over the low wall that circled it, but the fountain was running cheerfully.

The room inside the turret was round, taking up the entire top—or bottom—level. It was lined with book-filled shelves, and clay jars seemed to be crammed into every available space that wasn't occupied by the books. It smelled thickly of herbs and flowers, and sunlight from the wide window had faded the once-bright colors of the carpet and the chair covers.

Kade hopped down onto the wide stone window seat and then to the floor. She glanced back at Thomas as he was getting his first bemused look at the room. "Not what you were expecting?" she asked.

He stepped down from the window seat after her. "If I'd ever considered it, I wouldn't have expected to see the place and still be in any kind of condition to comment on it. You were a deadly enemy of the crown not so long ago, remember?"

"I'd forgotten." She crossed over to the shelves on the far wall. "Well, it doesn't look like the abode of a wicked fay sorceress, but this is where it's all done—all the plots, all the nasty little tricks." Kade ran a hand along the shelves, and selected a large dusty volume.

She flipped through the book until she found the page she wanted. He watched her as she stood on the lower shelves to take down several of the clay jars. He asked, "How did you find this place?"

"It belonged to my mother. She had others, but she lived here most of the time. After I left the convent, I looked for her. I looked so long and so hard she eventually had to let me find her."

Kade dumped the armful of jars on the draw table. "She wasn't a very nice person, not exactly what I was hoping for. But she was taken with the idea of having a daughter . . . for a while, at least." She paused in dumping the herbs and powders out of their containers and smiled at some memory. "She gave me a fayre ointment to take the mortal scales off my eyes, so I could see through fayre glamour. She had more people here, fay and humans, all of them bound to her somehow." She went back to her task. "She had Boliver locked up inside a stone in the garden. He's a phooka, and he likes to change into horses and dogs and fool people, but he's mostly harmless, and he wasn't very happy inside a rock. I broke it and let him out, and Moire threw a terrible fit, but she didn't really do anything about it. That's when I realized that I didn't have to do what she said. I knew sorcery, and she was wary of it."

While she tossed ingredients into a bowl and muttered to herself, Thomas paced the room. After a time, she stopped to glare at him and he took the hint and settled into the window seat. As he looked out into the bright air of Knockma, the realization of what Grandier and the Host had done to the city struck with renewed force. If Ravenna and the others hadn't reached Bel Garde safely . . .

It wasn't long before Kade said, "Now we wait until it works." She ran her hands through her hair. "If it does."

"If it does," Thomas said. "The keystone's place was in the largest undercellar of the Old Palace, in the base of the fourth pillar from the north side on the third row." At her look of surprise, he explained, "I wasn't comfortable being the only one alive besides Urbain Grandier who knew that."

Kade came to stand next to him at the window seat, looking out into the garden. She was blushing, and he wondered why. He said, "What happened after you released Boliver?"

She lifted a corner of the faded gold curtain and looked at it as if she had never seen it before. "I disobeyed her frequently. She pretended not to care. Then the Unseelie Court tricked her and she had to go to Hell, and I inherited everything. Most of her people ran away as soon as she was gone. Boliver stayed because he's feckless and hasn't anything better to do, and a few others stayed because they haven't anywhere better to go." She was quiet for a moment, looking out at the overgrown comfortable garden.

It was hard to believe that Boliver had ever been imprisoned out there, or that anyone but Kade had ever lived in the quiet dusty peace of this room. Thomas said, "Or maybe they liked it well enough where they were, once your mother was gone."

Kade looked down at him, her gray eyes serious. "I think you like me a little bit, even if it would half kill you to admit it."

"It would not half kill me to admit it." The sunlight, muted and changed by the layer of illusory water above, transformed the color of her hair to the same dusty gold as the drape. After a moment, he said, "I know what Ravenna told you, that night in the Guard House. She was oversimplifying the case. She does that when she's trying to get something she wants very badly."

Kade clapped a hand over her eyes, reeled around, and half fell into one of the wooden chairs. "Do you know everything?" she demanded.

"No. If I knew everything, we wouldn't be in this situation." He smiled. "But I suppose I should be flattered that she considers my presence an inducement."

Kade shifted uncomfortably. "I told her I didn't want the blasted throne."

"I know. If you'd accepted, it would have been a rare disaster. Exciting, but a disaster all the same."

"Well, that's what *I* thought." She hesitated a long moment, drawing a design with the toe of her boot on the floor. "Do you trust me?"

Tell her no, he thought, *and whatever it is that's happening between us will end.* But he didn't want it to end. He wanted to see what would happen next, to follow it to its conclusion. He wanted it more than anything else he had wanted in a long time. He said, "Yes, oddly enough, I do."

She bolted back across the room, stood for a moment in front of the shelves, then took down a white-and-blue-banded jar. She wandered back, and not looking up at him, she said, "This is the fayre ointment my mother gave me. It will let you see through glamour. Not all the time, because fay can use glamour to fool each other, but if they don't know you're there, or that you can see them, they won't know to hide from you. I mean, if you want it."

There's more to this than just that, Thomas thought. *It will make some kind of tie between us, and then what will happen? Anything or nothing.* He pulled off his glove and held out his hand.

———

The room was cold and still, windowless, a single candle sparking color from the bloodred fabric of the walls, leaving all else to fade into the gray-black of shadow. Urbain Grandier sat at the table, the polished wood chill under his hands, his face turned toward a framed parchment map of Ile-Rien. The southern border with Bisra was marked in red, Umberwald and Adera to the north and east in blue, and the compass rose and the faces of the four winds were rendered in precise and loving detail. Grandier could not possibly decipher the ornate script that described towns, rivers, and borders in the wan flicker of the single candle, but his eyes were as intent as if he treasured every faded brown scratch of the artist's pen.

There was noise outside, voices, then an alarmed shout. The door banged open, revealing Dontane and an Alsene trooper, half carrying, half supporting the young Duke of Alsene between them. Denzil's shoulder and left arm were soaked with blood, his doublet and buff coat torn aside to reveal lacerated flesh. There were more troopers out in the brightly lit anteroom, and one of the young lords of Alsene who had arrived with the duchy's troop that day was shouting at them. Grandier rubbed his eyes under Galen Dubell's gold spectacles and said mildly, "Put him on the daybed. And for heaven's sake, shut the door."

Grandier stood and winced. He still felt the old pain, his mind tracing the path of injuries that this body had never known. He lit the other candles in the room as the two men took Denzil to the couch and gently let him down on it. The Duke's face was bleached white, fierce with pain. One of his young pages had followed them in and now knelt anxiously beside the couch. "How did it happen?" Grandier asked, watching them.

"The Gallery Wing," Dontane replied. He stepped back from the couch, breathing hard from exertion, sweat gleaming on his forehead. "Someone was there, and fired at us from cover. It woke the fay sleeping in the walls, and they overran the place so quickly we didn't have a chance to pursue him."

Grandier tut-tutted under his breath, taking his leather-covered apothecary box out of a cabinet. "To be expected."

Dontane stared. "Expected . . . ?"

"Of course. It would be a very great mistake to think our opponents are fools. They were bound to investigate at some time."

"Then they know the Alsene troop is here." Dontane's sharp features were fearful.

"I would imagine so, yes."

Dontane strode for the door, gesturing for the trooper to follow him. Denzil watched him go, perhaps knowing as Grandier did that Dontane would take this opportunity to order the Alsene troops and officers, using the Duke's authority. Denzil was in no position to object; his blond hair was soaked with sweat, and he was biting his lips until blood came from the effort to not cry out.

And bleeding like a slaughtered pig on good furniture, Grandier thought. After the poverty of his early life in Bisra, the abundance of first Lodun and then Vienne and the palace had astonished him. Ile-Rien had little understanding of its own wealth, of how valuable was the flow of goods from the foreign vessels flocking to its trading ports, of the surfeit of arable land that allowed any peasant with enough coins in his pocket to own a patch. Of how this wealth would affect those who did not possess it. His voice dry, he told the kneeling page, "You may go. This won't take long, and he can do without the necessity of adoration for a short while."

The boy was too afraid of Grandier to argue. He left without protest but with several longing backward glances. Denzil took a breath, brow furrowed with exertion, and whispered, "Jealous, sorcerer?"

It did not surprise Grandier that the Duke would make the effort to say something vicious despite his agony. Grandier examined the large wound in Denzil's shoulder where the pistol ball had penetrated and frowned at the visible bone splinters. "Oh, yes, terribly," he answered. "It affects my judgment, you see." He turned back to the apothecary box to select the necessary powders. Dontane had been the messenger in the forging of the alliance between Grandier and the Duke of Alsene in Ile-Rien, and that alliance had never been anything but uneasy. And Grandier did not like the accord he saw at times now between Dontane and Denzil.

"Your affectation of superiority is amusing." Denzil gasped, closed his eyes briefly, then continued, "I hardly think you can take the high moral ground in this situation."

"I, at least, am not a traitor. My homeland turned against me long before I returned the sentiment." Grandier came back to Denzil's side. On the panel supporting the daybed's canopy was a painted scene of nymphs, satyrs, and human shepherds enjoying each other's company in several ways that would have been displeasing to the Bisran Church. The casual displays of sensuality and the acceptance of it in Ile-Rien had also been a surprise. Like the acceptance of sorcery. Grandier had heard about it, about the university at Lodun, but he had not really credited the rumors until he had seen the reality. *I wish I had come here as a young man,* he thought. *So much might have been different.*

"And what excuse do you make for your betrayal?"

"Attempting to excuse the inexcusable is always a mistake," Grandier said. "Why not simply admit that greed overwhelms loyalty, affection, and common sense?"

"I have no affection or loyalty for Roland," Denzil said, voice grating with pain. "He serves my purpose."

"I wasn't speaking about you," Grandier said. Denzil might have grown to hate the young King because of the power Roland held over him, even though as Denzil's friend and patron Roland had never exercised that power. Grandier understood this all too well. He knew the danger of allowing any individual, any state, any force of whatever kind, to hold one in its power, to control one's actions. "This is going to hurt, but I can't think why you should mind. You seem to enjoy the pain of others."

Denzil's chuckle was weak, but it held real amusement. "You mean that as a taunt, but even you would be shocked at how accurate your assessment is."

For an instant, Grandier hesitated. He knew Denzil to be a smiling killer, as excellent an actor as the hags who lured children to their deaths with their own mothers' voices. No, that was not quite the analogy he was searching for. *He is not a monster,* Grandier thought, *but forces beyond his control have warped him past reason. Even as they have me.* "Perhaps I would," he said, actually enjoying Denzil's presence for the first time in their short acquaintance. "We are both in good company."

CHAPTER FOURTEEN

"ROLAND, I WANT you to come with me." Ravenna stood in the doorway, her look of determination as grim as the faces of the Queen's guards accompanying her.

Her son looked up at her nervously. He sat in an armchair holding a small lap desk, though the paper on it was still blank. The room would have been light and airy in the summer, but now the wooden winter shutters covered the large windows and the fire in the hearth could not dispel the cold. There was no one with him but his personal servants; Ravenna had made sure she would not have to do this under the eyes of any courtiers or hangers-on.

Roland turned the pen over in his hands and got ink on his fingers. "Why?"

She said, "I have something to show you."

Roland stood reluctantly. "Has something happened?"

Ravenna knew he wasn't interested in anything besides news of Denzil's whereabouts and that he would realize she would not be the one to bring such news to him. "Take your cloak; we'll be going out on the wall."

Immediately an impassive servant brought a thick fur-trimmed cloak from the bedchamber. Roland stood still for the man to arrange it around his shoulders. "Where's Renier?"

"Downstairs, attending to the guard placements."

"Oh." He followed her through the other rooms in the suite and out to a landing on the grand stairwell. Ravenna could tell Roland was uneasy, even though the four knights guarding the door to his chamber followed them and she was accompanied by her gentlewoman Elaine.

They went up the stairs to a lesser-used floor, then waited as one of the Queen's guards unbolted a door and forced it open against the wind's pressure. They walked out onto the wall, which was sheltered by a shoulder-high parapet, and the wind tore through the crenellations like a mad creature.

Ravenna and Elaine each held onto a guard's arm to steady themselves, and Roland forced himself to walk along unaided. Ravenna held her head down and tried to breathe the shockingly cold air, knowing she would pay for this ordeal later with coughing fits. In the face of everything else, it was a minor consideration.

The sun was making a brief appearance, though dark clouds were visibly building up in the distance. To the north, if one could have forced oneself close enough to the parapet to take in the view, were several miles of snow-covered fields and then the rise of the city, like a man-fashioned mountain range. The wind had torn away much of the haze of wood and coal smoke that normally hung over it, and the snow made it appear pristine and empty. The other side of the wall looked down on the inner court, where Denzil had hosted gatherings in the summer and displayed the little fortress's wealth and elegance. When they had arrived yesterday, they had found the usual garrison depleted, and the steward had said that the Duke of Alsene had ordered most of his men to one of his other estates to quell some tenant problems over taxes some weeks ago. Messengers had been sent on to the Granges, a day's ride to the south, to General Villon.

Ravenna wondered if Thomas was alive.

There was no other man she had ever felt closer to, or who had actually understood how her mind worked without condemning her for it. When he had first been accepted into the Queen's Guard it had not been his political astuteness or his wit that had attracted her, though from the occasional flashes of ironic humor she had witnessed, she had suspected that he might possess those qualities. No, most of that she had discovered later, and that discovery had added more meaning to what had been one of the most pleasurable times of her life.

You're getting old, my dear, Ravenna told herself. Old and frail and helpless. It was the constant underground war of intrigue that had beaten her down. She and Thomas had once found such subtle battles exhilarating, but now . . . Palace power struggles had always been intense, but since Roland's maturity, the battles had escalated into full-scale wars with no clear victors. Denzil had much to do with it, but it was also that the wolves sensed Roland's weakness. And her options to remedy that were severely limited.

She forced her mind back to the present. Grandier had rendered the court's tenuous balance of power a matter for future academics to consider. If Thomas was alive, he would come to her when he could. If he wasn't . . . That would be for her to face alone.

They headed toward the old keep, a rough square tower more than seven stories high. It had been the center of the fortress before the bastion behind them had been built.

They reached the door into the side of the tower, and two of Ravenna's guards split off to post themselves at it. The others went inside, and Ravenna shivered gratefully. The keep felt warm after the wind. A guard stopped to light a candlelamp with flint and steel, and Ravenna saw that the Albon knights were standing stiffly together as if anticipating an attack they could do nothing to prevent. Roland saw it, too. His voice strained with nerves, he said, "What are we doing here, Mother?"

Ravenna didn't answer immediately. She started up the stairs, the guard with the lamp going on ahead, and there was only room for Roland to walk beside her. Finally she said, "I've made allowances for you, where Denzil is concerned."

She could see he was slightly shocked that she brought this up in the presence of her guards, let alone Elaine. In an effort to outdo her effrontery, he said, "Allowances? You've been trying to turn me against him with lies for years."

Ravenna stopped and looked at her son for a moment. As always, it hurt that he found her eyes hard to meet. She said, "My dear child, I didn't think you had noticed."

Roland stared at her. "You admit it?"

"Of course. Recent developments have made it possible."

She continued on up the stairs, and Roland followed her, bewildered. He said, "I don't understand."

"That man has made a fool of you."

"He has been my only friend—"

"He has used you to accumulate power and wealth beyond his reach under ordinary circumstances."

"He's been the only one who cared for me; I gave him all those things—"

"Of course you gave it all to him, Roland; that's the way these people work."

Ravenna stopped on a landing and faced him. Roland was out of breath and must have forgotten that he was King and able to order her to be silent, if he could enforce it. He said, "You certainly never showed me any affection. You never gave a damn for me."

"Perhaps you are right," Ravenna said. "You look too much like your father, and God knows I never gave a damn for him." She took a key out of her sleeve and handed it to a guard, who unlocked the door and pushed it open.

"Go in there," Ravenna said.

Roland didn't move. He was trembling, and his eyes were dark with hatred. *He isn't stupid*, Ravenna thought. *He must know his cousin's protestations of eternal love are not sincere. But perhaps he thinks he can earn his respect by doing everything Denzil asks.* It made her feel sick at heart, though her expression betrayed nothing. *The world doesn't work in that fashion, and Denzil is not interested in respecting you, my foolish son.* The guard with the lamp stepped into the room but stayed close by the wall. Finally Roland went through the doorway.

Inside was a large shadowy room, dark wood a rough veneer over the stone walls. The back half was filled with wine barrels and other boxes stacked to the high ceiling. "You wanted to show me this?"

"Why would anyone store wine here, Roland, away from the livable portions of the fortress, high up where the air is so very dry, in a place more fit for the storing of other things?" Ravenna nodded to one of her guards. "Open one."

He went forward and carefully knocked out the bunghole in a barrel at the bottom of a stack. Something dark flowed out. Roland started toward it, stopped when the odor reached him, but still went to kneel and touch the dark granular substance. "It's powder," he whispered.

Ravenna said, "The four floors above us are as well stocked as this one. The supply does not quite rival the city armory, but I'm told that it approaches it. More than enough to stage a palace coup."

Roland lifted his head, saw the pity on the face of the guard who had opened the barrel, then looked back at Ravenna. She knew her expression showed only weariness. She folded her arms. "Surely you are not going to say we brought it with us."

He shook his head mutely. He stood and walked the length of the row. The lid had already been pried off one of the long boxes, and he lifted the coarse wood to see matchlock muskets packed in heavy cloth.

Ravenna said, "There is another store of powder and shot, a small one, enough to supply the garrison for a few months, set where it should be near the gate. There is only one reason for all this."

Roland began to tremble. "He will have an explanation."

"Undoubtedly."

"I'm going back now." He strode past her and down the stairs.

His knights came to his side, Ravenna's party following. They reached the landing where the door led out onto the parapet, and Roland stopped, waiting. Ravenna reached him and regarded him quietly, then nodded for one of her guards to open the door.

As the door swung back she caught a glimpse of the sky and saw it seemed inexplicably dark. Then she saw the body of a man lying half in front of the threshold, before the guard slammed the door and braced his weight against it. "Run," he said breathlessly. "Something's out—"

A force struck the door half off its hinges.

Ravenna ran, pushing Elaine in front of her, all thought for the moment purged from her mind. She saw Roland dragged by one of his knights, half flung up the stairs, shoved on when he stumbled.

Below them, the door flew off its hinges and smashed into the wall. Someone fired a pistol and the noise seemed to galvanize Roland and he ran up the stairway with them to the landing. Ravenna grabbed the door there and flung it open, and Elaine stumbled inside. Then Ravenna stopped and looked back. She saw that the guards and knights were trying to hold the stairwell; there was already blood on the floor. There was screaming, and something roared, the sheer volume of sound making the ancient walls tremble.

Roland stood and watched, blank faced, in shock. He stood there until Ravenna seized his arm and pulled him into the chamber.

Elaine held the candlelamp, trembling and wild-eyed with fear. Ravenna shut the door and bolted it, then stepped back, looking around the room and rubbing her hands together. Roland leaned against the wall, watching her helplessly.

There is a way out, Ravenna thought. There was always a way out. She had never been trapped yet, and by God, she wouldn't be now. "This is a corner room," she muttered to herself. "There must be . . ." She took the lamp from Elaine and set it carefully down near the wall, then went toward the back of the room, trying to make her way past the boxes and barrels of powder. "Roland, damn it, help me."

After a moment he joined her, wrestling a box out of her way but moving stiffly, as if terror had frozen his blood. "What are you looking for?" he gasped.

"This, perhaps." It was made to look like part of the roughly paneled wall, but Ravenna's fingers found the edges and Roland helped her lift it away in a shower of cobwebs and dust. It concealed a small wooden door set back into the stone wall. Roland tugged on the iron handle and it came open with a protesting squeak.

Dank freezing air flowed out. It was a well within the outer wall of the tower, and handholds had been carved out of the stone, leading down into darkness below.

"For sieges." Ravenna nodded to herself. "It will lead all the way down to the bottom floor, with an opening on each level."

Roland looked down and bit his lip. Ravenna knew what he was thinking: it would not be a pleasant climb for him, let alone the two women hampered by court dress. He said, "Do you think you can make it?"

"Of course not," Ravenna said flatly. She knew someone would have to stay to close the door and draw the cover over it or the fay would have them within moments. "Go on. You'll have to help Elaine."

"But—" Roland automatically reached for the girl's arm as Ravenna pushed her toward him. "You can't—"

Elaine said, "No, I'm staying with you." She twined her arms around Ravenna with unsuspected ferocity. "I won't leave you."

Ravenna tried to pry her loose. "Damn you, you silly child, I—"

Roland protested, "Mother, you can't stay here, they'll kill you, at least try to—"

The door cracked as something heavy struck it. "Roland, go on!" Ravenna whispered furiously.

He stepped onto the little ledge, then cautiously felt for the handholds. He looked back and said, "I—"

"Climb," she ordered and swung the panel closed. Elaine helped her with the cover, and they wrestled it back in place, moving away from it just as the door gave way.

Ravenna put her arm around Elaine's shoulders and the girl clung to her as the fay poured into the room.

There were a dozen at least of varied shapes, bogles with distorted grinning faces, some hulking things with no faces at all, a delicate winged creature that looked something like both a demon and an angel. One had blood spattered on its mouth; Ravenna wondered if it was from one of her guards, and it was rage, not fear, that turned her to stone. They scampered or strode through the room, disarranging the boxes, searching, for the moment ignoring the two women. Ravenna wondered if they would casually toss a barrel onto the lamp; they did not seem to have any fear of the powder.

Another fay entered. This, Ravenna knew, was the leader. He was tall and slight, human in shape but blue skinned, with a face of childlike attractiveness and a horrible leering smile. He bowed mockingly to her. "Greetings, Queen of Nothing. I am Evadne, a prince of the Unseelie Court."

"What do you want?" she asked. She felt cold down to her bones, and it had nothing to do with the temperature of the room, but her voice was still hard.

"Your boy-king; why else would we go to this trouble?" He looked around the room. "You've hidden him, of course."

Ravenna felt Elaine quiver slightly beside her. She said, "He isn't here."

One of the troll-like creatures left off its search and grunted something at Evadne. He glared at it, then said to Ravenna, "We saw him come into this tower. You will tell us where he is."

"He did not come into the tower. You can see that for yourself. Whoever saw him must have been mistaken." She didn't look around at the other creatures but she could tell they had stopped searching. They would have looked harder, she knew, if they had really been positive that Roland had been here. They must have observed from a distance, and Evadne had taken the chance.

Evadne paced across the room, glaring at the other creatures, who shrank back or snarled at him. He stopped and thought for some moments, his smooth brow wrinkling, then leaned down and spoke to the other fay. Ravenna could tell that some of them did not seem happy with his decision, whatever it was.

He turned and came back toward the two women. "You will tell your men to bring him to us, or we will kill you."

How daft, she thought. *This thing doesn't understand us at all, does he?* But it gave her an idea, and she thought she knew how to manage him now. She said, "I can't do that."

"You can. You will."

Ravenna pretended to falter. She thought she did it well; she raised a shaking hand to her brow, and said, "Please . . ."

Evadne leered at her. "A King or a Queen, what is it to be?"

"I . . ." She managed a fairly creditable sob. "I'll send the message."

Evadne sneered in triumph. He snapped his fingers and a small winged creature with a hideous face produced a gold-chased quill, inkpot, and a ragged piece of parchment out of the air. It set the things down on the box in front of her.

Ravenna gently disentangled Elaine's hands from her arm until the girl stood alone shivering, and sat down on the box. She picked up the pen and dipped it, then paused to frame her thought. She wrote, *Accede to no demands and keep everyone away from the tower. By my hand, Ravenna Fontainon Regina.*

She hesitated. The fay didn't ask to see the note and had made no attempt to watch her write. He couldn't read, then. It made sense. Why would a fay read?

Except for Kade, of course. Ravenna would have given quite a bit to have Kade at her side rather than Elaine, whom she had to protect.

But would Renier and the others obey the note? Without Thomas here, there was no way to be sure. How could she make sure they would do it? There wasn't a way.

Evadne snapped, "Hurry, old woman."

Ravenna knew the expected response and tried to compose her features into something like fear. She had spent so much of her life concealing her fear that she had forgotten how to show it. She felt she looked more confused than afraid, but it apparently satisfied the fay. She said, "I'll have to seal it, so they will know I wrote it."

"Go on, then."

She folded the note and Elaine took the candle out of the lamp and handed it to her without being told. Ravenna looked up and saw the girl's expression, and knew she had read the note over her shoulder. There was both fear and trust in her eyes. *She thinks I have a way out of this.*

Ravenna took the candle and dripped the wax onto the paper, then pressed her ring into it. Her personal seal, the crescent moon embossed by the family symbol of the salamander. It was not until then she realized she had signed herself Queen, not Dowager. *Damn. Well, let them put that in their history books.* Elaine reached for the candle but Ravenna set it down on the crate, grinding the base into the wood so it would stay upright. Now for the next part. She handed the note to Elaine and said, "Take this to Renier, dear."

With an awful childlike smile, Evadne said, "I'm not sure I want to part with so lovely a hostage."

The paper crackled a little in Elaine's grip. Ravenna said, "Perhaps you would take the message yourself, then. No doubt my guards would like to meet you."

He looked amused, enjoying Elaine's fear. "I suppose you're hostage enough for their good behavior. The girl may go."

And you need no hostage for my good behavior? Ravenna thought. She resisted the urge to kiss Elaine goodbye and merely said, "Go on, dear."

Elaine looked down at her, bit her lip, then turned and hurried to the door. *I taught her not to cry before enemies and she doesn't.* Ravenna nodded to herself, satisfied. *That one turned out well.*

Evadne watched the girl go, but made no attempt to stop her. Ravenna waited until she heard Elaine's steps on the stairs, then relaxed a little. She settled herself more comfortably on the box and watched Evadne.

The fay said, "He told me you would be weak. I see he was right again."

It surprised her. "Who told you that?"

"Our pet sorcerer, Grandier. He had leisure to study you."

Your pet sorcerer! Your pet snake is more to the point. She said, "He doesn't like you very well, does he?"

"He is a human, and therefore a fool."

She inclined her head. "I see."

The time passed slowly. Ravenna counted her heartbeats and stared at the candle flame. It kept her mind off wanting something to do with her hands. She saw Evadne grow impatient. He began to pace again, snarling at the other creatures. To distract him, she said, "I thought your kind could not attack during the day, only your servants and the lesser members of your court."

He grinned at her implied insult. "Our sorcerer has made the sky darken for us, made the clouds turn black so the sun does not disturb us. Even now, one of our great ones perches on the outside of this tower, ready to destroy your men in the courtyard." He glared down at her. "Why don't they send out your king, old woman?"

"It will take them some time to persuade themselves that there is no alternative."

Evadne's stare turned curious, and she realized she had spoken with a smile. She thought of trying a fearful expression again, but it was too late for that. *Oh, I'm leaving everything undone. Roland, learn from this if nothing else.* Probably Elaine had unintentionally helped matters by telling Renier that Ravenna had some plan of escape. Roland had had more than enough time to climb to the bottom of the tower. *Or fall to it, God help him,* she thought.

"They take too long. I think I'll tell my friend outside to kill a few humans down in the courtyard, to hurry the others along."

Ravenna said, "I think you won't."

Evadne laughed.

She said, "I may be old, but not too old to deal with you." She stood, and before he could think to come at her, she tossed the lit candle into the nearest broken barrel of powder.

The blast blew gaping holes in the outside wall, and brought the upper floors and the roof down on top of them. The flying creature perched on the side drifted to the ground in a ball of flame, keening most of the way.

—◆—

When Roland's reaching foot touched solid stone he gasped in shock, then leaned against the rough wall and sobbed in relief. His arms were shaking and his fingers had begun to bleed. A hundred times he had seen himself falling to the bottom of the narrow well, bouncing off the walls, dying in filth and darkness. But the most painful thoughts did not concern his own death. *He'll have an explanation. Powder and shot hidden in the tower, enough for a small army, and the fay have come and he isn't here, and wherever he is, he's taken Falaise with him . . . He will have an explanation.* After a moment, Roland rubbed his sleeve over his face and began to feel for a door in the pitch darkness.

Roland found a catch but the door was stiff from disuse. He managed to push it open a crack, enough to let in a breath of air, but no further. He hesitated, afraid to make too much noise. If the fay had taken all of Bel Garde, if they had won past the gate Braun's apprentices had said was sealed against them . . . *Then we'll all die, Mother and Elaine in the tower, everyone down here, and when they catch me . . .*

But then he heard voices, rough human voices, the familiar city accent. A woman asked some inaudible question, and a man's louder tone replied, "That's what I said, but they're looking for the King down here, and why he's down here I—"

"In here!" Roland yelled. "In here! I'm here!"

There was consternation outside, more voices, then lamplight fell through a crack in the top of the door, and Roland looked up into it gratefully. He saw a brown human eye gazing at him in astonishment. "I'm here," he said again.

The eye withdrew, to the accompaniment of startled cursing. Then the door was pried open, the wood bending at the center and cracking under the pressure. Roland saw why he had not been able to push it any further. A wooden floor had been built up to it at about waist height, probably dividing an ancient high-ceilinged room into two usable compartments. The man outside had to break the wood to get it open, and Roland reached upward and was drawn out by strong arms in a rough homespun shirt.

The man, who was large enough to be a blacksmith, set him on his feet, then steadied him when his legs tried to give way. The room was a storeroom or pantry, shelves on the walls, piled with bags and barrels. A group of people bundled into worn coats against the cold and several wide-eyed children stared at him in astonishment. "God," one woman said loudly, "it's the K—"

She was leapt upon by several of her companions, one ripping an apron off and shoving it against her mouth. "Those demons are in the tower overhead," another woman hissed. "Who d'you think they're looking for?"

"He's all over blood," someone else whispered. "They've tried to kill him."

"No." Roland looked down at his hands and winced. "I was climbing. I have to get to Renier. I have to tell him—"

"I'll go and fetch him, Your Majesty," the man who had pulled him out said. "Best you stay here; the beasts could be anywhere."

"Yes, you're right." Roland leaned against the wall and watched the man pick up a musket and hurry out. A voice in his head whispered, *Denzil lied to you all along. His friendship ended the day they put the crown on your head.* Roland thought, *But he saved my life. He did save my life, that wasn't a lie. But he was a boy then, and he wasn't my heir. He needed a live prince. But a dead king is a different matter entirely.* One of the older women came forward with a scarf and, without meeting his eyes, started to gently wipe the blood from his hands. "Thank you," he said automatically.

The woman who had tried to scream had been released and allowed to take the apron out of her mouth. She said in an audible whisper, "Now he seems a nice lad, not like what they say at all."

Roland started to laugh. He knew they thought he was being brave, or hysterical, but he was laughing at himself. *I must have always known what Denzil was, but I didn't care, I didn't care, and now he's going to kill me.*

Then the door opened again and two of his knights stood there, gaping at him.

And Ravenna and Elaine were still in the tower. The memory jolted Roland back into his senses and he started toward the knights. "Where is Renier? We have to—"

The pure shock of the explosion knocked him to his knees. There was screaming, and Roland knew past his own fear that the others in the room were reliving the moment of the explosion in the palace, when the nightmare had started. One of his knights stood over him, as if the man could shield him from falling stone and timber with his own body. Dust settled around them, but no stones fell.

Roland caught the knight's arm and pulled himself up. He felt pitifully weak from the long climb, from fear, from everything else. The others were still huddled on the floor, and he heard someone weeping. "It's all right," he said, then repeated more loudly, "It's all right." He saw Renier then, standing in the doorway and staring at him. "What was that?" Roland asked. "What's happened?"

Renier came forward and led him out of the room to a narrow passage beyond, out of sight of the others. "What is it?" Roland asked again.

"Elaine said there was a gunpowder store in the tower." Renier's face was so pale he looked sick.

"Yes. Elaine's here, they escaped? Where's my mother?" Roland couldn't understand Renier's expression.

"She was up there with them."

And Roland knew. To the last he had fooled himself into believing he had been sent for help, not sent away from death.

But part of him still failed to comprehend, and that part said, "What was that noise?"

"That was the tower."

———

The cold was a shock.

Thomas shook his head and blinked hard. It was almost twilight in a gray world of muted color and dim light. They were in an open square in front of Aviler's house. The walls of other town houses rose up around them, and snow had buried the fountain in the center. Around him and Kade the new fayre ring appeared in the snow as a shallow trench in the shape of a perfect circle.

The corner of the house loomed above them, the shingled roof dusted with ice and thin gusts of smoke issuing from the chimneys. It was quiet, the dim glow of candlelight showing through the shutters on the upper floors. Thomas said, "I didn't realize it was this late."

"It takes time to travel through the rings. We've lost an hour or so out of the day," Kade said, but she was looking up and frowning. She folded her arms and shivered. "Though the sky is very dark."

Thomas started toward the house, thinking that one over, and Kade followed him. He supposed it made sense that time would be lost traveling from ring to ring, even if it didn't make sense that one was not aware of that time's passage.

The spell that Kade hoped would show her the location of the keystone had still been inert in its bowl when they had left. Once Thomas found out if Lucas was still here, Kade was returning to Knockma to see if there had been any result yet.

They moved around the side of the High Minister's house to the alley, and there Thomas stopped and loaded his pistols. In making the open attempt to kill Denzil, whether it had succeeded or not, he had crossed a line and there was no going back. As far as the rest of the world knew, he had committed treason, and he had to get to Ravenna and tell her what he had done before Roland learned of it.

There was a servants' door along the alley wall, and someone had taken the precaution of nailing iron cutlery to it to discourage fay. He listened at it for a moment, then tried the handle. It was locked, but the catch was not strong and he drew his dagger to pry at it. In the deep shadow of the alley the cold was far more intense, and Kade bounced up and down with her hands in her pockets in impatience. Thomas didn't comment; after the mild climate of Knockma, he was feeling the cold more as well.

The lock broke, and he slowly eased the door open.

Inside was a servants' passage with doors opening to either side. A candle-lamp on the wall was still lit, but the tallow collected in the bottom showed it hadn't been attended to for some time. Kade slipped in behind him and he closed the door silently.

She whispered, "Something's wrong."

He nodded. The house was far too quiet. Aviler might have left the city, though Thomas thought the High Minister had meant to hold out here until the last possible moment. If Aviler had abandoned the place, he had had good reason.

He whispered, "Wait here."

She drew breath to protest and he put his hand over her mouth and said, "Please."

After a moment, she nodded. He removed his hand and she said, "Just this once."

He gave her a smile, then went down the dimly lit passage. He found a half-open door, took a cautious look through to see the small room on the other side was dark. There was a curtained doorway on the opposite wall, light flickering just past it. Then he heard the low mutter of voices.

He tried to ease the door open only to find it stuck against something that lay on the floor. He shoved it open enough to see in and stopped.

It was Lucas.

Thomas felt the wood of the doorframe crack under his hand.

Lucas lay on his back, and he had been shot in the chest, probably just as he had come through the door. *He walked into a trap,* Thomas thought, *just as I have.*

The hesitation undid him. Armed men burst through the curtained doorway, shouting.

Thomas ducked back out of the room and into the servants' passage, then
halted when he saw more men running out of another narrow hall to block his
way. In the dim light he could see that they were dressed in the ragged buff
coats and mixed armor pieces of mercenaries or private troops. One drew a
pistol and Thomas ran into a dark scullery and out the opposite door, momentarily losing them. He hadn't seen Kade at the end of the hall behind them; she
must have slipped out the door.

They would expect him to stay on the ground level and look for an exit,
not to head for the upper floors. He found a narrow servants' stair behind
a curtained door and climbed it swiftly. He heard men pound through the
passage below, but they didn't come up. He reached the second floor and
made his way through a darkened salon and anteroom set, searching for a
windowed room at the back of the house. Climbing down the icy stone would
be a problem, but he would risk the drop.

There were more crumpled bodies on this floor, mainly city troops. Possibly
the civilian refugees had been allowed to escape, though small chance that
would be once night fell. Thomas was one room away from the family's private
staircase and could see it through the open doorway. He heard voices and
stepped back against the wall, half behind an arrangement of heavy drapes. It
was shadowy and ill-lit here, where most of the candles had guttered.

The men at the stair paused as someone gave orders, then spread out to the
surrounding rooms. The light from the lamp one carried clearly showed Thomas
the badge of the Duke of Alsene on their brown soldiers' doublets. It was a troop
from one of Denzil's manors.

There was a shout as someone saw him and Thomas turned and slipped
back through the salon. The darkness and confusion worked for him, but they
knew where he was now. He stopped in a darkened room to wind both his pistols. It would be dangerous to carry them like that but he was past that point
now. He checked the doors as he went through and closed the bolts of the ones
that had locks.

Thomas paused outside the door of the next chamber. The stairs down into
the stable court were just beyond it.

A quick glance showed him two men waiting in the beautifully appointed
room, both looking down toward the stairs. He pulled back as one started to
turn toward him, and drew his pistol.

Thomas stepped into the doorway and fired as the first Alsene trooper started forward. The ball struck the man in the chest at a range of no more than ten feet, sending him staggering backward into a row of lacquered cabinets.

Thomas dropped the first pistol and drew the other just as the second man reached him. He deflected the thrust of the soldier's rapier by hitting the narrow blade with his forearm and batting it away, almost managing to grab the blade and pull it out of his opponent's grasp. As the man closed with him, Thomas's pistol was knocked upward. It went off, the blast deafening him and scattering burning grains of powder down onto his attacker. The soldier faltered at the pain, giving Thomas time to shove him away and draw his main gauche. As the man rushed him again, Thomas stabbed him under the ribs.

He stepped back as the soldier collapsed, and in the sudden quiet he heard others breaking through the locked door into the room behind him. He grabbed up his other wheellock from the floor and tucked it into his sash with the second pistol. Drawing his own rapier, he took the dying man's discarded sword and went out onto the landing above the stables. There he shut the door and wedged the extra blade through the catch to keep it closed. It would not hold them for long.

He turned as the carriage doors below flung open and a large group of Alsene troops burst in. Thomas judged the odds and knew this was it. He stayed where he was, to let the narrow landing guard his back for him.

The first one to the top of the stairs came at him like a madman with something to prove. Thomas parried the first flurry of blows, then took the offensive, driving the man back a step. The lack of room worked to his advantage; with his bad leg he would not have been able to fight as effective a running battle. There were more waiting on the stairs below, and he knew he wouldn't have a chance to run.

His opponent tried an unsuccessful feint and Thomas drove his blade deeply into the man's side. The soldier stumbled backward and the man on the step below lunged past him, only to be speared through the neck. He collapsed on the top step, choking and bleeding copiously, and temporarily blocking the landing.

There was a brief moment of respite as the others below tried to wrestle their fallen comrades out of the way and Thomas hung onto the railing, panting. He could hear them battering away at the other side of the door, and it looked as if the thick wood around the wedged blade was beginning to give. The man with the neck wound made a loud strangled cry and collapsed.

Then Thomas saw a trooper on the stable floor below aiming a musket up at him. He flung himself back from the rail in pure reflex; this left room for another attacker to leap over the body blocking the stairs and come at him. Thomas parried the blows, letting himself be put on the defensive, trying to maneuver the man between himself and the musket. But moments passed and there was no impact or even the blast of a missed shot. They were trying to take him alive.

This realization energized him and he closed with his attacker, bringing their swords hilt to hilt and trapping the other blade in the quillons to hold it away from him. Pushed back, the man stumbled on the corpse behind him and Thomas shoved him down the stairs. He leapt after him into the momentary clear space, slashing at the men below who struggled to disentangle themselves. He caught one in the face, the point tearing through the man's eye and cheek before glancing off bone. The soldier fell against the wall, screaming.

Another struck upward at him, and he felt a tug and sudden pain as the point punctured his leather sleeve and stabbed into his arm. He cursed and tore himself free, falling backward on the steps now slippery with blood. The idiots were still trying to incapacitate rather than kill him. *No matter what their orders, I've given them enough provocation,* he thought in disgust.

Another man fought past his two fallen comrades in time to be stabbed in the chest, but Thomas's grip on the hilt was weak now and the point slid away instead of going deeply into the trooper's flesh. But it was enough to send his opponent reeling backward into the railing and Thomas struggled to his feet again.

Then he was struck from behind, between the shoulder blades, knocking him into the wall with stunning impact. He slid down it, unable to catch himself, blackness flowing in at the edges of his vision.

———

Waiting beside the door in the darkened hall, Kade kept her freezing hands in her pockets and tried to calm her thoughts. Anything to keep her mind off the man who had driven her half mad standing there on the green plain of Knockma being too much a gentleman to take any notice of what Boliver had said.

With effort she managed to drag her attention back to the immediate problem. She didn't think Grandier could really be helping Bisra. *Why not lure us into invading them?* She could shrug and say it didn't matter; she would kill him anyway for what he had done to Galen Dubell. *He was so like . . .*

The soldiers burst out of a door five short paces in front of her. Their backs were to her, and she instinctively searched for glamour to hide. There was hardly any in the dark hall, but the candlelight provided just enough for her to slip out the door unnoticed.

Outside she dropped the barely adequate illusion and ran down the alley to the front of the house. She would have to get in another way, use glamour from the snow outside . . .

The wall just in front of her exploded.

She hit the icy ground, more from surprise than any impulse to duck. When the building did not collapse on top of her she looked up. Several men crossed the square toward her, one carrying a musket, the glow from its slow match just visible in the dusk.

Shooting a poor little girl like me with something that large is hardly fair, she thought, dazed by the suddenness of it. At a distance and in bad light her red smock probably looked bloody. It wouldn't fool them at close range.

She dug in her pocket, hiding the movement in the snow, and managed to draw out a piece of guncotton stained with powder she had prepared earlier. She brought it up to where she could see it without having to turn her head and stared at it, trying to conjure a spark. Sympathetic magic—or unsympathetic magic as Galen had preferred to call it—was faulty and difficult to use. She might only burn her fingers. If she could call flame at all. *Damn it,* Kade thought, *a spark, just a little spark.* But she did her best work under pressure, and as the men came nearer, her mind stopped chattering and she reached the right level of concentration. The edge of the cotton began to glow.

Now. Just as the man with the musket suddenly shouted and raised his weapon, Kade sealed the concurrence spell. Every grain of powder within a ten-foot radius ignited.

The musket exploded almost over her head, there were screams and blasts as pistols went off, then a storm of little popping sounds as the scattered grains of powder from the musket's blast ignited.

Kade scrambled to her feet, her clothes dotted with someone else's blood. Three men lay dead or dying on the snow, two more running away around the corner of the house. She bolted after them, down the alley between Aviler's house and the next, into the street where they had fought the battle with the fay the day before.

Kade slid to an abrupt halt as she reached the street. She felt her heart hit the pit of her stomach. The carriage doors stood open and there were armed troops milling in front of them. She could tell by their dress only that they were not city or crown troops. It looked as though there were a hundred of them.

Someone saw her and shouted. She saw the slow match of a musket glow in the twilight; she darted back around the corner and ran.

———

"Where's the girl?" Dontane stood in the carriage doorway.

"Gone," Grandier said. He stood in the middle of the street, wrapped in his scholar's cope, thoughtfully studying the sky.

Dontane strode out and started around the corner of the house. "I sent five men after her. Damn it, she was running."

"Perhaps she wanted someone to chase her," Grandier said, and followed him.

On the other side of the house, they found the remains of the first group in the bloodstained snow. Dontane stared down at them a moment, then looked at the older sorcerer. Grandier hummed to himself and contemplated the sky again. Then Dontane saw what appeared to be a pile of rags on the snow farther into the square. He went toward it.

It must be the men he had sent after the sorceress, though all were dead and none was recognizable. They looked like corpses that had been left to mummify in some desert, dry desiccated husks.

Dontane started forward but then stopped, his attention caught by Grandier, who watched him with a speculative half smile. Dontane took a step back and said, "There's a ring here?"

Grandier nodded to a faint circular trough in the snow. He said, "It doesn't do to walk uninvited into Fayre. Or run, for that matter."

Dontane looked down at the pitiful remains of the Alsene troopers and wondered if Grandier would have let him walk unknowing into the ring. But he only said, "Good, we're rid of her, then."

"Oh, I think not." Grandier smiled and turned back toward the house. "We have something she wants, you see."

CHAPTER FIFTEEN

THOMAS WOKE WHAT must have been only a few moments later, lying on the steps in someone else's blood with one of the soldiers standing over him, slapping him awake. He had been disarmed and his head hurt incredibly, and he made a grab for the man's arm only to miss. They dragged him to his feet and he thought, *It can't last too long.*

He made them half drag, half wrestle him down the steps to the stable floor. Troopers wearing Alsene's badge moved around the enclosed court, stripping the weapons from the bodies of dead comrades as well as from those of the city troops who had tried to defend the house. The outside doors were open and cold air poured in as a smothering blast, temporarily lifting the thick odor of death that hung over the room.

Dontane waited at the bottom of the stairs. He had participated in the battle—the powder-stained buff coat and the pistols proved that—but the pallor of his face made him look half dead and his eyes were red-rimmed and haunted. He smiled at Thomas and said, "It seems I can now offer you my hospitality."

Thomas looked past him but couldn't see Kade, not as a prisoner and not as a crumpled little body on the flagstones. The pain radiating through his skull made it impossible to concentrate. He managed to focus on Dontane. "Really? And I was given the distinct impression that your position in all this was a subordinate one."

Dontane's expression tightened into anger before returning to a studied look of amused contempt. He glanced toward the open carriage doors where the daylight was beginning to fail, where Grandier must be waiting somewhere out of sight. His self-control had slipped since he had been in Lestrac's house, biding his time and waiting for that foolish young lord to die. He looked back at Thomas and said softly, "It was you who shot at us in the palace, wasn't it? How very foolish of you to go back there. The Duke of Alsene isn't dead, you see. He's very much alive. And you are going to regret that."

If they had caught or killed Kade outside, surely Dontane would brag of it.

"I have regrets already. I regret you weren't on our side of the siege doors when the Host attacked, where after sufficient persuasion you would have accused Denzil and informed us of Grandier's disguise. I regret I didn't spare the time today to blow your head off—"

He didn't even sense the blow coming. It rocked his head back and he sagged in the grip of the troopers as everything went black. He had time to hope that it would stay that way before the world slowly but relentlessly reasserted itself. The stable roof swam into hazy focus, and he swallowed blood and managed to lift his head. He said, "Careful, you might bruise your knuckles."

"Grandier wants you alive." Dontane stepped closer. "What does he want with you?"

Thomas heard the underlying tension in that cool, contemptuous tone and sensed a possibility opening up before him. If only he could pull his pain-scattered wits together enough to take advantage of it. "Ask him."

"It's easier to ask you."

"And I had the impression you two shared confidences." Thomas knew he was provoking the other man too much, losing what little control he had over the situation. He had the sudden impulse to goad Dontane further into rage, just because he could, just because it was so easy, no matter what the consequences to himself. It was astonishing how difficult he found it to suppress that urge.

Dontane struggled for calm and managed to lower his voice to say confidently, "Cooperate with me and it will go easier on you. Or do you really want to be handed over to that old madman?"

"If you've taken him as your master, you're far madder than he is."

Dontane snarled, "That's your last—" and Grandier's mild voice interrupted, "That's enough."

Grandier stepped into the circle of lamplight, appearing suddenly out of the dim cold twilight outside. From his tone he might have been encountering the younger man at a promenade or a market square, but Dontane whipped around to face him.

Grandier regarded him imperturbably. Dontane started to speak, thought better of it, and stepped back.

Moving forward, Grandier said, "An unexpected pleasure, Captain." He still wore the baggy black scholar's cope, still wore Galen Dubell's face.

That was the hardest part. *Now that I know who he is, he should look like a monster, not like . . . not like an old friend.* Thomas tried to pull free of the

troopers and was surprised when they allowed it. He stood on his own, swaying a little. "Are you getting what you want out of all this?" he asked Grandier.
About ten of the Alsene troopers were grouped around him; he thought about
fighting but his bad leg was trembling, threatening to give way, and the room
kept swaying. He thought about attempting it anyway.

Grandier regarded him silently for a long moment, his gray eyes calm as
ever. "Not yet. But soon."

At that moment it occurred to Thomas just why Grandier might want him
alive.

Grandier turned away, and while the troopers' eyes were on him, Thomas
dove sideways and slammed into one of the men, ripping the sword out of his
surprised grip and slashing upward at him. But a hilt cracked down on Thomas's head from behind, and in the end they took him alive.

———

Roland walked along a colonnaded porch open to the interior court of Bel
Garde, his knights surrounding him, feeling as if his mind were a rusty clockwork that hadn't been wound in far too long. Everything felt out of proportion,
and time seemed to move in fits and starts. He said suddenly, "The steward of
this place must have known about the powder store. Arrest him at once."

"Sir Renier has already done so, my lord."

"Oh. Good." *God,* he realized suddenly. *My mother is gone and there's no
one to think of these things.* He looked up, seeing the confusion in the court
for the first time, recognizing the figures in the center of the milling crowd of
servants and guards. It was Falaise, sitting her horse in her riding clothes with
Queen's guards around her, obviously just come through the gates.

Breaking free of his escort, Roland ran across the court to catch her bridle.
He had never made the effort to get to know Falaise very well, but he was glad
out of all proportion to see that she still lived. It seemed to promise that the
world as it was had not been completely destroyed. "Falaise, we thought you
were dead! Where were you?"

She looked down at him, startled. Her expression was frightened and there
were dark circles of weariness under her eyes. Her horse stamped and tried to
nibble Roland's sleeve. She said, "My lord, I must see Ravenna at once. There is
something I must . . . something I must . . ."

"My lady," he said, not quite recognizing his own voice, "my mother is dead."

Falaise turned white, the blood draining out of her face as if she were dying in front of him. Shocked, Roland called for help. Guards came to help the Queen from her horse; her ladies and servants appeared in the court. An Albon knight urged Roland away, saying, "My lord, you must come inside. It's not safe out here." Numb, Roland let the man lead him into one of the rooms off the court, thinking, *Something has happened. What is she so terrified of?*

The room was long, with many windows to look out onto the garden court, their lace curtains woefully inadequate to stop the drafts. Roland paced tensely, rubbing his cold hands together, ignoring his knights and unsure of just what he was waiting for.

Falaise appeared in the doorway, half supported by the Queen's Guard lieutenant Gideon. Past them, Roland could see two of the Queen's gentlewomen waiting outside, huddled together like children expecting punishment. Holding tightly to the lieutenant's arm, Falaise managed to cross the room, then collapsed at Roland's feet. He looked at Gideon in bewilderment, and the lieutenant bent over the Queen, saying, "My lady, you must tell him."

"Tell me what?" Roland said. Sickness hit the pit of his stomach suddenly, and he groped for the table to steady himself. He remembered that Falaise had disappeared at the same time as Denzil.

Falaise looked up at him, her face tear-streaked and frightened, but something in his expression must have encouraged her because she said, "My lord, I should have spoken days ago."

Roland listened in agonized silence to Falaise's story of more treachery, of how Denzil had deliberately kept the Queen from leaving the city so that she would be in his power. "Before this, he had offered me marriage if you were to die, Your Majesty. I . . . I don't mean to accuse him, but . . ."

"No." Roland had to stop her. He didn't want to hear how she had concealed treason out of fear of him. He understood her reaction to his mother's death now. She had been counting on telling this to Ravenna first, counting on Ravenna to protect her from him. *More nails in my coffin,* he thought. "It's all right, really. I don't blame you. There are . . . Other things have come to light which . . . Perhaps you should go to your ladies now."

The lieutenant led her away, and Roland stood at the table, staring at his own reflection in its polished surface. He had never loved Falaise, knew he never would, but this was the first time he had realized that he might have saved a great deal of trouble by simply making a friend of her. *When Denzil is with me it's as if I can't think.* His fist struck the table and the face in the reflection twisted. *Oh God, let him have an explanation.*

—•—

Thomas didn't remember much of the trip back to the palace. They bound his wrists and got him on a horse, and he leaned over the saddlebow, unable to sit up. The cold grew intense as night took the city in a dark wave and the freezing air was raw on his throat and lungs. His stomach was cramping with nausea, and dizziness kept overwhelming him.

He came back to full consciousness only when they were passing through St. Anne's Gate. He lifted his head and shook back the hood of the cloak someone had thrown over him.

They were passing between the Cisternan Barracks and the Mews, as he had days earlier bringing Galen Dubell into the palace for the first time. *I couldn't have been more helpful if I'd been in the plot with them,* he thought. He hadn't even been able to get them to kill him.

The barracks were a gutted ruin. The wooden panels over the three arched doorways had been torn open, exposing the dark pit of the interior and the piles of snow that had drifted inside. With the outer gate closed and guarded, the assault from within the palace would have caught the Cisternans completely by surprise. In the narrow corridors of the ancient stone structure, the attack by the fay must have had the devastating effect of a hunter blocking all the holes but one of a rabbit warren, and then releasing his ferrets.

The gates into the old siege wall stood open. As they rode through and toward the towering wall of the Old Palace, bogles dropped out of the eaves of the two long stone city armories across the court. Pale-skinned, ugly, distorted creatures, their yellow eyes gleamed in the gathering darkness. Each was short and squat, their arms hanging disproportionately long and their wide mouths grinning with rows of pointed teeth.

Sniggering in almost human voices, the bogles ambled toward them; the nervous horses shied away.

They stopped in the paved court beneath the bulk of the Old Palace, where lit sconces illuminated the high double doors of the westside entrance. Thomas managed to get off the horse on his own without falling. He held onto the saddle a moment while his head and legs became reconciled with the notion of standing. The troopers hung back from him now, watching him warily. He wondered if it was due to his unpredictability or his apparent familiarity with Grandier.

Inside the circular entrance hall the few lamps made hardly a dent in the shadows. This area of the Old Palace seemed remarkably undisturbed, the untouched rooms and short halls leading off into darkness and silence.

Grandier stood beside him suddenly, and Thomas was too weary to be startled. Grandier said, "This way."

Both Dontane and the sergeant in charge of the Alsene troops turned to look at him, but Grandier ignored their unspoken questions. He said to Thomas, "I want to show you something."

Grandier led the way down a lesser-used series of rooms, lit only by the lamps the soldiers carried, and to a staircase leading down to the lower levels. At the third turn of the stairs Grandier led them into an old stone-walled corridor, and Thomas realized they were going toward the same cellar where the keystone had been concealed. He looked at Grandier walking beside him, but the older man's features betrayed nothing.

As they moved through the cold rooms the flickering light revealed the sheen of sweat on a soldier's face, a white-knuckled grip on a sword-hilt or musket that told volumes about the troops' relationship with the fay invaders.

They reached a plain wooden stair leading down, and were now roughly backtracking the route they had taken away from the cellar the night of the attack, but heading toward the lower passageways they had been unable to reach because of the collapsed corridor. The strain of the fight had exacerbated the pain in Thomas's bad leg and it was protesting this treatment, but he managed not to limp too obviously.

The stairs led to an unblocked passage below the storerooms, and the stale air carried the fetid smell of death. Thomas's thoughts kept turning back to Grandier's shape-shifting ability. *Not that way. I don't want to die that way.* He had given up everything else—his honor, his right to say he had never killed a helpless opponent, his claim on his ancestral lands. Voluntarily or pushed to it by circumstance, bit by bit everything had gone to win a few years or a few months or a few days of political stability in a world where so few others seemed to care, and most of them were dead now. He was willing to die for duty's sake but the thought of giving up his identity turned his heart to ice.

There was light up ahead, from a place where there should be stygian darkness. Abruptly raucous noise, growling, and a high-pitched keening echoed off the stone walls. A few more uneasy troopers drew their swords.

The corridor turned, and the first thing Thomas saw was that a large chunk of the stone wall had been knocked out, allowing a view down into the cellar. Grandier moved to the edge, and after a moment Thomas followed him.

The Unseelie Court had found a home here. Fay with long emaciated bodies and huge leathery wings flew in lazy circles over the foul revelry below.
There were hundreds of them—bogles, spriggans, formless creatures like the
boneless that had attacked them in the street. The mockery and distortion of
human and animal forms was endless and infinitely varied. Thomas could see
them much more clearly this time, perhaps because they were not troubling
to conceal themselves anymore. The light came from a mist that crept up the
walls and wreathed around the giant columns supporting the ceiling.

This opening had been made at about the second level of the cellar, and the
wide pillars met the ceiling another two levels above them. Below were the remains of two flights of stairs and the narrow well that had enclosed them, now
a mound of broken stone and shattered wood. Corpse-lights flitted around the
stairs and the tops of the columns.

The unnatural light was bright enough to let Thomas see the dark openings
in the ceiling for the air shafts and the doors through which the larger siege
engines had been lowered. Chains and frayed ropes hung down from some
of those doors, the old system of block and tackle. Thomas said, "They fly up
those shafts."

"Yes." Grandier's gaze was on the unholy revelry below. "It protects them from
daylight, but gives them access to the surface." He turned back to the others and
said, "Dontane, they seem disturbed. Go down and ask them what's wrong."

Dontane moved forward, threw an unreadable look at Grandier, then
started the awkward climb to the bottom of the cellar.

"So he *is* a sorcerer," Thomas said.

Grandier glanced at him. "He's learning. He had been refused admittance
to Lodun, and in anger he came across the border to Bisra, and to me for teaching before my arrest. I refused him, because I felt he lacked moral character."
He smiled, amused, apparently, by this earlier self who had the leisure to make
such judgments. "Trust was a very important issue, among those of us who
practiced sorcery in Bisra. The merest suspicion of necromancy, or anything
else the Church could interpret as traffic with demons, was death. But after I
escaped from the Inquisition, I sought him out. I had discovered I needed a
man who lacked moral character. He was at Lodun with me after I was Galen
Dubell, but one of the masters learned he had been across the border, and became suspicious of him. The rumors that I had come to Ile-Rien had already
started, you see. So I sent him on to contact the Duke of Alsene for me, which
he did through our unfortunate and foolish Lord Lestrac."

Dr. Braun had visited Lodun frequently, Thomas remembered. "You killed Braun because he recognized Dontane."

"I would have had to eventually, anyway."

Thomas watched Dontane pick his way down the remains of the steps and said, "Are you sure he's not the one who turned you in to the Inquisition?"

"Oh, good try." Grandier smiled. "No, that man is dead."

Dontane had climbed halfway to the bottom, and now one of the winged sidhe flew to meet him, cupping its wings to hold itself in midair, gesturing and shouting at him in a high-pitched shriek. Dontane turned and waved at Grandier, his posture betraying irritation. Grandier said, "It appears this needs my attention." He nodded to the Alsene sergeant, then looked back at Thomas. "I'll see you shortly, Captain."

Without Grandier's presence, the troopers muttered nervously as they made their way back, but Thomas was too preoccupied to notice. *Why did he want me to see that? What did it accomplish?* A will-o'-the-wisp followed them part of the way, playing in the unlit wall lanterns and taunting them silently.

Thomas felt each step of the various stairways as a short stabbing pain. By the time they reached the upper floors of the Old Palace he was limping badly. They entered one of the smaller halls that had been set up as temporary barracks, now occupied by a few sullen troopers gathered around the hearth fire, and they passed through it into an attached suite. The last room had been stripped of furniture and wall coverings, and it was dark except for what light flickered uncertainly in from the lamps in the anteroom.

Thomas watched tiredly as one of them pounded an iron spike with a set of manacles attached to it into the wall. With respect for his unpredictability, one held a pistol to his head when they untied him to put the manacles on.

The chains were short but he was able to sit down against the wall. The troopers withdrew into the anteroom to huddle in a nervous knot near the hearth.

He tested the set of the spike in the wall to see if it could be worked loose, but it held firm. *Well and truly caught this time.* He rested his pounding head back against the cold wood, and tried not to think.

"I didn't believe they would let you live." It was Aviler's voice. Between the dim light and the distraction of various injuries, Thomas hadn't seen the other man chained to the opposite wall. The High Minister's dark-colored doublet was torn and bloodied, and from the livid bruises on his temple it seemed he had not been taken easily.

Thomas closed his eyes, damning the fate that had consigned him to be imprisoned with Aviler. Then he said, "Grandier wanted me alive, and if you imply I'm in league with him, I'll kill you."

At the moment it was a supremely empty threat, but Aviler answered, "Don't take me for a fool, Captain."

"I don't know what else to take you for." Thomas sat up and gingerly felt the back of his head. His hair was matted with blood, and there was a sizable lump composed of pure pain.

"You can take me for a man who did not acquire my power in a Queen's bed."

"Yes," Thomas agreed. "In her bed, on the daybed in the anteroom, on a couch in the west solar of the Summer Palace, and other locations too numerous to mention, and if you had the slightest understanding of Ravenna at all, you would know it never made one damn bit of difference as to whether she took my advice or not. And no, your father handed you your power wrapped in ribbon on his deathbed."

The High Minister looked away. After a long moment of silence, he said, "I expect it doesn't matter now."

Already feeling the bite of the manacles on his wrists, Thomas expected it didn't matter either.

Aviler rubbed his eyes, making his own chains jingle slightly. "Galen Dubell really is the sorcerer Grandier, then. Denzil told me something of it when he brought the Queen to me, but under the circumstances I don't place much confidence in his word."

"Dubell really is Grandier. He got a shape-changing magic from the fay, and he killed Dubell and took his place." The stab wound in Thomas's left arm was still bleeding sluggishly, though the pain of it hardly competed with that in his head. The thinner sleeve leather of his buff coat had absorbed some of the force but the blade had still penetrated a couple of inches, at least. He tore a strip of material from the tail of his shirt to use as a crude bandage. "Why are you alive?"

"I don't know. No one's bothered to say. What's your opinion on the subject?"

"He wants to keep his options open. He can't stay Dubell forever."

As Aviler considered the unpleasant implication, Thomas tightened the rag around his arm, taking malicious satisfaction in letting the other man in on his private terror. He knew he had more to worry about on that score than the High Minister did. Grandier hardly knew Aviler.

With Lucas dead—he hesitated in tying off the makeshift bandage, wondering who had done it, Dontane or some nameless hireling trooper—there was no one but Ravenna who knew him well enough to realize the deception immediately. He didn't think anyone could find a way through the complexities of his relationship with Ravenna, but that would only mean Grandier would have to kill her, the way he had coldly eliminated anyone who might have noticed that Galen Dubell had changed more than time could account for.

Then there was Kade.

Kade had done well enough leading her own erratic and dangerous life before Thomas had dragged her into this, talked her into staying with them past the point at which she could have left safely. And made her vulnerable. *The little idiot trusts me.* Lucas had been right. And he remembered that the last conversation he had had with his friend had been an argument; stupid thing to do in a war, and he would regret it the rest of his no doubt short life.

Kade was her own woman, and he was too old to bother lying to himself anymore and too young not to want her. But any chance of anything between them was wasted, as pointlessly wasted as Lucas, Vivan, and all the other lives lost and destroyed by Denzil and Grandier.

There was a stirring among the men in the anteroom, and after a moment Urbain Grandier appeared in the doorway, carrying a candlelamp and a short stool.

He set the lamp down on the scuffed floorboards, and glanced once, thoughtfully, at Aviler. Then he looked back to Thomas and said, "I felt I owed you more of an explanation."

Thomas had a sudden impulse to delay whatever the sorcerer had come to say. He said, "You have Dontane fooled. He thinks you're mad."

Grandier shook his head, put the stool he had brought just inside the doorway, and sat down. "I give him what he expects." He sighed, and looked like a tired old man. "He imagines himself to be subtle and dangerous, and I suppose he is, but there are things he fails to understand. Denzil, on the other hand, is rather like an incompetent copyist's version of you."

As the clear gray eyes met his, Thomas felt a stab of pure fear. *Worry about it later,* he thought. Grandier had probably noticed but there was no help for that. He said, "Do they know what you're planning? And there is a plan, isn't there?"

"Yes. I first conceived it in my cell in the Temple Prison at Bistrita. I had to think about something besides the torturers, and the death by fire that waited for me." He looked down at his hand and stretched the fingers, contemplating the unbroken skin as if he did not quite recognize it as his own.

And perhaps he doesn't, Thomas thought. He remembered the catalog of tortures the court documents had listed. Grandier was driven, dangerous, and intelligent. It was almost as if he had passed into another phase of being that was not madness or sanity but some lawless ground in between.

Across the room, Aviler shifted a little, breaking the silence with a faint clink of chain, and Grandier said, "Then an emissary of the Unseelie Court appeared with their offer, which you know about already. Part of a scheme on their part to suborn a human sorcerer, to make the Host more powerful in our world. It's a contest they have with the Seelie Court, their opposites in Fayre. Having a sorcerer at their beck and call would be a coup of sorts." He shrugged. "They thought me a likely candidate."

Thomas realized he was trying to control the conversation out of panic, and that Grandier was allowing him to do it. *Try to be a little less transparent,* he told himself. *You've helped the man enough already.* Grandier seemed to expect a comment, so he said only, "The more fools they."

"I thought so." Grandier smiled a little. "It's not entirely their fault, the trusting creatures. They are accustomed to Fayre, which bends to their will. The mortal world has sharp edges, bends to no man's will, and events occur with fatal finality. Mistakes are not suffered. Evadne was pressing me to give up this game and go on to something more entertaining. He was one of their self-proclaimed leaders, a very annoying character. He's dead now, of course. I rather thought someone might kill him eventually. And I meant to tell you, Kade escaped through the ring and is presumably in Fayre, at the moment."

That's one mercy. Thomas fought not to show relief and asked, "Why are you helping Denzil?"

"The Duke has offered me what I want. A war with Bisra."

"We've had a war with Bisra. It didn't turn out that well for anyone." But things began to fall into place. Ravenna would never have agreed to another war. They had been the victors of the last long conflict with their mortal enemies to the south only by a bare margin. Even if Roland had supported such a suicidal course, Aviler and the other High Lords and advisors would have prevented it at any cost.

"There *was* a war," Grandier conceded, "but I was not involved. And I have the Host."

Thomas thought of the monstrous turmoil in the undercellars. He said, "If you want to turn them loose on Bisra, be my guest, but why do you have to destroy us in the process?"

"I have no intention of destroying Ile-Rien. But I will have to alter it some-what. Denzil needs the war to cement his position as usurper. When word leaks out that Vienne is under a virtual state of siege by creatures of Fayre, Bisra will move to take advantage. They need Ile-Rien's wealth to maintain a balance of power with Parscia, on their southern border, and their Church fears any sorcery not under its control. Justifiably so.

"When the landed lords of Ile-Rien realize Bisra is marshalling its forces to attack, they will support any central authority that has a chance of orga-nizing a resistance. The Duke of Alsene will be that authority. Oh, that won't be all. There is to be some document of formal abdication, signed by Roland. Under what circumstances, I don't know." He looked over at Aviler, who had been listening in a kind of horrified fascination. "That explains your pres-ence. Your position allows you to deputize the King's seal on state documents during an emergency when the King has been removed for his own safety. I doubt the originator of that particular tenet of courtlaw intended documents of abdication to be included in that category, and it would be laughed off if Roland's supporters took power again, but Denzil intends to keep all his op-tions open."

Aviler looked away, his face grim. "I will not sign anything for Denzil, for you, or for the Prince of Hell himself."

"I know." Grandier nodded seriously. He turned back to Thomas. "Once the Bisran army crosses the border, and are no longer protected by their priests' defenses, the Host will help to harry them and they will be driven back. At that time, outrage against the Bisrans will be so high it will not be difficult to turn an army of defense into an army of offense."

Thomas shook his head in disbelief. "The Host participates in this out of the goodness of its collective heart? What did you offer them, the destruction of Lodun? What are they going to do when you don't keep up your end of the bargain?"

Grandier looked up, surprised and pleased. "Oh, very good. Go on."

"Denzil's motive is plain: he has to own everyone and everything around him. The Host wants the death of as many human sorcerers as possible. And you want Bisra. And I'd wager anything that you mean for no one to get what he wants except you."

"And how will I accomplish this?" Grandier asked softly, eyes alight.

"I don't know. But I don't think you'll let them destroy Lodun."

"No, I would not let them do that." For a moment his expression turned abstract. "Evadne was the one demanding I destroy Lodun. He is not a factor anymore."

Grandier hesitated, his face craggy and harsh in the candlelight. "I don't like Denzil; he is cunning and I will need help to manage him. But he will give me what I want, and so I must use him. Bisra will be struck by the might of your armies. Once their priests can no longer defend them from the fay, I can further the collapse. In time, there will be nothing left but to sow salt into the empty fields . . . and Bisra will cease to be. It will probably take many years, I know, but I have the time." He looked thoughtful, then shook his head. "I regret the necessity of a long war that will have ill effect on this land, but I really can't see any other way to start the process of collapse. You will agree that an all-out conflict can be particularly devastating."

Thomas just looked at him. There was nothing to be said. Grandier was setting forces in motion he couldn't possibly control. The old sorcerer might never see his goal accomplished, but he would see years of destruction.

Quietly, desperately, Aviler said, "What you are planning—dreaming—will never come to pass."

Grandier got slowly to his feet, as if the cold hurt his back. "I have ridden the tide of events for many years. I am quite capable of guiding it now."

Thomas looked up at him, and knew any argument was useless, but he said, "You're handing the kingdom to Denzil, and he doesn't give a penny damn for you or your plans."

"That remains to be seen."

In a tone of quiet rage, Aviler said, "I hope you burn in Hell with your damned fay allies."

Grandier chuckled. "I have already burned in Hell. You see the result. Heaven help us all if it happens again."

Thomas said, "Has Denzil noticed that anyone who gets in your way dies?"

"I don't think so. Not yet, at any rate. But then, you're not dead, and you were certainly in my way."

Not nearly enough, Thomas thought. "That's only a matter of time, isn't it?"

"It's what I'm told." Grandier regarded him silently, then said seriously, "There is one more thing. The Queen . . . The Dowager Queen Ravenna is dead."

Thomas felt the silence stretch, felt Aviler staring at him. Calmly he said, "You're lying."

"Not about this. She was trying to protect Roland. She succeeded and destroyed several important members of the Host in the process."

"You're lying." Thomas tried to stand and the chains jerked him back to his knees. He didn't notice.

Grandier closed his eyes a moment. "No. There are some things I regret, but this isn't one of them. She was too dangerous."

And then he knew it was true. "You fucking bastard!" he shouted at him.

Grandier turned to go and Thomas said, "You are a coward. You didn't have to do this."

His back to Thomas, Grandier paused in the doorway, but then continued out. Thomas sank back against the wall. Aviler said, "It is a lie, surely."

"No. No, it's not." It was the last thing he said for several hours.

CHAPTER SIXTEEN

KADE LANDED AWKWARDLY in the high velvet grass of the Knockma ring and rolled to her feet. She pressed her hands to her temples and tried to concentrate, feeling the lines of force radiating out from the ring around her. She reached out along them to open a ring in the maze court below the Old Palace. She opened her eyes and saw the green sward of Knockma, the menhirs standing around her in silent contemplation, and in the distance, the mist-shrouded column of the castle and its reflection.

She snarled, shrugged out of her coat, and tried again.

After four failures she knew it was no good; she couldn't form a ring inside the palace. *What did Grandier do?* He would have had to ward the palace against her, that would take . . . But traveling the rings from the palace to Knockma, to Aviler's house and back here, had distorted her sense of time's passage. By the sky, they had lost nearly an hour on coming to Knockma and returning to the city. Moving from the less powerful ring she had made at the High Minister's house and coming back, she could have lost more than that.

Grandier could have begun the spells against her when he was alerted to her and Thomas's presence in the palace. It would not have taken long if he used the wards already in place. No time at all if he had used another keystone prepared earlier when he had first known she was coming to court.

Kade knotted her hands in her hair until the pain stopped the rise of bile in her throat.

She opened her eyes. Boliver stood at the edge of the ring, watching her and scratching his bearded chin. He said, "What happened?"

"They have him," she said simply.

His eyes widened a little. After a moment he shuffled his feet, then said, "What are we going to do, then?"

"Wait here." She scrambled to her feet, touched the power in the ring, and took that step that carried her away.

The cold embraced her first. Kade had left her coat in the forever-spring of Knockma. She was outside the palace wall, near the Postern Gate where she and Thomas had got in earlier that day. The square with its broken fountain was still empty of life in the gathering dusk, the buildings staring down at her with gaping dark windows.

Kade stepped out of the newly formed ring in the snow and moved to the gate, and the hair on the back of her neck rose. Cursing, she dug in a pocket for some of the last of the gasçoign powder she had with her and rubbed it into the corners of her eyes.

The wards rose up from the ground in front of her in a corona of light, stretching up and curving over the wall. *He has put the wards back.*

High above, a razor-winged shadow dove out of the clouds, passed un-harmed through the corona it could not see, and disappeared among the palace towers. *That was a member of the Host. And it went through the wards.* Kade raised a hand toward the light and saw the gooseflesh spring up on her arm. *And I can't. He turned the wards against me, to let the Host in and keep me out.*

Kade stepped back, and felt the awareness of the wards' hostile presence recede. There was one other way in. She could go through the ring that already existed in the shattered remains of the Grand Gallery. *Yes, that way, the trap.*

Kade went back to the snow ring and took the turn that brought her into the Grand Gallery.

The cold was no less bitter for the shelter of the walls. The huge hall was dark and silent and a wind flung snow through the broken terrace windows.

A winged fay with blue skin and an angelic human face sat in the middle of the floor, picking its toes. It glanced up, saw her, and screamed.

As it fled the room, Kade lifted a hand to touch the edge of the ring. Just above the surface, she felt the heat of hostile force. The old ward around the ring was tied to the same etheric structure as the wards around the palace. She could not step outside it.

The floor was piled with chunky broken stone from the foundation, shat-tered wooden flooring, and dirt. She began to trace the outer edge of the circle, stepping up onto one of the larger pieces of foundation, leaping to the next. It took concentration. A recently formed ring would have hardly any mark on it at all. The Knockma Ring was ancient and well used, but it was a still pool of power. This ring was a whirlpool of conflicting forces, stirred up like a hornet's nest by the Host's recent passage. It had originally been her mother Moire's work and had rested atop the polished wooden floor of the gallery. Dr. Surete had sealed it off with spells long ago, and the pressure of the wards had even-tually pushed it down to this level, even with the foundation.

After some moments, Kade heard footsteps. She looked up to see Dontane and Grandier standing in one of the archways. Dontane was leveling a pistol at her.

She smiled grimly. He fired, the blast reverberating through the room, echoing off the high sculpted ceiling. Kade didn't see the ball until it entered the ring's sphere of influence, where it veered abruptly from its straight course and began to travel the ring's outer circle, orbiting around her like the philosophers claimed the sun orbited the earth.

Grandier said, "Don't waste your shot." He crossed the room to stand within a few yards of the ring's outer edge, and after a moment Dontane joined him. Kade had already resumed her halting progress around the outer rim. The pistol ball whizzed past her again, starting a breeze that stirred her hair.

To Grandier, Dontane snapped, "What are you waiting for? Kill her."

"She isn't here," Grandier said. "She is a breath away from a thousand other places, aren't you?"

Without interrupting her progress, Kade glanced up at Dontane. "Come and get me."

He took an impulsive step forward, then hesitated, looking at Grandier.

Ignoring him, Grandier said seriously, "I don't have to ask what you want here, Kade."

She had found the ring's pattern now and hoped her slight hesitation at the cardinal point would be put down to reaction to his remark. She said, "I want you dead."

"He's alive."

This time the hesitation was unplanned. She had not allowed herself to think Thomas might be dead, but from the sudden suffocating constriction in her chest, some part of her mind had recognized it as a very real possibility. She forced herself to step to the next rock. *I shouldn't have come.* This was what Grandier wanted, this was why he had not sealed this ring against her. Now he could ask her for anything he wanted, and she would have to give it to him. She thought about fleeing now, but it was too late. She took a deep breath, and continued her progress around the ring. Her head was buzzing, and she was going to have to leave soon to find somewhere private to be sick.

Dontane watched his master carefully.

Grandier said, "I want you to stay out of this, Kade."

She took another deep breath, but did not look up at him.

"I know it won't be easy—"

All the fear and panic inside her crystallized into an icy knot of pure rage.

Without betraying her intentions by the flicker of an eyelash, she tapped the fayre power in the ring and released the orbiting pistol ball. Grandier stumbled against Dontane, and the ball struck the far wall with a loud crack and a shower of plaster and dust.

Grandier reached up and touched his right ear, smiling ruefully when his fingers came away lightly spotted with blood.

Dontane had drawn his second pistol. "She missed you by a hairsbreadth," he hissed.

"On the contrary, she hit exactly what she aimed at," Grandier answered dryly, straightening up with an effort. "And I'll thank you not to toss her any more shot."

Kade waited for him to look at her. When he did, their eyes locked for a long moment. Then Grandier said, "Very well put. I will not patronize you again."

Dontane swore. "Are you going to let this mad creature get away with that?"

"Your appraisal wounds me to the heart," Kade said softly, before Grandier could answer. "Believe me, I shall fall down in agony at some more convenient time."

"She knows my death will not affect the wards that keep her out, or the presence of the Host, or any of the other plans I have set in motion." Grandier was speaking to Dontane, but his eyes went to Kade. "She has no choice but to cooperate."

There was a keening howl from outside the gallery, and a sudden eddy lifted a scatter of ice crystals from the floor.

"The Host is coming," Grandier said. "Perhaps you had better go. They will follow you."

"Will they?" Kade smiled. *No choice,* her thought echoed. *But appearances are everything.*

The Host streamed in through the doorways—the bogles, the grinning mock-human fay, the distorted animals, the hideous inhuman shapes, flying, crawling or running, bringing the stink of death. Dontane wheeled to face them, involuntarily moving closer to Grandier.

Kade waited until the first were almost to the edge of the ring, then stepped back into Knockma.

———

Thomas awoke leaning back against the wall, stiff and freezing. The candle-lamp on the floor had burned low, a pool of tallow collecting in its base. An iron brazier had been placed in the center of the room and was putting out just enough heat to keep them from freezing to death. He was surprised that he was alive at all. He had remembered that lapsing into sleep with a head injury was often fatal.

"Are you all right?" Aviler asked, watching him closely.

His head hurt so badly he didn't think he could move it, but he said, "Whatever gave you the idea I wasn't?"

Aviler was not fooled by this sally at all. He said, "Do you know where you are? Forgive my persistence, but we've had this conversation before."

"Oh." Thomas watched the flicker of light over the sculpted ceiling for a moment. He remembered who was dead. "Yes, I know where I am. Unfortunately. How long was I out?"

Aviler tried to shift his own position and grimaced in discomfort. "Several hours. I believe it may be near morning, but it's difficult to say."

Near morning of the third day since the attack. Not much time for travelers or refugees to carry word of the disaster. And if Ravenna was dead, what had happened to the rest of the court? Thomas tried not to care, and was surprised to find it impossible. There were Falaise and Gideon, Berham, Phaistus, his other men. If Denzil realized Falaise had betrayed what little she knew of his plans to Thomas, even if she had done it too late to be of any help . . .

He saw that Aviler was trying to loosen the heavy iron spike that held his chains to the wall with an air that spoke of several hours' familiarity with the process. Thomas shifted over enough to reach the peg holding him and started to work on it, for all that it felt absolutely immovable.

Another Bisran War. All the heroes of the last terrible years of war were gone. All the famous names that had passed into folklegend and ballads were the names of the dead. Aviler the Elder had succumbed to illness or possibly poison; the Warrior-Nun of Portier had been thrown from a horse; Thomas's old captain was killed at duty; Desero, who had been Renier's predecessor as Preceptor of the Albonate Knights, retired and passed quietly away in the country; and all the others had been killed in later battles or by the weight of years. For the last year or so there had only been Ravenna, Lucas, and himself, and they had come into the legend only at its triumphant conclusion. Now there was only himself, who had been the youngest of the lot, and who would not live to be executed by Roland for some imagined offense, or to see his skill degenerate from time and old wounds. It was the end of an age.

Thomas heard someone come into the anteroom, heard one of the troopers reply to some question. He glanced at Aviler, who looked grim, and he remembered that Denzil had wanted the High Minister to sign a falsified document of abdication.

After a moment, Dontane appeared in the doorway. He stood there, smiling down at them coldly. Thomas leaned back against the wall, relieved it wasn't Grandier. He couldn't find it in himself to feel anything but contempt for Dontane, for all that he was a sorcerer. After Grandier's example of how far one man could go for revenge, Dontane seemed nothing but a persistent gadfly of a schemer, not unlike the young nobles Denzil had used as cannon fodder in his plans.

"The Duke of Alsene has much to discuss with you," Dontane said then, and motioned to the soldiers outside. Two entered the room, one standing back with a drawn rapier and the other unlocking Thomas's manacles.

Thomas made no attempt to stand, letting the trooper jerk him to his feet. That was the only way he would've been able to get there; his leg had stiffened up again.

They led him out of the makeshift prison and down one flight of stairs into an area heavily guarded by more of the Alsene troops. Men were crowded into the disordered rooms, and every candle and lamp was lit to fight the darkness and the presence of the fay. The fear was palpable.

Dontane asked suddenly, "What did Grandier say to you?"

Thomas remembered Dontane's persistence in demanding why Grandier should want him alive when he had first been captured. He had suspected then that Dontane felt his position was insecure. Only a sane reaction, considering how many people Grandier had disposed of to further his goals. Thomas said, "He told us all his grand plans. Do you want to know if they included you?"

Dontane did not turn to look at him. Thomas sensed he was struggling to control a bitter anger, which was probably directed at Grandier almost as much as it was at him. After a moment Dontane replied, "If Denzil doesn't rid me of you, I'll just have to think of something myself, won't I?"

Dontane led the way through a suite piled with supplies, to where servants with the Alsene badge waited outside two large double doors.

Inside was a long low-ceilinged council room, decorated in blue and gold with a long draw table across the back wall. Three men stood with their backs to Thomas, consulting a map spread out on the table. Dontane went to lean against the wall, watching with folded arms, but the troopers stayed to either side of Thomas. The men wore the heavy velvet brocades of nobles, and two were blond. *Alsene lords?* he wondered. A couple of servants waited by the other door, with a dark-haired boy-page. Then Thomas saw that the man in the center of the group at the table had his left arm in a sling, and he forgot about Dontane and the others.

Denzil turned to face him, and Thomas said, "Pity I missed."

"Pity for you," the Duke of Alsene said, smiling as he came forward. "It was a good shot; it shattered the bone, but our fine sorcerer Grandier healed it." Thomas must have shown his disbelief because Denzil added, "Yes, I thought it impossible too, but it seems he's more skilled than most. Quite an advantage for me."

Quite an advantage. If not for Grandier, Denzil would have died, or lost his arm. One of the other nobles, watching from across the room, grinned and said, "So this is the one who gave you so much trouble, my lord; you didn't tell us—"

Denzil spun around and snarled, "Shut up!"

The silence became absolute. Thomas noted he was the only one in the room who hadn't started at the sudden transformation from urbane calm to nearly blind rage. He had always known Denzil was capable of that kind of anger; that the young Duke had hidden it from his followers came as no surprise.

Denzil turned back to him, again the cool, amused young noble. Smiling, he said, "Relatives are a necessary encumbrance."

"For now," Thomas agreed. He could see the family resemblance to Denzil in the other two men's features, the cold blue of their eyes. The one who had spoken looked resentful at being publicly chastened; the other was watching the scene with amusement, as if it were a play put on for his enjoyment. If Denzil succeeded, Thomas wouldn't have bet copper on the chances of either of them living out the year. He said, "Did you get Roland?"

"No." Denzil's eyes were very bright and he was flushed slightly from excitement. Excitement at the power. He was watching Thomas carefully. "Ravenna's dead."

"I know," Thomas said, able to keep his expression neutral and wondering if Grandier had told him first only to spoil his ally's fun.

Denzil was too good at this to betray even a flash of irritation. He only shook his head in mild regret. "Grandier again? And I was so looking forward to telling you myself."

At that moment Thomas knew for certain that Denzil had brought him up here to kill him. He had suspected it as soon as he had walked in, but now it was all there to be read in the younger man's face, the way he carried himself. He said, "You hide your disappointment well."

"Do you think so?" Denzil drew the main gauche from the sash at his back and touched the point thoughtfully. This wasn't the deadly toy with the serrated edge and extra rods for breaking blades. It was an elegant weapon with a long utilitarian blade and a gold-chased half-shell guard. Thomas watched Denzil's opaque eyes and tried to keep his mind blank.

Denzil said, "I don't suppose you're surprised by this," and stabbed him in the stomach.

For the first moment, Thomas only felt the force of the blow. It doubled him over, and as the blade pulled free and air reached his sliced flesh, the pain began. A wave of icy cold rose around him, and his legs gave way. He didn't notice that the troopers had let him go until his knees struck the floor. For a moment, he supported himself with one hand braced against the wooden planks, the other pressed to his stomach. The blood felt hot against the chill of his skin, and there was so astonishingly little of it at first. He was distantly aware of noise in the room, voices raised, but then his arm gave way and that was all.

———

Out of the warm darkness of fevered sleep, he heard voices.

Galen Dubell . . . No, Grandier said, "I don't have to justify my actions to you."

"Don't you? You're putting me on a throne, and I'm going to help you get your heart's desire, and you don't think you owe me a few words of explanation?" Denzil said, his tone soft and reasonable.

"Correct."

There was silence. Thomas managed to open his eyes. He lay curled on his side on a couch, and a large spot of the heavy damask upholstery was soaked with blood. He knew this because his left hand lay in it. His doublet had been unbuttoned and his shirt pulled aside. It was cold, though not as frigid as the room where he had been imprisoned. His limbs felt too heavy to move, and there was something about the absence of pain that was shocking.

Grandier's back was to him, and he could see Denzil across the room.

Denzil's brows had lifted in gentle inquiry, but when Grandier remained politely attentive, he said, "That man is my enemy."

"That isn't my concern."

Denzil was ominously still for a moment, though Grandier's reply had been in the same mild voice. He said, "Consider that you would do better not to antagonize me."

"Perhaps. But I have already antagonized you, it seems, so I see no point in not continuing on my chosen course."

"Very well. It means nothing then, but . . ." Denzil shrugged gracefully, only a slight tremor revealing his rage. "Do be more careful in the future."

Thomas closed his eyes, feeling darkness sweep up over him in a moment of dizziness, but he heard Denzil's steps cross the room and a door close.

He opened his eyes again and saw Grandier shake his head and turn around. The sorcerer smiled when he saw him awake and said, "Really, the man is driven mad by anyone who fails to succumb to his particular charm. But then, you are aware of this."

"Intimately." The sarcasm was automatic, and Thomas's voice slow and rusty. He winced at the sound of it.

Grandier turned away, and Thomas managed to lift himself a little on one elbow. Pain seized him for one sporadic moment, doubled him up, and let him go, leaving him breathless. His fingers found the small web of tight white scar tissue about five inches below his heart. That was all that was left of the puncture wound where the blade had entered, but his body remembered its presence all too well.

When he looked up, Grandier was watching him with a puzzled frown. "You are fortunate," Grandier said. "He could have injured you in a way less easily remedied."

Thomas took a deep breath, but the pain didn't return. The stab wound in his arm had stopped its insistent ache as well. He said, "You don't think he knew that?"

Grandier shook his head. "He was angry because I did not allow you to die."

"He was angry because you were so calm about it. Before he did it he was very careful to tell me how you healed his arm after I shot him."

Grandier hesitated a moment, eyes thoughtful. Then he said, "A valuable insight."

He sent Dontane to contact Denzil for him, Thomas thought. That had undoubtedly gone well for Denzil. *Might as well send sheep to bargain with wolves.* Grandier had crossed the room to a round table that held a number of jars and bottles, probably apothecary powders. He was tightening the stoppers and putting them back into a leather case. Thomas wanted to ask why Grand-

ier wanted him alive, but he suspected he would find that out anyway in a moment or two. He wished the damned Bisran priest who had heard Grandier's
confession in prison had asked for more specifics about the shape-changing
magic. How a potential victim could escape it, for example. But there was one
thing he wanted to know regardless of what happened to him next, and he
asked, "How did Ravenna die?"

Grandier paused, without turning, and said, "Evadne and a band of fay had
trapped her in the tower at Bel Garde, and attempted to exchange her for Roland. She fired a powder magazine Denzil had hidden there, killing Evadne
and the others. A few fay who had clung to the outside of the tower survived;
I had the story from them."

*Firing a powder magazine. God, woman, did you think about what you were
doing to yourself?* No, probably not, even if she could have considered it as
anything other than a means to an end. She would have given her own life the
same weight as anyone else's, done her best, and then proceeded on her course
with style. *Oh, but the bastards must have been surprised.*

When he looked back, Grandier was watching him thoughtfully. "You wondered why I felt the need to show you the Dark Host."

"Yes."

"It was not intended as a threat. It was a test."

A test I failed, Thomas thought suddenly.

"There was no light in that cellar," Grandier continued. "Or no light visible
to mortal eyes. The men with us heard strange cries and laughter, and caught
brief glimpses of foul things darting out of a wall of darkness. I could see the
Host, as could Dontane, because we have been touched by their power. How
was it that you saw them?"

Coming out of a wall of darkness, like the attack in the Old Hall. Wary,
Thomas answered, "If you knew enough to perform the test, then you must
already have a theory."

"She took you to Knockma, didn't she?"

Thomas said nothing. Kade's Fayre kingdom had been like an island of
calm reality in the midst of a nightmare. It had been easy to forget that the
pact he had made with her there would have an effect in the violent whirlwind
of the present.

Grandier said, "The change is noticeable, to those who know what to look
for. Perhaps even to those who don't. But she did more than take you there, I
think. She has opened the Otherworld to you."

"And what does that mean to you?"

"I could use your help. With the Duke of Alsene, for one example. As you have pointed out, my understanding of the way his mind works is woefully incomplete." Grandier closed the leather case and leaned back against the table. "Ravenna is gone, and Roland is alone. Even if you could free yourself and reach him, he wouldn't listen to you, not about Denzil's involvement. Those who might have organized resistance to the Duke's bid for power are either dead, scattered, or will not learn of it in time." He shrugged. "I agree with you. Denzil is dangerous, unamenable to my influence, and too clever to control. It will be a battle to make him carry out my wishes, at least until I no longer need him. You could help me win that battle."

Thomas's first impulse was to play for time. He knew what a flat refusal to cooperate might get him, and he wasn't willing to give up yet. He asked, "What about Kade?"

"She can no longer enter the palace, as I have turned the wards against her, but I spoke to her some time ago through the ring in the Grand Gallery. She is somewhat angry with me."

"You've tried to kill her at least twice."

"And was unsuccessful. You helped her in the Old Hall, and she handled my golem herself without much trouble." Grandier smiled a little, almost in pride, as if he'd been the one to teach her and not Dubell.

And Thomas thought, *I wonder if sometimes he thinks he is Galen Dubell . . .*

But the smile faded and Grandier said slowly, "He would never talk about her—how much he had taught her, what fay powers she had, where she was likely to be . . . He kept all her secrets, even at the end, when he became confused and told me what I needed to know about the palace wards."

Thomas thought of Dubell, who had been so trusting despite his occasionally acerbic wit. He had known him only through the faulty mirror of Grandier's imposture. But that imposture had fooled Kade, who had known the old man better than anyone, so much of it must have been accurate. He said, "Is that how you do it? Get someone's confidence, earn their trust, learn their secrets, and gradually draw every scrap of information out of them until there's nothing useful left?"

"Yes, in a way. It is a domination of the personality."

"You sound like Denzil."

"Perhaps I do."

"Don't pretend to delude yourself," Thomas said, too angry to stop the words, to play the game safely. "You're not like Denzil; you're not blinded by self-absorption or maddened by what the Bisran priests did to you, however much you'd like us to think so. You've calmly made the decision to take your revenge this way, and you're aware of exactly how much pain you're causing."

"Perhaps that is a sin of which we are all guilty—we sane men who participate in insanity for reasons of our own." Grandier was silent for a moment, then he said, "But you are wrong about my intentions. I do not mean to take you as I took Dubell. Your cooperation is more valuable to me than your body, for the moment. I don't suppose you will care to give me an answer yet. But I suggest you come to a decision soon."

———

Different troopers brought Thomas back to the makeshift cell and replaced his manacles. Aviler was still there, still relatively unhurt, except for the lines of strain and fatigue on his face, briefly visible in the light of the guard's lamp.

When they had gone, Aviler asked, "What happened?"

Thomas leaned back against the wall. On the walk back, he had discovered that the only wound that hadn't yielded to Grandier's unwanted healing had been the hole the elf-shot had left in his leg. He said, "I was offered a place in Grandier's glorious revolution."

Aviler considered that, then asked softly, "And where did all the blood come from?"

"Denzil stabbed me, and Grandier took care of the damage. Denzil intends to repeat the performance later. I could see him thinking it." Thomas looked away, glad of the darkness in the cold little room. He hadn't meant to say quite that much.

Aviler was silent for a time. Thomas wondered if he was thinking about the document he was supposed to sign. Then Aviler said, "An interesting demonstration of the consequences of refusal. What answer did you give Grandier?"

"I didn't give him any answer. It's called stalling for time."

"I see."

———

Kade sat down hard on Knockma's thick grass. She hoped the entire Host had flung itself into the ring after her, but she knew better than that. She had connected one cardinal point of the ring to the other, and any of the fay who followed her into it would find themselves caught in the ring's maelstrom, flung around and around until the connection broke, which it would do fairly soon. Rings were difficult to tamper with at best, and always sought to return to their original state.

Boliver was still waiting for her. He had settled on the grass outside the circle of menhirs and was smoking a white clay pipe. "No more than an hour," he said, answering her unspoken question. "Did you discover anything useful?"

Kade stood and stepped out of the ring so she could think without it singing in her ears. "Yes, but I made a mistake. I shouldn't have gone." She sat beside him and put her head in her hands. "Grandier was waiting for me. He knows that I— He told me Thomas is alive, and that I am to stay out of the way." She felt her mouth twist into a sneer. "He knows it will be difficult for me."

"Yes, you made a grand cock-up," Boliver agreed.

She rubbed her eyes and said sourly, "Your confidence in me is overwhelming."

Boliver sighed. "Is your Thomas that important to you, then? Has he said anything of the kind to you?"

She looked up and saw he was watching her gravely. She stilled the quick flare of anger. "Yes, he is important to me. And if he's dead I'll never know what he thinks about me." *And I wouldn't care if he hated me as long as I knew he was alive somewhere . . .*

"Then stop rushing about like a daft-headed chicken and do something," Boliver said suddenly, scattering her thoughts.

"I am not rushing about like a daft-headed anything," she said through gritted teeth.

He pointed the pipe at her. "Oh, you're not weeping or fainting, but you're running about in circles, letting this damned human wizard point you any way he wants you."

"I am not—"

"By Puck's pointed ears, woman, you're the Queen of Air and Darkness. Act like it!"

Kade was on her feet and Boliver was scrambling for cover when it occurred to her that Thomas had said much the same thing to her. He had said it on that cool rainy night on the loggia, when they had listened to Denzil twist Roland's friendship into slavery.

She supposed she should feel like dying. What she felt was a cold numbness centering around her heart, as if she were already dead. Kade turned away and started to cross the field toward the castle. Reaching the edge of the garden, she climbed the steps and entered her turret workroom. She stood for a moment in the quiet with the sweet smell of herbs and flowers. Then she saw that the bowl on the table was glowing softly. It was the spell she had tried to make to reveal the location of the keystone. She had forgotten it.

Holding her breath, Kade went to the table. The water at the bottom of the bowl had formed an image: a hazy translucent image of a room. And she recognized the room.

"Gods above and below take that canny old bastard," she whispered, almost reverently. "It was there all the time."

Then she had an idea.

CHAPTER SEVENTEEN

THE SUN WAS shining here, too.

Kade and Boliver stood in an open court, bordered on all sides by a low wall and a sheer drop to the sea. The wide blue vault of the sky stretched over them, and the stiff breeze had the tang of salt and dead fish. Kade went to the edge of the ring, which resisted her for a moment before she stepped free of it. The power swelling it had almost the same force as the Knockma Ring, but it was far more turbulent. But then, this ring saw a great deal more use.

She went to the wall and looked down. They were atop a pillar of rock that stood a hundred yards or so above the sea that tore at its base. Leaning out, she could see the stairs that climbed it, leading up from a bare stone dock, and the stern of the fantastically painted ship that was moored there.

On the opposite side of the court, two identical fay with golden skin, red-pupiled eyes, and long amber hair guarded an archway twined with carved oak leaves leading to a narrow delicate bridge. It led from their pillar over the channel of gray-green churning water to the cliff tops of a rocky section of coast. A massive structure grew out of the end of the bridge, with heavy octagonal towers the warm brown of sandstone from the faraway deserts of Parscia. Squinting at it in the afternoon sunlight, Kade saw that light glittered off it at regular points, as if it were adorned with a pattern of jewels, or small round windows. She looked back at Boliver, who watched the bridge guards warily and was cleaning out his pipe onto the immaculate flagstones. "This is the place."

She went up to the guards, who were dressed in cloth of gold and glittering gems and armed with slender swords of silver. They were both watching Kade and Boliver with disinterested amusement, and one said, "Your name and your errand, fair lady, before you pass."

The words "fair lady" had no doubt been applied facetiously. She answered, "I'm Kade Carrion, the Queen of Air and Darkness, and I'm here to see Oberon."

The two exchanged an opaque glance that might have concealed more amusement, or surprise, and the other said, "Then pass gladly, lady."

She walked down the bridge, Boliver padding behind her. Ahead they could see two large wooden doors surrounded by stonework carved into waves and bubbling seafoam. Closer, and the sun brought out the faint tint of rose in the brown stone; closer still, and she saw that the small round windows that studded the tower were not windows but eyes, with dark iris and blue pupil, and that some were watching them, others staring off to sea.

Boliver stage-whispered, "We're being watched!"

Not in the mood for jokes, Kade ignored him.

Another fay guard, identical to the two at the bridge except for the graceful amber-glazed wings on his back, pulled open one of the heavy doors for them.

Inside was a high stone gallery, floored with white tile, airy and cool. They went down it and into the perfect silence of the place. Corridors branched off at intervals, but they might have been the only living creatures inside.

Thinking over what she had to do—what she was forced to do—Kade was conscious of a curious numbness that might be shock. She was beginning to recognize it as the feeling of anger taken to such a level it was no longer possible to separate it from any other emotion or thought. In a way, it was a liberating sensation. The attitude of the fay guards, or what she suspected was their attitude, would have bothered her very much under any other circumstances; now it seemed the most minor of considerations. Anger this intense defined everything into the goal, and the obstacles that must be overcome to reach the goal, and it would make it very easy to make the decisions to dispose of those obstacles.

It was probably quite close to how Urbain Grandier felt when the Bisran Inquisition had finished with him.

As they neared the end of the hall, they could hear a thread of harp music, and voices and laughter.

"We're going to be roasted," Boliver said, with gloomy relish. "And eaten."

"Stop sniveling," Kade muttered. Boliver had driven her out of her despair with arguments that she should do something constructive; now that she had embarked on a plan, he was arguing against it. Typical fay perversity.

The hall made an abrupt turn, and stairs spilled down into a large roofless court that must be at or near the center of the fortress. More of the amber-skinned guards lined the porticoes, lazy but watchful, armed with gold-bladed pikes.

Most of the Seelie Court was gathered here.

Lake maidens dripped water and glamour from their gowns like pearls. Beautiful ladies wore clothes of flowers, gossamer spangled with dew, silvery gauze, or were covered only by their long hair. There were men of the same ethereal beauty as the guards, in more flowers, or velvets, fine lace, and gold-shot brocade. Here and there a wing as delicate as a butterfly's and more beautifully hued rose above the crowd. The bright sunlight in the open court made so much glamour the air glowed, and a troupe of gaily dressed fay tumblers performed feats impossible for humans. Most of those here were shape-changers.

Kade went down the steps and through the crowd.

They parted for her. There was no stink of unwashed flesh under the perfumes, as there would be in any human gathering. Her faded and dirty smock, her dragging petticoat lace, her page boy's boots, were violently out of place here, and she caught many sidelong glances. She could have used glamour to make herself more pleasing to the eye; several here had done so. But she didn't need to be told that that would have been a mistake.

Titania lay on a leopard-skin couch under a canopy of ostrich feathers, cool shade under the bright light. A small woman, smaller than Kade, the fayre queen wore a mantua heavily laden with pearls and silver embroidery, and her hair was the color of gold, true gold, and her features were much more beautiful than even Queen Falaise's. But Falaise's face had been touched by fear, worry, and care, and Titania's was as perfect as a carved goddess's; Kade suddenly preferred Falaise, for all that lady's wavering will.

Two fay pages with the appearance of fair young boys waited on the fayre queen, one holding a wine carafe, the other her fan. They watched Kade with matched expressions of sly mockery. But seated at her feet was a human boy with warm brown skin and dark curly hair, whose gaze remained locked on the tumblers.

Kade did not curtsey to Titania. She was a queen here in her own right.

Titania's shrewd sapphire eyes considered her. She held a silver wine goblet beaded with moisture, and ran a thoughtful finger over the rim. "Oberon is not here, my sister." Her voice was like harp strings stirred by the wind.

"But you are." A few days ago Kade would have replied *I am not your sister*, but she couldn't afford to be driven now.

Titania laughed. "And what have you come for?"

"A favor." Kade looked down at the human boy, and when his brown eyes met hers curiously, she asked him, "Do you want to go home?" The magic in this place was such that she couldn't rescue him unless he consented to leave.

There was an almost soundless gasp from the assembled fay, the music ceasing and the tumblers staggering to a halt.

The boy smiled and shook his head. "No, lady," he said into the silence. His voice was a little husky, but still a child's.

Kade looked back at Titania, who smiled. "I love him," the queen of fayre said.

"The sad thing is," Kade found herself replying, "you probably do."

Titania shook her golden head in irritation and set the goblet down on a low jade table. "You always ruin our pastimes, Kade."

"Good." Kade paced a few idle steps away from the bower, to avoid showing her rabid impatience, to keep Titania from knowing how every passing moment grated. She saw the smaller sprites at the edge of the crowd back hastily away. She was hardly surprised; she probably looked like she should be standing over a battlefield piled with corpses with a raven on one shoulder. She had been right not to try to put on a pleasing appearance with glamour; that would have been catering to their whims. She looked like herself, fey and eldritch even in this company.

Watching her with perfect brows lifted archly, Titania said, "I only tolerate your interference because of my affection for your mother."

Words, no sentiment. Copied from some human. Kade smiled at her feet. She couldn't think why she had ever feared Moire, or Titania, when she had spent much of her early life sparring with Ravenna, who could have effortlessly handled both fay queens were she completely incapacitated. Kade said, "*I* am the Queen of Air and Darkness."

Titania accepted a fan from her page and drew the delicate ivory construction through her fingers. "You do not know what that means."

"Someday I'll find out." Kade looked up and smiled. "And here you will be."

"And what must I do about that?"

"Make me happy."

Titania laughed again, this time in genuine amusement. Or at least genuine for her. She waved the two fay pages away, but let the human boy remain. "What do you want?"

Kade sensed the crowd behind her begin to relax. The clear note of a harp sounded, and the jugglers began to perform again. The boy's eyes strayed in their direction. Boliver was around somewhere; she could smell his pipe. "The first, the power to shape-change."

"Ah." Titania must know every movement of the Unseelie Court, and she did not ask why. "Best tell me what else you want, for I cannot give you that."

"You mean, you won't give me that."

Titania's perfect brow creased in annoyance. "I am not a fool; I can't hand you that much power."

Kade knew it would come to this. "What if I were to offer you a power in return?"

Titania shook her head, consideringly. "You are very desperate."

"Yes. And I am very dangerous, when I am very desperate." That was as close to a threat as she wanted to come. Threats she did not have time to make good on. Kade was at a severe disadvantage. All she had was bluff and Titania's greed.

"What would you offer?"

Kade felt as if she were about to step off a precipice. After this, there was no going back. She took a deep breath, and jumped. "Knockma." Somewhere in the crowd, she heard a thump: Boliver hitting the floor. He had known what she meant to do, but his sense of the dramatic had gotten the better of him.

Titania stared, honestly shocked. Kade waited, forcing herself to smile lightly. Then Titania shook her head, her expression of honest consternation making her look more human, and, Kade thought, more beautiful. "I cannot do it, not even for so great a prize. I cannot give you that much power."

Kade sighed. *I know. If I were you I wouldn't do it either. But I was hoping you'd be too blinded by greed to care. So forget the first plan and try the second.* With Knockma dangling before her like a diamond in the sun, Titania would break down eventually. "We can bargain."

Titania tapped her fan on the fur couch, watching her. "Bargain. Very well. But why are you doing this?"

Kade smiled and met Titania's eyes. "For love." The queen of fayre looked frankly disbelieving, but the human boy grinned up at Kade.

———

Kade met an anxious Boliver at the portico above the court. "How went it?" he asked, nervously hopping from foot to foot.

"Not as good as I hoped; not as bad as I feared." Out of her pocket, she drew one of the concessions she had wrested from the fayre queen. It looked like a well-crafted glass ball, only a few bubbles marring its perfection. Boliver peered at it closely, and she turned it in the light to show the lines of fire glowing ghostlike within. "It will turn a shape-changed being back to its original form." She pocketed the powerful little construction carefully, and they started up the hall toward the entrance.

"Is that all? What will you if it doesn't do its work?"

"What will I? I'll die, that's what will I. Gods below, Boliver, don't ask me these questions at a time like this." Kade had hoped to get the power to shape-change at will from Titania, hoped to get it without having to kill people right and left as Grandier did, but the fayre queen had refused her and she would just have to do it the hard way. *It's the only way to get anything done lately.*

"I'm sorry, lass. But one transformation is not much. And you'll need that to get in. You'll be going against all the Host."

"Yes." She hated to lose Knockma, but it was a tie to the past, to her mother, and to the Seelie Court and all their wrangling. And if the Host did cross into Knockma, she would never be able to defend it and find Thomas at the same time. Titania would defend it now, with every resource at her disposal, and the Unseelie Court would never have it.

It was also the only home she had ever had. Besides the palace, and that had been taken away. But Knockma had not been taken away, she had given it up, and the difference was important.

And if it would help her destroy Grandier and Denzil, then it was well given.

Kade put a hand in her pocket to touch the glass ball. No, losing Knockma she could live through. It was the next part she had doubts about.

———

Thomas had worked steadily at loosening the spike in the wall and was rewarded by feeling it begin to shift a trifle. If it wasn't his imagination; his hands were numb with cold. "Any luck?" he asked Aviler.

"No." Aviler left off his own efforts and leaned back against the wall. "I think you should accept Grandier's offer."

Thomas kept working on the spike, without answering. He supposed he should be flattered that Aviler had not automatically assumed that he would leap at any way out.

If he did . . . Grandier would not let him interfere with his plans to start a war. And once that war was started, Thomas would have no choice but to do his best to help win it. Grandier was well aware that Thomas would not be a willing participant, and Grandier had a talent for influencing people, working his way into their thoughts, bringing them unwillingly over to his side. It was how he wrested the needed information out of his victims before he killed them and took their shapes. There was the possibility that after a year or two of helping Grandier, Thomas would find that he no longer wanted to oppose him.

And then there was Denzil.

Movement out in the anteroom jolted Thomas out of his thoughts. Aviler looked up, puzzled, and they both listened. It sounded as if the troopers who were guarding them were gathering their weapons and leaving. After a long moment of silence, there was a faint shuffling sound from outside the door, and a low deep snarl.

Dontane had said he would have to think of something else. Aviler swore softly, looking around hopelessly for something to use as a weapon. Thomas gathered himself to move.

A fay appeared in the doorway, the torchlight gleaming from its jaundiced yellow skin. It was perhaps five feet tall, human shaped but with clawed hands and long powerful arms dangling almost to its knees. Its mouth had a wide evil grin revealing far too many sharply pointed teeth, its face distorted by round red eyes and a nose that was an ugly ragged hole.

It sprang at Thomas too quick for thought. He threw himself sideways as far as the chains would allow, flinging up an arm to shield his face. He felt the hard grip on his wrist, the claws tear through the leather of his sleeve, a pressure that nearly tore his arm from the socket. Then its hand came in contact with the iron manacle around his wrist and it shrieked and leapt away.

He rolled over and looked back. The fay staggered, keening in rage, its hand dripping burned flesh, the stink of it filling the room. Thomas's shoulder felt dislocated but as he tried to push himself up he realized the chains had far more slack now. The spike holding them to the wall had been pulled half out by the force of the fay's grip.

The creature turned on Aviler, snarling, and he scrambled back against the wall, swinging a loop of his chains at it. Thomas stretched and hooked the brazier with his bootheel, bringing it closer with a frantic kick and grabbing the handle. He flung the brazier at the fay's back just as it leapt again at Aviler.

The iron struck the fay and it staggered.

Thomas got to his feet and leaned his whole weight on the chain in one solid jerk. With a spray of wood chips and plaster, the spike came out of the wall.

He grabbed the spike just as the fay reached him again. Its claws sank into his shoulder and it hauled him up and almost off his feet before it felt the tip of the iron in its chest. It tried to shove him away, its other hand finding his throat. With instinct greater than sense, he grabbed its arm and fell against it, driving the iron spike through its thick skin. It fell backward, dragging him down. From the blood on his hands he knew he must have given it a killing blow, but it still had the strength to snap his neck.

Then Thomas fell against the wooden floor. The fay had vanished. He tried to sit up, looking around, braced for it to appear somewhere else. Then he saw the heavy gray dust that covered the floor, the spike, his hands, and that even the creature's blood had disappeared. It had vanished, but in death, dissolving into dust.

His buff coat had protected his shoulder, but his neck was covered with shallow scratches from its claws; he was lucky it hadn't managed to tear his throat out. Aviler started to speak and Thomas shook his head hastily. Dontane would not have sent all the guards away, only those not bribed to silence.

After another moment, Thomas managed to stand. He gathered the chains up and quietly moved along the wall to the door and stood beside it, waiting tensely. Without having to be told, Aviler slumped against the wall, trying to look like a corpse. In the dim light, and for a few moments only, it would fool someone; Thomas would not have long to move. Moments crept by, and Thomas thought impatiently, *You can't sit out there forever; you have to see what happened. Come on, damn you.* There had to be at least one man out there, to make sure that the fay had done its work. The difficulty was that the one last guard didn't have to sit out there forever, only until Dontane returned with reinforcements.

Then Thomas heard a low scuffling in the anteroom, someone cautiously approaching the door. He flattened back against the wall and stopped breathing. The swordpoint came first, and there was a hesitation; the trooper had seen the spilled and battered brazier, and Aviler's apparently lifeless form. He stepped inside, and Thomas slipped the loop of chain around his neck.

The trooper made the mistake of dropping his sword to grab onto the chain. He staggered forward, trying to slam Thomas against the wall. Thomas held on grimly, feeling the strain in his shoulder. The man fell to his knees abruptly, dragging Thomas with him. He felt something give way under the chain and the trooper collapsed. Thomas held on long enough to make sure the man was dead, then glanced back to check the anteroom. It was empty and the fire was guttering in the hearth.

He searched the trooper's corpse thoroughly and savagely, keeping one eye on the door. Besides the rapier, the trooper had a main gauche with a half-shell guard and a small dagger. He would be armed again, at least. After more searching he angrily shoved the body away. "It *would* be the one without the goddamn keys."

"What now?" Aviler asked, grimacing.

Thomas took the trooper's narrow-bladed dagger and began working at the lock of his manacle. *It's been a long time since I've done this,* he thought. After a long tense wait, the manacle gave and he shook it off and started on the other.

The chains holding Aviler were of a slightly different make and took longer to open. After Thomas had worked over the first one for some time unsuccessfully, Aviler said grimly, "It's not working. Get out of here before they come back."

"I," Thomas said through gritted teeth, "do not have time for theatrics."

Aviler stiffened, but didn't voice any more objections.

The manacles came free finally, and Aviler got to his feet in relief.

Thomas slipped the plain leather baldric of the trooper's rapier over his head and handed Aviler the main gauche. They passed through the anteroom quickly, hesitating only to make sure the troopers had left behind no other weapons.

As Thomas stepped out the doorway onto the landing, he knew he had made a mistake. He heard Aviler gasp an incoherent warning and Thomas dove forward, rolling. This didn't help any of his various bruises and when he came to his feet, he staggered. But Aviler struggled with the trooper who had waited for them beside the door. As Thomas reached them, Aviler managed to plunge the main gauche up into the other man's rib cage. The soldier collapsed with a choked-off gasp and Thomas and Aviler rolled the body back into the anteroom. Breathing hard, Aviler explained, "He moved just as you went out and I saw him. Was he there all along?"

"No, he could have easily taken me when I was strangling the other one. Probably came looking for him when he didn't come back for the others." Thomas cast a look back to check the landing, which stretched quietly into darkness in either direction, doorways leading off it and the staircase opening directly in front of them.

Aviler stripped off the soldier's baldric and tossed the extra main gauche to Thomas. The High Minister slung the baldric over his shoulder and picked up the trooper's fallen rapier. Something that jingled as it hit the floor fell from the trooper's baldric and Aviler nudged it with a boot. "This was the one with the keys," he said, with an ironic lift of an eyebrow.

Thomas snorted. "My luck."

They stepped out onto the landing. Hesitating a moment to get his bearings, Thomas saw the bob of lamplight on the stair below. "This way," he said, and led Aviler down to another doorway. It opened onto a progression of rooms that, if Thomas was where he thought he was, would eventually give onto another staircase. The rooms were as dark as the pit, but they had been meant to be viewed as a set, so the doors were all in the same position on the left-hand side of the hearths and were unblocked by furniture, making it relatively easy to cross them even in almost complete darkness. They had made it through the third room when they heard a shout of alarm and running footsteps from the landing.

They stopped to listen, but no one came in their direction. Aviler whispered, "I don't suppose they're going to think that thing ate both of us, killed the two guards, then wandered off."

Thomas smiled grimly. "They could try to tell Denzil that, but I don't think it would be very well received."

They came to the last room, and through its open door, Thomas could see the landing of the other stairwell, lit wanly by one candle in the silver and rock-crystal chandelier hanging above it. Across the threshold was the body of a young woman, the gray and brown of her skirts marking her as a servant. Thomas stepped over her without bothering to pause. He was growing used to seeing dead women and had stopped looking for familiar faces; since it was likely he would be killed at any moment himself, it hardly seemed to matter. After a moment, he heard Aviler follow him.

Just as they came out onto the landing, the muffled explosion of a pistol shot destroyed the silence. They both instinctively dove for the stairs. They reached the landing below and cut through another dark suite back the way they had come. The first room was unlit and crowded with dark shapes of furniture. Soldiers pounded down the stair behind them and Thomas could not find the doorway. He stumbled on a low table, then turned and put his back against the wall. The men coming after them would have oil lamps, and the light would be momentarily blinding. Then there was a muffled thump and Aviler gasped in pain, then said harshly, "Over here, a door."

Thomas made his way toward Aviler's voice and found the edge of a narrow door. Aviler whispered, "It's a servants' stair." He climbed down a few steps, and Thomas stepped inside, closing the door after them.

In the unfamiliar room, it was doubtful the Alsene troopers would find the stair, which had a door meant to blend into the paneling, but Thomas didn't breathe easily until he heard them clatter through the room, cursing and knocking things over, then retreat. After some moments of silence he said lightly, "I won't comment on your clumsiness since it saved our lives."

"Someone else wasn't so lucky," Aviler replied out of the dark. "There's a body down here."

Yes, there would be fay roaming here. *This is not going to get any easier,* Thomas thought, straightening up and feeling for the wall to guide him down.

"He didn't come down here without a lamp," Aviler was muttering. Before Thomas could point out that he might very well have, Aviler said, "Yes, here it is."

After more fumbling, Aviler found the man's tinderbox and managed to light the lamp. "Good God," he said softly, standing up and looking down in disgust at the corpse the wan light revealed. "What could have done that to his head . . . ? No, don't speculate; I'd rather be surprised."

They heard footsteps in the rooms overhead and voices from below, and moved a few steps down the narrow stairs. But the door with its heavy covering of carved paneling and flocked paper cut much of the noise from outside.

Aviler looked around, lifting the lamp high. The original stone of the wall was to one side, radiating cold like a block of ice, and the wooden bones of the lath and plaster facing to the other. The air was stuffy and thick with dust. This was technically a servants' passage, though it had probably been installed more with an eye to moving about quickly and unobtrusively in the event of a palace coup. The years before the reign of Ravenna's father had not been calm or untroubled.

"We're on the west side of the Old Palace," Aviler said quietly. "We could get out through the siege wall into the Old Courts. . . ."

Thomas sheathed the rapier and drew the shorter main gauche, which would be more effective in these close surroundings. "If we can get there. The King's Bastion is probably still sealed off from the other side. Most of the troops are quartered right below us." He took a soft step down the narrow stairs, careful of the creaking boards that would betray their presence.

The bogle dropped from above. It landed on Aviler, knocking him forward. He dropped the candlelamp and the flame guttered wildly, threatening to leave them in darkness. Aviler stumbled into Thomas, who caught himself against the wall. He turned, getting a grip on the thing's greasy skin below its neck and dragging it off the other man. It turned on him swiftly, claws flailing, and he stabbed it with the main gauche. It dropped and he saw that Aviler had gotten it from behind with their late guard's dagger. It struggled wildly on the steps, its claws scrabbling on the wood, a random swipe of one long arm sending Thomas staggering back into the wall. Then it froze into immobility.

They stared at one another, breathing hard, then Aviler wiped the blood from the scratches on his forehead. He said softly, "That was rather a noisy episode. Do you think anyone heard?"

After listening for a moment, Thomas shook his head. "No, they'd be hacking through the wall by now." He leaned back against the stone, considering their options. They would have to make for one of the rooms along the outside wall. And they could go no lower than this floor: the levels below had no windows. And what was Kade doing now? That she was planning something he had no doubt. Fortunately, Grandier would have as little chance to guess what it was as he had. Kade made her strategy on the run, which was poor planning in a chess game, but in real life tended to make opponents waste time bumbling around wondering what in hell she was thinking. The only problem was her inclination to the dramatic. Would Grandier consider that?

He looked up to find Aviler watching him narrowly. At his look of inquiry Aviler said, "You haven't yet pointed out that I was wrong about Denzil and you were right."

Thomas said dryly, "I thought the consequences so obvious that calling further attention to it was unnecessary."

Aviler snorted and shook his head. "Even though you've saved my life, I can't seem to bring myself to like you."

"That's probably just as well." Thomas was thinking of ways to rooms with outside windows, and that the nearest could only be reached by using this wall passage to travel directly through the part of the palace Denzil had made his stronghold. *And why not? They won't be searching for us there. And there's less chance of running into more fay.* There was also another possibility in that direction to be explored. "Did you know about the spyhole near the third-floor council chambers?"

Aviler's eyes widened. "No, I did not."

"Denzil doesn't either. When Dontane took me to those chambers, they had their maps laid out, so it must be where they plan their troop movements, at the very least."

He could tell the notion appealed to Aviler. "You think it would be worth it, for what we might hear?"

"Perhaps not, but it is on our way."

———

There were voices coming from the direction of the faint glow of light. "Why you?"

It's my plan, Thomas started to say. Instead, he put a properly sardonic note in his voice and said, "Another noble impulse? You're the only one who has a chance of convincing Roland of any of this; don't you consider that a little more important than your pride?"

They were crouched in the narrow darkened wall passage, beside a gap in the baseboard just large enough for an agile spy. But someone had been through this servants' passage at some point strewing the floor with iron filings, so they couldn't afford to waste time here. The hole in the baseboard had an extra helping of iron sprinkled around it, but there was no sign that its real purpose had been discovered.

Aviler glared, and gestured reluctantly. "All right, damn you." As Thomas bent to scramble under the lintel, Aviler added, "Eventually that little tactic is going to fail, then what will you do?"

Thomas grinned to himself. "Hit you over the head."

From inside the cramped spyhole, he could see the gap carefully cut into the planks below the wall, leading into a narrow crawl space below the first council room. They were there, right enough. He recognized Dontane's voice, but it was impossible to distinguish individual words. He would have to try to get over to the next room.

The crawl space was perhaps two feet high, the bottom made of planks supported by the thick wooden rafters of the room below, lit by soft candlelight finding its way through the cracks in the floorboards above. On the far side, where the wall of the second council room had been erected, another hole had been torn in the baseboards, allowing access to the crawl space below the next room. That was where the voices were coming from. *Well, it would be,* Thomas thought. He sat back, pulling off and laying aside the baldric and rapier, which would be far more trouble than it was worth in the narrow space. He hesitated over the main gauche, which would be equally unhandy at his back where it could catch on things or in the front of his sash poking him determinedly in the stomach. He settled for wedging it down into his boot, though he knew if he encountered anything more hostile than a rat, he was a dead man.

He worked his way slowly across the crawl space, trying to keep from choking on the dust, gasping in pain when his bruised ribs encountered the sharp corners of a rafter.

About halfway across, something sharp bit through the leather of his glove and he jerked his hand back. It was only a nail loose on the planks. Then he took a closer look and saw the boards of the crawl space were sprinkled with them. They must have fallen down through the cracks from above. Denzil did not trust his fay allies at all.

Thomas edged closer to the gap. The voices were distinctly louder here. And louder. *Damn them,* he thought, *they're coming in here.* There was no time to move as a door squeaked open nearly overhead. He froze as heavy footsteps sounded on the floorboards of the room above and Denzil's voice said, "God, you're such a fool."

"I didn't have to tell you," Dontane replied, his tone surly.

You prick, you've been so splendidly stupid, why did you have to ruin it by thinking? Thomas had counted on Dontane being fool enough to try to hide their escape from Denzil as well as from Grandier.

"You did if you wanted to live. You idiot, I would have gotten rid of him in time." Footsteps paced overhead, a long winter cloak brushed the floor. Thomas winced as Denzil came to stand by a dark area that must be a cabinet or other large piece of furniture, the Duke's boots almost directly over his hiding place. He was cramped and his shoulders were aching, but he dared not shift his position.

"They can't escape," Dontane protested.

"Of course they can. Boniface knows the palace very well; he's been spying on everyone in it for years."

"I'm not a fool, damn you, I was—"

"It doesn't matter, not at this point." There was a hesitation, then Denzil asked softly, "What position do you want when I take the throne? Court Sorcerer?"

Ah. I should have known Denzil would contrive to sell everyone to everyone else, Thomas thought. *He's lured Dontane away from Grandier, that was why our mercenary friend was so afraid.*

"Will the nobles accept me?" Dontane spoke slowly, diverted by visions of the future.

"They will if I order it."

They might at that. Anything to keep Denzil away from home and family.

The door opened again, and a young man's voice, shy with hero worship, said, "My lord, there's a message."

"Thank you." Denzil's voice warmed, probably out of habit. He would keep no one close to him who was not his absolute slave. How it must gall him that Grandier remained his own man. Dontane had probably been an easy conquest.

Paper crackled, then with a smile in his voice, Denzil said, "Villon has reached Bel Garde."

Thomas caught his breath.

"No." Dontane sounded horror-stricken. "The cavalry—"

"The siege engine cavalry," Denzil corrected gently.

"How could he get here so quickly?"

"If the messages went to the Granges yesterday, if Villon left his Train of Ordnance behind and traveled through the night, it could be done easily."

"Without Grandier's help I couldn't possibly hold him off."

"Yes, if Evadne hadn't failed I'd have Roland by now." Denzil was silent, possibly calculating the time as Thomas was. It would have been impossible to conceal the cavalry's movement up the plain to Bel Garde; they would have been spotted easily from the city wall. But it would have taken time to send the message through the dangerous snow-choked streets. And Villon was a cautious general, preferring maneuver and siegecraft to pitched battle. He had taken Bel Garde as a base from which to stage his attack.

Denzil said, "It's unfortunate. If I can't keep Bisra from attacking us in what they will perceive as our weakness, Lord General Villon would be useful. But he won't deal with me. I hope he has more amenable officers. You'll have to send the Host against him."

"Grandier won't allow it. He's counting on Villon to help lead the attack against Bisra."

"And counting on me to convince Villon to support my claim to the throne. But I can't . . . I won't do that. He is an old friend of Ravenna's, you see."

Denzil was not going to allow a war with Bisra. He wouldn't want a kingdom locked in struggle, war torn and poor. And he really didn't need a war to put him on the throne; he only needed the threat of it. *He's going to hold Bisra off somehow. If he can. If he gets past Grandier,* Thomas thought.

"I want you to speak to your friends in the Host and persuade them to attack Villon tonight," Denzil said.

"I'll go now, but—"

"Don't go now; wait until dusk. I don't want Grandier to learn of it. We can scarcely ask him to arrange the cloud cover for us, so they will have to wait until dark anyway." Footsteps crossed the floor to pause near Dontane. "Take care. Everything depends on you."

Does it? Thomas thought. *Does it really?*

He heard them move toward the door. As soon as it closed he rolled away from his painful position over the rafter and began to work his way back toward the hole in the baseboard, half-formed plans turning in his head. He had almost reached it when there was the thump of a chair pushed aside, hurried steps crossed the floor, and the door banged open.

Thomas swore and scrambled through the opening into the spyhole. Dontane and Denzil had departed, but he had never heard the messenger boy leave. He grabbed up his sword and baldric and ducked under the lintel back into the passage.

"Well?" Aviler demanded.

"Move. Someone heard me."

They made their way through the twists and turns of the passage and up a narrow flight of rickety stairs. "Villon's reached Bel Garde," Thomas said.

"Thank God. The court got through."

"It's not over yet. Denzil's sending the Host against him tonight—despite Grandier's orders to the contrary. Villon will have to be warned."

They came to a door with a thin line of chill daylight leaking under it. Thomas listened at it, then carefully prized it open. It was a long formal dining room lit by slanting gray morning sunlight from tall windows opening onto a portico. It was undisturbed except for a little snow that had blown in through a window left carelessly open; the scene had the strange still quality of a painting.

Thomas crossed the room and opened the window further, stepping out onto the portico. The tiled floor was heavily laden with ice, and he held carefully to the light railing and looked out on a view of the garden courts and the siege wall, the bastion rising up beyond. To the north was the open land of the park, and cut off from sight by the side of the Gallery Wing would be the Postern Gate. The ground was two stories down from the bottom of the portico. He stepped back through the window to lift a heavy velvet drapery cord. "Think you could make it?"

Aviler nodded. "Of course."

They started to tear down the drapes, pulling loose the cords and discarding the ones that had gotten wet from the open window and had stiffened with ice.

Aviler tied off a section and tested it, then said, "We can secure it to the table. It's heavy enough to support a dozen men, so—"

"It won't have to. Just you. I'm staying here."

Aviler frowned at him. "What do you mean?"

Thomas tied off two cords and reached for another. "There's barely enough time for you to make it across the city to Bel Garde by nightfall on a good day. I'm going to try to stop them here."

Aviler looked incredulous. "How?"

"I don't know," Thomas snapped. He didn't want to give Aviler the chance to talk him out of this. He controlled himself with effort and said more calmly, "Apparently Dontane's the only one who can talk to the Host besides Grandier. If I can stop him—"

"That would help immeasurably, of course, but Villon is hardly going to be unprepared for an attack by night. That he's here now means he knows what's happened. He will realize the danger."

"And with Ravenna dead you're the only one who knows for certain that Denzil is a danger. Even if the attack on Villon fails, all Denzil has to do is ride up to Bel Garde tomorrow and ask to speak to Roland alone."

Aviler hesitated. Thomas could see him turning over that image and not liking what he saw. But Aviler shook his head. "Outright assassination would hardly serve his purpose—"

"It wouldn't have to be that. But it's hardly politic to allow the man who's near destroyed a city so he can usurp the throne unlimited access to the King."

"All right, all right." Aviler shook his head impatiently. "I'll go on. But I think you're only going to succeed in killing yourself."

"Probably," Thomas admitted.

They finished the makeshift rope and tied it off, and Thomas told Aviler the way over the canal and through the Postern Gate that he and Kade had used.

They secured the rope to the table, and with Thomas to hold it steady, Aviler started to climb. The High Minister disappeared over the portico with no more than a whispered "Good luck" and Thomas was grateful, loath to countenance any attempt at sentimentality at this point. When Aviler had reached the snowy ground and vanished into the shelter of the garden walls and frozen hedges below, Thomas pulled the makeshift rope up and bundled it into the bottom cabinet of one of the sideboards. With luck the tangled draperies would look like an aborted attempt at looting. He closed the window and slipped quietly out of the room.

CHAPTER EIGHTEEN

ROLAND COULD NOT stop shivering. He sat near the fire in a window-less interior chamber at Bel Garde. A salon meant for entertaining, its walls were softened by cloth-of-gold draperies and the overmantel and borders delicately painted with black grotesques on gilt backgrounds. Fretfully looking around the room, Roland's eyes lit on a silver-and-gold-filigreed perfume burner he had given Denzil some months ago, and it occurred to Roland just how isolated he had become from the others in his court. He had no other close confidant or advisor but Denzil; most of those who had surrounded him were his cousin's companions, not his, and he had no wish to see any of them.

Lord General Villon had arrived with his men not long ago, and the walls of the little fortress had almost trembled from the cheers of the other guards. After Ravenna's death their situation had seemed hopeless, and now for the first time there was a chance for revenge and victory. Roland had been just as glad as the others to see them, but he was nervous of Villon, knowing the General's opinion of him was not a high one. And having to greet the old warrior with news of the Dowager Queen's death . . .

Behind Roland, in the center of the room, Villon and his officers, their cloaks still steaming from melting snow, met with Renier and the Queen's Guard lieutenant who had brought Falaise. They were talking intently, pointing to the maps laid out on the round table, making some plan. Roland had no wish to join in their council. They all thought him a coward, or a fool, and perhaps they were right.

A new voice made Roland look up, and he saw that Elaine had been brought in again. The hem of her skirt was torn and dirty, and her face was a pale oval in the candlelight. Her only companion was an Albon knight standing at her elbow as if she were a prisoner, and Roland wondered if she had been left to sit in some cold anteroom, without even a maid to accompany her. Such treatment suddenly reminded him of one of Fulstan's subtler tricks, when Roland had been left alone in a bare room to contemplate his fate for hours, only to discover later that the King had left the palace and that there would be no punishment after all.

"Hasn't anyone even sent for a lady to care for her?" Roland interrupted. All heads turned toward him, and he wished they would stop looking at him as if he were mad, or had just grown an extra limb. "God, just let her alone. Your damned questions are worthless."

"At once, m'lord," someone said. Roland found himself meeting General Villon's expressionless gaze and quickly looked away. Elaine still stood shivering in the center of the room and he motioned her to come over by the fire. She came obediently, taking a low cushioned stool near his chair, moving stiffly as if the cold and shock had solidified her muscles. Roland felt more at ease in her presence. Here, at least, was someone who knew he could not have disobeyed his mother's order, who did not think him a coward. If he had stayed in the tower he would be dead as well, or Bel Garde overrun by fay and they would all be prisoners. But he wondered if he would have had the courage to order his own child to safety while he met death. *I will never know, because we'll all die here and I will never live to have a child . . .*

There was more quiet talk, but the council seemed to be over. Roland stared into the fire, trying not to see images it hurt to think about. Since hearing Falaise's tale, he had sunk deeper into grief and pain, and he felt powerless to help himself. He heard Renier move up behind his chair, and he said the words he had been living on since that moment in the tower. "He will explain himself. There will be some reason."

"Yes, my lord," a soft voice answered. "But if he meant to betray you, wouldn't he also have a reason, a clever lie?"

Roland looked down at Elaine, startled, and heard Renier gasp. He glanced up and saw that his Preceptor looked as shocked as if a pet cat had spoken. But Roland knew that his mother would not have had women close to her who were fools; they had been at the focal point of the court with her.

Renier stepped forward to take Elaine's arm and Roland motioned him away, irritated at the interruption. He wanted to talk, and the young woman's eyes were red and bruised from crying and the expression in them anything but cruel. "If he loved me, how could he betray me?" he asked, hearing the tears in his own voice.

"If he loved you, he couldn't," she whispered.

Roland hesitated. If his mother had asked it of her, this woman would have flung herself off the roof of the highest tower in the city. She would believe whatever Ravenna had told her to believe. But Ravenna was not here to tell her what to say now. If Elaine was repeating his mother's views, it was only because she believed in them herself.

"You were close as boys," Elaine persisted. "I remember it. But didn't he change?"

Didn't he? Roland asked himself. Had the teasing turned to mockery? *I know he has a cruel streak. God, he could hardly hide it.* "That was because . . ." Roland began, and thought, *Because after I tried to die, he knew how much I needed him, and he thought me pathetic, and it made him feel powerful.* He felt anger stir in him, old tired anger. "Yes, he changed."

They sat in silence for a time, until a matron who had been one of Ravenna's gentlewomen came for Elaine. She let the older woman lead her away, but reluctantly, with a worried glance back at Roland.

———

The frigid wind tore at Kade's hair, blowing it into her face, and she shook it away irritatedly. "You'll be ready?"

The gold-and-amber fay leaned on his pikestaff and looked down at her with a smile. "If you can flush the birds, my lady, we can chase them."

It was late afternoon, the sky a low solid gray like the polished surface of an ancient shield, the housetops around them still sheathed in ice and snow. Kade had left Boliver at Knockma, to help the others pack what was necessary and to take them through the ring to Chariot, another of her mother's enchanted castles. She hadn't been to it for years, so it would not occur to the Host to search for her there. She had little memory of what it was like, except that it was big and old, and hidden rather prosaically in the hills of Monbeaudreux, a province in the south. It was protected from the Bisran border by steadily rising mountains that were too high and rugged to cross except on foot. The summer and spring lasted longer there, and they grew olive trees. At the moment, it sounded like heaven.

The fay from the Seelie Court, with his white blond hair, delicate features, and the embroidered satin of his doublet and cloak, was unreal in this world of gray and white. "Chase them far," Kade told him. "I don't want them turning back on us. I've paid enough for it."

"To the ends of the earth, and that will be a pleasure." The fay swept a bow to her, and suddenly a golden hawk glittered in the air beside her, and with a powerful sweep of its wings, it shot toward the sky.

Kade watched him until he disappeared into the clouds. She couldn't afford mistakes, and she wasn't at all sure of herself. She had been lax over the last few years, using what she could of the swift instinctive fay magic, depending on glamour and illusion. Swift, and in the end ineffective against the sorcery that was practiced so painstakingly, using as poor a tool as letters from a dead language's alphabet to symbolize concepts that passed understanding. With fay magic it was impossible to attempt something beyond one's skill; with sorcery it was all too possible, and all too deadly.

Kade hugged herself and shivered. She hadn't given sorcery the long hours of study it needed. Her efforts seemed so ungainly compared to the elegant and involved work of sorcerers like Galen Dubell and Dr. Surete. *Both of whom are dead now,* she thought, savagely, *and at least I'm alive.* But it all came home to rest in the end, and she had taken the easy way out far too often.

Kade knew she should have returned to make up with Roland at once after their father had died. She would not have had to stay long, and it might have made the difference in so many things. If she went to him now to tell him about Denzil, he would never believe her.

The glass ball Titania had traded her was in a deep pocket of her smock, and when it brushed against her she could feel the warmth radiating out of it even through all her layers of clothing. *God, I hope it's contained,* she thought. *I hope it's not sapping my strength or power, or leaking something into the ether that's going to interfere with the spell.* She was not at all sure that what she was attempting would work. She had bought the Seelie Court's help with Knockma, and they would hound the Host from the city, but she would have to stir the creatures out of the palace herself.

Kade heard something at the edge of the roof, then saw a small fay with ugly wizened features and cornflower blue hair peering at her over the edge. Its narrow eyes widened at her, and she snarled, "Bugger off." It vanished, and she stretched, easing the tension in her tight shoulders. She was a little shocked to realize it was not the cold that was making her tremble. *It's going to work,* she told herself. *It's not going to work,* a little voice answered. *I'm going to die.*

She took out a pinch of the gasçoign powder and rubbed it into her eyes. Looking toward the palace's towers, she could now see the corona of shifting light that played over them, colors touching and fading into one another. There should still be gaps between the wards high in the air above the palace; there hadn't been time for them to draw all the way together, and the higher they were in the air, the slower they would move. *Here I go,* she thought, and flung herself into the sky.

Kade had wings, and for a moment only, an unfamiliar instinct told her to use them. Colors changed; blurred outlines in the distance became sharp and clear. Her vision was incredible. Shadows had edges like razors, and her eyes found movement—the flutter of a curtain's edge through a broken window, the slight rustle of a frost-covered tree's branches in a garden court—that she would never detect with human sight.

Kade realized she was gliding in a circle over the High Minister's house, then she realized she was flying. For a moment, human thought and hawk instinct clashed, and her wings flapped frantically. She dropped like a stone. Kade forced herself to let go, to let the unfamiliar senses guide her, and her wings made the correct angle and she caught the wind again.

She thought she had the trick of it now. One had to exercise enough control to keep one's memory and purpose, but had to give the hawk enough rein to control the body. She made a slow circle to face toward the palace, watching the ground rush by below in impossibly fine detail and trying not to think about what her wings were doing.

Kade had not taken this form lightly. She knew that hawks, who could dive from hundreds of feet in the air and pluck a mouse off a forest floor, would have good eyesight and that with the gasçoign powder she would have a chance of finding the gap in the wards. The smaller body would make slipping through easier as well. Also, if she failed, this wasn't a bad way to spend one's last hour. But she had chosen better than she could have guessed. She could see the wards as fine shadings of gray mist moving almost imperceptibly above the walls.

And just a moment ago I thought gray a dull color, she thought, amazed. Who had known that one bland color would have so many distinctions?

A few powerful strokes of her wings took her higher and she flew toward the palace, astonished again at the power and strength of such a small body. She had risen above the wards and almost overshot the palace before she caught herself and turned back. It was no wonder human sorcerers lost themselves when they changed shape. If her sense of urgency hadn't been so strong, it would have been easy to play on these wind currents until she forgot who she was. *Is that what happened to all the human sorcerers who tried the shape-changing experiment? Did they keep saying, "I'll just stay out a little longer," until all the words faded from their minds?* If only she could afford that kind of self-indulgence.

Kade found the gap close to the high point where the edges of the wards met above the palace. It was an irregularly shaped hole, a bare four feet wide at its largest . . . and closing fast. Hawk instinct seized her and, pushed on by her fear, she dove for the gap. She had forgotten how fast she could move if she tried, and found herself safely through and frantically cupping her wings to slow herself as the sloped roof of the Queen's Tower rushed upward at her.

Elated, Kade controlled her dive and slipped sideways, catching the wind current around the tower and letting it steer her toward the North Bastion. She hadn't felt a thing when she rushed past the wards, and now she knew she was going to beat that Bisran bastard at his own game.

Kade made one slow circle above the King's Bastion for curiosity's sake. Along the top level, she could see the staining on the stones above the windows where smoke had poured out from the sporadic fires there the night of the attack. Then a play of light over the dark tiles of the multipitched roof caught her attention. It looked almost like a ward.

Yes, it is a ward. She didn't think it was a new one of Grandier's design; it lay on the roof like a discarded scarf. Kade circled again, losing altitude in her effort to see it more clearly. It could be Ableon-Indis, the ward she had called to rout the Host in the Old Hall. Her spell might have pulled it out of the etheric structure entirely, and that was why it was still here instead of with the other wards above. It might not have been affected by Grandier's conversion of the other wards at all.

Kade saw the black shape out of the corner of her eye, and her hawk's body twisted away, reacting before her human mind had grasped the danger.

It was a black spraggat, its leathery wings stretched above her, claws raking. She dove again, slipping in and out of the currents, but it followed her, its stronger wings overpowering the wind and forcing itself closer to her.

Kade slipped sideways and it overshot with a scream of rage. She flapped her wings frantically, trying to gain height and take advantage of its mistake, then she heard its screaming turn from anger to pain. She risked a look and saw it rolling and scrabbling across the roof of the King's Bastion, its leathery wings smoking and bursts of flame appearing over its dark body. It had fallen into Ableon-Indis. *I'm right,* she thought with great satisfaction. *But it's much weaker than it was without its keystone, or it would have burnt that thing up at once.* She had one ward on her side, and she would have to think carefully about the best way to use it.

She turned, making for the North Bastion. Then claws raked her back, and the force of the blow sent her tumbling, her wings frantically beating the air. The second black spraggat dove toward her again and struck at her. She wheeled and turned desperately to escape. The wall of the North Bastion seemed to spin, all the while rushing closer and closer.

The instincts Kade had fought off earlier took over in force, letting her right herself and fight her way toward the flat mountain looming in front of her. Her claws grasped stone, and there was a rush of air behind her as the spraggat stooped for the kill. She felt herself fumbling, trying to remember what she had to do now, her thoughts overwhelmed by the hawk's fear and its terrible desire to turn and throw itself at the spraggat in a hopeless attack. With the last bit of herself, she stretched out with her mind and touched the spark of light within her feathers that in another existence was a fayre queen's glass ball. She shattered it.

Then her fingers were digging into the weathered pits in the stone face, her boots slipping on the ledge. The spraggat screamed its confusion, suddenly confronted with a human larger than itself and the bright painful backwash of a powerful spell. It swung away in fright. Half sobbing with exhaustion, Kade clung to the stone and kicked at the catch of the window. Once, twice, then it sprang open and she fell through.

She lay on the wooden floor of a cold empty room, gasping, then reached into her pocket. Titania's glass ball was in shards, still faintly warm with the force of the contained spell. *Well, I'm not doing that again soon,* she thought, sitting up awkwardly. The fay's claws had torn through her coat, leaving two long tears in her back that sluggishly leaked blood. Her shirt and smock hadn't been torn, only snagged aside, and distractedly she searched her pockets for a pin to pull the fabric of the coat back together. Then Kade saw where she was: the walls covered with gilt-trimmed bookshelves, the large windows, the beautifully carved partners desk still piled with paper, more books, and an upset inkwell.

In her confusion, Kade had all but forgotten which room she was making for. She had meant to approach cautiously and make sure the rooms were empty first. She climbed to her feet, inwardly cursing herself and listening hard for any sign of occupation. *Stupid, stupid, have you ruined it all now? Is he still using these rooms? Did you go through all that just to be caught?*

She steadied herself against the wall because her legs were still trembling, and crept to the door. But the next room, a small parlor with furniture buried under more books, was cold and unoccupied as well. She ventured through the rest of the suite, feeling her heartbeat begin to steady. She could hear nothing but the wind against the windows, and the rooms were cold, the candles and hearths unlit. Grandier had not come back here, then.

Kade returned to the study and started her frantic search. The simplest hiding places were the best. It seemed like a year ago, but the morning that she had stood on the windows and spoken to him, he had been planning to let the Host in that very night. *It wasn't Galen who betrayed you,* she reminded herself. *It was Urbain Grandier the murderer.*

She went to the desk and opened all the drawers and looked through the first layer of papers. They were covered with crabbed half-completed calculations, none of which she could follow for more than a few steps. The books on the desk were *Theater of Terrestrial Alchemy* and *The Black Keys*; nothing illuminating there.

She moved around the room, scanning the shelves, shifting books, looking under chair cushions, then turned to the leather-bound chest on the floor. It had books stacked atop it but not much dust compared with the rest of the room, and she remembered that he had just finished putting something in it when she had come to the window the first time.

Kade kneeled beside the chest and lifted the books from the top. It wasn't even locked. She opened it and was disappointed by the sight of perfectly ordinary folded linens and fustian blankets.

Then she moved the top layer aside. It lay on a bed of cloth, a stone from the bottom of some streambed, rounded and smoothed by water, small enough to fit comfortably in her two cupped hands. The keystone was inert and silent now.

She picked it up, marveling at the symbols, letters, and equations incised into its surface. They started out blocky and large enough to read, then shrank as they wound around the stone, some obviously formed by different hands, becoming so tiny they might have been carved with a jeweler's knife, ultimately shrinking until they disappeared from sight. Kade blinked and shook her head, dizzied. She could follow the sense of it for no more than a few turns of the stone, if that.

Well, Kade thought, rolling it from one hand to the other. *So I've got it. Now find Thomas, and take this down to its place in the cellar.*

She bundled the keystone up in the bag she had brought in a pocket and tied it securely around her waist, then started out of the suite.

Kade listened at the heavy wooden door a moment, hearing no betraying sounds, then opened it cautiously. The next room was dark, but she had expected that. There was the smell of must and dampness and, far away and barely detectable in the frozen air, of death.

Kade hesitated, one hand on the doorframe. The hackles on the back of her neck lifted.

If the black spraggat outside had been a guard, there would be a guard inside, as well.

She crossed the anteroom in three light-footed leaps and reached the opposite door. Let whatever it was come for her, then; she had found the keystone. She could do anything.

Stretching before her was a suite of rooms, filled with silent shapes, distorted by shadows.

Kade slipped through the first room, sweat freezing on her back, the heavy lump of the keystone bumping her familiarly in the leg. In the second room she stopped. The cold had changed consistency. She felt it moving over her like a mist, clinging to her face and hair, her clothes.

There is something here. She touched the wall to keep her orientation, straining her eyes in the darkness and slipping the bronze knife out of the scabbard at her belt. Then something moved. She couldn't tell if she was seeing it with her eyes or inside her head.

Kade eased back against the wall, her heart pounding. Whatever it was would attack her in a moment. She didn't want to give it an advantage by bolting out of the room screaming.

The whisper almost made her jump out of her skin. It came from across the room, and she tightened her grip on her knife. The voice was low and harsh, and she couldn't make out the words.

Kade hesitated, aware of precious time passing. Sweat was freezing on her forehead and she didn't know whether to be afraid or angry, to try to push her way past the thing or retreat. Maybe that was its purpose, to keep her here while something else—

The voice was getting louder, and though she still couldn't make out the words, it trembled on the edge of her memory, recognition barely a breath away.

Then she remembered that *The Black Keys* contained spells for necromancy.

Her father's voice said, "Little bastard, why did your bitch of a mother bother to drop you? She didn't have to leave you to devil me."

Kade didn't remember running; she wasn't aware of anything until she was slamming the door of Grandier's study behind her and leaning against it, shuddering. Her knees hurt and one of her gloves was ripped, and the burn in her palm had torn open. She must have gone over or through a piece of furniture, though she didn't remember it.

Kade went to the desk, picked up the book on necromancy, and slung it through the window. It hit the open casement and smashed the glass, then tumbled out of sight. It was the first time in her life she had ever mishandled a book.

She paced the room because the liquid fire of fear and anger was in her veins and it hurt to stand still. She smashed an astrolabe and turned over the globe, and dug her fingernails into the open wound on her hand until she stopped sobbing. Then she asked all the old pagan spirits to visit their curses on Grandier, and the Church God to strike him down.

Kade stopped in the middle of the room finally, pressed her hands together, and thought. It was a test, a trick, a challenge. Grandier meant her to fail. Had he set the ghost here outside these rooms, or had it wandered the palace, to be drawn to her presence if she won a way inside?

The latter made more sense. But then . . . *But then it could come in here.* Kade was at the window in a moment.

She climbed out onto the sill, then stepped to the broad ledge. The black spraggat was no longer in sight, though it might come back at any moment. She was in a poor position to defend herself.

The frigid wind ripped at her, tearing the air out of her lungs. Kade edged her way along, fingers clinging tightly to the stone. She hadn't pinned her coat together again and the cold air poured down her back. She would have to cross the siege wall to get to the Old Palace anyway. *Can I do it from the outside?* Another laborious ten feet and Kade saw that she couldn't, not without falling to her death. She would have to enter the North Bastion to reach the walkway along the top of the wall.

Finally, Kade could stand the cold no more. She reached a set of windows she could push open, then almost fell through them onto the floor of a small bedchamber. Sitting up on the rug that was stiff with frost, she realized she had not even bothered to glance in first to see if the room was unoccupied. She could have landed headfirst among a whole tribe of spriggans, or a troop of Alsene soldiers.

She buried her head in her hands. *He has you on the run. You're playing into his hands again.*

Kade pushed to her feet and went through the doorway to the next room. It was a beautifully arranged parlor, the wallpaper and upholstery of rose and gold. She didn't know who this suite had belonged to or where she was, except that she was near the corner and would have to find the stairs that let out onto the siege wall. The light from the window in the bedchamber made no inroads on the shadows in the corners. The next room would be dark as pitch.

Kade dug in her pockets and finally came up with a tinderbox. She would light one of the candles in here and take it with her. She would have to do that anyway if she didn't want to run into walls and step on bogles. *Coward,* she thought as she fumbled with the flint. *Bloody coward.*

It refused to catch, and she pried the candle out of the lamp, sat down on the floor with it, and tried to light it with a spell. Her heart was pounding too fast, distracting her, but finally the wick began to glow gently with spell light. It was beginning to yellow to real flame when it went out, as if invisible fingers had snuffed it. "What?" she said aloud, and looked up.

It was there, in the darkest corner, looking at her. She could feel its gaze with the inner eye of her own sorcery. Her skin turned to ice and sweat dropped into her eyes. Then it whispered, "I could have you killed tomorrow and no one would notice. Perhaps I will—"

Kade was through the bedchamber, slamming the door behind her, and poised on the windowsill like a bird about to take flight before her wits caught up to her. She made herself stop, grinding her injured hand against the frozen metal of the casement, forcing herself to think. She could climb out and enter through another window, go around it. But it had taken so little time to find her. It would just follow her again. How could she find Thomas with the damn thing following her and freezing her blood—

Had it gone after Thomas, too? He had helped Ravenna kill Fulstan. But Thomas had never been particularly impressed with Fulstan when the old king was alive; Kade thought it unlikely that he would be concerned about him now that Fulstan was dead.

It was coming after her because it could make her afraid.

Kade hesitated, considering the idea. Fulstan had been nothing in life and was even less in death. Thomas and Ravenna had disposed of him with less regret than a farmer would feel when putting down a rabid dog. Kade nodded to herself.

That was the key to it.

She had not let the old bastard stop her from living her life. She was not going to let him stop her now.

Kade pushed away from the windowsill and crossed the cold room to the door. Her legs trembled; her hand on the doorknob trembled. That was all right. She could shake, cry, scream, as long as she didn't break and run. There was no one who mattered here to see her.

Outside the door, she could hear the muttering of the voice. She opened it and stood on the threshold.

Light from the room behind her fell only a short distance, then seemed to hit a wall of blackness and stop. The voice rose, ranting at her, words of darkness forming all the old terrible nightmares she remembered. "Little lying bitch, my punishment from God for my sins."

Anything to stop that. She said, "You're nothing."

It had no effect. The voice rose in volume. "Do you think your pathetic little brother could help you? He'd kill you himself if I ordered it—"

Roland do something you ordered? Kade found herself thinking. "Who's the liar now?" she said. "He hates you more than I do." And suddenly the words were just words. They hurt, but not with the sting of truth. They were the same words Fulstan had always flung at her, but she was not a child now. Perhaps she had not needed to return to the city of her birth to face her brother. Perhaps she had needed to return to face this. Her voice gaining strength, she shouted, "You're nothing! Galen Dubell was more a father to me than you ever were. Thomas is more a husband to Ravenna than you ever were." The voice went on, louder, and Kade's voice rose to a shriek, drowning it out, all thought of concealment forgotten. "You were nothing to her, you're nothing to me! She killed you because you got in her way and she wouldn't put up with your stupidity anymore. Roland's King now and he curses your memory whether he admits it or not. You're nothing and you always were!"

On the last word she stalked forward—not running, not blundering in the dark—until she barked her shin on a chair. Cursing the pain, she fell against the other door, opened it, and stumbled through into the next room.

It had an open door leading into the stairwell, and wan yellow candlelight came down through it from somewhere above. The silence was complete.

She looked back and could see the gray daylight from windows of the bedchamber through the open door of the salon. It was just a room, cloaked in shadow, no colder than the stairwell.

"And don't come back," Kade muttered, leaning against the doorframe. Then she heard heavy footsteps from the floor above, and she started hastily down the stairs. If there had been anyone or anything in the bastion, her idiot screaming would bring it running.

In the next hour, Grandier or the Host or Denzil could kill her. But Kade had never felt freer in her life.

CHAPTER NINETEEN

THERE WAS A CLANK somewhere in the passage below, as if hollow metal struck stone. Thomas paused on the edge of the gap in the floor and thoughtfully fingered the hilt of his rapier. He had seen Dontane come down the stairs from the council rooms, and he had taken the chance on going ahead into the lower passages and catching him here.

This was the large passage Grandier had shown him yesterday, the only unblocked way to the cellar where the Unseelie Court had established itself. Thomas had found a spot where a weak place in its ceiling had partly given way, spilling some debris down onto the floor and creating a hole into the space above. Climbing up through the gap, he had found another narrow corridor that was blocked on one end by a collapse of its own. It led only to more disused rooms and a now-rickety stairway up to the floor above.

A dim light fell down the stairs, slightly alleviating the darkness. Moving silently, Thomas poised on the edge of the gap, listening as the faint noise below became the footsteps of at least two men. Then Dontane passed below, with two Alsene troopers trailing reluctantly behind him. Thomas felt a rush of both relief and tension; he hadn't been certain until now that he would have his chance. Dontane could have brought twenty troopers with him, but the need to conceal his activities from Grandier must have won out over caution.

Thomas quietly stepped down to a fallen rafter half blocking the gap, then leapt onto the back of the second trooper.

His weight slammed the man into the hard stone floor. He rolled off the inert form and came to his feet against the opposite wall, ducking the flailing sword of the other trooper. Thomas parried the second wild blow, feinted, and put his point through the man's neck. The trooper sunk back against the wall, clawing at the wound and gasping, then slid to the floor.

Dontane had turned, whipping his sword free of the scabbard. He recognized Thomas and stopped, eyes widening in disbelief. "You're still here—"

Thomas moved toward him, making it look like a casual stroll. He doubted he could catch Dontane if the sorcerer bolted toward the cellar. "Afraid of Villon? Things not going quite according to plan?"

He saw the realization of where those things had been said pass over Dontane's frozen expression, and an awareness of just what else had been said. "So that was you. I thought the boy dreaming when he said something had moved in the floor."

Dontane rushed forward. Thomas started to bring up his sword to parry, but saw the blue flame of spell fire flickering down Dontane's blade. Instead of locking their weapons together he swept his sword around, deflecting the deadly blade and disengaging. Even then the shock of contact with that power was enough to send a jolt down his arm.

Dontane laughed, but sweat ran down his face and he held his sword en garde, not pressing the attack immediately. Thomas steadied himself against the wall. He thought, *Damn, this could finish me.* It had taken a moment or so for the blast of power to travel down the long rapier blade to his hand, long enough for him to parry and break contact. If he had connected with the shorter blade of a main gauche he would have a useless arm now. Stupid not to realize that the young sorcerer would have an arcane defense against attack. But Dontane had seen the battle at Aviler's house and knew he was outclassed in swordplay; Thomas could almost smell the fear on him.

Thomas eased away from the wall. "I hope that isn't all you've got," he said softly. "It's not going to be enough." He circled to the side, trying to get between Dontane and the cellar.

Dontane backed away, preventing him from blocking the passage. Thomas lunged, pulling the tip of his sword up and over Dontane's parry, nicking him in the opposite shoulder. Dontane cried out and his blade swung wide, the flat of it catching Thomas's sword arm. The force of the spell fire on the blade sent Thomas staggering. Dontane stumbled back and lost his grip on his sword. Pressing a hand to his wounded shoulder, he turned and bolted down the passage.

Cursing at the pain and forcing his almost-numb fingers to hold onto his sword-hilt, Thomas ran after him.

Around the corner he could see the gap in the wall. The unearthly light of the Host had faded, leaving a well of darkness in the old cellar. With the waning daylight outside, the Host must still be quiescent. But Dontane was just disappearing down the stairway and would have every intention of waking them.

Thomas plunged down after him. Dontane moved more slowly, still holding one hand pressed to his bleeding shoulder. He turned as Thomas reached the landing and swung a fist at him. They grappled, struggling across the narrow landing. His sword arm pinned, Thomas forced Dontane toward the edge, then felt the stone give way under his boot; the next instant they were both falling.

———

Kade had found enough glamour to make it difficult for human eyes to focus on her. She had made her way silently through the cold dark rooms to the Old Palace. Now she crouched in the concealing shadows beneath one of the grand staircases, watching the Alsene troops rush about. Most carried lamps and all seemed to be shouting at each other. They had sprinkled more of the cursed iron filings around the areas on the third and fourth floors where they seemed to have made their main encampment. It was the place where Thomas was most likely being held, but Kade's glamour wouldn't last there, not in such close quarters with the lights and so many wary men.

Kade was torn between staying here to look for Thomas and continuing on her way to replace the keystone. Frustrated, she gnawed on her thumbnail and tried to consider her options rationally.

Spells might alert Grandier or some member of the Host. The ether was disturbed enough as it was; Kade didn't want to stir it up further and give them the idea that she was about somewhere. She couldn't afford to be caught until she had at least replaced the keystone and driven the Host out of the palace to the waiting Seelie Court.

A page boy in a slashed doublet and heavy fur cloak came down the stairs and stopped a few feet from her hiding place. He rested one small hand on the newel post and watched the frantic activity of the men.

Kade's ears pricked. She needed information. Here was someone to get it from who was small enough for her to overpower.

For a moment, the landing was almost empty. She waited for the last trooper to step through an arch into the next room and then darted forward.

Kade wrapped her wiry forearm around the page's throat and dragged him back into the shelter of the darkened stairwell. His choked cry broke off as she put the tip of her bronze knife below his jaw. She hissed, "Be quiet."

She pulled him farther into the shadow and whispered, "Quietly now. Grandier has a prisoner, the Captain of the Queen's Guard. Where is he?"

She eased the pressure off the boy's windpipe enough to allow him to talk.

He drew breath to scream and she pressed the knife down just enough to draw a bead of blood. After a moment the boy whispered, "The prisoners escaped."

Well, that's just fine, Kade thought in irritation. *How am I going to find him now?* "When?"

"Earlier today, sometime, I don't know exactly—" His voice was rising, and she prodded him with the knife again to remind him to be quiet.

There was no way to tell if Thomas had left the palace yet or was still trapped inside. Kade decided she would just have to replace the keystone and improvise the rest.

The page was trembling under her arm, but Kade sensed he was angry enough to try to come at her when she released him, instead of the far more sensible act of running away and shouting for help. She shoved him away. As he turned back to lunge at her, she threw a handful of glamour into his eyes. He gasped and stumbled to a halt, staring at her, his eyes widening until they were almost all pupil. She said, "You had a dream. A confusing dream. A jumble of images."

He was still staring straight ahead when Kade slipped around him and started down the stairs. That should confuse his story long enough for her to accomplish her goal. It would only take a few moments to replace the keystone.

———

Thomas lay facedown, cold gritty stone against his cheek. He levered himself up a little and shook his head, too stunned to think. He caught his breath at the unexpected pain of a hundred new bruises. Then memory returned. He was on the flagstone floor of the cellar. He had fallen down the last flight of stairs.

Thomas rolled over and sat up. His sword was near his hand; he must have held onto it in instinctive reflex until he struck the pavement. Dontane lay sprawled perhaps twenty paces away.

And the Host was stirring around them.

Thomas looked back to the stairs. A dark winged fay with a sleek narrow dog's head had settled on the landing. It looked down at them with brilliant red eyes. The cellar's soft light grew brighter as corpse-lights climbed the walls. Creatures slunk from under the piles of discarded wood and trash, or seemed to rise out of the floor. All were uniformly hideous but no two were alike, with grotesquely distorted heads, jagged teeth, long clawed hands, ratlike tails, or bat's wings. One of the columns looked as if it had grown fur; Thomas realized it was covered with a troop of brown and dun-colored spriggans. The smell of the place was as foul as the bottom of a bog, and the creatures were still coming out of hiding.

Three misshapen bogles leapt to the ground between him and Dontane, drawn by the smell of blood. Thomas looked for cover, or something else to use as a weapon. To his right he saw a long heap of broken wood, an old scaling tower lying on its side. While its supports and platforms had been made of wooden beams, the pulleys and chains that extended them and the plates that had protected the troops manning it were of iron, and there were no fay near it. While their attention was on Dontane, Thomas snatched up his sword and limped to the broken tower. He crouched next to it, his back against a large rusted iron plate propped up by the rotting wood.

As more fay gathered, the growling mutter of their talk grew louder. Thomas scraped up the bolts and metal scraps scattered nearby into a handy pile. Most of the creatures moved toward Dontane, drawn by the blood and possibly by the young sorcerer's magic. But one small fay covered with fiery red scales and straggling hair crept toward Thomas. He waited until it was close enough, then used the tip of his sword to flip it back and away.

Incredibly light, the creature sailed back a good twenty feet before bouncing against the flagstones. It leapt up and yelled, "Hey, 'e saw me!"

Hell, now they know, Thomas thought. The Host could conceal themselves from him now that they knew he could see through glamour. *Idiot.* It was the second time he had betrayed himself that way.

But the fay were distracted again as Dontane stirred. The sorcerer rolled over, moaning, and the Host drew closer. A chorus of hags, their bodies emaciated, strands of grizzled hair clinging to their skulls, gathered around, laughing at Dontane's efforts to stand.

Dontane staggered to his feet and stared around, realizing he was trapped. He had lost his sword in the corridor above, and Thomas could tell from the way the blood drained from his face that he knew his danger. But with more bravery than Thomas would have given him credit for, Dontane said hoarsely, "Listen to me! We have more mortals for you."

The stubborn bastard still means to send them after Villon. Thomas knew his chances of reaching Dontane now were poor at best. Still, he had to try. He gathered himself to move.

The assembled fay seemed to be listening, or at least they hadn't attacked Dontane yet. Dontane pivoted, watching them warily. He licked his lips and said, "An army is outside the city gates—"

Screeching from up in the ceiling drowned out Dontane's voice. Thomas looked up as with a clatter and bang several fay tumbled out of an air shaft. They drifted or cartwheeled to the floor, one landing on the far side of the cellar with a fatal-sounding splat. The odor of burning meat and peat moss descended with them.

One drifting form reached the floor, landed lightly, and strode toward Dontane. Its tall body had a human shape but that was where the resemblance ended. Its skin looked as rough as gnarled wood, but as it moved closer Thomas could see that it had been burned. It still carried raw red wounds in its flesh.

As it neared Dontane, a smaller fay with a flattened head and limbs with too many joints hopped out of the watching crowd to greet it. The little creature danced around the large wounded fay, singing in a piping, clearly audible voice, "He's here, we told! The human wizard! He's here!"

The tall fay watched this performance, then leaned down and slapped the little creature out of the way.

Dontane took a few stumbling steps backward as the fay came toward him. It looked down and said in a harsh croak, "You don't know me? Surely you must. I'm Evadne."

"But—" Dontane stared up at it, growing fear in his eyes. "The others said you didn't come back, there was an explosion in the tower—"

"Yes, I saw the explosion. I saw it from the inside. I have only just returned with these few, for it took us this long to drag our poor selves back." The hissing voice rose to a shriek. "Your master sent me to my death, you lying human fool!"

"No, he couldn't have, he knew Denzil wanted to take the King prisoner—" Dontane said, taking another step back. He halted in confusion when he realized the other dark fay were creeping closer to him.

He sees it now, Thomas thought. Grandier hadn't trusted Dontane and Denzil either.

Evadne moved nearer to the sorcerer, and Dontane begged, "Wait—"

The fay prince paused, staring down at Dontane with burning eyes in a ruined face. The others had gone silent in anticipation.

Dontane hesitated, then with fatal desperation in his voice, said, "I didn't know—"

"You admit it," Evadne snarled. Dontane clapped his hands together, shouting something. A blue glow of sorcery grew over his head just as Evadne lunged forward.

One long clawed hand caught the front of Dontane's doublet, jerking him up off the floor. The sorcery evaporated harmlessly as Dontane panicked, struggling to break Evadne's grip.

Evadne threw Dontane down, slamming him into the hard stone floor. Thomas started at the clearly audible crack of breaking bone.

Dontane twitched once, then lay like an unstrung puppet.

Evadne stared down in satisfaction at the silent form, then slowly lifted his head. *My turn,* Thomas thought, and shifted his grip on his sword-hilt. Evadne's hot eyes found him and the fay grinned. "You are human as well, but you see through glamour. What are you?"

"Does it matter?" Thomas answered. He heard something move behind the heap of wreckage and gathered the bare handful of iron scraps he had collected.

"Perhaps not." Evadne shrugged, strolling toward him.

The dark fay gathered again, drawn by this new promise of entertainment. *This is not going to be pretty,* Thomas thought. Then something slammed into the rotten wood of the tower behind him. Before the heavy mass could come down on top of him he rolled forward, then he was in the midst of them. Thomas flung the handful of bolts at the closest, momentarily clearing himself a path. He made it almost ten paces toward the stairway before a pack of bogles blocked his way. The others closed around him again and he swept his sword around, scattering them back.

A squat troll creature leapt at him wildly and he lunged at it without thinking. It fell on his sword, ripping the weapon out of his grip. He was struck from behind and he staggered forward and caught himself. He turned around, waiting to die.

———

Kade arrived at the top of the stairway down into the cellar in time to watch the burned fay kill Dontane. She hadn't recognized Evadne until he spoke and his appearance shocked her. *What happened to him? I hope it hurts as terribly as it looks.* Then she saw Thomas trapped against the broken siege tower and panic sent every other thought out of her head.

She started forward to the steps, about to plunge down into the cellar. She caught herself, one hand on the wall, and forced herself to be rational. *This is no time to be an idiot.* The Host was in force here and it would be a fight to the death she could not win.

Kade knelt on the cold stone of the passage floor, ripped a piece of fabric from her skirt, and shook out the handful of ash she had collected from one of the fireplaces, thinking, *I only need a little time, just a little time; don't get yourself killed.* She had already gotten the candle lit before coming down here, thinking the cellar would be dark, and that saved precious moments. Dripping the wax onto the fabric and ash, she whispered the powerful words and begged Ableon-Indis to listen.

She completed the spell and hesitated. If Ableon-Indis had drifted farther away or dissipated . . . There was no time for that. Kade leapt to her feet and stepped out onto the stairs, shouting "Evadne!" at the top of her lungs.

All eyes turned to her and the various voices of the Host stopped their singing and howling. They had forced Thomas away from cover and surrounded him, but he was still on his feet. He looked toward her, but she bit her lip and didn't betray any sign that she had seen him. If Evadne had any idea she meant to help him, then they were both dead and that was that. She reached the first landing, and the large flighted fay that squatted there edged away from her, angling its narrow head to watch her surreptitiously. From below Evadne called out, "What are you doing here, sister? Have you come to join us?"

"I . . ." She spoke slowly, and wondered if it was as obvious as it seemed that she had no idea what to say. Inspiration struck and she finished, "I lost Knockma to Titania, and I want your help to get it back." She started down the last flight of steps, holding the scrap of spell-patterned fabric behind her back. The creature on the landing could see it, but it would have no idea that it was anything but a rag.

Evadne turned suddenly to look down at Thomas. "It wouldn't be because of this human, would it?"

"No." Kade sounded shocked that he would even think such a thing. Her heart wasn't pounding quite so hard now, and it was a little easier to think.

"That isn't what I was told," Evadne said slyly.

"Told by who?" Kade pounced on the admission. "By Grandier? By Dontane?"

Evadne hesitated, his eyes bright in the dusky cellar, contemptuous of her but growing doubtful.

"Do you think that was the only lie they told you?" Kade persisted.

"I don't think it is the only lie *you* told me."

She was almost to the bottom of the steps. *Where is the damn thing?* she thought desperately. The sweat from her hands was soaking into the scrap of fabric. *Why is it taking so long?* She had to get closer to Evadne. "But you expect that from me. I never pretended anything else. I never sent you off to your death with a false promise." *I am, however, about to destroy you now if I can just get this damned ward to—*

Behind her the fay who guarded the stairs shrieked in agony. Kade turned as if she were as surprised as the others. The creature staggered and tried to leap into the air, its flesh melting away like hot wax.

Ableon-Indis had finally arrived.

The ward had grown weak, and Kade thought her spell would only hold it for a few moments before it drifted back up from the cellar. More of the Host screamed and fled as the ward fell among them. A burst of hot air from the motion of their wings struck her and Kade stumbled and sat down hard on the bottom step. As the nearest gang of bogles burst into flame, a roar of mingled disbelief and fear from the assembled creatures deafened her. Kade clapped her hands over her ears. The fay remembered the battle in the Old Hall too, and now they realized what she had done. Evadne charged toward her, his mouth open in a silent scream, but he was swept away by the rush of his fleeing companions.

Kade got to her feet and ran into the chaos.

———

Thomas took advantage of the confusion to recover the rapier from the body of the troll that had taken it. He turned around as Kade reached him. She shouted, "Are you all right?"

"I'm better," he told her. One of the flighted creatures flew low over their heads, howling, and Thomas caught Kade around the waist and pulled her to him.

She had never stopped talking. "I found it! The keystone. Look." She struggled to unwrap a round stone covered with delicate carving. "It was right there in his rooms."

Now we have a chance, Thomas thought. He saw Evadne fighting his way free of the milling fay, coming toward them. He said, "I'll distract him, and you put it back in its place."

Kade shook her head, adamant. "No, you have to do it. You couldn't hold him off long enough and I can."

He stared down at her. Other fay joined Evadne, and there was no knowing whether the fay prince realized that they had the crucial keystone, or was only coming after them in a blind rage. Kade shrieked, "There's no time! Go on. I'd do it for you!"

She was right. He said, "Damn you," took the keystone out of her hand, and ran.

Thomas ducked around the milling creatures still panicked by the ward, forcing himself not to look back. He found the right pillar in moments and saw that the clay seal a foot or so above its base had been recently replaced. He reached down just as something struck him from behind. Claws dug into his back, parting the leather of his buff coat. He spun and slammed the creature and his full weight into the stone pillar. Its hold loosened and Thomas wrenched away. Turning, he stabbed the dazed spriggan and shoved it out of the way.

Dropping to his knees, Thomas broke the clay seal with the heel of his hand. He dug into the soft dirt and his fingers found the stone buried within, but it seemed to slip away as he tried to get a grip on it. He swore, and shifted against the pillar to reach deeper into the niche. Finally he caught the stone and pulled it out. Flinging it away, he shoved the old keystone into the niche, wondering if it was going to struggle to escape, too. But it seemed to slide out of his hand and into the proper spot of its own volition. Thomas sat back, breathing hard. Then he realized that the entire room had gone silent.

He looked up. In that whole great chamber it seemed that not a single fay moved. All were arrested in midaction by a sound or a sight only they could hear. All except one.

Evadne came toward him, shoving his motionless companions out of the way.

Thomas picked up his rapier and stood.

———

Kade led Evadne and the others in a chase toward the opposite end of the cellar, stopping only when she could put one of the pillars at her back. She had felt Ableon-Indis's withdrawal and knew she hadn't much time. She threw a handful of glamour at the nearest snarling bogle to give herself room, then whispered a spell of blinding. The sorcery had greater effect on the creatures of Fayre than it did on humans, and the nearest of the Host screeched and stumbled away as the mist of sightlessness settled over them. The mist dispersed rapidly. As a large and hideous water-fay bore down on her, Kade thought frantically for another spell.

Then her ears popped and she felt the ether tremble around her. The nearest fay stared at her, the others gazing about in astonishment. *He did it,* she thought in relief. The old keystone was taking control of the wards, and the

Host could feel the enmity in the etheric structure re-forming around the palace. To those nearest her, Kade said, "You'd better leave, before you're trapped here forever. If you aren't already."

The dark fay erupted into sound and motion as one, plunging away from her, taking to the air, running screaming across the floor toward the steps. Kade leaned against one of the pillars, weak from relief, then realized Evadne was nowhere to be seen.

————

The Host was dispersing in panic. Some charged up the stairs while the flighted fay rose into the air, running into the pillars and each other in their confusion.

Thomas couldn't see Kade. He put his back against the pillar. If Evadne tore the keystone out, this would all be undone.

Evadne broke through the milling fay and charged at him, his long arms reaching. Thomas ducked and swept his sword up. Evadne was too quick and dodged back, aiming a fist at him.

The blow caught Thomas in the shoulder and knocked him sprawling onto the pavement. He rolled over, tasting blood, dazed. Evadne stood over him. The fay's burned flesh hung in ribbons and the death's-head grimace of his mouth below the childishly petulant eyes was terrible. Evadne hesitated, obviously torn between the desire to kill Thomas immediately and the need to rip the keystone out of its niche. Thomas struggled to stand and got no further than his knees.

Something distracted Evadne. He cocked his ruined head, then turned in a crouch. Urbain Grandier stood at the bottom of the steps. Thomas had not seen him come down either; the old man might have materialized out of the air.

Evadne straightened his tall frame slowly. "You betrayed me, sorcerer."

Grandier started toward them, his steps unhurried. "Did I?"

"But I betrayed you."

Grandier stopped. His expression had not changed, but something in the very stillness in which he stood there was daunting.

Evadne's grin was terrible. "I bargained with your creature Dontane to destroy you. The human prince you sought to put on the throne would have given me everything I wanted."

Grandier sighed. "That hardly surprises me."

Evadne's look of disappointment would have been comical on any creature less injured. Thomas crawled back to the pillar and leaned against the niche concealing the keystone. Grandier would have no difficulty in killing him and taking it away, but he meant to keep it in place as long as he could. If Kade hadn't managed to kill herself for him, it would give her more time to escape. The fay wheeling around in the air overhead moved with purpose now. At the far end of the great cellar they were whipping themselves into some kind of frenzy, flying in a great circle around one of the pillars. A wind rose out of nowhere in the chamber.

Grandier shook his head, his features twisting in disgust. He said, "And what has your scheming gotten you?" His voice rose. "There is an army at the gates! A human army with iron and sorcerers to destroy you, and an army of the Seelie Court waits for you in the air."

Thomas realized it was the first time he had ever seen Grandier show anger. Evadne snarled, "They cannot destroy—" The pillar the fay were circling on the far side of the chamber suddenly shattered into dust. More fay were joining the circle and others on the floor below were swept up into it. And disappearing. The Host was forming a ring, Thomas realized, and remembered the broken foundation in the Grand Gallery. *They're going to bring the ceiling down.*

"Command your Host, then; gather your court!" Grandier gestured contemptuously at the fleeing creatures, at the ring forming in the air. "Could you not control your greed for a few days? Could you not have waited until we won to betray me?" He turned his back, as if he were unable to look at the product of his own folly anymore.

He's speaking to Denzil, Thomas thought. Denzil, who was very good at causing chaos but not so practiced at bringing order out of it. Grandier had betrayed Evadne as well, or tried to; he must know he had no right to expect loyalty from a prince of the Unseelie Court. It was the defection of his human allies that maddened him. And if Thomas was correctly interpreting the expression on the fay's maimed face, Evadne didn't understand one word in three.

Evadne shook his head, "Lies again. I made you, sorcerer." His voice dripped contempt. "And I'll destroy you."

Evadne started forward. Grandier turned, his hand moving suddenly. Evadne started back in surprised anger, raising his arms to protect his face. Yes, Grandier still kept his pocket of iron filings.

Then Grandier raised his hands, speaking softly.

Evadne shook his head and raked a hand across his cheek, leaving bloody streaks where the filings had touched him. He sneered, "And what do you intend to do to me, old man?"

This creature has no sense of self-preservation, Thomas thought in wonder.

"I'm going to turn your blood to iron," Grandier told him, and his voice held no anger. "It's a spell I prepared for just such an occasion as this, a derivative of a common alchemical process, which you would know if you studied sorcery."

"I gave you your power," Evadne said. He smiled at the old man. "Destroy me and you will lose it. You will be trapped in this shape forever."

Grandier hesitated. Then just as Evadne made to move forward, Grandier gestured sharply. Evadne froze. Grandier walked toward him, and as he moved past the silent fay, he pushed Evadne's arm. The corpse toppled and fell, breaking into dust as it struck the floor.

The Host was disappearing rapidly now, the ring a wild circle of airborne stones, splintered wood, mangled fay bodies, and other debris. Thomas leaned back against the pillar and looked up as Grandier reached him. "Well?" Thomas said. "What now?"

"I still have no regrets." Grandier smiled. His seamed face showed all the weight of his own years as well as Galen Dubell's. "Except perhaps my choice of allies."

"And your choice of enemies?" Kade was leaning next to the pillar at Thomas's side. He hadn't seen her approach and felt a surge of relief so intense it was painful.

Grandier watched her a moment, then said gravely, "Yes, that as well."

"So, Villon's troop is here," Thomas said. Trying to keep his attention on Grandier, he didn't look up at Kade.

Grandier nodded. "Denzil thought the General would hold Bel Garde and attack from there. He did not. He entered the city late this afternoon and is now attempting to force St. Anne's Gate."

Aviler got through, and Villon decided to risk an assault rather than be trapped in Bel Garde, Thomas thought. *And you think he's forcing St. Anne's Gate, but Aviler can tell him that with the Gate House unmanned, the Postern is indefensible.* Raising his voice to be heard over the howling wind, he said, "Why aren't you trying to stop him?"

"I came to stop Kade from replacing the keystone, and to summon the Host." Grandier could still take the keystone, but he made no move to do so. The wind tore at their hair, taking their breath away. Grandier squinted into it, then shook his head regretfully. "I fear you and the High Minister were correct. Despite all my experience with violence and treachery, I am still politically naive."

Thomas couldn't see Galen Dubell in that lined and weary face anymore, as if it were no longer a disguise. As if Grandier himself was actually completely present in that shell for the first time.

Kade eyed him, unimpressed. "You killed one of my only friends, and I'll never forgive you."

Grandier's calm gaze went to her. "I cannot argue with that sentiment."

Still wary, Thomas asked, "What will you do now?"

Grandier looked startled. Then his knees buckled and he started to collapse, his thin form giving way like an empty sack. Thomas caught him as the old man sagged against the flagstones. As Grandier slumped over forward, he saw the bloody gaping hole in his back.

He looked up, automatically tracing the line of fire. Denzil stood on the second tier of steps, handing a smoking musket to an Alsene trooper. They had heard nothing; the musket's blast had been carried away in the wind caused by the ring and the Host's departure.

Kade crouched beside Thomas, her face white and drawn in the rapidly shifting light. The trooper handed Denzil another loaded musket. Thomas pushed Grandier's body aside and stood, dragging Kade with him, putting the pillar between them and Denzil's line of fire. "They'll come after us. We have to—"

Kade shook her head. "It's too late." He could barely hear her over the growing roar of the wind.

A crash reverberated through the stone beneath them. The swirling mass of the ring seemed to lose its structure as the last of the Host winked out of existence. It flung out a deadly hail of rocks and splintered wood, then it drifted crazily, moving sideways toward them across the large chamber. The troopers on the stairway panicked, bolting back up to the entrance. Looking back around the pillar, Thomas saw Denzil hesitate, cradling the fresh musket, before the rain of debris moved nearer and he too retreated up the stairs.

They couldn't escape that way without being felled by the flying rubble. Even the keystone pillar was no longer providing decent cover. Thomas winced as a stinging deluge of splinters struck them. He pulled Kade closer and felt her arm go around his waist.

A section of the ceiling collapsed almost above them, and fell into the ring, pulverized into dust instantly. The pillars shuddered as the ring brushed against them, the forces that drove it pressing outward at the stone, and chunks began to fall out of the far wall. The ring tilted on its axis, falling toward the cellar floor, directly over their heads.

Then they were in the empty cold silence of the Grand Gallery. Thomas stumbled and caught himself on one of the broken boulders. He would never get used to this form of travel. He let Kade steady him, and they made their way to the edge of the ring and climbed out onto the cold dirty tiles.

Kade sat down abruptly, as if her legs had suddenly given out, and after a moment Thomas sank to the ground beside her. Out the broken windows of the terrace they could see Alsene troops running awkwardly in the deep snow across the park. There was a burst of pistol fire and two of the men fell, roses of blood growing around them in the snow.

Thomas looked at Kade, sitting so close, with her hair in wild disarray, and wondered what it would be like to kiss her when he didn't think he was going to die. So he took her chin gently and turned her face toward him and did.

He had started to draw back when her hand in his hair stopped him. Her mouth stopped his chuckle.

There were shouts and musket fire from somewhere inside the Gallery Wing now.

Kade jumped to her feet. "Come with me."

Thomas looked involuntarily toward the silent fayre ring in the Grand Gallery's floor. He decided that with sufficient motivation he could grow used to anything. Then he noticed that his hands were still speckled with Grandier's blood and thought of Denzil, and Ravenna. *Not now,* he thought. For a moment, the words stuck in his throat, then he said, "I can't."

He hadn't expected her to react like anyone else, and she didn't disappoint him. She smiled. "It's not that easy." And she stepped back into the ring and disappeared.

CHAPTER TWENTY

THE WIND HAD changed direction and emptied the night sky of clouds; stars were visible for the first time in days.

Lord General Villon had set up a command post on the siege wall of St. Anne's Gate, under the light of lamps and torches placed all along the high crenellated battlement. Thomas leaned on an embrasure and watched as the old General paced up and down, consulting with his officers through the couriers continuously reporting in. The snow and ice were melting rapidly and it was warmer now than it had been at twilight.

Villon had wanted to bring Roland back into the city as soon as possible. His men were clearing the palace of any remaining fay and Alsene troops, with the help of the sorcerers from Lodun who had arrived at nightfall just after Villon. It was Grandier's manipulation of the weather that had drawn their attention and brought them to investigate. Lodun had never received any of the messages Ravenna had sent out before the attack.

Thomas didn't know where Roland was and hadn't asked. He knew the young King had been taken to some secured place inside the city wall. Falaise was at the Bishop's Palace; he had approved Gideon's suggestion that she be taken there a few hours ago. Some of the court at least had returned, and the rest of his own men and the Albon knights were here helping to hunt down the last of the Alsene troops.

Fire occasionally blossomed in the dark canyons that were the streets of the city below: the lamps and torches of patrols or of townspeople hesitantly venturing out. They expected reinforcement in the form of the royal garrison at Portier to arrive sometime in the morning. Villon had learned that frantic messengers from the mayor of a village on the trade road had been sent there and to the Granges, bearing confused tidings of a massive attack.

Thomas had deliberately removed himself from the action. He had been with Villon for the past few hours, answering questions and directing him to the areas where Denzil's men might be concealed. Now he was merely waiting.

Recently he had noticed that time seemed to be passing in short stretches bordered by periods of less-than-coherent thought, and that his only support was the rough stone of the battlement. At one point he noticed that Berham was standing next to him, and had apparently been there for some time.

There was a new flurry of activity along the wall as Villon's cornet officer arrived with Dr. Conadine, one of the Lodun sorcerers. After a long consultation with them, Villon turned and came toward Thomas. The General was a small man, half a head shorter than Thomas, with graying dark hair. He had been one of Ravenna's oldest friends, having grown up with her on her father's country residence. Villon said, "They've taken our good Duke of Alsene. He's confessed to Aviler."

Thomas was not so far gone that he misinterpreted the General's expression. "And?"

"He's embellished somewhat, trying to make it look as though it were a misunderstanding." Villon's expression became deeply ironic. "That's to be expected. But he also says he killed the sorcerer Urbain Grandier. Conadine truth-tested him, and he's not lying."

Thomas looked at the night-shrouded city that was slowly creeping out of hiding. "I know."

Villon nodded, letting out his breath in resignation. "Of course, we look at it and say he's cutting his losses. It's only sense for a man to dispose of his confederates when a plot like this goes wrong. But the boy won't see it that way."

Roland had always been "the boy" to Villon. Still looking out at the city, Thomas said, "Denzil sent the Unseelie Court to take Roland prisoner and kill Ravenna."

"No, Grandier did." Villon was not arguing the point, but stating the facts as Roland would see them. "But he made a mistake in not killing Aviler. There's no getting around the point that Denzil brought a private troop into Vienne for the purpose of forcibly removing a High Minister from his home, killing a number of city guardsmen engaged in their rightful duty, not to mention a great lot of folk who were driven out into the street and killed by those demon creatures. And he didn't put that troop at the King's disposal, but used it for his own business, which involved imprisoning warranted officers of the crown." Villon shook his head. "If Ravenna were alive I'd order the scaffold built. As it is . . . There was only one hope, but too many people saw us take him alive. He made sure of that."

Thomas felt Villon expected a response, so he said, "He would."

Villon's gaze went to the city. "You can't help us anymore tonight. Go back to the Guard House."

After a moment, Thomas smiled. "You're bringing Roland back to the palace and you want me out of the way."

"She taught you everything she ever knew, didn't she? Everything the boy should have learned." Villon sighed. "Do you think you can control your desire for martyrdom and let me manage this?"

Desire for martyrdom? Thomas thought. "I don't have to be here, you know. I had two better offers."

"That's not an answer."

"Of course it is." Thomas pushed away from the wall and turned to leave.

"The boy won't think so," Villon called after him.

Thomas decided to walk along the wall as far as he could before going down to the courts below. The sky was beautiful. Berham followed him, and Thomas noted the servant still had the two pistols he had given him the night of the first attack. When they had walked awhile Thomas said, "I'm going to send you and Phaistus over to Renier."

"Respectfully, Sir, I'm a forgetful man, and I don't think I could remember that I was Lord Renier's servant after all the years of being yours, so if I were asked"—Berham shrugged—"I would just have to speak my mind."

"That was a very gentle threat." Thomas smiled to himself.

"I don't know what you mean, Captain."

The wind picked up, cool but without the frozen edge that took the breath away. They walked along in silence for a time, then Thomas suggested, "You could get yourself up as a highwayman and terrorize the trade road."

Berham chuckled. "There's a thought; there's a thought indeed."

———

Even though the Old Courts had been taken over by the Host shortly after the evacuation, the Queen's Guard House had not been much disturbed. Thomas wondered if the sigils Kade had put on the cornerposts had been more effective than she had realized. As he came into the entryway, he could see that the lamps were lit in the practice hall, and there were Queen's and a few of the remaining Cisternan guards there. Out of the original hundred and twenty men in the Queen's Guard, over seventy had survived, and that was more than he had expected. Deciding to avoid the occupied areas of the house, Thomas trudged wearily up the side stairs.

Phaistus was in the anteroom, building up a fire in the hearth. The bed-chamber beyond was musty and cold. Thomas stripped off his buff coat and what was left of the doublet beneath, left them in a ragged bloodstained pile, and sat down on the bed. After a moment, he fell over backward and stared at the underside of the tester.

He fell into a kind of half-conscious doze, only dimly aware of Berham and Phaistus rustling familiarly around the room and laying a fire in the hearth.

He said, "Ouch" quite distinctly when Berham pulled his boots off. The servant leaned over him a moment, then said, "Is there something you want us to see to?"

Thomas shook his head. He heard the door shut as the two left, and in moments he was asleep.

It must have been hours later when he opened his eyes and Kade was kneeling on the bed, leaning over him. She grinned. "Surprise."

———

Eventually, Thomas brushed a tendril of hair back from her forehead and said, "It's a long time since I've been with a woman who giggles."

Despite the awkwardness of mutual bruises, cuts, and claw marks, they were good together. There wasn't any other woman he would have felt comfortable making love to in this condition, but there wasn't any other woman he had ever met who would have pounced on him like that now either. He had been trying to decide what would be worse: a taste of what the next twenty years could have been like, or never knowing at all. He was glad she had taken the decision out of his hands.

"Don't brag," Kade said, smiling. "I know there have been hundreds of others."

"Not quite hundreds."

There was a scratch at the door and Berham's voice whispered harshly, "Captain, there's a couple of Albons downstairs. They were sent to tell you the King's giving an audience and he wants you there."

Couldn't he have waited one damn day? was Thomas's first thought. Reluctantly, he rolled off the bed, found his clothes, and started to dress.

Kade sat up and pulled her smock on over her head, then watched him quietly. When he sat down on the bed to get his boots on she said, "Leave with me."

One boot halfway on, Thomas stopped. The words "All right" were on the tip of his tongue. "I can't."

"Ravenna's gone. There's nothing left for you here."

"I have that lovely offer from Falaise."

She grimaced. "Listen to yourself. You know she's afraid of you."

He finished pulling his boots on. "That makes the situation perfect, then, doesn't it?"

"That's not what you want."

He couldn't ask her how she knew what he wanted, when it was all too obvious that she did know.

After a moment, Kade said, "I don't know exactly what I'm going to do, after giving up Knockma. I have other places and my household—well, you met Boliver; they're all mostly like that, except some of them are human. We argue sometimes but we never try to kill each other, and no one's terribly ambitious, which is why they live with me, I suppose. What I'm trying to say is, it wouldn't be like here at all, if you're as sick of this place as I think you are, and I hope you are, because I think I'm going to have some difficulty living without you."

"I'm not going to make any promises I can't keep." There was a muffled crash from the next room. Thomas grabbed the scabbarded rapier hanging over the bedpost and went to the door. He opened it a crack and saw Berham and Phaistus looking out the far door onto the landing. Thomas stepped out. "What is it?"

"Nothing, nothing." Berham looked back. "One of the Albons thought he should deliver his message in person, Sir, but some of the men pointed out that he was mistaken."

"Did they throw him down the stairs?"

"A little, yes."

Thomas shook his head, stepping back into the bedroom. Kade was gone, and one of the high windows was open, the morning breeze stirring the curtains.

———

The court was held in a hall on the ground floor of the King's Bastion. It was relatively undamaged, except for marks of smoke and water on the high sculpted ceiling. Massive paneled paintings hung on the walls, views of the canal city of Chaire. Standing in the center of the room was like standing on the Mont Chappelle and looking down at the beautiful ancient city.

The audience was small: Villon's officers, and men from the city troops that had come out of hiding, the courtiers who had returned from Bel Garde with Roland. Thomas was glad to see the Count of Duncanny in attendance. His

party had not been able to make it out of the city, but had taken refuge in one
of the fortresslike great houses and survived almost intact.

Albon knights lined the walls and were posted next to the doors. Thomas
went to join Villon. Without looking at him, the old General said, "Don't expect much."

A worn and haggard Aviler paced in front of the chair prepared for Roland. Falaise was already present, seated in an armchair near the front of the
room but to one side, so the focus was on the tapestry-draped chair waiting
for the King. That was Aviler's touch, Thomas was sure. Renier would not have
thought of it.

Gideon and Martin and several other Queen's guards stood around the
Queen's chair. Thomas knew from the way Gideon kept trying to catch his
eye that they were wondering why he didn't join them, but he was not going to
unless Falaise ordered it.

The door at the front of the room opened and Roland and Renier entered,
followed by more Albons. Thomas was surprised to see Ravenna's gentlewoman Elaine in the King's entourage, but only for a moment. She had learned
survival from the best.

As Roland took his seat, Aviler stepped back to the side, waiting with folded
arms. At the King's nod, he motioned to one of the knights.

Roland's eyes were dark hollows in his drawn face. He held his cloak pulled
around him tightly, though the hall was almost warm.

There was a stirring at the back of the room, then the crowd parted for a
group of Albons. Thomas felt his nerves go taut.

The knights were escorting Denzil, of course.

They crossed the room in silence except for the click of their boots on the
parquet floor, stopping before Roland's chair. The Duke of Alsene wore a court
doublet in somber colors, and his arm was no longer in a sling. He looked less
weary than Roland, but then, after his capture, Denzil had probably been able
to sleep through the night.

Surprisingly, Roland spoke first. He said, "It was all true." His voice was soft,
but clearly audible in the room so silent a loud heartbeat could have been heard.

Denzil said, "My lord—"

"I did not give you permission to speak."

Denzil waited, watching Roland.

"You plotted with the sorcerer Urbain Grandier." Roland closed his eyes.
"Against me."

The gesture might have looked theatrical, to someone who didn't know the actors. Roland was in real pain. He looked up suddenly. "My mother was killed."

For the first time there was a response from the crowd, a low whisper of comment that was hardly more audible than a wind stirring summer leaves. Thomas knew they were thinking that it had broken Roland. Aviler swayed as if to move forward, then stopped himself. It was a curiously moving gesture of restraint; the High Minister was going to trust that Roland hadn't lost his senses, and would not attempt to control what the King said in an open audience.

Roland fingered the carved chair arm, and his eyes went to Denzil. "Many people were killed. Someone should die for that."

Thomas realized he was holding his breath.

Denzil was as still as a statue, and almost as pale, but he didn't look away from Roland's hollow eyes. Thomas knew that people were remembering the two had grown up together, though Denzil was older.

Roland shifted in his chair suddenly, looking away. "The sorcerer Grandier is dead. Most of the traitors are dead. The charter of the troop of the Duchy of Alsene is to be torn up, the survivors disbanded, their arms taken, and they will not be allowed to form again under those colors on pain of death. The men who hold officers' commissions in the Troop of Alsene will be ordered executed as traitors, for the act of treason against the crown and the Ministry. Any of the lords of Alsene found in the palace taking part in the conspiracy will be ordered executed as traitors, on the same charge. Denzil Fontainon Alsene, Duke of Alsene, is . . . is ordered . . ." Roland did not look at Denzil, or anyone else. His gaze was locked on the pastel haze in a painting of a harbor skyline. The silence stretched, but no one in the crowd made the slightest sound of inattention. Roland closed his eyes to shut out some vision other than the painting. "Is ordered banished from our borders—" He hesitated again, as if he heard himself speaking and wondered at it. Then he continued, "Forever. On pain of death."

Thomas realized that Villon had moved to his other side and was now companionably holding his sword arm. It wasn't necessary. He didn't move.

Roland stood and left the room in a flurry of robes, his attendants closing in around him. The crowd began to talk and mill around, speaking softly at first and then more loudly as tension began to ease. Villon said, "For a moment I thought—" He shook his head, wry bitterness in his eyes. "My days of service won't last much longer, and I can't say that I'm sorry."

Villon had released Thomas's arm, so he started making his way up toward the front of the hall. Halfway there, Aviler met him. The High Minister looked haggard but also energized. He had probably done more of his life's work in the past day than he ever had since first taking office. He said quietly, "Denzil has three days to leave the city. That's not much time. We need to talk."

"No," Thomas said.

Aviler looked blank. "You mean, not here?"

"I mean, not at all." Before he could move on, he saw Renier coming toward them, using his bulk to part the milling crowd.

He reached them and said, "The King wants a private audience with you, Thomas."

"Good." He followed Renier to the front of the room, conscious of Aviler and Villon watching him.

The door at the back of the hall led to a short maze of old council rooms, all crowded with Albon knights, servants, and court functionaries. Thomas recognized no one, conscious of them only as blurs of color and noise. Eventually they reached a chamber with wide double-panel doors standing open and another contingent of knights guarding it.

Thomas followed Renier inside. It was a large parlor with arabesque wallpapers, thick carpets, and heavy brocaded furniture. There was a fire in a hearth with a mantel supported by two carved nymphs, and all the candles were lit. Roland sat in one of the armchairs, staring unseeing at the far wall.

Renier said, "My lord."

Roland looked up, his eyes focusing. "Thank you. Everyone else go."

Some of the knights stepped out immediately, but the others lingered, looking to Renier for direction. Thomas knew they were not easy with the idea of leaving him alone with Roland, and was almost amused to see that Renier apparently shared their opinion. What surprised him was that Roland realized it as well.

As Renier started to speak, Roland stood suddenly and shouted, "Get out!"

The other men moved reluctantly, and Roland crossed the room and flung the heavy carved doors shut after them. The sudden movement seemed to almost exhaust him, and he dropped into the nearest chair and buried his face in his hands.

Thomas simply stood there, not discomfited by the display, and waited for Roland to recover himself. He looked around the room and was startled to notice a portrait of Fulstan in the far corner. It was a good likeness of Roland's father in his early middle age, and it had probably been moved from some other more prominent location and buried away here, as all the portraits of Fulstan were eventually buried away somewhere.

Roland looked up and noticed what had caught Thomas's attention. He stared at the portrait for a long moment himself, then said, "He hated you."

"He hated everyone," Thomas answered.

Roland sat very still for a time, then looked away. He said, "My Queen has given me to know that she wishes you to remain as captain of her guard. I agree."

Roland would allow Denzil to return. Not today, or this month, but perhaps before the year was out. If Denzil had killed Ravenna with his own hands, if Roland had actually seen him casually ordering the destruction of Villon's troops, then it might have been different. But the ties between them were too strong, Denzil was too seasoned a manipulator, and Roland was still too enmeshed in self-hatred to break the link for good. The boy had proved that to himself and everyone else in the audience hall. But now he knew what his life-long friend was capable of, and in time he might manage to break free.

But Roland was a king, and could not be allowed the time.

"That won't be necessary, Your Majesty," Thomas said. "I'm resigning my commission."

Roland's head jerked up. His hands trembling on the arms of the chair, he asked sharply, "Why?"

Thomas needed to get away now, before Roland changed his mind. He said, "Your mother would have wanted it this way," bowed, and went out, closing the door behind him. Roland made no attempt to call him back.

Thomas passed Renier without speaking and made his way back through the passages. Roland already knew what was going to happen. The only one who thankfully hadn't realized it was Kade. She had been away from court too long and must have believed that Denzil would die for his crimes. *And so he will,* Thomas thought. *So he will.*

Denzil was still in the hall. The knights were grouped loosely around him, and he was watching the crowd with folded arms, smiling faintly.

Thomas went up to him, ignoring the knights who tensed watchfully and the stares from the others in the room. He said, "We have a long-delayed appointment." All Denzil had to do was refuse. Refuse and walk away alive, free to use all the persuasive powers at his command on an oversensitive boy-king who had lost his only companion and his mother in one blow, to trade on old love and loyalty to work his way back into Roland's trust. *But he has always been greedy,* Thomas thought, *and he wants me badly.*

Denzil hesitated, watching Thomas, weighing chances, opportunities, desires. If Roland could have seen that look in the eyes of a man who should be nearly broken by the sentence of banishment from a childhood friend . . . But that was something Denzil would be far too clever to allow. He nodded. "Is that how it is?" he asked lightly. "Do you want to challenge me or should I challenge you?"

The room was silent now. "It doesn't matter," Thomas said, and thought, *Now I've either gotten what I wanted or handed him the pleasure of killing me on top of all his other victories.*

"Very well, then. Now, no seconds, and out in the court."

"Agreed."

Thomas started for the double doors at the end of the room without waiting to see what Denzil did. There was a rising murmur of comment among the people still in the hall. Gideon caught up with him on the steps and said, "Captain, what's—"

Thomas interrupted, "The Queen will give you the appointment. You know as much as I can teach you now; the rest you'll do on your own. Just be careful and don't trust anyone, especially Falaise."

He went out into the wide paved court between the bastion and the Mews. The clouds had drawn over the sky again and it was raining a light drizzle. It slicked the paving stones and covered everything with a fine coating of moisture.

Denzil and his escort came out into the court, but they still had to wait while Denzil's swords were sent for. Thomas paced to keep bruised and strained muscles loose and felt a tense excitement building in him.

He thought of Roland sitting alone in that beautiful unused room, waiting for the news. The young King would not stop the duel. But if Thomas won, and that outcome was much in doubt, he would not forgive him for it either. *Burn the bridges after you cross them, not before,* Ravenna would say. He had lied to Roland; he didn't know if Ravenna would have wanted it this way or not. To the end, she had always been capable of surprising him. But with Kade or without her, he couldn't live with himself if Denzil survived this.

A crowd was gathering of Albons, Villon's men, Queen's guards, the servants and courtiers who had returned with Roland and Falaise. A servant brought Denzil's weapons finally, a swept-hilt rapier and main gauche. Both were utilitarian dueling weapons, with silver-chased hilts and no ornamentation.

Thomas waited while Denzil examined the blades, then drew his own weapons and moved out into the open area of the court. Denzil wore a tight smile; he had nothing to lose by this and he knew it.

They circled each other. The first exchange of blows was light, testing. Denzil was strong and quick, and he had excellent instincts.

And excellent training. Thomas countered a feint and lunge that should have punctured his shoulder and left his sword arm useless. Wanting to see if something unorthodox would rattle the younger man, Thomas parried the next thrust with a broad sweep of his rapier and stepped in to attack with his main gauche. It surprised Denzil but he recovered in time to parry with his own offhand weapon.

They were both more careful after that, and in the steady exchange of blows that followed, Thomas felt the duel taking on a rhythm. They were evenly matched, but he felt the fatigue of the past four days, and the knot of scar tissue the elf-shot had left behind in his leg was starting its persistent ache. If Denzil felt any lingering effects from the pistol wound in his shoulder that Grandier had healed, he didn't reveal it.

Denzil made a hard lunge and Thomas struck the blade away. He realized an instant later that the parry had not been strong enough as he felt the steel slip past his right side. Denzil whipped the forte of the blade against Thomas's ribs and pulled sharply back. Thomas felt the cut opening in his side even as he stepped away and brought his sword up in a thrust.

In his eagerness, Denzil had overbalanced himself and stumbled, his parry turning into a desperate block with the hilt. The tip of Thomas's rapier caught in the bars of the swept hilt and was trapped for an instant. Thomas slipped on the wet cobblestones and fell as Denzil wrenched the hilt free. Denzil recovered first and lunged at Thomas's chest as he tried to stand. Thomas twisted away and the point struck the ground behind his back. He rolled back onto the blade, jerking it out of Denzil's grip, his weight snapping it.

Thomas rolled to his feet. Denzil backed away, wiping his face with his sleeve, then he looked at the watching crowd and yelled, "Another sword!" His glove was torn and his hand bled from where the point had caught him.

Thomas picked up his own rapier and saw that the tip was broken off. He walked back toward the crowd, shaking the rain-soaked hair out of his face, trying not to press a hand to his side where he could feel the blood soaking through his shirt. The blade hadn't bitten too deeply, but it was more than enough to slow him down.

He handed the broken weapon to Berham and took the cup-hilted rapier Gideon was holding out to him. Their stricken expressions said it all.

There was some movement in the crowd, someone pushing through the group of anxiously watching guards. Then suddenly Kade stood in front of him. She was barefoot again, and with her ragged dress and disarrayed hair, she could have been some wilder variety of nymph. Except her gray eyes were too human, angry and afraid at the same time. Thomas said, "I thought you'd gone."

She said, "I'm half fay, but I'm not a fool. I've been up on the roof of the Guard House. I was going to wait you out, but Phaistus came and told me."

Thomas glanced up in time to see the young servant quickly retreating behind Gideon. He looked back down at Kade.

Almost pleading, she said, "Can't you just let me kill him, or have someone shoot him, and then we could go?"

"No. I have to do this."

"But I could—"

He put a finger over her lips. "No. It has to be this way. You said you'd do it for me, remember?"

She shook her head, anger temporarily winning out. "Fine. If I'd known you were going to do something like this, I'd have let you stand there and take on all the Unseelie Court and be killed."

"Fine. But if he wins, I want you to hurt him very badly before you kill him."

"I will. Very badly."

He turned and walked back to the center of the open area. Denzil was waiting for him with an unguarded expression of grim rage. *Good,* Thomas thought. *He's angry; that'll help.* Thomas was only exhausted and bleeding. Denzil had probably never faced an opponent in a serious duel who was as good or better than he was, and the young Duke was responding to it with anger. Falaise had come out onto the steps of the bastion and to watch with her ladies, her guards around her. She lifted a hand to him, and Thomas saluted her with his sword, then turned back to Denzil.

Denzil came at him furiously, but was not foolish enough to leave himself open. For a time Thomas was aware of nothing but his screaming muscles, of the flickering danger of the blades, of the blood pounding in his ears. He could see that Denzil's face was white and strained, that he was tiring, too. The rain was coming down harder now and they were both slipping on the wet stones; Thomas knew another fall would finish him.

Then they both lunged at the same moment. Thomas disengaged and circled his rapier around Denzil's blade, twisting his wrist as he sent the point home with his remaining strength. He felt the point of the other rapier graze his arm even as he moved, felt it open a line of fire across his biceps as it went toward his chest; then it dropped away. It wasn't until he stumbled back and felt the resistance on his own blade before it came free that he realized what had happened.

Denzil was on his knees, one hand pressed to his chest with blood spreading between his fingers. Thomas stepped back, waiting.

It had been a clean blow, right to the heart. Denzil tried once to take a breath, his cold eyes fixed on nothing and already going blank, then he slumped forward onto the wet pavement.

Thomas dropped his sword and walked back to where Kade and the others waited. He stopped in front of her, trembling with exhaustion and feeling cold and empty. She shook her head, ran a hand through her tangled hair, and looked up at him. Meeting her gaze, the emptiness fled.

Impatient, her voice weak with relief, Kade said, "Now can we go?"

"Yes, now we can go."

The DEATH
of the
NECROMANCER

CHAPTER ONE

T he most nerve-racking commissions, Madeline thought, *were the ones that required going in through the front door.* This front door was simply more imposing than most. Lit by gray moonlight, the monumental façade of Mondollot House loomed over her, studded with lighted windows. High above the street the pediment was a passionately carved relief of the hosts of Heaven and Hell locked in battle, the shrouds of doomed saints and the veils of the angels flying like banners or hanging down to drape gracefully over the stone canopies of the upper windows. A quartet of musicians played from an open balcony somewhere above, entertaining the guests as they arrived. Glass sconces around the doorway had been an unfortunate modern addition; the flicker and peculiar color of gaslight made it look as if the door was meant to be the mouth of Hell itself. *Not a serendipitous choice, but the Duchess of Mondollot has never been singled out for restraint or taste,* Madeline thought, but kept an ironic smile to herself.

Despite the frosty night air and the chill wind off the river, there were other guests milling around on the wide marble portico, admiring the famous pediment. Madeline tucked her hands more firmly into her muff and shivered, partly from the cold, partly from anticipation. Her coachman received his instructions and urged the horses away, and her escort, Captain Reynard Morane, strolled back to her. She saw the flakes of snow on the shoulders of his caped greatcoat, and hoped the weather held until later tonight, at least. *One disaster at a time,* she thought, with an impatient shake of her head. *Let's just get inside the place first.*

Reynard extended an arm to her. "Ready, m'dear?"

She took it with a faint smile. "Very ready, sir."

They joined the crowd of other guests pressing toward the entrance.

The tall doors stood open, light and warmth spilling out onto the scuffed paving stones. A servant stood to either side, wearing the knee breeches and silver braided coats of old-style livery. The man taking the invitations wore the dark swallowtail coat of fashionable evening dress. *I don't imagine this is the butler,* Madeline thought grimly. Reynard handed over their invitation and she held her breath as the man opened the linen-paper envelope.

She had come by it honestly, though if she had needed to she could have gone to the finest forger in the city: an old man nearly blind, who worked in a dank cellar off the Philosopher's Cross. But she could sense something stirring in the eaves overhead, in the dimness high above the reach of the gas lamps. Madeline did not look up and if Reynard was aware of it he betrayed no reaction. Their informant had said a familiar of the sorcerer who protected the house would guard the door, an old and powerful familiar to spy out any magical devices brought in by the guests. Madeline clutched her reticule more tightly. Though none of the objects in it were magical, if it were searched, there was no way a sorcerer of any competence whatsoever could fail to recognize what they were for.

"Captain Morane and Madame Denare," the man said. "Welcome." He handed the invitation off to one of the footmen and bowed them in.

They were ushered into the vestibule where servants appeared to collect Madeline's fur-trimmed paletot and muff and Reynard's greatcoat, cane, and top hat. A demure maid suddenly knelt at Madeline's feet, brushing away a few traces of gravel that had adhered to the hem of her satin skirts, using a little silver brush and pan specially designed for the purpose. Madeline took Reynard's arm again and they passed through the entryway into the noisy crush of the main reception area.

Even with the carpets covered by linen drapers and the more delicate furniture removed, the hall was opulent. Gilded cherubs peered down at the milling guests from the heavy carved molding, and the ceilings were frescoed with ships sailing along the western coast. They joined the crowd ascending the double staircases and passed through the doors at the top and into the ballroom.

Beeswax, Madeline thought. They must have been at the floors all night. Beeswax, and sandalwood and patchouli, and sweat, heavy in the air. Sweat from the warm presence of so many finely clothed bodies, and sweat from fear. It was all so familiar. She realized she was digging her gloved nails into Reynard's arm in a death grip, and forced her fingers to unclench. He patted her hand distractedly, surveying the room.

The first dance had already started and couples swirled across the floor. The ballroom was large even for a house this size, with draped windows leading out onto balconies along the right-hand side and doors allowing access to card rooms, refreshment, and retiring rooms along the left. Across the back was a clever arrangement of potted winter roses, screening four musicians already hard at work on the cornet, piano, violin, and cello. The room was lit by a multitude of chandeliers burning expensive wax candles, because the vapors from gas were thought to ruin fine fabrics.

Madeline saw the Duchess of Mondollot herself, leading out the Count of . . . *of something,* she thought, distractedly. *I can't keep them straight anymore.* It wasn't the nobility they had to be wary of, but the sorcerers. There were three standing against the far wall, older gentlemen in dark swallowtail coats, wearing jeweled presentation medals from Lodun. One wore a ruby brooch and sash of the Order of Fontainon, but even without it Madeline would have known him. He was Rahene Fallier, the Court Sorcerer. There would be women sorcerers here too, more dangerous and difficult to spot because they would not be wearing presentation medals or orders with their ball gowns. And the university at Lodun had only allowed women students for the past ten years. Any female sorcerers present would be only a little older than Madeline herself.

She nodded to a few acquaintances in the crowd and she knew others recognized her; she had played the Madwoman in *Isle of Stars* to packed houses all last season. That wouldn't affect their plans, since everyone of any wealth or repute in Vienne and the surrounding countryside would be in this house at some time tonight. And of course, someone was bound to recognize Reynard. . . .

"Morane." The unpleasantly sharp voice was almost at Madeline's left ear. She snapped her fan at the speaker and lifted an eyebrow in annoyance. He took the hint and stepped back, still glowering at Reynard, and said, "I didn't think you showed yourself in polite society, Morane." The speaker was about her own age, wearing dress regimentals of a cavalry brigade, a lieutenant from his insignia. *The Queen's Eighth,* Madeline realized. *Ah. Reynard's old brigade.*

"Is this polite society?" Reynard asked. He stroked his mustache and eyed the speaker with some amusement. "By God, man, it can't be. You're here."

There was a contemptuous edge to the younger man's smile. "Yes, I'm here. I suppose you have an invitation." It was too brittle for good-natured banter. There were two other men behind the lieutenant, one in regimentals, the other in civilian dress, both watching intently. "But you always were good at wiggling in where you weren't wanted."

Easily, Reynard said, "You should know, my boy."

They hadn't drawn the eye of anyone else in the noisy crowd yet, but it was only a matter of time. Madeline hesitated for a heartbeat—she hadn't meant them to become conspicuous in this way, but it was a ready-made diversion—then said, "You'll excuse me a moment, my dear."

"All for the best, my dear. This would probably bore you." Reynard gave her all his attention, turning toward her, kissing her hand, acting the perfect escort. The young lieutenant nodded to her, somewhat uncomfortably, and as Madeline turned away without acknowledging him, she heard Reynard ask casually, "Run away from any battles lately?"

Once away she moved along the periphery of the dancers, heading for the doors in the left-hand wall. A lady alone in the ballroom, without a male escort or other ladies as companions, would be remarked on. A lady moving briskly toward the retiring rooms would be assumed to require a maid's assistance in some delicate matter and be politely ignored. Once past the retiring rooms, a lady alone would be assumed to be on her way to a private tryst, and also be politely ignored.

She passed through one of the doorways leading off the ballroom and down the hall. It was quiet and the lamps had been turned low, the light sparking off the mirrors, the polished surfaces of the spindly-legged console tables and the porcelain vases stuffed with out-of-season flowers. For such a luxury the duchess had her own forcing houses; the gold flowers Madeline wore in her aigrette and on her corsage were fabric, in deference to the season. She passed a room with a partly open door, catching a glimpse of a young maid kneeling to pin up the torn hem of an even younger girl's gown, heard a woman speak sharply in frustration. Past another door where she could hear male voices in conversation and a woman's low laugh. Madeline's evening slippers were noiseless on the polished wood floor and no one came out.

She was in the old wing of the house now. The long hall became a bridge over cold silent rooms thirty feet down, and the heavy stone walls were covered by tapestry or thin veneers of exotic wood instead of lathe and plaster. There were banners and weapons from long-ago wars, still stained with rust and blood, and ancient family portraits dark with the accumulation of years of smoke and dust. Other halls branched off, some leading to even older sections of the house, others to odd little cul-de-sacs lit by windows with an unexpected view of the street or the surrounding buildings. Music and voices from the ballroom grew farther and farther away, as if she was at the bottom of a great cavern, hearing echoes from the living surface.

She chose the third staircase she passed, knowing the servants would still be busy toward the front of the house. She caught up her skirts—black gauze with dull gold stripes over black satin, ideal for melding into shadows—and quietly ascended. She gained the third floor without trouble but going up to the fourth passed a footman on his way down. He stepped to the wall to let her have the railing, his head bowed in respect and an effort not to see who she was, ghosting about Mondollot House and obviously on her way to an indiscreet meeting. He would remember her later, but there was no help for it.

The hall at the landing was high and narrower than the others, barely ten feet across. There were more twists and turns to find her way through, stairways that only went up half a floor, and dead ends, but she had committed a map of the house to memory in preparation for this and so far it seemed accurate.

Madeline found the door she wanted and carefully tested the handle. It was unlocked. She frowned. One of Nicholas Valiarde's rules was that if one was handed good fortune, one should first stop to ask the price, because there usually was a price. She eased the door open, saw the room beyond lit only by reflected moonlight from undraped windows. With a cautious glance up and down the corridor, she pushed it open enough to see the whole room. Book-filled cases, chimneypiece of carved marble with a caryatid-supported mantel, tapestry-back chairs, pier glasses, and old sideboard heavy with family plate. A deal table supporting a metal strongbox. *Now we'll see,* she thought. She took a candle from the holder on the nearest table, lit it from the gas sconce in the hall, then slipped inside and closed the door behind her.

The undraped windows worried her. This side of the house faced Ducal Court Street and anyone below could see the room was occupied. Madeline hoped none of the Duchess's more alert servants stepped outside for a pipe or a breath of air and happened to look up. She went to the table and upended her reticule next to the solid square shape of the strongbox. Selecting the items she needed out of the litter of scent vials, jewelry she had decided not to wear, and a faded string of Aderassi luck-beads, she set aside snippets of chicory and thistle, a toadstone, and a paper screw containing salt.

Their sorcerer-advisor had said that the ward that protected Mondollot House from intrusion was an old and powerful one. Destroying it would take much effort and be a waste of a good spell. Circumventing it temporarily would be easier and far less likely to attract notice, since wards were invisible to anyone except a sorcerer using gasçoign powder in their eyes or the new

Aether-Glasses invented by the Parscian wizard Negretti. The toadstone it-self held the necessary spell, dormant and harmless, and in its current state invisible to the familiar who guarded the main doors. The salt sprinkled on it would act as a catalyst and the special properties of the herbs would fuel it. Once all were placed in the influence of the ward's key object, the ward would withdraw to the very top of the house. When the potency of the salt wore off, it would simply slip back into place, probably before their night's work had been discovered. Madeline took her lock picks out of their silken case and turned to the strongbox.

There was no lock. She felt the scratches on the hasp and knew there had been a lock here recently, a heavy one, but it was nowhere to be seen. *Damn. I have a not-so-good feeling about this.* She lifted the flat metal lid.

Inside should be the object that tied the incorporeal ward to the corporeal bulk of Mondollot House. Careful spying and a few bribes had led them to expect not a stone as was more common, but a ceramic object, perhaps a ball, of great delicacy and age.

On a velvet cushion in the bottom of the strongbox were the crushed rem-nants of something once delicate and beautiful as well as powerful, nothing left now but fine white powder and fragments of cerulean blue. Madeline gave vent to an unladylike curse and slammed the lid down. *Some bastard's been here before us.*

———————

"There's nothing here," Mother Hebra whispered. She crouched in the brick rubble at the base of the barred gate, hands outstretched. She smiled and nodded to herself. "Aye, not a peep of a nasty old sorcerer's ward. She must've done it."

"She's somewhat early," Nicholas muttered, tucking away his pocket watch. "But better that than late." Tools clanked as the others scrambled forward and he reached down to help the old woman up and out of the way.

The oil lamps flickered in the damp cold air, the only light in the brick-lined tunnel. They had removed the layer of bricks blocking the old passage into Mondollot House's cellars, but Mother Hebra had stopped them before they could touch the rusted iron of the gate, wanting to test to see if it was within the outer perimeter of the ward that protected the house. Nicholas could sense nothing unusual about the gate, but he wasn't willing to ignore the old witch's advice. Some household wards were designed to frighten potential intruders, others to trap them, and he was no sorcerer to know the difference.

The tunnel was surprisingly clean and for all its dampness the stale air was free of any stench. Most inhabitants of Vienne thought of the tunnels beneath the city—if they thought of them at all—as filthy adjuncts to the sewers, fit for nothing human. Few knew of the access passages to the new underground rail system, which had to be kept clear and relatively dry for the train workers.

Crack and Cusard attacked the bars with hacksaws and Nicholas winced at the first high-pitched scrape. They were too far below street level to draw the attention of anyone passing above; he hoped the sound wasn't echoing up through the house's cellars, alerting the watchmen posted on the upper levels.

Mother Hebra tugged at his coat sleeve. She was half Nicholas's height, a walking bundle of dirty rags with only a tuft of gray hair and a pair of bright brown eyes to prove there was anything within. "So you don't forget later . . ."

"Oh, I wouldn't forget you, my dear." He produced two silver coins and put them in the withered little hand she extended. As a witch, she wasn't highly skilled, but it was really her discretion he was paying for. The hand disappeared back into her rags and the whole bundle shook, apparently with joy at being paid.

Cusard had cut through several bars already, and Crack was almost finished with his side. "Rusted through, mostly," Cusard commented, and Crack grunted agreement.

"Not surprising; it's much older than this tunnel," Nicholas said. The passage had once led to another Great House, torn down years past to make way for Ducal Court Street, which stretched not too many feet above their heads.

The last bar gave way, and Cusard and Crack straightened to lift the gate out of the way. Nicholas said, "You can go now, Mother."

The prompt payment had won her loyalty. "Nay, I'll wait." The bundle of rags settled against the wall.

Crack set his end of the gate down and turned to regard Mother Hebra critically. He was a lean, predatory figure, his shoulders permanently stooped from a term at hard labor in the city prison. His eyes were colorless and opaque. The magistrates had called him a born killer, an animal entirely without human feeling. Nicholas had found that to be somewhat of an exaggeration, but knew that if Crack thought Hebra meant to betray them he would act without hesitation. The old witch hissed at him, and Crack turned away.

Nicholas stepped over the rubble and into the lowest cellar of Mondollot House.

There was no new red brick here. Their lamps revealed walls of rough-cut

stone, the ceiling arched with thick pillars to support the weight of the structure above. A patina of dust covered everything and the air was dank and stale.

Nicholas led the way toward the far wall, the lamp held high. Obtaining
the plans for this house, stored in a chest of moldering family papers at the
Mondollot estate in Upper Bannot, had been the hardest part of this particular
scheme so far. They were not the original plans, which would have long since
turned to dust, but a builder's copy made only fifty years ago. Nicholas only
hoped the good Duchess hadn't seen fit to renovate her upper cellars since
then.

They reached a narrow stair that curved up the wall, vanishing into darkness at the edge of their lamplight. Crack shouldered past Nicholas to take the
lead and Nicholas didn't protest. Whether Crack had sensed something wrong
or was merely being cautious, he had learned not to ignore the man's instincts.

The stairs climbed about thirty feet up the wall, to a narrow landing with
a wooden ironbound door. A small portal in the center revealed that it would
open into a dark empty space of indeterminate size, lit only by the ghost of reflected light coming from a door or another stairwell on the far wall. Nicholas
held the lamp steady so Cusard could work at the lock with his picks. As the
door groaned and swung open, Crack stepped forward to take the lead again.
Nicholas stopped him. "Is something wrong?"

Crack hesitated. The flicker of lamplight made it even harder than usual to
read his expression. His face was sallow and the harsh lines around his mouth
and eyes had been drawn there by pain and circumstance rather than age. He
wasn't much older than Nicholas's thirty years, but he could have easily passed
for twice that. "Maybe," he said finally. "Don't feel right."

And that's the most we'll have out of him, Nicholas thought. He said, "Go on,
then, but remember, don't kill anyone."

Crack acknowledged that with an annoyed wave and slipped through the
door.

"Him and his feelings," Cusard said, glancing around the shadowed cellar and shivering theatrically. He was an older man, thin and with a roguish
cast of feature that was misleading—he was the nicest thief that Nicholas had
ever met. He was a confidence man by vocation and far more used to plying
his trade in the busy streets than to practicing his cracksman's skills underground. "It don't half worry you, especially when he don't have the words he
needs to tell what he does think is wrong."

Nicholas absentmindedly agreed. He was wondering if Madeline and Reynard had managed to leave the house yet. If Madeline had been discovered interfering with the ward . . . *If Madeline had been discovered, we would surely know by now.* He pushed the worry to the back of his mind; Madeline was quite capable of taking care of herself.

Crack appeared at the gap in the doorway, whispering, "All clear. Come on."

Nicholas turned his lamp down to a bare flicker of flame, handed it to Cusard, and slipped through the door.

Hesitating a moment for his eyes to adjust, he could see the room was vast and high-ceilinged, lined by huge rotund shapes. Old wooden tuns for wine, or possibly water, if the house had no well. *Probably empty now.* He moved forward, following the almost weightless scrape of Crack's boots on the dusty stone. The faint light from the opposite end of the chamber came from a partly open door. He saw Crack's shadow pass through the door without hesitating and hurried after him.

Reaching it, he stopped, frowning. The heavy lock on the thick plank door had been ripped out and hung by a few distended screws. *What in blazes . . . ?* Nicholas wondered. It was certainly beyond Crack's strength. Then he saw that the lock had been torn out from the other side, by someone or something already within the cellar room. The angle of the distended metal allowed no other conclusion. *That is hardly encouraging.*

Nicholas stepped through the door and found himself at their goal. A long low cellar, modernized with brick-lined walls and gas sconces. One sconce was still lit, revealing man-high vaults in the walls, each crammed with stacked crates, metal chests, or barrels. Except for the one only ten paces away, which was filled with the bulk of a heavy safe.

The single lamp also revealed Crack, standing and watching Nicholas thoughtfully, and the dead man stretched at his feet.

Nicholas raised an eyebrow and came farther into the room. There were two other bodies sprawled on the stone flags just past the safe.

Crack said, "I didn't do it."

"I know you didn't." Engineering Crack's escape from the Vienne prison had been one of the first acts of Nicholas's adult criminal career; he knew Crack wouldn't lie to him. Nicholas sat on his heels for a closer look at the first corpse. Startled, he realized the red effusion around the man's head wasn't merely blood but brain matter. The skull had been smashed in by a powerful blow. Behind him, Cusard swore in a low voice.

Exonerated, Crack crouched down to examine his find. The dead man's suit was plain and dark, probably the uniform of a hired watchman, and the coat was streaked with blood and the filthy muck from the floor of the cellar. Crack pointed to the pistol still tucked into the man's waistband and Nicholas asked, "Are they all like this?"

Crack nodded. "Except one's had his throat torn out."

"Someone's been before us!" Cusard whispered.

"Safe ain't touched," Crack disagreed. "No sign of anyone. Got something else to show you, though."

Nicholas pulled off his glove to touch the back of the dead man's neck, then wiped his hand on his trousers. The body was cold, but the cellar air was damp and chill, so it really meant little. He didn't hesitate. "Cusard, begin on the safe, if you please. And don't disturb the bodies." He got to his feet to follow Crack.

Cusard stared. "We going on with it, then?"

"We didn't come all this way for naught," Nicholas said, and followed Crack to the other end of the cellar.

Nicholas took one of the lamps, though he didn't turn the flame up; Crack didn't seem to need the light. Finding his way unerringly, he went to the end of the long cellar, passing all the boxes and bales that contained the stored wealth of the Mondollot family, and rounded a corner.

Nicholas's eyes were well adjusted to the dark and he saw the faint light ahead. Not pure yellow firelight, or greasy gaslight, but a dim white radiance, almost like moonglow. It came from an arched doorway, cut into a wall that was formed of old cut stone. There had been a door barring it once, a heavy wooden door of oak that had hardened over time to the strength of iron, that was now torn off its hinges. Nicholas tried to shift it; it was as heavy as stone. "In here," Crack said, and Nicholas stepped through the arch.

The radiance came from ghost-lichen growing in the groined ceiling. There was just enough of it to illuminate a small chamber, empty except for a long stone slab. Nicholas turned the flame of the lamp up slowly, exposing more of the room. The walls were slick with moisture and the air stale. He moved to the slab and ran his hand across the top, examining the result on his gloved fingers. The stone there was relatively free of dust and the oily moisture, yet the sides of the slab were as dirty as the walls and floor.

He lifted the lamp and bent down, trying to get a better angle. Yes, there was something here. Its outline was roughly square. Oblong. *A box, perhaps,* he thought. *Coffin-sized, at least.*

He glanced up at Crack, who watched intently. Nicholas said, "Someone entered the cellar, by a route yet undetermined, stumbled on the guards, or was stumbled on by them, possibly when he broke the lock on the older cellar to search it. Our intruder killed to prevent discovery, which is usually the act of a desperate and foolish person." It was Nicholas's belief that murder was almost always the result of poor planning. There were so many ways of making people do what you wanted other than killing them. "Then he found this room, broke down the door with a rather disturbing degree of strength, removed something that had lain here undisturbed for years, and retired, probably the same way he entered."

Crack nodded, satisfied. "He ain't here no more. I'll go bank on that."

"It's a pity." And now it was doubly important to leave no trace of their presence. *If I'm going to be hanged for murder, I'd prefer it to be a murder I actually committed.* Nicholas consulted his watch in the lamplight, then tucked it away again. "Cusard should be almost finished with the safe. You go back for the others and start moving the goods out. I want to look around here a little more." There were six other men waiting up in the tunnel, whose help was necessary if they were to transport the gold quickly. Crack, Cusard, and Lamane, who was Cusard's second-in-command, were the only ones who knew him as Nicholas Valiarde. To Mother Hebra and the others hired only for this job, he was Donatien, a shadowy figure of the Vienne underworld who paid well for this sort of work and punished indiscretion just as thoroughly.

Crack nodded and stepped to the door. Hesitating, he said again, "I'll go bank he's not here no more. . . ."

"But you would appreciate it if I exercised the strictest caution," Nicholas finished for him. "Thank you."

Crack vanished into the darkness and Nicholas stooped to examine the floor. The filth and moisture on the pitted stone revealed footmarks nicely. He found the tracks of his own boots, and Crack's, noting that the first time his henchman had approached the room he had come only to the threshold. In the distance he could hear the others, muted exclamations as the new arrivals saw the dead men, the rumble of Crack's voice, a restrained expression of triumph from everyone as Cusard opened the safe. But there were no footmarks left by their hypothetical intruder.

Kneeling to make a more careful survey, and ruining the rough fabric of his workman's coat and breeches against the slimy stone in the process, Nicholas found three scuffles he couldn't positively attribute to either Crack or himself, but that was all. He sat up on his heels, annoyed. He was willing to swear his analysis of the room was correct. There was no mistaking that some object had been removed from the plinth, and recently.

Something that had lain in this room for years, in silence, with the ethereal glow of the ghost-lichen gently illuminating it.

He got to his feet, meaning to go back to the guards' corpses and examine the floor around them more thoroughly, if the others hadn't already obliterated any traces when carrying out the Duchess's stock of gold.

He stepped past the ruined door and something caught his eye. He turned his head sharply toward the opposite end of the corridor, where it curved away from the vaults and into the older wine cellars. Something white fluttered at the end of that corridor, distinct against the shadows. Nicholas turned up the lamp, drawing breath to shout for Crack—an instant later the breath was knocked out of him.

It moved toward him faster than thought and between the first glimpse of it and his next heartbeat it was on him.

A tremendous blow struck him flat on his back and the creature was on top of him. Eyes, bulging because the flesh around them had withered away, stared at him in black hate out of a face gray as dead meat. It bared teeth like an animal's, long and curving. It was wrapped in a once-white shroud, now filthy and tattered. Nicholas jammed his forearm up into its face, felt the teeth tearing through his sleeve. He had kept his grip on the lantern, though the glass had broken and the oil was burning his hand. He swung it toward the thing's head with terror-inspired strength.

Whether it was the blow or the touch of burning oil, it shrieked and tore itself away. The oil set the sleeve of Nicholas's coat afire; he rolled over, crushing the flames out against the damp stone.

Crack, Cusard, and Lamane suddenly clustered around him. Nicholas tried to speak, choked on the lungful of smoke he had inhaled, and finally gasped, "After him."

Crack bolted immediately down the dark corridor. Cusard and Lamane stared at Nicholas, then at each other. "Not you," Nicholas said to Cusard. "Take charge of the others. Get them out of here with the gold."

"Aye," Cusard said in relief and scrambled up to run back to the others. Lamane swore but helped Nicholas to his feet.

Cradling his burned left hand, Nicholas stumbled after Crack. Lamane had a lamp and a pistol; Crack had gone after the thing empty-handed and in the dark.

"Why are we following it?" Lamane whispered.

"We have to find out what it is."

"It's a ghoul."

"It's not a ghoul," Nicholas insisted. "It wasn't human."

"Then it's fay," Lamane muttered. "We need a sorcerer."

Vienne had been overrun by the Unseelie Court over a hundred years ago, in the time of Queen Ravenna, but as far as the superstitious minds of most city people were concerned, it might as well have happened yesterday. "If it's a fay, you have iron," Nicholas said, indicating the pistol.

"That's true," Lamane agreed, encouraged. "Fast as it was, though, it's miles away by now."

Perhaps, Nicholas thought. Whether it had actually moved that quickly, or it had afflicted him with some sort of paralysis he couldn't tell; his mind's eye seemed to have captured an image of it careening off the corridor wall as it charged him, which might indicate that its movement toward him hadn't been as instantaneous as it had seemed.

This was the lowest level of the Mondollot wine cellars. The lamplight revealed cask after cask of old vintages, some covered by dust and cobwebs, others obviously newly tapped. Nicholas remembered that there was one of the largest balls of the fashionable season going on not too many feet above their heads, and while a large supply had undoubtedly already been hauled upstairs, servants could be sent for more casks at any moment. He could not afford to pursue this.

They found Crack waiting for them at the far wall, near a pile of broken bricks and stone. Nicholas took the lamp from Lamane and lifted it high. Something had torn its way through the wall, pushing out the older foundation stone and the brick veneer. The passage beyond was narrow, choked by dust and filth. Nicholas grimaced. From the smell it led straight to the sewer.

"That's where he came in." Crack offered his opinion. "And that's where he went out."

"Ghouls in the sewers," Nicholas muttered. "Perhaps I should complain to the aldermen." He shook his head. He had wasted enough time on this already. "Come, gentlemen, we have a small fortune waiting for us."

———

Still inwardly cursing, Madeline took a different stairway down to the second floor. They had planned this for months; it was incredible that someone else would scheme to enter Mondollot House on the same night. *No,* she thought suddenly. *Not incredible.* On every other night this place was guarded like the fortress it was. But tonight hundreds of people would be allowed in and she couldn't be the only one who knew of a good forger. This was an ideal time for a robbery and someone else had seized the opportunity.

She reached the ballroom and forced herself to calmly stroll along the periphery, scanning the dancers and the men gathered along the walls for Reynard. He would expect her back by now and be where she could easily find him. He wouldn't have joined a card game or . . . *Left,* she thought, with a wry twist of her mouth. *Unless he had to. Unless he got into a fistfight with a certain young lieutenant and was asked to leave.* He would not be able to insist on waiting for her, not knowing where she was in the house or if she had finished with the ward. *Damn.* But with the ward gone, it would be possible to slip out unnoticed, if she could get down to the first floor . . .

Madeline saw the Duchess of Mondollot then, a distinguished and lovely matron in pearls and a gown of cream satin, heading directly toward her. She stepped behind the inadequate shelter of a tall flower-filled vase. In desperation, she shielded her face with her fan, pretending to be screening herself from the lecherous view of an innocent group of older gentlemen standing across from her.

But the Duchess passed Madeline without a glance, and in her relief she found herself closely studying the man trailing in the older woman's wake.

He was odd enough to catch anyone's attention in this company. His dark beard was unkempt and though his evening dress was of fine quality it was disarrayed, as if he cared nothing for appearances. And why come to the Duchess of Mondollot's ball, if one cared nothing for appearances? He was shorter than Madeline and his skin appeared pale and unhealthy even for late winter. His eyes glanced over her as he hurried after the Duchess, and they were wild, and perhaps a little mad.

There was something about him that clearly said "underworld," though in the criminal, not the mythological sense, and Madeline found herself turning to follow him without closely considering her motives.

The Duchess strode down the hall, accompanied also, Madeline now had leisure to notice, by a younger woman whom Madeline knew was a niece and by a tall footman. The Duchess turned into one of the salons and the others followed; Madeline moved past, careful not to glance in after them, her eyes fixed farther down the hall as if she were expecting to meet someone. She reached the next closed door, grasped the handle, and swung it open confidently, ready to be apologetic and flustered if it was already occupied.

It was empty, though a fire burned on the hearth and a firescreen was in place, shielding the couches and chairs gathered near it in readiness for ball guests who desired private conversation or other amusements. Madeline closed the door behind her carefully and locked it. All these rooms on this side of the corridor were part of a long suite of salons and there were connecting panel doors to the room the Duchess had entered.

The doors were of light wood, meant to swing open wide and interconnect the rooms for large evening gatherings. Madeline knelt beside them, her satin and gauze skirts whispering, and with utmost care, eased the latch open.

She was careful not to push the door and the air in the room swung it open just enough to give her a view of the other room's carpet, and a thin slice of tulip-bordered wallpaper and carved wainscotting.

The Duchess was saying, "It's an unusual request."

"Mine is an unusual profession." That must be the odd man. His voice made Madeline grimace in distaste; it was insinuating and suggestive somehow, and reminded her of a barker at a thousand-veils peep show. No wonder the Duchess had called her niece and a footman to accompany her.

"I've dealt with spiritualists before," the Duchess continued, "though you seem to think I have not. None required a lock of the departed one's hair to seek contact."

Madeline felt a flicker of disappointment. Spiritualism and speaking to the dead were all the rage among the nobility and the monied classes now, though in years past it would have been feared as necromancy. It certainly explained the man's strange demeanor.

She started to ease away from the door but with fury in his voice the spiritualist said, "I am no ordinary medium, your grace. What I offer is contact of a more intimate, lasting nature. But to establish that contact I require something from the body of the deceased. A lock of hair is merely the most common item."

Necromancy indeed, Madeline thought. She had studied magic in her youth, when her family had still hoped she might demonstrate some talent for it. She hadn't been the best student, but something about this pricked her memory.

"You require a lock of hair, and your fee," the Duchess said, and her voice held contempt.

"Of course," the man said, but the fee was clearly an afterthought.

"Aunt, this is ridiculous. Send him away." The niece, bored and faintly disgusted with the subject.

"No," the Duchess said slowly. Her voice changed, quickened with real interest. "If you can do as you say . . . there seems no harm in trying . . ."

I wouldn't be too sure of that, Madeline thought, though she couldn't explain her uneasiness with the whole idea, even to herself.

"I have a lock of my son's hair. He was killed in the Parscian colony of Sambra. If you could contact him—"

"Your son, not your husband?" The spiritualist was exasperated.

"What does it matter to you whom I wish to contact, as long as your fee is paid?" The Duchess sounded startled. "I would double it if I was pleased; I'm not counted stingy," she added.

"But your husband would be the more proper one to contact first, surely?" The man's tone was meant to be wheedling, but he couldn't disguise his impatience.

"I don't wish to speak to my husband again, alive or dead or in any state between," the Duchess snapped. "And I don't understand what it could possibly matter to you who—"

"Enough," the man said, sounding disgusted himself. "Consider my offer withdrawn, your grace. And the consequences are your own concern." Madeline clearly heard the hall door slam.

The Duchess was silent a moment, probably stunned. "I suppose I'll never know what that was about. Bonsard, make sure that man is conducted out."

"Yes, my lady."

I'd do more than that, Madeline thought. *I'd summon my sorcerer, and make sure my wards were properly set, and lock away any relics of my dead relatives. That man was obsessed, and he wanted something.* But it wasn't her concern. She eased away from the door, waited a moment, then slipped out into the hall.

———

The safe had yielded to Cusard's ministrations and proved to hold nearly sixty small gold bars, each stamped with the royal seal of Bisra. Nicholas's men had already packed them on the sledges they had brought and started back down the tunnel under Cusard's direction when Nicholas, Crack, and Lamane caught up to them.

Nicholas motioned them to keep moving, lifting one of the heavy bars with his good hand to examine the crest. The Duchess of Mondollot maintained a trading business with one of the old merchant families of Bisra, Ile-Rien's longtime enemy to the south. This fact was little known and in the interest of keeping it that way, the Duchess did not store her gold in the Bank Royal of Vienne, which Nicholas knew from experience was much harder to break into. The Bank would also have expected the great lady to pay taxes, something her aristocratic mind couldn't countenance.

Mother Hebra clucked at his burns and made him wrap his scarf around his injured hand. Lamane was telling the others something about the sewers being infested with ghouls and in such a nice part of the city, too.

"What do you make of it?" Cusard asked Nicholas, when they had reached the street access of the maintenance tunnel, which opened up behind a public stable across Ducal Court Street from Mondollot House. The other men were handing up bars of gold to be stored in the compartment under the empty bed of the waiting cart. The street boys posted as lookouts worked for Cusard and thus for Nicholas too, as did the man who ran the stables.

"I don't know." Nicholas waited for the men to finish, then started up the bent metal ladder. The cold wind hit him as he climbed out of the manhole, the chill biting into his burns, making him catch his breath. The horses stamped, restless in the cold. The night was quiet; the men's hushed voices, the distant music from Mondollot House, and the clank of soft metal against wood as the gold was packed away in the special compartment under the wagon bed all seemed oddly loud. "But I'll swear it removed something from that room Crack found," he said as Cusard emerged.

Cusard said, "Well, I don't much like it. It was such a sweet little job of work, otherwise."

Someone brought Nicholas his greatcoat from the cart and he shrugged into it gratefully. "I don't either, that you can be sure of." The wagon had been loaded and he wanted to look for Reynard and Madeline. He told Cusard, "Take the others and get home; we'll draw attention standing here."

The driver snapped the reins and the wagon moved off. Nicholas walked back down the alley toward Ducal Court Street. A layer of dirty ice and a light dusting of snow made the streets and alleys passable; usually they were so choked with mud and wastewater that pedestrians had to stay on the promenades or use the stepping stones provided for street crossings. He realized Crack was following him. He smiled to himself and said aloud, "All right. It didn't go at all well the last time I sent you away. But no more ghoul-hunting tonight."

At the mouth of the alley, Nicholas paused to remove the small hairpieces that lengthened his sideburns and changed the shape of his mustache and short beard, and rubbed the traces of glue off his cheeks. The touches of gray in his dark hair would have to be washed out. He never appeared as Donatien except in disguise: if any of the men who had participated on one of these jobs recognized him as Nicholas Valiarde it could be ruinous. Maintaining the masquerade wasn't much of a hardship; in many ways he had been practicing deception for most of his life and at this point it came easily to him.

He buttoned and belted his greatcoat, took the collapsible top hat and cane from one of the pockets, and tugged a doeskin glove onto his uninjured hand. With the other hand in his pocket and the coat concealing everything but his boots and gaiters, he was only a gentleman out for a stroll, a somewhat disreputable servant in tow.

He paused across the wide expanse of street from Mondollot House, as if admiring the lighted façade. Footmen stood ready at the door, waiting to hand down late arrivals or assist those making an early night of it. Nicholas moved on, passing down the length of the large house. Then he spotted their coach, standing at the corner under a gas streetlamp, and then Reynard Morane waiting near it. Nicholas crossed to him, Crack a few paces behind.

"Nic. . . ." Reynard stepped down from the promenade to meet them. He was a big man with red hair and a cavalryman's loose-limbed stride. He took a close look at Nicholas. "Trouble?"

"Things became somewhat rough. Where's Madeline?"

"That's the problem. I had the opportunity to provide a diversion for her but it went too well, so to speak, and I found myself asked to leave with no chance to retrieve her."

"Hmm." Hands on hips, Nicholas considered the façade of the Great House. For most women of fashionable society, getting out of the place unnoticed would have been an impossible task, but Madeline had studied tumbling and acrobatics for the more active roles in the theater and she wouldn't necessarily need a ground-floor exit. "Let's go around the side."

Mondollot House was flanked by shopping promenades and smaller courts leading to other Great Houses and it was possible to circle the place entirely. The shops were closed, except for one busy cabaret set far back under the arcade, and all was quiet. There were no entrances on the first floor of the house except for an occasional heavily barred carriage or servants' door. The terraces and balconies of the upper floors were all later additions: originally these houses had been impenetrable fortresses, frivolous decoration confined to the rooftops and gables.

They made one circuit, almost back to Ducal Court Street, then retraced their steps. Reaching the far side, Nicholas saw the panel doors on a second-floor terrace fly open, emitting light, music, and Madeline.

"You're late, my dear," Reynard called softly to her. "We've been looking everywhere for you."

"Oh, be quiet." Madeline shut the doors behind her. "I've had to leave my best paletot behind because of you."

"We can afford to buy you another, believe me," Nicholas told her, concealing his relief. He should know her abilities too well by now to worry much about her safety, but it had been a disturbing night. "And it's well earned, too."

Madeline gathered her delicate skirts and swung over the low balustrade, using the scrollwork as a ladder, and dropped to land in a low snowdrift just as Nicholas and Reynard scrambled forward to catch her. She straightened and shook her skirts out, and Nicholas hastened to wrap his coat around her. She said, "Not so well earned. I didn't have a chance to distract the ward because someone had beaten me to it."

"Ah." Nicholas nodded, thoughtful. "Of course. I'm not surprised."

"He never is," Reynard said in a tone of mock complaint. "Let's discuss it somewhere else."

CHAPTER TWO

When they were sheltered from the wind inside the well-upholstered coach, Nicholas had Madeline tell her part of the incident and gave the others his description of the unexpected encounter in the Duchess's vaults.

Reynard swore softly. "Do you suppose someone sent it after you, Nic? You know we have old acquaintances that wouldn't mind seeing you dead."

"I thought of that." Nicholas shook his head. The coach jolted along the uneven stones of the street, making the tassels on the patent leather window shades dance. "But I'm certain it took something out of that room Crack found. A room which isn't on any of the house plans that we were able to obtain either. I think that was why the creature was there. It was only as an afterthought that it tried to kill me."

Madeline tucked the woolen lap rug more firmly around her. "And the key for the house ward had already been destroyed. I think it was that awful little man who wanted a lock of the late Duke's hair. What sort of spiritualist asks for something like that? It's too much like necromancy."

What sort of spiritualist indeed? Nicholas thought. "I wonder why the creature was still there? It was already in the wine vault; it didn't have to attack me to escape. If it successfully removed something from that room, why was it coming back?"

"For the gold?" Madeline suggested thoughtfully. "Though that isn't exactly common knowledge."

Nicholas had deduced the gold's existence from investigation of the Duchess's trading concerns. Someone else might have done so as well, but . . . "Possibly," he said. *Possible, but perhaps not probable.*

Reynard leaned forward. "What's that muck on your arm?"

Nicholas had given his greatcoat to Madeline and was making do with one of the lap rugs. In the musty darkness of the coach, the sleeves of his workman's coat bore a green-tinged stain that faintly glowed. Nicholas frowned. At first glance it looked like ghost-lichen, but he couldn't remember brushing against the walls of the room where it had grown so profusely. He remembered the ghoul's fingers, strong as iron bands, gripping him there, and the way it had shone with a dim unhealthy radiance in the dark cellar. "I believe it's a memento from the ghoul." It made him want to return to Mondollot House to make an examination of the corpses of the three watchmen in darkness, to see if their clothing had the same residue. He didn't imagine Madeline and Reynard would be amenable to that suggestion.

When the coach stopped outside the fashionable Hotel Biamonte where Reynard kept rooms, Nicholas said, "I suppose you're going out to celebrate."

"I would be mad not to," Reynard replied, standing on the snow-dusted promenade and adjusting his gloves. Behind him the doors and fogged windows of the hotel spilled light and warmth, music and the laughter of the demimonde.

Worried, Madeline added, "Take care."

He leaned back into the coach to take her hand and drop a kiss on the palm. "My dear, if I was careful I would not have been cashiered out of the Guard and we would never have met. Which would have been unfortunate." He tipped his hat to them and Nicholas smiled and pulled the coach door closed.

He tapped his stick against the ceiling to signal the driver, and Madeline said, "I worry about him. Those bucks at Mondollot House were holding grudges."

"They may talk, but they won't act. If they were in his regiment they know what Reynard is like with sword and pistol. He can take care of himself."

"I wish I could say the same of you," she said, her voice dry.

Nicholas drew her close, inside the circle of his arms. "Why my dear, I'm the most dangerous man in Ile-Rien, its provinces, and all the Parscian Empire combined."

"So they say." But she said no more on the subject, and their thoughts quickly turned to other things.

———

It was a relatively short ride to Coldcourt, which stood in one of the less fashionable quarters just outside the old city wall. They drew up in the carriageway and Nicholas helped Madeline out as Crack jumped down from the box.

This was the house that had been Nicholas's first real home. The walls were thick natural stone, built to withstand the Vienne winter. It was only three stories at its tallest, sprawling and asymmetrical, and boasted three towers, one square and two round, all with useless ornamental crenellations and embellishments in the style known as the Grotesque. It was ugly and unfashionable, and not terribly comfortable, but it was home and Nicholas would never give it up.

Sarasate the butler opened the door for them as the coachman drove the horses around to the stables in the back. They entered the house, glad to get out of the weather.

Coldcourt was also as drafty as its name implied, but the spacious hall felt warm and welcoming after the chilly night. The straight-backed chairs along the walls and the sideboard were well used, though still in fine condition, relics of the time when Nicholas's foster father had lived here. The carpets and hangings were new, though in a restrained style in keeping with the rest of the house. They only had gas lighting laid on in the main rooms on the first two floors and the kitchen. Nicholas didn't like vulgar display and Madeline's taste was even more particular than his. Still, the plaster above the dark wainscotting was looking a little dingy and he supposed they might afford to have it redone now.

Madeline headed immediately toward the stairs; Nicholas supposed her patience with delicate and cumbersome evening dress had reached its limit and she was going to change. His own progress was more leisurely. His ribs ached from the encounter with the ghoul, or whatever it had been, and he felt singed and three times his age. He shed coat and makeshift bandages as he crossed the hall and told Sarasate, "Warm brandy. Hot coffee. And Mr. Crack will be staying the night, so if his usual room could be prepared, and a meal . . . if Andrea hasn't gone to bed?"

"He thought you might want something after such a late night, sir, so he prepared a bit of veal in aspic and a chestnut soufflé."

"Perfect." Sarasate and the coachman Devis were the only Coldcourt servants who knew anything about Nicholas's activities as Donatien. Sarasate had been at Coldcourt for at least thirty years; Devis was Cusard's oldest son and almost as reliable as Crack. Nicholas saw the butler collecting the ghoulstained coat with an expression of distaste, and added, "That coat's ruined, but don't dispose of it. I may need it later." That was Sarasate's one fault as a butler—he understood nothing about the sometimes vital information that could be gleaned from objects that otherwise appeared to be rubbish.

Nicholas went to the last door at the end of the hall and unlocked it with the key attached to his watch chain. The room was chill and dark and he spent a moment lighting the branch of candles on the table. There were gas sconces on the yellowed plaster walls, but gas fumes could damage oil paint, and it was very important that the work of art in this room not be altered in the slightest degree.

The flickering light of the candles gradually revealed the painting on the far wall. It was a large canvas, almost six feet long and four feet wide, set in a narrow gilt frame. It was a copy of a work by Emile Avenne called *The Scribe*, which purported to be a depiction of palace life in an eastern land. It showed two robed women lounging on a couch while an aged scholar turned the pages of a book for them. Nicholas knew the scene came from nowhere but the artist's imagination. Experts had long maintained that the styles and colors of the tiles on the floor and walls, the detail of the fretted screens and the textiles draping the couches were not common designs known in Parscia, Bukar, or even far Akandu. But it was a subtle, masterful work and the colors were rich and wonderful.

The original hung on the wall of the library at Pompiene, Count Rive Montesq's Great House. Nicholas had sold the painting to the Count, who had affected to believe that he was doing a favor for the foster son of the man whose work he had once sponsored. Nicholas's public persona was that of an art importer and he used his inheritance from Edouard to act as a patron to several young artists of notable talent. He was more of a patron than most people realized, having once anonymously retrieved some paintings stolen from the public gallery at the old Bishop's Palace museum and punished the offending thieves severely. He didn't believe in stealing art.

Nicholas dropped into the velvet upholstered armchair that had been carefully placed at the best point for viewing the work and propped his feet on the footstool. In the long-dead language of Old Rienish, he said carefully, "Beauty is truth."

The colors in the painting brightened, slowly enough at first that it might have been a trick of the eye. They took on a soft glow, obvious enough for the watcher to tell this was no trick, or at least not a natural one. The painting then became transparent, as if it had turned into a window opening onto the next room. Except the room that it revealed was half the city away, though it appeared just as solid as if one could reach out and touch it.

That room was dark now, just a little faint light from an open door revealing bookcases, the edge of a framed watercolor, and a marble bust of Count Montesq sculpted by Bargentere. Nicholas glanced at the clock on his own mantel. It was late and he hadn't expected anyone to be about. Again in Old Rienish, he said, "Memory is a dream."

That scene faded, became washed in darkness, then formed another image.

The artist who had painted this work had known only that he was copying an Avenne for Nicholas's own home. He had believed that the paints he was using were special only in that they were the same mixtures Avenne had used, necessary to duplicate the marvelous soft colors of the original. This was true, but the paints had been personally mixed by Arisilde Damal, the greatest sorcerer in Ile-Rien, and there was even more sorcery woven into the frame and canvas.

The library appeared again, this time in daylight, the curtains drawn back at the windows and a parlormaid cleaning out the grate. That image ran its course, followed by views of other servants coming into the room on various errands, and once a man Nicholas recognized as Batherat, one of Montesq's Vienne solicitors, evidently coming to pick up a letter left for him on the desk.

The beauty of the painting as a magical device was that if Montesq had a sorcerer in to search his home for evidence of magical spying, as he had twice done in the past, the painting on his library wall would be revealed as what it was—only so much canvas, paint, and wood. The magic was all contained in the copy of it.

Montesq had believed the purchase of the original painting a cruel, private joke, an amusing favor for the family of a man he had caused to be killed. But cruel, private jokes were the ones most apt to turn on the joker.

Nicholas heard a voice he would have known anywhere and sat up suddenly.

The painting now revealed the library at night, lit by only one gas sconce. Nicholas cursed under his breath. It was too dim to read the clock on the library wall, so he couldn't tell what time this had taken place, except that it must have been earlier this evening. Count Montesq sat at the desk, his face half shadowed. Nicholas's memory filled in the details. The Count was an older man, old enough to be Nicholas's father, with graying dark hair and a handsome face that was fast becoming fleshy due to too much high living.

The solicitor Batherat stood in front of the desk, a nervous crease between his brows. Any other man of consequence in Ile-Rien would have invited his solicitor to sit down, but though Montesq was charming to his equals and betters, and in public showed admirable condescension to those beneath him, in private his servants and employees were terrified of him. In a tone completely devoid of threat, Montesq said, "I'm glad you finally succeeded. I was becoming impatient."

Nicholas frowned in annoyance. They must be continuing a conversation begun out in the hall and he didn't anticipate gleaning much information from this exchange. If Montesq killed Batherat, of course, it would certainly be worth watching. The solicitor held his calm admirably and replied, "I assure you, my lord, nothing has been left to chance."

"I hope you are correct." Montesq's soft voice was almost diffident, something that Nicholas had learned from long observation meant that a dangerous anger was building.

When Nicholas had first put together his organization, it had been necessary to free Cusard and Lamane and several others whose assistance he desired from their prior obligations to the man who considered himself the uncrowned king of criminal activity in the Riverside slums. This individual had been reluctant to give up their services, so it had ended with Nicholas putting a bullet in his head. The man had been a murderer several times over, an extortionist, a panderer, and addicted to various sexual perversions that would have startled even the knowledgeable Reynard, but he was the rankest amateur at villainy compared to Rive Montesq.

The Count stood and circled around the desk to stop within a pace of Batherat. He didn't speak, but the solicitor blinked sudden sweat from his eyes and said, "I'm certain, my lord."

Montesq smiled and clapped Batherat on the shoulder in a fashion that might be taken for amiable comradeship by a less informed observer. He said only, "I hope your certainty is not misplaced."

Montesq walked out, leaving the door open behind him. Batherat closed his eyes a moment in relief, then followed.

That was the last image the painting had absorbed and now the scene faded as it returned to its quiescent state, becoming merely a static window on some faraway household. Nicholas sighed and ran his hands through his hair wearily. Nothing of note. *Well, we can't expect miracles every day.* Twice the painting had revealed pertinent details of the Count's plans. Montesq moved among the financial worlds of Vienne and the other prominent capitals, bribing and blackmailing or using more violent means to take what he wanted, but he was careful enough to preserve his reputation so he was still received at court and in all the best homes.

But not for much longer, Nicholas thought, his smile thin and ice cold. *Not for much longer.*

He got to his feet and stretched, then blew out the candles and locked the door carefully behind him.

As Nicholas crossed the central foyer to the stairs there was a tap on the front door. He stopped with one hand on the bannister. It was too late for respectable callers, and the not-so-respectable callers on legitimate business wouldn't come here at all. Sarasate hesitated, looking to him for instruction. Crack reappeared in the archway to the other wing, so Nicholas leaned against the newel post, folded his arms, and said, "See who that is, would you?"

The butler swung the heavy portal open and a man stepped into the foyer without waiting for an invitation. He was lean and gaunt and over his formal evening dress he wore a cape and opera hat. The gaslight above the door gave his long features and slightly protuberant eyes a sinister cast, but Nicholas knew it did that to everyone. The man ignored Sarasate and looked around the hall as if he was at a public amusement. Piqued, Nicholas said, "It's late for casual callers, especially those I'm unacquainted with. Would you mind turning around and going back the way you came?"

The man focused on him and instead moved farther into the hall. "Are you the owner of this house?"

One would assume it, since I'm standing here in my shirtsleeves, Nicholas thought. His first inclination was that this was some curiosity seeker; it had been years since his foster father's death, but the notoriety of the trial still drew those with morbid hobbies. People with a more conventional interest in the old man's work also came, but they were usually more polite and presented themselves during the day, often with letters of introduction from Parscian universities. This visitor's appearance—his cravat was a dirty gray and the pale skin above it unwashed, his dark beard was unkempt, and his cape was so ostentatious it would have looked out of place on anyone but a March Baron at a royal opera performance for the Queen's Birthday—suggested the former. "I'm the owner," Nicholas admitted tiredly. "Why? Is it interfering with your progress through the neighborhood?"

"I have business with you, if you are Nicholas Valiarde."

"Ah. It can't wait until tomorrow?" Nicholas twisted the crystal ornament on top of the newel post, a signal to Sarasate to summon the servants more experienced at dealing with unwelcome guests. The butler shut the door, turned the key and pocketed it, and glided away. Crack came noiselessly into the room

"It is urgent to both of us."

The man's eyes jerked upward suddenly, to the top of the stairs, and Nicholas saw Madeline stood there now. A gold-brocaded dressing gown billowed around her and she had taken the dark length of her hair down. She came down the stairs slowly, deliberately, as elegant and outré as a dark nymph in a romantic painting. Nicholas smiled to himself. An actress born, Madeline could never resist an audience.

The man brought his gaze back down to Nicholas and said, "I would like to speak to you in private."

"I never speak to anyone in private," Nicholas countered. The butler reappeared and Nicholas gestured casually to him. "Sarasate, show our guest into the front salon. Don't bother having a fire laid, he won't be staying long."

Sarasate led their unwelcome visitor away and Madeline stopped Nicholas with a hand on his sleeve. In a low whisper, she said, "That's the man who spoke to the Duchess tonight."

"I thought it likely from your description." Nicholas nodded. "He may have recognized you. Did he know you were listening?"

"He couldn't have. Not without everyone knowing." She hesitated, added, "At least that's what I thought."

He offered her his arm and together they followed their guest into the front salon, a small reception room off the hall.

The walls were lined with bookcases as the room served as an adjunct to the library, housing the volumes that Nicholas found less use for. The carpet had been fine once, but it was old now and the edges were threadbare. There were a few upholstered chairs scattered about and one armchair at the round table that served as a desk. The stone hearth was cold and Nicholas waited for Sarasate to finish lighting the candlelamps and withdraw. Crack had followed them in and as the butler left he drew the door closed.

Their visitor stood in the center of the room. Nicholas dropped into the armchair and propped his boots on the table. Madeline leaned gracefully on the back of his chair. He said, "What was it you wanted to discuss?"

The man drew off his gloves. His hands were pale but work-roughened. He said, "Earlier tonight you entered the lower cellars of Mondollot House and sought to remove something. I was curious as to your reason for this."

Nicholas allowed himself no outward reaction, though the shock of that statement made the back of his neck prickle. He felt Madeline's hands tense on his chair, but she said nothing. Crack's eyes were on him, intent and waiting with perfect calm for a signal. Nicholas didn't give it; he wanted to know who else knew this man was here and, more importantly, who had sent him. He said, "Really, sir, you astound me. I've been at the theater this evening and can produce half a dozen witnesses to that effect."

"I'm not from the authorities and I care nothing for witnesses." The man took a slow step forward and the candlelight revealed more of his gaunt features. The shadows hollowed his cheeks and made his strange eyes sink back into their deep sockets.

How appropriate for a spiritualist, Nicholas thought. *He looks half dead himself.* "Then who are you?"

"I am called Dr. Octave, but perhaps it is more important who you are." The man laid his hat and stick on the polished surface of the table. Nicholas wondered if he had refused Sarasate's attempt to relieve him of them or if the butler had simply not bothered, assuming that the unwelcome visitor was not going to survive long enough to appreciate the discourtesy. Octave smiled, revealing very bad teeth, and said, "You are Nicholas Valiarde, at one time the ward of the late Dr. Edouard Viller, the renowned metaphysician."

"He was not a metaphysician, he was a natural philosopher," Nicholas corrected gently, keeping any hint of impatience from his voice. It had occurred to him that this might very well be Sebastion Ronsarde in one of his famous or infamous disguises, but now he dismissed the thought. Ronsarde and the rest of the Prefecture knew him only as Donatien, a name without a face, responsible for some of the most daring crimes in Ile-Rien and probably for a good deal more. If Ronsarde had known enough to ask Donatien if he was Nicholas Valiarde, he would have asked it in one of the tiny interrogation cells under the Vienne Prefecture and not in Nicholas's own salon. Besides, Ronsarde's disguises were exaggerated by rumors spread by penny-sheet writers who were unable to fathom the notion that the most effective Prefecture investigator in the city solved his cases by mental acuity rather than sorcery or other flashy tricks. Nicholas exchanged a thoughtful look with Madeline before saying, "And Dr. Viller was also a criminal, according to the Crown's investigators who executed him. Is that your reason for accusing me of—"

Octave interrupted, "A criminal whose name was later cleared—"

"Posthumously. He may have appreciated the distinction from the afterworld but those he left behind did not." Edouard had been executed for necromancy, even though he had not been a sorcerer. The court had found his experiments to be a dangerous mix of natural philosophy and magic, but that wasn't what had condemned him. Was this a clumsy blackmail attempt or was the man trying the same game he had played with the Duchess, and suggesting Nicholas pay him some exorbitant sum to speak to Edouard Viller? *Ridiculous.*

If Edouard wanted to communicate from the grave he was quite capable of finding some method for accomplishing it himself. Nicholas couldn't decide how much he thought the man knew about him, his plans. Did he know about Reynard or the others? Was he an amateur or a professional?

Octave's lips twisted, almost petulantly. He looked away, as if examining the contents of the room—the leather-bound books, the milky glass torcheres, a landscape by Caderan that badly needed to be cleaned, and Crack, unmoving, barely seeming to breathe, like a watchful statue.

Nicholas spread his hands. "What is this about, Doctor? Are you accusing me of something?" Behind him he sensed Madeline shift impatiently. He knew she didn't think he should give Octave this chance to escape. *I want answers first. Such as what he wanted in Mondollot House, what that creature was, and if he was the one who sent it.* Finding things out was the second driving force of Nicholas's life. "There are criminal penalties for making false accusations."

Octave was growing impatient. He said, "I submit that it is *you* who are the criminal, Valiarde, and that you entered the Mondollot House cellars tonight—"

Nicholas had slipped off his scarf to give himself a prop to fiddle with, and now pretended to be more interested in its woolen folds than in his visitor. "I submit that you, Dr. Octave, are mistaken, and furthermore, if I did enter someone's cellar it is none of your business." He lifted his gaze to Octave's dark, slightly demented eyes and thought with resigned disgust, *An amateur.* "I also submit that the only way you can know this is if you, or your agent, were also there. I suggest you think carefully before you make any further accusations."

Octave merely asked, "You still own Dr. Viller's apparatus? Is any of it here?"

Nicholas felt another chill. *He does know too much.* "Again, you show too much curiosity for your own good, Doctor. I suggest you go, while you still can. If you have some complaint to make against me, or some suspicion of criminal activity on my part, you may take yourself to the Prefecture and bore them with it."

Octave smiled. "Then it *is* here."

Nicholas stood. "Doctor, you have gone too far."

Crack, catching the change in tone, took a step forward. Octave reached for the walking stick still lying on the table, as if he meant to go. The gesture was entirely casual; if Nicholas hadn't already been on the alert he would never have seen the spark of blue spell light that flickered from Octave's hand as he touched the cane.

Nicholas was already gripping the edge of the heavy round table; with one swift effort he lifted and shoved it over. It crashed into Octave and sent the man staggering back.

Light flickered in the room, jagged blue light bouncing from wall to wall like ball lightning. Octave staggered to his feet, his stick swinging back to point toward Nicholas. He felt a wave of heat and saw spellfire crackle along the length of polished wood, preparing itself for another explosive burst. Crack moved toward Octave, but Madeline shouted, "Get back!"

Nicholas ducked as a shot exploded behind him. Octave fell backward on the carpet. The blue lightning flared once and vanished with a sharp crackle.

Nicholas looked at Madeline. She stepped forward, holding a small double-action revolver carefully and frowning down at the corpse. He said, "I wondered what you were waiting for."

"You were in my line of fire, dear," she said, preoccupied. "But look."

Nicholas turned. Octave's body was melting, dissolving into a gray powdery substance that flowed like fine hourglass sand. His clothes were collapsing into it, the substance flowing out sleeves and collar and pants legs to pool on the faded carpet.

The door wrenched open, causing Crack to jump and reach for his pistol again, but it was Sarasate and the two footmen, Devis the coachman, and the others who guarded Coldcourt gathered there. Their exclamations and questions died as they saw the body; everyone watched the spectacle in silence.

Finally, there was nothing left but the clothing and the gray sand. Nicholas and Crack stepped forward but Madeline cautioned, "Don't touch it."

"Do you know what it is?" Nicholas asked her. Madeline had some knowledge of sorcery and witchcraft, but she usually didn't like to display it.

"Not exactly." She drew the skirts of her robe off the floor carefully and came to stand next to him. "My studies were a long time ago. But I know the principle. It's a golem, a simulacrum, constructed for a certain task and animated by some token . . . probably that walking stick."

The stick lay near the body. Crack nudged it thoughtfully with the toe of his boot but there was no reaction.

"We should fold the whole mess up in the carpet, take it out to the back garden, and burn it," Madeline continued.

"We will," Nicholas assured her. "After we take a sample and go through its pockets. Sarasate, send someone for my work gloves, please. The thick leather ones."

"Nicholas, dear," Madeline said, her brows drawing together in annoyance, "I didn't say it was dangerous for the pleasure of hearing myself speak."

"I'll take great care, I promise, but since we can't ask our visitor any more questions, this is the only way we can find out who sent him."

Madeline seemed unconvinced. She added, "Besides, if whoever sent it had any sense at all, there won't be anything in its pockets."

She was right, but Nicholas never ignored the possibility that his opponent had overlooked something. Even the best went wrong; the trick was to be ready when it happened. Sarasate brought the gloves and Nicholas searched the clothing methodically, but found nothing other than a battered and much folded invitation to the Duchess of Mondollot's ball, tucked into the inside pocket of the frock coat. More to himself than to the others, Nicholas muttered, "It could be a forgery, but spiritualism is popular enough now that he may have been invited as a curiosity." A close comparison to Madeline's invitation note should decide it.

Madeline had taken a seat in the armchair, her legs curled up under her dressing gown. The other servants had gone to check the grounds for more intruders and to prepare a pyre for the carpet and their late visitor. Only Crack had stayed behind, watching worriedly.

"It didn't come in a coach, did it?" Madeline asked suddenly. "How did it follow us?"

"It didn't, apparently." Nicholas nodded to Crack, who shifted uneasily and explained, "Devis saw it walk up the road to the drive when he was coming back from the stables."

"So someone dropped it off earlier and it waited until it saw us arrive," she said thoughtfully. "I wonder, was that Octave at the ball tonight or was it this thing? No, that can't be right. The ward would have detected it, or the familiar above the doorway. It has the invitation, but the real Octave must have given the creature his outer clothes, and forgotten to take the invitation away."

"True." Nicholas took a sample of the gray powder, scooping it carefully into a glass vial. Crack came over to help secure the stopper with a bit of wire. "We'll take this when we visit Arisilde tomorrow and see what he makes of it."

"If he's of any help." Madeline rubbed her face tiredly. "There's no telling what state he's in."

Nicholas rested his arms on his knees. His back was aching and it had been a long night. "He's got to be of some help. Someone is taking an alarming sort of interest in us." He took the vial of powder back from Crack and set it on the table. It caught the candlelight as if it were more diamond dust than sand, but the reflection it gave off was the blue of Octave's spell light. "A very alarming sort of interest, indeed."

CHAPTER THREE

Nicholas gave Madeline his arm as she stepped down from their coach. She smothered an unladylike yawn, glanced around the street, and winced. Nicholas couldn't agree more. The Philosopher's Cross was not a pleasant prospect so early in the morning. Under the cold dawn light, with its customarily colorful inhabitants still abed, the place resembled nothing so much as a theater after a long night's performance: empty of magic, with all the tawdry underpinnings of the stage exposed, and the hall cluttered with trash left behind by the audience.

It was called the Philosopher's Cross because two great thoroughfares met here: the Street of Flowers and the Saints Procession Boulevard. The Street of Flowers ran all the way up to the Palace wall and down to the river, to intersect with Riverside Way, and the Boulevard connected the Carina Gate and the Old City Gate, at opposite ends of Vienne's sprawl. It had once been the only street that bisected the city, uninterrupted by canals or masses of decaying slums, failing to suddenly dead-end into a tiny alley, but the building projects of the last century had added a new bridge across the river and cut six new streets through crumbling neighborhoods.

Nicholas signaled their coachman to wait and Crack climbed down from the box to accompany them. It was barely after sunrise and the few people who were stirring were well bundled against the early morning cold and hurrying to their destinations. The remains of stone stalls under the promenades revealed there had once been a great market here, but the area had long since given way to cabarets, coffeehouses, mazes of small alleys, and decaying buildings. Some were ancient structures with a certain fallen grandeur, solidly built with chipped and weathered statuary along their gables. Others were new slapdash affairs of cheap brick, leaning slightly as if they meant to topple at any moment. All were darkened with soot and smoke. When the sun was well up, the streets would be crowded not only with old women hawking everything from herbals to hats, but with the beggars, musicians, poor sorcerers, witches, artists, and itinerant craftsmen that the area was famous for.

Crack went a short distance down the filthy alley and opened the door there. Nicholas and Madeline followed more slowly, picking their way carefully through the muck. There was no one watching the tenement's entrance; the stool in the tiny cupboard where the concierge would normally sit was empty, though the litter of apple cores and crumpled penny sheets around it showed the abandonment was only temporary. The cramped and dirty stairs were lit only by a shattered skylight, visible as a dim circle of light several stories up.

Madeline's mouth twisted wryly. "Poor Arisilde. But I suppose most of the time he doesn't notice."

Nicholas didn't comment. She was probably right and the reason why had been a nagging worry for some time. Arisilde Damal was undoubtedly the most powerful sorcerer for hire in Ile-Rien and he had the added distinction of often failing to remember what he had been hired for, so if he was caught and questioned his evidence would be next to useless. But Arisilde had been on a one-way journey for some years now and Nicholas knew it was only a matter of time before he arrived at his destination. With Crack going ahead to scout the way, they climbed the stairs.

They reached the narrow landing at the top floor and Crack knocked on the door for the garret apartment. The fact that the door was so readily available was a good sign and indicated that Arisilde was receiving callers. If he had been indisposed, the portal would have been far more elusive.

There was the sound of what might be furniture being shifted within, then the door was opened by the sorcerer's ancient Parscian servant. The man was wearing faded robes and a convincingly evil leer. When he recognized Crack, he dropped the leer and waved them in. Crack stepped aside to wait for them on the landing; he trusted Arisilde, as Nicholas did, but after last night extra caution was called for.

They went down a dingy low-ceilinged little hall and into a long room. The far wall was covered with windows, some draped with patchy patterned velvets and others bare to the dreary sky. In the yellowed ceiling were two small iron-rimmed domes, each a multipaned skylight. Faded carpets covered the floor and there were piles of books and stray papers, jugs, glass vials, bags, and little ceramic containers crowding every available surface. There were plants too, herbs growing out of various bottles and jars and vines that climbed the walls and twined up into the skylights. The room was warm and the air thick with the smell of must and foliage.

The most powerful sorcerer in the city, perhaps in all Ile-Rien, was seated in an armchair with stuffing leaking out of the cushions, gazing up at them with vaguely benevolent eyes. His hair was entirely white and tied back from a face that revealed his youth. Nicholas said, "Hello, Arisilde."

The Parscian man cleared a chair for Madeline by shifting the papers stacked on it to the floor. Arisilde smiled dreamily and said, "How very good to see you both. I hope your father is well, Nicholas?"

"Very well, Arisilde. He sends you his regards." As a talented student at Lodun, Arisilde had been part of the cadre of intellectuals who had surrounded Edouard Viller, and had collaborated with him on some of his greatest work. He had also been present at Edouard's execution, but Arisilde's hold on present reality had never been too firm and his dissipations over the past years had weakened it greatly.

"And the lovely Madeline. How is your grandmother, my dear?"

Madeline looked taken aback. Nicholas was surprised himself, though he didn't allow it to show. Madeline was nothing if not reticent about her family and her past; he hadn't known she had a grandmother still living. If, considering who was asking the question, the woman was still living. An odd expression on her face, Madeline managed to reply, "She's quite well, thank you, Arisilde."

The sorcerer smiled up at Nicholas again. His eyes were violet and had once held a lively intelligence. Now their only expression was one of vague contentment and the pupils were so small they resembled pinpricks. He said, "I hope you didn't come for anything important."

Nicholas had to close his eyes briefly, summoning patience and controlling the desire to swear violently. Arisilde must have forgotten about the Duchess's ball last night and their plan for her Bisran gold, even though he had been the one to investigate the house's sorcerous defenses and discover how to circumvent its ward. Nevertheless, Nicholas stepped forward. He drew out a swatch cut from the coat that had taken the brunt of the ghoul's attack and a glass vial containing a portion of the golem's remains. "This first. I wanted you to look at these and tell me what you thought." Among the clutter on the little table at the sorcerer's elbow were two opium pipes, an old-fashioned tinderbox, a thin iron bodkin fixed in a handle, and a small brass lamp. There was also a bowl of strawberries so soaked with ether that the stink of it in the air burned Nicholas's throat. They had been lucky to find Arisilde even this coherent.

"Ahh." Arisilde's long white fingers touched the fabric gently. "How very strange." He took the vial and held it up to catch the candlelight. "Someone's made a golem. A nasty one, too."

"It came to my home and behaved rather mysteriously," Nicholas said, hoping to engage the sorcerer's curiosity.

But the light in Arisilde's eyes was already fading. He lowered the vial slowly, setting it aside. "I'll get to it soon, I promise."

Nicholas sighed inwardly and said only, "Thank you, Arisilde." There was no point in arguing; Arisilde would either do it or not and that was that. Nicholas had held back other samples to take to practitioners whose talents were lesser but more reliable, but he had hoped to get Arisilde's opinion. He hesitated now, wondering whether he should broach the topic of the gold at all. *This was for Edouard, Ari. You could have remembered it. He was a father to you as well.* He said, "Do you remember what we were going to discuss today, Ari? I've got the gold stamped with the Bisran Imperial seal, and the forged documents are finally ready. Do you remember you were going to help me place them in Count Montesq's Great House?"

"Montesq." Arisilde's violet eyes darkened. In an entirely different voice, he said, "I remember Montesq."

Nicholas watched him intently. If destroying Count Montesq, the man who had destroyed Edouard Viller, would help bring Ari out of his daze, then it was doubly worth the risk. He said, "Yes, Montesq. Do you remember the plan we discussed?"

"That, yes, I've been working on that. Very powerful protective wards on that Great House. Found that out when I tried to burn it down, years ago, didn't I? Must be careful, mustn't leave a trace, going in or coming out. That's it, isn't it? We put the Bisran gold and the papers there, then tell the Prefecture, and Montesq is executed for treason." Arisilde looked pleased. The dangerous light had faded and he sounded more like himself. Nicholas didn't find it an improvement.

"That's vaguely it." Nicholas turned to Madeline for assistance, but Arisilde said, frowning, "While I'm thinking of it, you are looking into these goings-on, aren't you?"

"What goings-on?"

"Oh, you know, everyone is talking about it." The sorcerer waved a languid hand unhelpfully. Fortunately the servant understood the gesture and fetched a folded paper from one of the piles of debris and brought it to Nicholas. "Yes, he's right, it's in the front page of that," Arisilde explained.

It was the *Review of the Day,* the only one of the penny-sheet dailies—other than the *Court Record* or the *Lodun Literary Comment*—that was occasionally anything more than rabble-rousing nonsense. The title of the piece taking up most of the front page was "Strange Occurrence in Octagon Court."

It described a young girl called Jeal Meule, who had apparently disappeared as she walked home from her work at a dressmaker's. The strangest part of the "strange occurrence" seemed to be that the girl had vanished twice. She hadn't returned home from work and her mother had canvassed the neighbors searching for her, in greater and greater anxiety as the evening wore on. Yet some children and old people who inhabited Octagon Court during the day had reported speaking to Jeal the next afternoon. They said the girl had seemed to be in a state of terror and that no one could persuade her to go home. Some had seen Jeal speak to an old woman of vague description and after that the girl had vanished for good. The dress she had been wearing had been found in the stretch of parkland between the western expanse of the old city wall and the gas factory. *And everyone knows what that means,* Nicholas thought grimly. The family's only hope was that the body would be caught in the water gates and discovered before it washed out of the city.

The penny-sheet writer had tried to link the unfortunate event to the disappearance of three children from Seise Street, a poorer neighborhood on the far side of the city from Octagon Court. The children had been seen speaking to an old woman of roughly the same vague description before they had vanished without a trace.

Madeline had come to read over Nicholas's shoulder. She said, "It's terrible, but it's fairly common, Arisilde. If the man stays in the city, they'll hunt him down soon enough."

"The man?" Arisilde's brows rose.

"The person who lured the children away," she explained. "It's a man disguised as an old woman, obviously."

"Ahh. I see. Are you looking into it then, Madeline?"

Nicholas folded the paper. The date indicated it was several days old. "The Prefecture is looking into it, Arisilde. People who do that sort of thing are usually clumsy as well as violent. He'll make a mistake and they'll catch him easily."

"Oh, well, then. But . . ." Arisilde frowned, his violet eyes fixed on some faraway point.

"Yes?" Nicholas asked, trying to keep the impatience out of his voice. It was possible Arisilde had seen something in the smeared print that he and Madeline had missed.

"Nothing." The dreamy look was back. "Would you like to stay for coffee? It's a delicacy in Parscia, you know, and Isham is wonderful with it."

———

As they went down the stairs later, Madeline said, "Sometimes I think Arisilde believes you work for the Prefecture, like Ronsarde."

"He might," Nicholas admitted. "He knew that as a boy I admired Ronsarde. If he thinks Edouard's alive, then he might think anything."

———

The coach took them next to a street near the southern river docks, where all the various river cargo lines had their offices and tall warehouses with steeply pitched barrel roofs clustered behind the smaller buildings.

They had speculated about Octave's motives and possible accomplices or employers on the drive from the Philosopher's Cross, but it hadn't done them much good. *We need facts to speculate,* Nicholas thought, *and facts are something we're woefully short of.* "I want to find Octave again before he finds us," he was saying as the coach drew up at the end of the street. "I sent a message to Reynard this morning, asking him to try to get some word of the man. If Octave really is a spiritualist." He opened the coach door and stepped down. The street was moderately busy with midmorning traffic: horse-drawn vans and lighter passenger coaches trundled past, and clerks and shoremen crossed by along the promenade. The breeze carried the smell of the river, alternately fresh and foul, and brought to mind again the missing girl Jeal Meule, and her probable fate.

"And the Duchess accepted him as such," Madeline pointed out as she stepped down from the coach and took his arm, "or he wouldn't have been invited last night, and he certainly wouldn't have been able to speak privately to her."

Nicholas signaled the coach to continue. Devis and Crack would take it to its customary spot in the stables around the corner and then Crack would join them in the warehouse. He said, "Granted, but if he is talking to dead relatives for the aristocracy, his name should at least be mentioned in some of the circles Reynard still has entrance to. We haven't been much in society lately; that's probably why we hadn't heard something of him before." Nicholas had decided long ago not to risk entertaining at Coldcourt and he had no desire to maintain another house only for party-giving. Fortunately, among the few members of fashionable society that he maintained contact with, this reticence was ascribed to his sensitivity about Edouard Viller's death. Keeping a low profile also helped him maintain the Donatien persona, which was essential to his plans for Montesq.

"We should go to the theater tonight, then," Madeline said. "We can make more inquiries there. And besides, Valeria Dacine is performing *Arantha* and it should be marvelous."

They turned into the alley that led past the importers and cargo lines and down to the back entrance of a warehouse that was owned by Nicholas under the name of Ringard Alscen. Nicholas unlocked the deceptively strong door and they passed inside.

He had other strongholds, because he didn't believe in putting everything in one place, but this was by far the largest. The others were spread throughout the city and Madeline was the only one besides himself who knew the location of them all.

The door opened into an office where shelves stuffed with ledgers lined the walls and two men were playing cards on a battered trunk under the light of a hanging oil lamp. Much like the offices of all the other warehouses along the street. But one of these men was Lamane and the other was one of Cusard's sons. They both stood at Madeline's entrance.

Nicholas asked, "Is Cusard here?"

"Oh, aye," Lamane replied. "He hasn't stirred. He says it makes him nervous, and he just has to sit there, looking at it."

"Does he?" Nicholas smiled. "In a while he will be spending it, or at least part of it. I think he'll like that better."

They chuckled and Nicholas and Madeline went on through the inner door into the main part of the warehouse.

This was a massive chamber, several stories in height, with a vaulted ceiling that had been augmented by iron girders at some later date. Daylight entered through narrow windows high up in the walls and lanterns made pools of brighter light at intervals.

They crossed the stone-flagged floor between rows of trunks, crates, and barrels. The warehouse did real business for at least two of the smaller cargo lines along the river. Some of the things stored here were for businesses Nicholas owned under other names, though he was careful to keep Valiarde Imports from having any connection with this place. There were men working at the far end, loading a wagon that had pulled up to one of the large panel doors, and Nicholas spotted Crack among them, still keeping watch.

Nicholas stopped to unlock a door at the opposite end and they went through into a much smaller area. There were crates stacked here too, and shelves lining the walls and locked glass-fronted cabinets. There was also a safe about waist high, square and forbidding, which held nothing more exciting than the receipts from the warehouse's honest clients.

Cusard glanced up from the clerk's desk and tipped his cap to them.

"Any problems?" Nicholas asked.

"Not a one. Want to see it?"

Nicholas smiled. "I've seen it. Last night, remember?"

"M'lady hasn't seen it." Cusard winked at Madeline. "Want to see it?"

Madeline took a seat, laying aside her parasol and slipping off her gloves. "Yes, I want to see it."

"Very well." Nicholas surrendered, going to lean against the mantel. "But don't become attached—it's not staying long."

Cusard knelt and slid the braided rug aside—the rug was pure window dressing; this particular safe hole was hidden better than mere human ingenuity could manage—and pressed his palm flat against one of the smooth fieldstone blocks that composed the floor. A small section of the blocks seemed to ripple, not like a trick of the light, but as if the stone itself had become suddenly liquid.

It was one of Arisilde's old spells, cast before he had begun his retreat into opium. Nicholas knew there was not one sorcerer in a thousand who would have been able to tell that the spell was here, let alone to break it. Arisilde had explained something of the principle: the blocks were still the same fieldstone, but the spell caused them to change their "state" from solidity to something more malleable. It was set to respond only to Nicholas, Madeline, and Cusard. Reynard knew of its location but had claimed at the time to be too unreliable to be trusted with a key to the money box.

"Keep watch for a man calling himself Dr. Octave," Nicholas told Cusard while they waited. He described the man in detail, including the style of clothing the golem had worn. "He's probably a sorcerer, possibly a deadly one. And he seems to know somewhat more than is comfortable about us."

Cusard looked properly taken aback. "Don't that ruin my mood," he muttered. "I'll make sure the others are warned."

The section of stone was sinking down and rippling sideways, running like

water to vanish under the more permanent blocks. Revealed was a compartment lined with mortar, now filled with the small gold bars.

"Forty-seven of them," Cusard said, with great satisfaction. "That's what,
fifty thousand gold royals?" He fetched out a bar and handed it to Madeline.

Her arm sagged from the unexpected weight as she accepted it. "I didn't
realize it was so heavy."

"I also want you to pay everyone involved the bonus we discussed," Nicholas said. There was a penny sheet, *Review of the Day* again, lying on a nearby
table, and his eyes were irresistibly drawn to it. He picked it up and scanned
the contents.

"Today?" Cusard asked. "Before we're finished?"

"We're finished with their part."

Cusard hesitated, looking from Nicholas, who was now engrossed in the
penny sheet, to Madeline, who was smiling enigmatically and hefting the
small bar. He asked, "Is this one of those situations I'm not going to want to
know about, and wish I didn't know once I do?"

Nicholas turned a page and didn't answer. Madeline handed Cusard back
the bar, and said, a little ruefully, "It's most likely, yes."

"When did you get this, Cusard?" Nicholas asked.

"The pamphlet? My wife carries that about." Madame Cusard made lunch
for all the men who worked in the warehouse and came in daily to clean the
offices. It was important that Madame Cusard be seen by her neighbors to
work, to help explain the presence of the generous funds that fed and clothed
her and all the little Cusards.

"What is it?" Madeline asked.

"They found a body in the river. Washed up in the water gates."

Cusard snorted. "That's worth putting in a pamphlet? Happens every day."

"Not the missing girl Arisilde was interested in?" Madeline said, her brows
drawing together.

"No, not her. A young man. Not identified as yet."

"And . . . ?"

"And," Nicholas read, "'Attention was called to the ghastly occurrence when
the gatekeepers spied a spectral glow under the surface in the vicinity of the
water gate. When the working men drew near, the glow vanished. Upon further investigation, they discovered the young person's corpse.'"

"A spectral glow?" Madeline frowned. "You're thinking of last night. That
stuff that was on your coat."

"What stuff?" Cusard demanded.

"When that creature attacked me in the cellar, it left a residue on my clothing," Nicholas explained, preoccupied. "Once I was away from torchlight, in the darkness of the coach, the glow was plain to see."

Madeline stood and came over to take the paper. "When they drew near, the glow disappeared," she muttered. "This happened last night. They were carrying lanterns, of course."

"It bears looking into," Nicholas said, taking back the penny sheet and folding it. He smiled at Madeline. "You didn't have any plans for the afternoon, did you?"

———

"Sometimes I wonder about you," Madeline said. Her scalp itched under her cap.

"Why do you say that?" Nicholas seemed honestly surprised. They were standing in a corridor beneath the Saints Crossing Morgue, at the ironbound door that was the entrance to the lower levels, and he had just sounded the bellpull for admittance. Nicholas was dressed in a plain dark suit, with the short top hat and caped coat affected by professional men. He wore spectacles and Madeline had used a theatrical powder to tint his hair and beard gray. He carried a surgeon's bag. Madeline wore a plain dark dress with a white apron and had tucked all her hair away under a white cap. She had skillfully used makeup to change the long lines of her face from elegant to gaunt and to narrow her wide dark eyes. The floor of the hall was wet and filthy and the plaster was dank and smelled of carbolic.

"I think you'll do anything for curiosity's sake."

"I'm trying to establish foundation for a hypothesis."

"You're curious."

"That's what I said."

Madeline sighed and supposed it was her own fault for not voicing any real objections. There was no danger in coming here like this; Nicholas was adept at assuming different personas and she had faith in her makeup and her own acting ability. But she could think of better things to do with her afternoons than look at drowned young men. They would be starting rehearsals at the Elegante about now, she remembered, and then tried to put it out of her mind.

There was a thunk from the heavy door and the sound of bolts being pulled back, then it was opened by a man with thinning brown hair wearing an apron over his suit. He said, "Ah, Doctor . . . ?"

"Dr. Rouas, and my nurse."

Madeline dropped a little curtsey, keeping her eyes downcast. The other man ignored her, which was the attitude most physicians took with nurses and what made it such an effective disguise, almost as good as making oneself look like an article of furniture. He said, "You're here for our latest unfortunate from the river? It's this way."

He motioned them through and locked the door after them, coming forward to lead the way down. This hall was stone and stank even more strongly of carbolic. Madeline knew the heavy door and the size of the locking bolts were not current precautions, but holdovers from when this place had been part of the dungeons of the old prison that had once stood on this site.

The doctor led them down the hall, past ancient archways filled in with brick and modern wooden doors. Finally, they turned a corner into a wide chamber with something of both the laboratory and the butcher shop about it. There were shelves containing chemical apparatus and surgical equipment. There was also an air that led one to expect chains, torture devices, and screaming captives. *Perhaps it's only the weight of the past,* Madeline thought. Or her imagination.

In the center of the room was a steel operating table and atop that a limp form wrapped in burlap. There was another doctor present just now, an older man, with gray in his receding hair and in his neatly trimmed mustache and beard. He was washing his hands in the basin against the wall, his sleeves rolled up and his coat hanging on a peg nearby. He glanced up at them, his expression open and friendly. *There is something familiar about that face,* Madeline thought. He said, "I'm just going."

"Dr. Rouas, this is Dr. Halle," their guide said.

"Ah." The older man dried his hands hastily and came forward to shake hands with Nicholas. He nodded pleasantly to Madeline and this gesture of uncommon politeness on his part she almost met with a blank stare. She recovered herself in time to smile shyly and duck her head, but her mind was reeling. *Dr. Halle.* Of course she knew that face. Only once before had she seen it at such close range: two years ago at Upper Bannot when Ronsarde had almost uncovered their plot to steal the jewels in the Risais ancestral vault. This man was Dr. Cyran Halle, the good friend and colleague of Inspector Ronsarde.

She had been in disguise then, and far more thorough a disguise than she was wearing now. The other times she had seen him had been at a distance and in innocuous circumstances: the theater, the grillroom at Lusaude's, in a crowd outside the Prefecture. He couldn't be suspicious and indeed, he didn't seem so, but Madeline became acutely aware of a nervous flutter in the pit of her stomach.

With an expression of easy goodwill, Nicholas said, "Dr. Halle, I'm familiar with your work. It's an honor to meet you."

"Thank you." Halle appeared honestly pleased with the compliment. He nodded toward the body as he rolled his sleeves down. "You're here to make an examination?"

"No, I'm to attempt an identification only. One of my patients has a son who's gone missing—though the rest of the family believes him to have run away on his own. The mother isn't well and I agreed to come here in her place."

"A sad duty." There was real sympathy in Halle's voice. He put on his coat and took his bag from the stained table. "I'll be out of your way, then. Pleasure meeting you, Doctor, and you, young lady."

Madeline had to remind herself that this man was dangerous to them, even if he did have impeccable manners and was as genial as a favorite uncle. *If he knew who we were,* she thought, *if he knew Nicholas was Donatien, the man Ronsarde has been searching for all this time . . .*

Nicholas had moved up to the slab and turned the burlap sheet back. Madeline caught sight of a face, so distorted by water and decomposition as to be hardly recognizable as human, discolored as if it was some nightmare creature of the fay. Nicholas said, "He resembles the boy slightly, but I don't believe it's him." He shook his head, frowning. "I'd rather be absolutely sure. . . . Has his clothing been saved?"

"Yes, it has. Doctor Halle advised us to do so." The other doctor turned to open one of the cabinets and as he rummaged through its contents, Madeline took the opportunity to glare at Nicholas with a mixture of annoyance and exasperation.

He frowned at her. He hated to break character in the middle of a performance and normally so did she, but it wasn't every day that one encountered one's second most deadly opponent.

The doctor returned with a metal bucket, which he upended on the table. "There's not much left," he admitted. "Fragments of a shirt and trousers, the rags of a coat. No shoes. Nothing in the pockets, of course."

Nicholas used a pencil from the workbench to fastidiously poke through the damp stinking collection. "No, you're right, that's not much help." He tossed the pencil away and took the doctor's elbow, turning him back toward the body on the slab. "I take it you noticed these marks on his arms? What is your opinion on them?"

With the other physician's attention engaged, Madeline slipped a pair of sewing scissors out of her sleeve and quickly cut fragments from the torn and bedraggled coat and trousers. She folded the pieces in her handkerchief and tucked it away in the pocket of her apron, then turned back to the two men.

Nicholas took their leave shortly after that and within moments they were back out in the dank corridor on the other side of the ironbound door.

"Interesting that Ronsarde is taking notice of this," Nicholas said in an undertone. "He must have sent Halle—the man doesn't stir a foot from his house unless Ronsarde sends him."

Madeline wouldn't have put it that way; she had always found Cyran Halle the least objectionable one of the pair, but Nicholas had never forgiven the doctor for describing some of Donatien's activities as "the products of an hysterical and badly disturbed mind" in a letter to the current head of the city Prefecture. "'Interesting'? Is that the word for it?" she asked dryly.

"My dear, he suspected nothing."

They were nearing the stairs up into the main part of the building and Madeline was prevented from answering.

The dingy corridors on the ground floor were far more crowded and it was almost impassable near the public area. Here one of the walls was a glazed partition, behind which stood two rows of black marble tables, inclined toward the glass wall and each cooled by a constant stream of water. They held the bodies of the most recent unidentified dead, usually lost souls found on the street or pulled from the river. Each was left three or four days, in the hope that persons who were missing relatives or friends might come and claim them. Over half the corpses found in the city were eventually claimed this way, but Nicholas had told her that many were probably identified incorrectly. It was just too difficult for the bereaved to recognize even close relations under these circumstances.

They had expected to see the drowned boy on display, but had been told that they could find him in the examination room instead. Madeline wondered if it was Dr. Halle who had saved the nameless young man from this fate. As Nicholas forged a path through the crowd for her, she could see that few of the people here looked as if they were searching for loved ones; most of them looked remarkably like well-dressed tourists, drawn here by the grotesque nature of the display.

Once they were outside in the late afternoon light and relatively fresh air of the street, Madeline decided it was useless to argue. The day had grown warmer and the morning clouds given way to brilliant blue sky, incongruous after the morgue. The nights would still be cold, but the snow last night had probably been the last of the season and winter was in its death throes. She asked, "What were you saying about the marks on the boy's arms?"

"They were shackle galls. He was obviously held prisoner before he was killed."

"Killed, and not accidently drowned? It does happen, you know."

"Not in this case. His throat was torn out. It could have happened after death, if something in the river attacked the corpse, but Halle didn't think so. He had left some case notes for them on the table and I managed to glance over the first page."

Madeline considered that, frowning. They had to walk two streets over, to where their coach waited for them. Nicholas hadn't wanted it to sit in front of the building so that no one would associate it with the ordinary medical doctor and his nondescript nurse, and she was glad of it. Meeting Cyran Halle wasn't the same as running into Sebastion Ronsarde, but it was far too close a brush with the famous Inspector for her comfort. "Well, do you think this boy was killed by the same creature, or same sort of creature, that attacked you under Mondollot House?"

"I won't know that until I have the substance on the corpse's clothes examined and compared to the substance on my coat. I wish Arisilde . . . But there's no help for that."

"I could see there was something on the clothes other than river sludge; it was a sort of silvery grease. If it is the same, what does that tell us?"

"At this point, not much."

———

Nicholas leaned back in his seat, resigning himself to waiting. From the height of their private box he could watch the crowd swarming into the stalls below. Reynard was late, but then lateness at the theater was eminently fashionable. Nicholas had never managed to catch the habit of it himself. He had spent the first twelve years of his life in the Riverside slums, among decaying tenements and human misery, before Edouard Viller had taken him in. He still found the theater a delight.

Nicholas glanced at Madeline and smiled. She was watching the activity around the stage below with a jeweled lorgnette. She had started as a member of the chorus in the opera five years ago, working her way up to last season, when she had taken a leading role at the Elegante. It was only because of Nicholas's plans for destroying Count Montesq that she hadn't accepted a role for this season.

Members of the demimonde had wondered why a fashionable young actress had taken up with a restrained and often reclusive art importer, no matter how wealthy he was. Nicholas still wasn't sure he knew either. His original plans had never included Madeline at all.

Three years ago, he had sought her acquaintance on impulse, after seeing her several times in her first ingénue role. Before he knew it he was helping her extricate herself from a tangle involving a rather predatory lord who habitually stalked young actresses. Though by the time Nicholas had arrived, the only help Madeline had really required was instruction in the little known art of artistically arranging a body to make its injuries look self-inflicted. After making certain the lord's death would appear to be suicide, Nicholas had taken Madeline back to Coldcourt. At some point during their first night together, he had been shocked to discover that he had not only told her about his identity as Donatien, but blurted out his entire life story as well. He had told her things that only Edouard, or Nicholas's long-dead mother, had known. It hadn't just been a haze of lust clouding his brain; he had never had that kind of rapport with anyone before, never felt that kind of bond. He had certainly never expected to find instant camaraderie with a country girl, self-educated and come to Vienne to be an actress.

But Madeline had more than native wit. She had had no intention of staying in the chorus and had prepared for a career in classical theater by reading every new play she could get her hands on and studying the history behind the old period pieces. She had taught herself to speak and read Aderassi so she could take roles in the opera if she had to, but her real goal was the dramas and comedies played out on the stages of the big theaters of the fashionable district.

This theater was the Tragedian, one of the newest in the city. The wide sweep of the stage was lit by gas jets and the walls were delicately molded in white, pale yellow, and gold. The overstuffed seats in the boxes were stamped velvet of an inky blue, matching the plush seats of the stalls, and the curtains were yellow silk brocaded with flowers.

The curtain around the door was swept aside and Reynard appeared. He said, "Did you know the opera is absolutely full of thugs?"

"Well, there is a Bisran composer there," Nicholas said. Anticipating the request, he started to pour Reynard a glass of wine from the bottle breathing on the little table nearby.

Reynard leaned down to kiss Madeline's hand and dropped into the nearest chair. "Besides him. The place is stuffed with thugs from the Gamethon Club and they're blowing whistles, of all things. Of course, it doesn't help that the damn Bisran is crouched up on the stage, giving alternate signals to the orchestra. It's driving the conductor mad." Reynard was dressed much as Nicholas was, in black trousers, tailed coat, and straw-colored gloves appropriate for the theater. Reynard's black satin vest only had three buttons as was de rigueur for someone who carried themselves as a bit of a dandy; Nicholas's buttoned further up the chest, exposing less of his starched shirtfront, as befit his persona as a young though staid businessman.

Madeline lowered the lorgnette in alarm. "If someone blows a whistle during _Arantha_, I'll have him killed."

Reynard said, "My dear, I would be devastated if you did not demand the favor of dispatching such an undiscriminating character from me personally. But to continue, the reason I went to the opera was to speak to someone about your Dr. Octave."

"I'm relieved," Nicholas said. "Go on."

"Octave appeared on the scene in just the past month, but he's already done circles at three or four homes of the beau monde—not the sort of places I could get invitations to, mind." Reynard leaned forward. "Apparently, at one of the first of these exhibitions, the host hired a real sorcerer, from Lodun, to watch and to certify that Octave was not a sorcerer himself and that he was not performing any sort of spell. That's what made his reputation."

"That's odd." Nicholas shook his head. "There's a sorcerer in this business somewhere." He had taken steps through acquaintances in the Philosopher's Cross to meet with a spiritualist who might have an insider's view of Octave's activities, but real spiritualists were apparently elusive beasts and it would take a day or so to arrange the meeting.

"What do people say about him?" Madeline asked Reynard. "Are they afraid of him?"

"Not that I could tell. I spoke to several people and they all thought him a bit odd, but that's fairly normal for someone in his business. Though the people I questioned were friends of friends, you understand, not anyone who had been at one of these circles. But tomorrow night Octave is descending far enough in society to preside at a spiritual evening at Captain Everset's house. Everset used to be invited to court, but then there was that gambling scandal with the son of the Viscount Rale, so he's a member of the fringe at best, now. He's stark raving wealthy, though, which keeps him in company. The circle is being held at that new place of his a few miles outside the city proper. I managed to bump into him at the opera and coaxed an overnight invitation out of him."

"Was it his idea to invite Dr. Octave for a circle?" Nicholas asked. "If we're going to walk into the good doctor's lair, I'd like to have a little more forewarning than this."

"No, it was his wife's idea. From what I've heard, she's merely bored, sick of Everset, and trying to be fashionable." Reynard appeared to consider the matter seriously. "Everset is flighty, and not terribly clever. Not the type to be involved with this, I'd think." He sipped the wine and held the glass up to the light. "He's invited me along to liven things up, but I wouldn't have the man on a bet."

"Very good." Nicholas nodded to himself. "That should do nicely. I'll come along as your valet."

"Good." Reynard downed the last of his wine. "It'll be fun."

"It won't."

"And what do I do?" Madeline asked, her voice caustic. She lowered the lorgnette to eye them critically. "Stay at Coldcourt and roll bandages?"

"But my dear, if Nicholas and I are killed, who else can we depend upon to avenge us?"

Madeline gave him a withering look and said, "What if Octave recognizes you? He knew Nicholas, he might know you as well."

Reynard shrugged philosophically and made a gesture of turning the query over to Nicholas, who said, "That's a chance we have to take. Octave wanted something at Mondollot House and he was afraid that we had somehow discovered what it was. We have to find out how he knows about us." Madeline was right; spiritualists catered to people who knew nothing about real sorcery. Most were tricksters, fakes for the most part who couldn't attract a ghost in the most haunted house in the city. But speaking to the dead was dangerously close to necromancy.

Necromancy was primarily a magic of divination, of the revealing of secret information through converse with spirits and the dead. There were plenty of simple and harmless necromantic spells, such as those for identifying thieves, or recovering lost objects or people, that did not require the spilling of human blood. There were scarcely any apprentice sorcerers at Lodun—at least not when Nicholas had been studying at the medical college there—who had not used a simple necromantic spell to derive hidden knowledge from visions conjured in a mirror or a swordblade. The more powerful spells did require the use of a corpse, or the parts of a corpse, or a human death, and the whole branch of magic had been outlawed in Ile-Rien for two hundred years or more. If any of the spiritualists had really been necromancers, they would have found themselves on the wrong side of a prison wall long before now. That they were ignored by both the law courts and the sorcerers of Lodun showed how powerless they really were. Why would a sorcerer capable of making a golem bother posing as a spiritualist?

Nicholas turned his own glass to the light, watching the bloodred sparkle. His hand still ached from the oil burns, though they hadn't blistered. *You don't have time for this,* he reminded himself. Octave was distracting him from the destruction of Count Rive Montesq, his real goal.

Montesq had caused Edouard Viller's death, as surely as if he had personally fired a bullet into the gentle scholar's head, by making it appear that Edouard was experimenting with necromancy. Nicholas still didn't know the full story; he had been away finishing his education at Lodun when it had happened and Edouard had said only that he had regretted accepting Montesq as a patron and that he had discovered him to be dishonest. The only explanation Nicholas could arrive at was that Edouard had learned something about Montesq that the Count found dangerous. What that was, Nicholas had been unable to discover and Edouard had refused to tell anyone anything about his work during the last months of his life.

Nicholas had managed to convince himself that the why didn't matter; Montesq had done it and he was going to pay for it.

But Nicholas couldn't simply ignore Octave. *He knows we were in the Mondollot House cellars. If he also knows about the Duchess's Bisran-stamped gold, then we can't use it to frame Montesq.* And he couldn't afford to ignore the danger. *Octave could send another golem tonight, even,* he thought.

The house lights dimmed and the noise of the crowd swelled in anticipation before leveling off somewhat. It would never quite cease, but the performances of the actors and actresses in this play were absorbing enough that it would stay a background hum and not rise to drown out the dialogue entirely.

Any more discussion among themselves now, however, would cause Madeline to become agitated. And besides, Nicholas wanted to see the play himself. He said, "We'll work out the details at dinner tonight."

CHAPTER FOUR

The late afternoon air was chill, but Nicholas had lowered the shades on the coach windows so he and Reynard could view the approach to Gabrill House. The wide packed-dirt road led up through a stand of trees toward a triumphal arch, perhaps fifty feet high and wide enough for four coaches to pass through side by side. As they drew nearer Nicholas could see the stones were weathered and faded as if the thing was a relic of some long forgotten age. He knew it had been built no more than ten years ago.

"Strange choice for a garden ornament, isn't it?" Reynard said.

"If you find that odd, wait till you get inside. This place was built by a wealthy widow from Umberwald. She had two grown sons, neither of whom she allowed to inherit. She had smaller homes built for them—one on either side of the main building." Constructing opulent houses outside the city wall had become all the rage in the past few decades and they had passed many such, of varying degrees of size and wealth, along the way. It allowed for large gardens, and the dirt roads out here were wider and tended to have better drainage than the ancient paved boulevards within the city proper. "Before Everset bought it last year, the owners were selling tickets for people to come out and look at it."

"Yes, I'd heard that." Reynard adjusted the set of his gloves as their coach turned off the road and passed under the arch. "You're not a sorcerer, Nicholas. What do you intend to do if this Octave takes exception to your presence with something more than another golem?"

Nicholas smiled. "Only you would ask that question as we are actually driving up to the house where Octave is." Two cobbled carriageways led toward the house from the entry arch, splitting off to bridge a sunken garden where they glimpsed the tops of tall stands of hot weather ferns and flowering trees. The house had been built backward, so the façade facing them was a large colonnaded oval, which in other homes of this design would have given on to the back garden. But the architect had planned it well and the graceful columned portico had a mound of natural rock at its base, connecting it to the grotto of the sunken garden their carriage was passing over. It gave the whole front of the large house the look of an ancient temple in ruins.

"Oh, I've no sense of self-preservation," Reynard replied easily. "That's what I depend on you for."

"I suppose we should have brought Madeline, then, because that's what I depend on her for. But even your reputation wouldn't support a female valet."

"I don't know about that." Eyeing Nicholas thoughtfully, Reynard said, "Seriously. What if Octave resents your intrusion?"

"Seriously, I only mean to observe Octave. For now," Nicholas said. There had been no disturbances at Coldcourt or at any of his other headquarters last night, though several of his henchmen had kept watch with firearms just in case.

The hooves of the horses clopped on stone as the carriage passed under an arched opening to the right of the portico and into a well-lit stone-walled passage. They were going through the ground floor of the house itself now. One of the flaws in the backward-facing design was that this was the only practical way to reach the carriage entrance.

The passage opened out into the cool air and late afternoon sun again and their coach pulled up in the semicircular carriage court, overlooked by the elegant pillars of the back façade of the house.

Reynard collected his hat and stick. "We're on." He nodded to Nicholas. "Good luck. And don't embarrass me, my good fellow."

"If you'll do me the same favor," Nicholas murmured. A footman was already running to open the coach door.

As Reynard stepped down, a man appeared between the carved set of double doors and came down the steps toward him. *Our host, Deran Everset,* Nicholas thought, *and he looks quite as dissipated as Reynard said he would.*

Everset's clothes were foppish in the extreme, his waistcoat patterned with a loud design and his cravat tied in an elaborate way that seemed to interfere with any attempt to move his head, and his lanky frame wasn't well suited to the fashion. He was pale, with a long face and limp blond hair, and he was consulting a jeweled watch on a chain. "My God, you're late," he said, by way of greeting. "And since when have you kept a coach?"

"It's on loan," Reynard said, "from a very, very dear friend of mine." He clapped Everset on the shoulder, turning him back toward the house. "I hope you have a wild night planned for us."

"None of this was my idea—" their host protested, the rest of his answer lost as the two men passed inside.

Nicholas stepped out of the coach himself. He stretched, keeping one eye on the doorway into the house as a real valet would, in case a butler appeared. "Can we take down the baggage?" he asked the waiting footman.

"Yes, your man's the last guest to arrive, so there's no hurry." The man scuffed one polished shoe against the clean-swept stones of the court, obviously bored. The house livery was dark green, with gold piping on the coat. "Need a hand?"

Crack, dressed as a coach outrider, had hopped down from the box. "No," Nicholas told the footman. "Thanks the same, though."

There was stabling for the horses and coaches built into the walls of the court. Some of the carriage doors still stood open and Nicholas counted at least three town coaches. Reynard had wangled the invitation so quickly there had been no opportunity to find out about the other guests. A terrace ran along the top of the wall; he could see urns of potted flowers and benches facing out into the rest of the garden. He knew the elevated terrace extended out from the back of the carriage court, crossing over the garden to reach a small pavilion built to resemble yet another classical temple. It was isolated from the main house, but easily reached along the terrace by guests in evening clothes; if they meant to hold the circle anywhere else, Nicholas would eat his hat.

He took Reynard's single case as Devis handed it down and exchanged a nod with Crack. Crack and Devis would be quartered out here with the coach for the night and would probably be too closely watched to slip out and be of any help to him. Hopefully, he wouldn't need them.

The footman led him up the steps and through the open doors. Nicholas caught sight of an airy high-ceilinged vestibule, floored in what was probably imitation marble. The classical theme continued in frescoes with nymphs and graces that climbed the walls above a grand staircase. The footman showed him a servants' door and Nicholas climbed a narrow plain staircase up two floors, hoping this would provide him an early opportunity to scout around.

But as soon as he reached the top, he almost walked into one of the upstairs maids, who directed him to the chamber assigned to Reynard.

The room was well appointed and the eccentricity of the rest of the house hadn't been extended to the bedrooms, or at least not the guest bedrooms. Heavy damask draperies of pale yellow framed the windows, matching the ivory silk–paneled walls and the cushions and covers on the couches, overstuffed chairs, and the delicate little tables. The bed hangings made up for this restraint with embroidered garlands, silk blooms, and a crown of ostrich feathers.

Nicholas had never employed a valet himself and was able to unpack Reynard's case with speed and efficiency. While the guests were at dinner, maids would be in and out of the rooms, freshening flowers, filling the basin, and making sure the sheets were aired, and he didn't want the room to look out of the ordinary. Finishing up, he took out his pocket watch—a cheap one, without any ornament, that he kept for this sort of disguise—and gauged the time he had until Reynard came up to dress for dinner. That would be an ideal opportunity to get an initial report on the other guests and whether Octave was present in the house yet. The more information he had to act on, the better.

He slipped out into the hall and shut the door behind him. It was quiet, except for the faint hiss of gaslights inside their porcelain globes and muted voices echoing up the grand stairwell. He moved down the hall, quietly but purposefully, and without furtive caution. In a house of this size, with as many servants as this one had, and with the additional confusion of an overnight party, anyone who looked as if they knew where they were going was not too likely to be questioned.

He found the servants' stair at the far end of the corridor and went down it quickly, coming out in a narrow low-ceilinged hall that ran toward the back of the house. As he passed an open door someone called out, "Wait, there, whose are you?"

Nicholas stopped obediently. It was a pantry, a small room lined with glass-fronted cabinets, with china and silver plate gleaming inside. The man who had addressed him was gray-haired and stout, dressed in a dark suit and clutching a bundle of keys. *The butler, obviously,* Nicholas thought. There was a woman in the room too, a respectable-looking matron in a gray gown and an apron. Nicholas said, "Captain Morane's, sir."

"Ah, go on, then." The butler turned back to the agitated woman in the flour-dusted apron. "No, tell Listeri that's my final word."

"No, you tell him! I'm sick of his Aderassi chatter and you can—"

Without even having to deliver his carefully prepared excuse concerning gloves left behind in the carriage, Nicholas reached the arch at the end of the passage and the argument was lost in the greater clatter of the kitchen. The stove was a monolithic monument stretching across the far wall, copper fish kettles steaming on the burners. A long plank table was weighed down with molds, baking trays for meringues, and stone dishes for pies. Dressers standing against the brick-lined walls held the plain china and an array of silver pots for chocolate and coffee.

The cook, sweating under his white cap, slammed a pot on the range, and shouted an amazing Aderassi profanity. From the hearth, an aproned woman turning spitted capons over a sheet metal scallop shouted, "What do you know about it, you dirty foreigner?" The door in the far wall banged open to admit two scullery maids struggling with a tub of water. Nicholas hurried to help them guide it in and deposit it on the tiles near the table, then left them to join their colleague in battle. He escaped through another pantry and out the door into the kitchen garden.

He made his way down a dirt path, past geometrically laid out beds for melons, cabbages, and endives, and wooden racks for climbing vegetables. The wall to his left was lined with skeletal pear trees and bordered on the carriage court. There was a wooden door, a back entrance to the stables, but it was fortunately closed. On his right, over the top of the garden wall, he could see the side of one of the two outbuildings the widow had constructed for her sons. The gray stones were overgrown with climbing vines, but it looked as well kept as the main house. Both were probably used for extra guest and servants' quarters.

He reached the trellised gate in the back wall and opened it to enter the garden proper. He hesitated, taking his bearings. This was dangerous territory; he could explain his presence in the carriage court and the kitchen garden. Any servant except a gardener would be forbidden this area.

It seemed deserted. Rambling roses, quince trees, and willows obscured the walls that ran down to terminate in a slight dip and another high wall. Tangled greenery that would flower in the spring hung out of the beds and threatened the cobbled pathways. A fountain with a nymph trapped in winter-dry vines played near the center.

Nicholas jogged the length of the wall, over which he could see the carved balusters of the terrace enclosure. At the end of the garden the terrace formed a wide square platform. Overgrown brush screened him from the house now, and he was able to dig fingers and boot tips into the cracks in the rough stone wall. He hauled himself up and slung one leg over the balustrade, hoping the moss stains wouldn't show too badly on his dark clothes.

The temple was in the center of the platform. It was a simple design, an open circle of columns supporting a carved entablature. The stones were artificially weathered, as the triumphal arch was, giving the little place a look of aged dignity. A fine wooden table had been placed in the center, surrounded by eight chairs.

The great spreading mass of several oak trees, each large as a small hillock and far older than the house itself, blocked the view on three sides of the platform, and the only clear line of sight was straight down the connecting stone bridge to the carriage court terrace and the back of the main house. Huge flower urns and classical statues of various faunal gods stood around the edges of the platform and provided some cover, but the little temple would be clearly visible to anyone standing on the farther terrace. No one seemed to be out so Nicholas left the sheltering statuary and approached the temple cautiously.

He crouched to examine the underside of the table for wires, or mechanical or magical devices. There seemed to be none, and no secret compartments either. The table was also heavy and sturdy, impossible for a clever spiritualist to rock with their boot tips, which was one of the more common tricks. He moved on to the chairs, checking underneath them and palpating the seat cushions. Next was the temple itself.

Finally, he had searched as much of the place as he was able to without a ladder. Nicholas went to sit in the concealing shadow of an oversized urn. It was getting late and darkness was gathering in pools under the winter-stripped trees and in the thorny brush. No preparations had been made for the kind of show people such as Captain Everset and his lady would expect for their money.

Is that really a surprise? Nicholas asked himself. *You know Octave has real power, or at least access to real power.* If he had found the table prepared with flashpowder and false-bottomed drawers, it would only have obscured the issue further. He would simply have to wait and see what he could discover during the circle.

———

Nicholas made it safely back to the room to find Reynard already dressing for dinner.

"There you are," Reynard said. He was tying his cravat in front of the mirror. "I was beginning to wonder. Did you find anything?"

"No, as I expected. Is Octave here? Who are the other guests?"

"I didn't see Octave. Madame Everset talked about him as if she expected him to descend on us out of the ether at any moment, though. Whether that means he's in the house now or not, I couldn't tell you." Reynard swore, tore the cravat off, and discarded it over his shoulder, selecting a fresh one out of the open drawer. Nicholas caught the bit of cloth before it could flutter to the floor and put it away. Reynard continued, "As to the other guests, they're what you'd expect. Amelind Danyell, the obsessive one who's been dangling after what's his name, the unpleasant poet who's an opium addict—"

"Algretto?"

"That's it. He's here too, of course, and he's brought his wife along to play off Danyell. There's also Danyell's escort, a pimply-faced bit who has propositioned me twice already and I'm old enough to be his father, for God's sake. There's Vearde and his current mistress, Ilian Isolde the opera singer, and of course Count Belennier, who couldn't get invited to a salon party on a sinking ship since he was caught in that Naissance Court scandal."

Reynard was about to ruin another cravat. Nicholas impatiently stopped him, turned him around, and finished tying it himself. The company was uniformly scandalous, but then no one would have invited Reynard to any other kind of occasion. He had gained a reputation for casual behavior before he had taken an officer's commission in the Guard, but the worst scandal by far was the one that had lost him that commission and made him Count Montesq's enemy.

Reynard had been conducting an affair with a younger officer, a member of a noble family, at the same time as the young man was also seeking an engagement with a young woman of an even nobler and far wealthier family. Montesq's solicitor Devril, who had a second career as a blackmailer, had managed to buy an incriminating letter written by the young man to Reynard, which had been stolen out of Reynard's kit when their regiment was stationed on the Tethari peninsula. The young man had paid the blackmail at first, paid it until he had exhausted his personal funds, but Devril's demands had continued until finally, on the day before the wedding, Devril had made the letter public through intermediaries. The scandal and the pressures of his position and, possibly, the belief that Reynard had given the letter to Devril himself, worked on an excitable temperament, and the young man had killed himself. Reynard had returned to Vienne shortly thereafter to find his friend dead and most of the beau monde of the belief that Reynard had driven him to suicide. The feeling against him was so high his commanding officer had trumped up some charges against him in order to cashier him out of the Guard.

The part of the story that no one else but Nicholas and Madeline knew entirely was that Reynard had tracked down the unscrupulous batman who had stolen the letter and killed him after extracting Devril's identity. Montesq's men had discovered that Reynard was on Devril's trail and planned to eliminate him, but Nicholas had been following the situation as well and managed to contact Reynard and warn him. Together they had rid the world of the blackmailing solicitor Devril, and Reynard had worked with Nicholas ever since.

Nicholas finished tying the cravat and Reynard examined the result in the mirror carefully. "You did that well. Did they teach it at Lodun when you were there?"

"They teach everything at Lodun." The other guests were familiar names, except for one. "Vearde—do you know him by sight?"

"Yes, I've met him on several occasions. Just an acquaintance, though." Reynard turned to regard him quizzically, with a hint of a smile. "You think he's really Ronsarde in disguise?"

"No, I do not think that." Damn Reynard for being so astute, anyway. Nicholas didn't want to seem like a nervous fool, but Ronsarde was the one enemy he wasn't completely confident that he could outwit. He put away Reynard's old suit, knowing a real valet would never leave clothing on the floor. Well, maybe Reynard's valet might, but it would excite comment among the other servants and he didn't want to call attention to himself. "We did see Halle at the morgue, you know."

"When you went to look at that drowned boy? I thought Madeline said there was no connection to Octave?"

"Not yet." Nicholas hadn't heard back from the practitioners he had given the samples to. He would probably have to go to Arisilde again himself and remind him. "There were only eight chairs around the table."

"Well, Everset said he wouldn't be joining us for Octave's little show. I assume some of the others have also made their excuses. Do you think that matters terribly?"

"No." Nicholas considered a moment. "Do you think Everset will be suspicious that you haven't made an excuse?"

"I've mentioned that I haven't seen one of the things yet and I'm curious. That should do it. No one in this group is going to suspect anyone of anything except sneaking off to debauch on the sly."

"You're right, of course." Nicholas had learned early that one of the chief problems in deception was the tendency to try to overexplain one's actions.

The truth was that people did the oddest things for the most inconsequential reasons and elaborate justifications only made one look guilty.

———

Like most parvenu households, the Eversets had paid a great deal for an excellent Aderassi chef and since they had no real taste, had managed to hire only a mediocre one. Nicholas watched the chaos from the safety of the kitchen doorway, with one or two of the other upstairs servants who were resting now that the guests were settled. Earlier, from the shelter of the stables, they had all watched Octave's coach arrive. The spiritualist had brought no baggage and no one to accompany him except the coach driver.

The chef, Listeri, carried on dinner preparations as if the kitchen were a besieged citadel that would inevitably fall to superior force, and this entailed a great deal of banging, breakage, and profanity toward the scullery maids.

Nicholas shook his head over the choice of an inferior grade of wine for a sauce, then left his indolent pose in the doorway and made his way toward the dining room. Nicholas had made it a point to see all the servants brought in by the guests and to make sure that they were all—as far as he could tell—what they appeared to be. Crack had orders to do the same with the coachmen and outriders quartered in the stables, and Nicholas knew if his henchman had discovered anything suspicious he would have found a way to send word by now. It was only the guests he was worried about.

It proved impossible to get close enough to the dining room to overhear the conversation. The only possibility was a small anteroom used by the butler to marshal the footmen who were serving the courses and it was always occupied. Nicholas grudgingly returned to his position in the kitchen, where Listeri seemed about to collapse due to rage.

Not that casual conversation over the plates was likely to provide much illumination, though Nicholas knew that Algretto the poet was associated with Count Rive Montesq. Last month, Nicholas had been at Contera's with Reynard and Madeline, when the Count had come in with a large party that had included Algretto. There was nothing particularly damning in that. Algretto's current popularity made him a much sought-after guest with all levels of society.

But after a time Nicholas had become aware of the particular attention being directed at them from the neighborhood of Montesq's party. It might be due to Madeline's presence; as a feted actress she often drew attention. Or it might be due to Reynard, who tended to draw his own share of notice.

"We're being observed, my dears," Reynard had said. "Out of jealousy, it's obvious." He had betrayed absolutely no discomfort; Reynard loved challenges.

Madeline had laughed and lifted her glass to him as if he had said something extremely witty and cutting about the people watching them. "God," she murmured, "I must have a guilty conscience. I'm afraid he knows."

She meant Montesq, who was straightening the black opal studs on his cuffs as he leaned over to speak to one of the women in his entourage. Just that day Nicholas had obtained the rest of the builder's plans for Montesq's Great House, which they would need to plant the Duchess of Mondollot's incriminating Bisran gold. "Guilty?" he said, raising his own glass.

"Not guilty, precisely. An occupied conscience, perhaps." She touched her hair ornament in a gesture of flirtation and without moving her lips, said, "He's coming over here."

Out of the corner of his eye Nicholas had seen Montesq excuse himself to his party and stand. "He knows nothing," he said.

"And that's Enora Ragele with him," Madeline added, in a more audible voice. "The woman's such a whore."

"Now Madeline, you sound like an actress," Reynard chided her gently.

The exchange had been a bit of playacting for Montesq's benefit. The Count reached their table on the tail end of Reynard's comment and Nicholas stood to shake hands with him.

"It's been a long time, Valiarde. I had thought you left the country," Montesq said, easily. He looked every inch the noble of Ile-Rien, from the sober cut of his tailcoat to the impeccable grooming of his oiled hair and closely trimmed beard. His smile didn't reach his flat black eyes.

"I'm not much in society, my lord." Nicholas turned to introduce Madeline and Reynard. The knife-edge of tension that went through him when Montesq formally kissed Madeline's hand surprised him, but it was made up for as he watched the Count pretend he had never heard of Reynard Morane before. *Though he probably loses track of the people he orders his men to kill; there are so many of them.*

The introductions done, Montesq turned back to Nicholas. "Edouard Viller was a great loss to philosophy, Valiarde. I'm sure Lodun feels his absence."

"We all feel his absence," Nicholas said quietly. He was finding that being offered condolences, even long after the fact, by his foster father's murderer was an almost enjoyable experience. The fact that Montesq had not yet tired of his grotesque private jokes was a sign of weakness. *He isn't aware who the joke is on—yet.*

Montesq's face betrayed nothing. He said, "You are still an art importer?"

"Yes, I am." Nicholas made his expression one of polite interest. Montesq might be fishing, though he couldn't think for what.

"Really, and I thought my company was considered scandalous by the beau monde." The speaker was the poet Algretto, who had come up behind Montesq. He looked as if he had just rolled out of bed, his clothes disordered and his cravat hanging loose around his neck, his blond curls in disarray. The poet had given this same impression every time Nicholas had seen him so he strongly suspected it was a deliberate affectation. "Take care, my lord, this is almost too much."

Nicholas barely managed to conceal his amusement. There was no mistaking what Algretto was referring to. As an attempt to please his patron it backfired badly; Montesq's connection to his blackmailing solicitor had almost been exposed during the incident that had won Reynard the shame of the beau monde, and from the Count's expression he obviously remembered it with no fondness either.

"True," Reynard said to the poet, his voice amused. "Your company should be scandalous enough. Any more would be a surfeit of riches."

Algretto started to speak but then glanced at Montesq. He must have read impatience in the set of his patron's jaw, because he contented himself with an ironic bow, as if acknowledging the hit. Montesq smiled, too well bred to acknowledge the coarseness of the demimonde he had found himself surrounded by, and said, "My agent will contact your men of business, Valiarde."

"Of course." Nicholas smiled, gently.

When Montesq had taken his leave and gone back to his table, Madeline said seriously, "Sometimes your self-control frightens me."

"Thank you," Nicholas said, lifting his glass to her, not that he thought she had meant it as a compliment.

"I thought you were as subtle as a ground adder myself," Reynard commented dryly. "What did I miss?"

"If I had been too obliging, he would have become suspicious." Nicholas swirled the contents of his wineglass. "He knows I hate him. He just doesn't realize to what extent I've acted on it."

"So he was testing you," Reynard said thoughtfully.

Madeline idly shredded a flower petal from the table decoration. "I wonder why."

Nicholas had smiled, with a razor edge that was anything but gentle. "Perhaps he has an occupied conscience."

Algretto was a connection to Montesq, but not to Octave. And it was Octave's appearance on the scene, in the middle of the plan to destroy Montesq, a culmination of years of effort, that worried Nicholas the most. The chef, Listeri, suddenly became aware of his audience and flung a pot at the wall near the doorway. Nicholas and the other servants hastily scrambled for cover, and Nicholas's thoughts went abruptly back to his current role.

———

After dinner had been served, the apparently chronic confusion in the servants' hall allowed Nicholas to fortify himself with a bowl of gamey stew before slipping out of the house to take up a position near the circle.

Colored lamps had been hung at strategic intervals throughout the formal garden, making the trip out to the platform somewhat more interesting, but he managed it without incident. Once there, he scouted the area for any other watchers before climbing up to the balustrade again. A glass candlelamp had been placed in the center of the table and more lamps had been hung from some of the pillars. The shadows among the statuary at the edges of the platform were even darker for these yellow beacons, so he retired behind the large urn with some confidence.

It was cold, though Nicholas had taken the precaution of bringing dark gloves and a scarf to wrap around his throat. The wind had died down since earlier in the day and the quiet of the night was the heavy silence of the country. Nicholas was even able to hear a late carriage go down the road in front of the house, passing Gabrill's triumphal arch and continuing on toward the even grander parks farther away from the city.

Not long after, the doors to the terrace from the main house opened and he heard talk and laughter. Lamps had been lit along the bridge of the terrace and he was able to see the guests making their way toward the temple platform.

Amelind Danyell was in front, her shoulders bare in a gown better suited to a warm salon, escorted by a young man not quite her height with a waistcoat of such startling pattern Nicholas could make it out even in lamplight at this distance. At her other side was Count Belennier, who seemed to be paying

Danyell more attention than was quite necessary for a woman who already had one male arm to steady her. Behind them he recognized Algretto, who had come out in his shirtsleeves, possibly in an attempt to encourage an attack of tubercle that would make him even more attractive to women like Danyell. He had given his arm to Madame Everset, his hostess, who had bundled up in a paletot and wrapped a scarf around her head, showing far more sense than most of the others present. Possibly she was more interested in the circle itself than she was in being seen to have it by these people. Nicholas wondered if Octave had solicited some relic of a dead relative from her for tonight.

Behind them was Algretto's long-suffering wife, a rather plain woman in a dress of muted color under a long shawl, escorted by Reynard. He was paying her all the courteous attention due a lady of her station, despite attempts from the more boisterous members of the party to distract him. Nicholas smiled to himself. Reynard, despite his protests to the contrary, was a gentleman to his bones.

Behind them trailed Octave.

He wore a plain dark suit, without the ostentatious opera cape this time. If he had recognized Reynard, he might have given some sign by now. The man they had encountered at Coldcourt the night before would have, Nicholas thought, but there was no knowing how closely the golem's personality had matched the real Octave's.

He seemed to be the last member of the party. Everset had already told Reynard he intended to stay behind. Vearde must have opted out as well, and as an opera singer Ilian Isolde could not afford to expose her throat to the night air.

The first group reached the temple and Amelind Danyell called out gaily, "Does it matter where we sit, my dear?"

Madame Everset glanced back at Octave, but he gave her no indication, one way or the other. She answered, "No, dear, it doesn't matter."

Two footmen were stationed a short distance down the terrace to answer any calls for service. The guests found seats with a great deal of shuffling back and forth and some subtle jockeying for position on Belennier's part. Octave reached the temple and stood framed in the entrance, a slight contemptuous smile on his pale face. His appearance was subtly disreputable: frayed cuffs, a cravat that was distinctly gray in the lamplight. Nicholas wondered whether the effect was intentional. Octave stroked his unkempt beard and stared at the people around the table.

It wasn't until everyone was seated that he came forward into the temple. Most of the guests seemed to regard him as a hired entertainer; they chatted among themselves, Belennier flirting with Danyell, Danyell punishing Algretto with subtle jibes for ignoring her, Algretto parrying with a faintly superior smile, and Danyell's young escort fighting for some sort of notice from someone. Crouching in the darkness behind the solid bulk of the urn, cold and damp seeping up through his boots from the stone flags, Nicholas was still reminded of why he didn't much care for society. It had its own predators, just like the streets of Riverside, but they dealt their blows with words, gestures, expressions. Here there were no allies, only enemies, and yet everyone conducted themselves as though they were the dearest of companions. Nicholas hadn't been oblivious to it, but he had felt as if it all took place on another plane of existence that he could view but not interact with. Not that anyone in their right mind would wish to. He preferred the world where enemies were enemies and war was war, and the blows cut to the bone.

Madame Everset was clearly torn between attending her guests and keeping one eye on Octave; it was obvious she was anxious for the circle to start. Reynard kept one eye on Octave also, but in a far more subtle fashion, while carrying on a light conversation with Madame Algretto.

Madame Everset, her voice pitched a little too high from anxiety, said abruptly, "Do we begin, Doctor?"

The others looked toward her, some startled, some amused.

Octave said, "We begin, Madame." He stood behind his empty chair now, facing the others, his back to the wide gap between the pillars that marked the entrance to the temple.

Algretto, probably resenting the sudden cessation of attention to himself, drawled, "I, personally, am an unbeliever in this sort of fantasy, Doctor. Do you really propose to make our good hostess's late brother appear among us?"

Madame Everset winced and Nicholas made the mental note, *Discover the history of the dead brother.* Her face was white in the lamplight and the skin beneath her eyes bruised by fatigue. Nicholas had assumed any signs of strain were due to being married to Captain Everset; now it was obvious Madame had other concerns. It seemed less and less as if she had sought Octave out simply for the societal coup of holding a circle at a salon party. He wondered if perhaps Octave had sought her out, instead.

The doctor said, "Belief is unnecessary." His voice was almost the same as the golem's, perhaps a trifle lower in pitch. Nicholas reminded himself again that this might be an entirely different person from the golem he had met. Its reactions were nothing to judge the real man by.

"Is it?" Algretto smiled, prepared to enjoy baiting Octave and plaguing his obviously anxious hostess. "I thought it essential to this sort of . . . enterprise."

"Your thought was inaccurate." Octave was unruffled. He was in his own element and confident. He had his hand in the pocket of his frock coat and there was something about his stance that was not quite natural. Nicholas might have suspected a pistol, but somehow he didn't think Octave would carry a weapon. Or not that sort of weapon.

Algretto was not accustomed to being parried with such unconcern. Eyes narrowed, he said, "If you would care to word it thus. Your tone is insulting, Doctor. Though what you are a doctor of, exactly, has never been specified."

Madame Algretto sighed audibly, Amelind Danyell tittered, and Belennier looked bored. Madame Everset tried to interject, saying, "Really, I'm sure no harm was meant."

"Really, Algretto," Reynard said, managing to sound as if the subject both amused and wearied him. "Poetry is your field of expertise. Why don't you stick with that and let the good doctor carry on?"

Algretto's eyes went hooded. There was nothing of outright insult in the words, but Reynard was a master of insinuation. The poet said, "I hadn't thought you were the type to be interested in poetry, or this spirit nonsense, Morane."

"Oh, I don't know poetry, but I know what I like."

"Then why are you here?"

"I'm here because I was invited. I often am, you know. Everset and I are the dearest of friends. Why are *you* here?"

Octave was obviously enjoying the confrontation, a smile playing about his pale lips. Belennier said, "Gentlemen, surely it's not—"

Watching his opponent intently, Algretto said, "Perhaps to lend a badly needed air of artistic integrity to the proceedings. But I suppose, after hearing what is said of you, you are unfamiliar with the subject of integrity."

"Perhaps," Reynard agreed, smiling gently. "After hearing about your performance of your latest epic at Countess Averae's literary evening, I think you might be better qualified to lend advice on farcical posturing."

Algretto came to his feet with a curse, knocking back his chair.

With reflexes honed by years of dueling, Reynard stood just as abruptly, his elbow knocking Dr. Octave's arm and sending the spiritualist stumbling back a step. In an unconscious gesture to keep his balance, Octave's hand came out of his pocket.

Nicholas was smiling to himself, thinking, *Good old Reynard,* when Octave's hand came up and he saw the object the spiritualist clutched. There was only time for a moment's glimpse, before Octave hurriedly stuffed it back into concealment. Reynard was saying to Algretto, "Sorry, old fellow, didn't realize you'd take it personally. My apologies."

Algretto was hardly appeased but it would have been the worst manners to refuse the offered apology. He managed to nod grudgingly and sit down. Reynard gravely excused himself to Octave for jostling him and took his own seat again.

Nicholas's smile had died. The object had appeared to be a metallic ball. It had looked very much like one of the models of Edouard Viller's apparatus, except it was much smaller.

It can't be, he told himself. *The others were destroyed.* He had seen the Crown Investigators smash them to bits himself. It had been Edouard's last experiment in combining natural philosophy and magic, begun from a desire to communicate with his dead wife, whom Nicholas knew only as a portrait in the main salon at Coldcourt. By itself, a device for speaking to the dead, whether it worked or not, was not necromancy. But Count Montesq had made it appear as though Edouard had murdered a woman in an attempt to perform magic, fulfilling the legal definition of necromancy. And when the court had discovered what the device had been meant to do, Edouard had looked all the guiltier.

But how had Octave gotten his hands on one of the devices? Every bit of Edouard's surviving work—his notes, his journals, the last intact models of the apparatus, everything the Crown hadn't burned—was at Coldcourt. Nicholas cursed silently. *Perhaps there was some sort of prototype we never knew about.* Arisilde Damal would know, if anyone would. He had worked most closely with Edouard in the initial studies at Lodun. The only alternative was that Octave had recreated that work and developed the same theories independently.

If he hadn't, if he had somehow stolen Edouard's research . . . *He won't need a device to speak to the dead,* Nicholas thought. *He will do it quite comfortably from his own grave.* He would rather see all of Edouard's work burned by the Crown of Ile-Rien than let Octave use it for some filthy trick.

Octave recovered his composure as the other members of the party resettled themselves. He nodded at the still sullen Algretto and said, "To answer the
original question, I am a doctor of the spirit. Any student of sorcery will tell
you of the etheric plane. It is possible to use the ether to reach the souls that
dwell beyond it, who were once part of our world. To communicate with them.
To bring them—temporarily—back to the living. Now . . ."

Octave let the silence grow, until the only sound was the wind moving gently through the oaks. His eyes seemed to go blank, then roll up into his head.
A tremor passed over him and he moaned softly.

Theatrics, Nicholas thought in disgust. *And not very good theatrics at
that.* Octave must still be rattled from Reynard's near-battle with Algretto.
He wasn't the only one who found the performance less than convincing. He
could see an expression of quite open skepticism on Madame Algretto's refined features. But if the spiritualist was using a device that Edouard had some
hand in making, he was playing with power indeed.

A sudden loud rasp startled everyone. Someone gasped. The rasping noise
came again and Nicholas realized it was the sound of wood scraping painfully
against stone. Then he noticed what the others had already seen—the heavy
wooden table was rotating; slowly, ponderously, rotating.

Algretto said, "It's a trick."

Reynard pushed back from the table to look beneath it. Nicholas writhed
inwardly, wishing he had thought of a way to make himself a member of the
party, now entitled to jump up and examine the table for himself. Reynard
said, "It's not a trick. He's not touching it." He scraped at something with one
boot. "And there are splinters on the pavement."

"Then it's sorcery." Algretto smiled. "Such a thing wouldn't even amuse the
market crowds, Doctor. Though I can see why you found this way of earning
your bread more amenable than working as a hedgewitch in the Philosopher's
Cross."

The lamps all flickered once and simultaneously, as if a hand had briefly
lowered over the flame of each. Without dropping his pose of rapt concentration, Octave said, "Believe what you wish. I am the key that unlocks all doors
between our world and the next."

"Necromancy," Madame Algretto said clearly, "is punishable by death, aptly
enough." Her hands hovered over the still moving table, not quite touching it.
That she was beginning to find the proceedings distasteful was obvious.

"But not before the party is over, I hope," said Amelind Danyell slyly.

A trace of irritation in his voice, Octave said, "This is not necromancy, not ghost-summoning or grave robbing. This is communication of the highest form."

"This is a table moving," Algretto pointed out, rather cogently Nicholas had to admit. "We've seen nothing but—"

Octave held up a hand for silence. Behind him a man stood framed between the pillars of the temple entrance. Nicholas caught his breath. He had glanced in that direction a bare instant before and there had been nothing there.

The man was young, dressed in a naval officer's uniform. Nicholas stared hard, trying to memorize details.

The others were silent, those facing the other direction whipping around in their chairs to see. Even the table had stopped its halting clockwise progress. Madame Everset came to her feet as if she had levitated out of her chair. Octave didn't turn, but he had abandoned his apparently trancelike state and was watching her with avid attention.

It isn't a projection from a picture-lantern, was Nicholas's first thought. Its eyes were moving. Bloodshot, as if from salt water or lack of sleep, its eyes went from face to face around the table. It might be an illusion: sorcerous illusions could move, speak. Arisilde was capable of illusions that even seemed solid to the touch. It might be a living accomplice but he didn't see how anyone could have gotten past the servants stationed down the terrace without being remarked.

Madame Everset tried to speak and failed, then managed to gasp, "Justane . . ."

Or how Octave acquired an accomplice Madame Everset would recognize as her brother, Nicholas thought.

Then Octave murmured, "Ask him, Madame. You remember our agreement."

Reynard started, his gaze jerking away from the apparition to Octave, and Nicholas knew he wasn't the only one to hear those discreet words. None of the others seemed to take notice.

Madame Everset nodded, swayed as if she meant to faint, but said, "Justane, your ship. Where did it go down?"

The young man's searching eyes found her. His face was not corpse white, Nicholas noted, but tanned and reddened from the sun. Somehow he found that point more convincing than anything else. The apparition licked its lips, said, "Off the southern coast of Parscia, the straits of Kashatriy." His voice was low and hoarse. "But Lise . . ."

He was gone. There was no gradual fade, no dissolve into mist. He was gone and it was as quick as a door slamming between one world and the next. Madame Everset screamed, "Justane!"

In the suddenly vast silence of the night, there was one sound. It was the *click, click, click* of bootheels on stone.

Nicholas felt himself seized by something, some invisible force that seemed to stop his heart, to freeze the breath in his lungs. It was very like the moment when the ghoul had rushed him in the Mondollot cellars and he had been momentarily trapped, powerless to move.

At first nothing was visible. Then the shadows between the lamps resolved into a dark figure walking at an even, unhurried pace up the bridge of the terrace toward the temple. Nicholas squinted, trying to see the face, and realized he was shivering; the normal dank chill of a late winter night had suddenly turned bitter cold. It was as if the temple platform was made of ice; his hands burned with cold inside his gloves. Something scraped across the roof of the temple, as if the wind had dragged a tree branch against it. Nicholas managed to move, jerking his head to stare up at the deeply shadowed edge of the roof. There were no trees overhanging the temple.

He looked at Octave.

The spiritualist stared with grim concentration at the table. He hadn't turned to look at the approaching figure, but something told Nicholas he was more aware of it than any of them. Octave wet his lips nervously and muttered, "Not yet, not yet. . . ."

That worried Nicholas more than anything. *Good God, the man can contact the dead, and he doesn't know what he's toying with.* The figure drew inexorably closer. Nicholas tried to recognize it, to study its features, anything to understand what was happening, but something seemed to obscure its face. Even though he should be able to see it clearly at this distance, his eyes seemed to slide away when he tried to focus on its features. He concentrated harder; Arisilde had told him it was a way to penetrate the most clever of sorcerous illusions, but it didn't seem to work. The constriction in his lungs and his heart pounding like a train engine didn't help either.

The figure was two paces from the temple entrance. It stopped. Nicholas caught a glimpse of dark clothing, the swirl of a garment, a cloak or coat. Then it was gone.

Nicholas found himself gripping the balustrade and trembling. The members of the circle still sat or stood like statues, like carvings of yellowed marble in the candlelight.

In the breathless silence, Octave said, "We are finished, Madame." He bowed briefly to Madame Everset and walked out of the temple and down the terrace.

Madame Everset tried to protest, but her legs seemed to give way and she sagged, gripping her chair for support. Belennier jumped up to grasp her arm and Algretto said, "Get her to the house—"

"Wait," Reynard interrupted. He called out, "Footman! Get down here with a lamp!"

He's thinking of our underground ghoul, Nicholas thought. And the scraping across the temple roof. He leaned back against the balustrade until he almost tumbled headfirst backward over it, but saw nothing. With the shadows moving across the weathered stone, there might be any number of ghouls crouched up there.

A confused footman brought another lamp and Reynard snatched it from him and moved back down the terrace, holding it high, trying to see if there was anything waiting for them on that roof. Nicholas could see he was questioning the footman, though he couldn't hear the low-voiced inquiry; the man shook his head as he answered.

Reynard said, "All right, bring her out this way."

The others didn't question him. Even the irrepressible Amelind Danyell was gripping Algretto's arm and shivering. Madame Algretto had gone to Madame Everset's side; their hostess seemed to have recovered a little, though she was obviously dazed and shaken. With Belennier's assistance she stood and the entire party made for the terrace.

It was more than time for Nicholas to go as well. If Everset had any sense he would turn half the household out to search the gardens and the surrounding area. If Nicholas hurried, he might manage to be one of the searchers. He climbed over the balustrade and dropped the rest of the way down, landing somewhat noisily in piled leaves and an unfortunate bush.

His own descent was so noisy that he almost didn't hear the corresponding crash of dried twigs and leaves from the nearest of the ancient oaks. He tried to fling himself toward cover, stumbled and fell sprawling. A few feet away something dropped to the packed dirt beneath the tree, stumbled, and caught itself on one of the massive lower branches.

There was just enough light to see it had the outline of a man, dressed in a scarf and a hunter's coat. Startled out of all thought, Nicholas automatically said, "Pardon me, but—" at the same time it said, "Sorry, I—"

They both stopped, staring at each other in astonished and somewhat embarrassed silence. Then the other man said, "Good day to you," and bolted for the outer garden wall.

Nicholas scrambled to his feet and stumbled toward the relative safety of the kitchen garden, cursing under his breath. He knew that voice. He remembered it from ten years ago at Edouard's trial, testifying in the witness box, so calm, so confident, so damning. He remembered it from the Crown Hearing that had rescinded the conviction months too late to save Edouard's life, equally calm, despite the deadly mistake it was admitting. He remembered it from all the close calls, the other trials, when he had been carefully in disguise.

He had spoken to Inspector Ronsarde before, but this was the first time since he was a young man barely out of Lodun that he had used his own voice.

———

In all the confusion Nicholas managed to get into the formal areas of the house. Servants were running everywhere, and it was easy to look as if he had been summoned.

The guests were gathered in the largest salon, the one with enormous bay windows in the front of the house, that overlooked the grotto and the sunken garden and the triumphal arch, all lit by colored lamps now and as strange in that light as something out of Fayre.

The room was yellow—yellow brocaded fabric on the walls, the firescreen, yellow silk upholstery on the scattered couches and chairs, yellow gowns on the nymphs in the woodland scene in the painted medallion on the high ceiling—and guests and servants were scattered throughout. Madame Everset was draped on a divan like a dead woman, her pale features blue-tinged from shock. A maid hovered over her, trying to persuade her to sip a glass of brandy. Everset stood nearby, ineffectual and bewildered.

Reynard was saying, "Dammit, man, you've got to turn the servants out to search."

Algretto paced impatiently. Danyell was collapsed on a sofa but still the center of a little whirl of activity, with her escort and the opera singer Isolde and a small cluster of maids in anxious attendance. Belennier seemed to be describing what had occurred to a tall, Parscian man who must be Vearde. One of the tables bore wineglasses and a scatter of cards from an interrupted game. As evidence for how Vearde, Everset, and Isolde had occupied themselves while the others were at the circle, Nicholas couldn't accept it at face value. He would have to pry more information out of the servants in their remaining time here. He wasn't willing to dismiss the notion of accomplices, not yet.

Octave was nowhere to be seen.

Everset shook his head, baffled. "Why? Search for what?"

Reynard stared. "For accomplices, of course. The weasel frightened your wife out of her wits, you've got to find out if those . . . if those men were what they seemed to be or compatriots of Octave's."

Reynard, Nicholas thought wryly, *you've been keeping company with me too long and it's beginning to show.*

"What's the point? The bastard's leaving with his fee. They're bringing his coach round in the court."

"Leaving already?" Algretto said, turning back toward them and unexpectedly siding with Reynard. "That's damned suspicious, Everset. You ought to detain him at least until you've had a chance to inventory the plate."

. . . Coach round the court. Nicholas was already slipping out of the room. He found the nearest servants' door and bolted up the stairs to the third floor, digging in an inside coat pocket for notepaper. In the guest room he scribbled a line hastily and stuffed it in the pocket of Reynard's spare coat, then he was dashing back down the stairs.

He made his way to the front of the house, cutting through the formal rooms since anyone of note was gathered in the salon. He reached a conservatory with a wall that was formed entirely of glass panes in a wrought iron framework, lit only by moonlight now and looking out on the grotto and the sunken garden. He ducked around cane furniture and stands and racks of potted flowers, boot soles skidding on the tile floor. Down the steps to the lower part of the room where a fountain played under a draping of water lilies. Yes, there was a door here for the gardeners.

He unlocked it and stepped out into the chill night air, closing it carefully behind him. He was at the very front of the house, at the head of a stone path cluttered with wind-driven leaves that ran along the edge of the sunken garden and toward the triumphal arch. The stone of the grotto entrance was to his right, the archway that led under the house and to the carriage court to his left. He needed to be on the opposite side.

A brief scramble over the rock left him glad of his gloves. It was made of dark-painted concrete and not much softened by time. He was too near the side of the house to be seen from the windows in the salon; there was a possibility someone would spot the unorthodox method that he planned to depart in, but it would be too late for them to do anything about it and he would probably be taken for one of Octave's hypothetical accomplices. Nicholas climbed down the side of the grotto entrance and took up a position flat against the wall next to the exit archway for the carriage court.

He had only been there a few moments, barely long enough to calm his breath, when he heard quiet footsteps in the carriage passage. He sank back against the wall, into the thick shadows.

A man stepped out of the passage, stood for a moment in the light from the lamp above the archway, then turned suddenly and looked right at Nicholas. It was Crack.

His henchman swore under his breath. Nicholas smiled and whispered, "I was here first."

Crack slid into the decorative hedge bordering the path. A moment later, his apparently disembodied voice said, "Ain't I your bodyguard? Ain't that my job?"

"Two of us hanging onto the back of the coach would be noticed. On my own I'll be taken for a groom." Nicholas was only fortunate that Octave kept a private vehicle. Hire coaches often had a harrow installed beneath the groom's step, to keep children and anyone else from snatching free rides. A private coach wouldn't be equipped with that deterrent. "And I doubt even Reynard could conceal two servants abandoning him in the middle of the night. Someone has to keep an eye on him."

Crack snorted, possibly at the idea that Reynard needed guarding.

"And more importantly," Nicholas added, allowing a hint of steel into his voice, "because I said so."

Crack had a tidy mind and tended to dislike it when others questioned Nicholas's orders. The implication that he was guilty of this himself seemed to subdue him. One of the bushes trembled and there was some low muttering, but no further outright objections.

Hooves clopped on the pavement, echoing down the passage. Nicholas moved closer to the edge of the arch and braced himself.

Two pairs of harnessed chestnut horses, then the side of Octave's dark coach whipped past. The window shade was down. The coach had slowed to navigate the passage but it was still traveling at a good clip; knowing he couldn't afford to miss, Nicholas took a step forward as it passed and then leapt.

He caught the rail the grooms used to hold on and in another instant his feet found the small platform. Clinging to the handhold, he looked back up at the salon window. No astonished figures were outlined there. He had made his leap unnoticed.

A whip snapped and the coach accelerated as it passed under the arch and reached the road. Gabrill House receded rapidly behind.

CHAPTER FIVE

Trees rose up on either side of the road, turning it into a dark canyon, but Octave's coach barely slowed. This was far too fast a pace for night travel, even with a moon. The lamps at either side of the driver's box swayed, the frame shuddered as the wheels struck holes, and Nicholas huddled against the back, trying to keep a solid grip on the outrider's handle. Fortunately, the coach was a sizable one and he wasn't large enough to make the vehicle draw heavy behind; the chances of reaching the city unnoticed by the driver were good.

Trees gave way to manicured hedges, garden fronts empty and ominous under the moonlight. Greater and lesser houses stood on either side of the road, some still lit for late-night guests, others closed and dark. The coach slowed for nothing, even when they passed other traffic; somehow the driver managed to keep his vehicle upright and out of the ditches.

He had to slow as they neared the old city wall. The road grew narrower, buildings clustered more closely to it and each other, and there were more obstacles to dodge. The wall materialized out of night mist and shadow suddenly, as if it were forming itself out of the ground and growing larger as they drew nearer. Gaslights and lamps from a nearby brandy house threw wild shadows on the ancient stone, each weather-stained block larger than the coach Nicholas clung to. Then they were through the immense gates and under the shadow of the old square towers. Cobblestones clattered under the horses' hooves as they turned down Saints Procession Boulevard.

There was still heavy traffic on the boulevard, even this late at night. The crested coaches of the nobility jostled the smaller vehicles of the merely well-to-do and the little hire cabriolets fought for space to pass. The promenades on either side of the wide street were almost choked with pedestrians at times and the tree-lined verge down the center was often just as crowded; there were a number of theaters on this end of the city and the shows had let out not long ago. Nicholas stood more upright, casual and relaxed, as a groom huddled against the back of the coach and hanging on for dear life was sure to draw attention.

They turned off the boulevard and down a narrower, less frequented street. The houses were dark here, huge structures that blotted out much of the moonlight, as though they rolled down a steep-sided canyon. Nicholas thought the driver was avoiding the theater traffic but the coach didn't take any of the cross streets that roughly paralleled the boulevard.

Gas streetlamps grew less and less frequent and Nicholas wondered if they were taking this street all the way down to Riverside Way.

It was one of the oldest neighborhoods in the city and had once been the bankers' district, but now it was a notorious thieves' kitchen. *For a nondescript address Octave couldn't have chosen better,* Nicholas thought. *Even the Prefecture doesn't enjoy coming down here.*

The buildings were high and narrow, stretching up four and five stories to peaked garrets. Shadows concealed the entrances to courts, though Nicholas knew most of them were impassable from trash and debris. The streetlamps, tall iron poles topped by ornate grillwork, had disappeared altogether and were replaced by oil lamps and torches, usually above the entrances to penny theaters or cheap brandy shops and cabarets. Crowds gathered around the lighted fronts of these establishments, laughing, calling out to friends, breaking off in apparently amiable groups that suddenly tumbled into fistfights. There were more ordinary businesses here: cafés, tanneries, clothing and dye shops, but from a nighttime view the place looked like nothing but a den of iniquity.

The coachman took the sharp corner too abruptly and Nicholas lost his footing on the platform, his legs swaying dangerously out from the coach before he managed to haul himself up again. *The driver must have felt that,* he thought, shaking his head to keep the hair out of his eyes. The coach springs weren't good enough to conceal what must have been an odd shift in the balance of the vehicle. *Perhaps he isn't the observant sort.*

But one of the revelers on the corner staggered toward the street and called out helpfully, "Hey, there, skite! Slow down, you almost lost your groom."

Oh, hell. Nicholas closed his eyes briefly. *He didn't hear that.* The coach lurched under him, abruptly gaining speed as it barreled dangerously down the dark street. *No, he heard it all right,* he thought grimly.

The coach swayed sharply to the right, then again to the left. Nicholas clung tightly, glad of the gloves protecting his sweat-slick hands. Occupied with keeping a grip on the fast-moving vehicle, he didn't see the next corner until the coach took it at an alarming speed.

His feet slipped and he slammed against the back of the coach. He felt his legs strike the left wheel and hauled himself up desperately before he became tangled in the spokes. He barely found his footing again when the coach careened around another corner.

He had to get off the damn thing. Nicholas leaned out dangerously, getting a glimpse of what they were heading into. He saw the rows of buildings seem to come to an abrupt end not far ahead and suddenly recognized the street. They were on Riverside Way again and about to cross the river.

The buildings fell away behind them and a chill wind swept over him as they broke out into the open. Across the black chasm of the river he could see the lights of the far bank, the docks and warehouses of the shipping district. The coach barreled down a steep incline in the road and the lip of an ancient stone bridge appeared in the erratic light of the lamps.

Nicholas braced himself. The coach hit the bottom of the incline with a crash of springs and abused wood and he leapt into darkness. The breath was knocked out of him as he struck the ground, landing on the grassy verge instead of the stone roadway more by luck than design. He rolled into a foul-smelling muddy flat, gasping for breath.

He propped himself up, shaking his head to clear his senses. The coach had stopped at the top of the bridge above him, the horses trembling with exertion, their sides steaming in the cool air. The coachman climbed from the box as the side door swung open.

His eyes accustomed to the torchlit streets, Nicholas was almost blind in the heavy dark along the river. He scrambled down the bank until he felt the ground crumbling under his hands. There must be a drop-off here where the dirt had eroded away, though he could see little but moonlight limning the water below. The coachman had lifted one of the coach lamps out of its holder and would be down here in moments.

Nicholas ripped off his already torn coat and flung it over the edge of the drop-off, then rolled sideways to leave as little intelligible imprint in the wet ground as possible. He reached a more solid surface covered with patchy grass and struggled upright, and groped his way toward the arch of the bridge.

Above him the light bobbed, suggesting the coachman had started down the steep bank, following his progress through the disturbed mud and dirt. Nicholas worked his way under the low stone arch, blundering into pockets of stinking mud and bruising himself on broken bricks and metal debris. Cursing silently, he slid down and managed to fetch up against the first support pillar and crouched against it, waiting.

He heard their footsteps over the lapping of the water and the distant hum from the busy neighborhood. Their lamp appeared and Nicholas edged quietly around to the far side of the pillar. The light shifted erratically as the coachman investigated, then a voice said, "I think he fell over here. There's a bit of cloth caught on a bramble down there—looks fresh."

"You think." It was Octave's voice. "You didn't think. It would have been better to summon a constable than to draw attention with that ridiculous display."

"If he's dead, then he can't follow us," the coachman muttered, sullen.

Octave said, "If he's dead," and Nicholas heard grass rustle as footsteps retreated up the bank. In another moment, the lamp and coachman followed.

Nicholas let out his breath. He listened to the coach make an awkward turn on the bridge, then head back up the incline at a more sedate pace. He gave them time to get up the slope, then climbed back to the road.

He paused there, his breath misting in the cold damp air, and saw the coach passing between houses. He grimaced, then started to run up the sloping road after it. This night's work was not turning out exactly as he had hoped.

Fortunately, the coach kept to a more restrained pace as the coachman tried to make it look like a completely different vehicle from the one that had just torn so violently through the neighborhood. Nicholas kept to the side of the street, dodging in and out of groups of noisy revelers, avoiding the infrequent pools of lamplight. Hatless, coatless, and with his good servant's clothes muddy and torn, he fit in among the crowd and no one accosted him.

He kept up the whole distance down Riverside Way and through two turns onto shorter cross streets, but after a long straight stretch he began to fall back. The coach turned left down another intersecting street and Nicholas put on a burst of speed to reach the corner, his lungs aching. This was Gabard Lane, even narrower and more crowded than the other streets of this warren. The coach forged its way through at a good pace but was stopped at the end of the street by a cart that was trying to make a late delivery. It had managed to strew barrels down the middle of the lane and block all traffic.

Nicholas leaned against an alley wall, breathless, while the coachman shouted, the carter threatened, and spectators took sides. They were near the edge of the Riverside Way area, almost on the border of the Garbardin Quarter. It was run-down too, but not as gone to hell as its nearest neighbors.

The carter summoned helpers out of the nearest brandy house and the barrels were removed. Nicholas pushed off from the wall, his brief respite over.

The coach turned at the end of the lane and Nicholas reached the corner, only to stop short and fall back against the wall.

The coach had halted in front of a large building that had more the look of a fortress than a private home. It was several stories tall, with towers sprouting from the pitched roof. It was a Great House, a very old one, fallen on hard times as the neighborhood around it had decayed. As Nicholas watched, the doors of the carriage entrance swung slowly open and the coach passed inside. The windows on the upper floors were apparently lightless behind their heavy shutters and the house had a deserted look.

Nicholas knew little about this particular area, though he was far too familiar with its immediate neighbor Riverside. He stepped around the corner, moving casually down the street toward the only source of light—a small brandy house operating out of what appeared to be the old stable of another Great House, long ago torn down for tenements.

The front wall was open to the street, revealing a high-raftered interior packed with people, noise, and smoke. Outside, a few regulars were loitering and an old man was serving from an open barrel, for the patrons who didn't care to fight their way in.

"It's a penny for a drink, unless you don't got your own cup, then it's two," he said wearily, as Nicholas sat down on an overturned trough.

"It's two," Nicholas answered, tossing the coins over. The old man caught them and passed him a cup.

He took a cautious sip and managed not to wince. It burned all the way down his throat, with a faint aftertaste of kerosene. It brought back a host of disagreeable memories, of the one tiny room he and his mother had occupied in a tenement unpleasantly similar to those throwing their shadows over the street now.

The old man was still watching him. The only other patrons nearby were passed out entirely, huddled up against the wall of the old stable or staring vacantly into space. Nicholas was in no mood to fence. He said, "Whose house is that?"

"I saw you watching it." The old man grinned, caught Nicholas's expression, and added hastily, "There's nothing there. Just old people. Nothing to steal."

"Their name?"

"Valent. It's Valent House, or it used to be. Just old people live there."

Nicholas tossed him another penny and stood. He started to dump the

brandy in the street but instead handed it off to the most conscious of the huddled figures and walked away.

He went to the opposite corner. It intersected a street where late-night coach
and wagon traffic still traveled and several raucous establishments spilled cus-
tomers into the gutters. He went down a short distance until he found an alley
that led between two high, featureless brick walls back in the direction of Valent House.

He followed it with difficulty, finding his way past one dead end and two
other intersecting passages, and finally came out into a carriage court that had
been orphaned by the demolition of its original owner: none of the structures
crowding close around opened on it and it was piled high with rubbish. There
were windows looking down on it but all were closed or darkened; this entire
side of the street seemed completely deserted. Nicholas fought his way through
debris, bruising his shin on a broken dogcart axle in the process, and reached
the far wall.

He climbed it in a shower of loose bits of mortar and looked over the top
into a dingy little court that had once been a garden, now choked with weeds
and long abandoned. Looking up, he saw the outline of gables against the dark
sky and knew this was the back of Valent House. The windows in the upper
floors were all securely boarded shut and there were, of course, none in the
ground floor and only a single door to allow access.

He struggled over the top of the wall and dropped softly down into the remains of a flower bed. The shadow of the house blotted out much of the moonlight and he had to feel for the steps and then the door. He tried the handle
cautiously and found it securely locked and far too solid to force. He cursed it
silently and stood back to look up at the house again. There was not a hint of
light or sound from within, but these walls were thick, and one or a few people,
moving quietly and with hand lamps, would not be noticeable from outside.

More searching turned up an alley that led off the garden court and back
to the street at the front of the house. There seemed to be no other ground-
floor entrances but the garden door and the front, which he was not quite fool
enough to try.

Nicholas had prepared tonight to pose as a manservant, not act as a house-
breaker. He needed to send a message to Cusard. This meant a walk back
to Riverside and his older haunts, where he could find a reliable messenger
among the street boys who worked for the old thief.

He made his way back to the noisy side street with some difficulty and paused at the corner, to look toward Valent House again. Octave might think the night's work was over, but it was just beginning.

———

In a thieves' kitchen in Riverside, Nicholas found a street boy who worked occasionally for Lamane and who could take a message to Cusard. It would be an hour at least until Cusard could receive it and respond. He used the time to walk back up to Saints Procession Boulevard where there was an office of the Martine-Viendo Wire that stayed open all night, mainly for the convenience of the foreign embassies in the district that began across the street. There he sent a telegram to be delivered to Madeline at Coldcourt.

Both messages were cryptic and not readily to be understood by anyone who might intercept them. The message to Madeline had said only "E's storeroom—ascertain security of inventory." He might have waited on that until he could do it himself, but he was impatient and if Octave had found a way to get to Edouard's research without alerting them, he wanted to know as soon as possible.

He caught a hire cabriolet on the boulevard and took it as far back down toward Gabard Lane as the driver was willing to go and walked the rest of the way. He waited on the upper corner, comfortably out of sight of the street where Valent House lay, stamping his feet against the cold. He would have liked to keep watch on the house but wasn't so dead to common sense as that— Octave would be suspicious at best after the performance on the riverbank.

Fortunately, there were few prostitutes working this street and most were easily fended off. The district seemed to be quieting a little as the night wore on, but he had to keep moving to avoid suspicion. The ostler's wagon with Cusard on the box was a welcome sight. Even more welcome were Reynard and Crack, who climbed down as soon as the wagon reined in at the curb.

"How did you make it here?" Nicholas asked.

"After I found your note, I made my excuses and got the hell away," Reynard explained. He had changed out of his evening clothes and, with the somewhat battered greatcoat he wore, looked sufficiently enough like someone who would be riding in an ostler's wagon in this part of the city. "We went to the warehouse to see if you'd gone back there and met Cusard." He glanced around the street. "Lovely neighborhood."

"I brought these." Cusard finished tying off his reins and pulled a leather satchel out from under the bench. He handed it down to Nicholas. "Everything there we might need. I checked it myself. Who's staying with the wagon?"

"You are," Nicholas said, taking the satchel. "Did you remember the oil?"

"Of course I remembered the oil." Cusard was affronted at being left behind. "I'm the only official cracksman here and I taught you everything you know. It was a lie, the charge they laid against him." He gestured at Crack, who rolled his eyes in annoyance.

"I know that," Nicholas said with asperity. "I'll work the doors myself. Someone has to wait with the wagon and he'll have to keep sharp in this patch. You think on that." In another moment, Nicholas reflected, he would be speaking entirely in backstreet Vienne thieves' cant. This night was bringing his past back to him in unpleasant detail.

"All right, all right, have your own way, that's the young for you." Cusard gave in with poor grace. He handed Crack a dark lantern and Nicholas waited impatiently as it was lit.

"What happened to the coach?" Reynard asked as they started down the street.

"The driver realized I was on the back and I had to jump off and follow on foot." He led them to the corner and took Crack by the shoulder, pointing out the dark bulk of Valent House. "Octave drove into the carriage door of that house. See if you can tell if he's still there."

Crack slipped around the corner. Nicholas leaned back against the wall, feeling through the contents of the satchel Cusard had brought him.

"Your note was incoherent, by the way," Reynard said, regarding him thoughtfully. "What did you see at the circle that I didn't?"

"That item that you so adeptly forced him to reveal."

"Yes?"

"Edouard's last work. Did you ever know what it was?" Nicholas hadn't known Reynard then and he was well aware his friend had had his own troubles at that time.

"Not really." Reynard shrugged. "I heard rumors, none of which made much sense."

Nicholas suspected Reynard was exercising tact, something he only did with close friends. The rumors at the time had been explicit and damning. "It was a mechanical device that would allow someone who had no sorcerous ability to direct sorcerous power, in a limited fashion."

"Ah. That would tend to explain some of the events at the circle, wouldn't it?"

"Yes. It took the help of a sorcerer to make it work at first. That's why Edouard and I lived at Lodun for so long. He worked on it with Arisilde for a time." He looked back at Reynard. "When one of the devices is completed, it's in the form of a metal sphere, like the one Octave had."

"I see why you chased him over half the city. But how did he get his hands on Viller's work? Didn't the Crown have it destroyed?"

"We managed to get to Lodun before the Crown did. The University authorities weren't amenable to having a scholar's property seized, and their resistance gave me enough time to remove most of the important papers—" Nicholas realized he was saying far more than he had meant to. The conversation was moving away from the security of the bare facts of Edouard's work and the events surrounding his trial and into the dangerous ground of his own actions, thoughts, and feelings at that nightmarish time. He looked away up the street and added only, "I couldn't save anything from the workroom he kept in Vienne where he was arrested." In the last months of his life, Edouard had moved his experiments from Coldcourt to a hired studio on Breakwater Street in Vienne. It had been an odd thing for him to do, since previously he had worked only at his home or his quarters in Lodun. The prosecution at the trial had made much of this, suggesting that Edouard was trying to hide his activities from his family and servants.

One morning, Edouard had unlocked the studio to find a woman, very obviously and messily dead, on the table in his workroom. His reaction had been to run out into the street, shouting for help—not the act of a guilty man, as his counsel had pointed out. She had been a beggar who sold charms and flowers on the street and the prosecution gave evidence that Edouard had been seen to give her money, suggesting this was how he had lured her into his rooms. Edouard was found guilty of trying to use her death to power his magical device and had been executed only a week later.

Nicholas had learned later that Inspector Ronsarde had never been happy with the case. Six months after Edouard's death, the Inspector had penetrated the deception and discovered that the woman had been murdered by a local thug named Ruebene. Ruebene had been killed when the Prefecture attempted to arrest him, leaving Edouard's name cleared, but the Crown investigation had gone no further. Nicholas had taken up where Ronsarde left off, working for months until he found the link to Edouard's old patron, Count Montesq. The evidence was poor and since the chief witness was one of Montesq's lower-class mistresses who had been present when the Count had hired Ruebene, and who was then dying of syphilis, he knew it would never go to court.

Besides, Montesq couldn't be accused of necromancy, only of hiring the death of a beggar.

Nicholas wanted him to suffer far more than that. He took a deep breath and made himself think of the present and not the past. "I don't know how Octave could have gotten his hands on any of it. And I don't think I can make myself believe he was able to duplicate Edouard's work from his own inspiration."

"No," Reynard agreed. "He didn't seem the inspired type, if you know what I mean. I think I detected an air of the professional confidence man about him."

"That wouldn't surprise me." Reluctantly, Nicholas added, "And we have another worry. Ronsarde was at Gabrill House tonight."

Reynard was badly startled. "That's not funny."

"I'm not joking. He was in the garden, watching the circle. I spotted him as I was leaving. He saw me too, of course, but not close enough to recognize, considering it's been years since he's seen me without a disguise of some sort." Nicholas had avoided contact with Ronsarde after the trial, at first because he had been planning to kill him, later because he was building the Donatien persona.

"Damn." Reynard folded his arms. "That could complicate everything enormously."

"I'm well aware of that." Nicholas's expression was sour. "If he realizes you're connected with Donatien, that's going to give him the answers to more than a few mysteries." Reynard had been the inside man for several of their early jewel robberies, when they had needed operating funds for the campaigns against Montesq. "But at the moment he has no reason to suspect Donatien's involvement."

Reynard wasn't ready to let it drop. "But what if he saw the sphere? He'll recognize it just as you did. That will give him every reason to suspect the involvement of a member of the Viller family. And if he connects *you* with Donatien . . ."

"We have to assume he did see it, and did know it for Edouard's work. He could be led straight to us." The looming walls of the tenements around them seemed to be closing in and Nicholas told himself this was shadow and imagination. He took another look toward Valent House and saw Crack coming back up the street. "We'll just have to get to Octave first, and remove the evidence."

Reynard shrugged philosophically, apparently satisfied with letting the problem rest there. Nicholas wished he could be so sanguine.

Reaching them, Crack said, "There's an alley with slatted windows looking into the stable. No horses, no coach. Been there recently, though."

Nicholas swore, resisting the urge to kick the foundation of the nearest wall. "I don't know if he realized it was me on the coach, but he knows someone is after him."

"He's cautious." Reynard scratched his beard thoughtfully. "The house is still worth looking at."

Nicholas agreed. Nothing was keeping him out of that house. "Yes, he had to leave in a hurry, if he wasn't just visiting someone. There may be something left behind. Let's try that door I found earlier."

They went down the quiet street, keeping a wary eye on the brandy house in the old stable, the only possible source of interference. But the patrons who had crowded it earlier seemed to have retired and even the old man serving from the barrel had retreated inside. Several bundled forms were still stretched out on the walk in front, but they seemed dead to the world and disinclined to interfere.

They reached the corner of the house and turned down the narrow alley that led directly to the garden court, Crack in the lead. As they made their way across the dry overgrown grass, Reynard swore softly and stopped to scrape something off his boot.

Nicholas followed Crack up the steps to the door he had tried earlier. In the muted light of the dark lantern, he examined it cautiously. It was solid mahogany and barely weathered at all. "New," he whispered. "And in the last month."

Crack nodded agreement, taking the lantern as Nicholas fished a leather tool case out of the satchel. He selected a bit and fitted it to a small steel brace, then knelt on the step to work near the keyhole.

Frequent application from a small bottle of oil kept the drilling reasonably quiet. He could hear nothing but their own breathing and an occasional fidget from Reynard. The house might have been empty.

It took almost thirty separate holes and the better part of an hour before Nicholas could wrench out the lock and push the heavy door open.

Crack handed back the lantern and slipped in first, Nicholas and Reynard following. The air smelled of damp and rats and something even more foul, as though meat had spoiled and been left to rot somewhere inside.

They crept down a short hall, the lantern illuminating fragments of rooms, the wire-mesh meat safe of a servery, once-white tiles coated with dust and filth, an open and empty coal bin. Crack pushed silently through a door at the end of the hall, then leaned back to motion Nicholas to shut the slide on the lantern entirely. He complied, then followed his henchman through the door, Reynard behind him.

They were in the central foyer. Some light entered through the cracked glass windows above the deep shadow of the front entrance. Nicholas could tell that this had once been a very fine house. The staircase had a grand elegant sweep, splitting into two midway up its length to lead into the separate wings. Torn and rotting fabric that had once been draperies still clung to the walls and paper and paint had peeled away in the damp. If people were living here, as the old man had said, they must carve out a miserable existence in one or two rooms, probably on the ground floor. The rest of the place was like a tomb.

Crack whispered, "No one's here. No one alive."

Nicholas glanced at him in surprise, supposing he was succumbing to a heretofore unexpressed religious streak. Then Reynard said softly, "You smell it too, hey? I can't tell where it's coming from; seems to be everywhere."

"Smell what?" Nicholas asked, puzzled. "The rats?"

Reynard's mouth twisted, not in amusement. "You've never spent a long period of time in a war—or a prison. That's not rats."

Nicholas accepted the statement without argument; he was beginning to realize just what it was they might find here. He said, "Crack, look for the cellar door. We'll search this floor first."

Crack vanished into the gloom and Nicholas and Reynard turned toward the doors off the entrance hall. The first had been a reception room. Nicholas raised the slide again and lifted the lantern, revealing spiderwebs like lace stretching from the ornate cornice and floral frieze out to the broken remnants of the chandeliers. The carpet had been worn to rags and he could clearly see that it and the heavy layer of dust on the floor had been recently disturbed. What was once a fine table still stood in the center of the room, its surface long ruined by damp, but not as heavily covered in filth as it should have been.

Reynard called softly from another doorway, "Signs of life, here."

It was a library. The walls were lined with empty shelves and the floor was bare, but a large secretaire stood against one wall, with a straight-backed chair nearby.

Nicholas went to it, holding the lamp close to examine the scarred surface. There was hardly any dust at all and the lamp that stood on the shelf above was still half filled with oil. The drawers stood open and one had been pulled all the way out onto the floor.

"Left in a hurry," Reynard commented softly.

They searched the desk without having to discuss it, each taking one side. Nicholas found nothing but broken pens, an empty ink bottle, and a deserted mouse nest, and Reynard's haul wasn't nearly so promising. Nicholas pulled out the other drawers and crouched down to reach farther back into the cabinet, disturbing a flurry of spiders and something that skittered noisily away. He was rewarded when his hand brushed paper.

"There's something back here," he muttered.

"Hopefully not a rat."

"Someone pulled out that drawer," Nicholas argued, "because something was stuck and he didn't want to leave it." It felt like a sheaf of torn paper fragments, wedged into a crack.

"Or because he was in a hurry and clumsy."

"Well, that, too." The paper gave way without tearing and he was able to withdraw his arm. In the dim light, he could see the scraps were covered with handwriting. He reached for the lamp, just as Crack's voice came from the doorway.

"Found something."

"Found what?" Reynard asked, as Nicholas stood and shoved the paper fragments into his vest pocket.

"What you thought," Crack elaborated and vanished back into the hall. Reynard turned to Nicholas, brow raised, for a translation.

"The not-rats," Nicholas explained, already moving toward the door.

Crack led them to an alcove under the staircase. Going down, they found themselves in a hall with bare plaster walls, with various closed doors leading off it, probably to such places as the stillroom, the wine storage, the butler's pantry, and the bedrooms for the upper servants. Crack turned right and opened a door. The smell warned Nicholas what to expect. It had grown stronger as they neared this room and as the door swung open he nearly gagged. Crack took the lantern out of Nicholas's hand, knocked the slide all the way up and held it high.

In the center of the room a makeshift table had been fashioned out of planks and overturned tubs. Stretched across the planks was the corpse of a man. The chest and abdomen had been ripped open, the ribs pried back. Most of the organs had been removed and were littering the flagstoned floor, along with a great quantity of blood and other bodily fluids. The entrails were still attached but had been pulled out and dangled to the floor.

Nicholas heard himself say, "I wasn't expecting this."

"There's more," Crack said, his soft raspy voice grimly matter-of-fact. "But this is the worst. That room there, closest to the stairs, I checked it first. There's a hole knocked in the back wall with six of 'em crammed in it."

Reynard turned to him, aghast. "Six?"

"Kids," Crack added. He looked at Nicholas earnestly. "There's more, I know there is. I could find 'em all for you if you need it."

"That won't be necessary just at the moment." Nicholas stared at the carnage. Whether Crack had sensed it on a visceral level, or observed signs that led him to that conclusion, he knew it was true. Bile was rising in his throat and he had to turn away for a moment and rest his head against the doorframe. Reynard stepped down the hall a few paces and stayed there, cursing under his breath.

Nicholas forced himself to turn back and look at the room again. He had, for a time, trained in the physicians' college at Lodun, though he had given up the courses after Edouard died. He could recognize a dissection when he saw it, and this was not one. This was a vivisection.

He made himself take a step farther into the room, confirming the theory. There was no reason to tie down a corpse and the man's wrists and ankles, practically the only intact flesh still left on the body, bore terrible galls from straining against the bonds. One of the eyes had been gouged out and the face cut and disfigured. *He wasn't alive through much of it,* Nicholas told himself. *He couldn't have been.* But the moments the victim had lived through had been terrible enough.

He looked down at the debris on the floor. The remains were that of more than one person.

He almost turned and walked out of the room then, certain he was going to be ill. Nothing had ever affected him this way before. He was not squeamish: anatomical studies, the morgue, or the surgeries he had watched had never disturbed him. This was different. This was foul in a way almost past comprehension. He knew what Crack was seeing here, why the other man was

so certain they would find more corpses if they searched. This was not something one did once. This was a crescendo, worked up to with time and much
experimentation.

Nicholas forced himself to look around the room again and this time saw
something else. The whitewashed plaster on the walls, where it wasn't stained
with blood or some other fluid, was melted.

"What the hell . . . ?" he said softly, so intrigued by the anomaly he almost
forgot the butchery around him. He stepped to the wall nearest the door,
where he could reach it without having to move anything aside or step into
a puddle, and probed the affected area. It was not only the plaster that was
melted, but the wood beneath it. It was fused, the two disparate materials running together, forming glassy textured lumps. Nicholas swore again. This was
something he had learned at Lodun too, but not in the medical college. This
was something sorcerous; the result, perhaps, of uncontrolled power.

He should search for more telltale signs of sorcery, but he found himself
suddenly unable to turn and look at the rest of the room again. He stepped
out and nodded to Crack, who dimmed the lantern and pulled the door shut.

They climbed the stairs in silence. Once back in the hall, Reynard turned
immediately to the passage that led outside.

Nicholas caught his arm. "We still have to search the rest of the house. We
can come back tomorrow to investigate further, but we have to make sure
there's no one still hiding here."

Reynard hesitated. He was badly disturbed and doing his best to conceal it.
"Yes," he said finally. "You're right. Let's finish it."

They split up to make quicker work of it. Crack had already scouted the
basement, which seemed to contain nothing but the bodies and the instruments that had been used to torture and kill. They found repeated evidence
that the house had been inhabited and recently. The ground floor was barren,
except in the kitchen, which still showed signs of meals prepared and eaten at
the deal table. Stores of candles, lamp oil, and various foodstuffs had been left
behind. The dust and dirt coating the remaining carpets took footprints easily,
though it didn't hold enough of the shape to make identification of the type of
shoe possible.

On the second floor, Nicholas found a bedroom that had seen recent use and
a search of the drawers and cupboards in the remaining furniture turned up
a slim stack of notebooks, covered with elegant, spidery handwriting. He fell
on those eagerly, but as he flipped through them they seemed to be nothing but

verbatim notes out of a book of sorcerous instruction. It was mildly encouraging that the type of sorcery discussed was necromancy. That was patently obvious from the first page, which went on about all the uses of dried human skin. It was the type of notes a student would make, from a book he was allowed to use but not remove from a master's library. Nicholas took the notebooks anyway and found nothing more of use.

In the last room at the far end of the left-hand wing, the now familiar smell of mortal decay stopped Nicholas in the doorway. It was a bedroom, more completely furnished than the others he had searched. His gaze went to the dressing table, where brushes and combs and a few cut-glass bottles stood under a heavy layer of dust. He moved reluctantly to the heavily curtained bed and drew back the tattered drapes.

This, at least, was peaceful death. An old woman lay on the counterpane, dressed in a faded gown of a style out of fashion for twenty years, her feet in delicately beaded slippers. Her eyes were closed and her arms folded on her breast. Her flesh was deeply sunken and decayed; she must have lain like that for a year or more.

He let the drape fall back. It was unlikely the usurpers of her house had ever known she was there. He hoped that last loyal servant, who had dressed her in her best and laid her body out and drawn the bedcurtains, had followed those actions with packing their things and locking the door behind them, and had not lingered to become part of the collection in the basement.

Nicholas kept them searching as long as he could, but with only the three of them and lamplight, there was only so much they could do. Finally, Reynard collared him.

"Nic, there is nothing more we can do tonight. We need a medical doctor, and a sorcerer, and enough men to look in every cabinet, cubby, and mousehole in this house. Besides, you aren't going to find a message scrawled in blood on a wall that says, 'I did this, come find me at such and such address' no matter how hard you look. Leave it for now. We can come back in the morning with help."

Nicholas looked around at the silent hall and the disturbed dust hanging in the damp air. Finally, he said, "You're right, let's go."

They left the house by the garden door. Nicholas was hoping the outside air, remarkably clean and fresh after the fetid humors inside, would revive him, but he didn't get two paces down the broken path before he found himself braced against the garden wall, being messily sick.

When he straightened up he saw Crack had gone ahead, probably to scout the street. Reynard waited for him, arms folded, staring at the silent house.

Still leaning weakly against the wall, unable to help himself, Nicholas said, "It doesn't make sense. What does this have to do with spirit circles? You heard him ask Madame Everset's brother about his ship. It was so obvious that he was after the cargo, probably valuable if they were coming out of a Parscian port. He was after hidden wealth, not . . . What does this have to do with it?"

Reynard looked at him, frowning. "But you thought he had something to do with those disappearances, that boy you went to look at in the morgue?"

"There was evidence, I couldn't discount it, but I thought it would turn out to be some sort of coincidence. This doesn't make sense."

"Madness doesn't have to make sense." Reynard turned away from the house and took Nicholas's arm. "Let's get away from here."

———

They found Cusard waiting up the street and climbed aboard the wagon. After a brief whispered explanation from Crack, Cusard whistled and said, "Next time I moan about being left behind, remind me of this."

Nicholas and Reynard settled in the wagon bed, Crack climbing back to join them as Cusard urged the sleepy horses into motion.

They were silent for a time, watching the darkened houses pass by. The night was winding down in this part of the city and the loudest sound was the clop of hooves on stone.

"What do we do now?" Crack asked.

That's the first time he's ever asked, Nicholas thought. *No matter what was happening.* It was too bad he didn't have an answer.

"That's simple enough," Reynard told Crack. "Tomorrow night you and I will go out, find Octave, and commit his remains to the river."

"That's the one thing we can't do," Nicholas said. "Octave couldn't have done all that alone. There must be others. There's his coachman, for one." The coachman wasn't the one Nicholas was worried about. There was someone else in this, someone who wasn't interested in Octave's spirit circles.

Reynard returned his gaze steadily. "Are you sure we can afford to wait?"

Nicholas didn't look away. "No. But if there's even one other, he's got to be found. Octave knows too much about us. His colleagues must also."

"That wasn't the reason I was thinking of," Reynard said quietly.

"I know." Despite the devil-may-care persona Reynard had carefully constructed, his sense of morality was better suited to the officer and gen-tleman he had once been. His impulses were always in the right direction. Nicholas's impulses were usually all in the wrong direction and it was only the intellectual knowledge of right and wrong painstakingly instilled in him by Edouard that allowed him to understand most moral decisions. But some-thing in that room had struck him to the heart. He would stop it, but he had to do it his own way.

Reynard said nothing for a time. The wagon boards creaked as Crack shifted uneasily, but the henchman didn't venture an opinion. Finally, Rey-nard sighed.

"He's clever, Octave or whoever helps him, to take so many and not be caught, not start some sort of panic. He could keep at it for years."

Nicholas was staring at the street moving past. It was necromancy, obvi-ously. Octave and his followers were performing—committing—some sort of necromantic magic. There was a memory, just on the edge of recall, that would seem to explain much if he could just capture it. He said, "I think I've seen something like that room somewhere before."

Even Crack looked to him in astonishment. Reynard snorted. "Where? In a slaughterhouse?"

"Not in person," Nicholas explained with a preoccupied frown. "In a book, an illustration in a book. I used to read the most appalling things as a child, my mother . . . My mother bought torn-up, broken books by the stack for me, at the old shops near the river, and she didn't always have the leisure to look at what they were." He shook his head. "That's all I can recall of it. I'll look in Edouard's library—he used to read appalling things, too."

Reynard said grimly, "Whether he's committing plagiarism or he's thought it all up on his own, Dr. Octave's got to die."

CHAPTER SIX

Madeline wasn't able to sleep. It was for no rational reason: Nicholas had done far more dangerous things than pose as a servant at a house party. At least, she thought he had. Dr. Octave was such an unknown quantity.

Unable to reason away her sleeplessness, she sat up on the chaise in the bedroom, wrapped in her dressing gown, with a glass of watered wine and a book she was unable to pay proper attention to.

It's not as if Octave is the first sorcerer we've had to deal with, she thought for perhaps the third time, tapping one well-kept fingernail on the page before her and staring into space. They had once burgled the townhome of a sorcerer called Lemere and found their way through a bewildering maze of magical protections. But Arisilde had been more active then and well able to cope with any attempt at retaliation. *If Octave is a sorcerer.* Perhaps it was the unknown that disturbed her.

She wished she could tell if it was ordinary nerves or some long-buried sense trying to warn her. Nearly all the women in her family had strong talents and inclinations for witchcraft. Madeline had given all that up for the stage and, in truth, she didn't miss it. Her real talent was for acting, and the roles she played in pursuit of Nicholas's goals were just as thrilling as lead ingénue at the Elegante.

She shook her head at her own folly. Life was safer at the Elegante. Any fool could see Nicholas was obsessed. With destroying Montesq mainly, but also in a broader sense he was obsessed with deception itself. And obsessed with playing the part of Donatien to Vienne's criminal underworld, and dancing in and out of Inspector Ronsarde's grasp, and a dozen other things to varying degrees. And now with stalking Octave, for all she knew.

Lately the obsession had been gaining the upper hand. Madeline supposed that if she were of literary bent she would see Donatien as a separate, distinct personality that was fast consuming Nicholas. That, in fact, would make a good play. *Davne Ruis could play Nicholas,* she thought. *And I could play me.*

Or maybe his mother; that would be a good part, too. But she knew it wasn't the case. Nicholas and Donatien were too obviously the same personality; at heart and everywhere else that counted they were the same man, with only cosmetic differences to fool the onlookers. They both wanted the same things.

But then sometimes she wasn't sure she knew Nicholas at all. She suspected Reynard might know him better. He had been helping Nicholas with his various plots for about six years or so and Madeline had only been involved for half that time.

Not long after Nicholas had first taken her into his confidence, Madeline had had a tête-à-tête with Reynard, over brandy on the veranda of the Café Exquisite. She had asked him, point blank, if he and Nicholas had ever slept together, wishing to get that question resolved before she embarked on any deeper relationship with him. Sensing her seriousness, Reynard had replied, immediately and without baiting, that they hadn't. "Not that I didn't inquire once if he was interested, not long after we first met." After a moment he admitted, "I had the feeling that if I had pushed the issue, he would have given in. If you can imagine Nic giving in on any point whatsoever, which I admit is rather difficult."

"But you don't push issues," Madeline had said, swirling the warmed brandy in her glass.

"No, I don't. He didn't want me, he wanted affection and understanding. I didn't really want him, I just wanted to try to learn how his mind worked. Neither of us would have gotten what we wanted and we both already had more trouble than we could handle."

"You can't find out who someone is by sleeping with them," Madeline had pointed out.

"Thank you for the words of wisdom, my dear," Reynard had said, dryly. "Now where were you twenty years ago when the advice would have done me some good?"

Reynard had been of some help, but instinct told Madeline that both of them knew exactly as much as Nicholas wanted them to know and not one hint more.

Such speculations were pointless. Madeline shifted restlessly and tugged her dressing gown more firmly around her. There was a soft scratch on the door. As she put her book aside it opened and Sarasate peered in. "Madame, there's a telegram."

"Is there?" She stood hastily, tightening the belt of her gown. She had forgotten her slippers and the stone-flagged floor was cold. "That's odd."

She took the folded square of paper and read it, frowning; Sarasate didn't quite hover. She said, "Nicholas wants me to make sure the attic storeroom hasn't been disturbed."

"The attic? The old master's things?" Sarasate had been a manservant here when Edouard was alive.

"Yes, I'd better go up right away."

"I'll get you a lamp, Madame. Would you like me to accompany you?"

"No, that won't be necessary." She took a moment to tie back her hair and find an old pair of shoes at the bottom of the armoire, while Sarasate brought her a hand lamp.

Madeline climbed the stairs up to the third floor and opened the door of the library. She caught a faint scent of pipe tobacco and hesitated. It wasn't the type that Nicholas or Reynard used, but she recognized it just the same.

She smiled to herself and said softly, "Hello, Edouard."

There was no answer but she hadn't really expected one. Edouard Viller wasn't haunting his old home in the sense that most people understood the term, he was simply there. The way the beamed and coffered ceilings that made the upper floor rooms both oppressive and cozy were there. The way the odd-sized spaces and the old inelegant furniture were there. Edouard's personality lay over Coldcourt like a fine damask cloth.

There was nothing to fear from this haunting. Madeline had never met Edouard when he was alive and she knew he had been executed for one of the most heinous crimes under Ile-Rien law, but the traces of him that were left had convinced her of his innocence without a review of the facts of the case.

She paused to light the lamp on the round table near the center of the room, revealing book-lined walls and two overstuffed chairs, a secretaire with letter-scales, inkstand, and blotter, a faded Parscian rug on the floor and cretonne curtains cloaking the windows. She crossed to the bookcase against the far wall and selected the correct volume, placing her palm flat on the cover. It was, appropriately enough, *The Book of Ingenious Devices*.

The section of the bookcase in front of her slid backward, then lifted up into the air, accompanied by much squeaking of gears and wheels. A cool draft, smelling of must, moved her hair and fluttered the skirts of her gown.

She set the book aside. This portal was one of Edouard and Arisilde's earliest collaborations. Only the key, a spell imprinted on the cover of the book, was true magic. The mechanism that lifted the door was one of Edouard's mechanical contrivances.

The section of bookcase rose up into the high ceiling of the chamber beyond it, revealing a narrow stairway curving up into dimness. Madeline gathered her skirts and started to climb.

The stairs curved up and around, reaching a heavy wooden door. The key was in the lock. Long ago, Nicholas had taken the key from the drawer where it was kept and left it up here, explaining that if the house was ever searched, a key that fit no obvious lock was sure to be remarked, while if anyone managed to get past the concealed entrance to the stair, an ordinary door was not likely to stop them, locked or not. Madeline thought the Vienne Prefecture unlikely to be quite so astute, but she had long since given up arguing those points with Nicholas; as far as she was concerned, she was in charge of costume and makeup, he was in charge of paranoia.

She opened the door, which creaked a little, and stepped into the room beyond.

There was a little light already in the large chamber—moonlight, falling through three little dormer windows high in the opposite wall. The roof stretched up overhead, the beams beginning just above the windows and vanishing into darkness in the peak somewhere above. A platform about twelve feet in height cut the room in half: it was just below the windows, with a narrow stair at one end giving access to it. There were trunks and boxes piled atop it, though most of the space it afforded was empty. It was there to disguise the real purpose of the attic; if you looked in through the dormer windows from the roof, you saw only a rather odd-sized box room. Edouard's experiments occupied the lower half of the chamber, under the platform.

Madeline made her way forward, sneezing at the dust. The area below the platform was like a cave; her lamp seemed hardly to penetrate it at all. Shelves lining the back wall held notebooks and bound manuscripts—years of Edouard Viller's research, saved from destruction at the hands of the Crown Court. Piled around were various bits of machinery, pipes, gears, wheels, several large leather bladder-like things that were obviously made to hold air, but for what purpose she couldn't imagine. There was a sort of metal cage lying on its side that loomed overhead like a whale's skeleton and seemed to be connected to half the other odd things around it; it reminded Madeline of the book where the shipwreck survivors landed on an island, which turned out to be the back of an immense sea beast.

She had been up here before in the daylight, but it wasn't any easier to tell what anything was then, either. It was as if a blacksmith's workroom, a train yard, and a theater propmaker's shop had all been shaken together and the results carefully collected on the attic floor. But she knew Nicholas hadn't been concerned about any of these things. She pressed on, making her way toward the far wall.

In a cupboard at the very back of the space, she found her goal. Lined up neatly on one of the shelves were three spherical devices. They were small, each not much larger than a melon, and someone who knew nothing about either magic or navigation would have said they were tarnished armillary spheres. But instead of empty space each seemed to be filled with tiny gears and wheels, all linked together.

Madeline touched one and felt her fingertips tingle.

Though Edouard Viller had designed the spheres, each one needed a spark of real human sorcery, a spell of delicate complexity, to make it live and perform whatever its purpose was. The first one, the oldest one, had been brought to life by Wirhan Asilva, an old sorcerer at Lodun who had worked with Edouard while he was still perfecting his design. She touched Asilva's sphere; it was cold and there was no answering tingle of awareness. The spell had only lasted a few years, Nicholas told her. Asilva hadn't been very enthusiastic about Edouard's experiments and eventually he had refused to work with him anymore. But it had also been Asilva who had helped Nicholas save most of the important contents from Edouard's workrooms at Lodun, only a few steps ahead of the Crown officials sent to destroy it.

The other spheres had been built with Arisilde's help and he was the only one who knew anything at all about them.

She touched the third, partly out of thoroughness and partly because she liked that little thrill of power that seemed to course off the warm metal, and snatched her hand back in shock. The third sphere was vibrating. She reached for it again and a spark of blue light traveled along the spiral gears and winked out abruptly.

She lifted it off the shelf and, probably foolishly, tried to peer into it. *This is nothing for a lapsed and never-worth-much-in-the-first-place witch to be fooling with,* she told herself.

It didn't explode or blast her thoughts out of her head, but continued to shiver against her hands, like a frightened animal. She tried to see into the depths of it, to discover if any of the delicate works were damaged, but her lamp was no help.

Madeline tucked the sphere under her arm and carried it out of the confined space of the work area and up the narrow stair to the top half of the chamber. Moonlight flooded the platform, a clear, colorless illumination almost strong enough to read print by. She ducked her head under the low-hung beams and crouched near the middle window, balancing the sphere on her knees. Again she looked deep into it.

She couldn't see any damage, or parts shifting around, but deep inside, still following some invisible path, was the blue spark.

Madeline felt a cold spot between her shoulder blades, as if a breeze had touched her in the dead-still attic air. She lifted her head and looked out the window.

There was something crouched outside on the parapet, watching her. Tattered clothes, shroud-like in the wind, a skeletal head, teeth, clawlike hands grinding into the stone. She clutched the sphere to her chest and stood up in pure reflex, thumping her head on a ceiling beam.

The thing outside reared back, almost falling off its perch. The sphere shivered violently against her and the creature snarled and vanished over the wall.

Madeline was frozen, but only for an instant. She swore violently and leaned forward to see if it was still out there. She was careful not to touch the window, which was supposed to be warded. *It must still be warded,* she thought, *or that thing would have broken in and killed me.* She could only think it was one of the creatures Nicholas had seen in the Mondollot House cellars.

She looked down at the sphere she still clutched to her. The shivering had stopped and it was only tingling gently, as it always did, the outermost manifestation of the power trapped inside. The creature might have fled the sphere. If it was sensitive to human magic the way the fay were, the sphere would smell of Arisilde, who had been at the height of his power when he had helped Edouard build it.

Worry it out later, she told herself, making her way to the stair. She had to collect her lamp, get back downstairs, check that the ward stones were still there, and make sure everyone in Coldcourt was still alive.

———

Nicholas had Cusard drop him off at the Philosopher's Cross. He wanted to talk to Arisilde now, even if he had to wake him, and he wanted Crack and Reynard to go on to Coldcourt, to make sure all was well there and to tell Madeline what they had discovered.

The Cross was still lively and wild, even this late, but far safer than the streets of Riverside or the Gabardin, and many of the people promenading on the walks were of the beau monde. The cabarets and coffeehouses were still open, the streets well lit and comfortably crowded, and there were peddlers and beggars gathered on every corner, while a truly astonishing number of prostitutes waited on the after-theater crowd. It would be relatively easy to find a hire cabriolet when he was done, if he could manage to get aboard before the driver got a good look at the current state of his clothes.

Even Arisilde's normally quiet tenement seemed teeming with life. Nicholas edged past the concierge, who was bargaining room rates with a lady of the night and her top-hatted client. Climbing the stairs turned out to be a greater task than he had anticipated and he knocked on Arisilde's door greatly exhausted.

The door was thrown open with unexpected violence. Nicholas started back before he recognized Arisilde standing in the doorway. The sorcerer's eyes were red-rimmed and wild, his fair hair escaped from its braid and hanging in lank strings around his face. He looked like a member of the Unseelie Court from one of Bienuilis's more excessive paintings.

He stared at Nicholas without recognition, then said, "Ah, it's you." Glancing over his shoulder as if he feared pursuit from within the apartment, he leapt back down the little hallway into his rooms. "Quick, inside!"

Nicholas leaned his head against the dusty wall. "Oh, God." He was too tired for this. He thought of walking away, going back down to the street, and finding a cab. But wearily he pushed away from the wall and followed Arisilde, pausing only to pull the door closed behind him.

The candles had guttered in the room with the skylights and the fire had been reduced to coal. The curtains had all been torn down from the windows, exposing the little apartment to the night sky. Most Vienne dwellers, especially in the poor neighborhoods, kept their windows shuttered at night for superstitious fear of night-flying fay, though none had been spotted near the city since the railroad lines had been laid. Obviously that was not something Arisilde worried about. *And even in his present condition,* Nicholas thought, *he is probably more than a match for any creature the fay could produce,* That was one of the tragedies of it. No one would ever know what Arisilde was or how powerful he could have been.

Arisilde stood over the table, tearing through a pile of papers and books, scattering them onto the floor. Nicholas eased down into one of the torn armchairs near the hearth, wincing as his bruises made contact with the under-stuffed cushions.

Arisilde whipped around, ran a hand through his disordered hair, and whispered, "I can't remember what I was going to tell you."

Nicholas sank back in the chair and closed his eyes. He could already tell that getting any sense out of his friend, about the possibility of someone stealing Edouard's work or the connection between Octave and the disappearances, was patently hopeless, at least for tonight. But the climb back down the steep stairs of the decaying tenement was more than he could stand to contemplate just now. He said, "I'll wait. Perhaps you'll think of it."

He didn't realize Arisilde had crossed the room until he felt breath on his cheek. He opened his eyes to find Arisilde leaning over him, braced on the arms of the chair, his face scant inches away. A pitifully earnest expression in his violet eyes, he said, "It was important."

Nicholas said, "I know." He hesitated. That Arisilde was in a worse state than usual had already occurred to him. That perhaps he should not have ventured into the garret under these circumstances hadn't crossed his mind—until now. Cautiously, he asked, "Where's your man Isham?"

Arisilde blinked. For a moment, his expression was desperate, as if any concentration was painful. Then he smiled in weary relief and said, "At Coldcourt. I sent him to look for you."

"That makes sense." Nicholas told himself he was being a fool. When he had closed his eyes he had seen that room at Valent House again and it was making him imagine things; Arisilde couldn't bear to step on ants. *In his right mind,* a traitor voice whispered.

"Doesn't it?" Arisilde was suddenly elated. "That must be it, then!"

Nicholas pushed him back, so he could see his face more clearly, and asked, "Did you have more opium than you usually do, today?"

Arisilde said, "I didn't have any today," and tore away from him so abruptly Nicholas almost tumbled out of the chair. He stood, watching in bewilderment, as Arisilde swept the rest of the books and papers off the table and began rubbing his hands over the unpolished surface, as if he was searching for something hidden there. Nicholas said, "None at all?"

"None." Arisilde shook his head. "I had to be careful. I had to be very, very careful. But I found it out, I did, the thing I wanted to find out." He slammed his hands against the table, with a force that should have broken his slender wrists. "But now I can't remember what it was!"

Nicholas went to him, moving slowly so as not to startle, and tried to turn him away from the table. But Arisilde flung himself toward the opposite end of the room, upsetting a chair and careening off another table, sending a collection of little jars and plants crashing to the floor.

Nicholas took a deep breath. He had to get Arisilde's attention, keep him from turning that energy on himself. "Was it something to do with the things I brought you to look at, the ashes of the golem, maybe?"

Arisilde seemed to pause in thought, leaning on the far wall as if he had fetched up against it in a storm. The shadows were deep there and Nicholas could see nothing of his expression. "No," Arisilde said slowly. "It wasn't anything here. I went out today. Oh, damn." He slid to the floor, helplessly. "Next time I'll write a letter."

Nicholas went to him, stumbling a little over the scattered debris in the half-light. He knelt in front of Arisilde, who had buried his face in his hands. "Ari . . ." Nicholas cleared his throat. It was ridiculously difficult to speak. He wanted to say that if Arisilde had given up the drug for one day, couldn't he give it up for the next, and the next after that? But past attempts had taught him how useless any kind of remonstrance was; Arisilde would simply refuse to listen, or stop speaking to him at all.

The sorcerer lifted his head, took Nicholas's hand and ran a thumb along the lifeline, as if he was doing a palm-reading by touch, which he very well might be. He said, "I watched them hang Edouard, do you remember?"

Let's not do this, not tonight, Nicholas thought, too weary to do anything more than close his eyes in resignation. He had come to realize that the main reason he was uncomfortable in Arisilde's company was not his disgust for what the opium did to his friend, but the fact that sometimes Arisilde said things like this. *Do you remember when Edouard took us to Duncanny, do you remember that day at the river in the spring, do you remember . . . ?* When it was at its worst, it was like this: *Do you remember the day at the trial when Afgin testified, do you remember when Edouard was hanged?* Nicholas didn't want to remember the good times or the bad. He wanted to think about revenge, about Montesq paying for what he had done. He couldn't afford to be distracted. But he let out his breath, looked at Arisilde again, and said, "I remember."

"If I had stayed in Vienne with Edouard instead of going back to Lodun—"

"Ari, dammit, there was no reason for you to stay." Nicholas couldn't conceal his bitter anger. They had had this conversation before, too. "No one knew what was about to happen. You can't blame yourself for that." Sorcerers could gain knowledge of the present and the past, but only if they knew where to look.

"I was the family witness because you couldn't bring yourself to it . . ."

"That was a mistake." It also wasn't quite true, or perhaps Arisilde was being polite. They had kept Nicholas from trying to free Edouard or disrupting the execution by holding him down on a bed and forcibly dosing him with laudanum. When Nicholas had finally been conscious and coherent enough to realize the execution was over, he had broken every window, lamp, and glass object in the house, so enraged he had no idea what he was doing. But the rage had burned away and what it had left in its place was no less hurtful, but far more useful.

"What?" The light from the hearth behind them gleamed off the whites of Arisilde's eyes, but his voice sounded almost normal. "Do you think all this wreck and ruin came from that moment? Oh no, oh no, never think that. Watching a good friend hang is a terrible thing, but it didn't do this. I did this." Arisilde leaned forward. His voice dropped to a whisper but it was as intense as if he shouted. "I wanted to kill them all. It's not what they did, you see, it's what they didn't do. I wanted to pull Lodun down stone by burning stone. I wanted to destroy every man, woman, and child in it, I wanted to burn them alive and watch them scream in Hell. And I could have done it. They trained me to do it. But . . ." Arisilde started to laugh. It was an agonizing sound. "But I never could bear to see anyone hurt. Isn't it ridiculous?"

"That's the difference between us, Ari. You wanted to do it; I would have done it." But the words disturbed him. Arisilde had said some odd things under the influence of opium, but hearing him talk this way was almost shocking. Nicholas had never known why his friend had taken this path into ruin and despair. God knew he had seen it happen often enough before; in the teeming streets where he had spent his childhood, many fell into this same trap every day.

Arisilde rubbed his face until the skin seemed like to break and Nicholas caught his wrists and pulled his hands away, afraid that he was going to blind himself. Arisilde peered up at him urgently. "You knew I thought Edouard was guilty. You knew because I told you and we talked about it, and then later after the execution I came to you and I said you had been right and I had been wrong, remember? And it was proved later, of course, Ronsarde proved it later, remember?"

"Of course I do. That was when . . ." *I decided not to kill Ronsarde.* Nicholas couldn't finish the thought aloud, not even to Ari, who wouldn't recall this conversation by morning anyway.

"But I didn't tell you how I knew." Arisilde let the words trail off. Nicholas thought that was all he meant to say and tried to urge him to stand, but the sorcerer shook his head. His voice perceptibly stronger, he said, "I went to Ila-mires Rohan. He was Master of Lodun, then, remember?"

"Of course I remember, Ari, he tried to defend Edouard."

Arisilde stood up suddenly, dragging Nicholas with him. Ari was so slender, seeming so weak and languid most of the time, Nicholas had forgotten how strong he was. Ari's hands were buried in the front of his shirt, almost lifting him off his feet, and Nicholas didn't think he could free himself without hurt-ing him. Arisilde said, softly, terribly, "He didn't defend him well enough."

"What?"

"I went to see him in his study at Lodun. Oh, that beautiful room. I was afraid that my judgment was faulty because I had let Edouard fool me, and he said my judgment was not impaired. He said he knew Edouard was innocent. But he had let the trial go on, because a man of Edouard's knowledge was too dangerous to live."

"No." Nicholas felt oddly hollow. One more betrayal after all the others of that terrible time, what did it really matter? But as the words sank in, and Nicholas remembered the old man, Master of Lodun, sitting with them at the trial as if in sympathy and support, he was astonished to discover that it did still matter. It mattered a great deal.

Arisilde was saying, "Yes, the simple truth, after all the lies. I could have killed him."

"You should have told me," Nicholas whispered. "I would have."

"I know. That's why I didn't." Arisilde smiled, and Nicholas saw the other truth. Ari said, "But don't think he escaped unpunished. He loved me like a son, you know. So I destroyed something he loved."

Nicholas pulled away and Arisilde released him. The sorcerer was still wear-ing that mad, gentle smile. Nicholas walked back toward the hearth, not quite aware of what he was doing. The fire was nothing but glowing coals, wink-ing out as he watched. Behind him, Arisilde said, "And Rohan became such a bitter old man, who lost his greatest student, his hand-picked successor . . ." His voice broke. "That wasn't what I was going to tell you . . . I really have to remember that, it was very important."

Nicholas turned back as Arisilde slumped to the floor again, but the sorcer-er's wildness seemed to have died with the fire. He let Nicholas guide him to the big tumbled bed in one of the little rooms off the hall. The most powerful sorcerer in the history of Lodun lay there quietly, saying nothing more, until the old man Isham returned and Nicholas left him to his care.

CHAPTER SEVEN

It was still dark when Nicholas had the hire cab let him off at the top of Coldcourt's drive. He could see every window in the sprawling stone house was lit and there were a couple of servants with lamps patrolling the roof between the towers. It didn't look like there was trouble now; the wide sweep of lawn was an empty landscape of shadows, broken only by the one lone towering oak and the drive. He started toward the house, almost lame from exhaustion, the gravel crunching under his boots. When he entered the circle of light from the lamps hung on either side of the front entrance, the doors swung open and Madeline hurried down the steps to meet him.

Her embrace, in his current state, almost knocked him off his feet. She said, "I was getting worried. The others thought you would be right behind them."

"It . . . took longer with Ari than I thought," he told her. "What's happened here?"

They entered the welcome warmth of the entrance hall and Madeline paused to secure the doors, saying, "There was something—I think it was the same sort of creature that you saw under Mondollot House—up on the roof. It was peering into Edouard's old attic. Nothing seemed disturbed and no one was hurt, so perhaps it was only scouting us out. I don't know what it wanted."

"I don't know anything anymore." Nicholas laughed bitterly. "I suppose Reynard told you what we found."

"Yes." Madeline's face was drawn and harsh in the lamplight as she turned back toward him. "Could Arisilde tell you anything of use?"

Nicholas stopped at the foot of the stairs to look at her. Sometimes Madeline surprised even him. Most women—most people—would have had the decency to be shocked out of their wits, or to be made ill, or to invoke heavenly wrath on the perpetrators. He didn't know whether to attribute it to Madeline's general bloody-mindedness or the self-absorption and self-possession that usually characterized potentially brilliant actors. He ran his hands through his hair, trying to get his thoughts together. "I don't think Ari's going to be of much help."

Madeline winced. "The opium?"

"I think it's finally got the better of him. He was telling me things. . . ." Nicholas shook his head. "I don't know. Either that or he's finally lost his wits. Somehow Octave has had access to Edouard's work. That's how he's managing these spirit circles. He has a sphere, like the ones Edouard made with Ari and Asilva. Where that butchery in Valent House comes into it, I don't know. . . ."

Madeline linked arms with him and towed him up the stairs. "You're exhausted. Sleep until dawn, and then make plans."

"Damned optimist."

"Damned realist," she corrected with a weary smile.

———

Nicholas left Madeline to make the arrangements for a second, more thorough search of Valent House while he tried to sleep for what was left of the night. What he actually did was retire to his study on the second floor to lay out the notebooks and the scraps of paper their first search had brought to light.

The notebooks proved to be what he had originally thought, a student's copying from a probably forbidden text on necromancy. Reading through them, he couldn't see any evidence of the copyist inserting opinion. *He hasn't scribbled his name, present direction, and future plans for destroying the world in the margin either,* Nicholas thought sourly. *It's always helpful when they do that.* It might be illuminating to ascertain which text the notes had come from. Arisilde, of course, would probably recognize it at a glance . . . if Arisilde was in any state vaguely approaching sobriety. But Arisilde had been out of touch with Lodun for years and would no longer know who kept such books in their private libraries, so perhaps there was not much point in it. But to find out whose student Octave was, and when . . . Perhaps he would ask Arisilde anyway.

The scraps of paper from the desk were more intriguing, though not much more helpful. The fragments of words were indecipherable, though Nicholas wanted to say that he recognized something about the handwriting. It wasn't Edouard's, which would have been too much to hope for. Though perhaps it didn't matter either. He knew Octave had somehow re-created Edouard's work. Perhaps the method was immaterial. *Yes, keep telling yourself that.*

Speaking of method . . . Nicholas took down a heavy volume from the bookcase above the desk. It contained the memoirs of a very methodical man, the bureaucrat who had been responsible for cutting the new streets and plazas through the decaying slums of Vienne. It wasn't so much a memoir as it was a chronicle of work, describing in exacting detail the alterations that had been wrought on the ancient city. Nicholas had always found it extremely helpful since few completely reliable maps had ever been made of Vienne.

He flipped through the worn pages, looking for the section on Ducal Court Street. *And here it is. . . . Tearing down tenements, the old theater, what was left of the Bisran ambassador's home after the last time they burned it down . . . Ah.* "'I informed the Duke it would not be necessary to sacrifice Mondollot House'"—*I'm sure he was pleased*—"'but that its neighbor Ventarin House would have to be taken down.'" The bureaucrat, a man not entirely without finer feelings, had regretted this, finding that Ventarin House was more pleasing to the eye and would have made a better ornament to his street than Mondollot. Ventarin, however, was in the wrong place and presently occupied only by servant caretakers, the family having moved to a country estate to finish dwindling into obscurity in peace. They had not opposed the destruction. "'They had no need of the old place, having not indulged in public life for many generations. . . . One of their most illustrious ancestors was Gabard Alis Ventarin, a notable of some two centuries past . . . who held the position of Court Sorcerer under King Rogere.'"

Nicholas closed the book and sat for a while, staring at nothing, tapping one finger on the polished wood of the desk. So the chamber that Octave's ghoul had broken into had once been part of the cellars under the home of a former Court Sorcerer. Had the old Duke of Mondollot known what was there? Had he perhaps opened that door, seen what it guarded, and ordered it sealed up again? That was undoubtedly what Octave had wanted to know when he had tried to convince the Duchess to let him contact the late Duke. *Something was there, and Octave's ghouls took it away. But it wasn't right. Either it wasn't what he wanted, or something was missing from it.* One of the best uses for necromancy was the discerning of secret things, whether past or present. There were other ways for sorcerers to divine the hidden, but none so easy as necromancy provided. It also taught methods of creating illusions that were solid to the touch, ways of affecting the minds and wills of people, animals, even spirits.

In the end, Nicholas swept all the fragments together with the notebooks and carefully locked them away in one of the concealed drawers of his desk, and then trudged wearily to a bath and bed.

Nicholas managed to rest for only an hour, feeling the sun rise behind the heavy drapes over the window and listening to the mantel clock tick almost but not quite in time to his heartbeat. Madeline was sleeping deeply, her time in the crowded accommodations used by chorus performers having inured her to any amount of restless twitching on Nicholas's part. He kept having to fight the impulse to wake her, either to make love or to talk or anything to keep his mind off Octave's theft of Edouard's work. Finally, he got out of bed, half furious and half depressed, dressed and went down to the library.

It was a long room at the back of the house, the floor-to-ceiling shelves overflowing with books. Books piled on the warm upholstered armchairs and the rich Parscian carpet, books stuffed into the two boulle cabinets and the satinwood escritoire. *I'm going to need a bigger house,* Nicholas thought, looking at it. His gaze stopped at the tiny framed miniature on the desk. It was the only remaining portrait of his mother, painted to be placed inside a gold locket that had been sold when she had brought him to Vienne. His father had commissioned the piece not long after the wedding, when there had still been money for such things, though no doubt his family had made a great deal of trouble over the expense. They had not begun to actively plot against her then, but they would have argued over any money being spent on something not directly related to their own comfort. It was not a good likeness of her anyway, at least not according to Nicholas's memory. The portrait showed only a young, fine-featured woman with dark curling hair, and the artist had captured no nuance of expression or gesture that would have given the little image life. Of course, his father had probably paid three times what the painting had been worth and never knew he was being cheated. Nicholas looked away, banishing the old memories.

He meant to make a thorough search of the historical texts, both the dry scholarly and the lurid popular, for that trace of memory that had bothered him so at Valent House. The more he thought about it, or tried not to think about it, the more vivid that shadow picture became. *It was a woodcut,* he thought. *And the page was stained.* That didn't help. He didn't have any of his old books from childhood. All those had gone when his mother died, along with most of their possessions. The books in this room had been Edouard's or had been bought since Nicholas had come here years ago. But the history section took up the entire west wall of the room and from his earlier delvings into it he had high hopes.

He searched, thoroughly engrossed, barely noticing when Sarasate brought in a tray with coffee and rolls. Between Cadarsa's *History of Ile-Rien in Eight Volumes* and an ancient copy of *Sorceries of Lodun,* he stumbled on *The Pirates of Chaire,* a children's storybook with illustrations. "What in God's name is this doing here . . . ?" Nicholas muttered, flipping the much-battered book open to the flyleaf. There was writing there and he stared at it a moment, taken aback.

It was in Edouard's hand and it read *Don't you dare get rid of this book.*

Nicholas smiled. Edouard Viller had known him better than anyone.

The only reason Nicholas was alive now was that some forgotten benefactor had told Edouard that the Prefecture were always picking up stray children in Riverside. When Edouard had decided he needed a son to fill the lonely days after his wife died, he had gone down to the cells at Almsgate to look for one.

Nicholas barely remembered his own father and the moldering, disgraced, debt-ridden ancestral estate where he had spent the first few years of his life. His mother had brought him to Vienne when he was six and taken back her maiden name of Valiarde, preferring the slums of the great city to coexistence with her husband's relations. She had made her living by piecework laundry and sewing, and if she had ever had to supplement her income by the form of employment more common to destitute women in Vienne, she had never allowed him to find out about it. When he was ten she had died, of some congestive lung ailment that every year carried off hundreds of the poor who crowded into the broken-down buildings in Riverside and the other slums. Nicholas had already dabbled in thieving. After her death, he had taken it up as a profession.

He had been lucky enough to encounter Cusard, and before that worthy's second stint in prison, Nicholas had learned from him the pickpocket's and cracksman's skills that would give him an edge over the other street boys. By twelve, he had been leader of a local gang and had made them all wealthy and wildly successful by ambitious burglaries and by dealing with fences rather than rag and bone shops. This success brought the attention of the Prefecture. They had set a trap for him with the help of a disgruntled rival and Nicholas had ended his first illegal career in the filth of the Almsgate cells, beaten within an inch of his life and waiting to be hauled off to the real hell of the city prison.

He had been cursing the guards in fluent Aderassi, which his mother had taught him. There had been a fashion at the time for young gentlemen to learn the language so they could go to the court of Adera to complete their social education. She had never forgotten that his father's family had been noble, despite their poverty and well-deserved obscurity. Nicholas had discovered that he could call people the most terrible things in it and they would not understand him.

Edouard had come to the barred door and called, in the same language, "You have a very foul mouth. Can you read?"

"Yes," Nicholas had replied, annoyed.

"In what language, Aderassi or Rienish?"

"Both."

"Perfect," Edouard had said to the jailer. "I wouldn't want one I had to start from the beginning, you know. I'll take him."

And that had been that. Nicholas replaced the storybook on the shelf.

———

This time they entered Valent House through the front door. Nicholas was prepared to prove he was an estate agent for a firm on the other side of the river and that Cusard, Crack, and Lamane were builders, here to give advice on possible renovations.

For all these elaborate preparations, the street was deserted and no one demanded to know their business, though the builders' wagon standing outside was probably explanation enough for the curious.

Earlier that morning, when the sun was almost high enough to officially qualify as dawn, Nicholas had gone into the guest bedroom to waken Reynard. Waiting impatiently until the cursing stopped, Nicholas had asked him to make the rounds of the cafés and clubs today to find out when Octave's next appointment for a spirit circle was, and to delicately ascertain if the good doctor had asked any of his other summoned spirits about lost family wealth. To Nicholas's unexpressed relief, Madeline had decided she could be of more help finding out about Madame Everset's late brother, and what had been aboard his ill-fated ship that Octave had been so interested in, than as one more searcher in Valent House.

Standing now in the dust and ruin of the house's foyer, Nicholas was sure he was right about Octave's original purpose in holding the circles. It only remained to discover how and why Octave had turned from thievery to necromancy.

Cusard had also brought Lyon Althise, who had trained as a medical doctor but been asked to leave the College of Physicians because of a fondness for drink. He was well known in Vienne's criminal underclass as being willing to use his medical skills for almost any purpose as long as he was well paid, but Nicholas doubted even he had ever seen anything like this. Althise and Nicholas made another examination of the bodies while the others searched the house under Crack's direction.

They came up for air after what seemed an interminable time and stood in the kitchen with the scullery door open for the cool breeze. Nicholas was wearing one of his Donatien disguises, the one that made him look about ten years older. Althise didn't know him as Nicholas Valiarde and he intended to keep it that way.

Althise, leaning on the cracked counter, shook his head. "I can't do much more than confirm what you've already discovered for yourself. Yes, he was alive when it happened, though not for long. Whoever did it used a very sharp knife, and it probably happened no more than a day before you found him. The remaining eye is cloudy and the skin is discoloring. The others have been here much longer, some days, some weeks." He looked up at Nicholas wearily. He was an older man, his hair graying and his face marked by perpetual weariness and defeat. "I know I'm not being much help." Althise had been told what was basically the truth: that Donatien had been pursuing a man who had threatened him and stumbled on this house.

Nicholas shook his head. "I've begun to realize I may not be able to do much with this. We can't keep sneaking in here to investigate—someone is sure to report us." Althise had tried his best, but his best hadn't been good enough for the College of Physicians either. *Dr. Cyran Halle may be Ronsarde's mouthpiece and a pompous bastard, but I wish I had him here now,* Nicholas thought reluctantly.

A startled gasp from Althise brought him out of his own thoughts and he jerked his head toward the open scullery door. There was a figure framed there, between the shadow of the room and the wan light from the ragged garden. It took Nicholas moments to realize it was Arisilde Damal.

"Ari, I didn't think you'd come," he said, startled.

Althise sagged back against the counter, relieved that the apparition was evidently expected, and muttered, "And I thought my nerves were gone before I came here."

"Yes, well, Madeline's message said it was urgent." Arisilde came into the kitchen slowly, as cautious as a cat treading on unfamiliar ground. His greatcoat had once been of very good material, though now it was threadbare. He hadn't bothered with a hat and his fine hair stood up in wisps all over his head. He nodded a distracted greeting to Althise, then looked down at Nicholas, his violet eyes confused. "I'm not at my best today, I'm afraid. We don't know the people who live here, do we?"

"No, we don't. In fact—"

"That's good." Arisilde was relieved. Pale and battered and somehow otherworldly, he could have been mistaken for a particularly feather-headed member of the fay, but the size of his pupils was almost normal and his hands weren't trembling. "Because something terrible's happened here."

"Hey!" Lamane called from the foyer. "We found something else in the cellar!"

Nicholas refused to allow himself to speculate as he followed the man down the cellar stairs and into the stinking chambers below. Arisilde trailed after him but Althise stayed behind in the kitchen. Nicholas was glad of it. He had told Arisilde not to mention names in front of strangers, but it was simply better not to rely on his discretion. They turned down toward the opposite end of the hall, lit now with several oil lamps. As Cusard, Crack, and Lamane made way for Nicholas, he felt a cool rush of dank air.

The passage had appeared to end in a bare wall. Now a section a few feet wide and about half a man's height stood out from it, revealing a dark opening. Nicholas knelt to look inside and saw a rough tunnel supported by moldy brick walls, leading down into pitch blackness. Crack knelt beside him and said, "Look."

He held the lantern out over the floor of the tunnel, a mix of dirt and brick chips, then pushed the slide down. There was a faint glow emanating from the floor and walls. "Perfect," Nicholas said softly. "How did you discover it?"

Crack put the slide up again. With Crack, it was always difficult to tell, but Nicholas thought he was excited at the discovery. "We knocked on the walls. Cusard made the lock work."

Nicholas stood up to look as Cusard showed him the small hole on the outer side of the false door. "It's an old trick," he explained. "Slide your finger in that hole, push up on the lever, and snick goes the bolt." He added grimly, "You can open it from the other side, too. Lets you in and out, this door does."

Arisilde had taken Nicholas's place at the tunnel entrance, crawling half into it. He sat back now, closely examining some substance on his fingers. "Nic, this is the same stuff that was on that coat you brought me, and those pieces of fabric from that drowned boy's clothes. It's a residue caused by a type of necromantic powder that hasn't been used in Ile-Rien for hundreds of years. Isn't that odd? I can't think who would have made it."

Nicholas stared at him and Arisilde's vague eyes grew worried. He said, "That was you that brought me those things to look at, wasn't it?"

"Yes, of course, but—"

Arisilde sighed. "Thank God. I thought I was going mad."

"But I didn't think you'd looked at them at all. Why didn't you tell me last night?"

"You saw me last night?" Arisilde demanded. "What was I doing?"

"You don't remember— You said you had something important to tell me. Was that it?"

Arisilde sat down on the filthy floor and tapped his cheek thoughtfully. "It might have been. Did I give you any hints?"

Nicholas ran a hand through his hair and took a deep breath. "What about the powder from the golem? Did you learn anything from that?"

"The powder from the what?"

Nicholas looked sourly at Cusard, who was regarding the ceiling with pursed lips, and Crack, who stared down at the sorcerer with a puzzled expression, and gave in. "Never mind."

"Maybe I'll recall it, you can never tell." Arisilde was on his hands and knees now, crawling into the tunnel. "Let's see where this goes. I love secret tunnels, don't you?"

"My back's bad," Cusard said quickly.

Lamane immediately asserted that his back was bad, too. "I know, I know," Nicholas said impatiently. "I want to see it for myself, anyway."

Crack was already following Arisilde. Nicholas crawled after them.

"You don't need the lamp," Arisilde was saying, partly to Crack and partly to himself. "Well, I used to know how to do this." Light flared in the tunnel suddenly, soft and white. "There we go," Arisilde said, pleased. The spell light seemed to emanate from all over his body.

Nicholas's fear was that the tunnel would prove to be only a repository for more bodies, but that didn't seem to be the case. Crack glanced back at him and muttered, "I should go first, in case we run into something."

"It's all right," Nicholas told him. "Arisilde is more capable than he appears." In fact, the sorcerer was acting more like himself than he had for a long time. Nicholas added, "But thank you for not claiming a bad back."

"I like this," Crack said simply. Then, as if realizing that statement needed more explanation, added, "Finding things out. I like it better than stealing."

So do I, Nicholas thought, but he wouldn't say it aloud.

"The tunnel gets wider here," Arisilde reported cheerfully. "I think we found the sewer." In another moment this supposition was confirmed by the sound of trickling water and the fetid smell of sewage.

The tunnel widened and opened into a ledge, a few feet above a stream of putrid water flowing through a round, brick-lined sewer. Nicholas got to his feet, one hand on the damp wall to steady himself. Arisilde swept his hands over his battered coat, gathering the spell light into a ball, then set it in midair where it hung suspended by nothing and illuminated the tunnel. "Here we are," Arisilde said. "Is this where you thought it would lead?"

"It's where the one in the Mondollot House cellars led," Nicholas told him, thinking of the hole in the wall of the wine vaults that the first ghoul had fled through. He heard a scrabbling and put it down to rats. "I think—"

It came up from below the ledge, too fast for him to move, to shout a warning. He could only fall back against the wall as the claws grasped for his neck and the maw gaped in the withered, hate-filled face. Crack shoved an arm between them, trying to seize it around the neck, and its teeth started to sink into his arm. This gave Nicholas the chance to grab its head, to shove it away, but it was too strong. Then Arisilde was suddenly behind it to catch the thing from behind with a handful of its lank dead hair. The spell light flickered and suddenly the tremendous force pinning Nicholas against the wall was gone. He stumbled, caught Crack's arm, and steadied him as the other man almost fell backward over the edge.

The creature lying at their feet bore little resemblance to the ghoul that had whipped up from beneath the ledge and nearly torn them apart. Nicholas stared down at it, amazed. This thing was barely a pile of rag and bone, held together by shreds of skin and tendon. He managed to clear his throat and release Crack's arm. "One of the ghouls," he explained.

Arisilde squatted next to it, careless of his balance on the ledge, and picked up a bone thoughtfully.

Crack rubbed his forearm where the creature had planted its teeth. "Did it get you?" Nicholas asked, worried. Crack shook his head and showed his coat sleeve, unpunctured. "In another moment, Ari . . ." Nicholas found himself almost speechless, which didn't happen often.

"Yes?" Arisilde looked up inquiringly.

"Thank you."

The sorcerer waved it away. "Oh, no trouble at all, no trouble at all."

Nicholas looked around again. *They travel through the sewers, but we knew that already.* There didn't appear to be anything else here to see. *Octave, connected with this house, with the ghouls, with necromancy.*

"This isn't a ghoul, precisely," Arisilde said suddenly. "It's a lich. The necromancer obtains a long-dead corpse—very long dead, in this poor fellow's case—then animates it with a spirit that has been enchained to do the necromancer's bidding. Of course, the easiest way to obtain such a spirit is to kill an innocent victim in an act of ceremonial magic."

"Like that man who was killed in the cellar?" Nicholas asked.

"No, that was something else, another way to raise power." Arisilde glanced around the tunnel expectantly. "There's another aspect to the lich-making process. The remains that contained the enchained spirit still, um, hang about, you know. As revenants. Mindless, soul-dead creatures. I don't see any around here, though." Arisilde waggled his brows thoughtfully and frowned up at Nicholas. "Necromancy is such a messy business, and someone's been very busy at it. Very, very busy."

———

The woman who called herself Madame Talvera looked darkly at the passersby on the other side of the railing and said, "Communication with the spirits isn't a game. For those of us who embrace it truly, it is a religion."

Nicholas nodded encouragingly. Knowing he needed to question another practitioner of spiritualism about Octave, he had been working to arrange this meeting since the day before yesterday. He had found Madame Talvera by asking a couple of old acquaintances who he knew dabbled in the pastime and also in confidence work. Neither of them had heard of Octave before he had appeared on the scene this year, but both had recommended Madame Talvera as a reliable source of information.

The café was on the Street of Flowers, just within the borders of the Philosopher's Cross. Madame Talvera hadn't wanted to go any farther into that area, because she said she was afraid of witches. Nicholas was glad she didn't seem to know what Arisilde was; if she had realized that the vague young man sitting next to her and rendering cream pastries into their component parts before devouring them was a powerful Lodun-trained sorcerer, she might not have been as forthcoming.

He had been agreeably surprised that Arisilde had wanted to come with him. After crawling back out of the tunnel, he had had Cusard and the others close the door and leave Valent House. Before going, he had made Arisilde look at the oddly melted wall in the room with the vivisected body. All the sorcerer could tell him was that it had been done by a great release of power, definitely magical. When Nicholas had asked him what sort of magical power, Arisilde had replied, "Very bad power," and that was all he would say.

The other tables under the striped awning were occupied by tradespeople, but they were close enough to the vicinity of the Cross that no one cared too much about the state of their clothes, which had suffered greatly from the crawl through the tunnel. Nicholas had only had time to remove his Donatien disguise, which he didn't wear during the day in public if he could help it.

A wind stirred the trees in the strip of garden that ran down the center of the street and the strong scent of rain filled the air. Nicholas stirred his coffee and said, "Is it proper to use one's religion to earn money?"

"No, not at all. A gift is permissible, but it should be freely given and not more than the giver can easily part with." She made a sharp gesture. She was Aderassi, olive-skinned and hawk-featured, dark hair pulled back into a severe bun, serious dark eyes. She wore a black, plainly cut dress with a high collar and her hat had a small veil. "There are tricksters, who make tables rock with their toes, and imitate strange voices. You've heard of these things?" At his nod she shook her head grimly. "Such things are to be expected. There are men who make their living pretending to be priests, also."

She touched her glass thoughtfully. He had offered to buy her lunch, but all she would have was water. "It is not a thing of sorcery. The etheric plane is free to anyone who will strive to open their mind to it. The Great Teachers of spiritualism, the Sisters Polacera, have written of many techniques for schooling the senses to embrace it. Speaking to the dead is only a negligible part of what we do. Truly, taken altogether, it is a way of life."

It's a cult, Nicholas thought, *though a rather harmless one as cults go.* He knew about the Polaceras and the other intellectuals who had started the spiritualism craze. "Do you know of a man purporting to be a spiritualist who calls himself Dr. Octave?"

"Oh, him. Everyone knows of him." She looked disgusted. "I see why you wish to know these things. He has taken money from you, perhaps? From someone in your family?"

"He's been most troubling to me, yes."

"I first saw him six or seven years ago, when the Polacera Sisters still lived in Vienne. They live in the country now, outside of Chaire. Much more conducive to spiritual living, the country. And of course it's very nice there, near the sea.

But anyway . . ." Warming to her story, she leaned over the table intently. "He had been to circles held at other houses, by lesser devotees of the movement, but when he came to one of the Polaceras' circles at their old house in Sitare Court . . ." She shook her head. "Madame Amelia Polacera ordered him to go, saying his shadow in the ether was as dark as a well at twilight and she would give him none of her teaching. Many important people were there. Dr. Adalmas. Biendere, the writer. Lady Galaise. I'm sure it was most embarrassing for Octave, but . . ." She shrugged and admitted frankly, "I was glad she sent him away."

Madame Amelia Polacera may have something after all. Either that or she's simply a marvelous judge of character. Nicholas asked, "And you saw no more of him after that?"

"I heard he left the city and was studying privately with someone. It was not my concern, so I paid little attention. Then early this year, he returned and became very fashionable, holding circles for wealthy patrons. Many people are curious about spiritualism, but the true devotees will not hold circles for any but the pure and those who truly wish to learn. Octave does it as a party trick." Her lip curled. "The Madames Polacera will be greatly angered when they hear of it."

"Did Octave ever show any sign of knowing sorcery?"

She looked startled. "No, he was no sorcerer. Madame Polacera would have known, if he was."

Nicholas nodded. *Perhaps she would at that.* "There is just one more thing, Madame. If you wanted to contact a spirit, would you need something from the dead person's corpse? A lock of hair, perhaps?"

Madame Talvera frowned. "No, of course not. Hair, once it is cut, is dead. It would be of no more use than a cut flower. There is a technique that allows one to see visions of a person, living or dead, using something that they once wore close to their skin. Jewelry is best. Metal is very good at holding the impressions of the glow of ether that surrounds every living soul."

Arisilde was nodding agreement. "Hair, skin, bones are more useful in necromancy," he added.

Madame Talvera shuddered. "I have no knowledge of that and I wish none." She stood abruptly, collecting her little black-beaded reticule. "If that is all you wish to ask me . . ."

Nicholas stood and thanked her, and watched as she made her way through the tables and out to the street. A light rain had started, which she seemed not to notice. "I hope I didn't frighten her off," Arisilde said, worried.

"You may have, but she'd already told us everything she knew of use." Nicholas left some coins for the waiter and they strolled out onto the promenade. "She's bound to be nervous of being associated with necromancy."

"I see."

Nicholas had held off on questioning the sorcerer about Edouard's work, knowing that if what Arisilde had told him last night was the truth, then the less he thought about Edouard the better. *If Ilamires Rohan had known Edouard was innocent and still let him be executed, revenge was all well and good, but . . . But I'd rather have Arisilde,* Nicholas found himself thinking. "I know how Octave is contacting the dead," he said carefully.

"Oh, I must have missed that part. How?"

Nicholas felt some misgivings at further involving Arisilde in this. But he remembered how the sorcerer had destroyed the ghoul in the sewer, so casually, as if that display of power was not even worth comment. *I suppose he's in less danger from Octave than the rest of us are.* "He's using a device very like the ones Edouard made with you and Asilva. He must have had access to Edouard's notes to create it, but everything that survived the trial is at Cold-court and hasn't been disturbed. That leaves you and Asilva. . . ."

Arisilde stopped abruptly, heedless of the sprinkle of rain and the people hurrying past, the wagons splashing in the street. He stared into space, concentrating so hard that Nicholas thought he was performing a spell. Arisilde shook his head and gazed down at Nicholas seriously. "No, I don't think I told anyone about the spheres. I'm sure I'd remember if I had. And Edouard wouldn't have wanted me to, you see. No, I'm sure I'd remember that."

Nicholas smiled. "That's good to know, but I didn't really suppose you had."

Arisilde looked relieved. "Good. If you were sure it was me, of course I'd have to take your word for it."

They continued up the street, a torrent of water flung up from the wheels of a passing coach narrowly missing them. "I can't see Asilva telling anyone about them either," Arisilde added. "He didn't really approve of Edouard's experiments with magic, you know. It didn't stop him from participating at first—he believed very strongly in knowledge for its own sake, which is not a dictate that everyone at Lodun follows."

Nicholas glanced up at him and saw Arisilde's face had taken on a hunted look. He said cautiously, "You mentioned something about that last night, in connection with Ilamires Rohan."

"Did I?" Arisilde's smile was quick and not completely convincing. "It doesn't do to take everything I say too seriously."

Nicholas decided not to pursue the point. *He's more coherent today than I've seen him in the past year—I don't want to send him back to oblivion with prying questions.* It was safer to stick to the present. "That room in the cellar, where the man was killed. Have you ever seen anything like it?"

"I should hope not."

"I think I've seen a drawing, or a woodcut actually, in a book describing it. I'm wondering if it means that this was some sort of specific ritual of necromancy." Arisilde was frowning down at the wet pavement and didn't respond. Nicholas added, "If we could identify what our opponent was trying to do, we would be a little further along."

"I can't remember anything offhand—of course we both know what that's worth." Arisilde smiled a little wryly, then brightened. "I'll look for it. That will be my job now, won't it?"

"If you like." Nicholas wasn't sure what Arisilde meant to look for, but you never could tell. "We still need to know where Octave got his information and you know the most about Edouard's research. Was there anyone else who could have known enough to be of help to Octave?"

"That's the question, isn't it?" Arisilde wandered into the path of two well-dressed ladies and Nicholas tipped his hat by way of apology and took his friend's elbow, guiding him out of the middle of the promenade and closer to the wall. "It bears thinking about." His face growing serious, Arisilde said, "I'm glad you're looking into this, Nicholas. We can't really have these goings-on, you know."

———

Nicholas had arranged to meet Madeline at the indoor garden in the Conservatory of Arts. It was crowded as more people sought shelter. The rain trickled down the glass-paned walls and made music against the arched metal panels of the roof high overhead. Most of the little wrought iron tables scattered throughout the large, light chamber were full and it was hard to see past the hanging baskets of greenery and the potted fruit trees. He finally spotted her beneath an orange tree. She was dressed in burgundy velvet and a very extravagant hat and had simply managed to fade in with the fashionably dressed crowd.

"Did you discover anything about Madame Everset's late brother?" Nicholas asked as they took seats.

"Yes, but first tell me what you found out at that house." Madeline rested her elbows on the table and leaned forward anxiously.

Nicholas let out his breath in annoyance. She was always accusing him of not sharing his plans with her. "Madeline—"

Arisilde pointed at the remains of Madeline's iced fruit and said, "Are you going to finish that?"

She slid the china plate toward him and said to Nicholas, "Yes, yes, I know I'm a great burden. Now talk."

So as the light rain streamed down over the glass walls and the waiters hurried by, he told her about their morning at Valent House, the ghoul and the tunnel to the sewers, and what Madame Talvera had said of Octave's background.

"Another ghoul? How many of those creatures are we going to run into?"

"The dead brother, Madeline," Nicholas prompted. "What did you find out about him?"

"Oh, that. Yes, it was as you thought. The ship he was on went down with a very expensive cargo."

That confirmed his suspicions about what Octave's game was with the circles. *But using spiritualism to fleece the wealthy out of riches their dead relatives might have had some knowledge of is one thing; what we found in Valent House is another,* Nicholas thought.

"Also," Madeline continued, "I ran into Reynard and he wanted me to tell you that he spoke to Madame Algretto and she said Octave has apparently taken rooms at the Hotel Galvaz. Everset never did confront him about the odd events at the end of the circle last night, but that's to be expected, I suppose."

"The Hotel Galvaz, hmm?" Nicholas looked thoughtful. That was only a few streets over.

———

They obtained the number of Octave's room by a trick that must have been invented at the dawn of creation shortly after the building of the first hotel: Madeline fluttered up to the porter's desk and asked for her friend Dr. Octave. The porter glanced at the rows of cubbies for keys in the wall behind him and said the good doctor was not in at present. Madeline borrowed a page of hotel stationery to write a brief note, folded it, and handed it to the porter, who turned and slipped it into the cubby for the seventh room on the fifth floor. Madeline suddenly recalled that she would be seeing the doctor later at the home of another friend and asked for the note back.

As they climbed the broad stairs up from the grand foyer and the other public rooms, Arisilde used what was for him an easily performed illusion, obscuring their presence with a mild reflection of the available light. It caused the eye to turn away without ever quite knowing from what it had turned. It could be broken by anyone whose suspicions were aroused enough to stare hard at them, but in the middle of the afternoon at the Hotel Galvaz, with people streaming back from late luncheons to prepare for evening entertainments, there was no one whose suspicions were aroused.

The fifth-floor hall was presently occupied only by a basket of dried flowers on a spindly-legged console table and the light was dim. Madeline hung back at the landing to watch the stairs and give warning if anyone approached. Nicholas knocked first on the door, waited until he was sure there was no answer, then took out his lockpicks. He glanced at Arisilde, who was studying the vine-covered wallpaper intently, and cleared his throat.

"Hmm?" Arisilde stared blankly at him, distracted. "Oh, that's right." He touched the door with the back of his hand and frowned for an instant. "No, nothing sorcerous. Carry on."

That didn't exactly engender confidence, Nicholas thought. He looked down the hall at Madeline, who was rubbing her temples as if her head hurt. She signaled that no one was approaching and, holding his breath, Nicholas inserted a pick into the lock. Nothing happened. Breathing a trifle easier, he started to work the lock. There couldn't be too much danger; after all, members of the hotel staff would be in and out several times a day. But a very clever sorcerer could have set a trap that was only tripped if the door was forced or opened without a key. Either Octave's sorcerer was not very clever or . . . *There's nothing in the room worth the trouble to guard,* Nicholas thought grimly. After a few moments more he was able to ease the door open.

The small parlor just inside was shadowy, lit only by a little daylight creeping through the heavy drapes covering the window. There was a bedroom just beyond, also dark. Octave had been able to afford one of the better class of rooms: the furniture was finely made and well upholstered, and the carpets, hangings and wallpapers were of a style only recently in fashion. Arisilde slipped in after Nicholas and took a quick turn around the parlor, touching the ornaments on the mantel, bending over to poke cautiously at the coal scuttle.

Nicholas watched him with a raised eyebrow, but Arisilde didn't voice any kind of warning, so he continued his own search.

He went through the drawers and shelves of the small drop-leaf desk first, finding nothing but unused stationery and writing implements. The blotting paper revealed only past notes to a tailor and to two aristocratic ladies who had written thanking Octave for holding circles in their homes. Neither was from Madame Everset. Nicholas removed the blotting paper for a sample of Octave's handwriting, knowing the good doctor would assume the floor maid had done it when she refreshed the writing supplies.

Reynard had said that Octave seemed to have the air of a professional confidence man and Nicholas felt that supposition was confirmed by an examination of the doctor's belongings. He went through the suits and coats hanging in the wardrobe, carefully searching the pockets, finding the clothes were a mix of items well cared for but in poor quality and items of excellent quality but not cared for overmuch. *When he is in funds, he becomes careless,* Nicholas noted. The state of Octave's personal effects confirmed several of Nicholas's theories about the man's personality.

None of which disguised the fact that there was nothing of importance here.

Nothing under the bed, between the mattresses, in the back of the wardrobe, behind the framed pictures, and no mysterious slits in the cushions or lumps under the carpet. Nicholas searched the sensible places first, then the less likely, finally progressing to the places only an idiot would hide anything. *No papers, no sphere,* he thought in disgust, resisting the sudden violent urge to kick a delicate table. There were no books to be found, not even a recent novel. *He took this room for show; his real headquarters is somewhere else.* Somewhere in the city there was another Valent House in the making. *And he's using one of Edouard's spheres.* For a moment, rage made it difficult to think.

"Hah. Found it," Arisilde reported, leaning around the door. "Want to see?"

"Found what?" Nicholas stepped back into the parlor.

Arisilde was looking at the small framed mirror above the mantel. "It's a bit like that little job I did for you. The painting of *The Scribe.* This works on the same principle. I had the feeling there was something here, not something dangerous, just something . . ." He touched the mirror's gilt frame gently. "It's for speaking back and forth, I'm fairly certain, not spying. Hard to tell, though. It works like mine, with the spell all in the other end."

Nicholas studied the mirror, frowning. "You mean . . . You told me the painting was a Great Spell."

Arisilde nodded vigorously. "Oh, it is."

"So the sorcerer who did this is capable of performing Great Spells?" Not Octave. If the spiritualist had been so powerful he would have had no need for a confidence game. Madame Talvera had said that Amelia Polacera had sent Octave away because his shadow in the ether was dark. Perhaps it hadn't been Octave's shadow she had seen.

Arisilde nodded again, preoccupied. "Yes, I suppose that's the case. He's asleep right now, I think, or perhaps in some sort of trance state. Whatever it is, I can't tell anything about him. If he wakes and looks in the mirror, I can get a better sense of him."

Feeling a prickle of unease crawl up his spine, Nicholas took hold of Arisilde's arm under the elbow and urged him gently to the door. Resisting the impulse to whisper, he said, "But if he wakes, he could see us, Ari."

Arisilde stared at him in puzzlement, reluctant to leave this interesting problem. "Oh, yes, of course." He started. "Oh, yes, that's right. We'd better go."

Nicholas took one last quick glance around the room, making sure nothing was disturbed. *Perhaps I shouldn't have brought Arisilde.* The other sorcerer might be able to sense his past presence here the same way Arisilde had sniffed out the spell in the mirror. *But if you hadn't brought Ari, you would never have known about the mirror and you might have lingered too long, or tried to confront Octave here.* And there was no telling what might have happened then.

Nicholas closed the door behind them and locked it, leaving the mirror to reflect only the dark, empty room.

CHAPTER EIGHT

This particular private dining chamber at Lusaude's boasted a little bow-shaped balcony, and over its brass railing Nicholas had a good view of the famous grillroom below. The banquettes and chairs were of rich dark wood and red drapes framed the engraved mirrors. Women in extravagant gowns and men in evening dress strolled on the marble floor, or sat at the tables between stands of hothouse Parscian plants and Dienne bronzes, their laughter and talk and the clatter of their plates echoing up to the figured ceiling. The air smelled of smoke, perfume, salmon steak, and truffle.

Nicholas took out his watch and checked the time, again: the only nervous gesture he would allow himself to make.

The private chamber was small and intimate, its walls covered in red brocade and the mirror above the mantelpiece marked with names, dates, and mangled verses, etched onto it by diamond rings. On the white cloth of the table stood an unopened absinthe bottle and a silver serving set with the other paraphernalia necessary for drinking it. Nicholas normally preferred wine but for this night he favored the dangerous uncertainty of the wormwood liqueur. For now he was drinking coffee, cut with seltzer water.

He glanced up as the door opened. Reynard sauntered in, crossing the room to lean heavily on the table. "They've just arrived—they're getting out of the coaches now," he murmured.

His evening dress was a little disheveled and Nicholas could smell brandy on his breath, but he knew Reynard was only pretending to be drunk. In the doorway behind him were several young men and women, laughing, leaning on each other tipsily. One of the young men watched Reynard jealously. Nicholas pitched his voice too low for them to hear. "Very good. Will you be free to alert the others?"

"Yes." Reynard jerked his head to indicate his companions. "I'm about to shed the window dressing and head for the hotel." He took Nicholas's hand and dropped a lingering kiss on his fingers.

Nicholas lifted an eyebrow. "Reynard, really."

"It will make your reputation," Reynard explained. "I'm quite fashionable this week." He released Nicholas and turned to gesture airily to his audience. "Wrong room," he announced.

Nicholas smiled and sat back as Reynard left, pulling the door closed behind him. No one in the merry group would have the least bit of difficulty believing that Reynard had gone to an assignation when he disappeared from their company in the next half hour.

He lost his amusement as the main doors in the grillroom opened to emit a new party from the foyer. Several men and women entered, among them Madame Dompeller. On the fringe of the group was Dr. Octave.

One of the things Reynard had discovered today was that Octave would be performing another circle tonight at the Dompeller town residence near the palace. It was not a house Reynard could gain entrance to, but he had also discovered that Madame Dompeller meant to finish the evening with a late supper at Lusaude's, the better to advertise the fact that she had just hosted a spiritual gathering.

Nicholas tugged the bellpull to summon the waiter and with a brief instruction handed him the folded square of notepaper he had prepared earlier.

Below, the Dompeller party was still greeting acquaintances and foiling the majordomo's attempt to lead them to their private dining room. Nicholas watched the waiter deliver the note to Octave.

The spiritualist read the note, refolded it, and carefully tucked it away in a vest pocket. Then he excused himself to his puzzled hostess and moved quickly through the crowd, out of Nicholas's field of view.

In another moment, there was a knock at the door.

"Come," Nicholas said.

Octave stepped inside, quietly closing the door behind him. Nicholas gestured to the other brocaded armchair. "Do sit down."

Octave had received the note calmly enough, but now his face was pallid and his eyes angry. He moved to the table and put his hand on the back of the empty chair. He had removed his gloves and his nails were dirty. He said, "I know who you are, now. You're Donatien. The Prefecture has searched for you since you stole the Romele Jewels five years ago."

"Your source of information is good. Too bad you can't afford to tell anyone." Nicholas put his cup and saucer aside and reached for the absinthe. "Would you care for a drink?" After last night, he had expected Octave to discover his other persona sooner or later. The game was deep indeed and Octave wasn't the only player on the other side.

"And what is it that prevents me from speaking of what I know?" Octave was outwardly confident but sweat beaded on his pale forehead and the question was cautious.

He's wary now, too, Nicholas thought. *We've made explorations into each other's territory, and perhaps both of us have made discoveries that we had rather not.* "I've been to Valent House," Nicholas said simply. He opened the bottle and poured himself out a measure of the green liqueur. "You didn't say if you'd like a drink?"

There was a long silence. Nicholas didn't bother to look up. He busied himself with the absinthe, placing the perforated spoon containing chunks of hard sugar over the top of the glass, then adding a measure of water from the silver carafe to dissolve the sugar and make the intensely bitter stuff drinkable.

In one nervous motion Octave pulled the chair out and sat down. "Yes, thank you. I see we need to speak further."

"That's certainly one way of phrasing it." Nicholas poured out a measure for Octave, then took his own glass and leaned back in his chair. "I'll taste mine first, if that will make you more comfortable. Though I assure you that adding poison to absinthe is redundant."

Octave added sugar to his glass, his hand trembling just a little as he held the spoon and carafe. He said, "I realize now that I made a mistake in sending my messenger to you, the night of the ball. I thought you were attempting to meddle in my affairs."

"You're not a sorcerer yourself, are you? You didn't send that golem. Who did?"

"That's not your concern," Octave said, then he smiled, giving the impression of a man trying to settle a silly argument with a little cool reason. "I didn't realize your presence in Mondollot's cellars was due to the family jewels. I apologize, and we can consider the matter between us closed."

Nicholas's eyes narrowed. He tasted the liqueur. The bitter flavor was still intense, even watered down and sweetened. Drinking the stuff at strength or in quantity caused hallucinations and madness. He said, "It's too late for that, Doctor. I told you, I've seen Valent House. You seem to have left the place alive, which apparently isn't a feat that many people managed to accomplish."

"Then what do you want?" Octave leaned forward intently, his pose forgotten.

"I want him. The man who filled that house with corpses. His name, and his present location. I'll do the rest."

Octave looked away. For a moment, the expression in his protuberant eyes was hunted. "That may be more difficult than you think."

Nicholas didn't react. He had suspected that Octave had a more powerful partner and now the good doctor had confirmed it. "But that's not all I want. I must also know how you obtained enough access to Dr. Edouard Viller's work to enable you to construct one of his devices." *Mustn't place too much emphasis on that.* He didn't want Octave to realize how angry he was over that theft of knowledge. *If he realizes that, he'll know I can't possibly mean to let him escape.* "I must know that, and I must know that you will stop using it to fleece people out of their dearly departed's lost treasures."

Octave eyed him resentfully. He took the folded square of notepaper out of his pocket and dropped it on the table. On it was written *Marita Sun, carrying gold coins for deposit with the Bank of Vienne from the Sultan of Tambarta.* Octave said, "So this was not a bluff."

Nicholas lifted a brow, annoyed. "I don't bluff, Doctor." He picked up the note. "This ship sank last year. The fateful result of a complicated and rather dull transaction, involving an attempt to secure a loan from the Crown of Ile-Rien for the little nation of Tambarta. One lifeboat full of confused passengers and some debris survived. Only a crewman who went down with the ship could give an accurate enough description of her position to make salvage possible." He crumbled the note and met Octave's eyes. "You should have asked for longitude and latitude. The instructions he gave you were still too vague. It was too ambitious a project for you, Doctor. Better stick to Madame Bienardo's silver chests, stuck behind the old wine vault in the cellar, or the Viscount of Vencein's stock of gold plate buried in the garden by a mad grandfather—"

Octave struck the table with his fist, making the glasses jump and the silver spoons rattle on their tray. "So you know that much—"

"I know it all, Doctor." Nicholas allowed his disgust to show. "Edouard Viller found a way to meld machinery and magic, to create devices that would actually initiate spells on demand. His creations were so complex that no one has been able to duplicate them since he was framed for necromantic murder and hanged. No one except you, that is." His lip curled. "And you use them to ask the dead where they've buried the family silver, so you can come sneaking back and dig it up—"

Octave stood abruptly, knocking his chair back, breathing hard. His white face was shiny with sweat. "What do you care? You're nothing but a common thief."

"Oh, there's nothing common about me, Doctor." The words were out before Nicholas could stop them. He plunged on, knowing that to try to cover it would only draw more attention to his slip. "What of the ghouls? Are they a by-product of the process you use to communicate with the dead? And what of the man who needs to murder the way other men need this filth?" He set the absinthe down on the table, hard enough for a little of the green liqueur to slosh out and stain the cloth. "Is he a by-product too, or was he drawn to you by it? Can you get rid of him even if you want to?"

Octave drew back stiffly. "If you want to live, you'll stay out of my affairs, Donatien."

Nicholas rested his elbows on the table, smiling to himself. He waited until Octave's hand was on the doorknob before he said, "Perhaps I don't want to live as badly as you do, Doctor. Think on that."

Octave hesitated, then thrust open the door and stepped out.

Nicholas gave him a few moments' head start, sitting at the table and tapping the arm of his chair impatiently. Then he stood and slipped out the door.

He took the back stairs, passing a couple of heavily veiled women on their way up to assignations, and went down the narrow hall, past doors into the kitchen that disgorged fragrant steam and harried staff. He paused in the alcove near the rear entrance, to collect his coat and deliver a generous payment to his attentive waiter, then stepped into the back alley. The lightest possible rain fell out of the cloud-covered, nearly pitch-dark sky, and with any luck the fog was already rising.

The dark cabriolet waited near the mouth of the alley and one of the horses stamped impatiently as he approached. Crack was on the box with Devis, and Nicholas knew part of their plan, at least, had already gone awry. He tore open the swing door and leaned inside. "Well?"

Madeline was within, wrapped up in a dark cloak. "Octave's coach is under a lamp, right next to the front entrance of Serduni's. There's such a crowd there that if we take the driver now we might as well do it on the stage at the Grand Opera during the third act of *Iragone*," she reported, sounding annoyed. "But I did get a good look at him."

Nicholas swore. *I knew that was going to be a problem on this street.* There was no help for it. "You'll do it at the hotel, then, if he goes there," he said, and

swung inside the cramped cab, pulling the little door closed. The windows had
no glass, as was common on this type of conveyance, and it also made it far
easier to see out in the dark streets.

"It *will* be easier there," Madeline admitted. She began to readjust her costume for the next part of the plan, removing the dowdy hat she wore and stuffing it into the bag at her feet. Her cloak fell open, revealing that she was already
dressed in a man's dark suit. The cloak had completely concealed it and the
large hat had allowed her to scout out the spiritualist's coach without anyone
being the wiser. "Did you frighten Octave?" she asked, pulling a folded greatcoat out of her bag.

"He was already frightened." Nicholas scrunched over as far as he could to
give her room and looked out the window, though the alley wall cut off any
view of the front entrance of Lusaude's. Crack and Devis would be watching
for a signal from the man posted across the street. "Where do you keep family
jewelry?"

"In a strongbox in that little cupboard under the third-floor stairs. Why?"

"Not you personally, Madeline, but in general."

"Oh. In a safe, of course."

"Upstairs."

"Of course. In my dressing room, I should think. At least, that's where most
of the ladies I know keep theirs." Madeline fell back on the seat, a little breathless from wrestling with the voluminous cloak and the heavy coat in the confined space.

Nicholas glanced back at her. In the darkened coach, it was difficult to see
how well the disguise worked, but she had done this before and he knew how
convincing she could be. "Octave inferred we were in Mondollot House's cellars to steal the Mondollot jewels."

"That's ridiculous. Can you see the Duchess's lady's maid trooping down
to those dank cellars every time the woman wants to wear her emeralds to
dinner? Why, she goes to formal court at least seven times a month and she
has to wear the presentation pieces then or the Queen would be terribly offended. . . ." She tapped her lower lip, thoughtfully. "He didn't know about the
gold she was hiding, did he?"

"No, I don't think so. He hadn't even tried to persuade the Duchess to let
him contact the late Duke yet, so he didn't find out about any hidden wealth
that way. He was searching for something he already knew was there."

"Did he find it, I wonder?"

"Someone found something. There was that empty room that had been broken into, with the plinth that had been recently occupied. It was originally part of the cellar of Ventarin House, whose only claim on history is that it was once the home of Gabard Ventarin, who was Court Sorcerer two hundred years ago, give or take a decade or two."

"So he was after something buried under the house of a long-dead sorcerer?" Madeline's voice was worried. "That sounds rather . . . dangerous."

"It does, indeed." Nicholas leaned out the window, unable to contain his impatience. There was still no sign of Octave. "If he calmly sits down to dinner with the Dompeller party—"

"We'll feel very foolish."

Crack leaned down toward the window then and whispered, "He's out front, waving at his man."

Nicholas sat back against the cushions, relieved. "At last. He must have stopped to make his excuses to Madame Dompeller. It means he's not exactly panic-stricken."

"Then I don't suppose he's going to run straight to his accomplices."

"No, but that was a forlorn hope, anyway. If he was that incautious, he wouldn't have abandoned Valent House last night when he realized someone was following him." He heard the harness jingle and the cabriolet jerked into motion, moving out of the alley into the crowded street. He had reasoned that if Octave didn't immediately panic and head for his accomplices' hiding place, he would return to his hotel, leave his coach and driver, and go on foot.

Devis was adept at this game and his team quicker and more responsive than the nags that usually pulled hire carriages. He kept one or two other vehicles between the cab and Octave's coach while always keeping the quarry in sight.

Nicholas had no trouble recognizing the streets they were on tonight. "So it *is* to be the hotel." If his accusations had failed to panic the good doctor, what they were about to do would not.

Octave's coach reined in at the walk in front of the Hotel Galvaz's impressive gaslit façade. Devis followed his instructions, driving on by. Nicholas, shielding his face with a hand on his hat brim, caught sight of Octave hurrying between the dancing caryatids on either side of the entrance.

The cab turned the corner, drove past the hire stables the hotel used, and took the next corner into an alley. There it rolled to a stop. Madeline fished a top hat out of the bag at her feet and said, "I'm on. Wish me luck."

Nicholas caught her hand, pulled her to him, and kissed her far more briefly than he wanted to. "Luck."

Madeline slipped out of the cab and hurried back down the alley, Crack jumping down from the box to follow her.

———

Madeline adjusted her cravat, tipped her hat back at a jaunty angle, and lengthened her stride as she walked to the head of the alley. Her hair was bound up tightly around her head, under a short wig and her hat. Subtle application of theatrical makeup coarsened her features and changed the line of her brows, and pouches in her cheeks thickened her face. Padding helped conceal her figure under the vest, coat, and trousers, and the bulky greatcoat capped the disguise. As long as she didn't remove her gloves, she would be fine.

It was important that the coachman be removed without any sort of attention being drawn to the act. Octave might have accomplices within the hotel and they didn't want to alert them. She walked past the open stable doors, lamplight and loud talk spilling out onto the muddy stones. Behind her, she knew Crack would take up a position at the head of the alley.

She rounded the corner, passing under the weathered arabesques and curlicues of the building's carved façade. A large group was exiting a line of carriages in the street. She mingled with them as she climbed the steps and entered the hotel.

She made her way across the brightly lit foyer and up the stairs to the Grand Salon. The room was decorated with the usual profusion of carved and gilded paneling, with large mirrors rising to the swagged cornice. An enormous arrangement of plants and flowers dominated the center and reached almost to the bottom dangles of the chandelier. There were a number of men in evening dress scattered about the room in conversational groups. None of them was Octave.

Madeline made her way to the back wall, which was open to a view of the rear foyer below and the grand staircase. She had to make sure Octave left before she proceeded with her part of the plan.

Leaning on the carved balustrade, she didn't spot Reynard until he stepped up beside her. "He's gone up to his rooms," Reynard murmured. "If this is to work, he should be down again in a moment."

"It'll work," Madeline said. "He'll want to tell his friends that they've been found out." If Octave saw Reynard after the experience at the Eversets' circle,

the doctor would surely become suspicious, but no one else in their organization was as well qualified to idle in the salons of an expensive hotel as Reynard
was. Madeline, even in her respectable dark suit, was drawing some attention
from a porter who was crossing the salon. It was because she hadn't given up
her greatcoat to the cloakroom and so obviously wasn't a guest. She swore under her breath as the porter approached. This hotel had enough trouble with its
reputation, it couldn't afford to allow in a possible pickpocket or sneak thief.

Reynard spotted the man approaching and put a hand on Madeline's shoulder, drawing her to him. The porter veered away.

"Thank you, I—" She tensed. "There he is."

Octave hurried down the grand staircase, having changed his evening dress
for a plainer suit and cloak.

Reynard didn't turn to look. He was pretending to straighten Madeline's
cravat. "We have all the entrances covered, but I suspect he'll go for the back.
He doesn't strike me as being overly endowed with imagination."

Madeline leaned one elbow on the balustrade, standing as if coyly enjoying
Reynard's attentions, watching Octave until he disappeared below her level of
view. A moment or two, and the spiritualist appeared in the marble-floored
chamber below them, moving briskly toward the doors that led to the back
street entrance. "Right again," she said.

"I'll walk you out."

There was a crowd around the front entrance now and they drew several
curious looks. "You must tell me who your tailor is," Reynard said to her, as if
continuing a conversation, with just the right amount of amused condescension in his tone.

Madeline kept her expression innocently flattered and then they were out
on the street.

Madeline stopped at the stable door and Reynard kept walking. Nicholas's
cabriolet, with Devis at the reins, was already at the mouth of the alley. Madeline waited until Reynard had stepped inside and the cab turned up the street
before she casually strolled into the stables. She made her way past the carriage
stalls to the wooden stairs that led up to the second floor. The liveried hotel
servants ignored her, assuming she was someone's coachman or servant.

The stairs opened onto a low-ceilinged chamber that served as a common
room for the men quartered here. It was crowded and the air was warm and
damp and smelled strongly of horse from the stalls below. There was a dice
game in progress on the straw-strewn floorboards and Madeline circled it,

scanning the participants for Octave's coachman. She had gotten a good look at him in the street outside Lusaude's. He was a short, square-built man with coarse, heavy features and dead eyes.

He wasn't among the dice players. *Well, he didn't look the sociable sort.* No, there he was, standing against the far wall, alone. Madeline edged her way through the crowd, catching snatches of conversation in a variety of different accents, until she was near enough to her quarry for a few private words.

Much to Nicholas's consternation, she hadn't planned exactly how to lure the coachman into their clutches. She liked carefully planned schemes as much as he did, but with no prior knowledge of what the man might be doing, it was impossible to tell how best to proceed.

Besides, she did some of her finest acting under the pressure of desperation. "I have a message," she said, pitching her voice low and giving herself a faint Aderassi accent.

He eyed her, a sulky expression on his broad face. "From who?" he asked, suspicious.

Madeline realized she could say "From the doctor," but so could anyone else and she had no corroborating detail to give him. Nicholas had postulated the involvement of a powerful sorcerer, and Arisilde had confirmed it when he had found the enspelled mirror in Octave's hotel room. Taking a stab in the dark, she said, "The doctor's friend."

The man blinked and actually went white around the mouth. He pushed away from the wall and she led the way back across the room to the stairs.

She lengthened her stride as they reached the street, glancing back at him to motion him along, keeping her head down as if she feared pursuit. He quickened his steps to keep up with her.

She rounded the corner into the alley, passed a shadow hunched against the wall that she hoped was Crack. Blocking the alley was the back end of Cusard's ostler's wagon.

She turned, gesturing to it as if about to speak, saw the man's brows lower in suspicion. Then Crack moved, silent and quick, getting a forearm around the larger man's throat before he could cry out.

The coachman tried to throw his attacker off, then tried to slam him against the alley wall, but Crack held on grimly and the struggling only made the stranglehold work faster. The only sound was wheezing grunts from the coachman and the scrape of their feet on the muddy stones.

Madeline kept an eye on the mouth of the alley, but no one passed by. Finally, the coachman slumped limply to the ground and she hurried forward to help Crack haul him to the wagon.

Following a nervous man on foot wasn't as easy as following a nervous man in a coach and four. Nicholas had Devis keep the cabriolet hanging back as far as possible. He had chosen it specifically with this in mind, since it was an unobtrusive vehicle and tended to blend in to the city streets.

It didn't make waiting any easier.

"Really," Reynard said finally. "I'd rather you fidget than sit there like a bomb about to explode."

"Sorry," Nicholas said. The neighborhood they were entering was not quite what he had expected. The buildings were dark on either side of the wide street, the infrequent gas lamps wreathed in night mist, but this was a business district, heavily populated during the day. The traffic was light and they might have to get out and follow Octave on foot. "There's something wrong here."

"He didn't see me, and even if he had spotted Madeline in that getup, I don't see how he could have known who she was. I almost didn't recognize her and I knew what to expect."

"That mirror in Octave's room," Nicholas said. "If his sorcerer warned him through it . . ."

"But how would he know? Is he following us?"

"Damned if I know." Nicholas shook his head. "I wish I could hand this over to someone else. This is too complicated, too urgent for me to deal with when all our attention and resources should be devoted to the plot against Montesq."

"The sooner this is over with the better," Reynard agreed. "I'm a little confused as to how the Master Criminal of Ile-Rien ended up hot on the trail of a petty confidence man and his friend the murderer, and I was along from the first."

"Please don't call me a master criminal. It's overly dramatic. And inaccurate. And the bastard has one of Edouard's spheres, that's why I want him." *He's using Edouard's work to murder innocent people,* Nicholas thought. *I can't let that go on one moment more.* If Edouard were still alive he would have been leading the chase himself; he had never meant his work to be used to harm anyone.

Reynard was silent a moment, what little light there was from the street limning his strong profile. "I'm thinking of Valent House. Who could you possibly hand that over to? A sorcerer?"

Nicholas hesitated, though he wasn't sure why. "Inspector Ronsarde, of course. If he's good enough to almost catch us—"

"He's good enough to catch Octave and his friends. Of course. It's too bad you can't simply drop the whole matter on his lap, though I admit I would like to be in at the end."

It was too bad, but such a course was impossible. Octave knew too much about them. If Ronsarde found Octave, he found Donatien / Nicholas Valiarde, and if he found Nicholas, he found everyone else. Nicholas tapped his fingers impatiently on the leather sill of the cab window. *I want this done and over with. I want to concentrate on Montesq. We're so close. . . .*

Reynard added, "Though I'm surprised to hear you say it."

Nicholas frowned at him. "Why?"

"You do have a tendency to become . . . unduly consumed with certain things, don't you? Are you sure you aren't putting off that plan against Montesq?"

"What do you mean?"

"When Montesq is hanged—a laudable goal in itself—that means you no longer have an excuse."

"I don't need an excuse." Nicholas kept looking out the window, watching the damp mostly empty street, making sure that was still Octave stepping out of the shadows under the next lamp. Reynard was one of the few people who would say such things to him, but Reynard wasn't afraid of anything. And if Nicholas became "unduly consumed" with things, he felt Reynard erred in the other direction, by pretending not to care until it burned him away within. At least Nicholas wore his fire on the outside. "We all do what we have to do, don't we?"

Reynard was silent a moment, his face enigmatic in the shadows. He finally said, "I worry about you, that's all. All this can only go so far."

They reached a cross street that seemed completely deserted and Nicholas tapped on the ceiling, signaling for Devis to draw rein.

Nicholas waited until Octave turned the corner, then swung the door open and stepped out. He motioned to Devis to stay back here, where there were still a few passing coaches and people to explain the cab's presence. He and Reynard hurried down the dark street.

They saw Octave still moving away as they reached the corner and followed him cautiously, avoiding the infrequent pools of gaslight from the flickering streetlamps. This street was completely deserted, the buildings lining each side as silent and dark as immense tombs in some giant's mortuary. Nicholas's walking stick was a sword cane and for tonight's work Reynard carried a revolver in the pocket of his greatcoat.

They stopped as Octave crossed the street. Their quarry turned down an alley at the side of a tall, bleak building, a deserted manufactory that was solid and square, with dozens of unlovely chimneys thrusting up from the flat roof. Stone steps led up to a wooden double door, the street entrance, but Octave had gone down the alley. "It can't be," Nicholas muttered.

"I agree," Reynard whispered. "Too many people about during the day. Why, we're only two streets over from the Counting Row."

"The windows are boarded up," Nicholas said thoughtfully. "I don't think he saw us."

"Perhaps there's something behind it. We'd better move or we'll lose him."

I suppose, Nicholas thought. He smelled a trap. *Perhaps it would be best to spring it.* They crossed the silent street and Nicholas said, "He didn't see us, but still he knew he was being followed."

"Yes, dammit," Reynard said. "Someone could have warned him, but the only time he was out of our sight was when he went up to his hotel room. I suppose he could have been warned through that mirror thing you found, but how would they know about us?"

"If it was a sorcerer—a real sorcerer and not a damn fool like Octave—he'd know." And only a real sorcerer could have created that mirror. Nicholas had deliberately staged the meeting at Lusaude's to keep Octave from having any time to plan or prepare or think, but someone hadn't needed time.

They reached the side alley and went down it, ignoring the mud and trash their boots disturbed. The door was a small one, set into a slight recess in the stone wall. It was almost too dark to see it, the distant streetlamps providing little illumination in these depths. Nicholas touched the door lightly, with the back of his hand, but felt nothing. He did the same to the metal handle, again without effect. *I wish Arisilde were here,* he thought, and slowly tried the handle.

He exerted just enough pressure to find that it turned. He stopped and stepped back. "It's not locked," he told Reynard. "Fancy that."

"Oh, dear. The good doctor does have a gift for the obvious."

"But he set this trap under instructions from someone else. It's that person I worry about." Nicholas rubbed his chin thoughtfully, then felt in the various pockets of his suit and greatcoat, mentally inventorying the various tools he had brought with him. Whoever had arranged this trap hadn't had much time; he knew it took hours, often days for the casting of the Great Spells, even if the sorcerer already knew the architecture he was trying to create. *And that would be a terrible amount of work simply to eliminate us. Especially when they have other resources at their command.*

He found what he was looking for, a small holiday candle, ideal for causing mass confusion in snatch robberies in crowded places. "Step back," he told Reynard. "And watch the door."

Nicholas took out a box of matches and lit the candle. It sparked in the dimness, lighting the alley around them, its white light casting stark shadows on the dark walls. Then he flung the door open and tossed it inside.

The candle sparked, sputtered, and burst, emitting dozens of tiny flares that lit up a dingy foyer, floorboards thick with dust and spiderwebs depending from the mottled plasterboard. It also cast reflections into a dozen pairs of eyes, some crouched near the floor, some hanging from the ceiling or apparently perched halfway up the wall.

Nicholas heard Reynard swear under his breath. He heartily agreed that they had seen enough. He yanked the door closed, took out a short metal bar used for prying at reluctant locks, and thrust it through the handle to wedge it against the wooden frame. It wouldn't last long, but they only needed a short head start.

As they reached the street, Nicholas thought he heard the door burst open behind them and a frustrated snarl. That might have been his imagination. He knew the pairs of eyes, arrested by the brilliance of the sparking candle, had not.

The house was in an old carriage court called Lethe Square, off Erin Street across the river. It was only two stories and seemed on the verge of tumbling down. Surrounded by busy tenements with small shops crammed into the lower floors and right on the edge of a better district, it was an area where there were comings and goings at every hour of the night and the residents didn't pay much attention to new faces in the neighborhood.

The coach let Nicholas and Reynard off at the top of the alley, then headed for the stables at the end of the street. The infrequent gas lights turned the rising ground fog to yellow and cast odd shadows against the walls. There were other people in the street or passing through the alley to the courts beyond:

tradesmen or day workers hurrying home, a few prostitutes and idlers, a group that was obviously down here to slum among the cabarets and brandy houses, despite their dress and attempts at copying the manners of the working class. *Why don't they go to Riverside if they're so interested in seeing how the lower orders live?* Nicholas thought, as he and Reynard hurried up the alley. *I'm sure our neighbors across the river would love their company....* The answer, of course, was that this was a safe slum, filled with workers who couldn't afford better and those living in genteel poverty. Riverside was something else altogether.

They crossed the old carriage court, one side of which was occupied by a lively brandy house and the others by closed shops. Nicholas stopped at the stoop of the little house and knocked twice on the door.

After a moment it opened and Cusard stepped back to let them enter. "Any luck?" he asked.

"Yes and no," Nicholas answered, heading down the short hallway.

"Yes, we're still alive, and no, he didn't lead us anywhere useful," Reynard elaborated. "It was a trap."

Cusard swore under his breath as he locked the door behind him. "We've done a bit better. You won't believe what we been hearing from this poor bastard."

"I'd better believe it, for his sake." Nicholas opened the parlor door.

Inside was a small room, lit by a flickering lamp on a battered deal table. There was one window, shuttered and boarded over on the outside. Madeline was here, leaning against the dingy wall with her arms folded, still in male dress. She met his eyes and smiled grimly.

Lamane stood near the door and Crack, who was cleaning his fingernails with a knife, near the prisoner. Octave's driver sat in a straight-backed chair, blindfolded, his hands bound behind him.

Reynard pulled the door closed and Nicholas nodded to Madeline. She said, "Tell us again. Who killed the people we found at Valent House?" Her voice was low and husky. Nicholas would not have recognized it as hers, or even as female, if he hadn't known her. Sometimes he forgot how good an actress she really was.

"The doctor's friend." The driver's voice was hoarse from fear. Nicholas recognized it as the voice of the man who had driven Octave's coach last night, who had climbed down from the vehicle to search for him along the muddy riverbank.

"Why did he kill them?"

"For his magic."

Nicholas frowned at Madeline, who shook her head minutely, telling him to wait. The driver continued, "He needs it. It's how he does his spells."

Nothing we didn't already know, Nicholas thought. Arisilde's explanations had been more cogent. "And who is this man?" Madeline asked.

"I told you, I don't know his name. I don't see him much. Before he showed up, it was just the doctor and us." Beyond the fear, the man sounded sulky, as if he resented the intrusion of the "doctor's friend." "Me and the two others, his servants, I told you about them. The doctor held the circles for money. We started in Duncanny and he used that gadget he has."

Nicholas pressed his lips together. The "gadget" must be Edouard's device. Madeline asked, "How did he get the gadget?"

"I don't know. He had it before I came into it. He paid us well. Then his friend showed up once we were in Vienne, and everything changed. He's a sorcerer and you have to do what he says. I didn't have nothing to do with killing anybody, that was all him, for his magic."

Magic that was necromancy of the very worst kind. Nicholas remembered the melting of the plaster and wood on the walls in that horrible room and Arisilde's opinion on it. He had been trying to decide what to do with the driver once the man had told them everything he knew of use. *He was in that house. He knew what was happening.* These facts made the decision considerably easier.

"But Octave himself isn't a sorcerer," Madeline was saying.

"No, he just had that gadget. But his friend is. He knows things, too. He told the doctor Donatien was after him, and it was the doctor's fault, for mixing into things he didn't understand."

"Where are Octave and his friend now?"

"I don't know."

Crack reacted for the first time, snorting derisively. The driver flinched and protested desperately, "I don't. I told you. We split up after they said we had to leave Valent House. I been with the doctor. He knows, but he didn't tell me."

Nicholas glanced at Crack, who shrugged noncommittally. *It's very likely the truth,* Nicholas decided. It sounded as if Octave's former compatriots were being increasingly cut out of the scheme.

"What did he want in the cellars of Mondollot House?"

"I don't know," the driver said miserably, certain this further protestation of ignorance wouldn't be believed either. "I know he didn't find it. He told the doctor it must have been moved, when the Duke rebuilt the house."

That was why Octave had tried to arrange the circle with the Duchess. Octave's sorcerer must have entered the house first, to break the wards and allow the ghouls to breach the cellar and search it. Somehow the creatures must have communicated to him that the search was unsuccessful, so Octave was sent to attempt to arrange the circle to speak to the old Duke of Mondollot. But something had been removed from the plinth in that room and not long before he and Crack had arrived. *Did Octave's sorcerer friend have a rival for this prize, whatever it was? A rival who had also broken into Mondollot House that night? No, we would have seen signs of him.*

A sudden noise startled him, a muffled report like a pistol shot in the next room. Nicholas was the only one who didn't reach spasmodically for a weapon in an inner coat pocket. Reynard was closest to the door and tore it open to reveal Cusard, standing unhurt in the center of the outer room, his own pistol drawn.

"Was that you?" Reynard demanded.

Confused, Cusard shook his head. "No, I think it was from outside."

Muffled cracks and bangs erupted from the direction of the street door. "Stay here and keep an eye on him," Nicholas told Madeline. She nodded and Crack handed her his extra pistol.

Reynard was already heading down the short hall to the outer door, Cusard behind him. There was another outside door in the disused pantry at the back of the house. Nicholas motioned for Lamane to cover it and stepped to the center of the parlor so he could see down the front hall. Crack moved up beside him. Vienne lived up to its unsettled past at frequent intervals, but gunfire in the streets was rare; this was more likely to be a trap arranged by Octave.

Reynard opened the spydoor and peered through it. Cusard, standing behind him, craned his neck to look over his shoulder. "Well?" Nicholas asked.

"A lot of people standing about and staring," Reynard muttered. He unbolted the door and stepped out, moving a few paces into the court.

Nicholas swallowed a curse at this incaution, but no shots rang out. He stepped into the archway. Through the open door at the end of the dim hall he could see a few figures milling in the center of the court. "Hey there, did you hear that, too?" someone called.

"Yes," Reynard answered. "Did it come from the street?"

Suddenly, the floor moved under Nicholas's feet and he grabbed the wall for support. Reynard and the others standing in the court staggered. Nicholas felt splinters sink into his hand as the wood and plaster cracked from the stress of the shifting foundation. It was the most disturbing sensation he had ever experienced, as if something deep inside the earth had suddenly turned liquid. He thought of stories from far eastern Parscia and farther places, of the earth moving and cracking; he thought of the spell Arisilde had made to hide valuables in the warehouse. Then the sounds came again and this time he heard them clearly. Not muffled shots, they were cracks. The heavy stones that paved the court, snapping like twigs under some pressure from below. The sound came from behind him now, from under the house.

Madeline, Nicholas thought. He turned, plunged across the moving floor toward the parlor. He made it two paces before the floorboards in front of him exploded. He shielded his face as wood splinters and clods of dirt flew upward.

Sprawled only a few feet from the gaping hole in the floor, Nicholas felt cold air rush past. The single lamp winked out. The house shook and groaned as it shifted on the damaged foundation. Before he could try to stand, something massive shot up through the broken flooring and struck the ceiling.

Nicholas pushed himself away until his back struck the wall. All he could see of the thing was a dark shape against the light-colored walls, a deceptively large shadow in the dim light coming through the still-open door. He knew Crack had been standing near him, but he couldn't hear anyone else moving in the room.

The thing shifted and the wooden floor cracked in protest. *It's hunting for us,* Nicholas thought. Standing up in the small room would be suicidal. He edged along the wall, toward the archway that led into the entryway. If Crack was still here but unconscious, he would be near that narrow opening.

He didn't see the creature move but suddenly a more solid darkness loomed over him and Nicholas threw himself sideways, rolling away from it. He heard it slam into the boards just behind him, felt the tremor that traveled through what was left of the floor and upped his estimate of its size. He scrambled forward, knowing it would have him in the next instant. A door suddenly flung open, throwing light across the wreck of the room. Nicholas fell against the side of the archway and looked back.

He caught only a glimpse of gray skin, knobby and rough like stone. It moved, turning away from him toward the light. A figure appeared in the door and fired three shots, loud as cannon blasts in the confined space, then the light went out again.

The thing flung itself against the door. *That was Madeline firing at it, she's still in that room.* Nicholas staggered, grabbed a broken chair. He had to distract it to give her time to escape.

Someone caught hold of the back of his collar and flung him away, back toward the outer door. He was outside, staggering on the pavement in front of the house, before he saw that it was Crack.

People in the street screamed and ran. Nicholas tore himself free and looked through the door. He ducked back immediately. Dirt clods and shards of stone flew out of the interior of the house, striking the steps and the court. Crack caught his arm and tried to drag him away. "She's still in there!" Nicholas shouted, twisting his arm to free himself.

They both must have remembered the boarded-up window at the same moment and instead of fighting they were running for the corner of the little house, knocking into each other in their haste. Lighter on his feet, Nicholas reached it first and as he dug at the first board to rip it free he heard breaking glass from inside the room. *She's alive, she's breaking the window from inside,* he thought, tearing down the board. Crack was helping, then Reynard was there, taller than both of them and able to get a better grip on the top boards, then Lamane caught up to them.

The last board came free and Madeline launched herself through the window and into Nicholas's arms, the last glass fragments tearing at her clothes. Over her shoulder as he pulled her free he saw the body of the driver, lying in the open doorway of the room. One of the walls was bowed inward and as the lamp flickered and went out Nicholas heard the crash of the ceiling coming down. Then they were all running down the alley toward the street.

Nicholas realized Cusard wasn't with them. He knew the old man had gotten out of the house. He had been right behind Reynard. He wondered if Cusard had panicked and left them; he would've thought Lamane would break before the old thief.

They came out of the alley into the street. The din from the carriage court was audible and a few tradesmen and a couple of puzzled prostitutes had stopped to stare, though coach traffic was still moving. Others stood in doorways or peered out windows. Nicholas saw Devis on the box of their cabriolet heading toward them, and behind the smaller vehicle Cusard driving his bulky wagon. More relieved than he liked to admit, Nicholas thought, *Of course, he went to warn Devis we needed to make a quick escape.*

Nicholas pointed at the wagon and Lamane ran for it without further need of instruction.

"What happened?" Reynard was asking Madeline.

"I cut the driver loose," she said. She had lost her hat and when she tugged off her wig, forgetting for the moment her men's clothing, the dark curls tumbled down to her shoulders. "I wanted to give him a chance. It couldn't get in the door, but it started striking the wall and one of the beams hit him."

"Not here," Nicholas said, urgently. "Later."

The cabriolet drew even with them and they tumbled in.

CHAPTER NINE

I never got a good look at it," Madeline confessed. "Did you?"

"No, it was too dark." They were a good distance from the ill-fated court, almost to the river. Reynard had told them how Crack had been thrown out the front door when the creature had first burst through the floor; the henchman had kept the others from running back down the passage, creeping slowly down it himself to retrieve Nicholas. *And probably saved all our lives,* Nicholas thought. If anyone had run into that room with a lamp, none of them would have had a chance. For someone who had been accused of killing several men in an unprovoked rage, Crack was awfully good at keeping his head in a crisis. It was too bad the judges at his trial hadn't bothered to discern that fact.

Once they had crossed the river, Nicholas tapped on the ceiling for Devis to stop. They drew rein in an unoccupied side street, and he stepped out of the cabriolet to consult briefly with the coachman and to tell Cusard and Lamane to break off and return to the warehouse.

He climbed back into the little vehicle, noticing for the first time he had splinters in his hands from ripping at the board-covered window.

Madeline had heard his directions to Devis and now asked, "We're going to Arisilde?"

"Yes. We need to know how that thing found us." *We need help,* Nicholas thought. He settled back into the seat as the cab jolted forward. Cusard's wagon passed them, Lamane lifting one hand in a nervous salute as the cumbersome vehicle turned down a cross street. Nicholas had to assume everyone who had been in the house was now known to Octave's sorcerer; they had to keep moving until he could get Arisilde's protection for them.

"Is that worth it?" Reynard said. He had only met the sorcerer a few times in the past years, and hadn't known Arisilde when he was at Lodun and at the height of his powers. "I mean, will it be of any use?"

"He was well enough today at Valent House when he destroyed one of Octave's ghouls. We'll just have to hope he hasn't succumbed since this afternoon," Nicholas said, but thought, *Fond hope.*

"You think that thing is going to try again?" Reynard asked, watching him.

"It's the safest assumption to make," Nicholas admitted.

Madeline glanced up from her contemplation of the dark street. "I think it's the only assumption to make."

No word of the disturbance across the river had reached the Street of Flowers and the Philosopher's Cross, and all was as usual, colored lights lit over the market stalls and gay laughter and tinny music in the cool night air. Nicholas stepped down from the cab in the dark alley next to Arisilde's tenement and immediately felt something was out of place. He turned to help Madeline down and she gripped his arm, her dark eyes worried. "Something's wrong, can you feel it?" she asked.

He didn't want to answer her. He waited until Reynard had climbed out of the coach and then started for the door.

The concierge was gone again. Nicholas took the rickety steps two and three at a time.

Arisilde's door was in the right place and he banged on it peremptorily. He glanced back as the others reached the landing.

He heard footsteps in the apartment, then the door opened to reveal Isham, Arisilde's Parscian servant. For an instant, Nicholas felt a rush of relief, then he saw the man's face.

Isham had always seemed ageless, like a wall carving on one of the temples of his country, but now he looked old. The dark skin of his face seemed to sag, showing the network of wrinkles as fine gray lines, and his eyes were wretched.

Nicholas said, "What's happened?"

Isham motioned for him to follow and turned back down the little hall. Nicholas pushed past him, stopped at the door to the bedchamber.

The low-ceilinged, windowless room smelled of a bizarre variety of incenses, the tiny dresser and cabinet were crammed with books and papers, the carpet dusty and the wide bed disordered. Arisilde lay on that bed, a colorfully patterned coverlet drawn up to his chest. It was almost as Nicholas had left him last night, except that now Arisilde wasn't breathing.

Nicholas went to stand next to the bed. He touched Arisilde's hands, folded across the coverlet. The skin was still warm. This close he could see Arisilde was still breathing, but it was a slow, shallow respiration.

"I fear he will die soon," Isham said bitterly. Nicholas realized he had never heard the man speak before. "The drugs he took, they make the heart weak. I think it is only his great power that keeps him alive."

"When did it happen?" Madeline asked from the doorway.

Isham turned to her. "He seemed well this morning. He went out, I don't know where—"

"He was with me," Nicholas said. He was surprised at how normal his voice sounded. He touched Arisilde's face and then, moving like an automaton, he lifted the eyelids and felt for the pulse at the wrist. There had been times when he had wished Arisilde dead and thought it would be a welcome release from the torment the sorcerer put himself, and everyone close to him, through. But when he had stood in the doorway looking on what had seemed a lifeless body . . . *Maybe it's not fear for Ari,* he thought, bitterly. *Maybe it's fear for yourself.* Arisilde was the last vestige of his old life. If he was gone, Nicholas Valiarde, sometime scholar and only son of Edouard Viller, was gone too, and nothing would be left but Donatien. "Have you sent for a physician?"

"I sent the person who watches the downstairs door for one, but he has not yet returned." Isham spread his hands, resigned. "It is late and he will have difficulty convincing anyone to come tonight. I would have gone myself, but I thought I would have even more difficulty."

As a poor Parscian immigrant, Isham would be lucky to get a decent physician's servants to open the door to speak to him, especially at this time of night. And the concierge probably knew only the local quack healers. Even an honest hedgewitch would be better than that. Nicholas said, "Reynard . . ."

"I'll go." Reynard was already moving toward the door. "There's a Dr. Brile who lives not far from here. He's not a sorcerer-healer, but he's a member of the Royal Physicians College and he owes me a favor."

Nicholas looked down at Arisilde again as Reynard left. "Was it the drugs?" he asked roughly.

"I don't know." Isham shook his head. "When he came back today he seemed tired, but not sickly. He was pursuing his researches, so I went out. When I came back, I saw that he was in bed, with the lamps extinguished." Isham rubbed the bridge of his nose, wincing. "I didn't notice at first. I thought he was sleeping. Then I felt the spells, the wards, and the little charms, start to fade and grow cold. Then I came in and lit the lamp, and saw."

Nicholas frowned. "You're a sorcerer too?" he asked the old man. "I didn't realize . . ."

"Not a sorcerer. I am *interlerari,* for which there is no proper word in Rienish. I have some gift of power and I study the gift of those greater in power than I, so I may teach. I came here from Parscia to study with him." He looked up.

"I sent a wire to you at Coldcourt, but they told me it would not be delivered until later tonight. Did it reach you so soon?"

"No, we were already on our way," Nicholas answered, and thought, *How many years have you known Isham, and yet not known him at all?* Had he been that single-minded?

For a while there was nothing to do but wait. Not long after Reynard left, the concierge returned empty-handed, unable to convince even one of the local quacks to come. "They know what he is," the man explained with a shrug. He had a thick Aderassi accent and a philosophical outlook. "I tell them he's a good wizard, only a little crazy and not in a bad way, but they're afraid."

Nicholas had tipped him more generously than he had originally intended for that and sent him to the nearest telegraph station with a coded message for Cusard at the warehouse. If Arisilde could no longer protect himself, Nicholas didn't want to leave him unguarded. His own presence here was dangerous enough.

Madeline and Isham had gone into the other room and Nicholas sat alone on the edge of Arisilde's bed until an unfamiliar footstep startled him. An older man in a dark greatcoat carrying a doctor's bag stood in the bedchamber's doorway, eyeing the poorly lit room somewhat warily. He had the warm brown skin and curling dark hair that usually meant a blend of Parscian and Rienish ancestry. Then his gaze fell on Arisilde and the wariness changed to a professional blankness. Stepping into the room, he said, "What does he take?"

"Opium, mostly, isn't it?" Reynard said, following the doctor in and glancing at Nicholas for confirmation.

Nicholas nodded. "And ether."

The doctor sighed in weary disgust and opened his bag.

Nicholas waited tensely through the examination, leaning on a bureau in a far corner of the room. Isham had moved quietly to assist the doctor and probably also to keep a cautious eye on what he did to Arisilde, but Nicholas could tell Brile seemed more than competent. Reynard came to stand next to him and Nicholas asked, low-voiced, "How did you get him to come here?"

"Threatened to tell his wife," Reynard answered casually.

Nicholas regarded him with a raised brow. "Well, no, not really," Reynard admitted. "He was attached to my regiment and caught a bullet when we were in retreat from Leisthetla, and I stopped to throw him over the back of a donkey, or something, I can't recall, so he feels he owes me a favor. But the other makes a better story, don't you think?"

"Occasionally I forget that you're not as debauched as you'd like everyone to believe," Nicholas murmured.

Reynard pretended to seem disturbed. "Keep it to yourself, would you?"

Brile sat back, shaking his head. "It's not the opium. He doesn't have the signs of it. Oh, I can tell he's an addict and that it's destroyed his health, but it's not what's causing this, or at least it isn't directly responsible. This is some sort of seizure or catatonia." He looked up at them. "I'll need to send my driver to my surgery."

Reynard nodded. "Write down what you need and I'll take it to him."

More waiting, that meant. Nicholas walked out, into the main room, unable to hold still for another moment.

The curtains torn down during Arisilde's fit the other night had been replaced and a fire was burning, but the room still seemed cold and empty. Madeline sat in front of the hearth, near a writing desk overflowing with paper, books, pens, and other trifles. She looked up as Nicholas came in. "Well?"

"He says it doesn't appear to be the drugs, at least."

Madeline frowned. "I'm not sure whether to be cheered by that or not. It doesn't leave us with any comfortable options. Could it have been Octave and his sorcerer, attacking him as they did us?"

Nicholas shook his head. "I don't think so. If Arisilde had fought a battle, we would have known it." The entire city would have known it. No, he could see what had happened all too clearly. Arisilde had had a disturbing episode last night, then today, when he had seemed so much better, he had used his power as casually as when he had been a student at Lodun. "He hasn't been in the best of health for years, and after everything else he's done to himself, I'm afraid his body has just . . . given out." Isham was probably right in that it was only Arisilde's power keeping him alive.

Reynard came into the parlor and a moment later Isham followed. Nicholas asked, "Well?"

Reynard shrugged. "Brile said he's not getting any worse, but he's not getting any better either. There's no immediate danger and there's nothing else he can do tonight."

"Which means he doesn't know what to do."

"Exactly."

Nicholas looked away. *We need a sorcerer-healer,* he thought. *One who won't ask difficult questions. One who isn't afraid to tend a man who is probably far more powerful than he is and with a history of illness and instability.* It was a tall order. He said, "Isham, we have good reason to believe we're being pursued by another sorcerer. That's why we came, but we can't chance leading an enemy here with Arisilde in this state. I've set some men to watch the building and I want you to keep me informed of anything that occurs."

"I will do this," Isham assured him. "In what manner are you being pursued?"

Madeline had been turning over one of the books on the desk, her brows knitted in thought. "I think someone may have cast a Sending on one of us."

Nicholas frowned. "Why do you say that?"

"I know we weren't followed there, yet it found us so quickly. And there was just something about it. . . ." She glanced up and saw that he was regarding her skeptically, and glared. "It's only a feeling. I feel it to be so. I can't give you a hard and fast reason, all right?"

"Yes, but—"

"It is easily settled," Isham interrupted. "I can do a throwing of salt and ash to ascertain if this is the case."

As Isham lit two of the lamps above the mantelpiece, Reynard said, "I'm sure I don't really want to know this, but what is a Sending and why do you think it's after one of us?"

Madeline didn't respond immediately, so Nicholas answered, "A Sending is a spell to cause death. A sorcerer fixes it on a specific person, and then casts it. It exists until it destroys its target, or until another sorcerer destroys the Sending." He looked at Madeline. "I didn't know they could take on corporeal forms. I always thought they came as diseases, or apparent accidents. And I thought the victim had to accept some sort of token from the sorcerer before he could be made a target."

Madeline shook her head. "That's true now. But Sendings are old magic. Hundreds of years ago, they were far more . . . elemental."

"Very true," Isham agreed, lifting an embossed metal box down from one of the shelves. "Three hundred years ago, the Satrap of Ilikiat in Parscia had a sorcerer cast a Sending against the God-King. It was not necessary to send a token to the God-King, and indeed it would have been impossible to get such a thing to him through the defenses of his own sorcerers. The Sending destroyed the west wing of the Palace of Winds, before the great Silimirin managed to turn it back on the one who cast it. But that was three hundred years ago and sorcerers are not what they were then, for which the Infinite in its wisdom is to be thanked."

"Why not?" Reynard asked.

Isham had opened the box, taking out various glass vials. He started to clear a space on the table and Nicholas and Reynard helped him lift down the piles of books. The old man explained, "Such profligate outpourings of power can only come from bargains with etheric beings—Fay, for example. And such things have been shown to be more deadly to the bargainer than to any of his enemies."

Isham swept the dust off the table with his hand and began to lay out a pattern of concentric circles, using ash from the fireplace and various powdered substances from the glass vials.

Quietly, not wanting to disturb the old man's concentration, Nicholas asked Madeline, "But what makes you suspect a Sending?"

She sighed. "If I knew, I'd tell you."

Isham finished the diagram and now took a water-smoothed pebble from the box and placed it gently in the center of the lines of ash. He motioned them to gather around the table. As Nicholas stepped forward he saw the pebble tremble. When he stood next to the table, the pebble rolled toward him, stopping at the edge. *Damn it*, Nicholas thought. Whatever the test was, it seemed conclusive.

Brows drawn together in concentration, Isham nudged the pebble back to the center of the diagram. "It seems it is a Sending, and it is focused on you." He picked the pebble up and rolled it between his fingers. "What form did it take when it appeared to you?"

"We couldn't really see it clearly." Nicholas described what had happened at the house, letting Madeline tell what she had seen after Crack had gotten him out. That the Sending was attuned to him he had no trouble believing. He had been expecting it since Madeline had brought up the possibility. That might even have been the purpose behind the trap at the manufactory. He had been the only one to touch the door; the Sending might have focused on that.

"It reacted to the bullets from your revolver?" Isham was asking Madeline.

"It drew back, yes. It's what kept it off me long enough for the others to get the boards off the window." She frowned, twisting a length of her hair. "You think it could be something of the fay?"

"It could be. The most powerful Sendings are made from a natural or etherical force. For example, the Sending cast against the God-King was said to be made from a whirlwind that had formed on the plain below Karsat. I would think to use something of the fay would be even more complicated than that, not that I have the slightest idea how to go about it."

"This man is a necromancer," Nicholas said.

Isham hesitated, lost in thought. He said, "It occurs to me that there must be the remains of many dead fay buried beneath Vienne." The old man spread his hands. "I'm afraid I can't tell you any more than this. I am almost at the limit of my skill now."

"We need the help of a powerful sorcerer," Madeline said. She moved to stand in front of the hearth, the firelight casting highlights on her hair. "Who else can we go to?"

"It has to be a sorcerer we can trust," Nicholas added. "That's not as easily come by. . . . It will have to be Wirhan Asilva." Asilva had been a loyal friend to Edouard and maintained the connection with Nicholas after the trial, but he knew nothing of Nicholas's career as Donatien. He was also a very old man by now, but he was the only other living sorcerer whose abilities came anywhere close to being comparable with Arisilde's, and who Nicholas knew well enough to take a chance on. "He still lives at Lodun. He might be able to help Arisilde as well, or at least direct us to someone who can."

Isham had followed the conversation with a worried frown, and now said urgently, "I don't know much of this Sending, but I do know this: You will be in the most danger during the hours of the night. And if this is a remnant of some fay monster, cold iron will still be a protection. The iron in the buildings, the water pipes, the underground railways offer some safety. Leaving the city could be most dangerous."

Nicholas smiled. He wasn't beaten yet. "Not if I leave the city on the train."

———

Nicholas followed the others down the hall, but as he passed Arisilde's door, he found he had to take one last look. He stepped into the bedchamber.

The lamplight flickered on the sorcerer's wispy hair, his pale features. It was hard to believe this wasn't death. Then Nicholas noticed the book lying on the patched velvet of the coverlet, not far from the sorcerer's left hand.

It might have been instinct that made him return to the bed and pick up the book, or some latent magical talent, but it was more likely only that he knew Arisilde so well.

The volume was very old and not well cared for, the cover mottled with damp and the pages brown. The embossed letters of the title had worn away to illegibility and Nicholas opened it at random.

He was looking at a woodcut and for a moment he thought it depicted a modern medical dissecting room. Then he held it closer to the lamp and saw it was the scene from Valent House: an indistinct room, a man tied to a table, with his gut opened and his entrails exposed. But in this scene the victim was still terribly alive and the vivisectionist was still present: a strange figure, stooping and leering like a character in an old morality play, dressed in a doublet and a high-collared lace ruff, a fashion out of date for at least a century or two. The caption read *The Necromancer, Constant Macob, at work before his execution.* The date given was a little less than two hundred years ago.

The page was stained, just as in his childhood memory. He turned to the frontispiece and there, in faded ink and childish scrawl, was written *Nicholas Valiarde.*

I'm looking for a book. . . .

How like Arisilde. He hadn't found another copy. He had found the very one Nicholas had owned as a boy.

Nicholas closed the book and carefully tucked it into his coat pocket, looking down at Arisilde once more. *No, you're not dead yet, are you? Hold on, if you can. I'll be back.*

———

Vienne's central train station was like a great cathedral of iron girders and glass. Even at this time of night it was comfortably busy, if not crowded. People in all sorts of dress from every part of Ile-Rien hurried back and forth across the vast central area. Nicholas heard the distinctive whistle and checked his pocket watch, then moved to one of the bay windows that overlooked the main platform. The *Night Royal* was rumbling in, a huge cloud of warm steam engulfing the track ahead of it. Grinding to a halt, it was a black monstrosity with bright-polished brass rails and only about twenty minutes late.

Madeline should be back any moment, Nicholas thought. He refused to allow himself to look at his pocket watch again. She was sending the wires that contained his instructions to the rest of the organization and he knew that right now she was safer alone than with him.

Before they had left the others, Crack had handed Nicholas his pistol and now it lay heavily in the pocket of his coat. The henchman had not been happy at being left behind, but Nicholas had refused to argue the point; he didn't mean to get everyone he knew killed. *Just Madeline?* he asked himself wryly. She had been grimly insistent about accompanying him.

He moved away from the window and strolled back to the center of the main area. Sleepy families huddled on the benches against the wall, waiting for trains or for someone to meet them. There was a lounge for first-class passengers on the gallery level and every so often, past the mingled voices and the dull roar of the trains, he could hear the music from the string quartet that entertained there. Nicholas preferred the anonymity of the main waiting area, especially when something was trying to kill him.

His instructions had amounted to telling everyone to go to ground for the next few days. Reynard would watch Dr. Octave, but from a distance, and Cusard would do everything necessary to put off the plans for entering Count Montesq's Great House. Nicholas had sent a wire to Coldcourt, to warn Sarasate, and he only hoped Isham was right and that the Sending would concentrate on him and leave everyone else alone.

A delegation of lower-level Parscian nobility were disembarking from the *Night Royal,* their servants shouting, gesturing, and requiring the assistance of almost every porter on duty for the large number of heavy trunks. That would slow things down a little more. The *Night Royal*'s next stop was Lodun and Nicholas intended to be on it.

It would be better for Madeline if she didn't return in time, he thought wryly. The Sending had only turned on her when he was out of its reach, though, he had to admit, Lodun was probably the safest place for both of them. But if he left without her, she would only take the next train and be considerably put out with him when she arrived.

He saw a figure coming up the concourse then and recognized her walk. *No, it isn't her walk,* he realized a moment later. Madeline walked as if she had a heavy dueling rapier slung at her hip; it was the way the character Robisais walked, from the play *Robisais and Athen.* It was one of Madeline's first major roles, that of a young girl who disguised herself as a soldier to cross the border and rescue her lover from a Bisran slave camp, during the Great Bisran War. He wasn't surprised he recognized the walk; he must've seen the damn play twenty times and Madeline had been the only worthwhile aspect of it. She must be very tired, to slip from her character of Young Man to Robisais. Of course, she could probably do Robisais in her sleep.

She climbed the steps and nodded to him briskly. She had borrowed a hat from Reynard and gathered her hair back up under the wig, so there was nothing to reveal her disguise. "Everyone is warned, now. I suppose that's the best we can do," she said. She glanced around the waiting area. "Nothing's happened here?"

"No," Nicholas said. At the last moment he remembered to link arms with her as he would with a man and not take her arm as he would a woman's. "We'll have a little time. Not much, but a little. Our sorcerous opponent shouldn't have drawn so much attention to himself. The Crown will take notice of this. After tonight, he'll have the court sorcerers, the Queen's Guard, and everyone else after him."

"And they will all be looking for us too, if we're not careful," she pointed out.

"They can't trace ownership of that house, I've made sure of that. The driver's body can't be identified. We're safe enough." Nicholas felt the book in his pocket thump his leg as they strolled toward the platform and thought, *Safety is always relative, of course.*

Madeline's brows lifted skeptically but she made no comment.

The flurry of porters around the *Night Royal* had calmed, indicating the train was almost ready. In another moment, the bell above the booking area rang and the conductors began to call for boarding.

They took their place with the other passengers gathering in the damp cold air on the platform. Through persistence and not being encumbered by baggage they soon managed to successfully board the train.

Nicholas found them an empty compartment and drew the curtain over the etched glass of the inner door to discourage company. Sinking down into the comfortably padded upholstery, the gaslit warmth, the familiar smell of combined dust, coffee, and worn fabric, he realized he was exhausted as well.

Settling next to him, Madeline said, "I wonder if the dining car still has those cream tarts."

Nicholas glanced at her fondly. And this woman had the audacity to suggest that he was distanced from reality. He dug the book out of the pocket of his greatcoat and handed it to her. "Don't let this ruin your enjoyment of the trip."

He had left the page with the woodcut of Constant Macob folded down and she stared at it, then turned to the accompanying text.

Nicholas wiped the fogged window to look out at the gradually clearing chaos on the platform. He had read the section earlier, as he had waited for Madeline in the station. It briefly, and probably inaccurately, described Constant Macob's history as the sorcerer whose experiments with necromancy had turned it from a despised and barely tolerated branch of sorcery to a capital offense. *A capital offense, if you live until the trial,* Nicholas thought. In the past several sorcerers, most of them probably innocent, had been hanged in the street by mobs before the accusations could even be investigated.

Madeline closed the book and laid it back in his lap. "Dr. Octave's sorcerer friend is imitating this Constant Macob."

"Yes, or he believes he is Constant Macob. He is practicing the worst sort of necromancy, the spells that require pain or a human death to work, as Macob did. He is taking his victims from among the poorest class, apparently in the belief that the disappearances won't be noticed, as Macob did. And, like Macob, he can't tell the difference between beggars and the poor working class and occasionally takes a perfectly respectable dressmaker's assistant or some laborer's children and gets himself into the penny sheets." Nicholas turned away from the window. "Inspector Ronsarde must be very close to finding him."

"Yes, he was watching Dr. Octave at Gabrill House and he sent Dr. Halle to look at that drowned boy in the morgue. He studies historical crimes, doesn't he? He must have looked at all the disappearances reported to the Prefecture, and recognized Macob's methods. That means—"

"He's only a step or two away from us. When he takes Octave—and if he realizes Octave is involved with the creature that destroyed the house in Lethe Square, he might very well take him tonight—Octave will tell them everything he knows about us."

"And we can't dispose of Octave while he has this pet necromancer defending him." Madeline tapped impatient fingers on the seat.

"After what we saw tonight, I know we can't take the chance. Not now. Not without help. This sorcerer could be using Octave and Edouard's device to contact Macob, or at least he thinks he's contacting Macob. But it would explain where all their knowledge of necromancy is coming from." He shook his head. "If I can get this Sending disposed of . . ."

Madeline sat back in the seat, staring in a preoccupied way at nothing. Whistles and bells sounded outside on the platform and the compartment shook as the engine built up steam. "Why didn't you tell Reynard about this?"

"Because if the Sending follows us to Lodun and kills us, I didn't want him trying to avenge us."

"Then there won't be anyone to stop them," Madeline protested, brushing aside the idea of her own death.

"Yes, there will be. Ronsarde and Halle will stop them."

"For deadly enemies, you have a great deal of faith in Ronsarde and Halle."

"There are deadly enemies, and there are deadly enemies," Nicholas said. "Now let's go and see if the dining car still has cream tarts."

CHAPTER TEN

Lodun was a lovely town. Houses and cottages painted white, or ocher and blue, or a warm honey-color lined the ancient stone streets. Most had vines creeping up their walls and gardens or large courts with old cow barns and dovecotes, relics of the time when they were farmsteads in open country, before the town had expanded to embrace them. Nicholas remembered it as even more beautiful in the spring, when the flowers in the window boxes and the wisteria were in bloom.

Asilva lived close to the rambling walls of the university, almost in the shadow of its heavy stone towers. The house was on a narrow side street, flanked by similar dwellings, each with a small stable on the ground floor. The entrance to the living area was reached by a short flight of steps leading up to an open veranda on the second floor. Asilva's veranda was cloaked by vines and crowded with potted plants, some still covered for protection from the last of the cold weather.

Nicholas hadn't liked the implication of the tightly shuttered windows and when he had climbed to the veranda, his knocking at the blue-painted door had brought no response. A neighbor had appeared on the recessed balcony of the next house, to explain that Asilva had left over a week ago and that they didn't expect the old man back for at least a month.

Cursing under his breath, Nicholas went back down to street level and through the little stone barn beneath the house and into the garden. He knew that as Asilva had grown older, the sorcerer had come to find Lodun more and more confining and had taken to traveling for several weeks at a time throughout the year. *I expected my luck to hold,* Nicholas thought, disgusted at his own presumption more than anything else.

Madeline was standing on a stone-flagged path, almost hip deep in winter-brown grasses, contemplating an assault on the back of the house.

"He's gone for an indeterminate period," Nicholas reported. It was early morning and the air was mild; it would be warm later. He pushed his hat back, looking over the garden. "We can't stay here long." With a sorcerer living on practically every street there was breathing space, though not much. And if the Sending came after him here and was destroyed by any of the number of sorcerers whose attention it would attract, the questions raised would be impossible to answer.

Madeline rubbed her eyes wearily. They had had coffee and pastries in the dining car on the train and very little sleep. The overgrown garden around them was mostly herbs, dry and bushy from the end of winter. Herb gardens were everywhere in Lodun, grown not only for the benefit of cooking pots but for their magical uses and for the dispensaries at the medical college. Nicholas was conscious of movement in the undergrowth, quicksilver sparkles of light. Asilva had always allowed flower fay to inhabit his garden, another example of his eccentricity. The colorful little creatures, as harmless as they were brainless, were drawn by the warmth of human magic, apparently heedless of the fact that the owner of this garden could destroy them with a gesture.

"There's no one else, I suppose," Madeline said thoughtfully. "Asilva was the last of Edouard's old colleagues."

"Yes." Nicholas looked toward the towers of the university. Seeking help there meant explanations, discovery. "I haven't been here in years. He's the only one who might have helped us and kept quiet about it." Nicholas realized he was saying that he didn't know what to do next, an admission that would normally have to be forced out of him under torture. Yet he could say it to Madeline without a sensation of panic; it was odd.

A gossamer puff of blue-violet, with a tiny emaciated mock-human figure in its center, settled on Madeline's shoulder. He flicked it off and it tumbled in the air with an annoyed squeak.

"I might know of someone." Madeline became very interested in the dead weeds at her feet.

"Might know? Who?"

"An old . . . friend."

Nicholas gritted his teeth. Madeline's fellow artists in the theater mostly behaved as witlessly as the flower fay gamboling in the weeds around them now. Occasionally, when she was unsure of herself, Madeline imitated their behavior, apparently because it took up little of her attention, allowing her to devote her resources to finding a way out of whatever dilemma she was in. It drove Nicholas insane when she did it to him. He said, "Take your time. I do have all the time in the world, you know."

The look she gave him was dark, almost tormented. "I should let the dead past lay buried. It's a mistake to trouble still waters, but—"

"That's from the second act of *Arantha*," he snapped, "and if you're going to behave in this nonsensical way and expect me not to notice, you could at least do me the courtesy of not employing the dialogue from your favorite play."

"Oh, all right." Madeline cast her arms up in capitulation. "Her name is Madele, she lives a few miles out of town, and if anyone can help us, she can."

"You're certain?"

She let out her breath in annoyance. "No, I'm not certain. I thought a wild-goose chase would occupy us until certain death tonight."

Nicholas contemplated the morning sky. "Madeline—"

"Yes, yes, I'm certain." She added more reasonably, "We can get there by this afternoon if we hire a trap or a dogcart or something. We'd better get started."

"But . . ." *You never told me you knew any sorcerers.* He was beginning to realize why she had been so determined to accompany him to Lodun. She had known of an alternative to Wirhan Asilva all along but she hadn't wanted to suggest it until she was certain all other possibilities were exhausted. He knew she knew something of magic, but supposed she had picked it up somewhere the way he had, from simply living and studying at Lodun. He had the suspicion this was going to lead to a longer conversation than they could afford to have in Wirhan Asilva's fay-haunted garden with a Sending on their trail. He said, "Very well. Let's go."

———

Nicholas hired a pony trap from the stables on the street that led up to the university gates and they drove west away from the main part of the town.

The shop-lined streets gave way to laborers' cottages and summer residences with large garden plots, then finally to farmsteads and small orchards. This gave way in turn to fields of corn or flax, some standing fallow, all separated by earthen banks a few feet high planted with trees. The houses, whether they were tumbledown shacks or fine homes, all had runes set into the brickwork, painted on the walls, or cut into posts and shutters. A reminder that this was Lodun and it had seen stranger things than the Sending that currently hounded them.

It was close to noon and Nicholas was all too aware the hours of light left to them were limited. "Is it much farther?" he asked.

"We're almost there," Madeline said.

It was the first words they had spoken to each other since leaving Asilva's garden.

Finally, they reached a cart track that led off the old stone road and Madeline indicated they should follow it. It led them past gently rolling hills and through a copse of sycamore and ash, then out into cultivated fields again. On a rise overlooking the track were the remains of a fortified manor house. As the wagon passed beneath the tumbled-down walls, Madeline said, "There's a story Madele told me, that an evil baron lived here and that she did something awful to him, tricked him into turning himself over to the Unseelie Court or something." She added, "It couldn't have been a baron, of course. What's left of the house is too small. And I think this land is part of the County of Ismarne, anyway."

Nicholas smiled at her. "Perhaps an evil gentleman farmer," he suggested. The breeze lifted a few strands of Madeline's hair that had escaped from under her hat. "This could be very dangerous for your friend."

"I know."

"Do you think she would be able to do something for Arisilde, as well?"

"I hope so."

Could you be any less forthcoming? Nicholas wanted to ask, but he reminded himself that he was avoiding a quarrel.

There were a couple of farmsteads in the distance; Nicholas could see the smoke from their chimneys and hear the lowing of cows on the wind, but the area they were traveling through seemed deserted. Then the wagon track circled a hill and a house appeared as suddenly as if it had leapt out of the bushes.

It was of light-colored stone, two stories with a stable or cow barn tucked in below and an old dovecote rising like a tower to one side. Vines, dried and brown from winter, climbed the steps and the arches of the stables, and the whole was shaded by an ancient oak tree, far larger than the house it sheltered, its lowest branches as large around as wine barrels and so heavy they had come to rest on the ground. The windows had carved casements and paned glass and the doors and shutters were well made, though painted a dull brown. It was a substantial house; somehow Nicholas had been expecting a tiny cottage.

He drew rein in the dirt-and-graveled yard and Madeline jumped down from the box.

An old woman stood in the doorway where a set of stone steps led up to the second floor. Small and wiry, her gray hair knotted up in braids, her skin dulled by age, she was almost invisible against the weathered stone wall. She wore a smock and a dull-colored skirt: peasant clothes, oddly incongruous if she owned this prosperous house.

She put her hands on her hips and said, "So you've come to see me, hey, girl? You wouldn't if you didn't have to, I suppose. You reek of dark magic, I suppose you realize. If you'd stuck with your real calling you wouldn't need my help with whatever it is."

Madeline looked around, consulting an imaginary audience. "Has anyone got the time? What was that, one minute, two? How many instants have I been here before the same old song starts again? I suppose the rest of the family will be along to chime in on the chorus before the hour's out."

Nicholas sighed and rubbed the bridge of his nose, trying to discourage an incipient headache. *This is going well so far.*

The old woman sniffed. "You've brought a man with you."

"An astute observation." Madeline folded her arms. "I await further wisdom."

"And you've done something awful to your hair."

"It's a wig, Madele, a wig." She snatched it off and brandished it, scattering pins on the dusty ground.

"That's a relief. You could at least introduce me."

To the wig? Nicholas thought, stepping down from the wagon, then realized she meant him.

Madeline took a deep breath and said, "Madame Madele Avignon, may I present Nicholas Valiarde." She turned to Nicholas. "Madele is my grandmother."

For a moment, all he could do was stare at Madeline. As if sensing the trouble, the old woman coughed, and said, "I'll just step in and put some water on to boil, if you want to shout at me some more later."

She went back inside the house, leaving the door standing open. Madeline snorted. "She's listening to us, of course. She has the manners of a precocious child." She smiled faintly, and added, "But now you know where I get it from."

Nicholas didn't fall for this attempted distraction. He said, "Your grandmother is a sorceress?" An old friend, an old lover even, he had been prepared for.

"Well, yes, she is." She let out her breath, as if in resignation.

Nicholas looked away, over the rolling fields. "Why don't you go and tell her about our little problem, and I'll take care of the horse."

Madeline looked a little uncertain, as if she had expected a different response. "All right," she said finally, and went toward the house.

Nicholas unharnessed the biddable horse and led it into the little barn beneath the house. The mule and the two goats penned there greeted his appearance with enthusiasm, as if they expected every human they encountered to be delivering food. Upstairs in the house, he could hear metal cooking pots slamming around.

Arisilde had known, he supposed. The sorcerer had made some comment about giving his regards to her grandmother that had seemed to startle Madeline. It would be very like Arisilde to have somehow realized Madeline's antecedents years ago and during one of his drug hazes to forget that she obviously wanted it kept secret.

Nicholas finished tending the horse and went out and up the stairs. The front door was still standing open and he stepped inside to a long room, the walls limewashed a cerulean blue and the floor of patterned brick. A ladder led up to what was probably a sleeping loft and another door indicated at least one more room on this level. Madeline was nowhere to be seen.

Madele stood at the large cooking hearth, which held pots on hooks and a crane, trivet, and kettle. There was a settle inside, in good peasant style, and a cloth frill to help the chimney draw. She eyed him a moment, then gestured for him to take a seat. "Madeline says there's a Sending after you. Of course she doesn't know what she's saying." Her voice was raspy and harsh, as unlike Madeline's as possible. Any resemblance in feature was disguised by a profusion of wrinkles. "She could have been more help to you if she had followed her calling."

Nicholas took a seat on the bench at the deeply scarred table. Over the mantelpiece there was a clock with a garden scene on the enamel dial and a framed photograph of a stiffly posed family group, looking uncomfortable in their best clothes. There were two young girls in the group, either of which might have been Madeline, but the broad flowered hats made identification impossible. There were a few chairs, an enormous wooden dresser stacked with china, a shallow trough sink, a potager embedded in the wall, and a wooden drying safe hanging from the ceiling. Dried herbs and fragments of knitting littered the shelf below the window. There was absolutely nothing to indicate that Madele was a sorceress. No books, nothing to write with or on, and he was willing to bet the ceramic jars on the table contained only comfit and cooking oil. He asked, "What calling was that?"

Madele eyed him, almost warily, then as an apparent non sequitur muttered, "She's certainly found herself an interesting one, hasn't she?" She gazed out the window at nothing and answered, "The family calling. Magic. Or power, or whatever pretentious name it has at Lodun. All the women in my family have always had talent and they've all pursued it, except one. Well, except my cousin twice removed, and she was mad."

Nicholas managed not to comment. He was wondering if there was anything else Madeline hadn't told him.

Madele shook her head. "Let's see about this so-called Sending." She sat down across from him and took his hand. Her skin felt almost as rough and hard as the wood of the table. "Well, it is a Sending. A very powerful one." Her eyes, which were a warm brown and clear for her age, seemed to look straight through him. "It came at you in the dark, from under the earth. It took no form you could recognize. It was drawn from something that had been dead for some time, buried under the street, but the iron in the soil kept it from decay. It shuns the sun and seemed to withdraw from iron, but that was only because it remembers the fear of the cold metal from when it was alive."

Is she a sorceress or a fortune-telling hedgewitch? Nicholas felt more than a touch of impatience. Had Madeline completely lost her wits? Not only was she going to get herself killed when the creature came after him, but this old woman as well. He asked, "If the Sending follows us here tonight, can you turn it away?"

"Oh, I'm no Kade Carrion, I'm only a little hedgewitch, but I'll do," she answered cheerfully, as if she had read his thought. She pursed her lips and released his hand. "There's no if about it, you know. It will follow you here." Her gaze sharpened. "It's a very old sort of spell, this. Strange to see it used now. Strange to see that there is someone who can use it at all."

Nicholas hesitated, then took the book out of his pocket and opened it to the woodcut of the necromancer. "I think the man who is behind it is deliberately imitating, or believes himself to be, this person, Constant Macob."

Madele took the little book, fumbled for a pair of spectacles on a ribbon around her neck, and studied the illustration carefully, chewing her lip in thought. She ran her thumb over the page, as if testing the texture of the paper. "Believes himself to be Macob? Are you sure?"

Nicholas felt a flash of irritation. "No, I'm not sure of anything."

"I meant, it's more likely that he actually is Constant Macob."

"How can that be possible?" Nicholas said impatiently. "The man was drawn and quartered over two hundred years ago."

"I know that, young man." Her gaze was serious. "Anything's possible."

Madeline came out of the other room. She had changed into an old skirt and smock of Madele's and had brushed her hair and washed her face. She and Madele eyed one another warily.

Madele stood. "I've a couple of things to attend to outside."

As the front door banged shut behind her, Madeline said, "I suppose you want to talk."

Nicholas steepled his fingers. "Perhaps your supposition is incorrect."

"Nicholas . . ."

He had meant to be cold, but found himself saying, "Why didn't you tell me your family were all sorcerers?"

"Grandmama's been talking, I see. Why would my antecedents be your concern?" She looked up, caught his expression before he could conceal it, and said, "That's not what I meant." She gestured, exasperated, though at herself or him he couldn't tell. "I suppose I was afraid."

"Afraid of what?"

Madeline sighed and played with the fringe on her shawl. She said slowly, "I want to be an actress just a little less than I want to keep living. It takes all the time and concentration that I have. Studying this"—she waved a hand at the little room—"power, and all the varied ways of it, would take all the time and concentration that I have. I had to choose one. I did. Not many people understand that."

Nicholas folded his arms. *Be reasonable,* he told himself. They couldn't afford to fight now. And maybe it was none of his business; they weren't married. But he had told her everything. She was the only one who knew the whole story. "And you assumed I would be one of them?"

"Yes, I did." She met his eyes gravely. "I want to be an actress the way you want to destroy Count Montesq. I know what that kind of wanting is like. I could be much more of a help to you if I pursued magic instead of the leading role at the Elegante. Especially with Arisilde going to Hell in a handcart." She looked away. "I realized why I suspected it was a Sending. When it was trying to get into the room with me, there was a feel, a smell, something . . . When I was a child, Madele took me to Lodun once for the midwinter festival and while we were there some old enemy tried to kill her by slipping her an apple with a Sending of disease on it. She said it was a trick old as time and turned it aside, but she had me hold it first, so I would know how it felt, and know not to take anything that gave me that feeling. It was subtle, but it was there. It felt like wanting, like lust. It was frightening." She smiled briefly. "She didn't even bother to find out who Sent it to her. At least that's what she told me; for all I know he's buried under the house." She gestured helplessly. "I don't know. I've given up something that other people have begged, stolen, schemed for all through time. Maybe I'm mad."

"All my closest friends are mad." What that said about him, Nicholas didn't want to closely consider. He sighed and rested his head in his hands. "I wouldn't ask you to do something that you didn't like. Especially knowing it would do no good to ask."

"But if you had asked, I might have considered it." She smiled ruefully. "But that's not your failing, is it?"

Nicholas shook his head. He didn't want to discuss this anymore. It came too close to the bone. He said, "Do you think your grandmother can deal with this Sending? She's only a hedgewitch. There's no point in risking her life." He turned to look at her. "We still have time to get back to Lodun if we leave now."

Madeline's brows rose. She asked, "Did she say that? That she was only a hedgewitch?"

"Yes."

Madeline squeezed her eyes shut, briefly. "Her definition of hedgewitch is a little different from everyone else's." She looked up at him. "The name they called her was Malice Maleficia."

"Oh." The woman known by that name hadn't been seen for more than fifty years, but Nicholas had heard the stories of her exploits. Including the one about the evil baron, though he hadn't been a baron and he hadn't lived here. It had been the Bishop of Seaborn, who had tried to turn all the followers of the Old Faith out of the city and had reportedly ended up as a permanent fixture on the disappearing island of Illcay. "I see."

Madele banged in through the door, pausing to scrape the mud off her wooden clogs. "If you're staying for dinner, I'd better pluck a chicken."

———

They waited. Just before dusk fell, Nicholas helped Madele close the shutters.

He had forgotten what night was like in the countryside. It might be darker in the city, where gas streetlights were still sparse and crumbling buildings could blot out moon and starlight and leave the streets and alleys like little narrow ribbons of pitch, but it was never so silent as on an isolated farmstead. It might have been a great void outside, nothing stirring but the wind, an empty world where this little house was the only habitation of the living.

Madeline had fallen asleep on a chair and Nicholas covered her with a blanket from the bed in the other room.

Madele was knitting, her brow furrowed with the kind of concentration usually reserved for intricate mathematical calculation or perhaps surgery. Watching her, Nicholas smiled. She was acting, he realized suddenly. It shouldn't have taken him so long to see it, but this was really the first quiet moment he had had for real observation. She was playacting the role of an old, somewhat daft peasant woman, for an audience of one. God knew Madeline did it often enough, concealing her true feelings, character, or temper behind a role tailor-made for whoever she wished to fool. He saw now where she had caught the habit. To draw Madele out a little, he said, "So this is where great witches go to rest?"

Madele smiled. She was missing some teeth, but it was a remarkably predatory smile all the same. "She told you?"

"Yes. It gave me confidence."

She sniffed. "Well, I'm old, it doesn't change that. I haven't done a great magic or trafficked with the fay in a very long time. Can't hardly find the fay anymore; they're waning. But I've a few twists and turns left." She finished the row on her knitting, and said, "You're a thief."

Coming from Malice Maleficia, this was not so heavy an accusation. He said, "Sometimes. Sometimes not."

"Madeline didn't tell me," Madele added. "I saw it on your face when you came in."

"Thank you," Nicholas said, with a polite smile, as if she had complimented him.

Madele shot him a suspicious look from under lowered brows, but forbore to comment.

Outside, the wind had risen and Nicholas heard something heavy shift. He tensed, then realized it must be the huge oak that half embraced the house. He started to say something, then saw Madele's head had lifted and her eyes were alert.

Madeline woke with a start and sat up, the blanket sliding to the floor. The sound came again, less like a heavy tree branch lifted by the wind and more like earth moving. Madeline whispered, "Is that it?"

Madele motioned at her to be quiet. She stood, setting aside her knitting, and moved to the front of the hearth. Her head tilted to one side, as she listened with complete concentration to the night.

Nicholas got to his feet, glancing at the front door to make sure the lock was turned, for all the good that might do.

Madele frowned. "Can you hear it, girl? My ears aren't as good as they were."

"No." Madeline shook her head, her brows drawn together in frustration. "Nothing but the wind. You know I was never good at that."

Madele snorted in denial, but said only, "I need to know where it is."

Madeline went to the front window and Nicholas headed toward the back room. It was crowded with furniture, bureaus, chests, and an enormous cabinet bed. He blew out the candlelamp on the wall and opened the shutters on the single window, standing to one side of it in case something broke through. He could see nothing through the dusty panes but a moonlit stretch of empty ground and a clump of trees and brush swaying in the wind. He went back to the doorway.

Madeline had cautiously twitched back the curtain on the front window and knelt on the floor, peering out. "I can't see anything," she reported. "There might be something just behind the big oak, but the side of the house is blocking the view."

"I need to know," Madele gasped the words. Her face was pinched and drawn, as if she was in pain.

"I'll go out the back and look," Nicholas told Madeline. "See if you can find a length of rope; I'll need it to get back in."

Madeline started to speak, stopped, then cursed under her breath and got to her feet. Nicholas took that for agreement.

He opened the catch on the back window and raised it slowly, hoping the wind would cover any betraying noise and that the Sending's hearing wasn't keen. The outdoor air was dry and sharp, without any scent of the rain that the clouds and wind seemed to promise. He slid one leg over the sill, found footing on a wooden beam below, and slipped out to cling to the stone facing.

He dropped to the ground, landing on packed dirt. He couldn't hear anything but the wind roaring through the trees and the dry winter grass of the fields; it was like standing on the beach at Chaire when the tide was coming in.

Nicholas found the wooden half door and eased it open, slipping into the barn beneath the house. The docile horse stamped and snorted in its stall, agitated, and the goats were rushing back and forth in their pen from fear. He went to the door that led to the front yard and edged it open.

The wind swept dirt over the packed earth and made the oak tree stir and groan with the weight of its branches. The surrounding fields were empty in the snatches of moonlight. Nicholas pushed the door open a little farther, meaning to step out, when suddenly the mule in the barn behind him brayed.

He saw it then, just past the giant shadow of the oak, a piece of darkness that the moon didn't touch, the wind couldn't shift. He was astonished at the size of it. *The thing that came up through the floor of the house was only part of it,* he realized. The creature itself, whatever form it took, was taller than the tree that towered over Madele's house.

He edged the door closed for all the protection that might give the animals within and crossed back to the opposite door, giving the mule a pat on the neck as he passed.

Madeline had already dropped the rope from the window and tied it off to the bedframe. He scrambled up it easily. She stood nearby in the warm room, her arms folded and her face tense, and Madele waited in the bedroom doorway. "It's just past the oak tree," Nicholas told her, locking the window catch. "I couldn't tell what it was, except that it's immense—"

The roof creaked suddenly and a little dust fell from the beams.

"Ahh," Madele said. "That'll be it, then," and turned back to the main room.

Nicholas and Madeline exchanged a look and followed her.

The house started to shake. Nicholas put one hand on the table to steady himself. He wondered if it would come through the floor again. That seemed most likely. Or perhaps through the roof. This house was more sturdily built than the one in Lethe Square; more dust fell from the trembling roof beams but the walls still held.

Madele stared at the fireplace, kneading her hands and muttering to herself incomprehensibly. The iron pots and hooks hanging above the hearth rattled against the stone; the flames crackled as fine dust and hardened chunks of soot fell into them.

Something drew Nicholas's eyes upward. The stones of the chimney near the ceiling bulged out suddenly, as if whatever was within was about to explode across the room. Impossibly, the bulge traveled downward toward the hearth, the stones appearing almost liquid as it passed.

It burst out of the mouth of the hearth in a cloud of soot and ash, a giant hand, skeletal, yellowed by decay, too large to have fit through the chimney, larger now than the hearth behind it.

Nicholas thought he shouted, though he couldn't understand the words himself. He heard Madeline curse. Madele hadn't moved. She was easily within its reach, standing like a statue, staring intently at the thing.

It hung there and Nicholas saw it was formed as if human, five fingers, the right number of bones. Time seemed distorted; he wanted to reach Madele to take her shoulder and pull her away from it, but he couldn't move.

Then it withdrew, drawing back into the hearth, disappearing up the chimney hole that was far too small for it to fit through. The bulge traveled back up the stone chimney, vanishing as it climbed past the ceiling.

Nicholas realized his knees were shaking, that his grip on the table was the only thing keeping him upright. He thought he had imagined it, except the pots had been knocked to the floor and he had seen the thing's knuckles brush them aside when it emerged.

Madele's head dropped and she buried her face in her hands. Madeline pushed past him to catch her shoulders, but the old woman shook her off. Madele lifted her head and her eyes were bright and wicked. "Open the door," she said. "Tell me what you see."

Nicholas went to the door and tore it open. He saw nothing at first. The wind had risen alarmingly, making the house groan and tossing the branches of the oak tree. Then he realized that the tree was making far too much noise; a wind of the strength to stir those immense branches would have knocked the house flat. Thunder shook the stone under him and in the blazing white crack of the lightning, he saw the Sending.

It was white and huge, wrapped in the branches of the oak tree, struggling to free itself. He saw the hand that had reached down the chimney stretching up above the tossing branches, its clawlike fingers curled in agony. In the lightning flash of illumination, a branch whipped up and wrapped around the straining skeletal arm and snatched it back down into the tree.

The light was gone, leaving the yard to darkness and the rush of the wind. Nicholas slammed the door and leaned against it.

Madele was picking up the scattered pots from the floor, clucking to herself. "Well?" Madeline asked.

"The tree appears to be eating it," Nicholas reported soberly. He was glad his voice didn't shake.

"You're lucky you came here," Madele said. She straightened and rubbed her back. "That tree was a Great Spell. I made it years and years ago, when I was young and I first came to live here. The Sending isn't fighting me as I am now, old and withered and dry. It's fighting me as I was then, at my prime." She lifted her head, listening to the wind against the stones, and maybe to something else. "And whoever Sent it is far more powerful than I am. Then or now."

The wind didn't die down for another hour and after that Madele said it was safe to go outside. There was no trace of the Sending, except a scatter of broken twigs and detritus beneath the heavy branches of the guardian oak.

CHAPTER ELEVEN

I t's a lovely day not to be under a death sentence from a Sending," Madeline
said, as they came out into the morning light from the dark interior of
the stables. They had driven back to Lodun, starting before dawn to reach
the town in good time, and had just turned the hired horse and trap back
over to the owner. Madeline was in male dress again, Madele having nothing
suitable for town that she could borrow. They were both dusty, tired, and
somewhat the worse for wear.

Before they left Madele's house, Nicholas had told the sorceress about Arisilde and asked for her help. She had stood next to their pony trap while he
harnessed the horse and had said, "Arisilde Damal, hmm? And he studied at
Lodun? I don't think I've heard of him."

Nicholas thought that was probably just as well and didn't comment.

After a long moment of thought, she asked, "Is Ian Vardis still Court
Sorcerer?"

"No, he died years ago. Rahene Fallier has the position."

"Ahh," she said. "Don't know him. That's good." There was another long
pause and Nicholas devoted his attention to adjusting the harness. He wouldn't
beg her, if that's what she was waiting for. Finally she asked, "Is it a spell, or
just an illness?"

"We weren't sure."

Her brows lifted in surprise.

He hesitated, then said, "He's an opium addict."

Madele was now favoring him with one of Madeline's expressions of sardonic incredulity that seemed to question his sanity. It was worse coming from
her, since her thick gray brows heightened the effect. Stung, Nicholas said, "If
you feel it's beyond your admittedly failing skills—"

Madele rolled her eyes, annoyed. "He a thief, too?"

"Yes," Nicholas snapped.

"Then I'll come," she had said, smiling and showing her missing teeth. "I
like thieves."

Madele had promised to come to Vienne tomorrow, which would give her time for making various arrangements for the upkeep of the house and animals with her neighbors and extended family. Nicholas hadn't been sure she would really come, if he could really count on her help, but after Madeline emerged from the house to have a half-hour argument with her over what train the old woman would take from Lodun, he felt she did, at least, mean to travel to Vienne.

Now, here in Lodun, he could only hope she would keep her promise. "Can you arrange the train tickets, and check at the hotel to see if there's any word from Reynard or Isham?" Nicholas asked Madeline. He had left both with instructions to send a telegram in care of the railroad hotel if there were any new developments with Octave or with Arisilde's condition. "I need to pursue another line of investigation."

Madeline brushed road dust from her lapels. "Concerning how Octave became so intimately acquainted with Edouard's work?"

Nicholas's expression was enigmatic. "Yes, and how did you ever guess that?"

"Edouard performed most of his experiments here, didn't he?" She leaned back against the post and tipped back her hat thoughtfully, very much in character as a young man. The street was sparsely occupied, mainly by townspeople on errands or farmers' carts, with a few students in ragged scholars' gowns, probably just recovering from a night spent in the cabarets, hurrying along the walk toward the university gates. "I assume you don't suspect Wirhan Asilva, since we were going to him for help?"

"No, not Asilva." Asilva had helped Nicholas remove the contents of Edouard's Lodun workroom after the old philosopher's arrest, something that could have landed Nicholas in prison and put Asilva, as a sorcerer and subject to charges of necromancy, under a death sentence. He had also fought for Edouard's release up until the last moment, even as he had protested that Edouard's spheres were dangerous and should never have been created. He didn't think Asilva would betray his old friend, even years after Edouard's death. "There's something Arisilde said that has made me wonder about Ilamires Rohan. And if we eliminate Arisilde and Asilva, he's the only other sorcerer familiar with the situation who is still alive now."

"That we know of." Madeline looked doubtful. "Rohan was Master of Lodun and Arisilde's teacher. He could be extremely dangerous, to say the least."

"That depends." Nicholas took Madeline's arm.

"On what?"

"On whether he merely gave the information to Octave or if he is Octave's mad sorcerer."

Madeline was clearly worried. "If that's the case, it won't be safe to confront him. Are you sure—"

Nicholas said, "I'm sure of one thing. That 'safe' is not a state of being any of us are going to experience again until this is over."

———

Nicholas spoke to several old acquaintances at the café near the northern university gates and discovered that his quarry was not only in town, but that he would be at home later this afternoon entertaining guests. That was ideal for what Nicholas had in mind and it also gave him time to look for more information on Constant Macob.

For that the best place was the Albaran Library, currently housed in one of the oldest structures in Lodun. Standing in the foyer of that venerable building, in the smell of aged paper and dust and time, Nicholas's student days seemed only a short while ago, as if the intervening years had meant nothing. He dismissed that thought with annoyance. The past was the past, as dead as Edouard. But on impulse, he found one of the attendants and asked for Dr. Uberque.

The attendant led him to a room in the outer wall of the bastion that had once been part of an inner defensive corridor. There were still trapdoors high in the walls and the ceiling, originally placed there so boiling oil could be poured down on anyone who broke through the outer doors. But now the corridor had been partitioned off into half a dozen high-ceilinged rooms and the walls were lined with shelves. The narrow windows that had been crossbow or musket slits were now filled with stained glass. Dr. Uberque stood in front of a large table covered with books and papers. He waved away the attendant before the man could introduce them and said, "Nicholas Valiarde. Did you come back to finish your degree?" He was a tall man with sparse white hair and a lined, good-humored face. He wore a black-and-purple master scholar's gown open over his suit, as if he had just come from a tutoring session.

"No, sir." Nicholas managed not to smile. Uberque was single-minded in the extreme and was as unlikely to be curious about Nicholas's need for this information as if he was any other student trying to write a monograph. "I'm in town on business, but I need information about a subject I thought you could supply."

"Yes?"

"Constant Macob."

Uberque's eyes went distant. Nicholas had seen the same effect with storytellers in the marketplaces of Parscian cities. They were usually illiterate, but held thousands of lines of poetic sagas in their memories. After a moment, Uberque said, "One of the executed sorcerers from the reign of King Rogere. A disreputable character."

"The sorcerer or the King?" Nicholas asked, taking a seat at the table.

Uberque took the question seriously. "Either, though that is a different topic entirely. Do you want a reference on Macob?"

"Please."

Dr. Uberque stepped to the shelves and paced along them thoughtfully. "Everyone remembers Macob as a necromancer and nothing more. Before him, you know, necromancy was frowned on, but it was quite legal. It was mainly concerned with methods of divination, then. Seeing ancient kings on one's fingernail, and asking them for secret information." Uberque smiled. "Macob went on quite as any other sorcerer for a number of years. Then his wife and several of his children died in one of the plagues."

"It's certain they died naturally?" Nicholas asked, one brow lifting in doubt.

"Well, he was suspected later of causing their deaths, but I don't think he did. No, I don't believe so. Healing magic only goes so far and the apothecaries at the time were nearly useless. I think it was after his eldest daughter died that Macob . . . changed."

"He went insane?"

"It's hard to say. Judging from his actions, he must have done. But he didn't behave like a madman. He was more than clever, more than cunning. His work during this time period was nothing short of brilliant. He continually astounded the masters of Lodun, he was given honors by the King, and he carried on an utterly normal private life in his home in the city. And he killed people. He was caught, in the end, only by accident. The house next to his was sold and the new owners were adding a stables. A courtyard wall collapsed due to incompetence and it knocked down the wall of a wing of Macob's house. He was away at the time. When the builders hastened to repair the damage, they found the first of the bodies." Uberque shrugged and continued, "No one will

ever know how many he killed. Gabard Ventarin read Macob's secret journals before he burned them and discovered that Macob had been advancing
the frontiers of necromancy in quite a different direction from divination. He
had learned how to draw power from not only death, but pain." Dr. Uberque
paused, touching the spine of a book lightly. "'He called the dark fay allies and
conspired with everything of decadence and filth. He brought death to the innocent and concealed the traces of his passing with chaos. . . .' That's from *The
Histories of Aden Cathare.* You don't want that, it doesn't have anything helpful. *The Executions of Rogere,* that's better. It's only fifty years old and there's
half a dozen copies at least, so I can loan you one with a clear conscience." He
frowned at the shelves. "It's not here. No, it's not here. We'll go and have a look
for it, shall we?"

The Executions of Rogere secured at last and Dr. Uberque thanked, Nicholas
left the musty dimness of the old library. He crossed the open gallery to one of
the newer brick buildings that grew like mushrooms on the side of the older
structures. The view between the pillars of the gallery was of the towers and
courts of the medical college. The day was sunny and the breeze mild; another sign that winter was over for the year. Nicholas touched the pistol in his
pocket. He doubted his next appointment would end so congenially.

———

Ilamires Rohan, former Master of Lodun University, still spent most of the
year at his home on the university grounds. The house was four floors of tan-
colored stone that took on a golden glow in the afternoon light, with small
ornamental turrets along the roofline. It stood in the center of a large garden
surrounded by a low stone wall. On leaving the Albaran Library, Nicholas had
passed through a students' hall and picked up a reasonably presentable scholar's gown from the pile at the bottom of a stairwell, discarded there by young
students eager to escape tutoring sessions and enjoy the day. With that over his
somewhat dusty suit, no one gave him a second look as he crossed the various
college courts on the way to Rohan's house.

The university gardeners were preparing the flower beds for spring, and
none of them gave him a second look either when Nicholas walked in the back
gate and through the kitchen garden to the scullery door. It was long enough
after lunch that the kitchen and pantries were deserted except for a pair of
maids scrubbing pots, who acknowledged his passing with distracted head-
bobs and went back to their conversation.

Nicholas left the gown on the coat rack in the butler's sitting room and went through a baize servants' door that led out into the front hallway. The house was lovely from the inside as well. The hall was filled with mellow light from the dozen or so narrow windows above the main door, and the cabinets and console tables lining the hall were of well-polished rosewood, the rugs of an expensive weave from the hill country. But Rohan had always had exquisite taste, even when he had been a dean living in a tiny cottage behind the Apothecaries Guild Hall. *His star did rise fast, didn't it?* Nicholas thought. And for all its apparent peace, Lodun was a competitive world, especially for sorcerers. Nicholas investigated a few receiving rooms, finding them unoccupied, then heard voices and followed them into the large parlor at the end of the hall.

Several men and a few women were just coming in from the room beyond, talking amiably. They were all older, most dressed either in master scholars' gowns or impeccable afternoon visiting attire. One of the things Nicholas had discovered in his morning reconnaissance was that Rohan was giving a luncheon for several dignitaries from the town and the university this afternoon; he was glad to see his informant had not been mistaken.

"Master Rohan," Nicholas said lightly.

The old man turned, startled. His face, thin and ascetic, marked by harsh lines and pale from too much time in poorly lit rooms, changed when he recognized his new visitor. That change told Nicholas everything he wanted to know. Rohan said, "I didn't realize you were here."

The words had been almost blurted, as if from guilt at forgetting his presence, yet Rohan had to know the butler hadn't admitted Nicholas or he would have been informed of it. Stiffening with annoyance at the display of ill-mannered impudence and demanding to know why he hadn't come to the front door like a gentleman would have been more convincing. Nicholas smiled. "Which didn't you realize: that I was here in town, or that I was here among the living?"

Rohan's eyes narrowed, as if he suspected mockery but wasn't sure of the inference, but he said only, "You wanted to speak to me? I'm presently occupied." His voice was colder. In a few moments, enough of his self-control would have returned to allow him to confidently dismiss the intruder.

Nicholas strolled to the table, hands in his pockets, and met Rohan's eyes deliberately. "I had something to ask you about Edouard's Lodun affairs. You were doing such a marvelous job of handling them for me when I was younger, I thought surely you could assist me now."

The old man's gaze shifted. With a barely perceptible hesitation, he turned to the others. "You'll excuse me, please. An obligation to an old friend. . . ."

The others assured him that of course it was no trouble at all, and Nicholas followed Rohan into his study without pause. He had been seen by the Master of Doire Hall, three deans of the medical college, and the Lord Mayor of Lodun, none of them Rohan's fellow sorcerers. If Rohan wanted to kill him, he wouldn't be able to do it in his home this afternoon.

The study was spacious, the walls covered in green ribbed silk and lined with glass-fronted bookcases, interrupted only by a lacquered map cabinet and several busts of classical figures on carved pedestals. There was a landscape by Sithare over the marble mantel, a strong sign that Rohan was not having any difficulty with his finances.

Rohan moved to the desk and sat down behind it, as if Nicholas were a student called in for a dressing down. Not a very friendly gesture toward an old friend's son. He said, "I hope this won't take long. As you saw I am—"

"There's only one thing I still need to know; the rest is only curiosity," Nicholas interrupted. He let the old man wait a heartbeat. "The material you gave to Dr. Octave. Where did it come from? Did you take it from Edouard's laboratory?"

Rohan sighed. "I didn't steal it, if that's what you're implying." He leaned on the desk and rubbed the bridge of his nose. "Some of the notebooks were Edouard's, the rest were mine." He raised his head, wearily. "The sphere was mine. Edouard constructed it and I devised the spells."

Nicholas didn't allow his expression to change and kept his grip on the revolver in his pocket. This might be a trick. *Readily admit what you already know you can't conceal, and strike as soon as my guard is down.* He remembered the teasingly familiar handwriting on the scraps of paper they had found at Valent House; it must have been Rohan's. His voice deceptively mild, he said, "I didn't realize you had worked with Edouard. You said—"

"I said I didn't approve. I said what he did was nonsense." Rohan slammed a hand down on the desk, then took a deep breath, reaching for calm. "I was afraid. I made it a condition when I agreed to work with him that he tell no one of my involvement. Wirhan Asilva was an old man with no ambitions, even then. He could afford to be mixed up in such things. Arisilde . . ." When he spoke the name Rohan's voice almost broke with bitterness. "Arisilde was a precocious boy. No one could touch him and he knew it. But I was Master of Lodun, and vulnerable."

This sounded too much like the truth. Nicholas said, "He kept his word to you. He told no one. You could have testified—"

"He was a natural philosopher who wanted to talk to his dead wife and they hanged him for necromancy. I was a sorcerer in a position of power. What do you think they would have done to me?" Rohan shook his head. "I know, I know. Asilva testified and it did no good. I convinced myself that Edouard might be guilty, that he might have killed that woman for his experiment, that he might have concealed the true nature. . . . And I was afraid. Then Edouard was dead, and then Ronsarde proved it was all a mistake, and there seemed no point in dredging it up again." He rubbed his face tiredly, then spread his gnarled hands on the desk. "Octave wouldn't tell me what he wanted with the sphere. I suppose he went to you for the same purpose. I knew there were things missing from Edouard's rooms here when the Crown seized the contents and I knew you and Asilva must have taken them, but I didn't tell Octave that. That's not something that can be laid at my door. Did he threaten to expose you as well? Since Edouard was found innocent I don't think it would be a crime. . . ."

Rohan was speaking quickly, his hands nervously touching the things on the desk. Nicholas stopped listening. There was something tawdry and anticlimactic about it, to come here expecting evil and find only weakness. He asked, "What did Octave threaten you with?"

Rohan was silent a moment. "It wasn't the first time I had dabbled in necromancy." He looked up and added dryly, "I see you're not shocked. Most sorcerers of my generation have some experience with it, though few will admit it. Octave came to me here, two years ago. He knew. I don't know how. He knew about my work with it in the past, my work with Edouard, he knew everything. I gave him what he wanted, and he went away." Rohan winced. "I shouldn't have, I know that. Edouard meant it to be a method of communication with the etheric plane, but it never worked quite the way he wanted." Seeing Nicholas's expression he added, "I can't be more specific than that. Edouard built the thing; all I did was contribute the necessary spells. I know he wanted it to work for anyone, but it would only function for a person who had some talent for magic. It might be a small talent, just a bare awareness of it, but that was enough."

But how did Octave know you had it? Nicholas had the feeling that if he could answer that question then all the half-glimpsed plots would unravel. "Is Octave a sorcerer, then?"

Rohan shook his head. "He has a little talent, no skill. He isn't a sorcerer.

But with the sphere . . . I don't know. I can't tell you anymore." He sat up a little straighter. "If that is all you have to ask, please go."

It might all be an act but that seemed unlikely. This was Rohan's sole involvement with the plot, as the victim of blackmail for past crimes and disloyalties. Nicholas took his hand out of the pocket with the pistol and went to the door. He paused on the threshold, glanced back, and said, "I'm sure Arisilde would send you his regards. If he could remember who you were," and quietly closed the door behind him.

———

Nicholas found Madeline waiting at a table outside the little café where they had arranged to meet. She stood as he came near, saying, "There was a wire waiting at the hotel from Reynard. He says there's been a development and we need to return immediately."

———

Nicholas spotted Reynard in the crowd on the platform of the Vienne station as he and Madeline stepped off the train. Since they had no baggage to collect they avoided the congestion and were able to make their way over to him and withdraw into one of the recessed waiting areas, left empty by the arrival of the Express. It was a little room lined with upholstered benches, smelling strongly of spilled coffee and the steam exhaust of trains.

"What's happened?" Nicholas demanded immediately.

Reynard was as carefully dressed as ever but he looked as if he hadn't slept. He said, "Ronsarde's been arrested."

"What?" Nicholas glanced at Madeline, saw her expression was incredulous, and knew he couldn't have misheard. "What the devil for?"

"The charge is officially burglary," Reynard said. From his skeptical expression it was evident what he thought the likelihood of that was. "Apparently he broke into a house in pursuit of evidence and was careless enough to get caught at it. But Cusard says there's a rumor in the streets that he was assisting a necromancer."

The mental leap from housebreaking to necromancy was a long one, even for Vienne's hysterical rumormongers. Nicholas felt a curious sense of vertigo; perhaps he was more tired than he realized. "How did that get started?"

Reynard shook his head. "I should tell you from the beginning. The morning after you left for Lodun, the Prefecture found Valent House. Ronsarde was investigating the murders yesterday when he was caught breaking in to another house." Anticipating the question Nicholas was trying to interrupt with, he added, "And no, I don't know the name of the house. It wasn't in the papers and Cusard couldn't find out from his sources in the Prefecture either. Which makes it sound like a noble family, doesn't it?"

"An ignoble family, perhaps." Nicholas was thinking of Montesq. Octave's initial interest in Edouard Viller, his theft of the scholar's work, his knowledge of Coldcourt, even the way he had approached Ilamires Rohan—like footprints on wet pavement, they led back to Montesq. *Could he be at the root of it? Supporting Octave and his lunatic sorcerer? That would be so . . . convenient.* Convenient and in a way disappointing. He didn't want Montesq executed for a crime the man had actually committed. That would ruin the whole point of the thing.

"Wait," Madeline said, exasperated. "I've missed something. How did the Prefecture get the idea that Ronsarde was behind the murders at Valent House?"

"They don't have that idea, of course," Reynard told her impatiently. "He was done for burglary and whoever managed to pull that off must be damn high up in the ranks, that's all I can say." He gestured helplessly. "But this rumor that he's involved with necromancers is everywhere. There was a small riot last night in front of Valent House. Took a troop of City Guards to keep them from burning the place down."

"And half of Riverside with it, I imagine." Madeline's brow creased as she looked at Nicholas.

Nicholas dragged a hand through his hair. Several women and a porter laden with baggage passed the open doorway, but no one entered. He muttered, "Oh, he must be close. He must be right on top of them."

Reynard checked his pocket watch. "He's due to go before the magistrate in an hour. I thought it might help to hear what goes on there."

"Yes, we'd better go there at once." Nicholas turned to Madeline. "I want the other spheres removed from Coldcourt. Can you do that while we're at court?"

"Yes. You think Octave will try for them."

"No, but I may need them as bait and I don't want to risk going to Coldcourt again. I don't want their attention on it. Take the spheres to the warehouse and put them in Arisilde's safe. I wager even the real Constant Macob couldn't find them in there."

"I have the impression," Reynard began, his eyes grim, "that I'm underinformed. Who the hell is Constant Macob?"

"I'll explain on the way."

———

Madeline found a hire cabriolet to take her on her mission to Coldcourt, and Nicholas and Reynard went to the coach. Devis was driving and Crack was waiting on the box. Crack's greeting was a restrained nod. Standing so as to block any curious onlooker's view, Nicholas handed Crack back his pistol and touched his hat brim to him.

"It's very odd," Reynard commented, once he had seen the book and heard Nicholas's theory on their opponent, "to be rushing off to see Inspector Ronsarde arraigned before the magistrates. I always expected to be on the other side of the bench, as it were."

"'Odd' is a mild word for it," Nicholas said, his expression hard. Now that he had gotten over the initial shock, he was almost light-headed with rage at Octave and his murderous sorcerer. They had stolen Edouard's work, they had tried to kill himself and Madeline, and now . . . *And now Ronsarde.* He should be grateful to them for destroying the great Inspector Ronsarde, something that he had never been able to do. *Except I stopped trying to destroy him years ago.* He wasn't grateful, he was homicidal. It wasn't enough that they endanger his friends and employees, they had to attack his most valued enemy as well. "Where's Octave?"

"The night of our little upset in Lethe Square he moved out of the Hotel Galvaz and into the Dormier, using a false name. Some of Cusard's men are keeping an eye on him. Oh, and Lamane and I went back to that manufactory that Octave led us to. There was nothing there, just an old, empty building."

Nicholas grimaced in annoyance. Octave's behavior was inexplicable. He thought it would be greatly improved by a couple of hard blows to the spiritualist's head with a crowbar. "Octave should have left the city, at least until we were taken care of."

"Except that he has an appointment for a circle at Fontainon House. I don't think he wants to miss that."

"Fontainon House?" Nicholas didn't like the cold edge of prescience that simple statement gave him. Fontainon House was the home of the Queen's maternal cousin, an older woman of few ambitions beyond social achievement, but the house itself was within sight of the palace. It might even be caught in the edge of the palace wards. The idea of Octave holding a circle at Fontainon House didn't have the feel of another confidence game; it felt like a goal.

"Does that tell you something?" Reynard asked, watching Nicholas's expression.

"It makes a rather unpleasant suggestion. How did you hear about it?"

"I ran into Madame Algretto at Lusaude's. They've been invited. She wasn't keen on it after what happened at Gabrill House, but then she hasn't much choice in her engagements, from what I can tell," Reynard answered. He watched Nicholas sharply. "This worries you, doesn't it? Why?"

Nicholas shook his head. His suspicions were almost too nebulous to articulate. Octave had been working his way quickly up through Vienne's social scale. The Queen's cousin was practically at the top of that and there had been rumors for years about her odd pastimes. He said, "I never thought there was a plan. I thought Octave was out for what he could get and that this sorcerer was simply mad for power. But . . ."

"But this makes you think differently."

"Yes." Nicholas drummed his fingers on the windowsill impatiently. "We need Arisilde. If I'd paid more attention the last time I spoke to him, perhaps—"

Reynard swore. "You can't live on ifs, Nic. If I had burned the damn letter from Bran instead of keeping it in a moment of sentimental excess, if I'd become suspicious when I realized it was missing instead of shrugging it off to carelessness, the little fool would still be alive. And if I kept living those mistakes over and over again, I'd be as far gone into opium and self-pity as your sorcerer friend."

Nicholas let out his breath and didn't answer for a moment, knowing very well he had said something similar to Arisilde the night of the sorcerer's last fit. For a time, when they had first met, he had wondered if Reynard had loved the young man who had killed himself over the blackmail letter. He had decided since that it was not very likely. But the young man had been a friend and Reynard had felt protective of him and responsible for his undoing. Nicholas thought most of Reynard's excesses concealed an overdeveloped sense of responsibility. *I wonder what my excesses conceal,* Nicholas thought. Better not to speculate on that. Dryly, he said, "Don't worry on that account. If I succumb to self-pity I'll probably do something far more immediate and spectacular than a simple addiction to opium." That sounded a deal more serious than he had meant it to, so he added, "But I'll have to get Madeline's permission first."

Reynard's mouth twisted, not in amusement, but he accepted the attempt to lighten the mood. "I'm amazed that Madeline puts up with you."

"Madeline . . . has her own life and concerns." Maybe this wasn't such an innocuous topic after all.

"Yes, fortuitously so, since it makes her remarkably tolerant of aspects of your personality that would require me to thump your head against the nearest wall."

Nicholas said dryly, "When you meet her grandmother, it will give you an inkling of how she acquired her thick skin."

As their coach drew near the city prison, Nicholas saw no evidence of the unrest Reynard had spoken of. The streets of Vienne seemed busy as always, as calm as they ever were. He was sure the damage caused by the Sending in Lethe Square had stirred up some trouble, but Vienne had a long history and had seen far worse.

Then the coach passed the Ministry of Finance and entered the Courts Plaza.

The prison took up one side of the sweeping length of the open plaza. Its walls were of a mottled dark stone, several stories high, linking six enormous turreted towers. It had long ago been a fortification for the old city wall, and the places where the numerous gates had been filled in with newer stone were still easily visible. There were actually several entirely separate structures that made up the prison within those high walls, with a courtyard in the center, but they had all been interconnected and the court roofed over decades ago.

The last time Nicholas had been inside it was years ago, when he had first started to uncover some of Count Montesq's criminal dealings. He had discovered that a brutal murder that was the talk of Vienne had actually been committed by two men in Montesq's pay. The man who had been sent to prison for it had simply been in the wrong place at the wrong time and been framed by the actual perpetrators. Nicholas had had no evidence and little faith in Vienne's justice, so he had taken steps to obtain the innocent man's release. That was how he had first made Crack's acquaintance.

Engineering Crack's escape from the prison had been an unqualified success, especially since, as far as the prison authorities knew, there had been no escape. Officially, Crack was dead and buried in one of the paupers' fields in the city outskirts.

As their coach crossed the plaza, it passed the spot where an old gallows stood, a grim monument to Vienne's courts of justice. It hadn't been used for the past fifty years, since the Ministry had directed executions to take place inside the prison to prevent the gathering of huge unruly crowds. After Edouard's death, Nicholas had come every day to this plaza to look at that gallows, to touch it if he could do so unobtrusively, to confront it and all it stood for.

Ronsarde wouldn't be held in the prison itself, but in the offices of the Prefecture built out from the far side of the prison wall, extending halfway across the back of the plaza. The Prefecture's headquarters was a strange appendage to the grim prison and had many windows with carving around the gables and fancy ironwork. On the other side of the plaza were the Magistrates Courts and the Law Precincts. These structures were even more ornate, from the pillared portico over the entrance to the wickedly grinning gargoyles carved on the eaves and the depictions of Lady Justice wearing the regalia of the Crown of Ile-Rien above every entrance.

There was a massive fountain in the center of the plaza, with several statues of ancient sea gods spewing water from horns and tridents, and there were usually peddlers and penny-sheet vendors to cater to the constant stream of foot traffic. Nicholas frowned. Today the plaza was far more crowded than usual and the milling figures lacked the purposeful air of tradespeople or clerks moving to and from work. They were a mob and they were in an unpleasant mood.

Nicholas signaled for Devis to stop and he and Reynard stepped down from the coach. They had to keep moving to avoid being jostled and shoved by the crowd as Nicholas made his way along the edge of the plaza, trying to get closer to the end of the Justiciary closest to the prison.

The usual peddlers and food vendors were out but there was an angry group clustered around each one, debating loudly about necromancers and dark magic and taxes, and the failure of the Prefecture and the Crown to protect ordinary folk. There were a large number of idlers, but also clerks and shopworkers, women with market baskets over their arms and children in tow, house servants, and workers from the manufactories just across the river. He heard mention several times of Valent House, and also of Lethe Square. He supposed their adventure there hadn't helped the panic any. And there was no quick way to spread the word that that particular manifestation had been dealt with, except among the criminal classes.

Nicholas stopped at the steps that led down from the central fountain's dais, unable to make his way closer to the buildings. He was nearer the Courts than the prison and could easily see through the windows of the bridge that connected them on the second floor. Reynard stepped up beside him, muttering, "I'd like to know what the devil stirred up all this so quickly."

Nicholas shook his head, unable to answer. He had read *The Executions of Rogere* on the train ride, but what he thought of now was the fragment of *The Histories of Aden Cathare* that Dr. Uberque had quoted. *He concealed the traces of his passing with chaos. . . .*

Crack stood only a few paces away, watching the crowd around them with concentrated suspicion. Nicholas motioned for him to step closer and said, "Send Devis to tell Cusard to come here with as many of his men as he can bring. Hurry."

Crack nodded sharply and started back toward the coach.

Reynard stroked his mustache thoughtfully. "Are we anticipating trouble, or starting it?" he asked, low-voiced.

"Both, I think," Nicholas said. He raised a brow as uniformed constables forced some bolder curiosity seekers off the steps of the Courts. "Definitely both."

———

They waited. Crack rejoined them after sending Devis for Cusard, and through sheer persistence they made their way almost to the edge of the Courts' steps. Only one large foul-smelling individual objected to their presence: Nicholas gestured to Crack, who seized the man by the throat, yanked him down to eye level, and made a low-voiced comment that caused the offender to mutter an apology and back rapidly away when he was released.

The time scheduled for Ronsarde's hearing passed and Nicholas could tell they weren't opening the court yet, even for people who might have a legitimate purpose there. He thought that a mistake; they should have started as soon as possible and allowed anyone who could squeeze in to have a seat in the gallery. Then there would be no reason for most of the spectators to remain and they would drift off back to their own concerns. Delaying the hearing only fed the atmosphere of strained excitement.

The sky grew cloudy, but the morning breeze seemed to have died away completely. It was becoming warm and close in the plaza with so many bodies jammed into what was rapidly becoming a small area, which wasn't helping anyone's mood either. *He couldn't have chosen a better day for this,* Nicholas thought, whoever "he" was. *I'll have to remember to keep the weather conditions in mind should I ever need to start a riot.* He looked away from the Courts in time to see Cusard, with Lamane at his heels, making a path toward them. Reynard cursed suddenly and Nicholas snapped his gaze back.

At first he saw only a group of constables on the steps of the Prefecture. Then he swore under his breath. Ronsarde stood in their midst. On the steps of the Prefecture, not on the overhead bridge, where felons could be conducted across to the Courts out of the reach of angry mobs.

"There he is!" someone shouted and the crowd pushed forward.

Nicholas plunged forward too, shouldering aside the men blocking him, using his elbow and his walking stick to jab ribs if they failed to give way. He and Reynard had seen Ronsarde many times before and had both recognized him easily. That the troublemakers who had pushed their way nearest to the buildings had also recognized him, when their only exposure to him should have been as a fuzzy pencil sketch in the penny sheets, was a confirmation of his worst fear. Whoever had arranged Ronsarde's arrest was still at work and had no intention of allowing the Inspector to ever reach the magistrate's bench.

The steps were awash in people fighting, pushing. He saw one of the constables shoved to the ground and the others were already buried under the press of bodies. Nicholas paused to get his bearings and a man dressed in a ragged working coat seized his collar and jerked him half off his feet. He slammed the knob of his walking stick into the man's stomach, then cracked him over the head with it as his opponent released him and doubled over. Someone bumped into him from behind; Nicholas ducked, then realized it was Reynard.

More constables poured out of the Prefecture to vanish into the chaos and struggling figures pressed close around them. Everyone seemed to be shouting, screaming. Suddenly there was breathing space; Nicholas looked back and saw Reynard had drawn the blade from his sword cane.

That proves half these people are hired agitators, Nicholas thought. *Real Vienne anarchists wouldn't hesitate to throw themselves on a sword.* He had seen enough spontaneous riots in Riverside to know the difference. He managed to push his way up two more steps for a vantage point, Reynard close behind him. He couldn't see Ronsarde, but the nearest exit to the plaza was choked with people fleeing the fighting—sightseers escaping before the Crown intervened with a horse troop.

Crack tore his way out of the crowd and fetched up against them. "Can you see him?" Nicholas asked him, having to shout to be heard over the din.

Crack shook his head. "Maybe they got him inside."

Maybe . . . No, this was staged too carefully. *They wouldn't have allowed the constables to save him.* . . . Nicholas swore in frustration. "We need to get closer."

"There!" Reynard shouted suddenly.

Nicholas turned. Reynard had been guarding their backs, facing out into the plaza. Searching the press of bodies behind them, he saw the purposeful knot of men with Ronsarde among them. The Inspector threw a punch and managed a few steps back toward the Prefecture, then someone struck him from behind and he disappeared into the crowd.

They were taking him toward the prison side of the plaza. Nicholas started after them. Reynard caught his arm. "What are we doing, dammit?"

Nicholas hesitated, but only briefly. He had a dozen reasons for this, but the one that currently made the most sense was that someone badly wanted Ronsarde dead, the same someone who wanted them dead, and knowing the reason could tell him a great deal. "Find Ronsarde and get him out of here."

"I was afraid of that," Reynard snarled and whipped his blade up, abruptly clearing a path for them.

They fought their way forward, the crowd giving way before Reynard's weapon and their persistence. Nicholas couldn't see Ronsarde anymore but kept his eyes on the man who had struck the Inspector: he was a big man wearing a hat with a round crown and he remained just barely in sight over the bobbing heads around them. They broke through into a clear space and Nicholas saw there were at least six others accompanying Ronsarde's captor and that the Inspector was being dragged between two of them. They were taking him . . . *Toward the old prison gate? Why the hell . . . ?* Nicholas felt suddenly cold. *No, toward the old gallows.*

A firm shove sent him staggering forward a few steps; he sensed rather than saw the passage of something heavy and metal through the air behind him. He turned in time to see the tip of Reynard's sword cane protruding from the back of a man. The man's weapon, a makeshift club, fell to the pavement.

Nicholas pushed forward toward the gallows, hoping that Reynard and Crack could follow. The wooden trap had fallen in years ago, so if the Inspector's captors managed to hang him it would be slow strangulation rather than a quick snapping of the neck—that might buy Nicholas some time.

Another knot of rioters blocked his path. He plunged through them rather than going around and found himself ducking as a wild-eyed man swung a broken broom handle at his head. The man staggered and took another swing at him and Nicholas realized he was drunk.

Nicholas dodged around the obstacle, came up from behind, and seized him by the shoulders. The man obligingly kept swinging his club, apparently grateful for the temporary support. Nicholas steered his human battering ram in the right direction and the other combatants scattered out of his way.

Ronsarde's captors were taking the time to hang him because it was the sort of murder that would be attributed to a mob; if they had simply shot him someone might have been suspicious. *This wasn't Octave or his pet sorcerer,* Nicholas thought. Whoever planned this knew Vienne too well.

They broke through into another clear stretch of pavement. Nicholas aimed the drunk off to the side in case Reynard or Crack were making their way through behind them and gave him a push. The man staggered away in search of more targets and Nicholas ran.

Two of the men hauled Ronsarde up the steps of the gallows. One of the others spotted Nicholas coming and blocked his path. Nicholas saw the man's expression change from a malicious grin to sudden alarm. He reached into a coat pocket and Nicholas saw the glint of light on metal. He swung his walking stick, cracking the man across the forearm; the revolver he had been about to draw went skittering across the pavement.

The sight of the revolver made Nicholas realize he was somewhat unprepared for this particular undertaking and he dove for the weapon. He hit the pavement and grasped the barrel just as someone caught hold of the back of his coat. There was a strangled cry and his attacker abruptly released him. He rolled over to see Reynard withdrawing his sword cane from the man's rib cage, Crack guarding his back. Another man charged down the gallows steps toward them; as Nicholas struggled to his feet, he shouted to catch Crack's attention, then tossed him the walking stick. Crack turned and slugged the newcomer in the stomach with the heavy wooden stick, hard enough to puncture his gut, then caught him by the collar as he staggered and slung him out of the way.

Two down, Nicholas thought, *five remaining.* He plunged up the steps to the platform, which creaked ominously under the weight of the men atop it. Three wrestled with Ronsarde, who was still resisting despite a bloody face. One threw the rope over the scaffold and the other was standing and looking on. *The ringleader, obviously.* Nicholas motioned for Reynard and Crack to stay back, then pointed the revolver at the leader and said, "Stop."

They all stared at him, temporarily frozen. Ronsarde was on his knees, blinking, barely seeming conscious. His captors all had the rough clothing and heavy builds of laborers, but from the coshes they all seemed equipped with, they did precious little in the way of honest work. The very sort of men who worked for Nicholas. He smiled. "Let's be reasonable. Release him, and you can leave."

The ringleader took the smile for weakness. He grinned contemptuously and said, "He won't shoot. Go on—"

Nicholas pulled the trigger. The bullet struck the man in the chest, sending him staggering back into one of the heavy piers that supported the gallows. He slumped to the platform, leaving a dark stain on the old wood.

Nicholas moved the gun slightly to point it at the man holding the rope, the next likely ringleader candidate. Still smiling, he said, "Let's begin again. Release him, and you can leave."

The men holding Ronsarde dropped him and backed away, without waiting for a consensus from the rest of the group. The Inspector swayed and almost collapsed, but managed to stay upright. The one with the rope put up his hands nervously. Nicholas gestured with the pistol toward the edge of the platform. "Very good. Now run away and don't come back."

The men scrambled to the edge of the gallows and leapt down. Nicholas put the pistol in his coat pocket and crossed to where Ronsarde had slumped against one of the piers. As he pulled him up, Reynard stepped around to take the wounded man's other arm and said, "I hope you have some idea of what we're to do now?" His expression was skeptical. Crack, who hovered warily a few steps away, looked too nervous of Ronsarde to question Nicholas's next course of action.

Surveying the chaos around them, Nicholas muttered, "Why Reynard, you sound dubious." He couldn't spot Cusard and Lamane among the crowd; they must have been lost in the confusion. The riot seemed to be gaining momentum. More constables poured out into the plaza and their efforts to clear the area in front of the Courts were drawing an increasing number of previously neutral onlookers into the fray. Warders in dark brown uniform coats streamed around the gallows to join the fighting; Nicholas looked back and saw a small iron door now stood open in the prison wall behind them. The sunlight had been completely blotted out by heavy gray clouds; if it suddenly started to pour down rain, the situation might improve, but otherwise it was sure to get worse.

They could hand Ronsarde back over to the Prefecture, under the guise of good citizens preventing a mob murder. The problem was that whoever had arranged for Ronsarde to be exposed to the crowd in the first place had worked from within; they could be turning the Inspector over to the very man who had tried to kill him. "We can't give him back to the constables," Nicholas decided. That was as close as he wanted to get to admitting that he didn't know what to do next, even to Reynard. "Let's just get him out of here first."

"I couldn't agree more." This was so unexpected that Nicholas almost dropped Ronsarde. The Inspector's voice held only a little strain. His tone was as commonplace as if he were sitting in a drawing room instead of leaning on his rescuers, his face bruised and dripping blood onto their shoes. He smiled at Nicholas, and added, "I too lack confidence in our good constables at the moment."

Nicholas tried to answer and found his throat locked. Reynard must have been able to read something in his blank expression, because he said, "That's settled, then. Our coach is probably stuck outside the plaza. If we can just get to it—"

A sudden wind struck sharply: if Nicholas hadn't already been braced to support Ronsarde he would have stumbled backward. He gasped and choked on the foul taint in the air. The Inspector and Reynard coughed, too. Except for the worst pockets of fighting, the crowd seemed to pause. Stepping close to Nicholas, Crack muttered, "It smells like that room."

Not again, Nicholas thought. He said, "We have to get out of here." Not the same Sending, it couldn't be. It hadn't been able to come out in daylight and he had the evidence of his own eyes, besides Madele's word, that it was dead. This had to be something else.

He and Reynard got Ronsarde down the steps, then Crack grabbed Nicholas's arm, pointing at the opposite side of the plaza.

A mist rolled over the pitched slate roof of the Courts. It was thin enough that even in the dying light the shapes of the gargoyles and the gables of the building could be seen through it. But there was something about its advance that was inexorable, as if it was destroying everything in its path. It rolled almost majestically down the front of the Magistrates Courts, like a wall of water off a cliff, to pool on the steps at the base.

Then Nicholas saw movement behind it. Chips of stone fell from the gables, striking the pavement below. *It's going to destroy the Courts,* Nicholas thought, unable to see the purpose of it. The quicker-witted individuals in the crowd streamed toward the street exits of the plaza, though some pockets of fighters still seemed oblivious to what was occurring. Then something far larger than a stone chip landed on the pavement at the base of the building; the solid sound of flesh striking stone was audible even at this distance. Then it scrambled awkwardly to its feet and waddled out of the mist. It was large, gray, bent over like one of the orange apes from the jungles in the farthest parts of Parscia, but vestigial wings sprouted from its back. For an instant, Nicholas thought he was seeing a goblin, like some illustration in a book come to life. Then he realized it was one of the stone gargoyles from the building's gables, but it was stone no longer. In a heartbeat it was joined by two more, then a dozen, then another dozen.

It was too far across the plaza for them to reach the street exit, especially with Ronsarde as injured as he was. Nicholas looked around desperately, then focused on the prison wall behind them. The small door there was closed, but the guards had been running out that way only moments before. It might have been left unlocked. "Go that way." There was no other way to go. The prison had no other entrances on this side and the Prefecture was too far away to reach in time.

"It's obviously some sort of sorcerous attack, animating the decorative stonework," Ronsarde said calmly, as Nicholas and Reynard half carried him toward the door. "Who do you think it is directed toward?"

Reynard muttered, "I think I can guess." He glanced back over his shoulder. "They're coming this way—quickly."

"I didn't really want to know that." Nicholas motioned Crack ahead toward the door. The henchman reached it and pulled on the handle, then whipped a jimmie out of his pocket and jammed it into the lock.

Nicholas cursed under his breath and looked over his shoulder. The mist and the clouds had blotted out almost all the light: it might have been twilight rather than afternoon. People were still running away up the streets, but the ungainly gray shapes in the mist all moved this way. He gritted his teeth and resisted the impulse to tell Crack to hurry; the last thing he wanted to do at the moment was break the man's concentration.

Finally, Crack stepped back, shoved the jimmie into his pocket, and drew his pistol. He fired at the lock and on the fifth shot the door gave way with a whine of strained metal. Crack threw his weight on the handle, swung it wide open, and Nicholas and Reynard dragged the Inspector inside. The door wedged against the stone pavement when Crack tried to close it and he fought with it silently. Nicholas leapt to help him and together they tugged it closed, shutting out the approaching mist. Something outside howled angrily just as the door slammed shut. Reynard shoved the heavy locking bar into place.

Nicholas stepped back, reflecting that if one of the prison warders had thought to bar this exit then he and the others would be dead now. Reynard leaned against the door, looking annoyed more than anything else, and Crack wiped sweat from his forehead with his coat sleeve.

"This is a rather tense situation," Ronsarde said, conversationally. He was supporting himself on the wall, watching them thoughtfully. "What's our next course of action?"

CHAPTER TWELVE

Madeline walked the short distance from Coldcourt to the city gate and there got a ride on the public omnibus. She had learned from past experience that a public conveyance was always best when transporting valuable objects; even though it meant taking a more roundabout route to the warehouse, the omnibus was safer than a hire cab.

The spheres were in the carpetbag she held in her lap. Once at Coldcourt, she had taken time only to change from her dusty suit into a dress and jacket she thought of as Parlormaid's Day Out and stuff her hair under a dowdy and concealing hat. If she ran into any close acquaintances who recognized her as Madeline Denare, it would be easy enough to invent a story about some romantic escapade or wager. Most of her theater acquaintances were fools, and were sure to believe any lie as long as it sounded risqué enough. *You sound like Nicholas,* she told herself. *When did you become so cynical? Sometime after sorcerers started trying to kill me,* she answered. *Sometime after I met Nicholas.* She had also brought a muff pistol with her that was now tucked under her shirtwaist.

The omnibus was a long, open-sided carriage with bench seats accommodating about twenty persons if they were willing to become overfamiliar with one another. It was about half full now, and Madeline had managed to secure a seat not far behind the driver's box. She was staring abstractly at the people passing on the street, thinking of their current problem, when she noticed the sky. *When did it turn so dark?* She fumbled for the watch pinned to her plain bodice. It was still early afternoon. *Those clouds came in quickly; it'll rain in a moment.*

There was something happening in the street up ahead, people were running, shouting. Madeline sat up straighter, trying to see, and finally resorted to standing up and leaning out to see around the box. Other carriages, slowed by the sudden increase in foot traffic, blocked the way and the omnibus driver reined in.

Madeline frowned, tightening her hold on her carpetbag. The other passengers shifted and complained and one impatient man in a top hat got off to continue on foot. The driver was shouting for the other carriages to get out of his way or tell him what the devil was wrong.

"There's riot in Prefecture plaza!" one of the other drivers shouted. "Go around!"

"Not riot, sorcery!" A bedraggled man, his coat torn and his face bloodied, staggered out of the confusion of coaches and addressed the passengers of the omnibus and the other halted conveyances as though he was preaching to a packed hall. "Sorcery, ruin! Demons overrun the halls of justice. We are doomed! Flee the demons in the Courts Plaza!"

The omnibus driver watched this performance in silence, then took a piece of fruit from the bag at his feet, stood, and shied it at the speaker's head. Missiles from the other coaches and a few of Madeline's fellow passengers followed and the man ran away. The driver took his seat again, cursing, and began to try to turn the wagon. Madeline stepped off before this awkward operation could get underway and hurried across the crowded street to the promenade.

Demons weren't difficult to imagine after the Sending. *And the ghouls.* She supposed there were other people in Vienne who might currently be drawing that sort of sorcerous attention, but that they would also be visiting the Courts Plaza this afternoon was a bit too much for coincidence. No, it had to be Octave's pet sorcerer.

Madeline hesitated for only a moment. The warehouse was a mile or two away and the plaza was barely two streets over.

She cut through alleys until she reached Pettlewand Street, which paralleled the plaza. She passed enough people fleeing the other way and heard enough confused reports of mayhem to confirm that there was a riot, at least. She reached the avenue that would take her past the Prefecture building and the southern entrance of the plaza. It was ominously deserted, bare and colorless under the gray sky. She passed a darkened shop window and caught flashes of her own reflection out of the corner of her eye. She adjusted the strap of her carpetbag on her shoulder and kept walking. She could see the fanciful designs on the cornices of the Prefecture and the flight of steps flanked by two gas lamps in ornamental iron sconces. The sudden silence was so disconcerting it was almost a reassuring sight. Madeline told herself they were sure to know what had happened there, whether it was riot or sorcery, and if by some chance Nicholas and the others had been arrested . . . Well, it was the best place to find that out, too.

Madeline stopped abruptly as shouts sounded from up ahead. A group of people, uniformed constables and what appeared to be a mixed bag of court clerks, shopkeepers, and street layabouts tumbled around the corner of the Prefecture. Madeline stepped back against the wall of a shop, flattening herself against the dirty bricks as one of the constables pointed a pistol at someone just out of her line of sight and fired. She winced as the loud report echoed off the stone. If the riot moved into this street the Prefecture was likely to become a fortress under siege; she couldn't afford to be trapped there. She edged back toward the nearest alley.

The constable fired again and his target lurched into view.

Madeline swore, loud enough that one of the men glanced her way. The thing moving toward them was like a cross between a goblin and an ape, with a rictus grin and vestigial wings, its skin gray and pitted as weathered stone. It lurched forward again, moving with unexpected speed, and the constable who had fired at it dodged back out of its reach. *Well, my dear, it's definitely sorcery,* Madeline thought grimly, fumbling for her muff pistol.

Having the little pistol in her hand made her feel better, but she suspected the sense of security was only illusory. *Something of a higher caliber would be more comforting.* Through the heavy material of the carpetbag she felt one of the spheres start to hum and tremble, as it had when the ghoul had approached the attic window at Coldcourt. She clutched the bag to her chest, willing it to be quiet. *Not now.* The creature, goblin, whatever it was was a bare twenty paces away and she didn't want to attract its attention. It darted at one of the unarmed men and she raised her pistol, though she couldn't tell if bullets had any effect or if the constables who were already firing at it were just poor marksmen.

Something grabbed her arm and yanked her into the alley. She knew instantly it wasn't human, even in the semidarkness of the narrow, cave-like alleyway. The grip was cold, hard as rock, inescapable. Instinctively, she tried to throw her weight away from it, a move that would have sent a human attacker staggering, but the thing only gripped her arm more tightly. Her pistol went off as her fingers contracted at the pain. The little gun only held two shots; she gasped and barely managed to bring the lever back so she could try to fire again. Her throat closed from fear and shock; she couldn't even scream when the attacker squeezed her arm again and sent her to her knees.

Her eyes watering, she looked up at a creature similar to the one that menaced the men in the street. The body was the same but this one had horns sprouting from its broad forehead. It lifted its free hand in a fist; one blow would crush her skull. Madeline forced her numb hand to move, twisting the pistol down despite the bone-crushing pain and triggering it. The sound deafened her and a shard of rock struck her cheek, making her think she had missed and fired into the alley wall, but the creature roared in pain. It released her arm and she collapsed.

Do something—run, fight, get up. Her right arm was numb to the shoulder and she managed only to roll away. She came up against something soft and lumpy that buzzed like a beehive. Her carpetbag. *The spheres.* She awkwardly ripped open the bag with her one good hand and snatched out the topmost sphere.

The creature loomed above her and she thrust the sphere up at it.

The world went briefly white, overwhelmed by light. Time seemed to hang suspended. She could hear a great roaring and something seemed to tell her that she was seeing sound and hearing color. Then she blinked and time washed back over the alley.

The creature still stood over her but it was motionless, as if frozen into a block of ice. Cautiously, she reached up and touched the rough surface of its chest. *Not ice, stone.* Madeline lowered the still humming sphere to her lap. Now that she had leisure to study the creature, she could see it was a gargoyle. An ordinary roof gargoyle like the ones that guarded most of the private and public buildings in Vienne. She had an urge to push this one over and break it on the cobblestones. *Oh, for a hammer.* She started to stand and gritted her teeth at the pain in her right arm.

A loud bang sounded out in the street, followed by a peculiar thump of something heavy striking the pavement. Madeline groped at the alley wall and managed to get to her feet, moving forward enough to peer cautiously out.

There were three gargoyles in the street now but one had been turned back to stone and lay in pieces across the walk. As she watched, another suddenly halted in the act of seizing a constable and toppled over to shatter with a dull crash. Then she spotted the sorcerer.

The doors into the Prefecture building stood open and a spectacled young man in a frock coat leaned on the stair railing, staring at the last remaining gargoyle and muttering to himself. As he said his spell, the still restive sphere Madeline held shook violently.

She didn't wait to see the creature destroyed, but turned back to gather the other two spheres and tuck them hastily into the carpetbag. She had to get them away. If she could sense the power in them with her small talent, the Prefecture's sorcerer was sure to. She slung the bag awkwardly over her shoulder, still nursing her right arm. That was all she needed, to spend hours in a cell while court sorcerers determined that the spheres had nothing to do with the sorcery in the plaza, while Nicholas and the others were God knows where doing God knows what.

She stumbled out into the street only to be swept up in a wave of refugees heading for the Prefecture. Madeline tried to push her way free, but someone jostled her bad arm and she couldn't suppress a cry at the pain.

"This lady is injured!" someone called out. Madeline glanced around in confusion and realized he meant her. She was suddenly boxed in by a young constable and an elderly man, both staring aghast at her. Her sleeve was torn, revealing the discolored flesh of her forearm.

"No, really, it's just bruised," she managed to protest. "I must get home—"

They weren't listening to her. "There's a doctor inside," the constable said, urging her toward the Prefecture steps. The older man was helpfully gesturing at the others, exhorting them to look at what one of the horrible creatures had done to the poor girl.

Madeline planted her feet and started to express her wish to be let alone in no uncertain terms, then realized she was barely two paces away from the young sorcerer. She couldn't afford to draw his attention. She bit back a curse and let herself be guided up the steps and into the Prefecture.

The Prefecture's foyer was large but packed with shouting, pushing people. Coming into it suddenly from the daylight, Madeline was nearly blind in the gaslit dimness. One of her erstwhile rescuers took a firm hold of her good arm and guided her through the confusion. One could scarcely bludgeon someone in the foyer of the Prefecture and get away with it, crisis or not, especially when he was just trying to be helpful. Madeline decided she would have to let the doctor tend to her arm before making her escape.

A constable threw open the door to a room where the gaslight was turned up and high windows allowed in wan daylight. Madeline had barely a chance to focus on the group of men gathered around a table talking loudly before the constable said, "Dr. Halle, there's a lady injured here."

Oh, damn, Madeline thought weakly. Of course, Dr. Halle was in the Prefecture. Ronsarde had been about to go before the magistrates; where else would Halle be?

Dr. Halle swung around with an impatient glance that turned into a worried frown when he focused on her. He came forward to take her injured arm and Madeline found herself being ushered into a nearby chair.

One of the men standing around the table was Captain Defanse of the Prefecture. He was saying, "The attack is centered on the prison now, that's obvious." Defanse was a stout man with thinning dark hair. He was one of Ronsarde's chief supporters and had investigated Donatien's activities on numerous occasions, but most of the time without knowing it was Donatien he was after. If he recognized Madeline, it would be from seeing her on the stage at the Elegante.

"But the Courts—" someone protested.

"That's where the creatures came from. They were moving toward the prison," Defanse corrected, shaking his head.

"The important question, gentlemen, is who arranged for the sorcery?" The speaker was a tall man with graying hair and handsome if harsh features. *Oh, hell,* Madeline thought, light-headed from repeated shocks. *That's Rahene Fallier, the Court Sorcerer.* She wasn't sure how it could get any worse. *The Queen will be in here in a moment, I'm sure.*

Madeline shoved her carpetbag under the chair and put her feet on it. She was trembling from sheer nerves, but Halle would interpret that as reasonable due to her injury. She had never been this close to him before and this was his best chance to recognize her as the woman he had seen in disguise on other occasions, but his attention was torn between her injured arm and the men arguing in the other part of the room. Madeline allowed herself a small sense of relief; with luck he would never look more than cursorily at her face. "Nothing broken . . ." he muttered to himself, carefully palpating her forearm.

"No, just badly bruised," she whispered. She didn't want him to hear her voice. He was an avid theatergoer and she didn't want him to recognize her as Madeline Denare either. "I do need to be getting home—"

"One of the constables saw Ronsarde and the men who saved him from the mob go toward the prison," someone else said. He was another Prefecture captain; she couldn't remember his name.

Halle glanced back at the speaker, his lips compressed as if in effort not to make an outburst.

Defanse gestured in exasperation. "You think they were in league with the Inspector? Impossible!"

"You think this is all coincidence? To happen just as Ronsarde was being taken into the Magistrates Court?"

"The man was attacked by rioters and almost killed, surely you can't be-lieve this was somehow arranged as an escape attempt? I gave strict orders for the constables to escort the Inspector across the bridge, out of reach of the mob. I would ask them who countermanded those orders but all four men are dead."

"You suspect a conspiracy? Ridiculous!"

"Ronsarde would not use sorcery to cover his escape, not against his own con-stables," Fallier said suddenly. "Someone planned this without his knowledge."

"You're right, it's only bruised. You're lucky." Halle noticed Madeline's torn sleeve and looked up at the constable still waiting near the door. "Get this lady a coat so she can leave."

He was impatient to return to the argument and defend his friend Ronsarde but he still had time to think about her modesty. "Thank you," Madeline whis-pered, keeping her voice pitched low.

Halle met her eyes and hesitated, but said only, "You're welcome, young woman," and got to his feet.

Madeline grabbed her carpetbag, accepted the young constable's uniform jacket to cover her torn dress, and made her escape.

———

Nicholas knew they had to move now, while the prison was still in a state of chaos.

The room they stood in was bare and empty, lit by a solitary gas jet high in one limewashed wall, and obviously intended for no purpose other than as one more obstruction to the way outside. The floor was stone-flagged and there was one other door, a solid oak portal with heavy iron plates protecting the lock. Nicholas looked at it and felt a twist in his stomach. He didn't have the proper tools with him to drill through those plates, even if he had the hours necessary to do it. *If that's locked, we're done for right here and now.* He stepped forward and seized the handle, and felt almost light-headed from relief when it turned. He pulled it open, cautiously, and found himself in a corridor, narrow and low-ceilinged, lit by intermittent gas lamps and leading in one direction toward another heavy door and in the other roughly paralleling the outer wall.

"That's mildly encouraging," Reynard said in a low voice, stepping into the doorway after him. "That we're not trapped in here for the pleasure of whatev-er's after us, I mean. As to what we do now . . . ?"

Nicholas hesitated. Ronsarde's presence made the situation several times more problematic. "We could try the main gate, or throw ourselves on the mercy of the first official we meet, but . . ." He glanced back at Ronsarde.

The Inspector smiled grimly. "But explanations would be difficult? At the moment I also prefer a more unobtrusive exit." He would not be able to move with much haste. He was bleeding from a cut on the head, one eye was already swelling, and he limped with every step.

Very well, Nicholas thought. *Then we do it the hard way.* His eyes still on the Inspector, he asked, "Do you know this place at all?"

"No, only the public areas, unfortunately."

Crack watched Nicholas worriedly. Of all of them, Crack had spent the most time here, but his experience had been limited to the cellblock. Nicholas preferred not to get any closer to that section of the prison than absolutely necessary. "Give me a moment," he said, half turning away and shutting his eyes in an effort to concentrate. "I've been here before under similar circumstances." Not here, exactly, but on the upper floors.

He had committed a map of the place to memory when he had arranged Crack's escape, but that had been years ago. *Of course, you were dressed as a guard then, and you had keys to the connecting passages, and Crack was pretending to be dead.* Doing it without keys, a suitable disguise, or an apparently plague-ridden corpse to fend off casual interest would be considerably more difficult.

Sections of the map were coming back to him. He knew where they had to go; it was getting there that was going to be the problem. He said, "That open way looks easier, but it actually leads toward the warders, barracks, and the stairs up to the governor's quarters and the other offices. Straight ahead toward that door will take us to a point where we can get down to the level below this one, which will be much easier to move through." It was made up of the old cellars and dungeons, connected by a crisscrossing warren of corridors and passages. That was where they needed to go, where there would be far less chance of detection. The lower levels were inaccessible from the cellblocks and not well guarded. "The only problem is that past that door is likely to be a guard point."

"How many guards?" Reynard asked.

"At least two." Nicholas eyed the door. Crack's pistol was empty, its bullets expended on opening the outer door. The weapon Nicholas had taken from Ronsarde's abductors had only five shots left. "Do you have your revolver?" he asked Reynard.

"No. I didn't think it necessary in the Magistrates Court," he answered, glancing speculatively around the bare room. "Crack, hand me your pistol."

"It's empty."

"They won't know that."

While they were settling that, Nicholas took his scarf and tied it around the lower half of his face. He didn't want to make it too easy for the guards to recognize him later. He waited until Reynard had done the same, then he went to the door. "Get ready to force your way in behind me."

It was sheathed in heavy iron; there would be no way to force it with the materials they had at hand. Nicholas approached it quietly and listened but could hear nothing through the layers of wood and metal. He drew a deep breath and pounded on it. "Open up, quick, it's right behind us!" he yelled, pitching his voice toward the edge of hysteria.

He heard something from the other side, someone shouting about what the devil was going on, and he continued pounding and yelling. Moments passed, enough time for the men within to make a decision, to realize this door led away from the cellblocks, not toward them, and that this couldn't be an escape attempt, and to fumble with their keys. The door jerked and started to swing inward. Nicholas set his shoulder and slammed his weight against it.

The man on the other side of the door staggered back and Nicholas caught his coat collar and shoved the pistol up under his chin, snarling, "Don't move."

This was directed at the second man in the room, caught just standing up from a desk. Reynard pushed through the door behind Nicholas, caught the other guard by the arm, and slung him to the ground.

Nicholas stepped back so his man wouldn't be able to grab the pistol and said, "Turn around and lie facedown on the floor."

"What—What do you—"

He was an older man with thinning gray hair, gape-faced with astonishment. The one Reynard had flung down looked to be barely out of his teens. Nicholas found himself hoping he didn't have to shoot them. "Just do it," he snapped.

The two guards were unarmed, since unless there was some emergency, prison warders only carried clubs. When both men were lying facedown on the floor, Nicholas motioned for Crack and the Inspector to move on through the room. He tore the keys off the first guard's belt and handed them up to Crack as the henchman helped Ronsarde past.

"Their uniforms?" Reynard suggested.

"Yes, at least the coats," Nicholas said. "You take—" They both heard it at once, pounding footsteps echoing against the stone walls, coming from the corridor they had just passed through. "No time," Nicholas snapped. "Just keep moving."

Crack had unlocked the other door. Nicholas waited until the others were through and then backed toward it himself, saying, "Don't move, gentlemen, and no one will get hurt."

"You won't get away with this!" the older one said.

"You're very likely right," Nicholas muttered. He stepped back through the door and gestured for Crack to pull it to and lock it. Without the keys, the two guards would have to wait for their fellows before they could open this door again. Not that that was likely to be more than a few moments. Nicholas looked around, trying to get his bearings.

They were in another small dim antechamber with two more doors and another corridor branching off. Nicholas hesitated, thinking hard, then took the keys from Crack and stepped to the first door. He unlocked it and yanked it open, revealing a narrow staircase twisting down into darkness. He gestured the others ahead, then turned back to unlock the other door, the one that should, if he remembered correctly, lead to the long straight corridor to the lower cellblocks. He flung it open and turned back toward the stairs. Just let their pursuers believe they had taken that route, just long enough to let them lose themselves in the catacombs below. *They should have no trouble thinking us confused enough to go toward the cellblocks,* Nicholas thought, starting down the stairs and pulling the heavy door shut behind him. He shook it to make sure the lock had set again. *We're breaking into a prison, after all.*

He almost tumbled down the stairs in the dark, catching himself on the wall at the bottom under a barely burning gas sconce, and almost fell into Reynard. They were in a narrow, low-ceilinged corridor of dark stone patched with old brick, passages leading off in three different directions. There were a few gas sconces visible, obviously new additions, with their pipes running on the outside of the walls. Crack still supported Ronsarde. Nicholas motioned for them to be silent, though he doubted that would do any good if the guards decided to check down here.

The moments stretched. They heard a muted thump as someone tried the door above to make sure it was locked, then silence.

"It worked," Ronsarde said, quiet approval in his voice. "Simple but elegant."

Reynard looked at Nicholas. "Well, which way? Or do we flip a coin?"

Good question, Nicholas thought. He didn't know this level as well as the others. It had been a backup route for him in his original plan to engineer Crack's escape years ago, but he hadn't had to use it. "We'll try this way first."

The others followed, Reynard immediately behind him, with Ronsarde coming after, supporting himself with one hand on Crack's shoulder and the other on the slightly greasy stones of the wall. In the narrow corridor there was only room for one of them to help him at a time. That was going to tire Ronsarde more quickly and slow the rest of them down. *Worry about it later.* Keeping his voice low, Nicholas explained to Reynard, "What we have to make for is the southwest corner. That's the old chapel and mortuary and there's an outside door there for removal of the bodies. That's our only choice besides the entrance we came in and the main gate."

"Rather appropriate, if you think about it," Reynard commented, and Nicholas couldn't find it in himself to disagree. The farther away from the outer door, the staler the air became. Staler, and with a foulness under it that made the back of Nicholas's neck prickle.

His voice strained from the pain of his injuries and from trying to keep up, Ronsarde said, "If events turn any further against us, this may be our only opportunity to pool our resources. You saw the gentlemen who were pursuing me; I take it the sorcerer who animated the Courts' architecture is interested in you?"

"I suspect they may have been sent by the same person, whether they know it or not." Nicholas glanced back over his shoulder. "Do you know who arranged your arrest?"

"Within the Prefecture, no. Halle is currently attempting to uncover that intelligence, but since he can no longer risk trusting our former allies, it will be difficult. As to who ordered my arrest, I can only suspect Count Rive Montesq."

Nicholas stopped dead, for a moment all thought suspended, hearing that name. *Count Rive Montesq . . .*

Reynard thumped him in the back then, saying, "Escape first, revenge later."

Nicholas started forward again. *Careful, careful.* He would have to reveal a little to get more information, but he didn't want Ronsarde to realize how deeply he was involved. The Inspector must have recognized him as Nicholas Valiarde, or he would soon enough. If he recognized him as Donatien . . . *You would have to kill him.* As ironic as that would be, after risking his life as well as Reynard's and Crack's to rescue him. There would be no choice. Not when going to prison meant taking Madeline and the others with him. "Do you know anything about the sorcerer who is involved in this?"

"I know that there is one, that he is practicing necromancy, and that he is completely devoid of human mercy," Ronsarde said. "I might have discovered much more if I hadn't been interrupted so precipitously by my arrest."

"It's very possible he—" *believes himself to be Constant Macob,* Nicholas started to say, but the scream echoing down the corridor from somewhere ahead cut off the words.

They halted in startled silence and Nicholas felt for the revolver in his pocket, but the sound wasn't repeated. After a tense moment, Reynard said, "I know people must scream somewhat in the normal course of things in a place like this, but—"

"But not normally this far below the cellblock," Nicholas finished for him. "There shouldn't be anyone down here." Of course, Octave's mad sorcerer had gone to great lengths to get to them already, he wasn't going to let prison walls stop him.

There was another scream, startling out of the deep silence of the place, and Nicholas could tell it was much closer. "Back the other way," he said.

———

Madeline hurried down the street away from the Prefecture, but instead of turning toward the warehouse she took the other way, working her way closer to the plaza. When the official had mentioned the men who had run into the prison with Ronsarde, she had had a distinctly sinking feeling in the pit of her stomach. There was no guarantee it was Nicholas and the others, but . . . If he had sent someone for help, he would have sent to the warehouse only a few streets away, and that meant Cusard and Lamane.

She scouted the streets and alleys bordering the plaza, passing confused, fleeing people. Finally, she spotted Cusard's wagon on the roadside, the horses tied to the rails of a public water trough. She approached cautiously, but then she saw Cusard and Lamane, standing near the front of the wagon in agitated conversation.

They looked relieved at the sight of her and Madeline suspected that meant they were about to hand her a tricky problem. This thought was confirmed when Cusard greeted her with, "We're in trouble."

"Nicholas and the others?"

"In the prison."

Madeline swore a particularly vile oath, a luxury she usually didn't permit herself in front of people. Lamane even looked startled. She said to Cusard, "That's what I was afraid of. How?"

Cusard glanced toward a group of constables moving up the street, then gestured her toward the nearest alley. They moved a few paces down it, Madeline catching up her skirt out of habit to protect it against the filth-covered cobbles. The alley was open-ended and they could see a black wall across the street at its farther end. The prison wall.

"The Inspector was set on as they brought him out of the Prefecture," Cusard said. "There was a huge crowd gathered, a mob. Himself smelled a trap and he sent Devis for us, only we didn't get there in time to do nothing but watch."

"What did you see?"

"Some bullyboys took the Inspector off the constables and were going to hang him at the old gallows. I lost sight of where Nic and the captain and Crack went until they popped up there. They took the Inspector off the bullyboys and chased them away, and I thought, now they'll want a quick escape, but then the sorcery started."

"Those stone things off the buildings, yes, I saw those. Then what?"

"Then they ran in the prison, with those living statues right behind them. Just like Lethe Square, it's us this sorcerer's after, all right."

"Miss."

Madeline flinched and turned, badly startled. Not five paces away stood Dr. Cyran Halle. He must have waited just out of sight, around the corner of the alley.

"I heard your conversation," he said.

Lamane started to reach for something in his coat pocket and Cusard caught his arm. *No weapons, for God's sake,* Madeline thought. *We haven't done anything wrong, not that he's witnessed.* This was Ile-Rien, not Bisra, and thoughts and talk didn't count for as much. "What do you mean?" she choked out, trying to sound indignant.

"I followed you here from the Prefecture and I heard everything you said," Halle answered. His brow was furrowed with worry but his voice was calm. "I must speak with you."

"You can't prove nothing," Cusard spoke almost automatically. "It's your word against all three of ours."

Halle held up his hands, palms out, and Madeline wondered if he was asking to be heard out or showing he was unarmed. He said, "I recognized you. You were the nurse, in the morgue that day."

"That means nothing," Madeline managed to say. Her throat was dry. Pretending to be offended was no use. The circumstances were too suspicious.

Halle took a step closer, halted when Lamane shifted nervously. "I heard you just now," he repeated. "Your friends are the men who saved Ronsarde, who ran into the prison to get away from the sorcery. You want to get them out without the Prefecture being involved. I want to help you."

"Why?"

"You were in that room just now, you heard them. Someone arranged for that mob to be present and ordered the constables to take Ronsarde out on the steps instead of across the bridge, so the hired thugs could get to him. If he's taken by the Prefecture, it will just give whoever it was another chance to kill him." Halle hesitated. "If you are who I think you are . . ."

Madeline caught her breath. She felt as if someone had punched her in the stomach. Next to her, Cusard made an involuntary noise in his throat, but didn't react in any other way. She said, "Who do you think we are?"

"Ronsarde hypothesized your existence. He knew that this rogue sorcerer was encountering resistance from some person or group, and that there had to be something preventing that person or group from coming forward and reporting the sorcerer's activity. The incident in Lethe Square seemed to confirm this." Halle paused deliberately. "As to whatever it is that kept you from coming forward when the sorcerer attacked you, I don't know what it is and I venture to say that at this stage it hardly matters."

Madeline exchanged a look with Cusard. They were both too well schooled at keeping appearances to show relief, but he looked a little white around the mouth. Madeline turned back to Halle. *He doesn't know about Donatien—yet.* Ronsarde would recognize Nicholas as the son of Edouard Viller, but that would be all. *I need to come up with a story, something to explain what we're doing and why. . . . He doesn't want to know now, or thinks he doesn't, but he will soon. . . .*

"Please," Halle said urgently. "The streets are in confusion, the Prefecture is helpless, we need to do this now or we will lose our chance."

Madeline bit her lip. Her instincts said to trust him, but it was her instincts that she didn't trust right now. It came from knowing your enemy too well. She had heard all the stories Nicholas told, of Ronsarde and Halle at Edouard's trial; she had read Halle's accounts of the cases they had been involved in before that pivotal point, the cases since. The times she had tricked them her-self, the disguises she had worn or designed for others specifically to fool them, the plots she had participated in to circumvent them; she had become far too familiar with them. *God help me, I almost think of them as colleagues.* She had been startled when they had encountered Halle at the city morgue, but now standing here and speaking to him felt almost natural. *And you told Nicholas he wasn't wary enough; this man could have you sent to prison for the rest of your life.* She looked toward the dark stone wall, just visible through the open end of the alley passage. No, not that. She would put a pistol to her head before that.

Halle was watching her desperately. He said, "The only possible way in now is through the prison infirmary. I've assisted the surgeons there before. There are guards but I can get you past them without violence—"

"There's not been no violence, never, that wasn't self-defense," Cusard inter-rupted. "It was that sorcerer, whoever he is. Three, four times he tried to kill us with those ghouls and he killed all the people in that house—"

Madeline held up a hand to stop him. She said to Halle, "I'll need your word that nothing we say or do in the course of our association will be passed on to any official of the Prefecture."

"You have it," Halle answered readily. "But I'll need your word that no con-stables or civilians will be hurt or killed in what we're about to undertake."

She hesitated. "I can't promise that without reservation. If someone fires at me, I'll certainly shoot back, but I won't just kill someone for the sake of doing it, if that's what you mean."

Halle let out his breath. "That is satisfactory. I won't expect you to let your-self be shot for my scruples."

Madeline accepted that with a nod and turned to Cusard. "I'll need blasting powder. Go and fetch some for me."

Lamane looked as if he might faint. Cusard gaped at her. "Since when do you know how to set a charge?"

"You're going to show me how before we go."

Cusard closed his eyes, apparently in silent prayer. "Oh, no."

Halle said, doubtfully, "Blasting powder?"

"We can get in without violence, as you put it, but we won't get out, not with Ronsarde a wanted felon. We can't just steal a warder's uniform for him; too many of the constables have seen him, worked with him. We'll have to make our own way out."

"Young lady, you have a very . . . clear view of our situation." He took a deep breath and she realized this hadn't been easy for Halle either, that it was just as hard for him to trust her. *And he doesn't know as much about me as I know about him. He doesn't know I have a sense of honor, that I wouldn't break my word and shoot him as soon as I don't need him anymore.* He had been brave enough to approach her with Cusard and Lamane here; she knew they were cracksmen and housebreakers, not killers, but he didn't. He said, "We have no time to lose."

She nodded to Cusard. "You heard him. Hurry."

Cusard cursed, stamped his feet, and went.

"You won't regret this," Halle said, his eyes earnest.

Madeline nodded distractedly and began to pull the braid off her borrowed constable's jacket. *I regret it already,* she thought. *If this fails and I get us all arrested, I won't have to put a pistol to my head because Nicholas will kill me. And in all fairness I'll just have to let him.*

———

It was becoming more and more apparent that something hunted them through the darkened corridors of the prison.

Nicholas cursed when he saw their path blocked by another door. So far they had run into four locked doors that the keys Nicholas had taken from the guard upstairs refused to open, but two Crack had been able to force with his jimmie. Two had been too heavily plated to open with that method and they had had to change their route. There were not supposed to be doors blocking these passages; they must have been added in the last few years, perhaps as a response to more escapes.

He gestured Crack toward the door and leaned back against the dirty stone to let him pass. Ronsarde braced himself against the wall, his breathing harsh. Nicholas exchanged a worried look with Reynard. If they kept to this pace much longer they might kill the Inspector. Somewhere up one of the corridors a crash of splintered wood echoed, then a thump and a human cry, abruptly choked off.

"God, it's got another one," Reynard muttered. "How many does that make?"

"Four," Nicholas answered. He watched Crack work the door. This one looked like it might be forced, with luck, at least. When they hadn't been captured in the cellblock area, prison warders or constables must have been sent down to this level to search for them. Fortunately, the creature the sorcerer had sent after them was indiscriminate in who it killed. "If it knew where we were going, it would have had us by now. It's just . . . hunting."

"Maybe it's time to start hunting it," Reynard said.

Nicholas met his eyes, frowning. "What do you mean?"

"I'll slip back the way we came and try to kill it," Reynard explained. He looked back down the corridor. "That's the only course of action that makes sense. From what we've heard it moves fast; there's little chance of all of us outrunning it, not with an injured man and having to stop to break open doors every few minutes."

"You don't know the prison," Nicholas pointed out. He had considered taking this option himself but he was reluctant to commit to it until he could think of a sure way to destroy the creature that was trailing them. The most likely method he had come up with so far involved the gas jets the passages were lit with, but he couldn't think of a way to accomplish it without self-immolation and he didn't think the situation warranted that yet. "Even if you survived the encounter with this creature, you wouldn't be able to follow us out." *If we ever find the way ourselves, which is very much in doubt at the moment.*

"I don't have to find my way out. The Inspector is the one who is the fugitive from the Prefecture. Alone, I'm just another damn fool who ran in here to escape the sorcery."

"You'll need the pistol," Nicholas tried again. It would be certain death to confront the thing alone and he estimated he had until Crack forced the door to talk Reynard out of it. "And right now I've got it."

Reynard eyed him deliberately and smiled. "I bet I could persuade you to give it to me."

Someone else might have thought Reynard was threatening violence; Nicholas knew better. What did the leaders of other criminal organizations do when one of their men threatened to embarrass them into handing over a weapon? He lifted an eyebrow. "Not in front of the Inspector, surely. And besides, what would Madeline think? She'd have to challenge you to a duel." This was not facetious; Madeline had fought a duel before, using pistols, with a fellow actress who had insulted her. Reynard had acted as her second.

Crack hunched his shoulders, trying to divorce himself from the altercation. Ronsarde merely watched silently.

"True, and I would feel obligated to let her win," Reynard admitted, obviously torn. He knew Madeline's temper. "But still—"

The lock gave way with a creak and snap of old metal and Crack pushed it open.

Nicholas quickly offered the most pertinent objection, "We only have the one pistol, with only five bullets left, and if the creature gets past you, or you miss it in these corridors, we won't have a chance against it." This was what had stopped Nicholas from trying it himself, and until he perfected his theory concerning the gas jets, it remained the main objection. He gestured toward the now open door. "I suggest we get moving before this discussion becomes academic."

"True." Reynard looked convinced, for now, at least. "I hadn't considered that."

Nicholas hid his relief. "Perhaps we can find another horror for you to fight at a more convenient time," he said politely, as Reynard stepped toward the door.

"Oh, but I thought you had your heart set on us all dying together?"

Nicholas decided to let Reynard have that one and turned back to take the Inspector's arm and help him through. Ronsarde's expression had gone from quiet observation to quizzical amusement, which quickly shifted back to bland politeness when he caught Nicholas's eye. Nicholas was left with the rather nervous feeling that they had just revealed more about themselves than they should.

They made their way through the door, Crack shutting it and wedging it closed behind them.

Nicholas handed Crack the revolver without further comment from Reynard. Crack took the lead, with Nicholas assisting Ronsarde and Reynard following behind. About fifty paces down the dimly lit corridor, Crack lifted a hand to stop them. Nicholas waited, until Crack glanced back and whispered, "Smell that?"

Nicholas frowned, trying to detect something in the stale air besides the normal stink of the prison. Then he had it. There was an animal odor, a foulness like the one that hung around rat-infested buildings, but far worse and growing stronger.

"It's gotten ahead of us," Reynard whispered.

"We're so turned around we may have gotten ahead of it," Nicholas answered. "Can you see anything moving up ahead?" He could see the open area where the corridor joined another passage, this one with a lower ceiling and fewer lights.

"No. Can't hear anything."

"The other victims probably couldn't hear anything either," Ronsarde pointed out quietly.

Reynard and Nicholas exchanged a look. "He's fitting in well, don't you think?" Reynard commented, sparing a smile for the Inspector.

Nicholas decided he didn't have time to be annoyed. "Move forward—slowly," he said.

Crack reached the intersection first and held up a warning hand to halt them. They stopped, Reynard taking a firmer grip on his sword cane.

After a moment, Crack motioned them forward.

On the floor of the wider area where the two passages met, a man in a prison warder's dark uniform lay in a crumpled bundle, facedown, one arm twisted into an unnatural position, a spray of drying blood around him. A heavy steel door barred one end of the intersecting passage, the other led off to the left, the intermittent gaslights along its length revealing nothing but bare stone.

Nicholas could see the door was firmly shut and locked and he knew the creature hadn't come down the corridor they had just come up. He looked down the apparently empty passage. *It's there. It just doesn't know we're here. Yet.*

Nicholas motioned Crack to hand the revolver to Reynard, then pointed to the guard and mouthed the word "keys." Crack nodded.

Reynard took the pistol and stepped silently across the corridor where he could cover the open passage. He glanced worriedly at Nicholas, who knew what he was thinking. *We can be as quiet as we like, now,* Nicholas thought, *but it is going to hear that door open.*

Crack found the ring of keys on the warder's belt, then stepped to the door. He fit the key into the lock and carefully turned it. The tumblers clicked loudly in the silence.

There was no sound from the open passage.

Nicholas quickly helped Ronsarde past the dead prison guard and through the door. As Reynard turned to follow, a sudden rush of air dimmed the nearest gas jets. Nicholas let the Inspector go, his shouted warning instinctive and incoherent. It was enough for Reynard, who dove through the door, Crack slamming it shut almost on his heels.

Something heavy struck the thick metal with a thump that made the stones under their feet tremble. There was a pause, and then the handle jerked as it was pulled from the other side. "The keys?" Nicholas whispered, his throat dry.

Crack held up the bundle of keys and there was a collective exhalation of relief. If those had been left in the lock . . . Nicholas thought, *Well, our troubles would have been over much sooner.*

"Good man," Reynard told Crack. "Now let's get out of here before it finds another way past that door."

Nicholas took the bundle of keys from Crack. They could move faster now at any rate, and take a more direct route to their goal, if they could avoid the guards. He just hoped they could move fast enough.

CHAPTER THIRTEEN

The entrance to the prison infirmary was dangerously near the Prefecture, but Madeline hoped that the confusion that still reigned in the plaza on the other side of the building would keep anyone from noticing them. She and Halle waited on the opposite street corner, using the projecting bay window of a pottery shop to stay out of the prison guards' view. Even now, with people running everywhere, the guards might be alert for someone showing too much interest in their position outside the gate.

The infirmary door was set back in the dark stone wall, not as large as the main gate but still imposing, and there seemed to be four uniformed warders armed with rifles on duty all the time. Madeline smoothed down the front of her borrowed constable's coat; she had removed the braid from it so it was only a plain dark jacket. With her gray dress and the jacket covering the tear in her sleeve, she should make a passable nurse. She knew there were also cellblocks for women convicts; once inside she might be able to assume a wardress's costume and gain more freedom to search, but it was useless to plan when she didn't know what she would encounter once they passed those doors. She noted with annoyance that her hands were shaking. She always got stage fright before her best performances.

Halle paced nearby, his agitation evident, but he hadn't attempted to engage her in conversation. She was glad of that. She saw Cusard approaching again and straightened expectantly, taking a deep calming breath. It was always worst right before the curtain went up.

Cusard stepped a little farther down the alley, drawing a brown paper–wrapped parcel out of his coat. "Here it is." He handed it to Madeline carefully. "You remember all I told you?"

"Yes. A fourth of a cap for a wooden door, a whole one for a steel door, at least four for an outer wall of stone and plaster, and a coffin full for a supporting wall, because that's what I'll need if I use it on one." She looked at Halle. "Can we put this in your bag, Doctor?"

Halle nodded, his face preoccupied. "Probably wise. If they searched you—"

"It would be disastrous." She waited for Halle to open the bag and lift out the top tray of instruments so she could place the small package carefully within.

Cusard eyed Halle thoughtfully, then said to Madeline, "And I brought you this, just in case." He handed her a six-shot revolver and a small tin box of extra bullets.

Madeline checked it automatically to make sure it was properly loaded, then started to put it in the bag. Cusard coughed sharply.

Madeline knew what that meant but shook her head firmly. "I can't carry a pistol into the prison in my pocket. They know Dr. Halle, they know he investigates for the Prefecture. If they find it in his bag the most they will do is take it away."

Halle looked toward the prison. "I fear my reputation won't be of much use to anyone after this." He glanced back at her. "But I'll worry about that later."

Madeline hesitated. There was something else she couldn't risk carrying into the prison in her pocket. She had given the two quiescent spheres in her carpetbag to Cusard to take back to the warehouse safehole. The active one, which she knew had been created with Arisilde's help, was wrapped in her handkerchief and currently weighing down her coat pocket. Both logic and instinct had said to hold on to it. *Witch's instinct,* Madeline thought. Not always worth listening to when you weren't one. Logic, and something she thought of as artist's instinct, told her to trust Halle.

She drew the sphere out of her pocket, carefully, feeling it thrum lightly against her fingers, and lowered it into the bag.

"What's that?" Halle asked, frowning.

Cusard looked puzzled as well. Knowing him, he had put the whole carpetbag in the safe without opening it. *Knowing Nicholas, Cusard was probably afraid Count Montesq's head was in it,* Madeline thought. She explained, "This is a magical device that may help us if we run into any more of those walking statues, or any other sorcery."

"Ah." Halle sounded relieved. "How do you use it?"

Good question, Madeline thought wryly. "I don't know. It works by itself."

Halle's expression was doubtful and Cusard rolled his eyes in eloquent comment; Madeline ignored both of them. She said, "May I carry your bag, Doctor? The guards know you, but I need a prop." That was true in more ways than one. She hadn't realized before what a calming effect donning makeup and proper costume had on her.

Halle closed the bag and handed it over.

As they hurried across the street toward the prison, Madeline wondered what Nicholas would say. *Nicholas damn well better not say a word,* she thought suddenly, remembering he had been the one to go into the damn place first, with Inspector Ronsarde of all people, and cause all this. Then they were in the shadow of the wall and under the arch that protected the entrance, the pavement damp underfoot and the stone radiating cold, and it was time to stop thinking entirely.

The man who stepped forward to stop them was a constable, not a prison warder. "There was a report of men injured here," Dr. Halle said quickly, before the man could speak. He managed to sound both out of breath and anxious, though undoubtedly the anxiety was real. Madeline thought his approach was ideal; guards from the prison had been involved in the riot and were sure to have been injured. No one could know if they had all been attended to yet or not.

The constable looked confused and mulish, but a prison warder came forward, saying, "I thought they was all took to the surgeons. They said—"

"No, there are more still inside," Halle interrupted. "I spoke to Captain Defanse not an hour ago."

The prison warder swore and gestured emphatically at the heavy iron door. There was a grill in the center where another sentry could peer through; it swung open with a creak and then Halle hurried inside and Madeline followed him.

They passed through at least three grim chambers each guarded by heavy doors, iron gates, blank-eyed men, existing only to prevent those inside from getting out. Madeline tried not to think about the getting out part. *Find Nicholas and the others first, then worry about the rest.*

The next ironbound door opened into a tiny gray-walled court, little more than a shaft to let in light and air. Then another door opened for them and she knew from the thick odor of carbolic that they were passing into the prison infirmary.

It was a high, stone-walled chamber, with a vaulted ceiling overhead, with still visible oval patches of newer stone high on the walls where windows had been filled in long ago. The farther end was walled off by wooden partitions, but the beds in the two long rows nearest them seemed to be mostly occupied by constables or warders. There were guards at the door they had just come through and a few women in dresses of the dull brown of the prison warder uniform: wardresses probably hastily pressed into service to tend the injured.

From the shape and size of the place it had probably once been an old chapel. Madeline saw another door at the opposite end that would lead farther into the prison interior. Then she spotted a man who must be the Infirmarian, a stoop-shouldered young man with a frazzled appearance and spectacles, dressed in an old suit with a stained apron over it. Halle saw him too, but apparently not quite quickly enough, because he made to dodge behind a curtained partition and stopped when the Infirmarian called, "Dr. Halle! I didn't realize you were here."

Halle glanced at her and stepped forward to shake hands as the younger doctor hurried toward him, saying, "We've had quite a day, as you can see."

"Yes," Halle said, "I've been called in to speak to the governor about something. I'm not sure if he'll still be able to keep our appointment in this emergency, but I thought I'd better—"

"Of course, but while you're here, could you look at this one case, just for a moment. . . ."

Halle's lips thinned in frustration but he allowed himself to be led away. Madeline kept her eye on him, making sure the Infirmarian was only leading him down the row of beds a little ways, though she supposed it was too early to suspect traps. Halle's explanation had been offered smoothly enough, though a little too readily; fortunately, the other doctor seemed too busy for suspicion. *And who would suspect Dr. Cyran Halle of as mad a plan as this?*

She should use the time to gather information and try to discover if Ronsarde had been recaptured and if there had been anyone with him. One of the prison wardresses stood nearby, washing her hands in a metal sink against the wall. Madeline started toward her.

"Madame!" someone said. Madeline was too well trained from stagework to jump guiltily or allow herself any other reaction. She ignored the preemptory summons and kept walking. Out of the corner of her eye she could see a man approaching her. *This is trouble,* she thought. He was older, stern-faced, dressed in a dark, very correct suit. Not another doctor. With the way her luck was running, it was probably the prison governor himself.

He came straight toward her and she had to stop and acknowledge him with a nervous little duck of the head, the gesture a woman in her position would be expected to make. The nervous part wasn't hard to manage. "Who are you?" he demanded.

"Dr. Halle's nurse, sir." That should quiet him and send him off. Dr. Halle was a frequent visitor here.

Instead the man turned, spotted Halle with the other doctor, and stared at him, his eyes darkening with suspicion. Madeline felt a coldness grow in the pit of her stomach.

Halle glanced up and saw him. He was too far away for Madeline to read his expression accurately, but she didn't think he looked happy. He excused himself to the Infirmarian and came toward them.

"Dr. Halle," the man said as he approached. "What are you doing here?"

Halle's expression was grim. He hesitated, then said, "Could we speak privately, Sir Redian?"

All Madeline felt was disgust at her luck. She didn't need to be told this was some high official of the prison, someone who wouldn't believe their hastily concocted lies. Redian eyed Halle a moment, then said, "Come this way."

Halle started after him but Madeline stayed where she was, trying to fade into the furniture. But Redian snapped, "Your nurse also, please."

Madeline swore under her breath. *Of course, I was always more accustomed to stealing scenes than to disappearing into the chorus.* Halle glanced back at her, his features betraying nothing, and she had no choice but to follow.

They were led away past a row of cubicles screened off by canvas partitions to a small office that must belong to the Infirmarian. It was cramped, the desk and shelves overflowing with papers, books, and medical glassware; not nearly grand enough for someone with a "Sir" in front of his name. Redian closed the door behind them and said, "Well?"

That single uncompromising word didn't give Halle much to work with and Madeline couldn't contribute without ruining her role. She stood with downcast eyes, her hands beginning to sweat on the handle of Dr. Halle's medical bag. The walls that blocked this office off from the rest of the infirmary were thin and would conceal no loud noises. She wondered if she would have time to get the pistol out of the bag if Redian called for help, and exactly what good that might do her. The little room had no windows to leap out of. No, if Halle couldn't talk his way out of this—and it seemed unlikely—their only chance would be to take Redian hostage. *And that's no chance at all,* she thought.

Halle said, "I'm not sure what the cause is for this suspicion."

It was evasive but it made Redian talk. Glaring, he said, "The reason for suspicion is that your colleague Ronsarde escaped from the constables under what I lightly call extremely suspicious circumstances. The last reliable report we have is that he entered this institution. Now I find you here."

"That's ridiculous," Halle said, incredulous and annoyed. "Ronsarde was abducted, almost killed, you can't accuse him—"

"I was on the steps when the riot started," Redian retorted. "I know what I saw."

Halle had managed to distract him into a side issue but he was still only playing for time. "I don't care what you saw." Halle turned, took the medical bag from Madeline, and opened it as if looking for something, then set it down in the chair she was standing next to, all the while saying angrily, "And if you knew anything at all you would realize the charges against him were complete fabrications."

Brilliant, Madeline thought and started to breathe again. He had placed the pistol easily within reach, almost directly under her hand. It wasn't quite as good as working with Nicholas but close, very close. Halle turned back to face Redian, shifting enough to the side that he blocked the man's view of both the bag and Madeline's right arm. That might give her the edge she needed; if she didn't manage to surprise Redian, he would have time to call for help.

"That is hardly the point," Redian was saying. "If Ronsarde had a hand in this riot—" He stopped, grimaced and added, "And that is hardly the point either. I want to know why you've come here, Halle. Do you have anything to do with the armed men who forced their way through one of the guard rooms after Ronsarde escaped?"

"I can't believe you are accusing me—"

"Oh, we haven't caught them yet, but we will. Now give me an answer or I'll have you turned over to the Prefecture on suspicion of collusion in an escape."

Madeline dropped her handkerchief and bent down to reach for it, reaching instead into the bag and finding the grip of the pistol. The door burst open and Halle started and turned. Madeline had a heartbeat to make the decision and stayed where she was, half bent over, her hand inside the bag. She looked at the door and saw a young man in constable's uniform standing there, and almost drew the gun, but he wasn't looking at her.

The constable breathed hard, his eyes wide. He said to Redian, "Sir! We found five dead men in the lower level."

"What?"

"They're torn apart—it's sorcery, like what was outside."

Forgetting Halle, Redian strode to the door, following the constable. Halle looked at Madeline, his face a study in mixed relief and consternation. "Follow him?" he asked softly.

"Yes," she whispered, and pulled the pistol out of the bag and slipped it into the pocket of her jacket.

Nicholas approached the archway carefully. Gas hadn't been laid on in the last few corridors and it was as dark as pitch. Their source of light was a stub of candle Crack had had in his pocket, lit from one of the last sconces. It was now dripping hot wax onto Nicholas's glove as he slid carefully along the damp wall. The curve of it and the way it was constructed suggested the prison sewer outlet was just on the other side. He hoped they wouldn't have ghouls to contend with as well, though he didn't see any way in from the sewer tunnel.

Nicholas reached the darker shadow across the wall that was the low opening of the archway. A current of air came from it, also damp, but just as stale and flat as the atmosphere in all the passages. It was not an encouraging sign.

Improvements in the walls, gas laid on, new doors, Nicholas thought. Let them not have had time to block in the catacombs that led up from the old fortress's crypt to the new prison's mortuary. Let fate grant him that one small favor.

No ghouls or other inhuman products of an obsessed sorcerer's craft leapt out at him and he slipped inside the archway. He lifted the candle.

The jumbled contents of the low-ceilinged chamber were in the disarray he remembered. Old bones, splintered wood from coffins, broken fragments of fine stone that had once sealed grave vaults, all heaped on the stone-flagged floor and covered with dust and filth. Except that a path had been hewn through it, pushing the jumbled mounds to the walls. At the far end, the passage that should have led upward was sealed with nearly new brick.

Nicholas was too tired to curse Fate at the moment. He would have to remember to do it later. *They must have had escapes, somehow.* He couldn't take credit for that. When he had broken Crack out a few years ago, he had left a reasonable substitute in the form of a recent corpse from the city morgue in his place; Crack was marked down in the prison records as dead. This debacle was the result of untidy persons who broke out on their own and left trails any fool could follow.

He ducked back out the archway and returned down the passage to where the others waited. "It's blocked. There's only one alternative."

"Steal guard uniforms and try to bluff our way out," Reynard said. His sour expression revealed how likely he thought the chances of success were.

Nicholas knew success was not only unlikely, but with Inspector Ronsarde along, wounded and sure to be recognized by any constable they might pass, it was damned impossible. At this point he was even desperate enough to risk the sewer, but they had no way to get to it. "I'm open to suggestions," he said dryly.

Leaning heavily against the wall, Ronsarde said promptly, "I have one."

"If it's the one you've had the last three times I asked, I don't want to hear it again," Nicholas said. He was aware his patience was wearing thin, making him more likely to make mistakes, but there was little he could do about it now.

Ronsarde only grew more determined. "You said yourself, if I am not with you it would be relatively easy to explain your presence. You could walk out of here with a blessing from the prison officials—"

"And leave you to bleed to death?" Nicholas interrupted. *What kind of man do you take me for?* He wanted to ask, and managed to hold it back just in time. Damn fool question to ask Ronsarde, when he didn't know himself.

"It is out of the question," Reynard said, but he said it in his cavalry captain's voice, very unlike the indolent tone of the bored sybarite that he usually affected. "Because it would be giving in to the bastard, whoever he is, who has gotten us into this with his damned sorcery. And that's what he wants us to do, so that is what must be avoided at all cost. That's elementary, for God's sake."

"This sorcerer wants you dead," Nicholas elaborated. He was grateful that Reynard was still supporting him; raised mostly in the slums among the criminal classes, among which he counted his paternal relatives, he wasn't accustomed to that kind of loyalty. "He went to an untold amount of trouble to arrange it. You must be close to discovering him. If you're taken by the authorities he'll move against you again, probably even more swiftly and probably taking quite a few other innocent bystanders down along with you."

Ronsarde, who wasn't used to being argued with so effectively, said heatedly, "You forget the most likely hypothesis is that the man is simply barking mad and has seized on me the same way he evidently has seized on you gentlemen, and he'll pursue us to the end no matter how close or how far we may be from discovering his identity or whereabouts."

Nicholas and Reynard both started to answer but Crack, having reached the end of his patience, snapped, "You're doing it again. You're standing still and arguing."

Nicholas took a deep breath. "You're right; let's keep moving." He turned and started back down the corridor.

Crack shouldered Ronsarde's arm despite the Inspector's mutinous glare and followed. Reynard caught up to Nicholas in a couple of long strides and asked, "Where are we going?"

"If I knew—" Nicholas began, speaking through gritted teeth.

Obviously feeling he had to make up for his earlier show of nobility, Reynard said, "Sorry, sorry. Just trying to think ahead again; I can't seem to shake the habit."

Nicholas said, "Try."

———

Madeline and Halle followed Redian out into the infirmary again. There was a stretcher sitting on one of the long wooden tables holding the body of a man. Madeline caught a glimpse of flesh torn away to the bone and grabbed Dr. Halle's arm. This was partly in relief that the body was that of a constable and not Nicholas, Reynard, or Crack, and partly to keep Halle from rushing up to it with the other doctors.

Redian stared down at the body of the constable, his expression sickened. He said, "Has there been any sign of Ronsarde, or the men with him?"

"No, sir, nothing." The young constable looked ill. There were bloodstains on the sleeve of his uniform. "We thought they were in the other wing so the search was concentrated there, and we only sent a few men down to the cellars."

Madeline drew Halle back from the frightened group around the stretcher and said, "Whatever did this is searching for Nicholas and the others."

He nodded. "There are a great many passages down in the lower levels. I don't know why they would have gone there unless they were forced to it. Wait, there was an escape using an old tunnel up from the crypt to the prison mortuary, so the tunnel was walled up. Could your friends have been making for it, thinking it was still in existence?"

Madeline bit her lip, considering. "When was it walled up?"

"Only last year."

"Yes, they could have thought it was still there."

Halle glanced back at Redian and began to move toward the corridor at the back of the infirmary, drawing her with him. "Then I suggest we try to find them before anyone or anything else does."

"My thoughts exactly," Madeline murmured.

———

Nicholas traced their path back, finding a narrow stairway leading upward. They approached it with great caution since it was the only way up in this wing and the searchers might be watching it. But the intersection of corridors near the stairwell was just as empty as the other tunnels.

Leaving the others at the bottom, Nicholas went up to the first landing until he could lean around the wall and see what lay at the top. The head of the stairs was barred with a metal door with an iron grill in the top portion. He could tell the room beyond it was lit, that was all. After a moment of thought, he decided to risk it and crept upward toward the top of the stairs, glad that they were scarred stone instead of wood and there was no chance of creaking.

He edged cautiously up to the door and looked through the grill. Another guardroom, with two warders and a constable deep in worried conversation. One of the warders had a rifle. *That can't be on our account, can it?* Nicholas thought. *We haven't even killed anyone yet.* No, it had to be for whatever was hunting them through this maze. *They must know about the creature by now, surely.* If the authorities killed the thing, at least it would be one less obstacle in their path, Nicholas decided, as he crept carefully back down the stairs. Of course it would also make it easier for the constables to hunt them. . . .

At the bottom of the stairwell the others waited anxiously. "Well?" Reynard asked.

"Two warders and a constable, well armed." Nicholas described the door and the guardroom briefly, then took a deep breath. This was not a good plan but it was all he could think of, and they didn't have the time to sit about waiting for him to turn brilliant. "Crack will pretend to be a warder, and fumble with the keys to open the door." Crack nodded, not bothering to question this. His coat was dark brown, close in color to the coats the warders wore and in the dim light of the stairwell, it would be temporarily convincing. "You'll have a wounded man in tow to add an air of urgency."

"I shall be the wounded man, I think," Ronsarde said. He pointed to his right eye, which was nearly swollen shut and surrounded by a large purpling bruise. "This is rather convincing."

"It'll do." It was too bad they couldn't manage some more blood but . . . Nicholas reminded himself not to get wrapped up in detail. "And once the door is opened, Reynard and I will push through and take them by surprise." *And then we shall all be shot and killed.* He looked at Reynard, expecting him to say something along those lines.

Reynard merely smiled and said, "It sounds perfect to me."

Just then, they heard raised voices from the upper reaches of the stairwell, echoing down from the guardroom through the grill in the door. A low mumble of male tones, then a woman's voice, the words muffled but clearly urgent. Frowning, Nicholas took an unconscious step up. It couldn't be. "That sounds like—"

"Madeline," Reynard finished, looking worriedly at Nicholas. "She wouldn't, surely she wouldn't."

Crack swore and clapped a hand to his forehead, the greatest emotional outburst Nicholas thought he had ever seen from his henchman. And it was all the confirmation he needed. He climbed the stairs to the first landing, listening.

From here he could pick out occasional words but nothing to make sense of this. He heard another man's voice with a more educated accent, saying something about medical attention. Ronsarde boosted himself up the last few steps and grabbed Reynard's arm for support. "That's Halle," he whispered, his tone incredulous. "What the—"

"Dr. Halle?" Nicholas asked, managing to keep his voice low, though what he wanted to do was rage.

"Yes, certainly."

Dammit, dammit. Nicholas gestured for the others to stay back and crept up to the door again. He flattened himself back against the wall and managed a quick glance through the grill. Madeline was in her dowdy nurse persona and carrying a doctor's bag, but the light in her eyes was dangerous and entirely her own. *She's distracted and slipping out of character—I'll have to speak to her about that,* he thought. *And a few other things.* He recognized the man with her as Dr. Halle and his mouth set in a grim line. *The nerve of the woman.*

All three of the guards faced away now, arguing with Halle. And Nicholas's irritation with Madeline's precipitous behavior didn't change the fact that they would never have a better chance to get past this door. He stepped back down to the others and said softly, "Yes, it's them. Now let's go, just as we planned."

They scrambled quietly to get into position, Crack and Ronsarde moving to the step just below the landing, Nicholas and Reynard behind them and ducking down so they wouldn't be seen. At Nicholas's signal, Crack banged on the door suddenly, shouting, "Open up, it's right behind us!" With Ronsarde moaning in pain, he stuck one of the keys in the lock and jiggled it, as if in his panic he couldn't make it turn.

There was shouting from the other side of the door, then the lock clicked and one of the guards jerked it open. Ronsarde pitched forward to collapse at the man's feet, immobilizing him and keeping the door from being slammed shut. Crack lurched forward, apparently stumbling over his wounded companion, then he knocked the startled guard flat. Nicholas and Reynard pushed forward before the other two men could react, Reynard catching the rifle barrel just as it lowered to cover them. He slammed the wielder back against the wall. Nicholas looked frantically for the third man and saw Madeline had him by the collar with a pistol shoved under his ear.

Nicholas stepped back, letting Reynard tell their prisoners to lay down on the dirty floor. When Crack removed the constable from Madeline's grasp, Nicholas said, "Well, this is a surprise."

"We found you," Madeline said, sounding quite pleased with herself.

Nicholas stared at her, not sure if he couldn't answer because he was furious or because he was merely exhausted. He glanced at Dr. Halle, who was trying to examine Ronsarde's injuries despite the Inspector's attempts to fend him off. "It's moderately helpful. Now there are six of us stuck in here."

Madeline's brows lowered dangerously. She opened the medical bag, burrowed in it, and produced a small paper-wrapped packet. "Did you think we would come in here with no notion of how to get out again?"

Reynard was tying up one of the warders with the man's own belt. He glanced up and laughed shortly. "*We* did."

Nicholas glared at Reynard, then said, "What's that?"

"Blasting powder. Cusard's special mix."

Nicholas gasped in relief. "Brilliant!" He snatched the packet from her.

"You're welcome," Madeline said with acerbity.

Then Nicholas saw what else was in the bag. "You brought one of the spheres? I told you to take them to—"

"I was," Madeline interrupted. "I thought it would be useful against all this sorcery—"

"Useful? How?"

Madeline lowered her voice to a hiss. "It's been doing things."

"Things?"

"Magical things. You saw those stone gargoyles that were chasing people all over the plaza?" At his nod she explained, "It turned one back to stone."

He took her arm and drew her out the door and down a few steps, out of earshot of the guards. He kept one hand on his pistol, mindful that they weren't alone in these corridors. "Just like that? You didn't do anything to it?"

"Just like that." Madeline gestured in exasperation. "Nicholas, this device is as far beyond me as the role of Elenge would be for my dresser. I don't know what it did, but it did it, of its own will, with no help from me."

"But it's never done anything before," Nicholas protested. He was unaccustomed to feeling foolish and he didn't like it much. He took the sphere out of the bag and examined it as best he could in the bad light. It looked no different than it ever had, a device of nested gears and wheels that apparently had no purpose, something that might be a child's toy.

"It was sitting on a shelf at Coldcourt. Maybe it never felt the need to do anything before."

That was true. Nicholas gave it back to her and ran a hand through his hair, trying to think how to handle this development. *Edouard, Edouard, couldn't you have stuck with natural philosophy?* "We don't have time to deal with it now, we've got to get out of here."

"How?" Reynard asked, coming down the stairs to them. He had the constable's rifle and Nicholas was relieved that they were a little better armed now. "Are you thinking of blasting open that blocked passage up to the mortuary? The whole place will know where we are and they'll be waiting for us at the other end."

"I know, that's why we're going out through the sewer. Once in it, we can take any direction, leave it at almost any street. They won't have any hope of anticipating our direction."

"Yes, perfect." Ronsarde seconded the motion. For one of the foremost representatives of law and order in the country, he seemed to be entering into lawbreaking with real enthusiasm.

"We're going to leave those men tied up?" Halle said, as they followed Nicholas down the stairs. "With that thing roaming these corridors?"

"We left it trapped on the other side of an iron door, it will have to find a way past that first," Nicholas said. "Besides, it won't go up to the ground floor while we're still down here—it wants us. Crack, pull that door to and lock it."

Nicholas led them back to the wall that adjoined the sewer. It was near the point where the corridor dead-ended into the catacombs, which meant they would be trapped down here if anything came in after them. *I hope that is actually the sewer behind this,* he thought, sitting on his heels to carefully unwrap the package and lay out the contents on the stone flags. If it wasn't, he was going to cause an awful commotion for nothing. He noted Reynard and Crack taking the weapons to guard the open end of the corridor. That would buy them a few moments if they were discovered, but much depended on Nicholas getting this right the first time.

The blasting powder itself was contained within a small glass vial, carefully stoppered with a cork. Most of the package contained the accouterments for it, including a long coiled fuse and small chisel to set the charge within a wall. Madeline knelt beside him, saying quietly, "Cusard tried to tell me how to do it myself if I had to, but I'm just as glad I don't."

"Watch carefully, in case you ever have to again." Nicholas squinted up at the wall in the bad light, trying to judge the best point to set the charge. He had chosen a spot between two heavy support pillars, hoping they would hold up the ceiling if he made a mistake. He only wanted to make a small hole, just large enough for a human body to pass through easily.

"If you need assistance, do say so," Ronsarde said.

Nicholas glanced back and saw that Halle had retrieved his medical bag from Madeline and was redoing their makeshift bandage of Ronsarde's head injury. That was good; if they were going into the sewer, the less odor of blood about them the better. The sewers had been their enemy's territory up until now; for that reason Nicholas hoped what they were doing would be unexpected.

Madeline watched as he chiseled out a hole in the damp pitted surface of the wall. "Are you going to shout at me later for allying myself with Halle?" She sounded more abstractly curious than apprehensive at the prospect.

Nicholas glanced back at the Inspector and the doctor again. They were just out of earshot and deep in their own conversation. He said, "I suppose I could, for all the good it would do, since you would simply stand there and nod, going over the soliloquy from *Camielle* in your head. Of course, I'd be a hypocritical bastard, since all this came about because in a moment of weakness I decided to rescue Inspector Ronsarde." Nicholas finished the hole, then reached for the glass vial. "Stop breathing for the next few moments, please."

Madeline held her breath while he measured out a small quantity of the powder onto a piece of the packing paper and carefully slid it down into the spot prepared for it in the wall. When he nodded that it was all right, she said, "A moment of weakness?"

Nicholas picked up the fuse. "Yes. We'll see how weak if I end up having to break all of us out of here again, this time from the cellblocks after our trials."

Madeline's expression was serious. "Do you think he'll do that? Turn us in?"

Nicholas let out his breath. It had been a long day for hard questions. "If you were him, you wouldn't. If I were him, I might, in the right mood. I don't know."

Madeline drew breath to speak, then made a startled exclamation instead. She lifted the sphere from her pocket, looking into it. "Something's coming."

Nicholas stared down at the sphere, frowning, then at the empty corridor stretching away in the half-light. "How do you know?"

"It's humming, it does that when it senses power. Touch it."

Nicholas hesitated, then reached down and touched the metal of the sphere with a fingertip. It was oddly warm. Madeline was right, it was resonating slightly. "We have a problem," Nicholas said, pitching his voice louder to get the others' attention.

Crack said suddenly, "Wait, do you smell that? It's here again."

"Yes," Reynard said, shifting his hold on the rifle. "That's it."

A foul odor drifted down the corridor, the same miasma that had hung over the area where they had found the mutilated warder. Nicholas turned back to the wall and attached the fuse, making himself work carefully; there would be no time to try again.

Madeline stood, still looking into the sphere, and moved up with Crack and Reynard. Reynard glanced at her and said, "My dear, really—"

"Hush, I know what I'm doing," Madeline said, then added, "I haven't the faintest idea of what I'm doing, but this thing seems to."

Ronsarde struggled to his feet with Halle's help, saying, "That is one of Edouard Viller's famous—or infamous—magical spheres. I hadn't thought to ever see one in use."

"I rather hope we don't have to see it now," Halle said. "Is there anything we can do to help?"

"I'm almost finished." Nicholas unrolled the fuse, then quickly packed up the remains of the materials, though he hoped they wouldn't need them again. Halle came to help him and to put the package back into his medical bag. As Nicholas stood to tell the others he was ready, he heard it.

A scratching, like heavy nails against rock, accompanied by a sibilant hiss, echoed down the corridor. Madeline and Reynard glanced at each other and

Crack stood like a stone, pistol held ready, waiting for whatever was out there to charge.

It can't be very big, Nicholas thought, *not and fit through these doors.* It couldn't be as powerful as the last Sending either, or they would all be dead by now. Maybe that had hurt their sorcerous opponent, to loose that great store of magical power and have it snuffed out by the Great Spell that protected Madele's house. Whatever it was, they couldn't see it yet, but that didn't mean it wasn't near. It had managed to kill at least several armed men so far.

Nicholas unrolled the fuse, backing toward where the others waited, laying the cord out along the floor. This gave them about twenty feet of clearance. He wasn't sure that would be enough, but moving any farther up the corridor was out of the question. Nicholas said, "I'm ready to set off the charge. When it goes off, the creature may come at us."

Leaning against the wall, Ronsarde said, "We've no choice."

"I'm aware of that," Nicholas said, managing to keep his voice mild and reaching for the candle.

Madeline shouted suddenly and Nicholas looked up to see the corridor ahead of them go dark, as if a wave of shadow rolled along it. He lit the fuse and shouted, "Cover your ears and get down!"

The blast was a shock, louder than Nicholas had expected. He fell against the wall, ducking his head as fragments of rock peppered his back and his ears rang. He looked up to find himself blinded by dust and smoke. "Everyone all right?" He could barely hear his own voice and the answering calls were unintelligble.

Nicholas groped along the floor until he found the candle, blown out by the force of the explosion, then got to his feet. He shook his head, which did absolutely nothing for the ringing in his ears, and stumbled back toward the wall. Between the dust hanging in the heavy air and the darkness it was impossible to see or breathe. He felt along the wall for the opening. He tripped on a chunk of blasted stone and almost fell through the hole. It was at waist height, larger than he had expected; the stone hadn't been as thick as it had looked. *Lucky I didn't bring the ceiling down on top of us.* "Here!" he shouted.

As he got the candle lit again, the others managed to find him. They were all covered with brick dust, their faces smudged with smoke, and he supposed he looked as bad as they did.

Madeline held someone's handkerchief over her face, the sphere tucked securely under her arm. "It's not humming as loudly now," she reported. "The explosion must have frightened that thing."

"For the moment, at least," Nicholas agreed. The dust was settling, aided by the damp air from the sewer. He lifted the candle. Through the gaping rent in the wall he could see a wide tunnel with an arched roof, lined with uneven stone blocks. Ledges ran along both sides with a stream of dark water running between. A stench rose off that water, striking him like a blow in the stomach. Ducking his head, he stepped through the hole.

Crack scrambled through after him, saying tersely, "Ghouls."

Nicholas tested his footing on the slimy stone. "I haven't seen any."

"Didn't see any last time either."

There was a minor altercation occurring in the corridor, as Halle and Ronsarde tried to make Madeline go next and she protested, "No, I have the sphere, I should go last to cover our escape."

"Gentlemen, it is useless to argue with her," Nicholas told them grimly. He helped Ronsarde step through, then moved back to give Halle room on the ledge.

Reynard solved the problem of who would go next by wrapping an arm around Madeline's waist and lifting her bodily through the gap, then stepping through after her. "If you'd seen what it did in the alley," she was saying, "you'd realize what I mean. It reacts to the presence of magic— Good God, what a stink."

"Half the prison knows where we are now," Reynard reminded them. "Which way?"

"Here," Nicholas said, moving forward to pick a path along the ledge. The sewer ran roughly eastward, toward the river.

They had only a short time before the constables followed the sound of the blast and swarmed down here after them. Two streets over would be as far as they could safely go. Fortunately, it would be growing dark outside and with every other odd thing that had happened in this part of the city today, people climbing out of the sewer would not be that much to remark on.

"The sphere is humming again," Madeline said, breathless at the stink and the effort of walking on the slick stone in her long skirts. "That creature didn't stay frightened for long."

Wonderful, Nicholas thought. *Perhaps it will stop and eat more constables.* He didn't think that was likely; there was no question it was after them.

They kept moving, muffled curses marking occasional stumbles. The sewer was a long tunnel, vanishing into darkness a few feet in front of their candle, dissolving into it behind them as they moved along. Vienne had literally miles of sewers, some new and easily traversed by the sewermen in sluice carts or boats, others old and so choked by refuse as to be almost impassable even by water. They were lucky that this was one of the newly built tunnels.

The filthy air made it hard to breathe, but Nicholas noted the odor of rats was growing stronger, though the sewer seemed strangely empty of the rodents. The ledge grew narrow in places and Nicholas caught Madeline's arm both to steady her and to reassure himself. Most of her attention was on the sphere.

The sphere's humming grew loud enough to hear from several steps away. Madeline held it nervously; she had taken off her gloves and her bare hands left traces of moisture on the stained metal surface. The rank, animal odor was more intense, combining with the effluvia of filth from the water below and making it difficult to draw a full breath. It was how intelligent the thing was that really mattered and how afraid it was of the sphere, Nicholas realized.

"How much farther?" Madeline said. Her voice was thick.

"Just far enough," Nicholas told her. "It would be a shame after all this to come up within sight of the Prefecture or the prison gates."

Madeline laughed, a short gasp that turned into a choking cough. *And if we manage to escape everything else that's after us, the stench may still kill us,* Nicholas thought.

"Nic," Reynard said suddenly. "There's something behind us."

"Keep moving," Nicholas said. Looking back, he caught a glimpse of a shadow shifting in the blackness, something that might be a trick of the light and his imagination. He knew it was all too real.

They managed perhaps another fifty yards down the sewer, before Nicholas said, "We've come far enough." He had been counting paces and even given a generous margin of error, they should be at least two streets east of the prison by now. "Look for an outlet."

"Thank God," Reynard muttered from behind him. "I thought we were going all the way to the river."

"There's a ladder up here," Halle said. Nicholas peered into the dimness ahead, then suddenly caught sight of it.

Nicholas handed Halle the candle and stepped up beneath the ladder, which led upward to a round metal cover in the curved roof. It was a street access for the sewermen. "Reynard, would you make certain we're in the right place?"

"The wrong place being the prison courtyard or the steps in front of the Magistrates Court, I presume." Reynard handed the rifle to Nicholas, then caught the lowest rung of the ladder and swung up. Nicholas faced back the way they had come, the gunstock sweat-slick in his hands. He heard the heavy metal cover slide over, grating on stone, then muted daylight suddenly washed down through the tunnel. Nicholas thought he saw a form scramble back to the edge of shadow. He had the sudden conviction that it had changed, that it had taken a shape more suited to this fetid underground river. "Hurry," he suggested from between gritted teeth.

"It's Graci Street," Reynard said from above. "Come on!" Halle came forward, half supporting Ronsarde, and Nicholas realized the Inspector was in far worse case than he had been before. In the wan daylight his face was gray and he gasped for breath. *He's old,* Nicholas thought suddenly. *He wasn't a young man when Edouard died, but I didn't realize how old. . . .* Halle climbed far enough to hand his medical bag up to Reynard, then reached down to pull Ronsarde up the ladder, apparently on strength of will alone. It was going to be slow. Nicholas told Crack, "Help them."

Crack hesitated and Nicholas gave him a push. "Go, dammit, help them." Crack pocketed his pistol and gave Ronsarde a boost from behind, climbing up after him.

Nicholas looked back down the sewer. The darkness was pressing close, a palpable barrier. He swallowed in a dry throat. The next few moments would make all the difference.

Crack was through the opening now and looking anxiously down at them. Staring into the sphere, Madeline said tensely, "Go on." Nicholas caught her arm. "Madeline, I'm not going to argue with you—" The darkness surged forward, blotted out the fading daylight from the opening overhead. A burst of white light flared with the strength of a bomb blast. Madeline cried out and they both fell back against the slick wall.

It took long moments for Nicholas's vision to adjust to the dimness again, to be able to see anything beyond the spots of brilliance swimming in front of his eyes. The light from the opening overhead showed him nothing but empty ledges, the water below, the brick-lined tunnel leading off into the dark. But he could see farther than he had before and there was nothing moving in those shadows but the flow of the stream. The others shouted down from above, demanding to know what had happened.

Madeline pushed herself away from the wall and made a futile effort to brush at the stains on her dress. The sphere she still held carefully in the crook of her arm was silent. "I told you so," she said, preoccupied. "Edouard built it for this, after all." She caught the rung of the ladder and swung up easily, one-handed.

I'm beginning to believe he did, Nicholas thought, and slung the rifle over his shoulder to climb after her.

CHAPTER FOURTEEN

It was full dark by the time they reached the warehouse, but Nicholas only meant to stop temporarily. The small offices there were fairly comfortless, and he wanted to avoid Coldcourt and every other place that Octave might have some knowledge of. So after greetings and exclamations of relief from Cusard and Lamane, he bundled everyone into Cusard's wagon and directed him to a safehouse they had some occasion to use in the past, an apartment on the third floor of a small limestone-faced tenement near the Boulevard Panzan. There was no concierge to ask awkward questions and few other tenants.

The wagon pulled into the carriage alley between the buildings and Nicholas climbed down to unlock the side door. The small lobby was dusty and undisturbed, but he sent Crack up to make sure the stairs were clear anyway.

Madeline swung down from the wagonboard and climbed the stoop to stand next to him. Her hair was in wild disarray and she looked exhausted. She said, "Ronsarde doesn't look well. We're lucky Halle is here."

"I suppose." Leaning against the ornamental iron railing around the stoop, Nicholas rubbed the bridge of his nose. His head still pounded from the explosion, and standing still for a moment had made him realize how very badly he needed a bath and a change of clothing. And to fall down on a bed for a week.

To fall down on a bed for a week with Madeline would have been even better. "This day is not going quite as I had originally planned."

"Quite." Madeline's expression was wry.

"Thank you for saving our lives."

Her mouth twisted. "You're welcome, I suppose."

Before Nicholas could question that comment, Crack appeared in the darkened hall and gestured for them to come up.

Nicholas went first to unlock the door and briefly check the apartment. It was a modest town residence with a salon and parlor, dining room, bedchamber and dressing room, maid's room, and kitchen. The air was stale and dusty and the windows were covered with thick draperies and shades, the furniture concealed under dust covers. He went through the small kitchen to check the back door, which gave on to an outer wooden stair that led down into a narrow alley next to the building's court; that and the small trapdoor in the pantry that allowed access to the roof were the chief reasons he had originally selected the place. After reassuring himself that all the outer doors and windows were securely locked and showed no signs of tampering, he returned to the front door and called softly for the others to come up.

He stepped back as Reynard and Dr. Halle helped Inspector Ronsarde inside. "Take him to the salon," Nicholas said, opening one of the doors off the small bare foyer. "There's a couch and the lamps are better."

Nicholas went down the hall and back to the kitchen, to lean against the cold stone counter and try to get his thoughts in order. He heard Crack rummaging in the pantry for the coal store, Madeline's voice giving instructions, the others tramping about.

Finally, Madeline came in, eyed him a moment, then leaned against the china closet. "Well?"

Nicholas took in her appearance thoughtfully. "You look like a charwoman. I don't suppose there are any roles at the Elegante next season which require that?"

"Thank you," Madeline said, inclining her head graciously. "I shall certainly keep it in mind." Her expression turned serious. "I gave my word to Halle, you know."

"Is that what this is about?" Nicholas couldn't quite manage to laugh. "They are the least of our worries."

Madeline hesitated. "This sorcerer . . ."

"Is determined to kill all of us, true, but that's not what I was thinking of. Donatien is dead, Madeline. It's over."

At the mention of the name, Madeline glanced reflexively at the closed door. "But they don't know—"

"I suspect Ronsarde does know. Whether he will act on that knowledge or not, I have no idea. After we saved his life, I think not. And he still needs our help."

She was silent a moment. "So it's over."

"Yes."

She looked away, as if she couldn't quite believe it. "Is that such a bad thing?"

Nicholas's jaw hardened. "It also means the plan for Montesq is over."

Madeline stared at him, startled. "I'd forgotten it. With everything . . . I can't believe I forgot about it." She shook her head, disturbed. "But we can't just let that go. Perhaps—"

It was Nicholas's turn to look away. That it all still meant something to Madeline was a relief but he wouldn't show it. "We can't continue with the plan. Ronsarde would know and that would destroy the whole point of it."

Madeline paced the cold tile floor, coming up with several objections that she started to voice and then reconsidered. Finally she stopped, hands on hips, and said, "So that's it. We're letting Montesq get away with it?"

Not necessarily, Nicholas thought. He would have to kill Montesq himself. It lacked the elegance of allowing the state to execute the Count for a crime he hadn't committed, but it would be accomplishing the same end, even if Nicholas himself didn't survive it. He said, "For all practical purposes."

Madeline did him the courtesy of looking worried instead of skeptical. She said, "Donatien would kill Ronsarde."

Nicholas pushed away from the counter. "You're the one who gets lost in your roles, my dear. Besides, Donatien isn't in charge anymore, I am."

"That's supposed to reassure me?"

Nicholas had no answer for that so he pretended not to hear her and went down the hall to stand in the open doorway of the salon. The lamps had been lit and Crack had gotten a fire started in the hearth, dissipating the cold dampness and making the room almost livable.

The dust covers had been pulled away from the broad divan and Dr. Halle was trying to tend to Ronsarde, who fended him off with acerbic comments about physicians who thought their services indispensable; Halle deflected the sarcasm with the air of long practice and continued treating the Inspector's injuries. Reynard leaned against the mantel, watching them. Nicholas waited until Halle had finished and was repacking the contents of his medical bag, then caught Reynard's eye. "I'd like a word alone with the Inspector, please."

"Of course," Reynard said easily, gesturing for Dr. Halle to proceed him out. Halle went but his face was guarded; Reynard was worried too, though only someone who knew him well would have been able to discern it. Nicholas smiled bleakly to himself. So Reynard was uneasy about what attitude Nicholas would take to their new allies as well.

The only person who didn't appear uneasy was Ronsarde himself, who smiled expectantly at him as Nicholas closed the door behind Reynard and Halle.

Ronsarde was still pale and had a swollen eye and a darkening bruise on his jaw, but with the wound in his forehead stitched and the dried blood cleaned away, he looked considerably better. He said, "You were saying?"

Nicholas hesitated, but couldn't for the life of him think what Ronsarde meant. "Excuse me?"

"About the sorcerer who is so intimately involved in this affair. We are still pooling our resources?"

Ronsarde was continuing the conversation begun when they had first taken refuge in the prison, as if all the intervening struggles hadn't taken place, or had meant nothing. Well, perhaps they hadn't. Nicholas said, "I was saying that it is very possible he believes himself to be Constant Macob. But you already knew that."

Ronsarde shook his head. "Young man—"

Nicholas fought a flash of annoyance and lost. "You know my name, sir, don't pretend otherwise." This was no time for masquerades.

"Valiarde, then." But the Inspector said nothing for a moment, only watched Nicholas thoughtfully. "I had heard you meant to become a physician," he said finally.

"Events conspired against me." Nicholas moved to the window and lifted the musty damask curtain just enough to give him a view of the street. "I recognized you that night at Gabrill House, though I don't think you recognized me."

"No, I did not," Ronsarde admitted. "I thought your voice familiar, but it had been too long since we last spoke."

"Since the trial, you mean." Ten years, eight months, fourteen days. Nicholas performed the calculation automatically. "You must have recognized the sphere."

"Yes, that I knew only too well. I would have come to you eventually, if you had not come to me, so to speak." Ronsarde hesitated, then said, "Count Rive Montesq has had such a run of poor luck since that time, hasn't he?"

Nicholas dropped the curtain and turned slowly to face the older man, leaning back to sit on the windowsill and folding his arms. Ronsarde's expression was merely curious, that was all. Nicholas smiled and said, "Has he really?"

"Oh, yes. He has had several large losses of funds and property in the last few years. Not enough to bankrupt him, of course, but enough to seriously inconvenience. And then there have been the losses among his staff. One of his chief financiers, a solicitor, and two personal servants, all vanished without a trace."

"How terrible," Nicholas commented. He was glad at least that Ronsarde didn't know everything; Montesq had suffered more losses than that. "But then perhaps it's simply a visitation by Fate."

"Perhaps." Ronsarde shrugged, then winced as if the motion pained him. "If I didn't know that the solicitor was a blackmailer of the worse stripe, who had ruined a number of individuals and provoked the suicide of at least one victim, that the financier was his ally in that enterprise, and that the two servants had second careers as thugs and extortionists, I might have been moved to do something about it. But somehow I never quite found the time."

And am I expected to thank you for that? Nicholas thought. He looked away. This cat-and-mouse game was not particularly to his liking, even though they both seemed to be taking the role of the cat. "Why were you watching Dr. Octave that night?"

Ronsarde accepted the change in subject gracefully. "Several weeks ago, a lady came to me for my assistance in a matter concerning Dr. Octave. Her mother was paying him to hold circles for her and produce various deceased relatives on command. I began to investigate the good doctor, but could prove nothing definite. He was very careful." Ronsarde stared into the middle distance, a rueful anger in his expression. "I realize now he was warned against me by this sorcerer whose necromantic activities he evidently supports. Sorcery gives the criminal an unfair advantage."

"There are ways to even the balance," Nicholas said, his voice dry.

Ronsarde's quick smile flickered and the good humor returned to his gaze. "I imagine you are quite familiar with them. But to continue, I managed to help the lady convince her mother to leave the dead in peace, but I still pursued Octave. I discovered that Lady Everset would be hosting a circle and that in all probability it would be held in her garden. This was the first opportunity I had to observe a circle at close range, when Octave had no knowledge that I would be present."

"That's why I was there, too," Nicholas said, without thinking, and then grimaced and reminded himself not to say too much. All these years of caution and concealment and here he was talking to Ronsarde as if he were as close a colleague as Madeline or Reynard. Being hunted by mad sorcerers and ghouls had obviously unhinged him. "You didn't realize he was connected with the disappearances."

It was Ronsarde's turn to look uncomfortable. He tugged the blanket more closely around him with a short angry jerk. "No, I did not," he said. "Halle had examined the three bodies that had been recovered at various times from the river and he drew my attention to the lichen. It is a variety that flourishes in the presence of magic. That, and the style of the injuries made before death caused me to believe someone was imprisoning these individuals and killing them in the course of necromantic magics. I noted the similarities to the murders of Constant Macob, committed two centuries ago."

Nicholas frowned in annoyance. He hadn't noted it, not until the scene in the cellar of Valent House, when it had become obvious. *The Executions of Rogere,* the book Dr. Uberque had lent him, had been even more illuminating. One method Macob had used to lure his victims was to poison them with an herbal mixture that caused symptoms anywhere from mild confusion all the way to unreasoning terror. How he had gotten his victims to ingest it was a mystery to the writer of the account, though Nicholas wondered if the stuff might be so potent it could be absorbed through the skin. It explained the confusion and odd behavior of Jeal Meule, as described by the penny sheet *Review of the Day,* and why her neighbors had been unable to convince her to go home before her second disappearance. She must have escaped her captor at some point but the poison had clouded her mind and kept her helpless, until he had been able to collect her again. Nicholas asked Ronsarde, "Why did it suggest Macob so readily?"

"Macob's crimes and his trial were well documented for the time and give much vital information regarding the mind of a person bent on mutilation and mass murder. I'd read the history of it before, but I found it especially useful three years ago in the case of the Viscount of March-Bannot, who was—"

"Cutting people's heads off and throwing them in the river. Yes, I vaguely recall it."

"Octave and his associates made the mistake of disposing of one body under the bridge at Alter Point and not into the river itself. The presence of the lichen marked it as part of the same case and not one of the many other unfortunates who are found dead every day in Vienne. Mud adhering to the pants legs indicated the edge of Riverside where it bordered on the Gabardin."

"Yes, I found Valent House as well."

"Before I did." Ronsarde smiled faintly. "Octave was frequently seen near the place, by a person who is at times my informant, who recognized the good doctor after he had been described to him." His expression turned pensive. "After the circle at Gabrill House, I knew someone else had Octave under observation. When I discovered Valent House two days ago, it also became apparent that someone else had discovered it first. The signs that my quarry had left in haste and that his lair had been thoroughly searched were unmistakable. I wasn't certain if I had a second opponent, but I knew that Octave did."

Nicholas didn't comment. It had been so very close. Ronsarde had been one step behind him, at the most. He said, "Surely you weren't arrested for breaking into Valent House."

"Oh, no," Ronsarde said, gesturing dismissively. "I was arrested for breaking into Mondollot House."

Yes, exactly. Nicholas kept his elation in check; there were still too many questions unanswered. "You wanted to look at a small sealed room in one of the subcellars. If you got that far, you found it empty, but there were signs it had not been unoccupied for long."

"Yes." Ronsarde watched him as intently, as if Nicholas were a suspect he was questioning. "In actuality the chamber belongs to Ventarin House, destroyed years ago when Ducal Court Street was cut through. I realized Octave had an interest in the Ventarins during the first circle I watched. The family whose deceased relatives he was currently interfering with had been a distant connection of the Ventarins, virtually the only people left in the city of any relation to them whatsoever. Octave questioned their dead on the old Ventarin Great House's location and its cellars. I believed at the time that he was only after hidden family plate or other trinkets. It wasn't until I made the connection with Macob that the facts took on a more sinister tone."

"Yes, two centuries ago Gabard Ventarin was King Rogere's Court Sorcerer and presided at Constant Macob's execution," Nicholas said. "Do you know what was there, in the large box that was removed from the chamber?"

"I have no idea," Ronsarde admitted. He shook his head. "We could draw the conclusion that this sorcerer, who seems to believe himself a reincarnation of the Necromancer Macob, had some reason to believe there were relics of his idol stored in the chamber and wished to retrieve them."

"We *could* draw that conclusion," Nicholas said reluctantly, "but we might also wonder why relics of a famous criminal were buried deep inside a sealed room beneath a powerful sorcerer's home, and not on display somewhere."

"It isn't encouraging," Ronsarde agreed. "Whatever it was, Ventarin seems to have felt that it needed to be concealed and guarded. And we must assume our sorcerer opponent has had it since . . . ?"

"Four days ago," Nicholas supplied.

Ronsarde gazed curiously at him. "How did you discover the chamber?"

"It was how I and my associates became embroiled in all this," Nicholas said, evasively. "Through an entirely coincidental ... occurrence." He was not going to tell Ronsarde he and Octave had both decided to rob Mondollot House on the same night. "Octave believed I had been to the room before him and removed something. Oddly enough, I hadn't. The room was empty when I entered it. Octave wanted to question the late Duke of Mondollot, I assume to ascertain if he discovered the room before his death and removed some part of the contents, but the Duchess refused to cooperate with him." Nicholas hesitated. "Why did you break into Mondollot House? Wouldn't the Duchess have given you access if you had asked?" *After she hid anything linking her to Bisran trading concerns, of course.*

"Possibly. After discovering Valent House, I realized how very dangerous my opponents were and, also, how very influential their friends." Ronsarde's expression was grimly amused. "It was intimated to me by my superiors, and I use the term lightly, that I just de-emphasize my investigation. To avoid panic, you see."

"Ah," Nicholas breathed. De-emphasize an investigation of multiple abductions and murders, to avoid panic. *Yes, that sounds like the Vienne Prefecture.* "Which brings us to Count Rive Montesq."

"Yes, he has been shown to have a pernicious influence on Lord Albier, who is currently acting head of the Prefecture." Ronsarde's gaze sharpened. "I am not surprised you knew that."

Careful, Nicholas reminded himself. *Very, very careful.* "My interest in Montesq is entirely academic," he said lightly.

"Of course. But all this aside, we must find this sorcerer, and to find him, we must question Octave." Ronsarde let out his breath in annoyance. "Unfortunately, when I was arrested, I lost track of his whereabouts."

Nicholas smiled. "Fortunately, I haven't."

———

Nicholas pushed open the kitchen door to find the others all gathered there, most of them standing and staring at the floor as if they were attending a particularly dreary wake. "Are you all just standing about in here?" he demanded. "What's wrong with you?"

"Everything all right?" Reynard asked, with an uncharacteristic air of caution.

"Of course." Nicholas ran a hand through his hair impatiently. "Madeline, we need to consult you on makeup and clothing for disguises, and Crack, you'll need to fetch Devis, and Reynard—"

"We?" Halle interrupted, his expression cautious.

"Yes, we. What are you all staring at?" Before anyone could formulate an answer, Ronsarde pushed open the door behind Nicholas. He was leaning heavily on the wall, an expression of grim determination on his features. "I see no reason why I cannot accompany you," the Inspector said, almost peevishly.

"Disguised as what?" Nicholas asked him. "An injured beggar selling matches?"

"That would be ideal."

"Until you have to run away!"

"I could sit in the coach," Ronsarde persisted.

"What would be the point of that?" Nicholas asked, exasperated. It was like dealing with a less sensible version of Madeline.

"He's right," Halle said, coming forward to take Ronsarde's arm and urge him back down the hall toward the salon. "You need rest if you're to be of any help. You can't go running about the city—"

Their voices continued, raised in argument, and Nicholas rubbed his hands together, his mind already on the task ahead. "I need to make a list. We're going to need Cusard for this, too." As he left the kitchen he heard Reynard's ironic comment, "Oh, good, now there's two of them."

After setting some of the wheels in motion and sending Crack for Cusard, Nicholas found the others gathered in the salon, looking at the sphere, which was set atop a pillow on a small table. It looked like nothing more than an odd sort of curio or ornament. Nicholas leaned in the doorway and folded his arms.

"How does it work?" Halle asked, touching the metal with cautious curiosity.

Madeline looked over at Nicholas, who shifted a little uncomfortably, and said, "We don't know."

"You don't know?" Ronsarde echoed.

"Edouard left no instructions," Nicholas explained reluctantly. "None of the intact spheres ever reacted to anything at all, until this one transformed one of the gargoyles back into stone when it attacked Madeline. It was pure chance she had it with her at all. There are two others, but one appears to be dead and the other didn't react to the gargoyles."

"You did nothing to cause this one to act?" Ronsarde asked, with a hard stare at Madeline. "You felt nothing?"

"I did nothing," Madeline replied, faintly exasperated. "I felt quite a number of things—fear, anger, the desire to shriek. I've felt those emotions before and never had magic spontaneously erupt." She shook her head impatiently. "I have a small talent for witchery which I've never tried seriously to cultivate, but I've helped my grandmother with spells and I know what working one feels like. That thing acted all on its own account."

"Madeline's grandmother is a witch of some repute," Nicholas said, smiling slightly at the understatement. "She's agreed to attempt to help us with our difficulties and will be arriving soon from Lodun." *We hope,* he added to himself.

"Is there no sorcerer currently in town whose opinion we could seek?" Ronsarde persisted. He added wryly, "There are some attached to the Prefecture but I can no longer command their assistance. In fact, they would be more likely to turn me in to the nearest constable at once."

Halle grunted agreement and Nicholas speculated that Ronsarde had made his opinions on sorcery known in no uncertain terms to the practitioners who worked for the Prefecture. "There is a sorcerer whose advice I would like to have. He was the one who helped Edouard construct this sphere," Nicholas admitted. "But he's badly ill, in a sort of paralysis."

"Arisilde Damal?" Ronsarde asked, brows lifting.

Nicholas nodded warily. He had forgotten how much Ronsarde had learned about Edouard's work during the Crown investigation and the trial.

"It was the opinion of many that he had left the country," Ronsarde said thoughtfully. "I was asked several times by persons at Lodun to locate him, but was always unsuccessful."

"That isn't surprising. If Arisilde didn't want to be found, it would be impossible to locate him even if you were standing in the same room."

"An unfortunate tendency of sorcerers," Ronsarde agreed. "He is ill?"

"Yes." Nicholas hesitated. "We thought at first it might have been caused by our opponent—it occurred at a rather inopportune moment."

Reynard snorted at the choice of words.

"But it's more likely the result of poor health and an opium addiction," Nicholas finished.

Halle cleared his throat. "Has he been attended? I could examine him."

Nicholas shook his head. "He's being seen by a Dr. Brile, who has already brought in other physicians to consult with. I don't think there's anything any-one can do."

There was a moment of silence, then Halle said quietly, "I know Dr. Brile. He's a very accomplished physician and your friend is in good hands."

Nicholas realized he had everyone's attention and that he must have be-trayed more than he meant to. He said, "But the point is, there is no other sorcerer I will risk taking the sphere to." He looked down at the apparently innocuous device. "It's too unpredictable."

———

Fontainon House itself was unbreachable, at least without Arisilde's help, and there was simply no possibility of any of their group receiving last-minute in-vitations. Taking Octave at his hotel would have been the best solution, but they had little time to make arrangements, and after a brief scouting mission Madeline reported that the prospects were not ideal. Octave seemed to realize his danger. He spent all his time either locked in his room or in one of the lounges surrounded by dozens of people.

The next best opportunity would have been late at night after the circle, when Octave was relaxed with his success and the other participants would be on the way home and the worse for the large quantities of wine and brandy consumed before and after the festivities. But for some reason he was not quite willing to articulate, even to himself, Nicholas felt it better not to allow Octave to perform the circle at all.

Madeline had questioned this in her usual fashion, during the long af-ternoon when Nicholas had been trying to work out details and make con-tact with the more far-flung elements of his organization. "Why should you care what happens to the woman, just because she's a relative of the Queen? I thought you said once that Ile-Rien could go hang."

"It can still go hang for all I care," Nicholas had replied with some acerbity. "It might be just another one of Octave's confidence schemes, but if it isn't, I don't want to give this fool who thinks he's Macob another victory."

Madeline had sighed and given up her game of trying to make him admit fond feelings for his home country. "If he was a fool, we wouldn't be in this mess, would we?"

"No," Nicholas had admitted. "No, we wouldn't."

At the first opportunity, he and Madeline had put together disguises out of the things she had purchased for tonight and, with Crack along for protection, gone to Arisilde's garret in the Philosopher's Cross. Nicholas had taken the sphere with him, out of a hope he didn't dare voice to anyone else. But he knew it was a foolish hope when Madeline sat on the edge of Arisilde's bed with it and the sphere did nothing but hum and tremble, the way it did in the presence of any magic.

"It's no good," Madeline had said, when he followed her to the door. "It must be a natural illness, as the doctor thought, and not a spell."

"It was worth a try," Nicholas said. "You and Crack go on and take the sphere back. I'll be along shortly."

She had hesitated, but in the end she had gone without questions.

Nicholas went back to the bedchamber and took a chair near Isham, who was patiently tending his friend. Arisilde looked the same as he had that first night, his face drawn and pinched, his skin pale as wax. "We've got some help for you. She should be arriving tomorrow," Nicholas told Isham, and explained about Madele.

"She will be much welcomed," Isham said. He was seated in a straight-backed chair at Arisilde's bedside and looked worn and tired. "The physicians say they can do nothing." Isham watched the sorcerer's still face for a time, then said, "I used to try to stop him, sometimes. I talked and talked, which did no good, and then I tried to hide his poisons, which was foolish. If I destroyed them he simply got more."

"Hiding things from Arisilde is rather problematic," Nicholas agreed. Isham was skirting the edge of something that had occupied his own thoughts. "I should have tried harder myself. He might have listened to me." Admitting even that much was an effort. Nicholas had never liked to give in or acknowledge defeat. Maybe if he hadn't been so afraid of failure he would have tried harder.

Isham shook his head. "We can only work with what we have."

On impulse Nicholas asked, "What did you make of the sphere?"

"I've never seen its like before." Isham had examined the device tentatively before Madeline had taken it away, but made no comment on it. "It's something Arisilde has made?"

"He helped make it. It's capable of working magic; Madeline used it once or twice but she isn't sure how. It seems to work if and when it likes."

"Rather like Arisilde," Isham observed.

"Rather like," Nicholas agreed, smiling.

Later, back at the apartment, they had held another council of war. They agreed that the only time to take Octave would be when he was on the way to Fontainon House. This was complicated by Reynard's discovery that the royal cousin meant to send her own coach for the spiritualist.

"You realize, of course, that we're all going to be executed as anarchists," Reynard had pointed out.

"It may be a royal coach, but there's not going to be anyone royal in it, and it won't be guarded as if there were."

"So we'll only appear to be anarchists to the untrained eye."

Nicholas rubbed his forehead. "Reynard . . ."

"If we succeed in capturing Octave, then what?" This was from Dr. Halle.

"Then we ask him where his sorcerer is." Nicholas leaned back against the escritoire and folded his arms, anticipating the next objection.

"And if he doesn't want to tell us?" Halle said.

Nicholas smiled. "Then we explain to him that it would be better if he did."

"I won't participate in that," Halle said flatly. "And I won't condone it."

"You saw Valent House," Nicholas said. "We know Octave condoned *that*. For all we know, he participated."

"And I won't lower myself to that level."

You can't talk to these people, Nicholas thought. "I doubt we'll have to go quite as low as that," he said, lifting a brow. "Octave doesn't seem the stoic type to me."

Later, Nicholas had been walking down the passage outside the salon when he heard Dr. Halle's voice from within and the words made him pause. "Are you certain you know what you're doing?"

Ronsarde's voice, preoccupied, replied, "You will have to be more specific, old man."

"I'm talking about Valiarde." Halle sounded impatient.

Ronsarde chuckled. "He's an ally, Cyran, and a good one. You and I are getting somewhat old for all this—"

"That's beside the point." Halle took a deep breath, then said quietly, "Have you looked into that young man's eyes?"

There was a moment's silence. Then in a far more serious tone, Ronsarde said, "Yes, I have. And I'm greatly afraid that I'm one of the men who helped place that cold opacity there. He wasn't like that before his foster father died."

"So you will, at least, be cautious."

"I'm always cautious."

"Now that's a damned lie. You would like to think yourself cautious, but I can assure you—"

The conversation devolved into commonplaces and after a moment, Nicholas walked on. None of it meant anything, of course. Neither one of them knew him at all. But it took an effort of will to avoid the mirror at the end of the passage.

———

The mist was thick, pooling heavily around the nearest street lamp like the creature of the fay called the boneless, which had once haunted the less well-traveled country roads. Arisilde and some of the sorcerers who had spoken of their craft at Lodun favored the presence of mist for the working of illusions; Nicholas couldn't help but wonder if it aided the working of more dangerous magics as well.

He paced along the stone walk at the edge of the muddy street, rubbing his arms for warmth. The neighborhood was blessedly quiet. Directly behind Nicholas was a block of upper-class apartments with a row of arabesqued lintels under the second-floor windows and an ornamental ironwork fence along the street level. The main entrance was on the cross street, and the inhabitants would mostly be out dining or at the theater at this time. Across from it was the massive, forbiddingly dark façade of an older Great House, closed for the season except for caretakers. On the upper corner was the side entrance of a quiet and highly respectable hotel.

There was little traffic except for the occasional passerby and the cabriolet parked near the walk. It was an older vehicle, purchased this afternoon for the purpose, and Devis was on the box, making occasional clucking noises at the two rented horses. Nicholas was dressed as a cabman too, in a slightly shabby greatcoat and fingerless gloves, and a round cap tipped back on his head. Together they must have made a convincing impression, since several people had tried to hire them, only to be told they had already been engaged for someone inside the apartments.

For all the apparent quiet of the neighborhood, Fontainon House was only a few hundred yards down the street. Nicholas could see the gas lamps illuminating its carriage entrance, and sometimes hear the voices of an arriving party. Everyone had had something to say about his choice of site for the ambush, but there had been no other place on the possible routes between here and Octave's hotel that was fairly quiet and that Nicholas was sure the coach would have to pass.

They would just have to be quick and not only for fear of the constables and the detachment of the Royal Guard attached to Fontainon House. They were only safe from the sorcerer while he believed Nicholas and Ronsarde to be dead. *After this, he's going to know we're definitely not dead,* Nicholas thought grimly. *Out of our minds and flailing about like idiots maybe, but not dead.*

One of the horses lifted her head and snorted and an instant later Nicholas heard the clop of hooves from an approaching vehicle. He and Devis exchanged a look and Devis straightened up and adjusted his reins nervously.

Nicholas stepped into the street to meet the cabriolet as it materialized out of the mist. It was his own vehicle, the one Devis usually drove, with Crack and Reynard on the box. Nicholas caught the bridle of one of the horses, stroking the anxious animal's neck as it recognized him and began to aggressively snuffle at his pockets for treats. "They're not far behind us," Reynard said in a low voice as he leaned down. "Two coachmen, one groom on the back, no outriders. And the coach doesn't have the royal seal, only the Fontainon family crest."

"So we're not technically anarchists yet," Nicholas said, in mock innocence.

"Not technically," Reynard agreed, smiling sourly. "But we have hopes."

Crack allowed himself a mild grimace at the levity. Then Nicholas stepped back. A couple had emerged from the side entrance of the hotel on the corner and were strolling down the street in their direction. It was Madeline and Dr. Halle, and their appearance meant they had just seen the Fontainon coach turn onto the cross street that was visible from the windows of the hotel's café. Nicholas said, "Get ready."

Reynard swung down from the box, pretending to be doing something with the harness, and Nicholas moved with apparent idleness to the front of Devis's cab so he could give him the signal.

In another moment, Nicholas heard a larger vehicle, heavier than a cabriolet. Then he saw its shape approach out of the mist. The coach drew nearer and he could see the liveried driver and footman on the box. Nicholas turned away, leaning casually against the side of the cab, and fished in his pocket for the round firework packet that was standing in for an anarchist's bomb. He struck a match and lit the fuse, then as the noise of the approaching coach grew louder, turned and tossed it into the center of the street.

It went off with a loud pop that echoed back from the buildings around them. Smoke poured out as the horses screamed and reared and the Fontainon coach jolted to a halt. "A bomb!" Nicholas yelled, and ran across the street.

Devis allowed his frantic team to rear and then turned them, letting them sling the cab half across the street in front of the coach and block its escape. Halted near the smoke, the frightened horses continued to rear and buck, looking as if they meant to tear the cab apart and further terrifying the coach's team.

Reynard leapt down off the cabriolet and ran around, yelling like a panic-stricken fool. On the far promenade, Madeline shrieked and fainted convincingly into Dr. Halle's arms. Crack stood up on the box, nearly tumbled off as his team tried to join the confused horses in the center of the street, then pointed down the alley next to the apartment block and shouted, "I saw him! He threw the bomb and went that way!"

When they had discussed the plan earlier today, Inspector Ronsarde had been especially fond of that touch.

Nicholas dodged through the growing wall of smoke and almost ran directly into the footman who had been riding on the back of the coach. The man's forehead was bleeding, as if he had fallen when the vehicle had jolted to a halt. Nicholas grabbed him and yelled frantically, "It was a bomb, go get help!" and sent him staggering away.

Nicholas reached the coach just as the door swung open and Octave fell out. Nicholas grabbed him by the front of his coat and threw him back against the vehicle. "Surprised?" he asked.

"What do you want?" Octave stammered. A flare from the sputtering firework showed Nicholas the other man's face: he was sickly pale in the white light, his staring eyes red-rimmed and his flesh sagging. Nicholas was bitterly glad the last few days had obviously not been kind to Dr. Octave, either.

"You know what I want—your sorcerer. Where is he?" They needed to get Octave into Devis's cab and away, but Nicholas could hear Reynard arguing with someone on the other side of the coach, saying something about an entire crew of anarchists running off down the alley. He considered trying to drag Octave to the cab alone, but if the spiritualist resisted at all and was seen, their plan would fall apart.

"I'll tell you. I'll tell you if you'll protect me— You don't know what he is—"

Nicholas shook him. "Where is he? Tell me, Doctor, it's your only chance."

"The palace . . . the palace on the river. He's been there—" Octave's voice rose to a sudden shriek. "There!"

Nicholas had only an instant to realize it wasn't a trick. Something gripped his shoulder and he was flung to the ground. He rolled over on the muddy stone, the breath knocked out of him, and saw a figure standing over Dr. Octave.

In the poor light and the haze from the firework, he first thought it was a man. He could see the skirts of a greatcoat, a shape that might be a hat, but then he realized how it towered over Octave, shaking him as if he was a child. It wasn't human.

Nicholas fumbled for the revolver in his coat pocket. He had brought it reluctantly, not liking the thought of one of the coach drivers or footmen accidentally shot, but not meaning this night's work to fail either. He drew the gun, aimed at the creature's head, and fired.

It turned toward him, still keeping a grip on the struggling Octave's coat, and snarled. Nicholas scrambled backward, took aim, and fired again, though he knew the first shot hadn't missed. *The Unseelie Court would be easier to fight,* he thought in exasperation. At least the fay were highly susceptible to gunfire; the creatures of human sorcery and necromancy obviously were not.

It dropped Octave and started toward Nicholas, moving slowly, its steps deliberate. Nicholas struggled to his feet and backed away. The concealing smoke still swirled around them and the coach blocked the yellow light of the streetlamp; he wanted to see what this thing was. Octave lay like a lump on the street, moving only feebly, and Nicholas cursed under his breath. Sacrificing himself so that Dr. Octave could escape a probably righteous and well-deserved fate hadn't been in his plans either, but he couldn't let the man be killed until he knew where the sorcerer was hiding.

The tall figure stalked him, stepping out of the shadow of the coach. Its face was that of an old man, with craggy, uneven features, but as the light shifted it became a death's-head, the skin stretched over it to parchment thinness. Nicholas kept moving back, luring it farther from Octave, who had managed to struggle to his knees and was trying to crawl away.

Octave must have made some noise, or perhaps it read something in Nicholas's expression, because it turned suddenly and bounded back toward the injured spiritualist. "No, dammit, no!" Nicholas shouted, starting forward.

It reached Octave in one leap and swung at him with an almost careless backhanded blow. Nicholas saw Octave fall back to the street, spasm once, then go limp. He stopped, cursing, then realized the thing had turned toward him again.

Nicholas moved away, raising the pistol, though it hadn't done him much good before. He saw Reynard come around the coach and waved him back. Reynard halted, surprised, then got a glimpse of the creature as it moved into the light again. He stepped back, reaching into his coat for his own revolver.

A shout and a loud clatter sounded from up the street. Nicholas couldn't risk a quick glance behind him but whatever was coming, the creature saw it and halted with a thwarted growl. Then it stepped back into the shadows.

Nicholas blinked, resisting the impulse to rub his eyes. The shape of the creature grew darker, harder to see, fading into the pool of shadow on the street until it was gone.

Nicholas stared at the darkness where it had been, then looked for what had alarmed the thing.

A horse troop came toward them from down the street, at least twenty men. Nicholas swore under his breath. A mounted troop meant only one thing: Royal Guards.

He whistled a signal that meant "cut and run" and the frantic activity around the coach grew more frantic as the cabriolet suddenly drove off. Nicholas stayed where he was. He was in the middle of the street, in the full light of the gas lamp. If he ran, the horsemen would chase him. The others were almost invisible in the shadows and the troop wouldn't be able to clear the wreckage of the coach quickly enough to chase Crack's vehicle.

Nicholas clicked on the revolver's safety, then dropped it into the street. As he turned back toward the coach, he casually kicked it into the gutter.

The smoke eddied in the still damp air as the firework sparked one last time and went out. Devis had vanished from the rented cab, leaving it and the confused horses to block the street. Madeline and Dr. Halle were nowhere to be seen, having had orders to retreat back to the hotel on the corner as soon as the confusion was well underway. He couldn't see Reynard either and hoped he had had time to swing aboard the cabriolet before it left. One of the Fontainon footmen sat on the curb, still stunned from falling from the box. The coachman had managed to calm his horses finally and now staggered around the side, stopping when he saw Octave.

He bent over the spiritualist anxiously, gripping his shoulder. Nicholas stopped beside him and saw the man needn't have bothered; Octave's head was twisted at an unnatural angle, the neck cleanly broken. He resisted an urge to kick the unresponsive body. "He's dead," the coachman said, suddenly realizing it. He looked up at Nicholas, confused. He had a shallow cut in his forehead that was bleeding into tangled gray hair. "Did you see what happened?"

Nicholas shook his head in bewilderment and in his best Riverside accent replied, "They said there was a bomb, but all I saw was that sparkler. Are you sure he's dead?" He sat on his heels beside Octave's body, flipping his coat open as if looking for a wound and unobtrusively searching the pockets. He was beginning to understand Octave's behavior. He had been afraid of being cornered by Nicholas, afraid of being caught by the Prefecture, but he had become even more terrified of his sorcerous ally.

"He looks dead," the coachman muttered, looking away and clutching his head. "I would've sworn it was a bomb."

Octave didn't have the sphere on him. *Damned fool,* Nicholas thought. *How was he going to perform a circle without it?* Unless this was the last circle and Octave had stayed for it only because he needed the money to flee. Lady Bianci wasn't a member of the demimonde, she was wealthy aristocracy, and would have paid the spiritualist for trying even if he hadn't been able to produce any messages from the dead.

Then the horse troop surrounded them. Nicholas stood and stepped back against the coach to avoid being run down. From their badges and braid they *were* Royal Guard, probably dispatched from the nearby Prince's Gate to help defend Fontainon House. The lieutenant reined in just in time to keep from trampling the injured coachman and demanded, "What happened here?"

"We were attacked and this gentleman killed! What does it look like?" the coachman shouted, standing up suddenly. Before the lieutenant could reply, the older man swayed, clutching his head, and started to collapse. Nicholas stepped forward hastily to catch him and ease him to the ground; he couldn't have arranged a better distraction himself.

There was more shouting and confusion, the two footmen and the groom were located, and the majordomo of Fontainon House and the corporal in charge of that Guard detachment appeared to add to the conflict. The coachman was revived enough to give his version of events, which disagreed with the footmen's version, to which Nicholas helpfully added conflicting detail, glad that the blustering Guard lieutenant hadn't the sense to split them up and question them separately. This resulted in the conclusion that there had been six anarchists, who had thrown a firework instead of a real bomb, and had probably meant to cause a Public Incident of some sort. Nicholas wasn't sure how they were defining Public Incident but reluctantly decided it was better not to call attention to himself by asking.

"But how was this man killed?" the lieutenant demanded, staring worriedly down at Octave. They had sent one of the Guards to bring Lady Bianci's personal physician from Fontainon House, but everyone knew it for an empty gesture. "His neck looks broken. Did he fall from the coach?"

Nicholas shifted uneasily and scratched his head in bewilderment along with everyone else. Then the Fontainon majordomo suggested, "The coach door is open. Perhaps he tried to step out and when the horses reared he was thrown down?"

"Yes, that could very well be what happened," the lieutenant said, stroking his mustache thoughtfully. There were nods of agreement among the Fontainon servants. Octave's death might conceivably have been blamed on them and this was a convenient out. "Yes, that must be it," the lieutenant concluded and there were relieved sighs all around. He looked up then, frowning. "But who was shooting?"

Nicholas rubbed the bridge of his nose, annoyed. *That should have been your first question, you idiot.* "Must have been the anarchists, to scare the horses," he muttered, low under his breath.

One of the footmen heard him and took up the theme. "They was shooting, sir, to scare the horses!"

"Yes, that was it," the coachman seconded, and there were more nods of agreement and surreptitious relieved sighs. Nicholas smiled to himself. With all this obfuscation, by morning no one would remember what he had seen or who had claimed to see what, and that was just as well.

There was a clatter behind the wrecked coach as another party arrived from Fontainon House, led by a man in evening dress carrying a doctor's bag, who must be the lady's personal physician. He fought his way past the horses of the milling Guard troop and demanded, "Whose vehicle is this blocking the street? It will have to be moved so we can bring in a stretcher for the injured."

While the corporal and the majordomo explained that haste was no longer necessary on the injured man's behalf, Nicholas touched his cap to the lieutenant and said, "All right to move my cab, sir?"

The lieutenant nodded and waved him away distractedly. Nicholas went immediately to the cab, freeing the reins from where someone had tied them to the lamppost, murmuring some soothing words to the still restive horses. It hadn't been necessary to claim the cab as his; everyone had simply assumed that the person who looked like a cabman belonged to the only empty vehicle.

Nicholas had grabbed the rail and was stepping up to swing into the box, when someone just behind him said, "Stop."

Nicholas hesitated for a heartbeat, then made a conscious decision to obey. He was close to escape and didn't intend to ruin it by panicking for no reason. He looked back and saw a tall gray-haired man in formal evening dress. *Someone from Fontainon House,* Nicholas thought first, then he recognized him. It was Rahene Fallier, the Court Sorcerer. Nicholas's mouth went dry. He said, "Sir?"

Fallier took a step closer. He said, "There was sorcery here tonight. Did you witness it?"

Interfering bastard, Nicholas thought. It was too late to change his story; the Guard lieutenant wasn't that much of a fool. "No, sir, I didn't see nothing of the kind."

The corporal from Fontainon House was coming over. He was an older man than the lieutenant, with more intelligent eyes. He said, "Sir, did you want to question this man?" To Nicholas he called, "You there, step down."

They were drawing the attention of the mounted Guards still half searching the area for nonexistent anarchists. Nicholas protested, "They told me to move the cab," but he stepped back down to the scuffed paving stones. Fallier might not be as suspicious as he seemed.

Fallier took another step toward him, standing only a bare pace away, so that Nicholas had to look up at him. He was frowning, concentrating. *Working a spell?* Nicholas wondered, keeping his face blank. He remembered powerful sorcerers could sense the past presence of magic. The Sending Octave's sorcerer had unleashed on him might leave some residue. Or Fallier might detect traces of Arisilde's powerful spells from the sphere Nicholas had held earlier today.

Then Fallier said, "The resemblance is striking. And you are younger than you look, of course."

Nicholas let himself appear puzzled. *He knows who I am,* the thought burned as cold as ice thrust through the heart. He had never met Fallier in his own persona, never seen him at closer range than across the crowded pit at the opera. *The resemblance is striking.* Fallier knew what he was, as well.

Fallier half turned to the Guard corporal. "We must detain this man—"

Nicholas moved, not toward the waiting circle of horsemen but back toward the cab, turning and diving under its wheels in the oldest street trick there was. He rolled under the vehicle, narrowly avoiding a crushed skull as one of the horses started and the wheels rocked back. He ducked out from under it and bolted away.

Shouts sounded behind him, the clatter of hooves, as he ran for the corner. Two turns away these broad, well-lit streets gave way to the crowded byways and overhung tenements of the old city, where there were alleys so narrow the horses couldn't follow him. But first he had to get there.

He heard someone riding up on him from the right and dodged sideways so the mounted trooper plunged past him before he could stop. The man wrenched his horse around sharply and the animal reared. Nicholas ducked away from the flailing hooves and ran for the corner again.

Suddenly, there was a solid wall not ten feet away, rising out of the lingering mist. Nicholas slid to a stop, baffled, then cursed his own stupidity as he realized what it must be. He flung himself forward but a riding crop cracked across his shoulders, sending him sprawling headlong over the raised curve of the promenade.

Before he could scramble up, hands grabbed the back of his coat and dragged him to his feet. He was flung up against a wall—a real one, this time, not Fallier's illusory creation that was already fading gently away into the damp night air—and his arms were pinned behind him. Someone roughly searched his pockets.

He heard the Guard lieutenant saying, "Where do you want him taken? The nearest Prefecture is—"

Yes, the Prefecture, Nicholas thought, a sudden spark of hope blossoming. Being imprisoned as an anarchist was a better fate than some things that could happen, and Fallier might not want to drag up ancient scandals. And he knew there wasn't a prison in Ile-Rien that could hold him for long. *Fallier might not know as much as he thinks he does. . . .*

"Not the Prefecture, the palace," the Court Sorcerer's voice said.

Well, that's that. Nicholas laughed, and the two Guards pinning him twitched as if startled. He said, "But really, the palace? Isn't that rather melodramatic?"

Someone must have gestured because he was jerked away from the cold stone and turned to face Fallier and the lieutenant. The Court Sorcerer didn't even have the grace to look triumphant. His expression was merely cool. The lieutenant looked a little wary, probably at Nicholas's sudden change of accent and voice. Then Fallier said, "It hasn't been a very well-fated destination for members of your family. I can only hope history repeats itself."

Nicholas smiled in acknowledgment. "The least you could do is tell me how you knew."

"No," Fallier said, "that is not the least I can do," and gestured to the Guards to take him away.

CHAPTER FIFTEEN

Madeline took the stairs up to the apartment two at a time. She reached the door and fumbled with the key, cursing herself when she saw how badly her hands were shaking. Finally, the lock turned and she flung the door open.

Lamane stood in the doorway to the salon, staring blankly at her. "Did Nicholas come back here?" she demanded.

He shook his head. "No, no one's come. What's happened?" Inspector Ronsarde appeared in the doorway past him, a blanket draped over his shoulders.

Madeline shut the door behind her. "No telegrams, messages?"

"No, there's been nothing." Lamane looked a little unnerved. Madeline didn't imagine her expression was terribly reassuring at the moment. She leaned back against the heavy wooden door. This had been her last hope. If Nicholas had been unable to meet them for reasons of his own, he would have come here or sent a message. She rubbed her temples, trying to massage away the ache of tension.

Ronsarde let out his breath in exasperation and came forward to take her arm and draw her inside the salon. The fire burned brightly and a card game was laid out on one of the little tables. Ronsarde led her firmly to one of the well-upholstered couches, saying, "Sit down, calm yourself, and tell me what has happened."

Madeline sat down, glaring at him. "Don't treat me like one of those stupid women who come to the Prefecture because they think their neighbors are shocking them with electric current—"

"Then don't act like it," he said sharply. "What has gone wrong?"

She looked away. It wasn't his fault and the last thing they needed to do now was argue. "I think Nicholas was caught."

Ronsarde's face hardened. "By whom?"

Madeline drew breath to speak and then hesitated, remembering who and what he was. *No, we're in this too deeply to hold back now,* she thought, exasperated at herself. *And Halle knows already.* But she trusted Halle more than she did Ronsarde. She said, "A detachment of the Royal Guard rode up as the others were leaving. Nicholas was trapped in the middle of the street and couldn't slip away." She quickly told him everything Reynard had witnessed during the carriage wreck concerning Octave's death and the intrusion of the sorcerer again. "The others are still searching for Nicholas, trying to discover if he was taken to the Prefecture or the palace. . . ." Madeline was the only one who knew what that might mean, that there was a reason other than the crimes he had committed as Donatien that the palace might be interested in Nicholas.

Ronsarde threw the blanket off and paced. Lamane had found a walking cane for him somewhere and his limp didn't seem to slow him down much, as if some of the old energy Halle had described in his articles was return-ing to him. He said, "This sorcerer's ability to anticipate our movements is distressing."

"He can't have put another Sending on us," Madeline protested, gesturing around her at the apartment. "We would all be dead."

"Oh yes, if he had been able to fix his power on one of us, we would never have gotten through the sewer alive and we certainly wouldn't have been able to take shelter here unmolested for so long. No, it was Dr. Octave he was fol-lowing, watching somehow, knowing our next step would be to accost him." Ronsarde stopped in front of the hearth, staring into it, eyes narrowed. "He unites the ferocity of an obsessed maniac with the cognitive ability of the sane; this is not a pleasant combination."

"What about Nicholas?" Madeline said, running a hand through her hair wearily. She wasn't accustomed to feeling helpless and it wasn't a sensation she found agreeable in the least.

"If he has been taken to the palace, I can help," Ronsarde said. His mouth twisted wryly. "I should say, I can try to help. Appealing to them directly was an avenue I meant to take once we had obtained more solid evidence for our theories. It's always risky to approach royalty, especially after one's just es-caped from prison—you never know the attitude they are going to assume. But even without official assistance I can still secure entry to the place, at least for the present."

Madeline exchanged a look with Lamane, who shrugged, baffled. She thought Ronsarde was babbling and with everything else that had gone wrong, it didn't much surprise her at all.

The outer door rattled again and they all tensed, Lamane reaching for the pistol in his coat, but it was Crack who stepped through the salon door. He went immediately to Madeline, standing in front of her and breathing hard. He said, "It's the palace."

She swallowed in a suddenly dry throat. She hadn't believed it, not really, not until now. "How do you know?"

"The captain found somebody who seen the troop go back in through Prince's Gate. He was with 'em."

"Then we are committed." Ronsarde nodded to himself. "We will pursue the best course we can and hope we are not making a possibly fatal mistake." He looked around the room thoughtfully, as if marshaling nonexistent troops, ignoring the way the others stared at him. "I will need your help to obtain materials for a disguise, young lady."

——

Nicholas had never been to the palace before, not even in the areas on the north side that were open to the public during Bank Holidays. He had not thought it particularly politic, or sensible, to attend, even though there was said to be a museum display of items from the Bisran Wars in the old Summer Residence that he would have quite liked to see.

He did not think it was particularly politic, or sensible, to be entering the palace now, but then the choice wasn't his.

The plaza in front of Prince's Gate was lit by gas lamps and there were so many torches in the towers that the whole edifice looked as if it was on fire. The light washed the ancient stone blocks of the walls and the great iron-sheathed doors with a dull orange-red glow. There was a line of crested carriages waiting to enter the palace grounds for some occasion, with the usual crowd of idlers there to watch.

Nicholas was on horseback, one of the troopers leading his mount, the sound of the hooves muted by paving stones softened and polished by time. The Guards at the gate halted the carriages as the troop passed under the great arch of the Queen Ravenna Memorial. A few necks craned as the occupants tried to see who the troop was escorting, but Nicholas had been placed near the center and he thought no one could get a good view. They had bound his hands with a set of manacles held together by a lock that he would have found laughable under less serious circumstances. He had two pieces of wire sewn into the cuff of his shirtsleeve that would open it with little trouble. It was Fallier he was worried about.

The Court Sorcerer rode ahead in his coach, a fashionable vehicle with the royal crest on its doors. The gate Guard saluted as it went by. Nicholas watched the back of it even as they passed through Prince's Gate, more aware of it than the menace inherent in the battlemented walls and the armed men surrounding him.

Try as he might, he couldn't cast Rahene Fallier as Octave's mad sorcerer.

He didn't know much about Fallier personally, but everything he knew about his political career suggested a more subtle man than the sorcerer who had transformed the Courts Plaza into a battleground.

As they drew away from the gate, the torchlight faded and the shadows grew thick. The troop drew rein in a dark cobblestoned court whose uneven surface spoke of many years' use. Gaslight and other such modern innovations evidently had not come to this part of the palace; there were only oil lamps and the scattered illumination from the windows above to light the court. It was surrounded, turned into a deep well almost, by old stone and timbered buildings of elegant design, by massive stone edifices with fantastically carved pediments and new structures of brick, which seemed stark and ugly against the older work. Nicholas realized with a shock that they had passed within the wards, must have passed them at some point outside the gate. *And I didn't even turn to stone,* he thought.

He saw that Fallier's coach continued on, vanishing under a deep archway. This was one of the oldest sections of the whole walled complex, built to be a fortress and the center of Vienne's defenses. The newer section lay behind the ancient King's Bastion and was more open, designed more for comfort and entertainment, and less for defense. The old buildings crumbling around him were also the most powerful ethereal point in the city, perhaps in all of Ile-Rien, better warded and more powerfully protected than even Lodun.

Dismounting from the restive cavalry horse, Nicholas pretended to clumsiness, stumbling and letting one of the troopers catch his arm to steady him. Recovering, he looked around at the circle of armed men, all larger than he was. With a rueful expression he said, "Am I that dangerous? Why not draw up an artillery battery?"

One of the troopers chuckled. Walking ahead, the lieutenant glared back at them and snapped his riding crop.

Nicholas smiled to himself, looking down to conceal the expression. He wanted them to think him harmless and he might be succeeding. He had bruises from falling in the street and his shoulder was sore from having his arm wrenched around behind him, but it was nothing that should keep him from taking any opportunity that presented itself.

That was assuming an opportunity presented itself. *Oh, no,* Nicholas thought, as the troopers hauled him across the court, *I'm becoming an optimist. I've obviously been with Madeline too long.* That thought reminded him of how worried she and the others would be. Well, as far as sorcerous attacks went, there wasn't a safer place in Ile-Rien. It was all the other dangers he had to worry about.

They took him toward one of the older buildings, a stone-and-timber structure with three or four stories. As they approached it, Nicholas noted the heavy beams and frame around the door and the apparent lack of windows in the lower floor; it was a guard barracks, then, a very old one. He was hustled inside and through a high, timbered hall, empty except for a few Guardsmen talking idly. They glanced at Nicholas curiously as the group passed but didn't offer any comments. Nicholas marked potential exits and hazards as his captors led him up a flight of wooden stairs at the end of the hall, then down a short corridor.

They stopped before a door and one of the Guards fumbled with keys. They had shed most of the troop by now, either down in the court or coming up through the main hall of the barracks, but there were still five of them and that was about four too many.

The door opened finally and he was led into a small room, windowless, walled with dingy plaster with a plain wooden chair and table the only furnishings. One of them took the manacles off, which was a consideration he hadn't expected, but then this wasn't the Prefecture. He said, "Wait. I haven't been told why I'm being held here."

One trooper hesitated but then shrugged and said, "I haven't either," as he stepped out.

The troopers stood right outside, though they hadn't closed the door. There were quiet voices in the corridor, then Rahene Fallier walked into the room.

Nicholas took a couple of steps back, putting the table between them, suddenly overcome by the gut-level conviction that Fallier was Octave's sorcerer compatriot, no matter what logic said. He told himself it was ridiculous. Fallier didn't look mad and surely no one could be mad enough to commit those acts without showing it somehow, in his eyes or in his demeanor. Nicholas said, "Now that we are, I assume, unobserved, will you tell me how you recognized me?"

Fallier stood near the table, removing his evening gloves. His expression enigmatic, he said, "You are as dark as your infamous ancestor was fair. But I've seen the Greanco portrait of Denzil Alsene, which is very like seeing the living person, and there is a resemblance."

Simply from that? Nicholas frowned. *Could it be true?* It would be impossible to believe, except for the fact that Greanco had had the second sight and his portraits had tended to capture the soul of their subjects, and that Fallier was a powerful sorcerer, with perhaps more insight into those semi-magical works of art than most. *And of course there was a portrait,* he thought sourly. Denzil Alsene had been a King's Favorite a century ago before he had hatched his plot to take the throne, and Greanco had been the most celebrated portrait painter of the age. "You could be mistaken."

"But I am not." Fallier's gaze was calm.

Nicholas was aware his palms were sweating through his torn gloves, and he couldn't tell if he was successfully keeping his expression under control. He said, "I can't think why it's of interest to you. I have every right to be in this city."

"That is true to a certain extent," Fallier said. His face gave nothing away—not his motives, his intentions, and certainly no hint of how he felt about this encounter. There was nothing for Nicholas to grasp on to. The sorcerer continued, "I'll admit to some curiosity as to why you are in Vienne."

Fallier didn't sound very curious. Nicholas said, "I live here." The cold eyes didn't change and Nicholas found himself adding, "I'm only a scion of a disgraced family; I don't see why that piques your interest." The family was still technically of the nobility of Ile-Rien, though the charter of the duchy of Alsene had been revoked when Denzil Alsene had plotted to take the throne from the then King Roland. Nicholas's ancestry should be a historical curiosity, nothing more. Surely he wasn't the only person in Vienne at the moment who was descended from a famous traitor.

Of course you're not, Nicholas thought in self-disgust. *Now tell him you've had nothing to do with the Alsenes since your mother fled their moldering estate more than twenty-five years ago, that you use her maiden name of Valiarde, that you have a legitimate business as an importer. Then tell him why you're disguised as a cabman in the middle of an apparently anarchist attack on Lady Bianci's coach.* And Denzil's treachery hadn't simply been against his king. He had plunged the city into turmoil, caused countless deaths, exposed the people to attacks by the dark fay of the Unseelie Court, murdered enemies and allies alike. He was the most hated traitor in Ile-Rien's long history. His actions and subsequent death had turned the former duchy of Alsene into an enclave of hated outcasts, not that they didn't deserve that status on their own merit.

Fallier said, "That may well be true, but somehow I doubt it." A little sarcasm slipped through the stony façade. "I have previous engagements, so I'll leave you to think of a better excuse for your presence in the street tonight." The sorcerer stepped back, pulling the door closed behind him, the lock tumblers clicking into place with what Nicholas hoped was only symbolic finality.

He waited a moment, giving Fallier time to get down the corridor. *You idiot, you've done for yourself now.* He had trouble enough in the present without dragging the past into it. And the damnable part of all this was that he hadn't meant any harm whatsoever to the Queen's stupid cousin, he had only wanted Octave.

He knelt next to the door to carefully examine the lock. It was old and not terribly secure. He touched it lightly with the back of his hand, but there was no reaction. Fallier hadn't bothered to put any magical warding on it. He extracted the wires from his cuff, carefully inserted one into the lock—an instant later he rolled on the floor, clutching his hand to his chest and biting his lip to keep from crying out.

The pain faded rapidly and Nicholas lay on his back, breathing hard, carefully working his fingers to make sure the joints and muscles still worked. "You bastard," he said aloud. So Fallier *had* bothered to ward the lock.

After a moment, Nicholas sat up and looked around the room. There was a yellowed map of the city environs pinned to one wall, an empty bookshelf in the corner. This wasn't a cell, it was only an old, unused chamber. So why hadn't he been taken somewhere more secure?

All his knowledge of the palace came from what was available in the popular press and a few half-remembered tales passed down from his father's family, which were all at least a century out of date and probably lies to begin with. But he knew there were better areas for holding prisoners than this, probably in the King's Bastion. Why hadn't Fallier had him taken there?

Fallier was taking no chances. He didn't want anyone else to know Nicholas was here.

Nicholas edged back to the door and through painful trial and error managed to ascertain that the ward didn't extend beyond the metal of the lock. He pressed his ear to the wooden door, listening for noise from the corridor. He was willing to bet there was at least one guard outside, probably two. After a moment he heard a voice, transformed into an unintelligible mumble by the thickness of the wood, and another answering mumble.

He sat back. *Dammit.* Given time, he thought he could get past the ward on the lock. Pain wasn't as effective a deterrent as some other methods, such as the spell that caused you to be distracted by movement glimpsed from the corners of your eyes whenever you focused on the warded object. He could train himself to become accustomed to the pain long enough to work the lock, and the ward might not react to a splinter of wood as quickly as it did to a metal lockpick. But he couldn't get past the guards.

Nicholas stood and began to pace.

———

Looking at Ronsarde, Madeline had to shake her head in admiration. The Inspector was as adept at disguise as she and Nicholas.

It was cold and very dark and the air had the feel of the deep night well past midnight, when only those people and spirits up to no good were about. *Which includes us,* Madeline thought grimly. They stood one street over from the palace, in the open court of a closed porter's yard, using Cusard's wagon to shield them from casual view. Down the street Madeline could see the plaza in front of the Prince's Gate, the circle of gas lamps illuminating one side of the massive arch of the Queen Ravenna Memorial and the classical fountain at its base. The plaza had been busier earlier in the night, carriages carrying guests through the gates, peddlers hawking to the small crowd of sightseers, but it was mostly deserted now except for a coach or two passing by. Madeline knew that if this sorcerer who thought himself Constant Macob somehow found them now, they wouldn't have a chance of escape. *He was following Octave,* she reminded herself. *And Octave is dead.*

It had taken an hour or more to get them to this point. Ronsarde had a special pass that allowed him to enter the palace at any time of the day or night, for the purpose of consulting with the Captains of the Queen's Guard and the Royal Guard. Since it named the bearer only as a "senior officer of the Prefecture" he could still use it to get in without alerting anyone to his identity. It had been left in the desk in his study in his apartment on Avenue Fount, which was sure to be under observation by the constables. Cusard had had to burgle the apartment to get it, going in through the attic to avoid capture himself. And it had taken Ronsarde some time to assume his disguise.

He had used hairpieces to alter the shapes of his beard and mustache, and applied an unobtrusive scar just above the left eye that still served to focus the observer's attention. In clothes that fit the role, and with the bruises and cuts from the fighting outside the prison covered with makeup, he looked an entirely different person.

He stood carefully now, folding the pass and tucking it away in his coat pocket. Everyone had had to admire that document, which was only a sheet of good quality stationery finely written with the Queen's own hand. "A damn shame there's not time to get old Besim to make a copy for us," Cusard had commented sotto voce to Madeline. "Never know when it would come in handy." *The original is coming in damn handy now,* Madeline thought. To Ronsarde she said, "You did agree now. You're going to go in, get Nicholas, and get out, and no appealing to anyone official for help, correct?" *I sound daft,* she thought. *This is the palace, for God's sake.* She reminded herself they had broken out of Vienne prison earlier today, but then Nicholas had done that before, if not under quite so spectacular circumstances.

"I shall do as I think best," Ronsarde agreed complacently. "An appeal to Captain Giarde of the Queen's Guard would be a last resort, of course."

Cusard groaned, and Reynard and Madeline exchanged a look. Crack stood like a stone, but his jaw muscles tensed. Even Dr. Halle rubbed his face and sighed. Reynard said, tightly, "I thought we had agreed—"

Ronsarde held up a hand. "I will do nothing that endangers our mission—"

"Our mission?" Cusard commented to Crack. "What about us?"

"—but I will not fail to take any opportunity that presents itself." Ronsarde's gaze went to Madeline. The ebony cane he carried was no prop, he needed it to walk, but the prospect of action seemed to have cured him of any other injury. He said, "I will find him, my dear. I swear it to you."

Madeline closed her eyes briefly, wishing she was religious enough to appeal to something supernatural, either of the old gods or the new, without feeling like a hypocrite. She and Reynard had argued over this while Ronsarde was assuming his disguise, but Madeline could think of no other way to proceed, and when pressed, neither could Reynard. She said, "Just remember that if this ends with all of us spending the rest of our lives in prison, he won't thank you for it."

Impatiently, Halle said, "Just get on with it, old man, you're driving everyone to distraction."

Ronsarde gave him an aggrieved look and adjusted the tilt of his hat. "Please,

I'm concentrating." He nodded cordially to them all and walked out into the square.

There was nothing else to try, Madeline reminded herself. She didn't like the way Ronsarde leaned so heavily on the cane, but he might be doing it intentionally, to alter his customary step and mannerisms, which was the essential part of any effective disguise.

"He won't make it," Reynard said, voicing it for all of them. Madeline had never seen him so worried and it wasn't helping her nerves any, either.

But Dr. Halle said calmly, "Oh yes, he will. He helped them work out all their guard procedures several years ago and he knows the palace intimately. If anyone can break it, he can."

Reynard pressed his lips together and didn't appear convinced. He motioned for Madeline to step back from the others and when they had drawn a short distance away, he said, "I'm acquainted with Captain Giarde. He was in the First Cavalry before he was appointed to court and we were both stationed in the Bahkri."

"Well?" Madeline prompted.

"Well, he's a bastard, but he's a very discerning bastard. If Ronsarde encounters him, he will be extremely difficult to fool." Reynard eyed her a moment, his expression a little sardonic. "Is there something I haven't been told, Madeline?"

"Yes." Madeline rubbed her face wearily. She was tired of secrets. She was tired, period. "But it's not something you're going to care much about, if you understand me."

"But it's something others would care about?" Reynard persisted.

"Yes." She hesitated, then let out her breath in resignation. "Nicholas is related to a noble family who happen to be rather famous traitors to the Crown."

"That can't be all, surely? I'm related to a noble family of rather famous drunkards and it never hurt my standing at court. When I had one, that is."

"They weren't your run-of-the-mill traitors. Nicholas is related to the Alsenes, as in Denzil Alsene."

"Oh. That traitor. *The* traitor, I should say." Reynard's brows drew together as he turned over the implications. "Is there still an interdict about Alsenes leaving the old duchy? He's not committing a crime simply by being in the city, is he?"

"No, that was apparently revoked almost fifty years ago. But . . . it doesn't look good."

"No. No, I suppose it doesn't." Reynard looked down the dark street after Ronsarde. "Damn."

———

Nicholas had waited a long, tense hour, during which the guards had never left their posts outside the door and he had become increasingly frustrated. Then he heard steps out in the hall and the lock turning. He moved warily to the back of the room, but the man who entered wasn't Fallier. It was the guard lieutenant who had helped capture him.

The man closed the door deliberately behind him. Smiling, he took a seat in the chair at the battered table, saying, "I hope you find your quarters comfortable?"

"Comfortable enough," Nicholas replied. He folded his arms and eyed his visitor thoughtfully. He was a large man, strongly built, armed with a dress sword and a serviceable pistol. He obviously thought himself secure enough from an unarmed, slightly built man. "I only wish I knew why I've been brought here."

The lieutenant said, "Perhaps I could tell you, if you were to tell me who you are and why Rahene Fallier is so interested in you."

Ah, then you don't know either, Nicholas thought. He looked at the man's sly, curious face and a plan sprang to mind, complete in practically every detail. He took a deep breath, looking away as if about to reveal some uncomfortable truth, and said, "I'm his bastard son."

The lieutenant stared, then tried to hide his astonishment and appear offhand. "Not surprising."

Save me from amateur schemers, Nicholas thought dryly. If everything he understood from his checkered family history was true, then this man didn't stand a chance among the practiced plotters at work in the royal court. He said, "My mother is . . ." The Queen was too young, in fact she was several years younger than himself, so that wouldn't do at all. *Ah, perfect.* ". . . the Countess Winrie."

The lieutenant swore under his breath. The Countess Winrie had been a prostitute famous for the most outrageous practices before she had persuaded the aging but still hale Count to marry her. He had died a year or so after the marriage, leaving the wealthy Countess the unofficial leader of the demimonde and a perpetual thorn in the side of good society. "But . . ." The lieutenant was frowning in concentration.

"You see what this would do to his reputation," Nicholas prompted. He began to pace again, slowly, getting his quarry used to the sight of him moving about. "If it were to become known . . ."

"Ah." The lieutenant nodded sagely, finally picking up on the innuendo. "You've been threatening to come forward and he has been buying your silence."

Nicholas paused and glanced back at the man, managing a trapped expression, and swallowed as if in a dry throat. He wondered what Madeline would make of this performance. *She would probably say something sarcastic about the quality of my audience,* he thought. "I have no idea what he intends to do to me," he hinted hopefully.

The lieutenant assumed an expression of smug knowledge, which Nicholas felt safe in presuming meant he didn't have the slightest notion either. The man tipped his chair back, propping his booted feet up on the table, and said callously, "Keep you out of the way permanently, I suppose."

Nicholas felt a flash of anger on behalf of this persona he had just constructed, this powerless young bastard at the mercy of his sorcerer father, and reminded himself not to get too involved in the role. He said, "My father has paid me a great deal of money over the past years and the Countess, who feels some fondness toward me, is still quite wealthy. Anyone who helped me regain my freedom would be well rewarded."

The lieutenant's eyes shifted. He said, "I would need some guarantees. You can't expect me to trust you."

Nicholas read his expression easily. The man only wanted information to give him a possible advantage over Fallier; he wasn't quite foolish enough to oppose the Court Sorcerer directly. "Of course not," Nicholas agreed readily. "Perhaps if I show you this, you will realize my sincerity." He approached the table, reaching into his pocket.

The lieutenant watched him, trying to look arch but failing to cover his obvious greed. His eyes dropped to the hand Nicholas was withdrawing from the pocket of his old coat and Nicholas kicked the chair leg. Overbalanced, the lieutenant fell backward.

Nicholas stepped in and punched him, knocking the man's head back against the wall. The thumps hadn't gone unnoticed by the guards and he heard keys working frantically in the lock. He snatched the pistol from the dazed lieutenant's holster and leapt over the tangled heap of body and chair on the floor. He put his back to the wall just as the door flew open.

He pointed the gun at the lieutenant and both guards stumbled to a halt. "Any closer and I'll shoot him, gentlemen. And please don't call out," Nicholas said evenly.

The lieutenant gasped and made a garbled noise, trying to push himself up, and Nicholas kicked the supporting hand out from under him. He motioned with the gun. "Move away from the door, please."

The two men glanced at each other, then obeyed. As they moved out of the way, Nicholas stepped quickly to the door and backed out into the corridor. Two heavy bodies struck the door as soon as it swung to, pounding on it and shouting, but Nicholas was already turning the key in the lock. Experimentally, he took a couple of steps away, then smiled. The noise the captives made was inaudible more than two steps away from the door; that would buy him some time, at least. Nicholas pocketed the key and strode down the corridor away from the main staircase, turning the corner into the cross corridor. This was a barracks and there wouldn't be an unguarded servants' door; he would have to go out the way he had come in. Running now, he passed more closed doors, an open arch into an old practice room filled with wooden fencing dummies, more passages branching toward the back of the building. Around another corner he found a second staircase, smaller and less ornate than the one in the main hall. He hurried down it, keeping his steps quiet.

The stairwell led down into an anteroom, with an archway opening onto the main area. Nicholas paused at the edge of the arch, back against the wall, leaning around to get a view of the hall. The number of men there had greatly increased. Most were in Royal Guard uniforms but a few were in civilian dress. Nicholas cursed under his breath. *Of course, that was why the lieutenant had time to question me.* The guard was changing, with men going off duty and their replacements coming on. The confusion might make it easier—if Fallier was trying to keep his capture quiet, most of the men coming on duty might not have been informed there was a prisoner in the barracks. What he needed to do now was steal a uniform coat and . . . Nicholas's attention was suddenly caught by a man in civilian dress standing with his back to him, apparently studying the flags of old decommissioned guard troops displayed along the gallery, and engaged in animated conversation with a Royal Guard lieutenant. For a moment he thought he had recognized him. *But it couldn't be,* Nicholas told himself. *Not here.*

The man turned and Nicholas stared suspiciously at his face, his clothes. *It could very well be,* he thought grimly. The man was limping, he was the right height, the right build, about the right age, despite possible cosmetic alterations to his hair and features and— *And he is using an ebony cane with a carved ivory handle exactly like the one Reynard brought back from Parscia.* Nicholas resisted the urge to knock his head against the wall. *Damn them.*

There was a shout from the gallery. One of the guards Nicholas had left locked in his temporary prison careened down the stairs and ran across the hall, heading for the outside doors. The off-duty guards watched him go, some calling out questions. *He's going for Fallier,* Nicholas thought. *He must have ordered them to keep my capture secret.*

As the men in the hall went about their business, Nicholas snatched off his cap and ducked out into the milling crowd. Keeping his head down, he managed to fetch up against the old man with the cane. "Were you looking for me, sir?" he asked, in a Riverside accent.

Inspector Ronsarde actually had the audacity to smile. "There you are, my good fellow." He turned to the Guard lieutenant standing at his elbow. This lieutenant was older than the man who had helped with Nicholas's capture and his gaze was sharper. "I sent my driver here to see if he could locate Sir Diandre. No luck, then?"

This last was addressed to Nicholas, who shook his head and said, "No sir, no one here's heard tell of him." He kept his head ducked and fervently hoped Ronsarde had chosen the name of a man who was on leave or otherwise inaccessible.

"Ah, well, then. We'll keep at it. Simply must find him. . . ."

"Have you tried the Gallery Wing, sir? There is a ball tonight and he may be attending," the lieutenant said. He was choosing his words carefully and his expression was a little guarded. He did not appear an easy man to deceive. Ronsarde must have concocted quite a story to get this far.

"That's a thought. Yes, if he isn't here . . . I shall try there immediately, then, thank you very much." There was a flicker of suspicion in the man's eyes. Then Ronsarde paused and with a self-possession that Nicholas would have admired had he been less angry, said, "Could you accompany me or does duty call?"

The suspicion vanished and the lieutenant consulted his pocket watch. "No, I'm afraid I must stay here. I can assign someone to guide you if—"

"Oh, no, don't bother, I can find my way on my own. I was here for the Queen's Birthday, you know. Thank you again for your assistance. . . ."

The expostulations and goodbyes seemed to go on forever. Nicholas felt sweat run down his back. But finally Ronsarde exchanged one last handshake with his new friend and they made their way down the length of the hall. Nicholas stayed behind the Inspector, who kept to a steady pace despite his limp and the need to hurry. They were almost to the arch of the stone-walled foyer when a Guard corporal stepped forward to accost Ronsarde. "Sir, are you—"

Ronsarde flourished a folded paper. "Here to see Captain Giarde, young man."

At the sight of the seal on the document and the name of the Queen's Guard Captain, the corporal backed away, saluting for good measure.

Nicholas didn't breathe, didn't dare lift his head until they were out of the main doors and down the steps. Once they were in the cold windswept court and out of range of the lamps, Nicholas grabbed Ronsarde's arm and dragged him to a sheltered corner. "What are you doing here?" he demanded.

"Looking for you, my boy. Really, what did you think? I would've been here sooner, but it took me some time to find where they had taken you. Discovering it was the old barracks was somewhat anticlimactic; I had anticipated having to free you from the holding cells under the Gate Tower."

"I'm so sorry you were disappointed," Nicholas said, through gritted teeth. "I risk everything to get you out of that damn prison and you come here?"

"Of course." Ronsarde glanced around the court. There were groups of people crossing between the shadowy hulks of the buildings around them, laughing and talking, some bearing lanterns. They didn't look like search parties but in the dark it was hard to tell. The Inspector asked, "Do you know where you are?"

"Not particularly."

"You were held in the old Queen's Guard barracks, or what's left of it. It was expanded when the Royal Guard was chartered."

"Ordinarily I have a deep appreciation for historical curiosities, but at the present moment—"

"And that," Ronsarde continued, pointedly, "is the Albon Tower, which was enlarged to join the Old Palace, destroying much of the security provided by the old siege walls and bastions, but allowing us to make our way through the lower floors to the new section of the palace grounds, where there is a ball being given for the Lord Mayor in the Gallery Wing. Most of the guests will have left by now but St. Anne's Gate should still be relatively busy, and they will not be searching for you there."

"Then let's go."

The tower only lay across the court but Nicholas felt exposed and vulnerable as they made their way toward it. There was one guard on the door, standing under a lamp suspended from the mouth of a stone gargoyle. Ronsarde displayed his pass again and they were waved on.

Once inside, they found themselves in a large drafty hall, the curved ceiling supported by heavy square pillars. The place had an almost unused air and there were only a few lamps to light the way through. Ronsarde hesitated, getting his bearings, then said, "This way," and strode forward.

They were almost to the center of the large room when the doors behind them crashed open. Nicholas spun, drawing the pistol. Guards poured into the hall behind them. Ronsarde grabbed his arm and said, "No, it's too late."

Light flared behind Nicholas and he glanced over his shoulder. More Guards with lamps moved to block the only other way out.

CHAPTER SIXTEEN

"Stop where you are, please."

Nicholas stopped. From a doorway a man pointed a pistol at them. He was a little older than Nicholas, dark-haired, bearded, wearing evening dress. Nicholas thought at first it was one of the off-duty Guards, but then he saw the men behind him were in cavalry uniforms. No, not cavalry uniforms; the sashes were different. *Queen's Guard,* Nicholas thought, recognizing the style suddenly.

"Put the weapon on the floor."

Nicholas hesitated, but only for a heartbeat. The man's eyes told him that he would shoot without compunction. Keeping his movements slow and deliberate, he lowered the pistol to the floor.

"Very good," the man said. He stepped farther into the room, the gun never wavering from its aim. Nicholas watched him grimly. The Queen's Guard had traditionally been the personal bodyguard of the Queens of Ile-Rien, and since the current Queen ruled in her own right this made them the first armed troop in the palace, and more politically powerful than the Royal Guard. If this man was their captain, he would not be as easy to escape as the hapless lieutenants they had outwitted.

Ronsarde said, "Captain Giarde, how very good to see you."

The man stopped, stared hard at the Inspector, then glanced uncertainly at Nicholas. "I don't think I know—"

Ronsarde straightened up and deliberately began removing the extra hairpieces from his beard, mustaches, and eyebrows. "Flattering of you not to recognize me," he said in his normal voice. "I threw this together in something of a hurry."

"Ronsarde?" Giarde's lips thinned in annoyance. "Good God, man, how dare you come here like this?" He looked again at Nicholas. "That's not Dr. Halle, is it?"

"No, this is my protégé, Nicholas Valiarde."

Nicholas stared at Ronsarde in fury, barely managing the self-control not to voice an outraged denial. *Protégé?*

"How did you find us, if you don't mind my asking?" Ronsarde continued easily. "You know I am always seeking to improve my technique."

"I've been following Fallier's movements, actually, and was curious to see who it was he brought here in such secret." Giarde's gaze went to Nicholas speculatively. "Your protégé?"

"Our situation has become . . . complicated," Ronsarde admitted.

Giarde motioned them to back away, then moved forward to collect Nicholas's stolen pistol. As if aware this would not be over quickly, he leaned against the nearest pillar and said, "You know you're being hunted all across the city by your own men, of course, even if the charges do sound ridiculous. Why did you escape when you must have realized the Queen would intervene as soon as the Magistrates Court ruled? And what the hell are you doing here now?"

"I did not intend to escape from the Magistrates Court," Ronsarde said, as if it should be obvious to anyone. "I was seized, by men hired to insure my silence, and was about to be murdered when I was rescued by some friends and associates. We then spent the next several hours fleeing for our lives. That is the short version."

Giarde did not appear pleased. "I hope the long one is more illuminating."

Ronsarde cleared his throat. "Then, as we continued our investigations, Valiarde here was detained without cause and I came to retrieve him."

"Wait." Giarde held up a hand. He motioned one of the Guards over, spoke a moment, and sent the man away.

Nicholas stared at Ronsarde in mixed disgust and disbelief. "That's to be our story, is it? I was doing better as the illegitimate son of the Court Sorcerer," he said, keeping his voice low.

"Don't be alarmed," Ronsarde said, maddeningly. "The situation is well in hand."

Nicholas wished he had taken his chances with the pistol.

Giarde turned his attention back to them. He said, "It's odd that you claim this man is working for you, because my sources informed me the prisoner brought in by the Royal Guard gate troop was involved in an anarchist attack on Lady Bianci's coach." He looked at Nicholas. "Is that why Fallier had you brought here?"

Nicholas would have wagered anything that Giarde already knew why Fallier had brought him here, or at least that he had guessed most of the truth. "I was a witness to the attack. The driver and the footmen can verify that," he said. "I was not arrested by the troop." Nicholas hesitated, reluctant to say it aloud, but there was no help for it. And the sooner Giarde was distracted from the coach incident the better. Nicholas said, "I'm an indirect descendent of Denzil Alsene. Fallier was extremely interested in me."

Disgusted, Ronsarde said, "Was that all?" but the captain's face was impassive.

Giarde said, "You told him who you were."

Nicholas smiled. "No. Fallier told me."

Giarde was silent a moment more, considering. "How exactly did this come about?"

"I haven't been to Alsene since I was a child," Nicholas said. "I don't use the name and I have no desire to. I was about to leave the scene of the coach accident so I could report to the Inspector." He couldn't help throwing a dark look at Ronsarde, but the Inspector didn't seem to notice. "Fallier said he recognized me from the Greanco portrait of Denzil Alsene. I have no idea if he was telling the truth or not." He suspected it was true, but there was no harm in muddying the water a little. "He had me brought here quite against my will."

Giarde was thoughtful. "I see."

"All this aside," Ronsarde interrupted testily, "the city is being menaced by a criminal sorcerer, and if I"—he paused and corrected himself graciously—"if we are to do anything about it, I must have a pardon and some assistance, thank you."

"What are you talking about?" Giarde demanded.

Ronsarde waved his arms in frustration, causing the watching Guards to stir nervously. "The person who caused the disturbance in the Courts Plaza, the deaths in Vienne Prison, and Valent House. He is most certainly a sorcerer, he is most assuredly a criminal, and I would have apprehended him by now without all this deliberate interference."

"You know who he is?"

Ronsarde glanced at Nicholas. "Not yet, but we have our suspicions. I need a pardon, Captain. The situation is urgent."

Giarde's expression was difficult to read. He put his pistol into his coat pocket and said, "It's very late."

"She will be awake."

He can't mean who I think he means, Nicholas thought, shifting uneasily. This experience was surreal enough already.

Giarde hesitated. "You're not exaggerating this?"

Ronsarde's expression was grim. "I only wish I was."

"All right." Giarde tossed the pistol Nicholas had stolen to one of the Guards. "Follow me."

Ronsarde nodded as if pleased. Nicholas took a deep breath to calm his pounding heart.

Giarde led them through dark halls, farther into the tower. With the lamps of the Guardsmen sending shadows chasing up old stone walls that bore marks of fire, and at least one round impact that looked as if it could have come from a cannonball, they might have been passing back through time. Nicholas would not have been terribly surprised if they were leading him to one of the dungeons below these ancient floors. He thought about bolting down one of the cross corridors they passed but knew that would be useless; he didn't know the place and would probably be rounded up within minutes.

It was known there were areas in the lower levels of the palace still sealed off from when the Unseelie Court had occupied it for that short time over a hundred years ago. Corridors, storerooms, stairwells, huge echoing cellars, blocked off by falling walls and collapsed roofs, that had been left as they were with no effort expended to reclaim them from the earth.

But the double doors they eventually came to opened into an old if not ancient stairway, lit prosaically by gaslights. The gas pipes were mounted on the walls, since the plaster and wood panelling must be only a thin veneer over solid stone. Nicholas knew they had left the tower; this must be the King's Bastion.

They went up the stairs and through a few echoing halls with abrupt turns and occasional dead ends, until Nicholas realized he was thoroughly lost. He could tell they were approaching the more well-used portions of the palace when the floor underfoot turned from polished wood to white marble.

They passed several of the semipublic areas, seeing no one but a few quiet servants, then entered a reception room. Giarde said, "Wait here," and continued on, leaving the other Queen's guards with them.

Nicholas folded his arms, resisting the urge to pace. The room was small, chill, with a marble floor and mantels and a set of delicate giltwood chairs that looked as if they would burst apart if sat on. He knew he looked an odd figure here, dressed all in tattered black and with an expression of dark outrage. It was perhaps an appropriate appearance for the first Alsene to visit the palace of Ile-Rien in so many years.

Leaning on his cane, Ronsarde said conversationally, "I discovered your rather colorful antecedents when I was first investigating your foster father. I thought it of no consequence, however."

Nicholas looked at him, eyes narrowed. "You're not endearing yourself to me, you know."

Giarde reappeared and motioned them to follow. As they did, Nicholas noticed the Queen's guards remained behind. He glanced sideways at Ronsarde but couldn't tell if the Inspector seemed relieved or not. They went down another hall and then through an open doorway into a vast chamber.

An arched arcade ran all along the upper half and the floor was covered with parquet and very old Parscian carpets. An enormous chimneypiece of black-and-white marble would have dominated the room, except for the gold-framed mirrors, the elaborate floral designs of the figured ceiling, and the faded glory of the two-hundred-year-old tapestries. The furniture was all marquetry or vermeil, all in colors of old gold or amber, until the room seem to glow with it. Ronsarde nudged Nicholas with an elbow and pointed up. Three large gold lanterns of intricate design hung from the ceiling. "From the barge of the Grand Cardinal of Bisra, looted during the battle of Akis in the last Bisran War," he whispered. "The touch of the conquering barbarian among the splendors of civilization."

"I heard that."

There was a woman seated in an armchair near the massive hearth. She was small and her face was very young, a girl's face almost, except it was too thin to be entirely childish. Her hair was red and worn piled up under a very old-fashioned lace cap, and her dark dress looked plain and almost dowdy, until the lamplight caught it and revealed it as a deep indigo velvet. She was laying out cards in a game of solitaire on the little table in front of her and she hadn't looked up at her visitors.

She said, "You were arrested." A quick, almost furtive glance revealed she was speaking to Ronsarde. Her voice was light and unexpectedly girlish for someone with such a serious mien.

"I was, my lady," the Inspector said calmly.

Nicholas felt the back of his neck prickle. Traditionally in Ile-Rien, officers of the royal court and palace staff addressed royalty as "my lady" or "my lord" instead of the more formal and cumbersome "Your Majesty." That Ronsarde had been granted that indulgence showed he was closer to the Crown's confidence than Nicholas had previously suspected.

"Can't have that," the Queen muttered, as if to herself. She turned over a card and ran her thumb along the edge, lost in thought. "I know who you are," she said. Another quick glance showed she was speaking to Nicholas now. "It was distressing that Rahene Fallier brought you here without informing me."

"Distressing, but not entirely unexpected," Giarde added.

The Queen shot Giarde a dark look. She made an abrupt gesture, as if embarrassed by this admission. "Politics, you understand."

"I avoid politics, Your Majesty," Nicholas said.

She looked up at him then, for the first time, eyes narrowed as if she suspected mockery. She probably was mocked, to her face or to her back, by the more sophisticated ladies of the court and by those of her advisors who didn't appreciate serving a woman who appeared barely out of childhood. If he remembered rightly she wasn't older than twenty-four. Apparently satisfied that he had spoken in all seriousness, she said, "Wise of you," and looked back down at her game. She placed the card carefully in the array on the table. "There is a resemblance. I think it's the eyes." She turned over another card and studied it. "And I suppose your mother must have been the first new blood in that family for several generations."

She was speaking of his resemblance to the long-dead Denzil. Nicholas damned Greanco's skill. "Circumstance has made them insular"—he hesitated infinitesimally—"Your Majesty."

"It was a pretty damn deliberate circumstance," the Queen corrected, her voice dry. She glanced at him furtively. "When I was a child I met your aunt Celile once, at a garden party the Valmontes gave at Gardien-on-Bannot." She shuddered, not theatrically, but apparently in real horror at the memory. "Horrible woman."

"You should try having to face her over dinner." The words were out before Nicholas could stop them.

The Queen hesitated, her hand on a card. Her smile was so brief it might have been imaginary. She looked at him directly then, her large eyes utterly serious, and said, "I've seen the house, from a distance. It was horrible, too. What was it like there?"

Nicholas drew a breath but was temporarily unable to speak. He knew he needed to answer her but he hadn't expected this. If he had ever imagined this meeting, he would never in his wildest dreams have constructed it in this fashion. He thought of the decaying, faded glories of the Alsene Great House, the land meant to support it long gone, either sold off to pay debts or taken by the Crown as more punishment for Denzil's long-ago attempt to seize the throne of Roland Fontainon, who was this woman's great-great-grandfather. He said, "Mercifully, I don't remember much of it." There were details, long buried beneath the surface, that insisted on springing to mind. He added only, "My father died and my mother fled with me to Vienne."

She blinked, her expression unchanging. "Are we related?"

"It's a distant connection." He suspected she knew it very well; the purpose of the question had been to ascertain if he knew it.

She sat back in her chair. "By the charters of Old Vienne and Riverside, and the Council of Margrave and the Barons of Viern, there is a proposed line of descent that gives you a claim on the throne." One eyebrow quirked, but her face was serious. "I might have to marry you."

The shock wasn't mild but Nicholas realized immediately that he was being tested, in ways both subtle and blunt. *It explained what Fallier wanted of me,* he thought, feeling a sinking sensation in the pit of his stomach. Perhaps that was why the family seldom left the estate. His father had only left long enough to court his mother. And there were those who had never left the slowly rotting house, who had spent their whole lives living for the past. He was probably the first Alsene to come to Vienne in generations. He said, "The Council of Margrave and the Barons of Viern was invalidated by the later action of the Ministry, in their first convening in Vienne."

"That's true." The Queen slumped back in her chair suddenly, frowning. "I'd forgotten."

Thank you, Dr. Uberque, for a thorough grounding in the history of court-law, Nicholas thought, though he didn't believe for a moment the Queen had forgotten that obscure fact. It was like watching Madeline play a role, only underneath it all Madeline was harmlessly amusing herself and the Queen was anything but. *The woman uses candor like a loaded pistol.* He still thought her courtiers probably mocked her, but if they did it within her hearing, they probably didn't do it twice. In his peripheral vision he saw Giarde wincing and rubbing the bridge of his nose.

She sat up straight again and Nicholas suspected he was about to be dealt another roundhouse blow. She said, "But you're still the heir to the Alsene properties."

"Like being the heir to Hell, only less glamorous," Nicholas said, keeping his voice light. But this was almost a relief. He had never expected nor wanted to inherit anything from the Alsenes and indeed he doubted they had anything worth wanting. He bowed, ironically. "I renounce my claim, Your Majesty."

"Really? Because when you say it to me, you know, it's official." The Queen pointed this out somewhat diffidently, as if embarrassed by it.

He hadn't known. He hadn't lived at Alsene long enough to be taught all the vagaries of the landed noble's relationship with the Crown. Nicholas said, "I want no part of the family of Alsene. I am not the heir." There was a curious sense of freedom in saying it.

She glanced at Giarde and said, "We'll write that into the court proceedings, remind me, please."

Giarde sighed audibly and the Queen glared at him again. Nicholas would have given a great deal to know what their relationship was. Queens of Ile-Rien had always taken lovers among their personal guard; it was practically a tradition.

A large ginger cat suddenly leapt up onto the table and, with great deliberation, settled itself down on top of the card game. The Queen froze, card in hand, and stared at it with a grim set to her mouth. The cat returned her gaze with a challenging air and settled itself more comfortably. The Queen sighed, evidently conceding the point, and set the card aside. She leaned back in her chair and folded her hands, looking thoughtfully down at the carpet. "We were going on to that other matter. . . ."

Giarde evidently took that as a signal to continue. He cleared his throat and glanced at Ronsarde. "I've sent for Lord Albier. He's in charge of the investigation of the incident today. I thought he might benefit from this discussion."

Ronsarde and Nicholas exchanged a look. Lord Albier was the head of the Prefecture and no one had said yet whether they were under arrest or not.

"And I've asked Fallier to attend," Giarde continued. He smiled. "His reaction should be illuminating."

The Queen glanced up at him, her mouth twisting ironically. Her expression as she looked at her Guard Captain was much the same as when she had looked at her cat, holding both affection and resigned annoyance.

A butler caught Giarde's attention from the doorway and the captain motioned him forward. As the servant conferred with the Queen and Giarde, Nicholas said, low-voiced, to Ronsarde, "Well, are we for prison or not?"

"I'm not sure," Ronsarde admitted. "It's always so hard to tell what the dear child is thinking. Giarde has some influence on her but not as much as appearances suggest." He shrugged philosophically. "You've escaped from the Vienne prison twice now, haven't you? Don't most sorcerous formulae suggest the third time should be lucky?"

Nicholas rubbed his forehead, to conceal his expression from the others. "Oh, if I'm to be sent to prison I'd prefer it to be for bashing in the head of a Prefecture Inspector and leaving his body in a midden." He was beginning to feel a deep sense of sympathy for Dr. Halle.

Ronsarde chuckled.

The butler retreated and Giarde glanced at them and explained, "Fallier and Albier are here."

The Queen shifted uneasily.

"This should be interesting," Ronsarde muttered.

Nicholas folded his arms. "Interesting" was a good word for it.

It was Fallier who entered first, Lord Albier following. Nicholas knew the sorcerer was almost instantly aware of his presence even though he gave no sign of it.

Fallier paused, meeting the Queen's gaze without challenge but without apology either. She said nothing, merely looked at him with a light in her eyes that might have been contempt. It was the imperturbable Court Sorcerer who was the first to look away. Turning to Giarde, he said, "I was told this was a matter of some urgency, Captain?" His voice was cool.

"Inspector Ronsarde has some intelligence concerning the sorcerous attack on the Courts," Giarde said. He looked thoughtfully at the sorcerer. "That is all."

Fallier's eyes narrowed slightly and he looked from Giarde to the Queen. Nicholas saw that her hand, resting on the delicate chair arm, the jeweled rings incongruous next to bitten nails, was trembling. *She is seething,* he thought. He suspected this wasn't the first time Fallier had attempted politics, as the Queen had called it.

In the meantime, Lord Albier stared at Ronsarde, caught between astonishment and anger. He was a large, florid man, very much the type of the military officer. The state of his clothes suggested he had dressed hastily. "Captain, I demand an explanation. Inspector Ronsarde is a wanted man. What the—"

"The Inspector has reasons for his rather odd behavior," Giarde interjected, before Albier could commit the indignity of swearing in front of his sovereign.

Ronsarde smiled at Albier. "Have you been searching for me very hard, sir? If so, I suggest it's time for another review of the detective force, because I assure you I was not that difficult to find."

Albier reddened. He looked at Giarde and said harshly, "I should have been informed—"

"You're being informed now," Giarde interrupted, apparently tiring of Albier's discomfiture. "Have you made any progress on discovering who turned the Courts Plaza into a sorcerous spectacle yesterday?"

Albier retained his control with an effort. "We had nothing to investigate. The sorcerers we called in could find no trace of the identity of the person who caused the disruption." Albier was all but ignoring the Queen, which Nicholas thought was poor judgment indeed.

Giarde nodded to Ronsarde. "I believe the Inspector can shed some light on it. He and his . . . associate have been investigating the matter."

For the first time, Fallier's gaze came to rest on Nicholas. He allowed himself one small smile at the sorcerer's expense and Fallier turned his attention to Ronsarde, without reacting. *He is a dangerous man,* Nicholas thought. He was making another enemy tonight, that much was obvious.

Ronsarde cleared his throat and began to describe the events of the past few days, beginning with his investigation of Octave.

Listening to him, Nicholas was pointedly reminded of the current difficulties of his situation. Even his delight at Fallier's discomfort was dampened.

He had told Madeline that Donatien was dead, but perhaps he hadn't quite believed it himself until now.

The Inspector's quiet voice as he told their story was working on Nicholas's nerves like salt on raw flesh. *It has to be this way,* he told himself. To get this sorcerer, he would have to have help. He was running out of resources and time and, more importantly, they had him dead to rights. There was no other choice.

When he looked back he realized the Queen's eyes were on him, that she had read his reaction as plainly as if he had spoken aloud. Her gaze flicked away as if she was ashamed to be caught watching him.

Ronsarde told them all they had discovered so far, his deductions and Nicholas's, their individual and shared discoveries, making it sound as though Nicholas had been working under Ronsarde's auspices from the very beginning. He left out anything that might hint at less than legal activities on Nicholas's part. The Inspector made it sound as if he had known Nicholas all his life and that was, in a way, true, just not in the way Ronsarde was implying. *You should be grateful,* he thought, instead of standing here simmering with resentment. Sebastion Ronsarde, Inspector of the Prefecture, sworn to the Crown, was standing here lying like a market confidence trickster to save him. And he was telling those lies to the Queen, who was sitting there blinking solemnly and probably all too aware she wasn't hearing more than half the real story, but trusting Ronsarde anyway.

As the Inspector finished, Giarde and the Queen looked at Albier. He coughed and said, "I had heard some part of this before—"

"And believed none of it—" Ronsarde interrupted.

"You had no proof," Albier said heatedly, "only outrageous speculations!"

"I assume the destruction and death yesterday is proof enough?" Ronsarde's voice was icy, for one moment revealing the bitterness he must have felt at his warnings going unheeded.

"Of course." Albier gestured to Giarde. "But even the great Inspector can give us no clue as to this person's whereabouts."

This was too much for Nicholas's abraded nerves. He interrupted, "There is, in fact, one clue."

That got everyone's attention, including Ronsarde, who stared at him, frowning. Nicholas said, "Dr. Octave, before he was killed by his associate, said that the sorcerer was hiding in a 'palace on the river.'"

"There are a number of deserted or unused Great Houses along the river or on the islands," Albier muttered.

"And they will be searched," Giarde said. He looked at the Court Sorcerer, who said, "I will put my apprentices at the disposal of Lord Albier."

The Queen said suddenly, "You're dismissed."

Albier looked startled, almost offended, and actually looked at Giarde for confirmation, but Fallier bowed and turned at once to go, crossing the parquet floor to the doors.

It must have finally dawned on Albier that there were undercurrents of which he was unaware. He bowed to the Queen and to Giarde said, "I'll make you aware of any progress." With another dark glance at Ronsarde, he followed Fallier out.

As the doors closed behind them, Ronsarde shook his head. "I don't like to say it, but in light of what brought us here, I find I do not entirely trust Fallier."

Giarde glanced at the Queen and seemed to receive some quiet and almost imperceptible signal. He said, "Fallier may be Court Sorcerer, but he is not Her Majesty's only advisor in things sorcerous. The person who holds that position is a very old woman who lives in a corner of the main kitchen in the North Bastion. To consult with her it's necessary to go to the kitchen in question and crouch on a coal scuttle, but she is always correct, and her advice is untainted by political pressures of any kind. I'll put this before her and see what she thinks." He added, "She sent me a note a short time ago to tell me that within the past few hours there have been no less than three etherial assaults on the palace, all repelled by the wards."

"That . . . isn't unexpected," Nicholas said. *He's still after us,* he thought. *Killing Octave didn't satisfy him.* But how could the man be a sorcerer in Ile-Rien and not know the palace at Vienne was the most heavily protected place, both physically and etherically, in this part of the world? The wards that guarded it were woven into the very stones of the oldest parts of the structure, they had been created and maintained by the most powerful sorcerers in Ile-Rien's history, and some of them were so old they were almost self-aware. How could the man think he could strike at them past that magical barrier? *Except. . . .* "Fontainon House."

Nicholas looked up to realize everyone was staring at him. Ronsarde nodded and said, "Yes, the reason Octave stayed to perform his circle."

Giarde swore. "Fontainon House is inside the wards."

The Queen was frowning. She looked at Nicholas, brows lowered, and he explained, "During a circle, Octave would apparently materialize ghosts. It's possible he meant to open a circle in Fontainon House, within the wards, and open a way for something else to materialize."

"He leaves bodies strewn like discarded trash," the Queen said, suddenly. She stroked the now somnolent cat with a quick, nervous touch. "I take it we assume he is a madman?"

"The indications are there, my lady," Ronsarde said.

She subsided again, staring bitterly at the carpet.

"Well?" Giarde asked her. There was a stillness to his expression that brought Nicholas back from all thoughts of their sorcerous opponent. *He is asking her if we—I—should be released.* Ronsarde had done nothing except try to stay alive; Nicholas was the one who presented a problem.

The Queen's eyes lifted, met Nicholas's gaze shyly. *Shy doesn't mean weak,* Nicholas thought. It would be entertaining to live long enough for Fallier to realize that. She said, "You're certain?"

That one baffled him. "Your Majesty?"

"About the inheritance? About giving it up?"

It was such an ingenuous question, yet he didn't doubt her seriousness. "I'm

certain, Your Majesty. I was certain a long time ago." He found himself adding, "Of course, a true Alsene would say anything to get out of this, would
swear allegiance to the devil, even."

She sighed and looked at nothing in particular. Then she stood, gathering
her cat in one large ginger armful. She stepped close to Nicholas before he
could react, put her hand on his shoulder and said, gravely, "Your aunt Celile
still writes to me. If you fail, I shall give her your address."

Then she was making her way to the door, the cat's tail snapping with irritation at its interrupted nap, while the men in the room hastily bowed.

As the doors closed behind her, Nicholas felt something unclench around
his heart. He distinctly heard Ronsarde draw a relieved breath. Giarde shook
his head, as if in continued amazement at his sovereign's thought processes.
With an air of resignation he asked Ronsarde, "Is there any other assistance
you require?"

"Albier was correct on one point," the Inspector said. "We have to find this
sorcerer first. We can do nothing until we know where he is."

"The Prefecture will search the abandoned structures along the river with
the help of Fallier and his apprentices. Lord Albier will believe he is directing
the investigation, but he'll take my advice, and I'll take yours."

"A pardon, so I can continue my investigations without impediment, would
also be helpful," Ronsarde pointed out.

Giarde folded his arms. "Our influence with the Prefecture is not all in-
clusive. It will take some time to persuade the Lord Chief Commissioner that
your rampage through the lower levels of the prison was done in the Crown's
name." He added, "But I'm sure something can be arranged."

Ronsarde's bow was a trifle ironic. "In the meantime, I would prefer to stay
with my associates and contact the Prefecture through you or Lord Albier."

"That would probably be wise."

Giarde led them out, pausing in the reception room to say, "Take care, Ronsarde. You have powerful enemies."

"Yes, that had begun to dawn on me," Ronsarde confessed.

Giarde sighed and glanced briefly heavenward. "I'm serious. If you leave the
palace, I can't protect you."

"If I don't leave the palace, I can't catch him," Ronsarde said, patiently. "And
that would be too dangerous for all of us."

Giarde watched him narrowly, then nodded. "We can get you outside the
palace walls without drawing unwanted attention. There's a passage under St.

Anne's Gate that leads to the underground station on the Street of Flowers. My men will take you that far." He glanced at Nicholas, his eyes hooded, then said, "I think you are keeping dangerous company, Inspector."

"Oh come now," Ronsarde said, smiling indulgently. "That's a terrible thing to say about old Halle."

Giarde glared at him in exasperation. "I'm the only thing that's standing between you and a few nights in the Prefecture cells, so I'd think you could at least pretend to show me a little diffidence."

"I'm sorry." Ronsarde managed a contrite expression that fooled no one. "I will try to do better."

"Get out, before I change my mind."

Following their escort of Queen's guards down the opulent halls, Nicholas waited until they were a safe distance from Giarde and the royal environs, then said, accusingly, "You're enjoying this."

Ronsarde glanced at him, arching a brow. "And you aren't?"

There was no answer for that. Seething, Nicholas made no reply.

After a moment of silence, the Inspector said, "Don't be fooled by Her Majesty's rather unusual manner. Her habits of thought are devastatingly precise."

"Whatever gave you the idea I was fooled?" Nicholas said, coldly. "It was everything I could do not to accept her offer of marriage at once. I think we would have taken Bisra and half of Parscia within the year."

"A frightening thought." Ronsarde watched him alertly for a moment, then as they reached the head of the staircase, stopped Nicholas with a hand on his sleeve.

Their escort halted on the steps below, looking back up at them impatiently. Low-voiced, Ronsarde said, "We'll find this man. We'll find him because he doesn't know when to stop. He lacks the professional criminal's knowledge of when to cut and run." The expression in Ronsarde's eyes turned rueful. "That's why I never caught you. You knew when to stop."

Nicholas swallowed in a dry throat. He wanted to be away from here and pursuing the hunt so urgently it was almost a physical need. He wasn't sure he knew when to stop, not anymore. "He wants something," he said, starting down the stairs again. "He wants something and we have to know what it is."

CHAPTER SEVENTEEN

The stench rising up from the dark swirling water in the stone pit was truly hellish; the handkerchief Nicholas had wrapped around his mouth and nose did little to mask it. He managed to draw enough of a breath to ask, "But have you noticed anything unusual in the refuse lately?"

The oldest sewerman frowned and paused to lean on his broad paddle, which he was using to direct the flow of sluice water down the channel of the main sewer into the collector pit. "Some days it's hard to say what is usual," he said, which was a more philosophical answer than Nicholas was hoping for. The man's much younger assistant, wielding a paddle on the other side of the channel, only nodded in perfect agreement.

Nicholas nodded too, keeping his expression sympathetic. This was only partly because he needed the sewermen's cooperation to get the information he wanted. After only a few minutes down here it was easy to see that you either became philosophical about your vocation or you lost your senses.

It had been three long days since his interview at the palace. The Prefecture's search along the river had turned up nothing so far, at least according to the frequent bulletins from Giarde. Nicholas was uncomfortable with having his connection to the Alsenes known, even though Halle had been too polite to bring the subject up and Crack, of course, had ventured no opinion at all, and Cusard only worried that it would draw attention to them. Reynard had affected to think it amusing, and commented, "Now I know why you tried to hand the Duke of Mere-Bannot that bomb at the Queen's Birthday celebration two years ago."

"I was drunk, Reynard, that's why," Nicholas had reminded him tiredly. "And besides, Denzil Alsene wasn't an anarchist. He was a dedicated monarchist, he just thought it should have been him on the throne and not the legally crowned Fontainon who was currently occupying it. That he had to kill everyone in the country to accomplish that goal was immaterial."

Notices in the penny sheets had cautioned people about the sorcerer's method of obtaining victims and there had been some panic in Riverside and many false reports, all of which diverted constables from the search. Oddly, there had been no more verifiable disappearances in the past few days. Nicholas found that more ominous than reassuring.

He had kept up his own observations of the Prefecture's efforts, spying on them from various vantage points with Crack's help and employing Cusard and Lamane's network of street children and petty thieves to follow their progress. He brought the information back to Ronsarde, who pored over it, muttering to himself, and sent terse orders to Lord Albier through Captain Giarde. Nicholas felt this procedure was highly unsatisfactory; if directing a methodical search was all that was needed, Albier and his cronies were as good at organizing that as anyone else in authority. What was needed was Ronsarde's reductive abilities, his genius for ferreting out apparently unrelated clues and finding the relationship between them. He needed to be on the scene, where the constables could report their findings directly to him. It infuriated Nicholas that the Prefecture was probably even now overlooking important information, simply because they didn't know what they were looking at. He knew the Inspector felt this as deeply as he did.

They had discovered yesterday through a friend of Reynard's that the warrant issued for Dr. Halle's arrest had been formally rescinded. This had occasioned an almost violent argument, since Halle had wanted to join the search himself, hoping his experience with Ronsarde's methods would allow him to bring items of possible significance to the Inspector's attention that the constables and their officers might overlook. Nicholas had forbidden it on the grounds that their opponents knew Halle was a direct link to Ronsarde; if the doctor tried to take a visible role in the investigation, they would move against him as violently as they had moved against the Inspector. It was no accident that the Prefecture's principal investigator and the city's foremost medical expert in violent death had both been effectively stymied. There was at least one person behind all this who knew what they were about.

The argument had raged on until Madeline had stepped in to explain Nicholas's point of view, even though he had already explained it several times himself. Halle had grudgingly given in then and Nicholas had stormed out of the apartment to spend an hour kicking gutters in the Philosopher's Cross. He ended up sitting at Arisilde's bedside again, hoping for improvement. Part of his anger came from his suspicion that there were things Ronsarde wasn't telling him.

It was all being taken out of his hands, but they couldn't stop him from pursuing his own line of inquiry.

Which was why he was currently some distance below the street, squatting on a walkway above the stagnant waters of a sewage collector, talking to sewermen and ratcatchers. The lamplight flickered off the oily stone curving above, though this part of the sewer was well tended and relatively clean. There were pipes overhead, splitting to cross the domed roof of the collector, some carrying potable water that had been brought in from outside Vienne by aqueducts ever since the city officials had given up the charmingly naive belief that the river water was drinkable if pumped from the deepest current. "This would be within the past five days, say," Nicholas persisted. This was the fifth work group he had spoken to and he had learned he didn't want to offer suggestions for the items that might have been found, since the sewermen were often of the type of witness who tended to say what you wanted to hear, simply to be polite.

The oldest sewerman straightened, one hand on his obviously aching back, and hailed the two men aboard the small boat that was plying the waters of the collector. "Hey, is there any talk of odd things found in the pits?"

An adroit push from a paddle brought the boat within easy speaking range. There was some chin-scratching and due consideration from the two men in the boat, then one said, "We don't ever find much in the way of coin or valuables. That's a myth people tell, like the one about the big lizards."

"I found a silver piece last year," the youngest one commented helpfully.

"Perhaps I don't mean something unusual," Nicholas said, trying to think of a good way to explain. "Perhaps I mean an unusual amount of something you often find. Like a large concentration of sand, or bits of ironmongery, or—"

"Bones?" one of the boatmen suggested.

"Or bones," Nicholas agreed, concealing his reaction. "Was that the case?"

"Aye, the word was the Monde Street syphon came up full of bones two days ago. The Prefect figured a wall had broke through in one of the catacombs somewhere and that's where they come from."

"No," the oldest sewerman disagreed. "If that was it, the water level in Monde would drop and our collectors all down fifth precinct would go dry. There hasn't been enough rain to fill a catacomb."

The discussion abruptly turned highly technical, as water levels, drainage, rainfall, sluices, collectors, and connecting passages were all brought in as evidence for and against the catacomb hypothesis. Nicholas listened carefully. There were catacombs under Vienne and old covered-over rock quarries, and other places where a wily sorcerer could hide. It was a likelier place than an abandoned river palace, no matter what Octave had said.

The sewermen's lively discussion moved on to other topics and Nicholas interrupted long enough to bid them goodbye before he moved on to the next group. The sewers called for more research and he had many more questions to ask.

———

Madeline let herself into the apartment off the Boulevard Panzan, tired and cursing her luck. She had been following the progress of the Prefecture's search with the others but the frustration of being unable to participate actively was wearing on her. She would have preferred to be off with Reynard, who was pursuing Count Montesq's possible connection to their mad sorcerer, or Nicholas, who had been damnably uncommunicative about his pursuits.

Dr. Halle was in the salon, standing in front of the fire, apparently as preoccupied and discouraged as she was. He glanced at her as she flung herself down on the sofa and commented, "This inactivity rather grates on one, doesn't it?"

Madeline laughed ruefully. "I'm glad someone else feels it." She removed her hat, a plain gray affair to match her plain gray walking dress, an assemble guaranteed not to draw attention on the street and which did nothing to lift her flagging spirits.

Halle leaned on the mantel and cleaned out his pipe. "Ordinarily, when the Prefecture has no use for me I see patients at the charity hospitals."

Madeline nodded in agreement. "I feel fortunate that I didn't take a role this season; I wouldn't have been able to do a farce justice with my mind on this."

His brows lifted. "So you *are* that Madeline Denare."

"Come now, you knew that."

"I did, but I wasn't sure I should mention it." He hesitated.

"I'm sure you have questions," Madeline said, carefully.

Halle smiled gently and shook his head. "Only impertinent ones. Why Reynard Morane persists in presenting himself to society as a debauched and dissipated wretch when he's as sound as a young horse. How a wandering scion of the infamous Alsenes made the acquaintance of so many congenial thieves." He looked at her gravely. "And what you are doing here."

He would *ask a hard one,* she thought. She shook her head. "I'm not entirely sure of that myself," she admitted.

Halle didn't show surprise. He regarded her gravely. "How long have you known Valiarde?"

"Since my first real ingénue role, as Eugenie in *The Scarlet Veil.* I got into a bit of trouble and Nicholas helped get me out." She saw the expression that Halle hadn't quite concealed in time and laughed. "No, not that sort of trouble. I had gotten the attention of a rather terrible person called Lord Stevarin. Did you ever hear of him?"

"Vaguely." Halle frowned thoughtfully. "He took his own life at his country home, didn't he?"

It had been so long Madeline had almost forgotten that part of the story. She nodded and said, "Yes, I believe he did." She would have to judiciously edit the rest of her account. "He was a great theatergoer, but not quite in the way other people are. He would go to look at the actresses, and when he took a fancy to one he would have her abducted, keep her at his townhome for a few days—until he was tired of her, I suppose—then dump her out near the river somewhere, usually covered with bruises and too terrified to accuse him of anything. After all, they were only actresses, and he was a lord."

"Good God," Halle said softly. After a moment, he looked at her sharply. "Then one day he chose you."

"Yes. He had drugged champagne sent to my dressing room, and then sent his men to haul me off like I was a bag of laundry. Then—"

"You needn't tell me anymore if you don't wish—" Halle interrupted hastily.

"No, he never got a chance." She smiled. "I woke in a bedchamber in his townhome, he told me his intentions rather baldly, and I . . . brained him with a vase." She wondered what had possessed her to tell this story. *You should have made something up.* But she didn't like to lie to Halle and wasn't doing such a good job of it with a story that was mostly the truth. "I was climbing out the window into the inner court when I met Nicholas climbing up. He had seen me in *The Scarlet Veil* too, and also had the idea of making my acquaintance but in a more conventional fashion. He saw Lord Stevarin's men taking away what he thought was a suspicious bundle, discovered I wasn't in my room and that my dresser had no notion where I'd gone, leapt to a conclusion no one else in his right mind would have leapt to, and followed them. So I got away."

Halle looked at her a long moment, his gaze penetrating. "And Lord Stevarin killed himself in remorse?" he asked finally, as if he meant to believe her answer, whatever it was.

"No." Madeline hesitated, then shook her head. It suddenly seemed pointless to conceal it, what with everything else Halle knew. She said, "That wasn't quite true. It wasn't a vase. He had a gun, you see, and I took it away from him

and shot him with it. I wasn't afraid. As soon as I realized what he was, I knew
I'd kill him." That was the simple truth, though it sounded more like bragging.
Madeline knew herself well enough to realize it had more to do with a disbelief
in her own mortality than courage. *That could catch up to you at any moment,*
she told herself. *And you call Nicholas reckless.*

Dr. Halle shook his head. "A young woman, abducted and threatened? Not
a court in Ile-Rien would see it as anything but self-defense."

"Perhaps." Madeline shrugged. "I never had much to do with courts and
Nicholas had good reason not to trust them, after what happened to Edouard.
Stevarin had sent his servants away so he wouldn't be interrupted and so it was
very simple to take his coach and transport his body to his country home and
make it look like suicide. Nicholas knew how to make it appear as if Stevarin
had held the gun, and put powder burns on his hand and around the wound,
and all these other things I wouldn't have thought of if he hadn't mentioned
them. I found it truly fascinating."

Halle watched her a moment, a worried crease between his brows. "Valiarde
doesn't . . . use this against you, does he?"

"No, Nicholas only blackmails people he doesn't like." She bit her lip. She
really wanted to make Halle understand, but she wasn't sure she knew how.
She was an actress; she didn't make up those eloquent speeches she gave on
stage. "It's not like that. Nicholas isn't just a clever criminal. If Edouard hadn't
been killed, he would be a physician or a scholar or a dilettante or . . . But if
Edouard hadn't taken him in when he did . . . he would be a good deal worse."

"Yet you trust him?"

"I do. With my life."

Halle fiddled with his pipe a moment, then his eyes lifted to meet hers seriously. "Should Ronsarde and I trust him?"

Madeline smiled. "You ask me?"

"You strike me very much as a young woman who goes her own way."

"Nicholas is a dangerous man," Madeline said honestly. "But he's never betrayed anyone who kept faith with him."

There was the sound of the outer door rattling as someone opened it with
a key. Halle cleared his throat almost nervously and Madeline stood, fussing
with her hideous hat and unaccountably embarrassed, her face reddening as if
the conversation with the doctor had been of a far more intimate nature.

She forgot her embarrassment when Inspector Ronsarde appeared in the doorway, trailed by an expressionless Crack. Ronsarde waved a telegram and his eyes gleamed with triumph. "At long last, a development," he said. "Summon the others at once!"

———

Nicholas walked back to the Philosopher's Cross, threading his way through street vendors and the midmorning market crowd, until he reached Arisilde's tenement. He slipped past the concierge, who was arguing with a delivery boy, and started up the stairs.

Nicholas always approached Arisilde's garret cautiously, though it had remained under observation by Cusard's men and no one they didn't know had attempted to enter. Madeline had also visited here with Crack, though they were all careful to take different routes when they left to prevent anyone following them back to the Boulevard Panzan apartment. Nothing had happened here since Arisilde's illness and Nicholas was almost grudgingly willing to admit that it might be safe.

The door whipped open before he could knock. Madele stood there, glaring at him. "What, you again?" she demanded. "Don't you trust me?"

"Since you ask," Nicholas said, stepping past her, "not particularly." Madele was dressed in what she considered "town clothes": a shapeless black dress and a hat with somewhat wilted fabric flowers jammed on her head. He stopped in the hallway to take off his coat and boots, not wanting to take the sewer stink that clung to them into Arisilde's room. Madele stood and stared at him, her arms folded, her brows lowered in suspicion. "What have you done with Isham?" he asked her.

"He's out at the shops," Madele said, defensively. "I've got to live."

If Nicholas had only the evidence of his eyes to go by, he would have said Madele had done nothing since Madeline had met her at the train station except sleep and devour whatever food was brought into the apartment. But Isham had told him that Madele spent every night seated on the floor of the parlor in front of the fire, working with the herbs and other supplies he found for her during the day. She had made a healing stone by the second night but so far it had done no good for Arisilde. It had, however, cured various fevers, lung ailments, piles, and other illnesses throughout the tenement, including a case of advanced venereal disease on the first floor, simply by its presence in the building, so Isham had no doubt of Madele's power. Madele had also rearranged the furnishings in the apartment with special attention to the potted plants, mirrors, and glass bric-a-brac. She had pretended to Isham that she was doing it out of sheer eccentricity, but he had recognized it as a very old method of channeling etherial substance and suspected she was trying to use whatever of Arisilde's power remained in the apartment to help sustain him. Madele had used none of Arisilde's extensive collection of magical texts, and after some subtle observation Isham had concluded that she was illiterate. Nicholas had suspected it before and wasn't surprised to hear it confirmed. He said, "You realize you're 'living' enough for three or four old women, don't you?" and continued on to Arisilde's bedroom. Madele followed him, grumbling.

Nicholas stopped just inside the door to turn up the gas in the wall sconce. Medicine bottles and other medical paraphernalia littered the dresser near the bed, along with an incense burner and some bunches of herbs. "Did the physician come today?"

"Yes," Madele admitted, reluctantly. "Didn't do a damn thing. How much are we paying him?"

"'We'?" Nicholas sat on the bed. Arisilde's face was white, his eyes sunken in their deep sockets. Isham had kept the sorcerer clean, forced enough water and broth down his throat to keep him alive, followed the physician's instructions, but there had been no change. Madele had ventured no opinion as to whether Arisilde's condition had been caused by a spell or just the inevitable consequences of his much-abused health, but according to Isham she was exploring both possibilities.

One of the necromantic techniques for creating illness was to write an inscription in blood on a piece of linen or skin and bury it near the house of the victim. Isham had searched the neighborhood for anything of that kind with the help of a few hedgewitches of his acquaintance, but found nothing. Madele had looked again with the same result. *Can't you wake for a challenge, Arisilde? Wouldn't you appreciate the novelty of defeating a demon sorcerer in battle?* Nicholas thought. He said, "More than 'we' are paying 'you.' Are you asking for further compensation?" Madele had country sensibilities and her idea of compensation would probably be a new hat, which she certainly seemed to be badly in need of.

Madele sniffed and said nothing. Nicholas glanced at her and thought he read defeat in her expression. He looked away. Madele didn't have a Lodun degree but he suspected she was as knowledgeable as any sorcerer-healer they could find there. And she had been able to do nothing.

The day she had arrived in town, Madeline had brought her to the Panzan apartment and they had shown her the sphere. She had held it in her work-roughened hands for a long time, turning it over, watching the wheels within wheels inside it move. Then she had looked up at them with a baffled expression and said, "What in hell is this?"

Madele might have forgotten more sorcery and herbal medicine than most practitioners knew at their best, but the principles of natural philosophy that Edouard had used to construct the sphere were a closed book to her. She could sense the power within it but she had no notion of how to reach it.

There was a rattle from the hall as someone tried the outer door of the apartment. Madele darted out of the bedroom and Nicholas stood, reaching for the pistol in his inside jacket pocket. A moment later, he heard Isham's voice and relaxed.

Isham came down the hall, handing off a string bag of bread and onions to Madele, saying, "Take this to the pantry, please, you horrible old woman. Is . . . Ah, you are here." Isham fished a folded telegram out of his sleeve and gave it to Nicholas. "The concierge had this, it arrived only a few moments ago. It is addressed to me but it is surely for you."

Nicholas tore it open quickly. *Important news—come at once. SR.* "Yes," he said, feeling his first flash of hope in three days. "It's for me."

———

They came to the place from the river, aboard a small steam launch owned by a friend of Cusard's. Nicholas stood in the bow, ignoring the spray of foul river water. The light was failing but he could see the turrets and chimneys of the house they were approaching outlined against the reddening sky. It was a monolithic bulk, mostly featureless in the shadow, but swinging lamps lit the garden terraces above the river and the water gate.

Nicholas jammed his hands further into his pockets and braced his feet as a gust of wind tore at him. The air was cold and the water like black glass. The setting sun left the Great Houses lining this side of the embankment in darkness and lit the columns and classical pediments of the buildings on the far side with a pure golden glow. The Prefecture had found the house this morning and it had taken most of the day to convince Lord Albier that Ronsarde and Halle should be permitted to inspect the scene. The battle had been conducted entirely by telegram, with frequent missives fired off to Captain Giarde at the palace for support. In the end, Albier had given in with poor grace and Ronsarde and Halle were formally invited to give advice. Nicholas had not been invited but he was here anyway. Madele had not been invited either but she was the only trustworthy source of sorcerous advice they had at present, so she was now huddled in the cabin of the boat, vocal in her displeasure at being forced to cross running water. Madeline had invited herself and was in her "young man" disguise to help forestall questions from Albier and the other representatives of the Prefecture. Crack had not been invited but he was here to guard their backs.

The chugging engine of the launch abruptly cut off. Nicholas turned back to the cabin and saw the captain standing, staring worriedly at the water gate the boat still drifted toward. Nicholas glanced at it and saw that they had drawn near enough for the lamps to reveal the official markings on the launch already tied there and the uniforms of the men waiting at the gate.

"Constables," the captain said, and spat succinctly over the side. He was an old man, featureless under several layers of ragged coats and scarves, looking more like a dustman than a smuggler. Dr. Halle and Ronsarde exchanged a look, then Halle took a step toward the man.

"It's all right," Nicholas told the captain. "They're expecting us."

The captain grunted thoughtfully, then disappeared back into the cabin. A moment later, the engine came to life again.

Ronsarde stepped up beside Nicholas, his eyes on the house ahead. He said, "Albier has been here all day."

The boat drew up to the water gate with practiced ease, bumped gently against the pilings as Crack stepped over to the tiny stone dock to catch the lines. One of the constables hurried to help him tie it off. A young man in a dark coat and top hat stepped forward to greet Ronsarde. "Inspector, I'm glad you can assist us in this . . . matter." The lamps on the pillars of the gate were shaped into elaborate wrought iron lilies; by their light the young man's bland, handsome face looked ill. He said, "Lord Albier—"

"Lord Albier wishes me in Hell," Ronsarde said briskly. He gripped Nicholas's shoulder to steady himself as he stepped off the boat. Halle was immediately beside him, handing him his cane. "So I doubt he was pleased to hear my assistance would be inflicted upon him. I only hope he and his minions haven't destroyed too many vital traces."

"Ah . . . Yes, well." The man's eyes widened at the number of people piling off the boat. Nicholas had followed Halle, and Madeline was helping her grandmother. "These are . . . ?"

Ronsarde gestured sharply. "My associates." He started for the stone steps leading up to the house and the young man hurried after him.

"That's Viarn, Lord Albier's secretary," Dr. Halle explained to Nicholas as they followed.

The stairs climbed a terraced garden, cloaked in twilight and shadow, a constable's lamp illuminating small manicured hedges and stone flower urns. They passed the garden walls screening the entrance of the house from the river and found themselves on a broad court with benches and graceful statuary, lit by gas sconces framing the doorway. Nicholas looked up at the large windows on the second floor where lamps from inside the house revealed a conservatory filled with palms and hothouse flowers. Nicholas tried to think how many gardeners would have been employed to care for those tropical plants and for the gardens on the embankment. During the winter, and with the family at their country seat, surely only two or three.

The doors stood open as they probably never would had the house's real owners still been in command. A uniformed constable stood guard there. Ronsarde stepped into the foyer beyond, stopping abruptly as he realized there were muddy bootprints on the tiles. Then he saw the muddy boots of the constable at the door, swore violently, and strode into the house. Dr. Halle grimaced and hurried after him.

"This is Chaldome House." Madeline spoke in a low husky voice, part of her "young man" disguise.

In the man's suit, greatcoat, and hat she wore, and with her face subtly made up, she looked the role, but he hoped she would be able to maintain it once they saw what was sure to lay within. Stiffly, Nicholas said, "Are you certain you want to be here?"

Madeline looked at him, her dark eyes enigmatic, and followed Halle into the house.

Nicholas felt a tug at his coat sleeve and glanced down. Madele stood there, bundled up in several coats and shawls. She said, "Damp air is bad for my joints."

He offered her his arm. She took it, muttering to herself, and he helped her up the steps into the house.

The second floor of the entrance hall was open to the conservatory and air from the open doorway rustled in the heavy fronds and stirred the leaves, made the flames in the glass sconces flicker, brought the faint scent of the river into the house. Nicholas realized he had unconsciously braced himself for the heavy odor that had clung to Valent House. *But he wasn't here as long,* he thought. *There hasn't been time.*

He heard Ronsarde's voice and followed it through the open double doors at the end of the hall.

The sound led him to a ballroom, high ceilinged, with a row of marble columns dividing it from another conservatory, this one a glass-walled oval extending out from the side of the house. The torcheres along the walls and the chandeliers were meant to hold candles, so the room was lit only by the kerosene lamps of the constables. Most of it was in shadow but Nicholas could tell the walls were covered with paintings of tropical islands, with plants, birds, strange animals picked out in fine detail. Nicholas remembered that the current Lord Chaldome was a naturalist of some renown, a writer and teacher and member of the Philosophers' Academy.

Uniformed men were searching, pulling the dustcovers off the furniture in the salons that gave onto the ballroom, even unrolling the rugs that were stacked along the far wall. There were eight tarp-covered forms stretched out on the floor in a line. Lord Albier stood near them, with his secretary and another man in a frock coat and top hat, arguing with restrained, bitter violence with Inspector Ronsarde. Halle looked around at the shapes on the floor, shaking his head, Madeline standing near him.

Nicholas swore under his breath. "They moved the bodies. They destroyed the scene." He had dragged poor Madele and her bad joints here for nothing. He supposed it would do no good to explain to Albier that if they hadn't seen the murder room in Valent House as it was, they would never have realized it was necromancy, or known about the tie to Constant Macob.

Madele slipped her arm free of Nicholas's and moved away, studying the large chamber thoughtfully.

Madeline turned away from Halle and Ronsarde, and Nicholas went forward to meet her. "We may have come here for nothing," she said, low-voiced. "Albier is a complete fool."

"Is he?" Nicholas said. Albier was now pointing at them and gesturing to Ronsarde, obviously objecting to their presence. "Or did someone tell him to do this?"

"That's the question." Madeline glanced around. "Where is Grandmother?"

Nicholas turned, looking around the room. Madele was nowhere to be seen.

He let out his breath in annoyance. "We'll find her when she wants to be found. Try to see as much as you can before we're thrown out." Before boarding the steam launch, Nicholas had told Madeline their primary goal was to search for the sphere Octave had made. He hadn't mentioned this to Ronsarde and Halle.

Madeline nodded and moved away. An agitated party of people was being conducted into the room through the doors in the far wall: several men in business dress, one older woman who might be a housekeeper or upper servant. She saw the still forms lined up under the sheets and cried out in shock. Albier saw the newcomers, gave Ronsarde one last parting glare, then hurried across the room toward them.

Halle moved immediately toward the bodies and the other doctors who conferred near them, taking advantage of Albier's distraction. Nicholas approached Ronsarde. "Well?"

The Inspector leaned on his cane, with an expression of thwarted fury. His eyes still on the occupied Albier, he said, "The family is still in the country, but there was a small staff to maintain the house in their absence, including a housekeeper, maids, a footman, and two gardeners to keep up the grounds and conservatories. This morning a dairyman tried to make his usual delivery at the kitchen door. He was well acquainted with the house and when he realized it appeared to be locked and empty, he brought it to the attention of the local constable. That the servants were all found here, dead, is all I have been able to ascertain, and from the state of the place that is all I will ever be able to ascertain."

"Did he discover when any of them were last seen alive?"

"The dairyman made a delivery three days ago and found them all quite alive and healthy. There are constables speaking with the other merchants in the area and the servants in the houses to either side, hoping to obtain confirmation of that."

Nicholas stared around in irritation. "They were killed here?" The ballroom floor was marked only by the dirt and mud from Prefecture boots.

Ronsarde slanted a look at him. "So Albier says."

"Then where's the blood?" His recent research told him that there were some of Constant Macob's necromantic magics that could be performed by strangling or suffocating the victim, but that wasn't enough for the powerful spells their criminal sorcerer seemed to favor.

"A good question." Ronsarde looked at him, his eyes serious. "Albier claims that there is no need for haste or further investigation. He says he has the solution."

"Solution?" Nicholas looked around the ballroom again, baffled. "He's bluffing, trying to get rid of you."

"I fear that he is not." Ronsarde moved away, leaning heavily on his cane.

Worried, Nicholas watched him go. The new arrivals were being led over to the bodies, obviously to view them to establish their identity. Nicholas started to fade out of the way. He noticed, in the far corner of the ballroom, an unobtrusive set of panel doors, made obtrusive by the presence of two constables guarding them. This piqued his curiosity greatly, but he saw no way to discover what was there until Albier saw fit to reveal it. He left the ballroom through one of the attached salons.

He walked through the empty rooms, occasionally encountering constables who took him for one of the doctors or an aide to one of the inspectors present. The only sound was quiet talk from the ballroom, punctuated by the loud sobs of the older woman as she identified the bodies.

Albier is either a fool or a liar, Nicholas thought. If the sorcerer had been here at all, he hadn't been here long. The house was clean, freshly swept, ready for the occupancy of its owners at any moment. Most of the furniture was still neatly covered, paintings still on the walls, silver dining services neatly arranged in unbroken glass cabinets. Nothing had been looted, nothing disturbed.

The house wasn't very old. The design was too modern, with too many public rooms and windows on the first floor. The owners would probably wish they had bought one of the older, more fortress-like Great Houses instead of building for comfort. Still, there had to be a sorcerer hired to ward it against theft. Nicholas made his way down to the kitchens to check the pantries and found Madeline coming up from the cellars. "Did you go down there alone?" he demanded.

She gave him a withering look as she fastened the door latch again. "No, Nicholas, Lord Albier escorted me personally. The constables have already been through it and there's nothing down there. I was looking at the cisterns."

Nicholas pinched the bridge of his nose, regained his calm, and asked, "Were they topped off?"

"Yes." She waved a hand toward the main kitchen. "The fires were banked and then let to burn out and there were beds disturbed in the servants' quarters. They must have been attacked at night."

He nodded. "And the intruders didn't use any water while they were here. To drink, or to clean up the blood."

Madeline gestured in exasperation. "I don't see how those people could have been killed here."

"They weren't."

"Well, that clears everything up," Madeline said, annoyed.

Nicholas ignored the sarcasm and took the servants' passage back to the public rooms. It opened into one of the reception areas off the ballroom. Nicholas looked around at a room as clean and undisturbed as all the others, with jade figures ornamenting the mantelpiece, and swore aloud. He would have taken an oath on anything that no intruders had stayed long in this house. Just long enough to abduct the servants, then to bring the bodies back.

The voices from the ballroom grew loud and agitated, then Dr. Halle appeared, supporting the older woman who had been called in to help identify the corpses. She was gasping for breath and even in the dim light Nicholas could see her face was going blue. He tore a cover off the nearest couch while Madeline shoved the ornamental tables out of the way. Halle lowered the woman to the couch as another doctor bustled in, digging in his medical bag.

Nicholas and Madeline backed away to give the physicians room and Madeline whispered, "Why did they make her look at them now? Surely they don't always do it that way, not when the death was violent."

"No, the relatives aren't brought in until the victims are at the morgue and have been washed and prepared by the undertaker. For some reason, the Prefecture is in an unseemly hurry for identification." From the look of it, Halle would be busy here for a time. Nicholas went back into the ballroom, Madeline trailing him.

Ronsarde had cornered Albier again. As Nicholas drew near he heard him say, "I've been patient throughout this farce, Albier, now tell me what it is you think you have. Unless," Ronsarde added, smiling, "you are afraid it won't stand up to my scrutiny."

Albier returned the smile with the same lack of cordiality. "Very well. I was not trying to delay you, Ronsarde, only making sure of my facts. This way."

Albier led the way to the doors Nicholas had noted earlier, the ones barred by the constables. Albier nodded to the secretary Viarn, who hurried over, drawing a key out of his pocket.

Viarn unlocked the sliding panels, then pushed them open. The room within was dark, illuminated only by narrow windows high in the outside wall. Another gesture from Albier and one of the solemn constables brought a lamp.

Obviously as impatient with the theatrics as Nicholas, Ronsarde took the lamp away from the constable and held it high, lighting the room.

Nicholas caught sight of another body on the floor, this one left in situ as the others had not been. He pushed forward, elbowing Viarn out of the way.

The body was that of a man, young, with a lanky build and dirty blond hair, sprawled on the parquet floor amid markings of ash and black dust or soot. What many of the marks had represented was permanently obscured by blood, most of it pooled around the man's body. His throat had been cut and the lamplight glinted off a knife still clutched in one discolored hand.

"There is your sorcerer," Albier said.

Nicholas looked at Ronsarde, whose expression of stunned incredulity said everything, then back at Lord Albier, who complacently straightened his gloves. Since Ronsarde was apparently still speechless with rage, Nicholas cleared his throat and asked, "He killed everyone in the house, cleaned up after it, then cut his own throat, I suppose?"

Albier lifted his brows at this presumption, then noticed that everyone within earshot—constables, inspectors, their assistants, the doctors—was staring, waiting for the answer. He said sharply, "He was a sorcerer, called Merith Kahen, trained at Lodun and hired by Lord Chaldome to ward this house and the family estates in the provinces against theft and intrusions. I have been informed the remaining symbols on the floor of that room indicate the practice of necromancy. The conclusions are obvious."

"Are they?" Ronsarde's voice was admirably cool, the edge of sarcasm as sharp as a blade.

Albier's mouth tightened. "He was practicing necromancy at the house in the Gabardin and he became frightened when you discovered the place. He tried to eliminate you with the attack on the Courts Plaza. In the meantime, one of the unfortunate servants here also discovered some evidence of Kahen's activities, and perhaps confronted him. In his madness, Kahen killed every-one in the house, then—"

"Conveniently killed himself in remorse," Nicholas finished. "How very . . . tidy of him."

For a moment, Albier's eyes were dangerous, then he turned away with a muttered curse.

Nicholas smiled tightly to himself. Viarn and the constables posted nearby were all pretending not to have noticed the altercation. Ronsarde had been too caught up in his study of the dead man to notice, and now he handed Nicholas the lamp without looking at him and leaned down, studying the floor intently. Picking his spot with care, he took one step forward, then one more, so he could kneel awkwardly beside the body. Nicholas took his place in the doorway, holding the lamp so Ronsarde could see. He leaned in as far as he could, to examine the walls of the room. There was none of the melting that he had observed in the cellar chamber in Valent House where the necromancy had taken place. He would have been greatly surprised if there had been.

Ronsarde had carefully lifted the dead hand that was still clasped around the knife. Now he lowered it gently, and said, "Unfortunate young man."

"Did he cut his own throat?" Nicholas asked. "Not that it matters."

"He did. Not that it matters." In a tone of bitter disgust, Ronsarde added, "Magic."

Nicholas looked around the dark little room again. Albier wasn't a fool; if they could find any evidence that this scene was as stage-managed as a play at the Elegante, Albier would believe it, if reluctantly. But there would be no evidence. The young sorcerer had been enspelled to kill himself. From the traces of black dust on his hands, he had also been enspelled to draw the circle. *But was that simple expediency, or attention to detail?* Nicholas wondered. There was even a bucket of soot standing in the corner. *When they search his rooms, if they haven't already, will they find texts and notes on necromancy?* Their opponent was learning.

Ronsarde had come to the same conclusion. He said, "There is nothing of use here." He planted his cane and used it to lever himself to his feet, turning back toward the door. Nicholas stepped out of his way and handed the lantern off to the nearest constable.

There was an outcry from across the ballroom and the woman that Halle and the other doctor had been tending came running toward them. Her face was red and streaked with tears, and she gasped, "He wouldn't do it, he wouldn't do a thing like this, I swear it! You've got to believe—"

Ronsarde stepped forward and caught her hand, turning her away before she could get another look into the room. Nicholas quickly slid the doors closed and the secretary Viarn hastened to lock them.

"He didn't . . . he didn't . . ." the woman was still trying to say.

"I believe you," Ronsarde said to the distraught woman, his voice firm.

"Go to your home, mourn him and the others, and know that the accusations against him are vile lies, and in time he will be proved blameless."

The woman stared at him, as if she couldn't quite comprehend what he was saying, but her breathing calmed and her eyes were less wild. When the other doctor came to lead her away, she went without protest, only craning her neck to look back at the closed doors.

Halle had followed the woman in and now stepped close to Ronsarde. He said in a low voice, "She was the housekeeper here and the boy, the young sorcerer, was her son. When they discovered he had the talent for magic, Lord Chaldome paid for his education and sent him to Lodun. He was being paid well for his services here, enough so that his mother had no need to work. It sounds as if he had absolutely no motive to feel anger toward the family or the servants."

Nicholas cleared his throat and said, "His father . . . ?"

"I thought of that," Halle said impatiently. "His father was a barman at a local wineshop, who died only a few years ago. The possibility that he was a bastard of Lord Chaldome—"

"Is not worth considering," Ronsarde finished. He looked around the ballroom again, his expression dark. "I greatly fear that this . . . charade has been designed to throw off pursuit long enough for our culprit to move to another city and begin his work again."

Nicholas said nothing. He wasn't so sure that was the case. To throw off pursuit, yes, but not to cover an escape. He saw Lord Albier coming back toward them and murmured, "Watch out, gentlemen."

Lord Albier advanced on Ronsarde, saying, "Calming the woman's hysterics with platitudes does her no good. Facing the facts—"

"I gave her the facts," Ronsarde said coldly. "You are the one who is deluding yourself. If you would be the only one to suffer from it, I would be happy to let you have your delusion. But the killing will continue, if not here, then somewhere else."

Nicholas moved away, leaving Ronsarde and Halle to argue with Albier. Madeline, he realized, had also disappeared, probably to pursue the search through the rest of the house. He felt fairly confident that she would find nothing.

Doing his best to stay unobtrusive, Nicholas made his own brief examination of the bodies of the unfortunate servants. The wounds on two of them

were like those on the corpses found at Valent House, with the tattered, hideously stained clothing torn aside to reveal disembowelments, eyes gouged,
rope marks on wrists and ankles. *He chose one man and one woman,* Nicholas
noted. *Impartial bastard.* The others had been simply slaughtered, their throats
cut. Only one large man, who by his coat and mud-stained trousers might have
been one of the gardeners, had been killed by repeated blows to the head that
had finally crushed his skull. The man must have fought or tried to escape. *So
he used two for necromancy, and the others had to be killed because . . .* Because
they might have been able to swear to Merith Kahen's occupation with some
harmless pursuit during the time when he was supposed to be killing people in
the Gabardin or planning magical attacks on the Courts Plaza.

Nicholas dropped the sheet on the last corpse. He didn't know why he was
doing this; he wasn't discovering anything Halle wouldn't be able to tell him.

"What are you doing?"

Nicholas turned on his heel, but the words weren't directed toward him.
Rahene Fallier stood over Madele, who knelt on the floor, lifting a sheet to
peer at one of the bodies. Nicholas stood slowly, his back stiffening. He hadn't
known Fallier was here but he supposed it was inevitable. Despite his fall from
grace in the palace, Fallier would still be working with the Prefecture. Nicholas started toward them.

Madele looked up at Fallier, her bright eyes wary. Then she smiled, or at
least showed her teeth. She said, "Think again."

Fallier stared down at her for a long moment then, though Madele had done
nothing, or nothing obvious, he took a deliberate step back. Dressed in an impeccable dark suit and towering over the ragged old woman, he looked totally
in command and it seemed an uneven contest. But Madele would fight like a
feral animal when cornered and that wasn't taking her power into account.
The sorcerer adjusted his gloves, his expression revealing nothing, and said,
"Who are you?"

Madele said, "I came with Sebastion," and grinned at him.

Nicholas had no time to wonder when Madele had had the chance to get
on a first name basis with Inspector Ronsarde. Fallier growled, "That hardly
answers my question."

She said, "It didn't that, did it? Go on, now."

Fallier watched her a moment longer, his lips thinning with annoyance,
then he gave her an edged smile and tipped his hat to her.

Nicholas approached cautiously as Fallier moved away. He sat on his heels next to her and said, "I was racing to your rescue but since you seem perfectly capable of rescuing yourself, I thought I'd let discretion rule valor."

Madele turned from her rapt contemplation of Fallier's departing form to regard Nicholas with a raised brow. "If you were thirty years older or I was a hundred years younger—"

"I would run screaming," Nicholas assured her. "What have you found?"

Madele chuckled but she looked down at the sheeted body again and her face turned serious. She lifted the arm of the corpse. Nicholas noted it was a woman's arm, and that it was discolored and the stiffness had passed off, showing that it was at least a day or more since the death, but Halle would have already made note of all that. Madele gently lifted one of the fingers and Nicholas frowned. The corpse wore a ring, a plain dull metal band. "I don't understand."

Instead of the sarcastic response he half expected, Madele gently worked the ring up the finger, so he could see that the skin beneath it was blackened, burned. "What caused that?" Nicholas asked, frowning.

"A magic," she said. "Unfinished, and harmless." She tucked the arm back under the sheet, smoothing the cloth over it and giving it an absentminded pat, as if she was tucking in a child. "It makes me wonder if it was a second go."

"Can you be a trifle more obscure? I think I almost understood what you said that last time."

She shook her head impatiently. "He was making a magic, with the ring and this poor dead thing, but he didn't let it finish. Just a thought I had—I do have them occasionally. I need to ruminate on it a bit and take a look somewhere." She held out a hand and Nicholas helped her up.

Madele wandered away, her course apparently aimless. With Fallier here, Nicholas thought he might as well make himself scarce, at least for a time, and he headed for the way out of the ballroom.

Nicholas saw the secretary Viarn hovering near the outer doorway, an expression of tired resignation on his face. He greeted him with a nod and Nicholas took the opportunity to ask, "Lord Albier said the dead sorcerer was trained at Lodun. Who did he study with?"

"I believe it was Ilamires Rohan." The secretary shook his head. "After all the opportunities Lord Chaldome gave him, it's hard to believe the young man would betray him so. But madness knows no reason."

"No," Nicholas agreed. "No, it doesn't, does it?" He walked on.

Out on the stone court, the wind was in the right direction and the night air was fresh. The lamps flickered and the constables patrolled the grounds, end-lessly searching. Nicholas jammed his hands in his pockets and paced to the end of the court where he could see the river. Octave had said, "The palace . . . the palace on the river. He's been there—" *He's been there and gone,* Nicholas thought. *Is that what he meant to say?* Octave had known about this house. From the state of the bodies, they could have been killed that very night. If the spiritualist had lived for one more breath, one more heartbeat, would they have known about this place in time to save the occupants? He wasn't sure why that should be such a bitter thought; this was none of his business.

No, that wasn't true. What would Edouard have thought if he had known his work had been used in aid of all this killing?

And that wasn't true either. *Edouard's dead,* Nicholas thought. Might as well admit that as well, if honesty is everything. *None of this can hurt him.*

I want this sorcerer because I want him, there's no altruism about it. He has challenged me, he has interfered with me, and I'll see him in Hell if I have to escort him there personally.

Crack ghosted up and took a post at his elbow, and Nicholas put those thoughts aside for the moment. He said, sourly, "Lord Albier's solved our little mystery—to his satisfaction."

Crack grunted noncommittally.

"You know what that means, of course."

Crack muttered, "We're on our own again, that's what."

———

Madele burst through the door of Arisilde's apartment, shedding scarves and shawls. She found Isham seated in an armchair in front of the parlor hearth, a book in his lap.

She dropped her last shawl, still damp from the river spray, and said, "He was making a corpse ring!"

Isham stared. "What?"

"This sorcerer. He's killed another lot of folk, and on one's hand I found the making of a corpse ring."

Madele's excitement made her country accent thicken and Isham frowned in incomprehension, but he caught the last two words. "Corpse ring?" It was one of the oldest tricks of necromancy, a ring enspelled and left on the hand of a corpse for three days. When it was removed and placed on the hand of a liv-ing person, it would simulate death, or a state close to it. Isham shut his book and slammed it down on the table. "I already told you that that was the first thing I looked for! There were no strange tokens, nothing that was not his—"

Madele shook her head impatiently. "Looked with your eyes, or looked with your hands?"

Isham hesitated, then said something vile in Parscian and struggled to his feet.

Madele followed him to Arisilde's bedchamber, saying, "You said you went out and when you came back he seemed to sleep. Well, he must have gone to sleep, with a bit of his drug to help him along. And while he lay so it must have come in, whatever it was, and put it on him without waking him. . . ."

Still cursing his own stupidity in Parscian, Isham tore back the patched coverlet and grabbed for Arisilde's hands. He felt carefully around the base of each finger, moving upward slowly, deliberately turning his face away so he would have only the evidence of touch to go by. An illusion strong enough to hide a ring on the finger of a man who had been examined by physicians, who had been searched many times for any evidence of magical attack, could still be powerful enough to confuse the senses even when the searcher was certain it was there. He found nothing and shook his head in frustration.

Madele snatched the coverlet off the bed entirely and took Arisilde's right foot in one hand, feeling carefully along the toes. Isham watched, but the brief spark of hope was dying as she found nothing and moved on to the left foot.

Madele frowned, then her face went still suddenly, as her fingers reached the smallest toe.

Something else had occurred to Isham and he said urgently, "Madele—" She was already slipping the ring off Arisilde's toe. Once it lay in her palm the illusion dissolved and she could see it as well as feel it, a small iron band, grimly stained. She met Isham's anxious gaze, and grinned. "Isn't it always the last place you look?"

CHAPTER EIGHTEEN

It was late at night by the time Nicholas returned to the apartment off the Boulevard Panzan. The others had gone there directly from the docks while he had escorted Madele back to the Philosopher's Cross. The old woman had been preoccupied about something but he hadn't been able to pry it out of her. He had resolved to go over to Arisilde's in the morning to see if she was more willing to talk then.

The river spray and the damp had gotten into his clothes and he climbed the stairs up to the apartment wearily, cold to the bone.

It was a despondent group that greeted him in the salon. "I don't understand why Albier is persisting with this," Halle was saying, pacing agitatedly in front of the fire. Crack leaned against the wall near the doorway, Cusard was a dour figure huddled in a chair as far away from Ronsarde and Halle as possible, and Madeline was draped across one of the couches with her hat pulled over her face.

Ronsarde was in the chair near the window, smoking his pipe, with a serpentlike intensity to his gaze. He said, "The facts of the case are becoming known. Dozens of deaths in Riverside and the Gabardin and sorcerous attacks in the city make the Prefecture look ineffectual. He wants to produce a culprit, or at least pretend to produce one, to deflect criticism while the search for the real criminal goes on." He lifted one edge of the window curtain to look out at the dark street below. "It is nothing that has not been done before."

Nicholas paused in the doorway, feeling a twist in his gut. "We know," he said lightly, crossing into the room.

"Was Madele all right?" Madeline asked, sitting up on the couch and tossing her hat aside.

"Yes, only preoccupied."

She was trying to dig something out of her pocket and eventually produced a folded letter. "Sarasate sent a messenger with this. It came to Coldcourt this morning."

Nicholas took it from her and glanced at the address, then smiled. "Dr. Uberque." He sat down on the couch and tore the letter open immediately.

"Is that another sorcerer?" Cusard asked suspiciously.

"No, he's a doctor of history, at Lodun. I consulted him on Constant Macob and he was going to keep looking into the subject for me." He spread the closely written pages on his knees. Ronsarde's interest had been piqued at the name of the ancient necromancer and he came to stand at Nicholas's elbow.

The information Nicholas wanted had apparently led Dr. Uberque on a merry chase through the libraries of Lodun. But the historian seemed to combine an enthusiasm for the hunt with a detectival instinct to rival Ronsarde's, as well as an encompassing knowledge of his subject.

"He's discovered what was in the chamber buried beneath Ventarin House," Nicholas reported after a moment. "That's the room we found broken into from the Duchess of Mondollot's cellars," he explained for Cusard and Crack's benefit.

Cusard glanced uneasily at Ronsarde, who frowned down intently at the letter.

Madeline drew breath to expostulate at the delay and Nicholas continued, "It was Constant Macob's body."

"His body?" Ronsarde's expression was almost affronted.

"His bones, more probably, after this amount of time," Halle commented reasonably. "Did your informant discover the reason the corpse was concealed?"

"He believes Gabard Ventarin had the body sealed in the chamber as a precaution. He relates it to the custom present at the time for burying murderers at crossroads in case their predilection for bloodshed stemmed from an arcane source." Nicholas folded the letter and tapped it against his chin. Ronsarde captured the document and opened it to read for himself.

"I suppose that explains it," Madeline said, though she seemed troubled. "Octave needed a relic, a lock of hair or an old possession, of the dead people he wanted to speak to. His sorcerer wanted a relic of Macob so he could speak to him. After all this time Macob's bones must have been the best thing for it."

"After all this time," Ronsarde echoed. "Dr. Uberque explains that he obtained this information from a letter penned by Gabard Ventarin, who was then holding the post of Court Sorcerer. The letter was sent to the sorcerer who was at that time Master of Lodun and whose papers and books are stored in the university's oldest archives. A difficult task, even for a historian familiar with the Lodun libraries." He frowned. "How did Octave and our sorcerer know of the corpse's location?"

That question had occurred to Nicholas as well. But he remembered how Arisilde had found the book he had described to him and felt wary of constructing any theory that contradicted that incontrovertible fact. "Sorcerers," he pointed out, "can find things that have been lost for years with little difficulty. Without more information, the only conclusion we can draw is that we are facing a very powerful sorcerer. Something we already knew," he added dryly.

Ronsarde did not look satisfied.

Nicholas hesitated. Now would be a good time to bring up the subject of the sewers and what he suspected an investigation of them would reveal, and he had planned to do so. But Ronsarde's comment on the Prefecture's methods had awakened old, and not-so-old, suspicions. He said only, "I'm going out again," and stood.

Crack stopped him in the hallway. "Me with you?" he asked.

Nicholas shook his head. "No, I want you to stay here. Watch the others."

Whether Crack had received a subtle message from that, Nicholas didn't know. He scarcely knew whether he meant to convey one or not. But Crack made no protest, only nodded, and stepped back into the salon.

Nicholas went through the darkened bedchamber and into the dressing room, a small chamber with a table and a few chairs, a good mirror, and some inadequate lamps. It currently looked like it was being used by at least half the cast of an amateur theatrical.

Madeline followed him back to the dressing room, as he hoped she would. But before he could say anything she kicked the door shut behind her and said, "You're being somewhat uncommunicative."

Her tone, honed to an edge of expression from years of training, stung more than her words. Nicholas's patience wasn't inexhaustible to begin with and his temper was short from long hours of work and continual frustrations. He snapped, "I haven't anything to communicate."

"You mean nothing definite," Madeline corrected, folding her arms.

Nicholas turned away and dug through the chaos of clothing and disguises spilling out of the wardrobe and onto the floor, cursing under his breath. *It's my apartment and this was all my idea. You would think I could find my god-damned trousers.* "All right, nothing definite to communicate."

"You won't discuss it with me because you're afraid I'll tell Ronsarde and you don't want your thunder stolen."

"That makes me sound like a complete fool." He found the remnants of his cabman outfit, which had the merit of being dry, at least, and began to strip.

Madeline didn't disagree with that statement. She eyed him narrowly, then said, "Halle asked me today if he and Ronsarde could trust you."

"Halle asked you that?" Nicholas paused with his shirt half off.

"Yes."

Nicholas pulled his shirt on. "Ungrateful bastard."

"You're jealous," she said.

"On your account, I assume?" As soon as he said it he knew it was a mistake, but it was too late to snatch the words back. *Idiot,* he snarled at himself.

But Madeline only gestured in annoyance. "No, I'm not that much of a fool. On Ronsarde's account. Halle's worked with him all these years, been involved in the investigations of all these fascinating crimes, been his confidant and his partner. That's what you would have wanted."

"That's ridiculous," he snapped, slinging things out of the way as he searched for his boots in the bottom of the closet. He wasn't sure which charge was more demeaning: the accusation of professional jealousy or her obvious belief that that was the only kind of jealousy he could possibly fall prey to.

"Is it? That's why you won't tell anyone what you've been doing. You want to impress everyone."

Nicholas finished dressing in suppressed fury. Finally, he slung his battered black coat over his shoulders and pulled on the torn fingerless gloves. He grabbed his hat from the dressing table and went to pull back the curtains and shove the window open. He turned back and saw, from Madeline's expression, that she might regret what she had said, but it was far too late for that. He said, "I don't know what's worse: your inaccuracy or your patronizing attitude," and stepped out the window onto the ledge.

The decorative stonework let him boost himself up onto the roof where he could make his way down the outside stairs into the back courtyard.

———

It was too early for the appointment Nicholas had to keep, so he found himself in the theater district just off the Saints Procession Boulevard. He passed the façades of the Tragedian, the Elegante, and the Arcadella, with their well-proportioned columns and statues of the Graces and the patron saints of drama and the arts. The promenades were crowded with well-dressed patrons and the vendors and flower-sellers overflowed out into the street, impeding traffic. The carriage circle of the opera was almost choked with coaches with noble crests emblazoned on their doors, and the ornamental lamps around the fountains in the center crowned the confusion with a blaze of light and moving water.

Nicholas kept moving, skirting the busy promenades and the constables who patrolled them, ducking into the street where he had to dodge between the lumbering coaches and the faster-moving cabriolets and curricles. The crowding became even worse when he came into sight of the less expensive theaters and the music halls, an area that flirted dangerously with the edges of the Gabardin and Riverside. He paused outside the High Follies, a theater that specialized in grandiose epics with shipwrecks on fayre islands, exploding steamers in stormy seas, and volcanic explosions. As a boy he would have given, or stolen, anything for the coins to attend a show here. As an adult with freedom and money in his pocket, he would have thought the tawdry magic of the place would have palled. But it was amazing how tempting the doorway, framed by an enormous pair of gold-painted palm trees hung with giant snakes, still was. He reminded himself that the shows went for hours and he didn't have that much time to waste. *You can take the boy out of Riverside,* Nicholas thought ruefully, *but it's always in his blood.* Which showed you what fools the people were who believed heredity and bloodlines meant everything. His blood was of the pure aristocracy of Ile-Rien, which the Alsenes were still members of, even if their disgrace kept them from participating in it. This would have been a comforting thought if he hadn't had the suspicion that his infamous ancestor, Denzil Alsene, would have got along rather well in any place of violence and cutthroat competition.

Nicholas walked on until the theaters became little hole-in-the-wall affairs and the music halls became progressively smaller and dingier, and he was in Riverside proper.

There he found entertainment of a somewhat more active nature. He talked or traded insults with a wide variety of people, some of whom were old acquaintances, most of whom knew him by different names. He watched the robbery of a brandy house and ducked into an alley as the constables and the shouting owner ran past. He walked and thought and ended up sitting on what was left of the grand staircase of a ruined Great House with a street urchin, sharing a handful of hot chestnuts, when he heard the nearest clocktower ring the hour.

His goal was only a few streets up, back toward the boulevard, but the area was very different. The streetlights illuminated few passersby and most of the tall brownstone buildings were offices, closed for the night and dark. There was only one building with lit windows, a much more elaborate affair with columns and a polished stone façade. It was the office that housed the Prefect of Public Works.

Nicholas went round the back, threading his way through the alleys, until he found himself in the quiet carriage court behind it. He knocked on the door there and in a few moments the man who answered passed him a tightly folded bundle of documents, and Nicholas handed him an envelope of currency notes.

He went farther up toward the boulevard then, finding an open café whose lamps threw enough light onto a nearby bench, and he sat there to study his prize. He stayed there long enough that the waiter decided he was an eccentric and began to include him in his circuit, so Nicholas was able to order coffee without having to disturb the arrangement of the documents.

He had been there some time when a voice behind him said, "You're not easy to find."

Nicholas glanced up. Madeline leaned on the back of the bench, dressed as a young man, wearing a ridiculously emphatic blue-and-gold waistcoat and with her hat tilted at a rakish angle. He said, dryly, "That assumes I want to be found."

Madeline sat on the bench beside him. "Oh, I think you wanted to be found, just a little. You did leave a trail through Riverside, though I did have quite a time until I picked up on it." She frowned at the papers in his lap. "What's that?"

"Sewer maps from the Public Works office. I bribed a clerk to steal copies for me. Ronsarde could have got them just by asking, of course, but then it would be in the penny sheets by tomorrow. The clerks there are eminently bribable." The dregs of the argument still lay between them but at this time of night it seemed pointless to pursue, and Nicholas was disinclined to continue it.

"Hmm." Madeline looked like she badly wanted to ask what the maps were for, but managed, maddeningly, to restrain herself. She said, "Well, I actually had a reason for following you."

"Oh, good. I'd hate to be deluded into the thought that you were mildly fond of me."

Madeline's mouth twisted wryly. "A second reason. Reynard sent a telegram to the apartment; he wants you to meet him tonight. He has something important to tell you, I gather, unless there's something you haven't been telling me?"

"Madeline, you can't be jealous of Reynard; it's passé," Nicholas said, but he was already folding up the maps.

———

The first glow of dawn was lightening the sky to the east by the time they reached the Café Baudy. It was in the Deval Forest, a pleasure garden with wandering paths, streams, and picturesque waterfalls and grottos, always crowded in the warmer months. The café was built on two large firmly anchored barges in a small lake and reached by footbridges. In the summer, the water would have been cluttered with boaters and bathers, the rounded islands thick with flowers, but now it was still and dark, the banks shadowed by willows and poplars. Only the café was bright, colored lanterns lighting the balcony and the raucous diners crowding it, music drifting over the still black water. Nicholas noted the resemblance to a scene out of one of Vanteil's *Visions of Fayre* oils.

Nicholas and Madeline made their way over one of the narrow bridges to the terrace of the café. Reynard had chosen the spot well; their unconventional dress, which would have kept them out of any of the better hotels and restaurants, was here not even acknowledged. As the waiter led them among the tables, Nicholas saw that Madeline was by no means the only woman dressed as a man, or vice versa, in the crowd.

Reynard was seated at a table with its white linen littered with wineglasses and crumbs and the remains of a light meal. By the number of glasses, Nicholas suspected he had had to fend off numerous friends and acquaintances while waiting for them. This impression was confirmed when he greeted them with "Where the hell have you been?"

"We were detained," Nicholas explained unhelpfully and Madeline assumed an expression of innocence. While the waiter fussed with fresh glasses and poured more wine, she poked at the remnants of the food, finding enough pâté to spread on one of the leftover rounds of toast. As soon as the man was gone, Reynard said, "You were right. It was Montesq got Ronsarde arrested."

Nicholas leaned forward intently. "Money?"

"How else? I suspected he had Lord Diero in his pocket—"

"Diero, not Albier?" Madeline interrupted, pâté-smeared bread forgotten in her hand.

"Not Albier," Reynard confirmed. "My sources of information—and I'll admit, most of them are prostitutes, either professionals or amateurs—all believe Diero to be heavily in debt to Montesq. Last week, Diero was visited by Batherat, that solicitor you heard about last year—"

"Yes, the new one." Nicholas had been witness to a meeting between Montesq and Batherat via Arisilde's portrait at Coldcourt.

"And the next day, Diero gave a very private order to have Ronsarde's movements checked."

"How did you discover that?" Madeline demanded. "You have a source in the upper levels of the Prefecture?"

"One of Diero's subordinates is a friend of a friend. It's surprising how many people come to the same places for their entertainment. This rather vital piece of information was confided to me over a late supper at the Loggia, as though it meant nothing, and of course to the person who told me it did mean nothing. But if you know the rest . . ." He gestured eloquently.

"So Montesq is in league with our sorcerer," Madeline said. "But how did that happen? We watched him so closely. How—"

Nicholas's thoughts were going along the same path, but Reynard cleared his throat and said, "No, I don't think he is in league with our madman. I think he was after Ronsarde for an entirely different reason."

"What reason?" Nicholas had never forgotten that Ronsarde had advanced some suspicions of Montesq. He had wanted to follow up that tantalizing hint but had been afraid of exposing more about his own activities than Ronsarde could comfortably ignore. And there hadn't been time.

"Ronsarde apparently never dropped the case concerning Edouard Viller." Reynard advanced the topic cautiously, but Nicholas gestured at him to continue. As a victim of scandal himself, Reynard wasn't one to talk of rope in the house of the hanged, either literally or figuratively, and wouldn't mention it unless it was important. Reynard said, "This same person, Diero's subordinate, told me that Ronsarde had finally asked formal permission of Diero to reopen the court documents and interview witnesses officially, in front of a magistrate. Your name, Nic, was on the list of persons to be questioned in court."

The waiter arrived to pour more wine, appearing just in time to hear

Madeline utter an oath that disturbed a normally impenetrable demeanor to the point that the man actually cocked an eyebrow in reaction. They waited until he had moved on, then Reynard continued, "And that of course means nothing unless you know that Montesq arranged the evidence against Edouard Viller."

Nicholas smoothed the tablecloth, to keep his hands from knotting into fists. "Ronsarde said nothing about it."

"He wouldn't." Madeline was strangling her napkin in suppressed excitement. Her voice shook with it. "He never knew who arranged his arrest. Halle tried to find out but he couldn't discover anything. Ronsarde doesn't know Diero is connected to Montesq. If he had he would have gone over his head, to Albier or Captain Giarde or the Queen herself, he could easily do it."

"That's not all," Reynard said impatiently. "Montesq didn't only move against Ronsarde. Batherat met with someone else last week as well, in a cabaret. The man evidently believes the lower-class prostitutes that inhabit the place won't recognize men they must see every night at the theaters, getting out of crested carriages. He met with Fallier, Nicholas, Rahene Fallier."

"Ah." Nicholas leaned back in his chair, and the too-warm, noisy room seemed to fade. "Of course he did."

"I don't know what he has on Fallier," Reynard added. "Montesq has been in the business of blackmail so long, it could be anything. Debts, youthful indiscretions—"

"Necromancy, past or present," Madeline added.

"Exactly."

"Your informant didn't know what Batherat and Fallier discussed," Nicholas said, thoughtfully.

"No," Reynard admitted. "But I think it must have been you."

"Yes." Nicholas nodded. "It would explain Fallier's sudden interest in me."

"What do you mean?" Madeline demanded.

"Fallier may or may not have recognized my resemblance to Denzil Alsene from a Greanco portrait. In fact, I think he must have; he did know me when we came face-to-face in the street. But he already knew who I was and not from past researches to uncover possible usurpers to the Crown. He knew because Montesq had Batherat tell him." Montesq could have sought information on the Valiarde family easily enough. Nicholas's mother's family denied her existence now, but there would be old servants or far-flung relations who would readily admit that Sylvaine Valiarde had lived, married a disgraced Alsene, left her husband's family after his death, and dropped out of sight in Vienne.

Madeline nodded. "Montesq knows you hate him, knows you believe he destroyed Edouard. Maybe he even knows you've been sticking your nose in his illegitimate dealings."

"But he doesn't know much, or he would have moved against you before now," Reynard added. "He wanted to get Ronsarde out of the way so he had these charges trumped up, then stirred up a riot so he'd have done with him permanently. He also wanted to discredit you, so he told Fallier about your past history."

"But I'd left Coldcourt and Fallier couldn't find me until he was called to the contretemps outside Fontainon House." Nicholas's eyes narrowed as he followed that line of logic. "And our sorcerer knew Montesq's movements and took advantage of his machinations for his own purposes." And why had Montesq acted against Ronsarde and himself now, after all this time? *Obviously he's afraid Ronsarde has new information. Or that I have new information.*

"So he is in league with Montesq?" Madeline said, with the air of being determined to settle at least one point.

"No." Nicholas was thinking of the enspelled mirror Arisilde had found in Octave's hotel room. "Our criminal sorcerer has too many ways of finding things out. He is a necromancer, after all. But I would like to know how he knew where to look." He let out his breath. He hadn't wanted to discuss this with anyone, except perhaps Arisilde, who was too distanced from reality himself to find any theory far-fetched, no matter how outrageous it sounded. "I'm almost afraid that the reason he did know all this—"

A sudden shout from the doorway drew their attention. A raggedly dressed boy was at the entrance, gesturing urgently to a skeptical maître d'. Nicholas recognized one of Cusard's messengers and nodded to Reynard, who signaled their waiter over and said, "I believe the boy has a message for me; have them let him in, will you?"

In another moment, the boy stood panting at their table, much to the consternation and amusement of the other diners. "Captain Morane!" The boy held out a smudged square of folded notepaper. "This's for you."

Reynard handed the note to Nicholas and dismissed the boy with some coins and a couple of pastries from the table. Nicholas quickly scanned Cusard's hasty and almost illegible handwriting, swore, and got to his feet. "There's trouble. We have to get there immediately."

The cab let them off in the Philosopher's Cross, one street over from Arisilde's building. Without knowing what had happened, Nicholas wanted to be able to approach the place cautiously and on foot; Cusard's note had said only that there had been a "disaster" and that they must come to Arisilde's apartment at once.

The early morning light was gray and heavy, the air cold and damp. Nicholas was first down the alley and first to come within sight of the tenement.

He halted on the dirty paving stones of the promenade without quite knowing he had. Cusard had not exaggerated.

There was a hole in the upper stories of the old building, just where Arisilde's apartment was. It was a ragged, gaping cavity as if from a bomb blast, and had torn a section out of the mansard roof. But there was no mark of fire and no smoke hung in the damp air, though broken stone and shingles littered the pavement.

Behind him he heard Reynard curse, then Madeline made a strangled noise and pushed past him, running across the street. Nicholas bolted after her.

There were people in the alley, pointing up and discussing it in hushed tones, milling around. There were constables and men from the fire brigade going in and out of the entrance.

Madeline pushed through a pair of constables and plunged up the stairs. Nicholas would have been right behind her but someone stepped into his way. It was Cusard, having materialized out of the crowd of spectators like a wraith. He said, "Something you got to know."

Nicholas paused and Reynard fetched up behind him. "What?"

Cusard's shoulders were stooped and he looked very old in the gray morning light. He said, "Ronsarde and Halle was in there, too."

Reynard said, "No," and looked up at the rent in the building, his face aghast. Another brick fell, scattering the front edge of the crowd.

Nicholas's throat was tight. "How?"

"The Parscian sent a telegram for you, saying for you to come at once, that Arisilde was going to wake up. The Inspector told me to look for you and he and the doctor went off to here." Cusard hesitated, his face guilty. "I should've stopped 'em."

Nicholas shook his head. *If I had been there . . .* "Go on."

"I had to go to the warehouse to find a boy to send, but by that time Verack—he was watchin' here last night—come for me, to tell me what had happened."

"They're dead?" Reynard asked.

Cusard shook his head and gestured in frustration. "They wouldn't let no-body in. And I didn't want to give notice to the constables—but they ain't carried nobody out."

"They let Madeline in." Reynard looked at Nicholas.

"Her grandmother was in there." Nicholas caught Reynard's arm when he would have pushed on toward the building. "No, stay out here."

The constables tried to stop him but he told them that he was Madeline's husband and they let him pass. There were frightened tenants on the stair-well, crying children and people in various states of undress, and constables trying unsuccessfully to get them out of the building or at least out of the way. Nicholas wove his way past until he reached the landing that was just below Arisilde's apartment. The skylight over the stairs had been shattered and part of the ceiling had come down. The concierge stood on the landing, resisting all attempts to move him. He was arguing with a constable and an official-looking person in a frock coat.

"No," the concierge was saying stubbornly, his Aderassi accent thickening in his distress. "Do I look drunk nor mad? There was more than that—" He saw Nicholas and winced. "Ah, sir. The old woman, they got her in there."

Nicholas turned to the indicated doorway. It was the apartment below Aris-ilde's. The door had been knocked off the hinges and stood to one side, and the floor in the hall and front parlor was littered with plaster dust and pieces of molding. A frowsy-haired woman wrapped in a dressing gown appeared and gestured him through a pile of broken crockery to a back room.

A single lamp revealed a bedroom in tumbled disorder, with old furniture and blue-flowered damask. Madele had been laid out on the bed, her hands folded neatly, and Madeline sat next to her. Nicholas's first reaction was relief. Even though he knew there hadn't been time, he had been irrationally afraid that her body would have been used for necromancy. There wasn't a mark on her and except for the dust in her clothes and hair, she might have died in her sleep.

Madeline's face was utterly still.

The concierge stepped into the doorway behind Nicholas and touched his sleeve. He whispered, "Tell the lady we found her all curled up at the top of the stairs, like she was asleep. It took her so quick, whatever it was, that she didn't feel a thing. I don't want to say it to her now, but later, when she wants to hear it."

"Yes, thank you." Nicholas nodded. It would have had to take her quickly, a battle would have drawn too much attention. And there were other witches and sorcerers who lived in the Philosopher's Cross, though not powerful ones. If she had had a chance to fight, they might have come to help her. "Did you see it?"

"I heard it. An explosion, like a bomb, very loud, very sharp." The man glanced warily over his shoulder. "They think it was a gas explosion, but it was nothing like one and they don't know the wizard lives here. Wizards got enemies, everybody knows that."

The constable and the official in the frock coat were making their way through the shattered apartment toward them. "They were all killed?" Nicholas asked the concierge, speaking in Aderassi.

"That's just it!" The man switched to his native language automatically. "We found the old Parscian man alive, but not a sign of the others, and these bastards don't believe—"

The official interrupted, "Excuse me, what connection do you have to this affair?" If he knew he had just been called a bastard in Aderassi he gave no sign of it.

"My wife's grandmother was killed and I'm a friend of the tenant in that apartment," Nicholas answered, stepping back out of the bedroom so the official would focus on him and leave Madeline alone. To the concierge he said urgently, "Where's Isham?"

The man turned back down the hall and led him to another small, disordered room, the official and the constable still trailing them. Isham lay on the bed there, blood in his hair and on his face from multiple cuts on his forehead. The woman in the dressing gown was trying to bathe the cuts but the old man moaned, barely conscious, and tried to push her hand away. Nicholas forgot about their audience and went hastily to his side.

"Isham, it's Nicholas," he said. The old man's face was badly bruised, there were other cuts and scrapes, and the colors of his robes were muted by plaster dust. "Can you hear me?"

Isham's hand came up, grabbed his coat with surprising strength. Nicholas leaned down, his ear close to the injured man's lips. His voice a weak rasp, Isham whispered, "Madele freed Arisilde. It was a corpse ring, hidden by a spell. I thought . . . there might be danger—but she removed it and nothing happened so I sent for you. But he must have known when the spell failed and he came . . . He came for Arisilde . . ."

Isham tried to manage more but he started to cough, a racking, pain-filled sound, and Nicholas said, "That's enough, you've told me all I need to know." That was anything but true, but he didn't want the man to kill himself with the effort. He probed at one of the cuts gently, trying to determine the extent of the injury.

"Careful, there's glass," the woman cautioned him.

She was right. Dr. Brile's surgery wasn't far from here. He would have to make arrangements to have Isham moved there immediately. And he would have to claim Madele's body so it wouldn't be sent to the city morgue.

"Sir," an impatient voice behind him said. Nicholas twisted around and the official took a step backward, startled and wary. Nicholas made an effort to school his features into an expression less threatening. He realized the man had been trying to get his attention for some moments. He said, "Yes?"

The official regained his composure and said, "This person"—he indicated the concierge—"has said there were three others in the apartment but we can find no sign of them. Can you confirm this?"

No sign of them. "Yes," Nicholas said. "This man and the old woman were caring for the tenant, who was an invalid. Two of our friends were coming here early this morning." He looked at the concierge, who stood at the foot of the bed, his arms folded, frustrated and highly affronted at having his veracity questioned. "Did they arrive before . . . ?"

"Yes, the two men, gray-haired, one with a doctor bag, one with a cane? Doctors come all the time lately, I hardly notice."

"How long before?" Nicholas asked sharply, interrupting whatever pronouncement the official had been trying to make.

"Not long." The concierge narrowed his eyes, lips pursed in thought, anticipating the demand for a more specific answer. "I heard them go up the stairs, a door open and close. Then Cesar, from the market, came to argue about rent, but that was only for a moment and boom! It knocked us both down from fear. Things fell, dust came down the stairs in a great cloud. I thought the whole place would come down on our heads."

It was a trap, then. If Nicholas had correctly understood Isham, then the removal of whatever spell had imprisoned Arisilde had alerted their opponent, but instead of acting immediately he had waited to see who would come to Arisilde's side. But if Arisilde was waking, why hadn't he tried to defend himself? I have to get into that apartment.

"And what relation was the tenant to you?" the official asked.

Nicholas was glad he hadn't brought a pistol with him; he would've been tempted to shoot the man. But before he could answer, Madeline shouldered the bulky constable out of the doorway and shoved into the room. She stood, breathing hard, looking down at Isham. Nicholas saw the official look askance at her coat and trousers and he told the man, in a cold voice, "She's on the stage."

"Ahh." The official pretended to understand that statement and persisted, "I understand the shock of the situation but—"

Madeline lifted her gaze to Nicholas. "How is he?" she demanded.

Her eyes glittered and not from unshed tears. It was a dangerous light, uncertain and with an edge to it. Nicholas answered, "Not good. He needs to go to Dr. Brile immediately."

The concierge abruptly remembered his duty and said, "I get you a carriage," and pushed his way out past the constable.

Nicholas hesitated for a heartbeat, then put his faith in Madeline's quick wits. He stood and caught her hand, saying urgently, "You look faint!"

Her expression didn't change but she blinked and raised a suddenly trembling hand to her brow. Then she fell backward, boneless and apparently completely unconscious, right into the arms of the surprised official. He staggered under her sudden and unexpected weight and the constable leapt forward to help support her. The woman who had been tending Isham yelped in sympathy and scrambled around the bed to help.

Nicholas shouted something about going for help and slipped past them and out the door. He reached the landing again, saw the other tenants still milling below, and hurried up the stairs.

The doorframe in Arisilde's apartment was cracked and splintered and the door hung on its hinges, revealing the familiar hall choked with rubble and debris. He stepped through it carefully, making his way into the long parlor at the back of the apartment. The hole was between the two windows that had looked down into the alley, the edges ragged with broken stone and shattered wood. The floor was buried under plaster from the ceiling and broken glass from the windows and skylights, and the remnants of the curtains stirred gently in the cool breeze. Nicholas moved around the room, noting the familiar objects strewn about, the furniture broken or overturned, the scattered books and smashed plant pots.

A gas explosion, Nicholas thought in contempt. *Whoever came to that conclusion was delusional.* From the look of it all, it was immediately obvious that whatever had burst through the wall had done it from the outside coming in.

He left the wreck of the parlor and searched the rest of the apartment swiftly. The other rooms were not as badly disturbed, except for objects knocked off the walls and the cracks in the plaster. There was no sign of Ronsarde or Halle, no sign that anyone had been here.

Arisilde's bedroom was oddly undisturbed, as if it had been at the still center of a violent and destructive storm. The coverlet on the bed was thrown back and the impression in the soft mattress where Arisilde had lain was still visible.

He heard voices from below and knew he had run out of time. He moved quickly toward the door, but a glint of white wedged into the bottom of the splintered doorframe caught his eye. He knelt and worked it free.

It was a piece of ivory, carved into the shape of a Parscian hunting cat's head. It was the ornament from atop the ebony cane Reynard had loaned to Inspector Ronsarde.

The concierge had found a carriage to take Isham to Dr. Brile's surgery and Nicholas used that confusion to get down the stairs to the lower landing without anyone noticing. In the ensuing effort to get the injured man down the stairs without hurting him further, Nicholas managed to give some coins to the woman who had let her rooms be used as hospital and morgue, and to ask the concierge to send for an undertaker to take charge of Madele's body. He escaped into the street without further interrogation by constables or anyone else.

As he gave the coachman instructions and a note for Dr. Brile, he saw Madeline waiting across the street with Reynard and Cusard. He checked that Isham was settled as comfortably as possible, then sent the coach off and joined the others.

"Are you all right?" he asked Madeline.

"Of course," she snapped.

"Do we know anything of what happened?" Reynard asked, as if he didn't have much hope of an answer.

Nicholas shook his head. "From what Isham was able to tell me, Madele discovered what was wrong with Arisilde. It was a spell, not drugs or illness. But when she removed it, it somehow alerted the sorcerer. He waited long enough to draw a few of us into the trap." He stopped, compressing his lips, then looked at Madeline. "Why didn't she tell me she had discovered what was wrong with Arisilde?"

"She never told anyone anything. She probably didn't want to get your hopes up if she was wrong." Madeline knotted her fists and paced angrily. "Damn stupid old woman."

Reynard looked up at the ruin of the tenement's top floor. He said softly, "Now what?"

That wasn't a question Nicholas wanted to answer at the moment, even though he knew exactly what he had to do now. He looked around, struck by the sudden notion that he was missing something important. "Wait. Where's Crack?"

Reynard turned back and Madeline looked up. Cusard blanched and said, "He was with Ronsarde and Halle when I left. . . ."

Nicholas cursed and started back down the alley toward their coach. He would check the apartment but he knew he would find no one there. He had told Crack to "watch the others," and Crack would not have let Ronsarde and Halle leave the apartment alone.

CHAPTER NINETEEN

Nicholas read the telegram one more time in disbelief, then crumpled it into a tight little ball. The struggle to control rage took all his concentration for a moment, before he was able to turn to Reynard and say tightly, "I'm informed that any messages I send will not be delivered to Captain Giarde."

Reynard stared in disbelief. "Fallier?"

Nicholas considered it, then shook his head. The Court Sorcerer couldn't affect the delivery of private messages to the palace. No, that was the Prefecture's realm. "Albier. He thinks I'm trying to undermine him on Ronsarde's behalf. He has probably given orders to block messages from Ronsarde and Halle, as well." No one in the Prefecture knew that the two men had been in the shattered apartment in the Philosopher's Cross. Nicholas had sent his message from the telegraph office on the Boulevard of Flowers and then returned with the others to the Panzan apartment to find the place chill and empty, the fires gone out from lack of tending. As he had feared, Crack was nowhere to be found. Nicholas had sent Lamane over to check the warehouse, hoping against hope, but he knew Crack must have followed Ronsarde and Halle to Arisilde's apartment.

He threw the telegram into the hearth. Madeline was sitting on the divan near the window with her knees drawn up. She lifted her head and regarded him with a dark unflinching gaze, but said nothing. Cusard was pacing anxiously.

"But Albier's honest, or enough so for this purpose," Reynard said. "We could go to him and explain, ask for help."

Nicholas grimaced at the thought but as much as he disliked the idea of an appeal to Albier, it was the quickest way to get Captain Giarde's assistance. "Madeline will go to Albier." He hesitated, not wanting to drag Reynard into this. He had lost enough people to this sorcerer. *But I can't do it alone.* "You and I will go after the others."

Reynard stared hard at him. "You know where they've been taken?"

"It's only speculation." Nicholas found the folder of maps he had tossed onto a chair and dug out the one he needed. He spread it on the table. "This is the key. The Monde Street sewer."

"He's hiding in a sewer?" Cusard said, coming over to look, his doubt evident.

"For the past few days, the Monde Street sewer syphon has been subject to blockages, caused by bone. Human bone," Nicholas explained. At their expressions, he said, "No, it's not what you're thinking. These bones were years old; that was apparent from even a cursory examination. That was why the sewermen were not alarmed."

"Better start from the beginning," Reynard said, exchanging a dubious look with Cusard.

"From experience I know how difficult it is to find a reliable, safe hiding place in this city," Nicholas said patiently. "Considering that our sorcerer chose Valent House the first time, I found it unlikely that he would have tried to purchase or acquire property, and the Prefecture would be investigating any deserted buildings that were possibilities. So before extending the search outside the city walls, I wanted to see if he had gone underground."

"The Sending. Isham said it could have been the remains of a long dead fay, buried somewhere, didn't he?" Reynard tapped the map thoughtfully. "A catacomb?"

"Exactly. After speaking to the sewermen and looking over the maps from the Public Works office, it became apparent that a catacomb was being cleared, the bones dumped into the sewer somewhere above Monde where they were flowing down into the syphon."

Reynard asked, "But what if there's been a collapse somewhere, and the bones washed out of a catacomb naturally?"

"The sewer level would have dropped, since there hasn't been rain for days." Nicholas hesitated. It was all a tissue of suppositions, but he still thought his reasoning was sound. "It's only a theory. But I've thought hard about it and it's the most likely option."

Reynard eyed him. "How long have you known this?"

Nicholas glanced at Madeline, but though she watched alertly she still betrayed no reaction. "Since I looked at the maps I received from a clerk at the Prefect of Public Works office last night, before we went to meet you. I wanted to be sure it was possible for a catacomb to exist in the location it would have to occupy for this to work. There's been so much building in the past few decades and none of the original catacombs that are still accessible are very deep."

Reynard was nodding. There were catacombs that were still in use under the cathedral, and others in the older parts of Vienne that were opened occasionally for tours. "But this was a catacomb only our sorcerer knew about? The same way he knew about everything else, I suppose."

Nicholas nodded, distractedly. "Once we know for certain that this is the sorcerer's hiding place, we can return and direct Fallier and Giarde and his men to the exact location." He glanced at Cusard. "I'll need some things from the warehouse."

Cusard nodded and let out his breath in resignation. "Sewers. Ghouls. I'm glad I'm old."

"Let me be clear on one point," Reynard said. "The idea is to locate the sorcerer so he can be dealt with by Fallier and the other resources the palace can command, not take care of him ourselves."

"Correct. The situation doesn't call for suicide," Nicholas said, a brow lifting ironically. "But should we be cornered, there can't be that much difficulty. After all, I am related to the man who killed the sorcerer Urbain Grandier."

"As I remember the story, Alsene shot him in the back, from a distance," Reynard said dryly, folding his arms.

"That would be my preference as well."

"Hmm." Reynard stroked his mustache and said consideringly, "How does one dress for the sewer?"

Nicholas started to answer but Madeline stood suddenly, saying, "Nicholas, I'm going with you, not Reynard."

They both turned to her.

She seemed to realize she would at least have to clarify her position. "There are a number of reasons. One of which is that we know Edouard's sphere works for me and we don't know that it will work for anyone else, and there's no time to make a suitable test. I assume there will still be ghouls in the sewers."

She paused, as if to give him leave to interrupt at this point, but Nicholas kept silent. He had never been spoken to in this tone by anyone not holding a pistol trained on him and he found himself unwillingly fascinated. He wondered if she would mention Madele.

After a polite interval, Madeline continued, showing no sign of being disconcerted by his silence, "I could threaten, I could shout. I could follow you or delay you if you try to stop me. But I'm not going to do any of those things. I'm just going with you."

Nicholas waited but that seemed to be all. He cleared his throat. "That would mean Reynard would have to attempt to contact Albier and Captain Giarde."

Her mouth tightened. She must know Reynard had been acquainted with Giarde from his days as a cavalry officer and Nicholas had to admit it was a low blow. Dryly, she said, "I don't think Reynard's sensibilities are as delicate as yours."

Reynard and Nicholas exchanged another look. *I know she just insulted both of us but I'm not sure how,* Nicholas thought. He said, "You almost fainted from the stench when we went into the sewer from the prison." He was aware he sounded accusing. And ineffectual.

"You were ill when you saw the carnage in Valent House," she retorted. "I'd say that makes us even."

Nicholas took a breath for consideration, then looked at Reynard, who said immediately, "This is your decision. I'm not in the middle of this."

The problem was that she was right about the sphere. Once they found the sorcerer's hiding place they would certainly be pursued; it could mean the difference between getting out alive and perishing nobly. Nicholas wasn't fond of the idea of dying heroically, alone or in company.

"We're running out of time," Madeline said softly.

"There's something I need to tell you both first." Nicholas folded the map slowly. Regardless of which of them went, he wanted them to know what they might be facing. "I don't think this sorcerer is a man pretending, to himself and everyone else, to be Constant Macob."

Madeline frowned. Reynard looked confused. He said, "But I thought that was the conclusion indicated by everything we'd discovered."

"It is," Nicholas assured him. "But I think he actually *is* Constant Macob."

There was a moment of silence, then Reynard said, "He is Macob, but not in the flesh, you mean?"

Cusard groaned and covered his face.

"Not in the flesh," Nicholas agreed. "Not anymore."

"You mean Edouard's device brought him back to life?" Madeline asked. She shook her head doubtfully.

"Good. We'll all need it later," Cusard muttered.

"No, I don't think Edouard's device did that. Or at least, not yet." There was an uncomfortable silence as that sank in. "I think Octave must have been in contact with Macob before he obtained the sphere and the notes on Edouard's work from Ilamires Rohan. I think Octave contacted, or was contacted by,

Macob in one of Octave's earlier attempts at spiritualism. Macob used his sorcery to discover things of benefit to Octave. Necromancy is, after all, primarily concerned with divination and the discovery of secret knowledge. One of the things Macob discovered for Octave was that Ilamires Rohan still had one of Edouard's spheres. Octave blackmailed Rohan to get it, then must have used the sphere to strengthen Macob's connection with the living world." He paced away from the table. "Macob must be planning some way to make that connection permanent, to bring himself back to life. To do this he apparently needed to get his body, or whatever was left of it, out of that room below what used to be Ventarin House. He sent Octave to contact the Duchess of Mondollot, but he didn't quite trust his accomplice. It was, after all, in Octave's best interest to keep the business of holding circles and discovering hidden treasures going as long as possible. Macob must have realized that Octave never meant him to succeed. So Macob sent the ghouls he had made with his necromancy and they located and stole the corpse for him. But it must have startled Macob that we arrived in Mondollot's cellars almost in time to witness the retrieval of the body, because he sent the golem of Octave to question my motives. He was afraid I had discovered that Octave was using Edouard's sphere." He shook his head. "No, he didn't want Octave to know what he really wanted, not at that point. He was playing at helping Octave with the spiritualism confidence game. I think it wasn't until that night after the circle at Gabrill House that Octave began to suspect the truth. He wanted to tell Macob that someone had tried to follow his coach, so he went unexpectedly to Valent House. Perhaps he truly didn't know the extent to which Macob had returned to his old practices until then. I only know that when I saw Octave at Lusaude's the next night, he was very frightened."

"But Macob's had his body back for days," Madeline said, gesturing in frustration. "That can't have been all he needed."

"No, there is some other element still missing. Something that is presently in the palace."

"The palace?" Reynard said, frowning. "What does the— Wait, you said Fontainon House was inside the palace wards. So Macob wanted Octave to hold a circle there and that would let Macob inside the wards and into the palace?"

"I suggested as much to Captain Giarde," Nicholas agreed. "But there was no proof."

"But what does Macob want there?" Madeline asked.

Nicholas shrugged. "I don't have the slightest idea. The palace has been a home for sorcerers for hundreds of years. It could be anything. It might be something no one knows is there. No one except Macob." He regarded Madeline. "Do you still want to go?"

"You shouldn't have phrased it as a challenge," she said dryly.

———

Reynard had already departed for the Prefecture and hopefully a meeting with Lord Albier. If he couldn't convince Albier of the urgency of his errand, and if he avoided being thrown into a Prefecture cell, he would try an audience with Giarde directly. Nicholas had to admit that Reynard might be far more adept than Madeline at tackling the issue of Albier's bullheaded stupidity without infuriating the official to the point where he had him arrested.

After some hasty preparations, Cusard drove them in his wagon to the sewer entrance Nicholas wanted to start from. It was on a street with little traffic, lined with tenement apartments that were quiet during the day, with broad walks and potted trees that kept passersby at a distance. It was also very near to the Monde Street syphon.

The wagon drew up in such a way as to block the view of the manhole, and Nicholas checked through the waterproofed knapsack he had quickly packed, enduring Cusard's doleful inquiries about extra candle stubs and matches.

Madeline stood nearby, with the sphere wrapped in sacking and tucked under her arm. She looked more impatient to get started than anything else.

Cusard followed his gaze, and muttered, "Take care of her ladyship there. And find Crack. I didn't realize I'd gotten so used to the bloody bastard."

"I will," Nicholas told him. "And don't worry; if everything goes well, we shouldn't be in much danger."

"Don't say that," Cusard demanded. "You're tempting fate."

They pried up the heavy metal cover and Nicholas went down first to get the lamp lit, using the shaft of mild sunlight from the opening to navigate. Madeline climbed down after him and he motioned for Cusard to slide the cover closed.

As their eyes grew used to the darkness Nicholas could see this was one of the newest galleries. Their lantern revealed high brick-lined walls and a wide channel of dark flowing water. The walkway was clean and almost dry and there was only a faint trace of unpleasant odor.

The sluice cart was tied to a ring set into the walkway, the current tugging at

it. It was a small boat with metal plates mounted behind it that could be raised
or lowered to control water flow around the craft and a pierced metal shield in
front to flush the sewer channel. This cart was one used for inspections and
had had its shield removed so it would travel faster. Nicholas had bribed one of
his recent sewermen acquaintances to provide it. His explanation that he was
an investigator assigned to discover information detrimental to the Prefect of
Public Works had insured enthusiastic cooperation.

He held it steady for Madeline, who climbed into the front and immediately
unwrapped the sphere. "Anything?" he asked her.

"No." She shook her head, studying the sphere carefully. "It's still and cold."

As Nicholas retrieved the broad paddle from the walkway and stepped in
behind her, he noted she hadn't asked "What if you're wrong?" *If I'm wrong,
our friends are dead, and we're wasting time here.* But he didn't think he was
wrong.

Besides, there was more to worry about if he was right.

He untied the line anchoring the cart to the walkway and braced his feet
as the flow jolted the little craft forward. "Ho," Madeline commented, startled
at the speed. "We don't know what we're going into but at least we'll get there
quickly."

"Isn't that always the case?" Nicholas said, keeping his tone light. He was
relieved that she sounded more like herself, then silently cursed himself for
allowing it to distract him. He knew she blamed him for Madele's death and
justifiably so; if not for him the old woman would still be in peaceful retire-
ment outside Lodun. But there was nothing he could do about it now. After a
few false starts he used the paddle to direct the cart toward the gallery exit and
into the main sewer.

The cart slid into a channel that was only slightly larger than the metal
plates mounted behind it. Their speed increased somewhat, but there was no
need to steer and Nicholas laid the paddle down and crouched on the narrow
shelf at the stern of the cart. The ceiling was much lower here and the walkways narrower, and the lamplight reflected off the water pipes in the curved
roof. It bore a strong resemblance to the sewer channel they had entered from
the prison, but it was still far cleaner. Nicholas knew that would change as they
reached the older areas.

The cart carried them rapidly down the Piscard Street channel where they
passed through another high-ceilinged gallery and exited into Orean Street.
The walls and walkways grew dark with slime, the odor rising from the water

grew more noxious, and their cart encountered solid objects that Nicholas preferred not to look at too closely. Madeline dug in the knapsack for the dark-colored rags Nicholas had brought and they each tied one around their nose and mouth. The rags had been soaked in a strong Parscian perfume oil; the condensed scent was cloying, but it warded off the sewer stink admirably.

The new sewers were all long and straight, orderly channels with their flow controlled by syphons and galleries, though even these broad tunnels could be dangerous. They were lucky there had been little rain lately; sudden torrential downpours sometimes drowned sewermen. The older sewer, begun with the birth of the city and altered over hundreds of years, would be much harder to traverse. Nicholas said, "We're not far now." Orean Street would cross Monde, just below the syphon.

The lapping water made very little sound and Nicholas clearly heard voices echoing down the tunnel. "The lamp," he whispered urgently. Madeline hastily shut the cover on the dark lantern and lowered it to the bottom of the cart. Nicholas slowed their progress by stepping forward to the front of the cart and thrusting the broad flat of the paddle down into the muck at the bottom of the channel.

They drifted toward the end where an archway opened into the collector near the syphon. Nicholas could see the glow of lamplight ahead, hear voices. There must be men on the walkway above the syphon, conducting an inspection. He handed the paddle to Madeline, who took it with only a little fumbling in the dark. Nicholas stood, bracing his feet apart against the cart's motion. As they neared the arch more light became visible, illuminating the rounded wall of a high-ceilinged chamber, and a breeze moved the stale damp air in the tunnel. He raised his arms and a moment later felt the slimy stone of the arch strike his hands. He grabbed the lip of it and the cart jerked forward, almost knocking him off his feet. Madeline rose to a crouch and jammed the paddle harder into the accumulated muck at the bottom of the channel. The cart stopped, the water gurgling as it rushed past.

Straining to hold on, Nicholas was surprised they could stop the cart at all. The Monde syphon must be blocked again and the water level dropping.

The group on the platform in the next gallery was discussing a drainage problem. Shadows were flung on the wall opposite the archway as their lamps bobbed and Nicholas caught the words "silt," "clogged," and "dynamite." He hoped that last was indicative of someone's exasperation and not something they had to worry about immediately. He heard Madeline grunt from effort and felt the cart shift as she resettled the paddle.

The voices faded and the light died away. Nicholas waited another few moments, then whispered, "All right."

Madeline lifted the paddle with a gasp of relief and he let go of the arch, grabbing the sides of the cart to steady himself. They drifted into the collector, Madeline using the paddle to guide them in a wide circle.

Without the lamp they were in a vast dark pit, echoing and silent except for the lapping of water and a distant rushing from the other tunnels. Nicholas found the dark lantern in the bottom of the cart and raised its cover again.

The light revealed the high walls of the collector and the walkway around the edge. Nicholas could see from the marks on the walls that the water level was normally several feet higher. At the far side of the collector, on a broad stone platform, was the end of the syphon, a long pipe that drew water from one end of the sewer system to the other. All that was visible of it was a gaping hole in the platform, surrounded by an iron guardrail. Suspended above the pit was what looked like the top half of a circular cage. It was actually the holder for the wooden ball that was used to clean the syphon of obstacles. Nicholas took the paddle back from Madeline and guided the cart over to bump up against the stone footing of the platform.

Cold, fetid air streamed up from the pipe, making Nicholas shiver even in his greatcoat. The surface around it was covered with stinking lumps of silt and sand. Nicholas leaned on the paddle to hold the cart steady and picked up one of the lumps, scraping the silt off it. He handed it to Madeline, who crouched down to examine it in the light of the lantern. She had to break it and look at the inside before she could make sure what it was. "Yes, it's bone," she said quietly. "Old and stained but brittle, as if it hasn't been in the water long."

Nicholas pushed off with the paddle and guided them toward the exit into the next sewer.

They were well into the older tunnels now and the stench would have been overpowering except for the cloths treated with perfume oil. The lamplight caught furtive movement on the filth-choked walkways as rats traveled busily along and there was an occasional plop, as a spider or centipede dropped from the rounded ceiling into the stream. The sphere remained quiescent under Madeline's hands and Nicholas didn't know whether to be relieved or discouraged. They had had no time or means to test the sphere's range of influence, but if the necromancer was really down here, he thought it should have detected something before now. *If we're attacked by a ghoul while we're stuck in this cart, it will go badly,* he reminded himself grimly.

Finally, an archway sealed by rusted grating appeared at the limit of the light. "That's it," Nicholas said, dragging the paddle along the bottom to slow the cart. "We'll walk from now on."

Madeline grabbed the stone lip of the walkway and helped him swing the cart against it. "I could feign delight but I think I'll save that for when we encounter something really horrible."

"Then it won't be long," Nicholas told her. He wasn't looking forward to this part of the journey either. "This is the Great Sewer. It hasn't been drained in six hundred years."

Madeline muttered under her breath but made no other comment.

Nicholas tied the cart off to one of the metal rings sunk into the stone for the purpose and climbed up on the walkway to examine the grating. There was a lock that the Prefect of Public Works probably possessed the key for, but it was badly rusted. He pulled the pry bar out of the knapsack and set to work separating the grating from the stone at the weak points along the side.

As they had discussed already, Madeline didn't offer to assist but stood by with the lamp and the sphere, keeping watch. The ghouls couldn't be running rampant in the newer channels or the sewermen would have seen them. But Nicholas was aware that sewermen died all the time, from falls, from noxious vapors that built up in the lesser-used tunnels, from sudden deluges of rainwater; if more sewermen had been killed in the past months than usual it would be put down to bad luck and no one would think to search for some other cause.

The grating broke away from the stone in pieces and soon Nicholas had cleared enough of an opening for them to squeeze through. He slung the knapsack over his shoulder, collected the lamp from Madeline, and worked his way past the broken metal. On the other side he waited for Madeline to follow, holding the lamp up to get a look at the passage before them.

The ceiling was lower, the channel and the walkway narrower. The masonry was crumbled and cracked or coated with layers of filth and festooned with bizarre shapes of fungi. Ghost-lichen mixed in with the other growth threw sparkles of light back at the lamp.

Madeline squeezed through the opening behind him, clamping her hat down tight on her head and clutching the sphere against her side. "Anything?" Nicholas asked her.

She held the metal up against her cheek to make sure, then shook her head. "Not the slightest twitch. But there are water pipes all around us, aren't there? Maybe that's confusing it."

"Why would that confuse it?" Nicholas noted that she spoke of the sphere as if it were alive, as most sorcerers spoke of the Great Spells. He wondered if it was a habit picked up from Madele.

"Some complicated reason having to do with natural philosophy—how should I know? But the sphere is so light, it can't be made out of anything but copper or bronze or other metals that weigh hardly anything. Iron has magical properties; maybe it interferes with the sphere."

"Maybe," Nicholas said, grudgingly. There could be something in what she said. "That would be just our luck to haul the damn thing down here, confident that it would protect us, and then discover that it won't work." He started down the narrow walkway, choosing his path carefully.

"Though it did work in the other sewer," Madeline pointed out, following him.

"We're much deeper underground now." And this was one of the oldest sewers under Vienne, that anyone knew of, anyway. The fay had been much more virulent in the past. What if it had been imbued with forgotten magical protections that were interfering with Edouard's work? What if the old bones clogging the syphon had gotten into the water by a natural phenomenon and they were heading in the wrong direction entirely? *What if, what if, what if,* Nicholas thought, disgusted with himself. *Why don't we just give the hell up?*

Because he knew he was right. "Would you have followed me down here if you thought I was wrong?" he asked Madeline, out of perverse curiosity.

She snorted in disbelief at the idiocy of the question. "Of course not. What do you take me for?"

The channels here were almost choked at points with stinking mud. When the walkway disappeared for long sections into masses of broken stone, they had to stumble through the muck. Nicholas was glad he had bothered to get them both stout rubber-soled boots that laced up past the knee, and that their gloves were thick.

Branchements led off to both sides and Nicholas used the compass to find the first two turns they needed to take, but then the arches overhead became even more cracked and dilapidated and they encountered several blocked or abbreviated galleries that weren't marked on the map. After taking a wrong turn down one of these blocked passages, Nicholas had to stop, cursing, and look at the map.

"We should be close, almost too close," he muttered, kneeling on a relatively dry stretch of rock as Madeline stood over him with the lamp.

"We're somewhere," she said suddenly. "Look at that."

He looked up. There was a cavity hollowed out of the wall of the passage. Nicholas had thought it a partial collapse, but a closer look showed him that the walls were too regular. He stood and saw what had caught Madeline's attention. There were chains, heavily corroded but still clearly visible, mounted on the wall. He stepped closer and realized they weren't the remnants of some method to raise and lower dams in an ancient drainage system; they were shackles. He looked around but any other clues were hidden under years of filth. "This was a cell. They cut the sewer right through it."

Madeline held up the lamp and squinted at the other side of the passage. There were regular hollows in that wall as well. "I bet that's another. And that. Was there anything about an old prison on the map?"

"No, but . . ." He turned in a slow circle, visualizing the map, the streets above. "If we're under Daine Street, then this could be part of the old rampart. It was demolished two hundred years ago." It wasn't on the maps anymore, but neither was the catacomb they were looking for.

"Nicholas," Madeline whispered suddenly. He looked around and saw she gazed down at the sphere, her eyes intent. He stepped up and took the lamp so she could hold the sphere with both hands.

"Close, closer." Her brows drew together, then she shook her head. "No, it's fading, as if— It's stopped now." She looked up and studied the walls around them thoughtfully. "It was as if something it didn't like moved through a tunnel adjacent to this one."

Nicholas nodded to himself. That settled all doubts on the sphere's area of influence. "Back this way."

They made their way back to the last branchement and Nicholas hesitated, remembering that Monde Street ran roughly east to west and would have hit the rampart—if the old structure had still been there when the much younger street was cut—at an angle. It was difficult to visualize and he didn't want to examine the map again; the sewers paralleled the streets they serviced, and it wasn't those streets he wanted to see, but the narrow, barely passable roads and alleys they had replaced. "It has to be here. The catacomb must have been behind the rampart." He held up the lamp, studying the filthy, fungi-covered surface of the branchement wall.

Madeline probed the stone beneath the spongy growth with one gloved finger. "There could be any sort of hole or door under this stuff," she said thoughtfully. "Do we know which side of the channel it's on?"

Nicholas shook his head. The builders could have cut a sewer right through the catacomb the same way they had cut it through the cells beneath the old rampart. "You check that side, I'll take this one."

Nicholas kept the lamp since she had the sphere, and though this channel wasn't wide the light was inadequate and they had to search mostly by feel anyway. They had moved perhaps twenty feet down the wall, groping along it, when Nicholas stumbled. He felt the surface of the wall give and realized it was rotted wood, not stone. He tried to pull his arm back and felt a tug on his sleeve. He frantically flung his weight back, thinking something had caught hold of him, but his arm came free so readily he sat down hard on the walkway. His coat sleeve had been torn. As he got to his feet, he realized it must have been caught on the metal frame still holding the rotten wood in place. *Idiot,* he thought. But having a limb torn off by a ghoul would be most inconvenient at the moment.

"Are you all right?" Madeline demanded, struggling toward him through the muck of the channel.

"Yes, just startled myself." He gave her a hand up onto the walkway. He hesitated a moment, holding her gloved hand and looking at her. Her boots, trousers, and the skirts of her coat were covered in unspeakable filth, and with her hat pulled low and the rags tied around her mouth and nose, she looked like a grave robber. He knew he looked worse. He said, "If the ghouls hunt by sense of smell, we're in luck."

"Hmm." She recaptured her hand and cradled the sphere. "It's shaking again."

"Then we're on the right track," Nicholas said. He turned to the door. There wasn't much of it left. It was low, only about five feet tall, rotted to matchstick consistency and held together only by the rusted metal frame. Nicholas widened the hole he had inadvertently made so they could peer through and found a narrow passage, the walls slick with moisture from the sewer.

They broke away enough of the door to climb through and began to make their way down the passage. Scraping away some of the thick muck coating one of the walls, Nicholas could see it had been constructed with large cut stone blocks. The surface overhead seemed to be natural rock and the narrow corridor had been dug through it.

"Do you think this is a section of that battlement?" Madeline whispered. "It doesn't look like part of the sewer."

"Yes, I think this is all that's left of the lower course and we're in the passage that originally led to those cells."

"This sphere is about to shake itself apart," she said, sounding uneasy.

"Then we're close."

"Nicholas." Now she sounded exasperated. "This nonchalant attitude is beginning to wear."

"Would you prefer me to twitch hysterically?"

"If you could bring yourself to express such an honest and genuine sentiment as hysteria then—" She stopped and caught his coat sleeve. "Wait."

He waited, then heard it himself. A sharp knock, echoing from somewhere up ahead. It was repeated once, then silence. Nicholas moved forward a few steps, listening. He glanced back at Madeline, motioning that he was going to shut the lamp. She nodded and he pushed the shade down.

After a few moments, he could see the distinct glow of light ahead, a whitish, green-tinged glow, not natural daylight. He looked back toward Madeline and realized he could see her outline against the wall. "There must be ghost-lichen all through this muck," he said, quietly. "Come on."

The light grew—not brighter, Nicholas decided, but more defined. He could see an irregularly shaped opening ahead and there seemed to be more light beyond it.

They drew closer and Nicholas could see this passage dead-ended into a larger chamber. As he reached the opening he heard a rustle, as if old dry paper had been brushed against rock. He motioned Madeline to come forward and as she stepped up, he accidentally brushed his fingers against the sphere.

The metal was warm, an impossibility in the dank chill of the underground, and he felt a strange tingle in his fingertips, as if he had touched one of the electrical experiments displayed at the Exposition. He jerked his hand back and realized he had felt the contact through his gloves. *At least it's doing something.* He wished they had some notion of how to control it.

He edged up to the opening, drawing the pistol out of his pocket. The passage dropped off into a large cavernous chamber, more than twenty feet high, and the ghost-lichen clustering thickly everywhere revealed pillars and the openings of crypts hollowed out of the walls. A great many life-sized statues of saints with gloomy expressions gazed down forbiddingly from niches above the crypt entrances. Nicholas thought the winged Saint Gathre, its face like something out of a hellish nightmare, was a particularly appropriate companion with whom to view the scene.

They had found the catacomb. The floor was about a ten-foot drop from where the passage broke off, but there was a broken section of pillar just below that might be stable enough to climb. Nicholas started to step down to it when Madeline urgently thumped his shoulder and pointed.

Something moved on the floor of the grotto, a dark form drawing back into shadow. Nicholas squinted in the dimness and saw the tattered cloth and ragged hair, the glint of bone.

At least one ghoul, maybe two, moved in and out of the open crypts and darted under the collapsed arches. One of them crept around a fallen slab propped up on a broken column, poking at the dark area beneath it, as if trying to flush something. *They're hunting,* Nicholas thought, watching that surreptitious motion. *For us?* That didn't seem likely. *If they knew to look for us, they would know we hadn't reached the catacomb yet and they would be searching the sewer and the tunnel.* That meant—

The ghoul snarled suddenly and darted back from the slab, shielding its head. Nicholas saw the flying rock and the human arm that had thrown it; without stopping to think he leapt down onto the pillar and then to the catacomb floor.

The ghoul whirled on him, jaws gaping, its face little more than a bare skull. He raised the pistol before he realized; he didn't even know if bullets would hurt the thing. Madeline leapt down after him just as the ghoul darted forward. Light flared suddenly, a glow that washed out the dim radiance of the ghost-lichen and rendered the chamber in stark shadowless glare.

The last time the sphere had demonstrated its power the event had been too quick and violent for Nicholas to really see what had happened. This time he saw it all, outlined in a white haze of light. The ghoul scrabbled at the ground, its claws throwing up dust, trying to turn and flee. Before it got more than a step it seemed to fold in on itself, then it burst apart and dropped to the floor as a pile of yellowed bone and rags.

The bright light was abruptly gone, leaving pitch darkness in its wake. Nicholas, caught in the act of stepping forward, stumbled and cursed. Behind him he heard Madeline yelp. "Are you all right?" he asked in a tense whisper.

"Yes, dammit." She sounded more annoyed than frightened. "I hope it didn't kill the ghost-lichen, too."

He found her arm and pulled her close. There had been more than one ghoul in here. If the sphere hadn't disposed of all of the creatures he and Madeline were at their most vulnerable.

Time stretched agonizingly, but it was probably only a minute or so until the ghost-lichen's glow began to return. Nicholas blinked hard, staring around, gradually able to discern the shapes of the fallen pillars and the crypt openings again. Something stirred under the propped slab and he stooped immediately to look under it.

The face peering out at him was Crack's. He was bruised and filthy, but alive. Nicholas caught his arm and drew him out, demanding, "Are you hurt?"

"Not much," Crack admitted. His voice was weak and hoarse.

"Ronsarde and Halle? Arisilde?" Nicholas asked urgently.

"I ain't seen none of them, not since the wall broke open."

Madeline took his other arm and helped him sit back against the slab. "His wrist is broken," she reported, her expression grim. "How did you get here?"

"I don't know." Crack shook his head, his face tense with pain. "Something came through the wall from outside." He looked at Nicholas. "It was like the house in Lethe Square, that thing that came through the floor."

Nicholas nodded. He thought this was all more than Crack's powers of description could handle and knew he would have to ask better questions. "Did you see what happened to the others?"

"No, I got knocked in the head and I thought the ceiling come down on top of me, then the next thing I know I was here," Crack answered. Madeline had dug a relatively clean scarf out from under her coat and was trying to fashion a sling for his injured wrist. With his good hand he gestured helplessly. "Where the hell is here?"

"A series of old tunnels and catacombs off the Great Sewer," Nicholas said. "Were you here when you woke?"

"I was down there." Crack turned awkwardly and pointed down the length of the catacomb. "I came this way, away from the ghouls and those other things."

"What other things?" Madeline asked, with a worried glance at Nicholas.

"They look like people but they come at you like animals. I think they're those things our sorcerer talked about, that come when the ghouls are made."

"Revenants?" Nicholas frowned. He remembered Arisilde telling them how the necromancer would have made the ghouls, using a ritual murder to give life to the bones of some long-dead corpse. He had said the victim would still have a kind of life, but would only be a soulless remnant of the person it had once been.

"You can kill 'em," Crack said, rubbing his forehead wearily. "I used a rock."

Nicholas stood to look down the length of the catacomb. From this vantage point he could tell it went on for some distance, winding through the depths with the ghost-lichen throwing light on the fallen statues and broken crypts. "Was Arisilde awake when you got to his rooms?"

Crack looked up at him worriedly. "No, but the Parscian said he would be soon."

Nicholas nodded to himself. They should take Crack and return now, while they could. If the ghouls were here the necromancer was not far behind, and he knew enough now to find the location of this place from the surface. But if the others were here, perhaps injured and stranded only a little farther up the catacomb . . . He looked down at Madeline. "Well?"

She was watching him and had no difficulty following his train of thought. She nodded.

Crack was too injured to accompany them, but it wasn't that great a distance through the tunnel and back to the sewer. Nicholas sat on his heels next to him and pulled out the map. He found a stub of pencil in his pocket and wrote a series of directions in the margin. "If Reynard has been successful, he should be waiting at the top of Monde Street for me with Captain Giarde and a guard detachment." *If he isn't, at least Crack is well out of this.* "This will tell them where to look for the necromancer."

Crack took the map but shook his head. "You can't stay here. There's more of them things, a lot more."

"We've got to," Nicholas told him. "And right now you are a liability and will better serve us by taking yourself to safety so I don't have to worry about you."

"That ain't fair," Crack said, through gritted teeth.

"I feel no obligation to be fair," Nicholas said, hauling Crack to his feet and ignoring his snarl. "You should know that by now."

It took both of them to get him up to the tunnel opening and by the end of it Crack was almost ready to admit that he wouldn't be much help in his current state. He collapsed, panting from exertion and pain, at the mouth of the tunnel, and tried to convince them to come with him. "You shouldn't stay. There's more of them things, I tell you."

"No." Nicholas handed him the lamp. He and Madeline both had candle stubs and matches in their pockets, enough to see them back through the sewer. "Now get moving."

"I can't walk anymore," Crack said, not convincingly.

"I need you to take the message to Reynard or it will get a damn sight worse for us," Nicholas told him patiently.

Crack looked at Madeline in appeal. She shook her head. "I'm no help, I'm afraid."

Cursing both of them, Crack climbed to his feet. They watched him make his way down the tunnel. When he was out of earshot, Madeline jumped back down to the catacomb floor, commenting, "He's right."

"Of course he is," Nicholas said, following her.

"You really think we'll find the others in here somewhere?" she asked. "Alive?"

Nicholas stopped and faced her. "It's a trap, Madeline, obviously. If you don't like it, go with Crack."

She swore in exasperation. "I know it's a trap, that's the only reason to leave Crack alive. If we don't walk into it, you think Macob will kill the others?"

Nicholas pushed on ahead, finding a path through the tumbled stone debris. "I know he will."

"Of course, stupid thing to ask," Madeline muttered, following him.

Farther down, the tombs they passed were less elaborate, some mere hollows sealed with mortar. Many had been broken open over time and the floor was littered with smashed bones, moldering rags, and verdigrised metal. They had seen no more of the ghouls and none of the revenants who had attacked Crack, neither of which was a good sign. "I thought there would be some sign of them before now," Nicholas admitted.

"Maybe it isn't a trap, though that seems unlikely."

Nicholas paused to give her a hand over a rockfall that half blocked the path. Water seeped up through the cracks in the floor, he noted. "Yes. I hoped he would be incautious enough to leave one more of our friends along the way, but that doesn't appear to be the case." Nicholas hesitated again. The debris underfoot was becoming more varied and they were tripping over rusted metal and rotted wood. There was even something crammed up against one of the tombs that looked like the rusted skeleton of a siege engine. The catacomb was getting narrower too, and the ceiling was much lower overhead. He didn't like the look of it. *Could there have been another passage along the way, that we missed in the dark?* No, surely not. Surely the idea was to lure them into the sorcerer's stronghold, not decoy them off down some dead end.

"Look at that wall," Madeline said, pointing toward a projection that seemed to be breaking through the rocky side of the catacomb. It was made of cut stone and had a blocked-up gateway large enough to pass a carriage through. "Are we running into the lower part of the rampart again?"

"Possibly." He moved toward it for a closer look. Something dripped down the wall that didn't quite have the consistency of water. Pulling the perfume-soaked scarf away from his nose and mouth, he dabbed his fingers into the dark substance streaming down the wall and sniffed cautiously. "It's a good thing we gave Crack the lamp." There was no telling how thickly the fumes had penetrated the air in this passage.

"Oil?"

"Paraffin." He glanced up at the ancient stonework woven in with the rock overhead. "If I'm right, we're somewhere below the Bowles and Viard Coke-works. One of their storage tanks must be leaking."

"It's frightening that you know that," Madeline grumbled.

"It means we're where I think we are. The directions I gave Crack will be accurate."

They worked their way past the wall and almost stumbled on a set of broad steps, broken and chipped, leading down through an archway with elaborate scrolled carving. The angle of the steps and the slope of the ceiling made it impossible to see what lay beyond.

"There's light down there," Madeline said, low-voiced. "Torchlight."

They exchanged a look, then she sighed. "Well, we've come all this way."

Nicholas went down the steps first. Past the archway was a wide stone balcony with a broken balustrade, looking down on a bowl-shaped cave, almost twenty feet below the present level. It held a small city of freestanding crypts and mausoleums, many of fantastic design, with statues, small towers, and much ornamentation. The ghost-lichen hanging heavily from the stalactite-covered roof gave it an otherworldly glow, as if they were looking down on a city of fayre. But Madeline was right, there were torches.

The largest crypt was the round one in the center. It had a domed roof and had been made to look like a small-scale keep, with towers with miniature turrets. Smoky torches were jammed between some of the stones of its crenellations, casting flickering firelight on the bizarre scene. In front of it there was a broad, round stone dais, several feet high. It looked like the platforms

followers of the Old Faith often built in their holy places in deep forest clear-
ings or high in the hills.

Nicholas moved forward, almost to the broken balustrade. "Careful,"
Madeline breathed. He acknowledged the warning with a distracted nod. The
air was staler than in the upper catacomb and there was a sweetish, foul smell
under it. He could see there was a walkway or gallery, badly ruined in places,
running from the balcony and along the walls on both sides, entirely encompassing the cave and ending in a set of stone stairs that were covered with
rocks and debris from some earlier collapse. The stairs had led down to an
open space in front of the dais and the keep crypt. *Like a processional way,*
Nicholas thought. *Did they hold funerals there? Make offerings?* He knew very
little about the Old Faith.

There was no telling how old the place was. It might go back to the founding
of the first keep that had marked the original site of Vienne. From the martial
nature of the statues, these could be the tombs of the first knights and warlords
of Ile-Rien.

There was a clink from somewhere behind and above them, as if a rock had
fallen. Nicholas looked back, frowning; since they had left the ghouls behind,
the only sounds they had heard had been of their own making.

Madeline had heard something, too. She moved a step or two away, looking
at the shadows and hollows in the cave wall above them warily.

Nicholas motioned her back toward the stairs. He had his pistol and the
sphere had been proof against the ghouls up to now, but he had the feeling they
had come just a few steps too far.

He saw something luminously white on the edge of the balcony and for an
instant thought it was a lichenous growth or some underground parasite. Then
it moved and he realized it was a hand.

He shouted a warning to Madeline but it was already too late. They were coming up over the balcony in a silent wave. *People—no, not people,* Nicholas had
time to think. Their faces were characterless, the features slack, the skin pallid
and dull. Their clothes were ragged remnants but their bodies were so bloated as
to make them nearly sexless, and there was nothing in their eyes at all.

Light flared brighter and cleaner than the ghost-lichen's pale glow as the
sphere reacted, but there were too many. Nicholas fired into the thick of them,
again and again, but the bullets hardly seemed to slow them. The two nearest went down finally, their wounds bloodless, but there were still ten, more
like twenty; moving with inhuman determination, they pressed toward him,

stumbling over the bodies of the fallen, and he had to back away. He had lost sight of Madeline but the sphere flared again, telling him she was near the base of the stairs. He shouted at her to run.

Then something crashed into him from behind and knocked his feet out from under him. The last thing he saw was one of the revenants leaning over him before the light vanished.

CHAPTER TWENTY

Madeline was lost. *Utterly, irretrievably,* she thought. *I will wander down here forever.* No, forever was unlikely. She would surely be killed by something long before forever arrived.

She had been driven back by the weight of the revenants. The sphere had accounted for a number of them but they seemed less self-aware than the ghouls and they hadn't fled. She had heard Nicholas fire at them and hoped that meant he had been able to get away. No, she was sure of that. He had been closer to the stairs than she had. She would have made it herself if she hadn't slipped and fallen down through that damn crevice at the edge of the stairs. Between the bad light and the dark color of the stone, she hadn't seen it until it was too late. Now she was bruised all over and hopelessly lost.

She had found her way into a wide passage, the blocks in its walls regular and obviously shaped and set by human hands, the remains of a curving, dressed stone ceiling overhead. Whether it was part of the catacomb or some long forgotten underground level of the old fortifications, she couldn't tell. *And since I don't have the damn map of Vienne, underground and above, memorized, like Nicholas does, small good it would do me if I did know.*

Hopefully he had been able to get back to the relative safety of the sewers. Hopefully. It infuriated her that she was stuck down here, uselessly.

The ghost-lichen's light was just enough that she hadn't had to resort to her candle yet. She hadn't been attacked again but the ghouls couldn't be too far away; the sphere trembled, its insides spinning like a top.

She drew near the end of the passage and saw the regular walls deteriorated into tumbled rockfalls, though the opening still seemed to continue. She could tell the floor had a distinct slant downward, which was not encouraging. Madeline peered suspiciously into the shadows and the gaps in the rock at the end of the passage. She thought she could see the gleam of eyes and a surreptitious movement there. No, the ghouls weren't gone. She hoped they were only ghouls; she had reloaded her pistol from the box of spare ammunition in her coat pocket but it hadn't been too effective against them before.

Suddenly in the silence she heard footsteps. One person walking at a deliberate, heavy pace; the sound seemed to come from all around her. She hugged the sphere tightly, looking up and down the apparently empty passage. Her mouth was dry and she couldn't swallow past the lump in her throat. It wasn't Nicholas; she would have known the sound of his walk.

Out of the shadows at the far end of the tunnel a figure appeared. Madeline stared, too overcome with shock and sudden relief to react. It was Arisilde.

She made a motion to step forward but from the sphere in her arms came a sudden vibration, a pulse she felt deep in her chest. She stopped in her tracks. That had been a warning.

Arisilde came toward her. He looked as she would expect him to, very pale and thin, wearing a dressing gown of faded blue and gold. He smiled at her as he drew near and said, "Madeline, you're here. How very good of you."

"Yes, I'm here, Arisilde," she managed to say. The sphere felt like it was going to fly apart in her arms, its wheels clicking in furious motion.

"And you brought the sphere." A breath of air moved down the passage and lifted his wispy silver hair. He held out his arms to her. "Give it to me."

She could feel sweat running down her back despite the cold. She said, "Come and take it, Arisilde."

There was a hesitation, but his expression of slightly daffy goodwill didn't change. He said, "It would be better if you were to give it to me, Madeline."

She felt that strong vibration of warning from the sphere again, as if it had reached a tendril into her heart and touched her soul in fear. She drew a deep breath. *Maybe it is alive.* But how could a thing of metal, even imbued with magic, be alive? How could it think? Something that was alive and powerful wouldn't sit on a shelf in the attic at Coldcourt all this time and do nothing. Not unless it needed a person, a living being, someone who could sense magic, to live. Maybe it used the consciousness of the person who held it to think with. *Maybe that's why this sphere works for me, and the one Octave had worked for him. And if I give this one to a real sorcerer . . .* "You built this sphere with Edouard, Arisilde. Why can't you take it from me?" *Why doesn't it know you? Why does it tell me to be afraid of you?*

He hesitated again, then shook his head and spread his hands helplessly. "It's because I was the one who did all these things, Madeline. I was only pretending to be unconscious all that time. I called the Sending and transformed the gargoyles in the Courts Plaza, and sent the creature into the prison. But I would never have hurt anyone. I was trying to get revenge on the men who killed Edouard, but it didn't work." The violet eyes were distressed. "I think I've gone mad, I'm afraid. A little mad. But if I could hold the sphere, I think that would help me. There's a part of myself in it, a part of me from before I went mad. If I could take that part back . . . But you have to give me the sphere."

Madeline watched him for a long moment. Then her brows lifted and she said dryly, "Do you think all women are fools, or just me?" He looked like Arisilde and he had Arisilde's sweet smile, but he was never Arisilde. Even if one included Isham in the plot, Madele had examined Arisilde and the notion that her grandmother could have been deceived in such a way was ridiculous. That Nicholas could have been fooled in such a way was unthinkable. Nicholas was suspicious of everyone. She wouldn't have been surprised if he had considered Arisilde as the possible culprit already and discarded the idea as simply not feasible. He had said their opponent was Constant Macob and Madeline had to admit there was every sign in favor of it.

He stood there, expressionless, then her eyes blurred for an instant and she was looking at another man. She had never seen him before. He was young and very thin, with lank blond hair and a weak chin, his expression vacant. His coat and trousers were muddy and his waistcoat was torn open.

Madeline's brow furrowed. *Who the hell is this?* It might be one of Macob's victims, abducted off the street, but under the dirt his suit was a little too fine; Macob had preyed on the poor and street people he thought would not be readily missed. Then she remembered that Octave had had two other companions who had never been accounted for. Octave's driver had mentioned them before he had been killed. This man could very well be one of them. "I take it the driver was lucky," she said to herself.

He stepped forward and she moved back out of reach. Behind her she heard a frantic skittering among the rocks as the ghouls scrambled to get out of the sphere's range. There was no expression at all on the man's face; he might have been as mindless as one of the revenants. He took a sudden swing at her with his fist and she ducked away. She considered drawing her pistol, but she wasn't sure she wanted to fire it down here; there was no telling what else the sound would attract.

Watching him warily, she shifted the sphere to her right side, tucking it under her arm. His dead eyes followed it. He lurched forward and she let him grab her arm, then slammed the heel of her free hand up into his chin. His head snapped back and he staggered back a pace, tearing the sleeve of her coat.

She kicked out, striking him solidly between the legs. He collapsed onto the floor of the passage, obviously in pain but making no sound.

She moved away cautiously, making sure he wasn't about to jump back up again with inhuman strength. It didn't look like it. That maneuver had always worked well to discourage the attentions of importunate stagehands and actors; she was glad it worked on men ensorcelled to serve necromancers.

He rolled on the floor, making an attempt to stand and failing badly. She turned and ran up the passage, hearing the ghouls flee before her.

———

Nicholas realized first that he lay sprawled on his back on a damp, dirty surface, that the dampness smelled foul, that it was cold and firelight cast flickering reflections over stone walls. He drew a shaky breath and lifted a hand to push the hair out of his eyes. There was a clink and a tug on his wrist. *Not good,* he thought. He leaned his head back and saw both his wrists were manacled to a short length of chain attached to a ring sunk deeply into a stone flag. The chains were old but not rusty. Not disastrous, but definitely not good. He tried to roll onto his side, but stopped abruptly as a splitting pain shot through his head. He cautiously probed the tender knot at the back of his skull. His fingers came away bloody.

The chains were loose enough to allow for some freedom of movement and he sat up on one elbow, slowly. He was inside one of the crypts; from the domed ceiling, it was the one shaped to resemble a miniature keep that stood in the center of the cave. It was lit by smoky torches shoved into gaps between the stones, and some unhealthy radiance from the ghost-lichen came in through the large crack in the roof. The walls were covered with carving and inscriptions, obscured by layers of mold. It was not a family crypt; there was only one vault, a large, ornate, freestanding one in the center of the chamber. Atop it, carefully laid out as if for a wake, was a very old corpse.

Time had shrunken it to bare bones, held together by withered strips of skin and muscle, festooned with the rotten remnants of leather and cloth. Nicholas thought he must be gazing on all that remained of Macob's physical body. Except . . . *The skull is missing.* Either it had been removed for some purpose of Macob's or . . . *Or it wasn't in the room with the corpse when the ghouls broke in. That's what Octave wanted to question the old Duke about.* On the bier next to it lay Nicholas's pistol.

He squinted and sat up a little more, wincing at the pain in his shoulder and head. The missing skull was not the only oddity. There was a woven webbing or net hung from the ceiling of the chamber and suspended in it was something small and round, of dull-colored metal. For one bad moment he was afraid it was Arisilde's sphere, which meant Madeline had been caught as well, but then he realized it was far too small. *No, it's the other sphere*, he thought with relief. The one Rohan had constructed with Edouard, that Octave had obtained by blackmail.

Except for himself and the corpse, the crypt was ostensibly empty. Madeline was nowhere to be seen. *She escaped*, he told himself. There was no point in speculating on anything else. As long as she had the sphere, she was in far better case than he was.

The crypt might appear to be deserted but Nicholas didn't think he was unobserved. He pretended to test the strength of the chains, tugging on them and trying to work the links loose, while actually examining the locks. Someone had searched his pockets, but they hadn't found the picks sewn into the cuff of his shirt. He didn't want to risk using them now and betraying their existence to a hypothetical watcher. One mistake and he was dead. He was most likely dead anyway, but the tension engendered by pretending there was still hope would keep him alert.

After a few moments he noticed the quality of light in the chamber was changing, the shadows sharpening, the torches becoming dimmer and the sick glow of the ghost-lichen correspondingly brighter and more defined. Turning his head to look at the doorway, Nicholas caught a growing radiance out of the corner of his eye. It was in the darkest corner of the crypt. He continued to watch the doorway expectantly.

He had time to notice that the damp chill in the air was becoming more concentrated as well, the cold intensifying until his bones ached, and he could feel the bite of it in his fingers. There was a slight sound like a boot sliding over stone; a deliberate betrayal. Nicholas flinched as if startled and jerked his head toward the corner.

A figure stood there in the shadows. It was a tall man, dressed in an old-fashioned caped and skirted greatcoat and a broad-brimmed hat. His face was gaunt almost to the point of appearing to be a death's-head, and it was hard to get a sense of his features. His eyes were dark pits under the shadow of his hat brim, impossible to read.

He stepped forward deliberately and said, "You needn't introduce yourself, I assure you I know who you are."

The voice was an old man's, hoarse and raw, as if he had long suffered from throat afflictions. *Or been hanged,* Nicholas thought suddenly. That was how Macob had been executed. This was fascinating. Terrifying, but fascinating. The accent was a little off, too. It was still recognizably of Ile-Rien and particularly Vienne, but with odd twists in the pronunciation of some of the words. Nicholas hadn't decided what tack to take, but something in the man's confident manner made him answer, "Of course. You're Constant Macob. You know everything."

Macob took another step forward, the iron-gray brows drawing together. He hadn't expected that response.

For a shade he was terribly real, his wrinkled face and rheumy eyes that of a living person. *You would think he would have made himself appear young,* Nicholas mused, *he has either no imagination, or no vanity.* The former was a disadvantage for Macob, the latter a disadvantage for Nicholas and in direct contradiction to his theories. Surely only an infinitely vain, self-obsessed man would try to hold on to life like Macob had. But sorcerers had to be artists as well as scholars; Macob couldn't lack for creativity or he would never have managed to take himself so far.

An indulgent tone in his rusty voice, the necromancer said, "I suppose you want to know my plans."

"I already know them, thank you."

The eyes narrowed, then Macob evidently decided to be amused. "Gabard Ventarin wanted to know."

"Gabard Ventarin has been dust for two hundred years," Nicholas said, politely. "His name is known only to historians."

"A fitting end for him," Macob said, pleased. But there was something unconvincing about the manner in which he said it. Macob couldn't be too aware of the passage of time. Did he even really believe his executioner was dead?

What could it be like to cling to the world of the living this way? To refuse to move on, to remain chained to vengeance and old hates? *You might be lucky if you don't find out for yourself,* a traitor voice whispered, and Nicholas brushed it aside. Macob must live in the ever present now, all past and no future, never changing, never altering in the slightest degree. Never learning from his mistakes. He saw Macob was about to turn away and said quickly, "Why did you kill Dr. Octave?" He already knew the answer but he didn't intend to ask any questions to which he didn't already know the answers; this was no time to court surprises.

Macob's smile was slow and self-satisfied. "He . . . faltered. He became infirm in my purpose so I destroyed him."

It didn't change Nicholas's opinion on what had occurred. He still thought the initial scheme had been Octave's quest for an ideal confidence game and that the spiritualist had participated in Macob's murders only because he had been forced to it. But it didn't surprise him that Macob's perception of events differed from this. He said, "Very wise of you."

Macob's eyes glinted. "And why shouldn't I destroy you?"

Ah, now we get to it. Causing terror could be addictive. Nicholas had seen that before in a number of people who had considered themselves masters of Vienne's criminal underworld. It was a ridiculously exploitable weakness and one Nicholas could diagnose from the first exchange of fake pleasantries. Macob liked to terrify his victims. For all Nicholas knew, terror might be necessary to necromantic spells, but he thought the main motive was that Macob had learned to enjoy it. "Since you destroyed Dr. Octave, I would think you in need of more mortal assistance."

"Which you could provide." Macob said it without much evidence of interest.

"For a price." Macob seemed to have an air of preoccupation that Nicholas didn't like. Not only was it not terribly complimentary to himself, but it made him wonder what else was happening in Macob's little kingdom. Was it Madeline that was drawing the necromancer's attention, or Ronsarde and Halle, or Arisilde? He needed to do something to regain Macob's interest. "Despite all your sorcery, essentially you're just a criminal. A criminal who has been caught. I'm a criminal who has never been caught."

Macob's head lifted and his gaze returned to Nicholas. "I've caught you."

Give him that one or not? Nicholas made a swift mental calculation. *I think not.* "After I walked into your trap."

There was anger in Macob's eyes and something of frustration. "I wanted to bring you down here. I wanted to see what you were."

"And you wanted the other sphere."

Macob hesitated, then nodded to Rohan's sphere, suspended above the corpse. "That one is dying. It was never any good to me. Octave made it work for his ghost talking but it was never good to me." He gave Nicholas a sidelong look. "Not as I am."

As an attempt to elicit information, it was fairly transparent. *Not as he is? Not while he's dead, he means. And is that state likely to change?* Nicholas obligingly said, "It must have been one of the first constructed. And Rohan is powerful, but not as powerful as Arisilde." That was as close as he wanted to come to mentioning the others. If they were dead he couldn't help them, but if they lived, the last thing he wanted to do was direct Macob's attention back toward them.

"You know much of the spheres?"

"No." Macob would know if he made anything up.

"The woman." Macob hesitated. He knew he was betraying himself and it was making him angry. Dangerously angry. His voice became a low ominous growl. "Does she know of the spheres?"

So Madeline was free and causing great consternation. Nicholas smiled. "She knows all that she needs to." *Or at least she thinks she does.* He added, "I could engage to obtain the missing skull for you. That is the item you're in need of, isn't it? The one Octave wanted to question the late Duke of Mondollot concerning? I doubt the Duke's information would have been helpful; it was surely removed by Gabard Ventarin at the time of your death as a further precaution." He paused. He had Macob's rapt attention. "It was removed to the palace, was it not?"

"Yes. A trophy." Macob stared at him, the malevolent eyes narrowed. "I know where it is. I can obtain it myself. I would not engage you to do so. I would sooner engage a viper."

Nicholas's mouth quirked. Constant Macob, necromancer and murderer a hundred times over, thought he was a viper. He was not quite light-headed enough to thank him for the compliment, but said, "That's a rather unjust assessment in light of your activities, isn't it?"

"I continued my work," Macob said, but he wasn't much interested in defending himself, to Nicholas or to anyone else. He looked at the corpse again, his attention leaving his prisoner. "That is the only thing of importance."

Nicholas frowned. Vanity might not be the key to Macob's character after all. Was it obsession, instead? With his family dead from a swift and violent plague, he had not been able to stop—had he thrown himself into his work until it had achieved such an overwhelming importance that every other consideration fell by the wayside? It would explain a great deal. *And it makes him far more difficult to manipulate.*

Macob turned back to Nicholas and started to speak, but the necromancer froze suddenly, all motion arrested, his head cocked in a listening attitude. Without another word, he strode toward the door. As he reached the shadow across the opening, his form seemed to dissolve and it was impossible to say if he had walked out or vanished into the darkness.

Nicholas sat up and awkwardly rolled his torn coat sleeve back to get to the shirt cuff and the lock picks. He tore open the seam of the cuff with his teeth and shook out the picks. This explained Macob's preoccupation, at least. Nicholas might have preferred that Madeline had sought the safety of the surface instead of taking the sphere on some sort of rampage through Macob's hiding place, but he also preferred not to become the central element of the next necromantic spell.

Working the lock picks on his manacled wrists was difficult, but he had gotten himself out of handcuffs before and the manacles came off with only the sacrifice of some scraped skin. Nicholas stood too quickly and had to steady himself on the crypt wall as the floor swayed and his sight narrowed to a dark tunnel. He rubbed his temples as his vision cleared, thinking, *This could present a problem.*

As soon as he could see, he stumbled to the plinth and leaned on it. He checked the pistol that lay beside the body, but it was empty and the extra ammunition he had had in his coat had been removed, along with his clasp-knife and anything else that might serve as a weapon. They had left his matches and other articles that might possibly be of use, just not at the moment. He shoved the pistol into his pocket with a muttered oath, then looked up at the sphere, suspended in the net above the corpse. Destroying it would probably be a great disservice to the furtherance of human knowledge, but he wouldn't leave it for Macob.

There was a sound from the door of the crypt, a soft footstep. Nicholas looked up and saw a man standing in the doorway, pointing a pistol at him. He was a large man, about Nicholas's age, with greasy dark hair and a ruddy, rough-featured face, his once good frock coat ragged and dirty. *One of Dr. Octave's colleagues,* Nicholas thought. There had been two other men besides the driver. Perhaps Macob had taken the rest of the ghouls with him and left only this last human servant to guard his prisoner. He had to be running out of ghouls; there had been a limited number to start with and Arisilde's sphere seemed to go through them quickly.

The man's eyes were lifeless, dull, but the pistol didn't waver. Nicholas said, "I'm no good to him dead." That wasn't quite true, but this man didn't look as if he had access to all his faculties.

He motioned with the pistol, indicating that Nicholas move away from the bier. The corpse was obviously important to Macob; he had gone to a deal of trouble to obtain it and the missing skull still obviously worried him. While there was madness in the necromancer's method, it didn't rule him. He had reasons for everything he did. *Not what one would call "good" reasons, perhaps, but reasons nonetheless,* Nicholas thought, obeying the man's gesture and backing away toward the wall.

Nicholas reached the wall and turned suddenly, stretched up and grabbed one of the torches. The man's reflexes were slow, doubtless the result of whatever Macob had done to him to secure his obedience; he was just raising the pistol to fire when the torch landed on the corpse. The rags of rotted clothing caught immediately.

There was an instant of hesitation, then the man ran for the bier. He dragged the torch out, dropped it on the ground, then beat at the burning clothing, oblivious to anything else. Moving forward, Nicholas picked up a broken paving stone from the floor. The man turned just as he was within reach and brought up the pistol. Nicholas grabbed his wrist to turn the weapon away from him and they grappled.

Nicholas lost his grip on the stone, trying to keep the pistol from pointing toward his head. The man wasn't inhumanly strong but he fought like an automaton with no concern for his own safety. Nicholas managed to swing him around and drove him back against the wall of the crypt, when there was a shriek of rage from somewhere above their heads.

No, Macob hadn't taken all the ghouls with him. A quick glance upward showed Nicholas two of the creatures climbing through the crack in the dome and scrabbling headfirst down the wall. He wrenched an arm free and punched the man in the jaw, knocked his head sharply back and sent him sprawling. He heard the pistol strike the floor somewhere but the ghouls were almost on him and there was no time to look for it. He bolted for the door out of the crypt.

Once out in the half-light, he ran past the dais and plunged into the maze of passages between the crypts, with no time to get his bearings. The ghouls moved too fast and he only had a few moments' head start at best.

He could hear them behind him, careening into walls, screaming in high unearthly voices with all too human rage. He ran down between a row of crypts and saw an open passage into the rock wall. It wasn't until he had plunged into it and found himself in near total darkness that he realized he was too far down in the cave for this to be part of the catacomb, that he had hared off into totally unknown territory.

He couldn't go back now. He kept running, stumbling over half-seen ob-structions along the ground, bouncing into walls, knowing that if he fell they would be on him in seconds. He saw a darker pool of shadow across the pas-sage in front of him and knew it might be a hole in the ground. Claws scrab-bled on the rock behind him and he jumped wildly, not pausing to judge the distance or gather himself.

He hit the far side, lost his grip on slick stone, and slid down. He caught the edge of the fissure, his feet finding purchase on a slope littered with loose peb-bles and rock chips. The suddenness of it took his breath away; he hadn't really believed it was a hole until he felt the empty cold air beneath him instead of solid earth. The ghouls screamed almost directly over his head, so he released his tenuous hold on the edge and let himself slide down.

———

The ghouls had tried to attack Madeline again and the sphere had destroyed them. The things had come after her only reluctantly, as if they had been driven to it. Since then she had had no sensation of being followed.

She was almost ready to sob with relief when she found a tunnel that led upward. The slope was steep so she made a sling for the sphere out of her scarf and tied it around her neck. Makeshift and none too secure, it still freed both her arms and made climbing the upward passage much easier.

She came out above the cave with the standing crypts again on a reasonably whole section of the walkway, her legs sore from the steep climb. The entrance to the catacomb should be over to the right, above the balcony, if she had her bearings. She could see flickering firelight, greasy in the bad air, showing be-tween the cracks in the walls of the large crypt in the center. *What is Macob doing in there?* she wondered. *No, don't think of it, just go while you can.* The sphere didn't make her invulnerable.

She crept along the broken remains of the walkway, ducking to stay below what was left of the balustrade and moving slowly, despite her fear. As she drew closer to the place where she was certain the walkway met the catacomb, she saw something strange in the quality of light. After a moment, her eyes found the glow of another torch, burning at the entrance of a crypt on this side of the cave.

She kept moving but that torch worried her. She reached the ruined balcony and saw with relief the entrance to the catacomb appeared unguarded by revenants. A few steps up and she would be in it and running back toward the sewer. She hesitated. The ghouls didn't need torchlight. In fact, she rather thought they were afraid of fire, from what Nicholas had said. Firelight meant people.

Her hands were clammy and her back hurt from the fall and she didn't particularly want to die down here. But if Nicholas hadn't gotten away it might be him. Muttering under her breath, she carefully found her way past the broken arch that lay across the balcony and back onto the walkway.

The crypt with the torch was closer but there was an impediment. Part of the walkway had collapsed entirely, leaving a gap of a few feet. She was able to get a handhold on an overhang and step easily across, but it would not make for a quick getaway.

The walkway curved and she pressed herself as closely against the wall as she could. She could see the front of the crypt now. A large part of the pitched roof had collapsed but there were still statues of helmeted pikemen on either side of the intact doorway. The torch was jammed into a loose chink above the door and she could see the mortar and stones had been knocked out of it, leaving an opening into the crypt. More evidence: if the ghouls had wanted in, they could have climbed the wall; they had no need to open the crypt's door.

Speaking of ghouls . . . There were at least three of them, like bundles of dry rags and bones, seated in front of that gaping doorway. They weren't moving or making any sound and she would have missed them entirely if she hadn't been certain they were there somewhere. They looked like unstrung puppets, cast aside until they were wanted again.

She edged along the wall, cautiously. She could see down into the crypt itself now, but it was deep in shadow and the torch had dazzled her eyes somewhat, so the ghost-lichen's light was negligible. Staring hard, she thought she could discern movement inside. Then a form leaned across the shaft of firelight falling through the open door and Madeline's heart leapt. It was Dr. Halle.

That's all I needed to know. Moving back until she was above the doorway and the guardian ghouls, she studied the edge of the walkway. The wall had crumbled here, so if she was quick and sure-footed she could leap down to the flat spot there, and then to the floor of the cave. Not so hard. *Not as hard as hanging in that flying harness in* The Nymphs. She moved to the edge and readied herself, then hesitated.

What if she got them killed? Would it be more sensible to flee up the catacomb and bring help? Before she could decide, her foot dislodged a pebble and it struck the rocks below with a loud crack. All three of the ghouls reacted as one: their heads whipped around and the glazed, glaring eyes stared straight at her.

To hell with it, Madeline thought. She clutched the sphere tightly and leapt.

Being more used to humans who fled from them, her attack caught them by surprise. As she landed on the cave floor they started back from her, but she could already feel the sphere shaking. When the light burst from it an instant later, she turned her head away and shut her eyes tightly to keep from losing her night-sight.

The light faded and she looked back to see three heaps of bones, scattered as the ghouls had started to flee. No, four heaps of bones; there had been a fourth one against the wall of the adjoining crypt that she hadn't seen.

She stepped forward into the doorway, whispering, "Dr. Halle?"

"Good God, it's you," his voice answered reassuringly.

She stepped back and pulled the torch free, holding it so she could see the inside of the crypt.

Ronsarde lay on the ground, his head pillowed on a folded coat. His face was still and sallow, his eyes sunken back in his head. The wrinkles and age lines were brought out in high relief; she hadn't realized before that he was so old. Halle knelt next to him. Their clothes were torn and filthy and Halle's face was bruised but he didn't look as badly injured as Ronsarde.

"You'll have to carry him alone," Madeline told him. "I've got to hold on to this thing."

Halle was already lifting Ronsarde, dragging one limp arm across his shoulders and pulling him upright. It was only the two of them, she saw. No Nicholas, no Arisilde. "Have you seen the others?" she asked.

Halle half carried, half dragged Ronsarde to the doorway and Madeline stepped back out of his way and cast the torch aside. They didn't need it and she didn't have any spare hands. Halle said, "Your man Crack was with us—"

"We found Crack; there's a catacomb above here and he was in it. We sent him back for help. I hope he's found his way out by now." *I hope Nicholas isn't dead. And what did Macob do with Arisilde?* There was no time for speculation. She climbed up onto her rock step and took Ronsarde's free arm.

With Halle pushing and her pulling, they managed to get him up onto the first ledge. Madeline looked up at the walkway unhappily. She could make it and Halle could on his own, but . . . *But we're not giving up now.* She grabbed one of the balusters and swung up, ignoring the ominous crack from the stone and the wrenching pain in her arm. She reached down for the Inspector and caught movement out of the corner of her eye. Ghouls, several of them, leapt from roof to roof across the sea of crypts. And something else behind them, something dark, its form impossible to discern in the half-light.

Halle followed her arrested gaze and swore, loudly. Ronsarde picked that moment to come back to consciousness. He straightened in Halle's grasp and said, "What the devil?"

"Climb," Halle ordered succinctly. "Then run."

Ronsarde didn't argue, only reached up for Madeline's hand. She braced her feet and leaned back, and in another moment he scrambled up beside her. His breathing sounded labored and harsh but there was nothing they could do for him now. Madeline got to her feet and helped him stand as Halle climbed up beside them. "That way." She pointed toward the catacomb. "Hurry."

Halle caught Ronsarde's arm and hurried. Madeline followed, not taking her eyes off the approaching ghouls.

The creatures had stopped on the roof of the nearest crypt, watching with those staring eyes but not coming any closer. Their terror of the sphere was gratifying but the dark thing that her eyes just couldn't seem to focus on was still coming, flowing over the rooftops toward her, sometimes like an airy mist, sometimes like something far more solid and ominous.

They reached the gap in the walkway and Halle got Ronsarde across with difficulty. Madeline almost stepped backward into it, but her boot caught the edge and she recovered with effort, then turned and jumped across.

The dark thing was on the walkway now. A glimpse back showed Madeline its motion was more halting and jerky now, more like a man running. The sphere under her arm was ominously quiet. *If it can't stop that thing, we're dead,* she thought desperately.

They reached the entrance to the catacomb. Madeline caught Ronsarde's other arm and helped Halle pull him up the broken steps. She stumbled, barking her shins on the stone and barely noticing. The thing was almost on them; its proximity made her skin itch. She gave Halle a shove and shouted, "Keep going!"

She swung around in time to watch it cross the balcony and start up the steps toward her. It was a man now, she could see his shape in the obscuring cloud of shadow and firefly flickers of light. The sphere was silent in her arms. It wasn't going to help them. He was on the top step a handsbreadth away and she could see his face. An old man's face, but hideous with greed and somehow inhuman, like a death mask.

Then Madeline felt a concussion, and there was a searing white light. She blinked and found herself sitting on the step, staring at the cave of crypts, and everything rippled like a hot stone-paved street on an intense summer day.

The man was nowhere to be seen. An instant later, her eyes found that unnaturally dark blot of shadow and mist, tumbling back across the crypts, a leaf in a windstorm.

The sphere in her hands was hot and trembling a little.

Sense returned to her and she staggered to her feet and ran after Halle and Ronsarde.

The slope was steeper than Nicholas thought and he couldn't control his descent. He half tumbled to land hard on a shelf of rock. He blinked dirt out of his eyes and managed to push himself up, feeling bruised and battered muscles protest. He squinted up the slope toward the narrow opening at the top but the ghouls didn't seem to be pitching down after him.

He was on a ledge hanging above a deep, shadowed pit with sloped sides. There was ghost-lichen here, just enough to see by. The walls were rough stone, pocked with irregular cracks and fissures, and a pool of foul-smelling water had collected in the bottom. It was either the dim, unnatural quality of the ghost light or his blurry vision, but the dimensions of the pit were hard to judge and a fold in the rock cut off his view of a section of it. There was a crack in the wall nearby that seemed to open into a deeper fissure. He kept an eye on it warily as he staggered to his feet. It was the perfect lurking spot for ghouls or revenants.

The wall just above him was too steep to climb and he started to make his way along the ledge to where the slope wasn't so dramatic. There seemed to be an inordinate amount of debris from the catacomb down here. He stumbled on a pile of bones and disturbed a ragged heap of detritus that gave off an odor so sickly sweet it made him gag.

A scrabbling sounded above him, then a shower of pebbles rained down the slope as a revenant burst out of a crack and barreled straight for him. Nicholas reached for his pistol before he remembered it was empty. He flung himself back against the wall and grabbed up a rock. He had time to see the creature was an old revenant, its features distorted until they were barely recognizable as human, its clothing in rags, then it raced straight past him and flung itself into the deeper crevice he had noted earlier.

Nicholas stared after it, his brows drawing together. *That . . . was not a good sign.*

Down in the pit below he heard a shifting, something heavy moving and grating against the stone. Nicholas hesitated, but an awkward scramble across the ledge would just make him more of a target. It was better to face whatever it was here with the wall at his back. Then it growled.

It was a low rumble, sounding more like rock grinding but with an animal tone to it that was unmistakable. The sound reverberated throughout the pit like a distant underground train. *That isn't a ghoul, or a revenant.* Nicholas sank back against the wall and held his breath.

Something stirred below, creeping out of the deep shadow. At first it blended in against the mottled surface of the rock, then he made out something vaguely like a human head with patchy gray-green flesh. There was a scrambling in the rocks above him and Nicholas twitched minutely before he caught himself. He stayed motionless even when chips of rock and bone rained down on him. Then he saw a revenant burst from cover on the ledge above and skitter down the slope.

The thing below moved in a blur, suddenly resolving into a recognizably human shape. Its skin was horribly discolored and gaped open in places to reveal bare yellowed bone. Nicholas thought it was a larger version of the revenants until it started to climb the slope toward the one that was trying desperately to escape.

Seen in perspective it was far larger than any human, perhaps twenty feet tall. Moving with an uncanny swiftness, it climbed the rocky slope and snatched the revenant. What Nicholas had seen before was the bare crown of its head, and it had been standing farther down in the pit than he had thought. Its skull still bore ragged remnants of hair and it wore rusted chains wrapped around its upper body. The revenant had barely time for one shriek of terror before the thing tore it apart.

Slowly, Nicholas started to edge backward toward the fissure in the rock wall. It might be a dead end and teeming with revenants, but it was too small for that thing to fit into. It had to be another dead fay, like the one Macob had used for the Sending. Perhaps buried in the catacomb, long forgotten beneath the present-day city's foundations.

It was eating the revenant, or trying to. *It doesn't realize it's dead,* Nicholas thought. The sight would sicken him if fear hadn't already overridden every other emotion. He reached the end of the ledge and eased himself carefully to his feet.

It turned suddenly as if it had heard him. The one remaining eye seemed to be staring directly at him, though it was covered with a heavy white film; the other eye was an empty socket surrounded by bare skull. The mouth was open, revealing jagged teeth and the decaying lips were curled in a snarl. Nicholas leapt for the next ledge.

He heard it behind him as he landed and he swarmed up the jagged rocks. He felt a tug at his coat just as he reached the lip of the crevice and threw himself forward. The coat ripped and he rolled down over rough rock and foul-smelling debris. The thwarted roar of rage echoed down the narrow passage.

Nicholas crawled several yards farther down before he looked back.

It was digging at the edges of the fissure and pounding the stone, furious at losing its prey. The thing's face was even worse at close view, the dead tattered flesh revealing the bone beneath and the teeth jagged yellowed daggers. He could see the wound that must have killed it the first time, a gaping hole in the side of the skull that looked as if it had been made by a cannonball or a ballista.

That would have been an ignominious end to a checkered career, Nicholas thought, taking a deep breath to try to calm his pounding heart. His hand was burning and he realized he had ripped his glove and torn his palm open climbing the rocks. He found a handkerchief in an inner coat pocket and stanched the blood, then stood carefully, trying to ignore the fact that his knees were still shaking. Keeping his head down to avoid the low ceiling of the passage, he made his way deeper into it, stumbling a little on the bones and other unspeakable debris that littered the floor.

It was so dark, with only small patches of the ghost-lichen to light the way, that there could have been any number of revenants hiding in the crevices and gaps in the rock, but nothing attacked him. Nicholas thought he would be safe until the fay stopped clawing at the entrance and snarling its frustration. The revenants still active down here must have survived by learning when to go to ground; they would stay silent and still until the creature left.

There was a brighter patch of dimness ahead and Nicholas headed for it.

The passage grew narrower and he had to climb fallen chunks of stone and navigate narrow gaps. He struggled through the last crevice and almost fell out of it onto a paved floor. There was just enough light from the opening in the wall ahead to show him that this was a room built of regular-shaped blocks and not just a hollow carved in the rock. Another part of the old fortification, perhaps. The opening had been a square window but a chunk knocked out of the corner gave it an irregular shape. It was high on the wall and Nicholas had to look for hand- and footholds in the ancient mortar before he could pull himself up high enough to look out.

Outside lay another section of the pit about half the size of the area haunted by the fay. There was a gap in the side that must lead back to the other section and a round, regular opening overhead. Nicholas could still hear the creature growling and scratching at the other entrance to the crevice, so he was at least temporarily safe here. There were bones scattered on the ledges below and several corpses in a much more recent state of decay, still clad in rags of clothing. Nicholas squinted at a pallid form on the ledge several yards below and stiffened suddenly. The body lay facedown but the hair was almost shoulder-length and entirely white.

Nicholas had scrambled up onto the flat stone sill of the window before he realized what he was doing. He hesitated, listening for the fay, and heard another low rumbling growl echo through the crevice. He lowered himself as far down as he could, then let go and dropped to the ledge immediately below. Trying to move as silently as possible, he climbed down the rocky slope, cursing the small avalanches of pebbles his boots touched off. Closer, he could see the body was the right size, that it wore a dull-colored dressing gown. *If he's not dead,* Nicholas thought. If the fall down here or the cold dampness of the place hadn't killed him yet. He reached the outcropping and crouched near the motionless form, brushing the loose hair back from the face.

It was Arisilde. His face was white and there were dark bruises under his eyes—that was all Nicholas could tell in the light from the ghost-lichen. He looked dead. *But he looked dead before.* Nicholas rolled him over, gently lowering his head to the ground. There was dirt in his hair and his robe was stained and torn from contact with the damp stone, but Nicholas couldn't see any new injuries. If he was breathing it was shallowly, and Nicholas's own pulse was pounding too hard for him to detect Arisilde's. *Damn it, we're both going to be dead for certain in a moment.* But Isham had said Arisilde was waking.

Nicholas patted Arisilde's face and chafed his freezing hands while trying to think. Isham had also said something about a "corpse ring" that Madele had removed. Nicholas hadn't heard the term before but he remembered Madele's interest in the ring that had charred the flesh around the dead woman's finger at Chaldome House. Arisilde didn't appear to be wearing any kind of a ring now but he hadn't before either, when they had first found him in this condition in his apartment.

Nicholas felt each of Arisilde's fingers, wary of illusions or avoidance spells, then checked his feet. He felt a hard metal band around the smallest toe and almost didn't believe he had found it. He worked the band off and sat back on his heels, watching Arisilde hopefully.

There was no change, or at least no visible one. Nicholas looked at the ring he had removed. It was a plain cheap metal band, no odd inscriptions or glyphs inscribed on it, but he was careful to keep from inadvertently slipping it onto one of his own fingers.

Arisilde still showed no sign of waking and in the silence of the place . . .

Silence. I can't hear the fay, Nicholas thought. He shoved the ring into his pocket and grabbed Arisilde's arms, hauling him up and managing to sling him over one shoulder. He didn't know how long the creature had been silent; if he had any luck at all, it had been distracted by another fleeing revenant.

He managed to get Arisilde up the slope and to the ledge just below the window but it was slow and awkward going. Nicholas let him down, propped him up against the wall, and took a deep breath. He was going to have to climb the rock face to the opening with Arisilde a dead weight over his shoulder.

He started to lift Arisilde again but froze when he heard a skitter of pebbles from the other side of the pit. Nicholas lowered Arisilde and glanced around frantically.

There was a small crevice where the rock had broken through the old stone wall, with an overhang that provided some shelter. Nicholas found the pitiful and far too recent remains of the last creature to take shelter there and hastily flung it out, then worked his way as far back into the corner as he could. He dragged Arisilde in after him, pulling the limp body half into his lap and letting his head rest on his shoulder. They were in deep shadow here and it gave them more of a chance than being caught in the open.

Another rush of disturbed rock chips sounded, then stealthy movement at the far end of the pit. Nicholas stopped breathing, stopped thinking when the huge fay crept into sight. Its head swung back and forth, a seeking motion. It knew there was something alive in here or at least something that moved, and it hadn't given up yet.

Nicholas's hold on Arisilde had unconsciously tightened. Suddenly, the sorcerer drew a deeper breath. *He's waking,* Nicholas thought, stunned. What a time to prove Isham right. He leaned his head down to Arisilde's ear and in an almost voiceless whisper said, "Don't move."

The fay crossed the floor of the pit, the stumps that had been its feet stirring up a small cloud of dirt and debris. Arisilde gave no sign he had heard or understood but he didn't betray them with a quick movement. Nicholas could feel him breathing now, deep regular breaths, as if he was in a natural sleep. That might be some intermediate stage before real consciousness. There was no telling how long it would take Arisilde to wake or if he would be capable of performing sorcery when he did. *Think,* Nicholas told himself. *Come up with a clever way to kill that thing because it's not going to leave until it finds us.*

He watched it hunt for them along the lower reaches of the pit, kicking at piles of ancient bone, poking behind rockfalls, casting its hideous head back and forth like a hunting dog on the scent. *Cold iron and magic kill fay,* Nicholas thought, his mind racing. *And we have rocks and nothing.* He might try to cause a rockfall to crush it but he didn't see how; the loose stones were all far too small to hurt it and the large ones too heavy for him to shift. And it was so fast it might well duck out of the way. His pistol was empty and useless . . . and made of steel, which was still iron, as far as sorcery was concerned. Except if he tried to throw the pistol at the thing it would do nothing but further enrage it. *When it eats us, perhaps it will accidentally swallow it and that will cause some discomfort. . . . Now there's a thought.*

He looked at the revenant who had been the last occupant of their shelter. Its legs had been torn away but most of the torso was left. The fay was on the far side of the pit digging at a pile of filth, stirring up a cloud of dust. *Now or never.*

Nicholas shifted Arisilde over, propping him against the wall. He squeezed out past him and knelt next to the revenant, searching around for a fragment of rock with a relatively sharp edge. The fay whirled around, alerted by some faint sound. Nicholas froze, gritting his teeth, cursing the persistence of the damn thing.

It growled low but couldn't seem to pinpoint his location. After a moment, it turned back to digging at the side of the pit, slinging a small boulder out of the way in its annoyance.

The noise of the fall masked the slight sound as Nicholas rolled the revenant over. He used the fragment to tear the belly open and had to swallow hard to keep from gagging at the stench released.

The fay turned and came back toward this side of the pit, its head cocked, as if certain it heard or sensed movement. Nicholas slipped the empty pistol out of his pocket and forced it into the revenant's body cavity.

The fay moved closer, the low growl rising again. Nicholas waited until it was almost just below, then tipped the revenant off the ledge.

The fay dove for it instantly, clawing at the rock as the revenant bounced down the slope. Nicholas scrambled back into the shelter of the crevice thinking, *Come on, you greedy bastard, go after it.*

The fay pounced as the revenant rolled to the end of the lowest ledge and crammed the battered corpse into its maw.

Nicholas crouched against the wall next to Arisilde's limp body. *There now.* If it worked at all. If it worked in time.

———

Madeline caught up with Ronsarde and Halle only a little farther into the catacomb. The Inspector leaned heavily against one of the crypts. His eyes were closed but the lids fluttered as he fought to return to consciousness.

"He keeps blacking out," Halle explained as she climbed over some broken steps to join them. "He's had a bad knock on the head."

"We're all right for the moment but we've got to keep moving." Madeline was trembling so hard from fear and their precipitate flight that her teeth were chattering. She was relieved Halle was too occupied to take notice of it. She lifted Ronsarde's other arm and stretched it across her shoulders to get them moving again. This was going to be difficult. She was strong but she couldn't carry Ronsarde all the way out of here, even with Halle's help.

"The sphere destroyed that thing that was coming after us?" Halle asked as they made their way forward.

"It stopped it. I don't think it destroyed it." Madeline was still having difficulty believing what she had seen with her own eyes. The sphere must be alive to some extent. She certainly hadn't told it to lay a trap for Macob, if Macob that thing had been, luring him close enough and then letting go full blast. That had been no accident; this little metal ball had exhibited human cunning. "Nicholas should be up ahead of us here somewhere," she added. She only hoped he was still searching for her in the catacomb or the tunnel and hadn't decided to turn around and look for her back in the cave. "I've been lost for a bit."

"How did you know where to look for us?"

"Nicholas deduced it." Even in the bad light, she could tell Halle's face was strained and ill. "How were you brought here?"

"I'm not entirely certain," he admitted. "We were in the sorcerer Damal's apartment in the Philosopher's Cross and I had just started to examine him. He still appeared to be unconscious, though it seemed to be a natural sleep and not the state he was in before. Then something struck the outer wall of the building. I was knocked unconscious. We woke as prisoners where you found us and we've seen no one except the ghouls. Wait. Your grandmother and Isham, they were in the apartment," Halle said suddenly. He stopped, as if ready to turn back to search for them. "Were they—"

"My grandmother's dead." The dim light had given her a wonderful head-ache; she wanted to rub her eyes but with the sphere to hold onto and Ronsarde to support, she had no free hand. She didn't want to think about Madele's death. "Isham was badly injured but Nicholas had him taken to a physician, that was a few hours ago." At least she thought so; her watch had been pinned inside a coat pocket and been torn loose in one of the near misses. She had lost it and all track of time.

"I'm sorry. Your grandmother—"

She shook her head, warning him off. "Nicholas thinks this sorcerer, this man who's doing this to us, is actually Constant Macob himself, or his ghost or shade or something."

"Can that be possible?" Halle muttered, then shook his head, annoyed at himself. "What am I saying? Of course it's possible."

"Damn sorcery," Ronsarde said suddenly, in a weak voice. "Didn't consider that as a valid hypothesis. Tell Valiarde—"

"Sebastion, save your strength," Halle said urgently. "You can't tell him anything until we get out of here."

"Tell Valiarde," Ronsarde continued stubbornly, ignoring the interruption, "that Macob isn't mad. Conclusion I came to, studying the historical accounts. Halle, you know—"

"No, I don't agree, and you know it," Halle said, exasperated. "I think he is mad, but it's a strange sort of madness. Madmen are often cunning, but not so deliberate. Macob's madness didn't—that is, hasn't hampered his intelligence."

"And he's dead already, so killing him is problematical anyway," Madeline said. "It's all right, Inspector, we'll tell Nicholas."

Ronsarde stopped suddenly, let go of Halle, and with startling strength grabbed the collar of Madeline's coat. Ferocity lending force to his voice, he said, "Tell Valiarde that in my study in my apartment on Avenue Fount, under the loose tile on the right side of the hearth, there is a packet of documents. He must see them."

Halle recaptured Ronsarde's arm and urged him to move. The Inspector seemed to be losing consciousness again. He added, "I wanted him to see . . . Not pertinent to this matter, but he must know after this is over . . ."

"Do you know what he means?" Madeline asked Halle.

"No." Halle shook his head. "I just hope we last long enough to find out."

They made their way back through the catacomb with what seemed painful slowness, but fear kept them moving. There were three ghouls waiting for them at the entrance to the tunnel that led to the sewers, but the sphere disposed of them almost desultorily, as if it had faced a greater challenge and now found ghouls rather passé. *Next you'll be talking to it,* Madeline thought wearily.

The tunnel was difficult until Ronsarde woke abruptly again. He was able to lean on Halle, allowing Madeline to light one of the candle stubs she had in her pocket so they could see past the point where the ghost-lichen died out. As they made their way closer to the sewers the rising stench, fetid and familiar, was a welcome sign that they were almost free.

They reached the rotted door into the old sewer channel and Madeline was about to help Ronsarde through when they heard voices.

She and Halle stared at each other in the dim candlelight. "Crack got through," she whispered hopefully. But she didn't hear Nicholas's voice.

"I'll make certain," Halle said. "You wait here with Sebastion."

"All right." They eased Ronsarde down so he could sit against the wall and she handed Halle the candle. "Don't go too far. There are branchements and turns and you'll get lost."

Halle made his way up the broken path toward the voices and she sat next to Ronsarde. After a moment, she thought that was a mistake. Her legs ached from climbing and running in the damp chill, her muscles were strained from lifting Ronsarde, and her arms were sore from holding the sphere so tightly.

She leaned her head back against the filthy wall and closed her eyes; she wasn't sure she could get up again.

The candlelight faded as Halle moved farther away and they sat for a moment in the pitch dark. Then the sphere began to emit a dim, golden glow. Madeline stared down at it. The color of the light was very like flame, as if it imitated the departed candle. She glanced up to meet Ronsarde's gaze. He was still conscious and his eyes were sharper. He smiled and said, "Clever gadget."

She heard the voices again then, louder this time. She recognized Dr. Halle, who sounded relieved, and the person replying to him was . . . "That's Reynard!" she said to Ronsarde.

"Doctor, is the Inspector with you?" someone called out.

"And Captain Giarde," Ronsarde said, identifying the voice and sounding pleased. "Success may be at hand."

But where's Nicholas? Madeline wondered. *He must have been far ahead of us.* If he had realized she was behind him, he would have turned back to look for her and they would have encountered him in the catacomb or the tunnel. If he was ahead of her, she realized coldly. *But if he was behind me . . .*

The voices came closer as Halle led the rescuers toward them. "Yes, Crack told us," Reynard was saying. "Nicholas and Madeline are with you?"

Halle's answer was inaudible but she heard Reynard reply, "No, he's not with us, are you sure—"

More confused answers, then Halle saying distinctly, "But Arisilde Damal, the injured sorcerer, was taken prisoner also. He and Valiarde must still be down there."

The man Ronsarde had identified as Captain Giarde said, "Fallier and the other sorcerers are planning to collapse the underground chambers. If there's anyone left down there—"

"You can't leave them there," Reynard said, sounding furious. "You wouldn't know where the bastard was without Nic's help. I'll go down after him."

"I'll show you the way," Halle said.

"No." That was Giarde again. "We'd just lose the lot of you. I can hold Fallier off, give them time to get out, but if we wait too long, this necromancer will escape—"

More protests. It sounded as if Giarde had a great many men with him and Reynard and Halle were trapped among them. Madeline looked at Ronsarde.

The Inspector's expression was tired and vexed. He said, "I wish I could accompany you, my dear. You are a resourceful woman but a little assistance never hurts." He let out his breath. "I can contrive, however, to delay any possible pursuit."

"Thank you," she whispered. She leaned over and kissed him on the cheek, then got to her feet. "I'll be back."

As she stepped back through the door and into the tunnel, she heard Ronsarde whisper, "I hope to God you will."

CHAPTER TWENTY-ONE

Nicholas watched the fay stalk back and forth, clawing at its belly. It had lost interest in searching for them but refused to go away and perish somewhere else. The lost time was grating; he only hoped Crack or Madeline had reached the surface by this point to carry the word of Macob's whereabouts to the help that was, theoretically at least, waiting for them.

Crushed back into the crevice as they both were, it was hard to tell if Arisilde was showing any more signs of returning consciousness. If he didn't wake soon, Nicholas had no idea what to do with him. He couldn't leave him here in this condition. With the giant fay eliminated there was no telling what other inhabitants of this place would emerge, and if Arisilde wasn't conscious enough to defend himself, it would be murder to leave him here. "What am I going to do with you?" Nicholas muttered to himself.

"Might I move now?"

The voice was a weak whisper and plaintive, but as the first time Arisilde had spoken in days, it was entirely welcome. Nicholas could have shouted in relief but he confined himself to saying, "Yes, but slowly. It's still down there." He pressed back against the wall to give him room. "How do you feel?"

"Rather . . . horrid, actually." Arisilde managed to sit up a little. He blinked as if even the dim light of the ghost-lichen was too much for him. His face was terribly drawn and gaunt, but he was alive. "Rather confused, too."

"Do you know where you are?"

"I thought I was at home." Arisilde peered at the fay pacing below. It gave a high-pitched shriek of anger and clawed at its belly again, leaving wide tears in the putrid flesh. "Oh, my. That's awful, isn't it?"

"Mildly, yes," Nicholas agreed. "It's a fay or what's left of one. I tried to poison it, but since the creature is already dead it's taking much longer than I thought."

Arisilde greeted this information with a complacent nod. "I see, yes. Most inconvenient. Now, why are we here again?"

"The necromancer I was searching for enspelled you with a corpse ring—do you remember that?"

Arisilde's vague gaze suddenly sharpened. "Someone came to the door. Isham was out so I went to open it. There was a man, he handed me something . . . Oh, I'm a fool. That's the oldest trick in the world." He shook his head, his expression rueful. "He handed me a ring and said he wanted me to tell him where the person who had owned it was now. I said I'd work on it. He even paid me. People around the neighborhood bring me those sorts of commissions all the time. The ring probably had a charm, a simple, subtle one, that suggested I put it on. Where was I wearing it?"

"On your foot, oddly enough," Nicholas said. Arisilde's opium habit must have left him open to this. His power was proof against open assaults, but his failing senses left him vulnerable to more subtle, indirect attacks.

"That's quite a good idea, actually; Isham would have checked my hands. I don't remember putting it on at all. But if I was under the influence of a charm, I wouldn't." He sighed. "I failed you, Nicholas."

"We can assign blame later, Ari." Nicholas was thinking hard. Macob must have put the ring back on Arisilde and simply dumped his body down here with the unwanted revenants. It was infuriating but hardly surprising.

Nicholas considered the fay again. It seemed increasingly distracted and was staying at the far end of the pit. They might be able to make it back up to the opening into the fissure, and from there get through to the other side of the pit and reach the way out. "Can you stand?"

Arisilde frowned in concentration and tried to pull his legs up. With some effort he managed to bend his knees, wincing in pain. "Not yet. I'll keep trying. Is there a time constraint?"

"We can't afford to wait long." Nicholas drew a sharp breath. With so much time in an unconscious state Arisilde must be unbelievably stiff. He said, "Listen: this necromancer is Constant Macob and he's been dead nearly two hundred years. He has what's left of his corpse and he seems to be using one of the spheres—"

"Macob, the Necromancer, himself? That's not good," Arisilde interrupted, startled. "Is the corpse intact?"

"No, he's missing the skull," Nicholas answered. The expression on Arisilde's face was not encouraging. "What does it mean?"

"He's trying to bring himself back to life, that much is obvious. But how?"

Arisilde frowned into the distance. "The planets are in entirely the wrong configuration for that sort of— Wait, I wasn't unconscious for months, was I?"

"No, no. Only a few days."

"That's all right, then." Arisilde paused in thought again, then asked urgently, "You said he had one of the spheres? That Edouard made? Which one?"

"One that Ilamires Rohan helped him with. Dr. Octave blackmailed Rohan for it."

"Rohan helped Edouard? I didn't even realize . . ." As the knowledge sank in, Arisilde swore incredulously. "That bastard Rohan. He didn't even offer to testify on Edouard's behalf. I knew he was a hypocrite, but—"

"I know," Nicholas said, his mouth set in a grim line.

Arisilde ran a trembling hand through his hair, as if trying to get his thoughts in order. "What does the sphere do?"

"I don't know, Ari. I was hoping you could tell me." Nicholas's voice rose a bit in exasperation and he lowered it hastily, glancing at the fay to make sure he hadn't drawn its attention. It didn't look in their direction, entirely occupied with the iron in its belly.

"No, I haven't the faintest idea," Arisilde assured him. "I suppose it was an early effort. Rohan, hmm? Well, as long as it isn't that last one that Edouard made, the one I helped with. Even he thought that one was a bit much." Arisilde nodded to himself. "Now if this necromancer had that one, we would be in a real difficulty." He looked up and saw the expression on Nicholas's face. "Oh."

"It was the largest of the three at Coldcourt, with the copper-colored metal case?" Nicholas asked, reluctantly.

"Yes, that's it." Arisilde looked worried. "He does have it?"

"No, Madeline has it. She came down here with me but we were separated and she escaped. At least, I hope she did." Frustrated, Nicholas looked back at the fay. "I haven't had any chance to search for her."

"As long as this Macob doesn't have it. I don't suppose we should ever have made that one in the first place, but it's a trifle late for regrets, isn't it?"

"What does it do?" Nicholas demanded. He was glad Arisilde wasn't dead, but he was also ready to bang the sorcerer's head against the nearest rock.

"It's hard to say." Arisilde gestured earnestly. "A little bit of everything, I should think, from the spells Edouard wanted me to cast for it. At the time I think he knew more about sorcery than I did, for all he was never able to perform it. The spheres were meant to allow anyone to cast spells, even a person with no talent and no ability for magic. It was all based on Edouard's theories about how the etheric plane worked. He thought everyone had some ability to sense the presence of magical phenomena—"

"Even if it wasn't on a conscious level. Yes, he told me." Nicholas had heard it all at length before Edouard died. Edouard had believed that it was only the people who had a heightened perception of magic who could consciously sense it, who could learn to become sorcerers, but that everyone had some awareness of it. "And Rohan said the spheres will only work for someone who has some talent for magic, despite what Edouard wanted."

"Yes, Edouard was disappointed. They never turned out quite right. But Madeline has some talent, she should be able to control it. If she can give it some direction, it can do the rest." Arisilde looked thoughtful. "This Macob—he's dead, you say? He couldn't possibly remain on the plane of the living and use his powers without some sort of assistance. If there's no other sorcerer in the matter, then it must be the sphere he has that's keeping him here. If Macob used it the way it was meant to be used, it would be as if he had another living sorcerer performing spells but completely under his domination. If he manages to force his spirit to reinhabit his body, he won't need the sphere anymore but it would make him . . . well, terribly powerful." Arisilde said this apologetically, as if it was somehow his fault. "The spheres seem to give the bearer, in some measure at least, the power of the sorcerer who helped create it. I put all my best spells into that last one I helped Edouard with. Somehow, all that machinery inside it, those gears and things, remember the spells. Edouard explained it to me but I never fully understood."

Nicholas said slowly, "So if Macob brings himself back to life, the sphere he has now will give him all the same power of Ilamires Rohan, Master of Lodun, plus his own not inconsiderable abilities?"

"Well, yes."

"And if he gets his hands on the sphere Madeline has now, he will also have your power?"

"Well, yes, but not as I am now, you know. It will be as I was then, when I made the sphere. Before I had all my little difficulties, you know."

Nicholas was almost too distracted to notice that this was the first time Arisilde had ever referred, even obliquely, to his opium addiction. He said, "As you were then, at the height of your power?"

"Well, yes."

"But how can he possibly retrieve the skull from the palace? It's protected by the wards. Except . . ."

"Yes?"

Nicholas shook his head, frustrated. "Macob was apparently a genius at creating new spells. With all these dead fay around—"

Arisilde was nodding. "Yes, I wouldn't put it past him to have thought of some way around the wards."

For a moment, it was tempting to concentrate on finding the others and escaping, leaving Fallier and Giarde to deal with Macob. But that was a fool's choice; if Macob returned himself to life, he would not suffer anyone to live who had interfered with him. *And I'll be damned if I let him use Edouard's work to do it.* Nicholas swore under his breath. "Whatever he means to do, I have to stop him." He had the germ of an idea but he wasn't sure if it was even remotely possible. He dug the corpse ring out of his pocket. "Just how subtle is this spell, Ari? Could it fool Macob?"

Ari studied the ring, eyes narrowed. "It might. It's a very good spell, meant to fool a strong sorcerer. And if Macob was distracted, perhaps by working other difficult spells . . ."

Their eyes met. Arisilde's gaze was worried. He said, "You would have to be careful."

"Careful? You mean suicidally rash, don't you?" Nicholas asked, smiling lightly. "Will you be all right if I leave you here? There are ghouls and the revenants you told me about. Can you defend yourself?"

"Oh, I'll be fine." Arisilde gestured reassuringly, as if Nicholas was leaving him in a café on the Boulevard of Flowers and there might be some difficulty in securing a cab. "Do go on. I'll follow as soon as I can."

Nicholas eased out of the crevice and stood cautiously, keeping one eye on the fay. It was on the far side of the pit still, reeling drunkenly and snarling at shadows, well past taking notice of him.

"Nicholas," Arisilde said urgently. "Take care. He is a powerful sorcerer, but you know, I do think you're much better at scheming things than he is."

Nicholas had no time to sort that statement out. He nodded to Arisilde and started to climb the wall.

———

Nicholas had considered the possibility that the ghouls would still be waiting for him up in the tunnel, he just had no notion of what to do about it. With the giant fay still stalking distractedly around, it was impossible to search the pit for another exit.

He made it through the fissure into the other section of the pit and back to the ledge at the base of the slope. The crack at the top was visible as a darker patch in the rough stone above and there didn't seem to be any ghouls actually peering down at him from it. He started to climb.

His shoulders ached by the time he reached the top and his fingers bled through what was left of his gloves. It was too dark in this tunnel to tell if there were ghouls lying in wait or not but he couldn't hear anything moving around. He dragged himself up over the lip of the crevice and collapsed onto the floor of the tunnel, breathing hard. If the ghouls came now, there wouldn't even be a struggle. It was a moment before Nicholas could roll over and get to his feet.

He had to cross the crevice again to get out of the tunnel, but after a little fumbling around in the dark he found the far side had a large enough lip that he could edge along it with only the minor danger of pitching headfirst back down into the pit. That accomplished, he felt along the wall until the relatively brighter light of the ghost-lichen in the main cave became visible through the tunnel entrance. There he paused, concealing himself in a fold of the wall and trying to get his bearings.

He was on the wrong side of the cave for the catacomb entirely, he realized. The mold-covered walls of the nearest crypts blocked his view of the rest of the cave, but he could tell by the light reflecting off the roof overhead that more torches had been lit, probably around the central crypt. Macob must be preparing himself to act. *I need a view of what's happening over there.*

He worked his way around the edge of the cave back toward the catacomb entrance, climbing over the tumbled remains of broken statues. Reaching the other side, he found a low crypt near the wall where he could get a vantage point. He jumped until he caught hold of the stone coping along the roof and hauled himself up. From there he could see the central crypt.

Torchlight illuminated the miniature battlement and the delicate turrets, threw oddly shaped shadows on the great cracked dome. The dais was empty except for an odd pattern of shadow. *No, not shadow,* Nicholas thought. He felt through his pockets until he found his small spyglass. Looking through it, he could see Octave's servant standing near the doorway into the crypt, and on the dais itself . . . There were dark markings on the light-colored stone, perhaps of soot. Most of the pattern was lost in shadow but he could see enough to know that Macob was preparing for the working of a spell.

Displaced pebbles struck rock behind him and Nicholas twisted around, violently startled. There was a dark form above him, on the ledge just below the walkway, but it was gesturing agitatedly at him. "Madeline," he breathed. He didn't know whether to be relieved that she was all right or angry that she hadn't gotten herself out of here yet. He stood and made his way to the edge of the roof.

Madeline jumped and he steadied her as she landed, pulling them both down into a crouch. Their embrace was cut short when something hard and metallic thumped Nicholas in the ribs. He held her at arm's length and saw she had the sphere in a makeshift sling around her neck.

"We've been looking for you," she said breathlessly.

"We?"

Madeline glanced down at the sphere and shook her head in distraction. "I mean, I've been looking for you. I found Ronsarde and Halle and led them out."

That was a relief, at least. "Good. What are you doing back here?"

"I came to look for you, what do you think? We have to get out of here now. Fallier is going to collapse the cave."

Nicholas shook his head impatiently. "That won't work. Macob knows we sent Crack for help, he knows what Fallier will do. He probably wants them to destroy this place. Then everyone will assume that he's dead and he will be free to do whatever he wants."

"Nicholas, we have to leave now," Madeline persisted.

"I found Arisilde." He told her about the pit and the corpse ring. "He's said that Macob can bring himself back to life. With the sphere Macob already has, he could be more powerful than ever before."

"Dammit, Nicholas." Madeline swept her hair back angrily. Her face was badly bruised, he could tell that even in this light. She let out her breath in resignation. "And Macob will just come after us again, won't he? We know too much about him."

"He won't take all this interference kindly, no."

"I saw him, when I found Ronsarde and Halle and we were escaping," she admitted, sounding as if the memory wasn't pleasant. "No, he's not going to give up on us. Well then, just what are we supposed to do?"

"I have a plan." This was true. "I just don't know whether it will actually work or not." This, unfortunately, was also true. "Arisilde said you should be able to control the sphere if you try. He said if you give it the direction, it would do the rest. I need you to make it hide you with an illusion, one so strong Macob can't see through it or even know that it's there."

"But—"

"No, listen to the rest. Get inside that large crypt, where Macob has his body. Put the corpse ring on it, but not on a finger, on a rib." He only hoped Arisilde was right and that Macob would fail to detect his own spell until it was too late. "Then when he reinhabits his body—"

"The spell on the ring will take effect and he'll be a living corpse, like Arisilde was." She nodded impatiently. "And it will be inside him so a surgeon would have to remove it. But Nicholas, any sorcerer can see through an illusion. Even a layman can see through one if they know it's there, and Macob is going to be on the lookout for something like that."

"I know. I'll distract him."

Madeline sounded unconvinced. "How? By getting yourself killed?"

"There are some things up in the catacomb I can use to make a very suitable distraction."

Her voice was thoughtful. "That paraffin that was leaking down the wall?"

"Yes." It was hard to read her expression in the dim light, but she didn't sound very happy. "Can you make the sphere hide you with an illusion?"

"I know the spell. Madele taught it to me years ago. If the sphere works like Arisilde says . . ." She looked away. "I think so." She let out her breath. "But I don't like it."

"It's only the once," Nicholas said, and felt like a traitor. How many days ago had he said he would never ask her to use her magic if she didn't want?

"Just don't get killed and make it for nothing," she said dryly. "Here, take the pistol. I won't have a free hand for it."

While she was digging the spare bullets out of her pockets, Nicholas considered telling her not to linger here if his trick didn't work. He wanted her to run and not wait for Arisilde or himself. But he knew it would only be so much wasted breath since she would do whatever she liked, anyway. Annoyed at the truth of this realization, he said, "Let's just get it over with, then."

Madeline nodded, but as Nicholas started to stand, she grabbed a handful of his hair and kissed him. It was a hasty embrace and Nicholas lost his balance and sat down hard. Madeline let him go and crawled to the edge of the roof, swung over, and dropped to the ground with agile ease. Nicholas whispered after her, "Don't move until the distraction starts. And don't be so damn sentimental."

———

Madeline crouched behind a crypt, near the dais but out of sight of it. She leaned back against the mold- and filth-encrusted stone and pulled the sphere free of the sling. She held it in her lap and felt it hum gently. *All right, here we go,* she thought. She closed her eyes and began the spell of avoidance. She felt nothing. The incantation ran through her mind with no rush of power, no sense of gathering forces. *It's been too long,* she thought, as she finished the spell and there was nothing in her head but her own thoughts. *Too long for me.* Madele had been right, of course, when she had told her that if Madeline didn't use her skills she would lose what little power she had. She opened her eyes and started to stand.

She froze when dust moved on the floor around her, pushed outward as if by some unfelt breeze. Spells of avoidance wouldn't cause physical displacement. She concentrated, trying to get some hint as to what the sphere had done. For an instant she had it. She was surrounded by not just a spell of avoidance, but by obscura major and minor and various nothing-to-see-here charms, a complex mesh of them. *Damn, I wish we had known to try this before. It would have come in handy. Madele would have loved this. . . .*

Standing in that maze of power, feeling it under her control even though it was only through the sphere, she understood suddenly that Madele must have cared about magic with the same intensity as she herself cared about acting. Madeline had always seen power as a means to an end, and it had been an end she was not particularly interested in achieving; she had never thought of it as an art in itself.

She stepped carefully out of the shelter of the crypt, moving to a better vantage point. If she was lucky, Macob would never know what hit him.

———

Nicholas found a place to climb back up to the walkway and from there found the entrance to the catacomb again. After searching through the layers of stinking debris near the ruined siege engine, he dug out two wheels that he had noticed earlier, half buried under rusted metal and rotten wood. He was in luck and they were mostly intact. While they wouldn't support a wagon's weight anymore, they would do well enough for what he had in mind.

He filled the bottle he had used to hold the Parscian perfume oil with the paraffin leaking down the wall, and then quickly lashed the two wheels together with a length of rusted chain. His outer coat was too sodden with sewer water to be of use, so he wound his jacket through the spokes of the wheel, along with some fragments of wood and rags from one of the open crypts. After the spare bullets Madeline had given him were inserted into it at intervals and it was soaked with more of the paraffin, it was ready.

Nicholas dragged the wheel down the steps and back to the balcony. Crouching in the shelter of its broken balustrade, he checked the revolver one last time. He had saved enough bullets to reload it once, but no more. The diversion needed to be as diverting as possible and if it didn't work, he doubted there would be time for him to reload.

He took a cautious look over the balustrade and saw there was more activity on the dais. The remaining ghouls were collected on the crypt roof, like a brooding flock of particularly ugly doves. Down on the dais were two men, the one he had fought with earlier and a slighter, blond man who must be Octave's second missing servant. The larger man was simply standing near the circle drawn on the stone like the will-less automaton he had become. The blond servant disappeared into one of the pockets of shadow near the wall of the central crypt, then limped back into the light, carrying what appeared to be an old metal urn. He climbed the steps of the dais and set it down just inside the boundary of the outer circle, then backed away.

So Macob was making his preparations though there was no obvious sign of the necromancer's presence. This would be easier if Arisilde was here, but there was no sign of him, either. Nicholas felt a pang of worry, wondering if Arisilde had been struck ill again or attacked by something in the pit, but there was no time to look for him now.

Staying in a crouch, he rolled his wheel down the walkway until he reached the point in the gallery where it curved around and the balustrade dropped away. From here it led straight along the wall to the top of the pile of rubble that had been the stairs leading down to the dais. He crouched, bracing the wheel against the last steady baluster, and fished in his pocket for his matchbox.

Below on the dais, the torches flickered and almost died. The blond servant flinched and stared around but the other man didn't react; he simply stood there, numb and motionless. When the torches surged back to life, Constant Macob was at the head of the dais.

The shadows seemed to cling to the necromancer's coat like a living cloak of darkness, and his hat brim concealed his features. He took two carefully measured paces forward and stood before the circle. The blond man suddenly bolted for the edge of the dais as if he meant to run for safety through the ruined crypts. Macob lifted a hand and three ghouls leapt off the roof of the crypt and bounded after him.

They caught the fleeing man at the bottom of the dais steps and dragged him back up, struggling and shouting. Macob pointed at him without turning his head and the man's cries choked off to silence. The ghouls dropped him and retreated back to the roof, leaving their captive to lie in an unmoving heap on the dais.

This ceremony, whatever it was, was obviously going to require a sacrifice. *I suppose it's poetic justice,* Nicholas thought, bracing his wheel in the middle of the walkway and squinting along its path. If the man had helped Macob trap his earlier victims, then he surely knew what was in store for himself. Nicholas jammed the perfume bottle containing the paraffin between one of the spokes and the chain and removed the stopper. Madeline must be moving around down there somewhere, but Macob hadn't reacted to her presence. But to reach the inside of the main crypt she would have to cross the torchlit area between the entrance to it and the dais, and no matter how powerful Arisilde's sphere, this was her first time doing such a thing; she would need help.

The other servant, who had remained as unmoved throughout all this as one of the statues, now stepped forward. He crossed the dais toward the edge of the circle and stooped to pick something up. Nicholas caught the gleam of light on edged metal and knew it was a knife. It must have been one of the objects the other servant had carried up in preparation for the spell. *Nicely ironic touch,* Nicholas thought, *to force the man to lay out the preparations for his own murder.* But he doubted Macob had even considered that aspect, or at least not consciously; the necromancer would maintain a façade of indifference over his enjoyment of his violence.

Macob didn't appear to be doing anything, but the casting of a spell like this might not appear like much to a layman's eyes. Most of the work would be taking place in Macob's mind. The large servant had reached the other man and bent over him, and Nicholas judged Madeline had had enough time to get into position.

He stood and gave the wheel a push.

The two wheels lashed together gave the contraption some stability and it rolled down the walkway without wobbling overmuch. Before it reached the slope and gained speed, Nicholas struck a match and tossed it into the paraffin trail left by the open bottle. The oil caught readily and the flames traveled swiftly along it to the source.

The oily rags caught and the whole mass went up, just as the wheel reached the part of the gallery where it sloped down to the wrecked stairs.

The sound must have caught Macob's attention. His head jerked toward the gallery. The ghouls ran along the roof of the crypt, leapt down from it, but the wheel bounced down the stairs and landed on the dais near the edge of the circle. It spun and fell on its side, and the ghouls scattered back from the flames. Behind them, Nicholas thought he glimpsed a dark figure run across the lighted face of the crypt toward the door. Macob stood rigidly, fists clenched, glaring at the burning wheel and the shrieking ghouls. The servant who had been about to kill his comrade started back, shaking his head, looking around in bewilderment.

Nicholas was already running back along to the nearest break in the balustrade. He scrambled down over the rock pile to the cave floor. He had thought about firing at the dais to increase the confusion, but the last thing he needed to do at this point was accidentally shoot Madeline; she was going to have enough trouble when the flames reached the bullets embedded in the packing in the wheel.

Nicholas ran down past the crypts, came out in the open area before the dais just as the first bullet went off. With another nice touch of irony it almost struck him, tearing through his coat sleeve and ricocheting off the stone wall behind him. Nicholas dove away as other bullets struck the crypts, the floor, the dais. Ghouls shrieked louder, scattering at the onslaught.

It should only take Madeline a moment to slip into the crypt, put the ring on the corpse's rib, and slip out and back into the shadows. Nicholas got to his feet and bolted down one of the paths between the crypts, hoping the ghouls would chase him now that they had seen him, leaving the way clear for Madeline.

The ghouls were running, all right, but in all directions, confused and terrified by the fire and the popping explosions. Nicholas laughed and ducked down another pathway. Then something grabbed him by the back of the neck. He tried to wrench away but he was caught in the grip of an irresistible force. The scene in the street near Fontainon House flashed through his mind: Octave in the grip of that towering, terrifying figure, shaken and cast down like a child's toy puppet. Then he saw the nearest wall coming toward him and the blow was like being struck by a train.

He didn't lose consciousness, though the world fluttered in and out of existence and everything seemed set at an odd angle. Some snatches of reality were more real than others: the roughness of the stone he tried to grab onto as he was dragged past; the bruising impact on the bottom step of the dais.

At the top, he came back to himself enough to recognize the large servant leaning over him. He took a wild swing at him, landed a blow on the man's jaw, but the return punch knocked him over backward. He struggled to push himself up but the man grabbed his shoulder and shoved him down and he met the rough surface of the dais face-first. He had a confused view of Macob looking down at him and struggled to sit up. He was pushed down and held with a knee in his back, and despite struggling and cursing he couldn't prevent his wrists being tightly bound.

The weight left his back and Nicholas rolled over and managed to sit up. The ropes were rough and felt new and strong; he might work his hands loose eventually but not soon enough.

Macob looked down at him, his hat brim shadowing his expression. The necromancer seemed more solid than he had before and there was an air about him like the breath from an open grave, detectable even in this place of damp and cold and fetid odors. He said, "It wouldn't have mattered if you had run away. I would have found you."

"I know," Nicholas assured him. "You're predictable that way."

Macob was already turning away, his form wavering, drifting like smoke, then rematerializing into solidity as he stepped back to the edge of the circle. Nicholas worked at the ropes, though he knew it was hopeless. *This is damnably embarrassing.* He looked at the servant who was standing nearby, staring off into space, his eyes red-rimmed and empty. The other man still lay on the dais, motionless except for the rise and fall of his breath.

Macob must have the two men completely under his control, though how, Nicholas had no idea. He had never heard of a spell that could enslave the human mind in such a way. But Macob had used drugs to help render his victims suggestible; this might be any combination of drugs, mental suggestion, and spells.

Macob lifted a hand. The servant retrieved the knife where it had fallen and moved woodenly to where his comrade still lay insensible on the stone. *No, not insensible,* Nicholas saw. The man's eyelids fluttered. He must be aware of exactly what was happening.

From this close an observation point, Nicholas could see dust stirring within the circle, moved by the invisible forces Macob drew into it. The movement centered on the urn, and from the dust pattern it was as if the currents of power were spiraling down into it.

Macob gave no outward signal but there was a sudden strangled cry. Nicholas twisted around to see the servant grab his former comrade by the shoulder and stab him in the chest. Blood welled and the man clutched helplessly at the protruding blade. The other servant straightened, still no expression on his face. In the circle the urn trembled. It shook violently, fell on its side, and started to spin.

Over the clatter of the metal urn, Nicholas realized he was hearing something else. Something familiar. He turned his head, pretending to be wincing away from the sight of the man bleeding to death, trying to hear it more clearly. It was the humming, clicking whir the sphere made when it was in the presence of inimical magic. Nicholas swore under his breath. Madeline must be close, only a few steps away.

The urn was still spinning but now a dark gray substance poured out of it. It wasn't dust or ash, or at least not anymore; it streamed out in a solid mass, spiraling up until it made a spinning column almost five feet high. Now there was a shape forming out of it, as if a statue was buried in the center and the gray sand was streaming away to reveal it.

The sound of the sphere was closer and Nicholas watched Macob carefully for any sign of awareness. The necromancer stared at the circle and the thing forming out of the gray sand, all his attention apparently caught by it. One of the ghouls crouched near Nicholas sidled away, its wild eyes empty of anything like thought, as if some unseen force had gently nudged it aside. Nicholas took a relieved breath. He had been afraid the sphere would give itself and Madeline away if it came within striking range of one of the creatures, but either she had managed to restrain it or it knew what it was about. Nicholas sat up a little more, holding his bound hands out from his back. She must be almost there.

Then Macob turned toward him and he saw the gleam in his eye and the cold smile. Nicholas snapped, "He knows, dammit, run."

He heard boots scrape on the stone behind him but it was too late. Macob lifted a hand and light flashed; Nicholas fell away from a searing heat that singed his face. He twisted around to look, heart frozen in fear, but Madeline stood unhurt in the open space below the dais, still holding the sphere. He shouted, "Strike back at him, hurry!"

Madeline's head twitched. He had disturbed her concentration and Nicholas cursed himself for distracting her. Of course that was what she was trying to do.

Deliberately, Macob moved to the edge of the dais. He was still smiling. He said, "She cannot strike me. The device was only meant for defense."

Madeline and Nicholas exchanged a look. It might be a guess but it explained too much of the sphere's behavior. *And it would be just like Edouard to build in such a stipulation,* Nicholas thought grimly. "He can't attack you either," Nicholas told her. "If he does you can turn his own power against him. Just walk away." Macob could, however, threaten to kill him, but he was rather hoping that aspect of the situation would slip the necromancer's mind.

Madeline must have realized the other point that Nicholas hadn't dared voice aloud: that if she could bring the sphere within range of him, then Macob could hurt neither of them. She leapt forward, made it almost to the last step of the dais. Then she staggered back as if she had run into an invisible wall. She recovered her balance, swearing loudly.

Macob said, "The barrier is around us." He gestured, indicating Nicholas, the circle, and the thing now crouched inside it, the nervous ghouls and the castle crypt, the enslaved servant standing motionless, and the man who lay dead in a pool of blood. "It is also purely a work of defense. The sphere will not react."

He turned back to the creature inside the circle. It was a gray, wizened figure, its body human except for clawed hands and three-toed feet. Its head was a triangular wedge with predatory eyes buried in deep sockets. Macob gestured again and the creature disappeared.

"You sent it to the palace," Nicholas said. He was aware of Madeline storming up and down at the bottom of the dais, trying to find a way past the sorcerous barrier. *I'm going to have to do this the hard way,* Nicholas thought. He met Macob's eyes. *You don't think I'm capable of it, do you? You won't suspect anything until it's too late.* "It's a fay but it's already dead, so the wards won't stop it."

"Correct," Macob said. His expression was sane and quiet, almost peaceful. "I will have my life and my work. Everything that was taken from me. You have lost."

"You could say that," Nicholas said. *But you would be wrong. Even the best go wrong. The trick is to be there when it happens.*

In the circle, the dead fay winked back into existence with a suddenness that the eye almost refused to accept. Nicholas didn't realize he was actually seeing it until it stepped forward and handed Macob an ivory casket.

Macob opened it, not even bothering to watch as his messenger dissolved back into dust and ashes. The necromancer tossed the casket away and lifted up the object it contained, a yellowed skull with crystals set into the eye sockets. Macob lifted a brow and said, in the first thing close to humor Nicholas had heard from him, "His Majesty Rogere always did have execrable taste."

He turned and Nicholas's heart almost stopped. *God, no, he has to put it with the rest of his bones. He'll see the ring,* he thought. Then the servant stepped forward and took the skull from Macob and turned to carry it into the crypt.

As the man passed inside the dark doorway of the crypt, Macob looked at Nicholas and said, "I meant to use him for my final effort, but I think it would be better with both of you."

"Yes, I gathered that, thank you," Nicholas said bitingly, to cover his relief.

The servant returned, climbed the dais again, and stood ready.

Macob turned back toward the circle. He seemed to be using it as a focus, an anchoring point for the forces he was mustering. He made no gesture but the servant moved stiffly toward the body of his late companion, put his foot on the chest, and removed the knife with a jerk.

Nicholas realized then what had struck him when he had last looked at Madeline. She had been standing with her hands in front of her as if she held the sphere, clutching it protectively to her chest. But her hands were empty.

She had handed it to someone. Someone who had approached the dais unseen, passed through Macob's barrier without alerting him and now crouched nearby, aided by the relic created by the lost powers of his youth. Nicholas was never surer of anything in his life.

A faint whisper, barely a breath in his ear, said, "When he strikes at you, fall down as if you've been hit. I'll take care of the rest."

Arisilde's voice. Nicholas whispered, just as softly, "No."

There was no answer but he felt something brush against the back of his coat. Arisilde had shifted position. Nicholas drew a deep breath. The last thing he wanted to do was startle Arisilde, who must be at the center of a complex web of spells. One strand pulled at the wrong time and the whole structure might collapse, even with the sphere's help. He whispered, "If we're to be rid of him, he has to complete this spell."

Again there was no answer from Arisilde. *If I were him, I'd kill Macob's servant as Macob obviously intended to do before I conveniently turned up, and complete the spell for him that way,* Nicholas thought. *But then, it's a good thing I'm not Arisilde.*

The servant came toward him with the knife and everything seemed to happen far more rapidly than it should. Nicholas had no time to brace himself, no time for anything except to flinch back when the blade struck home. He fell backward, a roaring in his ears, a tearing pain in his gut.

A wave of darkness swept over him, then just as abruptly it gave way to bright sunlight. He was in the garden of the house they had lived in when Edouard worked at Lodun, sitting on the bench near the wisteria. Sitting next to him was Edouard himself.

Nicholas looked into his foster father's eyes and for a moment saw the same distance and determination that had marked Macob's gaze.

Edouard smiled, a little ruefully, and said, "Two sides of the same coin."

"No," Nicholas said. He didn't even have to think about it. "If you can see the trap, you're not likely to fall into it."

"Ah." Edouard nodded. "Remember that."

Somewhere far away there was a scream, compounded of thwarted rage and heartbreaking loss.

"That's done it," Nicholas told Edouard, though he couldn't have said what "it" was at the moment.

A cloud passed over the sun and the light started to die. Edouard leaned forward and said something else, but the words were hard to hear and his sight was blurred and . . .

Nicholas opened his eyes. The reality of the cave, the cold, the stink of death, hard stone under his back, was like a blow. His head was in Madeline's lap and Arisilde leaned over him. There was blood everywhere and his chest ached horribly. He took a breath and it was like being stabbed again.

Arisilde sat back on his heels. "That'll do," he said brightly. "Close, though, wasn't it?"

Madeline's face was bruised and pale, streaked with tears and dirt, her eyes huge and reddened from the smoke. He said, "Madeline?"

She shoved him off her lap. "You bastard! I could kill you."

She sounded serious. After a couple of tries, Nicholas managed to roll into a sitting position. "You're welcome," he said. His voice was hoarse and he cleared his throat. "Help me up."

It took both of them, since Madeline was more overcome than she appeared and Arisilde was scarcely in better case than Nicholas. The body of Macob's last servant lay nearby in a pool of his own blood, his throat slit. He must have done it to himself on Macob's command to increase the power of the spell.

Once Nicholas could stand, he started toward the crypt, Madeline following him.

Macob's body lay on the slab, still wrapped in the rags of its clothing and winding sheet. It had been restored to an appearance of recent death and the flesh, though bloodless and a little withered, was unmarked by time. The eyelids were open, revealing the crystals King Rogere had embedded in Macob's skull.

Nicholas leaned on the slab and pointed up at the sphere suspended above it. "Get that down, can you?"

One hand on his shoulder to steady herself, Madeline found footholds in the side of the slab and got enough height to reach the hanging sphere. She tore the net open on the second try, managed to catch it, and leapt down.

She handed it to him and Nicholas hefted it thoughtfully. It felt dead like the other two spheres that had been stored in Coldcourt's attic. Cold and silent and motionless. But he would have to make sure.

He put it down and found a loose chunk of stone from the plinth. He hefted the stone, checking its weight, then knelt and steadied the sphere with his free hand. He thought it would take at least several blows; he might not have been surprised if it had proved impossible. But the sphere shattered on the first impact.

Nicholas started back as odd fragments of colored metal scattered everywhere. Sparks of red and blue light splattered across the floor, rolling like marbles until they disappeared into the cracks between the stone flags. He realized there was a white light on his hand, clinging to it like a thick fluid. He was too startled to be worried and it wasn't painful. He shook his hand and the light dissolved into tiny sparks that vanished in the damp air. He thought he heard voices whispering, almost familiar voices. Rohan's? Edouard's? But the sound swelled and died away before he could identify them.

Nicholas stood slowly, looking at the remains of the sphere. It was only so much junk now.

Then he realized he was hearing something, a deep, rumbling reverberation echoing down from one of the tunnels. He looked back at Madeline, frowning, puzzled. He could tell by her expression she had heard it, too. She shook her head, baffled.

Then the ground started to shake. They stared at each other, both coming to the same realization at once.

Madeline said, "Dammit, it's—"

"Fallier," Nicholas finished for her. He started toward the door, staggered as the ground suddenly rolled under his feet. Madeline stumbled into him and they caught each other and almost tumbled out the doorway.

Arisilde had been kneeling beside the smudged circle and was just standing up as they came out. He swayed as the ground shuddered again. The last of the pediment cherubs on the crypt across the dais crashed to pieces against the rocks. Madeline paused to grab up their sphere, left forgotten on the dais. Nicholas steadied her as she stood and they plunged toward Arisilde.

He caught them, bracing them against the continuous jolts. His eyes were distant and he was muttering, "The structure is still here, yes, the dissipation hasn't been too great, I think I might . . ."

Nicholas grabbed the sorcerer's shoulder to steady himself, keeping an arm around Madeline's waist. There was a great crash as the balcony and most of the walkway cracked and folded away from the cave wall, smashing down onto the outermost ring of crypts. With forced patience, he said, "Ari, if you would . . ."

Madeline tried to comment and choked on the cloud of dust that rolled over them from the passages that had already collapsed.

"Yes," Arisilde was saying, "I think I might—" A portion of the roof went, striking the crypt with the armored knight and smashing it to pieces. "I think I'd better," Arisilde finished. "Madeline, the sphere, please."

She passed it to him. "Can it stop what Fallier is doing?"

"No." Arisilde held it out, one-handed. "But if this works, it won't have to."

The sphere reacted as it always did, the wheels inside spinning rapidly. *You would think after holding off Macob that long, it would be tired,* Nicholas thought, foolishly. Obviously the thing didn't get tired. If Macob had managed to take it . . .

Dust and small fragments of rock rained down on them. Arisilde tossed the sphere into the circle. Madeline cried out in protest but instead of smashing on the stone, the sphere hung in midair, buoyed up by the power gathered there.

It spun faster, inside and out, until Arisilde muttered, "It's not enough."

There was a crack loud enough to be audible over the shaking and crumbling of the walls around them. The sphere exploded, fragments of hot copper showering over them. Nicholas ducked, pulling Madeline closer. Even as the copper fragments struck them and the blue light flared, he felt an iron grip on his arm and Arisilde suddenly dragged them both over the boundary and into the circle.

Nicholas was seized by a sudden vertigo and then the sickening sensation of falling. An instant later, he realized he was falling, just as he landed hard on a smooth stone surface. *It didn't work,* he thought. *We're still here.* But the rumble of the collapsing warren was distant, a barely audible echo, and the shaking of the ground had become a mere tremble.

Nicholas pushed himself up on his elbows. It was pitch dark and he could hear water running. He said, "Madeline?"

There was a heartbeat of silence that stretched into eons, then he heard her say, "Unh," or something like it.

A warm white glow sparked and grew, revealing the rounded brick roof and flowing channel of black water of one of the newer sewers. Nicholas was sprawled on the walkway and Madeline was only a few feet away, sitting up and rubbing her head. Arisilde steadied himself against the wall. The light came from a jewellike orb of spell light suspended in the air over his head. He looked down at Nicholas and said, "That was close. Two feet to the left and we would have materialized inside the wall."

"Thank you for the precipitate exit, Ari," Nicholas said. His head ached and when he tried to sit up his stomach lurched threateningly. He was thinking he might have to lose consciousness now.

There were voices down the length of the sewer, the yellow glare of lanterns. "Now who's that, I wonder?" Arisilde said, mildly curious.

It was too late, anyway. *Arisilde and Madeline will just have to handle it,* Nicholas thought, and then he did pass out.

CHAPTER TWENTY-TWO

Nicholas drifted back to awareness, believing he was in his own bed. He rolled over under the tangle of blankets and reached out for Madeline. It was her absence that really woke him.

He sat bolt upright. The room was opulent. Heavy oak paneling inlaid with rare woods, a garden scene tapestry old enough to have been hung when Rogere was on the throne, equally antique and priceless Parscian carpets spread casually before the marble mantel as if they were rag rugs. He was in the palace, obviously.

Cursing, he slung the heavy coverlet aside and struggled out of the bed. He was dressed only in a linen nightshirt. As he looked around for his clothes, he caught sight of himself in the mirror above the mantel and gave a startled exclamation, thinking it was someone else. Bruises had turned the side of his face a dull green-black and his right eye was puffy and swollen. Yes, he remembered that. *This is bloody wonderful,* Nicholas thought sourly, continuing the search for his clothes. It was going to make assuming a disguise damned awkward.

As he was opening and shutting the array of carved and inlaid cabinets in a futile search, the door opened to allow in a very correct and disapproving upper servant, attended in turn by a very correct and expressionless footman. "Can I assist you, sir?"

Nicholas straightened up. "My clothes."

"We had to destroy most of them, sir. They were . . . not salvageable."

This was what he should have expected, but at the moment it only increased Nicholas's fury. Making sure to enunciate each word clearly, he said, "Then I suggest you get me something to wear."

The servant cleared his throat. He had obviously expected his charge to be somewhat more overawed by his surroundings. "The physicians felt it would not be wise—"

"Bugger the physicians."

They brought him clothes.

Nicholas dressed hastily in the plain dark suit that mostly fit and boots that were a little too small. He wasn't sure if the consternation of the servants was due to his refusal to accept his status as a prisoner, or that they had simply expected him to spend most of the day in bed, moaning. The place in his chest where he had been stabbed felt, and looked, like he had been kicked by a horse.

The servants didn't try to stop him but the majordomo hovered conspicuously as Nicholas stalked through the antechamber and salon and out into a high-ceilinged, pillared corridor. He paused there, noting the presence of two palace Guards who appeared startled to see him.

This might be the King's Bastion or possibly the Queen's. The carved paneling on the walls was certainly old enough and the marble at the base of the columns bore cracks and discolorations from age. He started to turn to the majordomo to ask where the hell he was when he saw Reynard coming down the corridor.

Reynard looked in far better shape than Nicholas but his brow was creased in a worried frown. They must have sent for him in the hope that he could exercise some sort of restraint over Nicholas.

"Where's Madeline?" Nicholas asked as soon as he was within earshot.

"She's all right, I've had word from her." Reynard took his arm and drew him behind a pillar where they could speak in comparative privacy, much to the consternation of the majordomo and the Guards. Lowering his voice, Reynard said, "She left before you and Arisilde were found by the Prefecture. She wasn't sure what our status was with the palace and thought at least one of us should be on the outside."

Nicholas nodded. "Good." A little of the tightness in his chest eased. *She's alive and she's well out of this.* He tried to get his thoughts together. "Is Crack here as well?"

"No, I thought it better if no one in authority got too curious about him. Once he gave us the map and told us where you were, I had him hauled off to Dr. Brile's surgery. Fortunately for the men who did the hauling, he was too exhausted to put up much of a struggle. I received word this morning that he's patched up and recovering nicely."

"And Isham?"

"He was well enough to sit up in bed and demand to know where we were and what had happened, Brile said, so he should be all right in a few days. He's a tough old man." Reynard hesitated. "It's too bad Madeline's grandmother—"

"Yes, it is." Nicholas looked away; he didn't want to discuss Madele. "Did Madeline say where she would be?"

"No, but there was something else she wanted me to tell you. This note was in our code, by the way, so it's not as if half the palace knows our business." Reynard glanced idly around, unobtrusively noted the location of the Guards, and lowered his voice a little more. "When you were down in the sewer and Ronsarde thought he wouldn't make it out, he told her he had some papers hidden under the floor in his apartment and that she was to make sure you got them. It can't be about Macob or he would have told us before this, surely."

Nicholas started to reply then stopped, arrested by a sudden memory. A memory of a moment that had never taken place. The garden at the old house at Lodun, and speaking to Edouard while he listened to Macob's scream of rage. The last thing Edouard had said was *If I had known it would worry you so much, I would have told you about the letter.* He said, "No, I think I know what it's about."

"Oh." Reynard was a little nonplussed. "Well that's good, anyway, because she went to Ronsarde's apartment last night to retrieve the papers and found the place had been ransacked. Whatever it was, it's gone now."

Of course it is. Nicholas closed his eyes briefly and swore. *Montesq runs true to type, as usual.* "Is Ronsarde here?"

"Yes, I was just over there, though I couldn't get in to see him. He's going to recover, according to the physicians."

Nicholas thought hard. An idea was beginning to form, though there were some things he had to make sure of first. He looked at the Guards loitering nearby, then turned back to Reynard. "Are you free to leave or are they watching you as well?"

Reynard hesitated, his expression hard to read. "Nic, Giarde has offered me a colonel's commission in a cavalry regiment, the Queen's First. As a reward for sounding the alarm over Macob, I suppose."

"That's a very prestigious regiment," Nicholas said. His throat was suddenly dry. He had known Reynard had never wanted to leave the cavalry. He was a military man at heart and would still have been in the service if he hadn't been unfairly driven out.

"Yes, service to the Crown and all that. Ronsarde apparently said some complimentary things, too." Reynard cleared his throat.

"Have you accepted it?"

Their eyes met and Reynard's mouth quirked in a smile. "Not yet."

"How coy of you." Nicholas paused, and suggested cautiously, "Before you do, can you get some messages out of the palace for me, without anyone knowing?"

"Well, I'm not a Queen's officer yet."

Ronsarde was ensconced in a suite of rooms in the King's Bastion and there were a number of physicians, upper-level palace servants, and officials of the Prefecture in attendance. Nicholas talked his way through the anteroom just as the inner doors opened and the Queen emerged with her train of attendants. Nicholas tried to duck behind a pedestal bearing a bust of some late bishop, but she spotted him and cornered him against a cabinet when he tried to retreat.

"You're awake," she said. She eyed him with that startling directness, then turned to study the porcelain ornaments in the cabinet. "Did you know where it was?" she demanded.

Nicholas was aware he hadn't properly bowed to her but it was impossible now as she had him backed into a corner. At least, he decided, she was armed with neither the cat nor Captain Giarde. "Did I know where what was, Your Majesty?"

"It was buried back in some salon, in a box no one had looked in for years." She glanced at him to see how he was taking it, and added, "That's odd, isn't it?"

He deduced that she was talking about Macob's skull and that she was not accusing him of knowing its location, but trying to impart it as an intriguing curiosity. "It wasn't as odd as some things that happened, Your Majesty."

She considered that judiciously, then nodded to herself. "Are you going to see Inspector Ronsarde?"

"Yes, I was, Your Majesty."

She looked up at the large and well-armed Queen's guard who had been standing at her elbow throughout the conversation. He turned and suddenly a path opened through the crowd to the door into the inner chambers of the suite. The Queen stepped back so Nicholas could get past and he made his escape gratefully.

It wasn't until he walked into the bedchamber that Nicholas realized that Ronsarde had been housed in a set of state apartments. The room was about the size of a modest ballroom, with two large hearths with intricately arabesqued marble chimneypieces. The enormous bed, hung with indigo curtains, was set up on a dais and had a daybed at its foot. Ronsarde lay in it, propped up by a mass of pillows with Dr. Halle and another physician standing nearby. Halle was pale and had a large bruise on his forehead but otherwise appeared none the worse for his experience. The Inspector, however, was too red-faced for real health. "I don't want to rest," Ronsarde was saying in a querulous tone. "It's ridiculous that— Ah!" He saw Nicholas and sat up straight. "There you are, my boy."

Nicholas walked to the foot of the dais. He wondered which kings of Ile-Rien had slept in this chamber. No recent ones, since the furnishings were too far out of date. *Rogere, perhaps?* With the current Queen's sense of humor that was all too possible. He said, "If I could speak to you alone . . ."

Ronsarde looked at Halle, who sighed and reached for his medical bag. "I suppose it would do more harm to argue with you," Halle said. He gestured the other doctor ahead of him and clapped Nicholas on the shoulder as he passed.

Nicholas stepped up to the bed. As the door shut behind the two physicians, he said, "Your apartment has been vandalized."

"Yes, I know." Ronsarde's welcoming expression faded a little. He said, "It was discovered when Halle sent for some of my things this morning. I knew it wasn't you, since your men would have known where to look." He paused, worried. "Madeline did escape the sewers, did she not?"

"Yes, but she didn't fancy palace hospitality."

Ronsarde let out his breath. "Sit down, at least, and don't stand there like an executioner. I can tell you what was in those documents."

Nicholas sat down on the edge of the bed, aware of the tension in his muscles and a headache like a stabbing needle in his left temple. Ronsarde said, "I never stopped investigating the case surrounding your foster father. I say the case 'surrounding' him, because in some ways I now believe he was incidental to it."

Nicholas nodded. "It was always difficult to keep sight of the fact that necromancy is a magic of divination and of the revealing of secret information."

"Yes," Ronsarde said, gently. "Count Rive Montesq was Edouard Viller's patron. Count Rive Montesq has been linked, through various circumstantial reports, to blackmail and illicit financial dealings. Two fields of endeavor in which the revelation of secret information would be of great benefit."

"And Edouard had a device, invented with Arisilde Damal, the most powerful sorcerer at Lodun at that time, that would allow a layman to perform magic."

"That was *intended* to allow a layman to perform magic," Ronsarde corrected. "As we know, and as Viller and Damal must have discovered almost immediately, the device did not function quite as anticipated and the wielder had to have some small gift of magic before it would work."

Nicholas looked down at his hands, avoiding Ronsarde's perceptive gaze. "Montesq must have asked Edouard to use the sphere for necromancy, to discover secrets."

"Viller refused, not only because it was a violation of law, but because he couldn't use it. He was not a sorcerer. Montesq, being a liar himself, did not believe Viller was telling him the truth. But Montesq wanted the power of the sphere. He is a man who craves power. It must rankle that he has to depend on hired sorcerers for magic." Ronsarde ran his fingers along the edge of the quilt thoughtfully. "He was Viller's patron and it would have been easy for him to obtain keys to the rooms Viller was using for his work. He entered them one night after Viller had gone and he tried to use the sphere."

"And it didn't work," Nicholas said.

"The failing could not be his, of course, so he tried again. He brought a hired thug, who took a beggar woman off the street for him, and he tried the necromantic spell in Macob's time-honored fashion. And it did not work. So he left and allowed Viller to take the blame."

Nicholas said nothing.

Ronsarde hesitated, then added carefully, "It helps to know why something occurred, when one is reconstructing a chain of events, but it can also cloud the issue. You can't be faulted for suspecting that your foster father had actually committed the crime he was executed for. The evidence was overwhelming and he was the only one directly associated with the situation who had a motive to use necromancy. His desire to speak to his dead wife was well documented during the trial. And he wouldn't talk. He wouldn't tell you what had happened. And you knew he was keeping something from you. The power of the 'why' obscured the 'how,'" His mouth twisted ruefully. "It can happen to anyone. It has certainly happened to me."

Nicholas shifted. His shoulders ached from tension. "What was in the missing documents?"

"They were sent to me a month ago. I was pursuing the matter from the only direction that was left to me: that Edouard Viller knew something detrimental to Montesq and that he did reveal this information to someone before he was executed. To that end I was tracing and contacting his correspondents. I had had no luck. Then I was sent a package of letters from Bukarin, from the daughter of a man Viller had corresponded with for some time, a doctor of philosophy at the Scholars' Guild in Bukarin. The man had died before Viller was executed. The daughter had received my request for information that was directed to her late father and sent me all Viller's letters that she could find among his papers. One was unopened. It had been sent only two days before the dead woman was discovered in Viller's workroom, but had arrived after the man it was addressed to had passed away. In it, Viller describes the curious incident of Count Rive Montesq's request that Viller use his device for necromancy."

"Why didn't he tell me?" Nicholas said. The words sounded oddly hollow.

"Montesq must have threatened your life to insure Edouard's silence." Ronsarde spread his hands. "It doesn't matter. We have all that we need. Montesq will suffer for his crime."

"You don't have the letters anymore." Nicholas shook his head. "Montesq knows. He's been preparing all this time while we were pursuing Macob."

Ronsarde's brows drew together.

"He sent Fallier after me and directed Lord Diero of the Prefecture to arrange your arrest," Nicholas explained. "He has known all along. He is well prepared by now to deal with a public accusation."

Ronsarde frowned. "It doesn't matter how well he has prepared. It won't help him."

"Don't be naive."

Ronsarde glared at him, but his expression turned worried when Nicholas got to his feet and said, "I assume I'm to be detained here."

"For your own good," Ronsarde said, watching him carefully. "Only until Montesq is formally charged."

Nicholas nodded. "I'm going abroad and my man Crack will be looking for a new position shortly. You need someone to watch your back, who could help with your work. Would you consider taking him on?"

"Crack would certainly be adept at frightening away any old enemies in search of revenge," Ronsarde admitted. "I assume he was innocent of the murder charges against him?"

Nicholas smiled, a trifle ironically. So Crack's real identity hadn't escaped

Ronsarde's notice either. "Any in-depth investigation of the extortion branch of Montesq's little empire will reveal that Crack was framed for those charges."

"All right." Ronsarde nodded, then asked sharply, "Where are you going?"

"You're the greatest detective in Ile-Rien," Nicholas said. He put his hands in his pockets and strolled to the door. "Figure it out."

———

His next visit was to Arisilde, who had been given a smaller suite of rooms on the same floor as Inspector Ronsarde. It was less difficult to obtain entry and Nicholas was soon sitting in the chair next to his bed. "How are you?" he asked.

"Oh, better, I suppose." Arisilde's long pale hands plucked anxiously at the coverlet. "Have you heard anything about Isham? No one here seems to know."

"He's at Dr. Brile's house, awake and recovering." He told Arisilde what Reynard had heard about the old man that morning.

"Good." Arisilde sat back against the pillows, more at ease. "I hope he's well soon enough that he can come and see me here. It would be terrible if we all visited the palace and he missed it." His violet eyes turned pensive and he added, "The Queen was here. She's very sweet, but she asked me if I wanted to be Court Sorcerer. I don't think she's very fond of Rahene Fallier. I told her I'd have to think about it. I'm not very reliable, you know."

"You were there when it counted, Ari."

"Well, yes, but . . . I remembered what I had been going to tell you, you know. That night I went so mad and charged all over the room."

"What was it?"

"I'd looked at those things you brought me. The fabric with the ghost-lichen on it and the remnants of that golem. There was the mark of an unfamiliar sorcerer on them. A very powerful sorcerer. But it went right out of my head until now."

"It wouldn't have mattered, even at the time." Nicholas hesitated a long moment. "I came to tell you that I'm going away for a while."

Arisilde brightened, interested. "Really? Where?"

"Abroad. I'll write you when I get there and let you know. If you like, you and Isham can move into Coldcourt while I'm gone."

"Ah, yes. They told me that Macob didn't leave much of the garret. That would be very nice. And you'd better write Isham instead of me. He'll keep track of the letter better than I would." Arisilde watched him a moment, his gaze sharpening. "Take care of yourself, Nicholas. I don't think I could manage to bring you back from the dead twice."

Nicholas stood, an ironic edge to his smile. "Ari, I hope you won't have to."

They were watching him, of course.

Nicholas sent two messages, one to Madeline and one to Cusard, both in code. Reynard got them out for him easily enough under the cover of an innocuous note to Nicholas's butler, Sarasate, at Coldcourt, asking him to send one of the footmen with some clothes proper for court attire.

Ronsarde demanded to see him again but Nicholas dodged the Inspector's questions and refused to elaborate on his future plans. He had to endure a court luncheon where the others in attendance all seemed to know his Alsene antecedents and to be present only to get a look at him. It did, however, provide Reynard—who now had the Queen's favor and Captain Giarde's powerful patronage—with an opportunity to be rude to a number of highly placed courtiers.

Rahene Fallier was also there, with a dour expression somewhat at odds with his usual implacable visage.

After the luncheon, Nicholas slipped away from the men assigned to watch him and followed Fallier. The sorcerer went through the wing that held the galleries and grand ballrooms and into the main hall of the Old Palace, which adjoined the newer, open sections of the structure with the older defensive bastions. At the top of the massive stone spiral stair that led to the King's Bastion, Fallier stopped, turned back, and said, "What do you want?"

Nicholas climbed the last few steps. Fallier's gaze was cold and not encouraging. "We need to talk."

"I think not." Fallier took his gloves out of his pocket and began to pull them on.

"I know you didn't do Rive Montesq's bidding of your own will."

Fallier hesitated, all motion arrested, then finished tugging on his glove. He looked at Nicholas and the expression in those opaque eyes was deadly.

Nicholas leaned one hand on the balustrade. "No, you don't want to kill me," he said, easily. "I have friends who wouldn't take it kindly. Especially Arisilde Damal, who is ordinarily the mildest of creatures. But he is suffering the effects of many years' overindulgence in opium and his temperament could be uncertain."

Fallier considered that. "Damal would be a worthy opponent," he said. "Perhaps . . . too worthy. What do you want?"

"I don't care what Montesq is holding over your head. I studied at Lodun myself, at the medical college. I know many student sorcerers dabble with the harmless minor divinatory spells of necromancy. Of course, with your position at court—"

"I understand you. Go on."

"You don't know what Montesq will ask for next."

"I can imagine," Fallier said dryly.

From his tone, Nicholas suspected Fallier had already been approached to aid Montesq in eluding Ronsarde's charges. But if he read Fallier right, that wouldn't be a problem. He said, "Then you wouldn't be adverse to helping me put Montesq in a position where he couldn't act against you."

Fallier actually unbent enough to sneer mildly and say, "If it was only a matter of giving testimony—"

"It isn't, and we both know it." Nicholas smiled. "I'm speaking of a way to stop Montesq from acting against anyone—permanently."

Fallier eyed him a moment thoughtfully, and nodded. "Then I think we need to speak in private."

———

With Reynard's help, Nicholas received permission to visit Dr. Brile's surgery to see how Crack and Isham were recovering. It was Ronsarde from whom the permission had come, he knew. He thought the Queen would have let him wander as he pleased and Captain Giarde, though always a dark horse, didn't have anything against him. It was Ronsarde who thought he needed watching.

He was transported in one of the palace coaches and delivered to the door of Dr. Brile's surgery. The doctor appeared bemused by the liveried Royal Guards who posted themselves on his stoop, but conducted Nicholas upstairs to where his patients were housed.

Nicholas saw Isham first, who was sitting up in bed though unable to talk for long without tiring himself. He reassured the old man as to everyone's safety and told him that Arisilde wanted to see him as soon as possible. But as he was taking his leave, Isham gestured him back with some firmness and said, "About Madele—"

Nicholas shook his head abruptly. "I don't want to—"

"She was not an old woman," Isham continued, ignoring the interruption.

"She was a witch, from the time when witches were warriors. She had done everything from curing plague to crawling behind the lines in border skirmishes with Bisra to assassinate their priest-magicians. She was very old and she knew she would die soon, and she preferred a death in battle. Do not look doubtfully at me. When you are my age you will know what I say is true."

"All right, all right," Nicholas said placatingly. Isham was looking gray about the mouth again. "I believe you."

"No, you don't," Isham said stubbornly, but allowed himself to be laid back in bed. "But you will, eventually."

Nicholas went next door to see Crack, who greeted him with an impatient demand for information. Nicholas spent more time than he meant, telling Crack what had happened in the caves and how they had defeated Macob.

He hadn't alluded to Madeline's current whereabouts, but Crack wasn't fooled. He said, "She was here."

"She was?" Nicholas tried to look mildly interested, but knew he wasn't fooling his henchman.

"The doctor don't know it—she climbed in through the window. Isham don't know it either, since he was asleep and she didn't want to wake him."

Nicholas gave in. "What did she say?" he demanded.

"Some things," Crack said. It would have been evasive, except Crack never was. He added, "She's worried at you."

Nicholas put it out of his mind firmly. He had too much to do now and he would know if she had received his message when he went to Coldcourt. "Never mind that now," he said. "I've spoken to Inspector Ronsarde about you working for him while I'm gone." He explained further.

Crack didn't like the idea and expressed his displeasure volubly. Patiently, Nicholas said, "It would only be until I returned, then you could decide if you wanted to continue with the Inspector or come back with me. You'll get your normal retainer from me, anyway. Sarasate will see to that."

"It ain't the money," Crack grumbled. "What about Montesq?"

Nicholas glanced at the door of the room, making sure Brile was out of earshot. "Montesq won't be a consideration anymore."

"He won't?" Crack sounded hopeful.

"No."

"Then I'll think on it."

And that was the most he could get out of Crack. Nicholas went out to the consulting room where Dr. Brile was sitting at his desk in his shirtsleeves, writing. The physician stood and put on his coat when Nicholas came into the room. "You saw both of them?" he asked.

"Yes." Nicholas hesitated. He had brought money to pay Brile for his services, but in light of his next request, it would look unpleasantly like a bribe, and he knew the physician wouldn't respond well to that. "Make sure they have whatever they want and send the bill to Coldcourt. I won't be there but my butler has instructions to arrange payment."

"I wasn't worried," Brile said mildly. "Are you going now?"

"Yes. Do you have a trapdoor to the roof?"

It was Brile's turn to hesitate. Nicholas saw him considering the presence of the Royal Guards at his door, perhaps weighing it with what he had seen of Nicholas's concern for his patients. He said finally, "There's a back door to the court behind the house."

"There is probably someone watching it."

Brile sighed. "I knew it would lead to this when Morane turned up at my door in the middle of the night. Will I be arrested if I help you?"

"I doubt it, but if you are, ask to speak to Inspector Ronsarde or Dr. Halle. They know all about it."

"Then I'll show you the roof door."

———

It was later that night, long after the streetlights were lit. Pompiene, Count Rive Montesq's Great House, looked down on the empty street, towering over the more modest town houses that clustered around it. Its original fortress-like façade had been modernized to make it current with fashion, and a number of generous windows and a second-floor terrace gave it an airy, fanciful appearance.

Across the street a figure stood in the shadows, muffled in a dark shabby coat and a hat with the brim pulled low. It wasn't raining but a damp mist hung heavy in the air and the flickering light of the gas lamps gleamed off the slick paving stones.

He crossed the street, moving toward the arcaded carriage alley at the side of the house. He avoided the pool of light from the single oil lamp that hung over the carriage doors and went instead to an inconspicuous portal farther down the alley. It was a servants' door and though it was heavy and well made, the inside bolts hadn't been shot. After some moments' work, the lock yielded to the picks.

Everything there was to know about this house, from its original floor-plan to its furnishings to the habits of its servants, he already knew. The door opened into a narrow dark hall, with the servants' stairs on one side and the entrances to the pantries and servery on the other. He slipped past these door-ways, hearing muted voices from the kitchens, and out the curtained door at the end and into the main foyer of the house.

The gas sconces and the chandelier were lit, revealing the house's main en-trance, a carved set of double doors framed by multipaned windows and a grand sweep of double staircase that led up into the public and private rooms. He took the right branch of the stairs, moved soundlessly down the carpeted gallery at the top, and paused at a door that stood partway open.

It was a room made familiar by long hours of watching, spying. It was dark but a fall of light from the hallway revealed bookcases and a beautifully carved marble mantel, and glinted off the frame of the watercolor and the marble bust by Bargentere. Across the room, above the large desk of mottled gold satin-wood, was the painting *The Scribe* by Emile Avenne, the large canvas taking up a good portion of the wall above the wainscotting. He crossed the room swiftly, stepped around the desk, and began to open drawers. Locating the one where Count Montesq kept correspondence, he took a packet of letters out of an inside coat pocket and placed it within. Shutting the drawer, he paused, lis-tening to a quiet step out in the stairwell. He smiled to himself and stepped to the other side of the desk and opened another drawer, pretending to search it.

That was how the light caught him when the library door swung fully open. Two men stood there and a voice said, "Don't move."

He stayed where he was, knowing at least one firearm was directed his way. A figure stepped into the room and lit the gas sconce on the wall. The light re-vealed a burly, rough-featured man standing in the doorway, pointing a pistol at him. Count Montesq adjusted the height of the flame in the sconce, then turned unhurriedly to light the candlelamp on the nearby table. He said, "You were foolish to come here." His voice was warm and rich and he was smiling faintly.

The man he knew as Nicholas Valiarde said, "Not foolish."

Montesq finished with the lamp and stepped back to take the gun from the wary guard, motioning him to step out into the hall. The Count pushed the door closed behind the man and said, "After you dropped out of sight, I thought you were dead."

"Oh, why the pretense?" Nicholas said, showing no evidence of discomfiture at being caught. "I'm sure Rahene Fallier told you that Inspector Ronsarde had surfaced again, that he extricated me from Fallier's clutches and used the episode as a chance to solicit Captain Giarde's assistance."

Montesq's eyes narrowed. "You know about Fallier."

"I know everything, now."

"Not quite everything."

"Fallier also told you that I approached him today and asked for his help to circumvent the wards on this house, so I could enter it tonight."

The smile on the Count's lips died. He didn't try to deny the charge. "But you came anyway? Why? What could you possibly hope to accomplish?"

"It was the only way."

Montesq had observed that something in the quality of his guest's voice was not quite normal, that there was a flatness in his dark eyes. "How disappointing," Montesq drawled, coming to the wrong conclusion. "I was hoping you weren't mad."

"It is a little tawdry, isn't it?" Nicholas agreed, watching him with an odd intensity. "Ending like this. There was one thing I wanted to ask you."

"Yes?"

"You did realize that Edouard was telling you the truth. The spheres never worked for just anyone; they had to be wielded by a sorcerer, or someone with at least a minor magical talent."

Montesq hesitated, but there was no harm in admitting such things to a dead man. "I realized it, after I killed the woman."

Nicholas nodded to himself, satisfied. "I'm glad you said that."

Montesq smiled, one brow lifted in a quizzical expression. "You don't think I'll shoot, do you?"

"No, I know you will," Nicholas said, quietly. "I'm counting on it."

They both heard the crash and a surprised shout as a downstairs door was flung open. Montesq's head jerked involuntarily toward the sound and Nicholas leapt at him, making a wild grab for the pistol. Montesq stumbled back and as footsteps pounded up the stairs, he fired.

Two burly constables of the Prefecture were first into the room, but Inspector Ronsarde was right behind them.

Ronsarde paused in the doorway, red-faced and breathing hard from the run up the stairs. The two constables had seized Montesq and taken possession of the pistol. The sight of the body on the carpet in front of the hearth broke the Inspector's temporary paralysis and he crossed over to it. He knelt and felt for a pulse at the throat, then jerked his hand back as if he had been burned. Ronsarde looked hard at the face, then slowly stood and turned to Montesq.

Their eyes met. Montesq's expression of bafflement turned to rage. In a grating voice, he said, "You bastard."

One of the constables reported, "When we came in, he was standing over him with the pistol, looking down at him, sir."

"Yes," Ronsarde said, nodding. "I'm sure he was."

Dr. Halle appeared in the doorway, more constables behind him. Taking in the scene, Halle swore and pushed past Ronsarde to the body. He knelt and ripped open his medical bag, then froze as he stared down at the face of the corpse.

The constables at the door made room for Lord Albier, who was trailed by his secretary, Viarn, and Captain Defanse. Albier summed up the situation with a swift glance and ordered Defanse to secure the house and detain the servants as potential witnesses.

Halle stood and turned a bewildered expression on Ronsarde. "This isn't— This man's been dead for—"

Ronsarde said, "Yes?" and stared hard at Halle.

After a moment, Halle cleared his throat and finished, "Moments, only. A few moments." He picked up his bag and retreated to a corner to gather his thoughts.

Albier stepped into the room now, glancing ruefully at Ronsarde. "Well, when you're right, you're right," he admitted.

Ronsarde's lips twitched. "Or vice versa," he murmured inaudibly.

Montesq had had a moment to recover himself. He said, "I was attacked by that man—"

"He's unarmed," Ronsarde interrupted. He hadn't bothered to search the body, but he was reasonably sure of his facts.

Albier nodded to Viarn, who went over and began to go through the corpse's pockets. "You won't find it easy to explain this away, sir," Albier said to Montesq with some satisfaction. "This wasn't a burglary. It's early evening, the lamps lit, your servants everywhere. You must have invited the man in."

Montesq almost bared his teeth in fury. "He entered without my knowledge, with sorcery."

Albier raised a skeptical brow. "If he was a sorcerer, why did he let you shoot him? Besides, Inspector Ronsarde had information that you would have an interview with a man whom you would attempt to murder tonight."

"I'm sure he did." Montesq turned his cold gaze on Ronsarde and said con-temptuously, "You violate your principles, sir."

"Do I?" Ronsarde said softly. "If you hadn't shot him, this would all have fallen to pieces. He laid the trap, but you didn't have to step into it."

Albier frowned. "What would have fallen to—"

"Sir!" The secretary Viarn was holding up a pocket watch with a jeweled fob. "Sir, he has several documents that should identify him, but they all seem to be in different names, and he has this!" He stood and handed the watch to Albier. "Look at the inscription on the back of the setting for that opal."

Albier squinted down at the jewel in his palm, half turning so the lamplight would fall on it. "Romele," he breathed. "This is one of the pieces stolen in the Romele jewel robbery." He and Viarn exchanged a significant look. "That man is Donatien."

From his corner, Dr. Halle made a muffled noise and Ronsarde rolled his eyes in disgust. Montesq said, "Donatien . . . ?" Slow understanding dawned in his eyes and he swore bitterly under his breath. "If I had known . . ."

Albier rounded on him. "If you had known? It looks a good deal like you did know, sir. That what we have here is a falling-out among thieves."

"No, does it really?" Montesq said acidly.

"There's something missing," Ronsarde said, his expression thoughtful.

"What?" Albier asked, startled.

"Direct evidence of the good Count's involvement with Donatien." Ron-sarde looked around the room appraisingly. He moved behind the desk and studied the array of drawers. All were firmly shut except one, which had been left open a hair. Ronsarde let out his breath. Since he had seen the face of the dead man, he hadn't known whether to laugh hysterically or shout and stamp. He opened the drawer and lifted out a pack of letters. "What are the names on those documents, Viarn?"

The secretary sorted hastily through the papers he had retrieved from the body. "Ordenon, Ferrar, Ringard Alscen—"

"Ah, yes." Ronsarde nodded to himself. "Here are letters from men of those names to Count Montesq. I'm sure this will provide the confirmation of your theory, Albier."

Albier was surprised and a little uncomfortable. "My theory? You told me to come here, Ronsarde, and you've been pursuing Donatien for years. I'm sure it was your work that led to this."

A muscle jumped in Inspector Ronsarde's cheek. "Oh, no," he said. "I can't take credit for this."

———

Later, as the Prefecture moved into Count Montesq's Great House in force, questioning servants, confiscating documents, collecting evidence, Ronsarde and Halle escaped outside. They moved across the street to where a gas lamp lit a circle of wrought iron benches with a small fountain in the center. It was a damp, cold night and a mist cloaked the pavement.

Dr. Halle stood with shoulders hunched and hands jammed into the pockets of his greatcoat. He said, "There's just one thing I'd like to make certain of—"

"I will check with the authorities at the city morgue tomorrow and discover that sometime yesterday afternoon a person answering to our friend Cusard's description claimed the body of an unidentified and recently deceased young man. That he perused all the available male corpses before making his choice, rejecting the ones that had been dead too long or been killed by some obvious means, such as stabbings or disfiguring blows to the head," Ronsarde said. "I will wager you the price of a dinner at Lusaude's grillroom that this is so."

"I won't take that wager," Halle said. After a moment, he chuckled.

"It's not funny," Ronsarde said stiffly.

"Of course you're right." Halle stopped smiling but he didn't give the impression of suffering any sensation of guilt. He noticed that farther down the street the colored lamps outside the café in the ground floor of the promenade were lit, signifying that it was still open for business. Halle knew Ronsarde shouldn't be out in this weather and steered their steps toward it, the Inspector following him by habit. After a moment, Halle said, "I understand it must have been a golem constructed in some fashion out of the corpse, and when Montesq destroyed the spell by firing the pistol into it, the rest of the thing dissolved, and left only the body. But who made the golem? Was it Arisilde Damal? He's been at the palace all day inside the wards. Could he control the creature from there?"

"It wasn't Damal," Ronsarde said, his mouth thinning. "It was Rahene Fallier, who had every reason to silence Montesq."

"Good God, Fallier," Halle said in wonder. He shook his head and chuckled again, then glanced at Ronsarde's face. "Sorry."

Ronsarde continued, "If the Count tries to reveal any of the information he was using to blackmail Fallier now, it will simply be more proof against him."

"Masterful," Halle said, admiringly. He caught Ronsarde's glare, and said, "Oh, come now. Valiarde played you expertly."

"Thank you for mentioning it. But he also counts on me not to expose him."

Halle stopped in his tracks. "You wouldn't."

"I could," Ronsarde said, grimly. "Damn that boy. He could have been a brilliant investigator." Then he relented and allowed himself a slight smile. "But I won't expose him. Did you see the look on Montesq's face?"

"Did I? When I first walked in I thought you'd struck him, he looked so shocked."

Laughing, the two men walked down the dark street toward the lights of the café.

———

The port city of Chaire smelled of dead fish and salt sea, or at least this portion of it did. It was long after midnight but the lower level of the old stone docks still bustled with activity when Cusard's wagon pulled in. The shoremen and carters were hauling last-minute cargos to and from the steamers preparing to leave the next morning. Nicholas jumped down from the wagon seat, dressed in work clothes and an old greatcoat, a battered leather knapsack slung over one shoulder. He usually preferred to travel light, but the trunk weighing down the bed of Cusard's wagon had to accompany him on this trip.

Cusard dropped the tail of the wagon and as they waited for the shoremen to get around to them, he sniffed and said, "You got all your papers and tickets?"

Nicholas rolled his eyes. Cusard was going to get maudlin. "Yes, Poppa. I'll remember to stay away from fallen women, too."

"Like my own son, you was." Cusard let out his breath in a gusty sigh. "Should'a beat you when you was a boy."

"Probably." Nicholas leaned back against the wagon. "For the love of God, Cusard, I'm going to Adera for a few months, not Hell."

"Foreigners," Cusard commented succinctly. He eyed Nicholas thoughtfully. "You'll miss the trial."

"That's for the best. Montesq is going to be convicted of murdering Donatien, his partner in crime. I don't want him to have the opportunity to prove that Donatien is alive and well and living under the name Nicholas Valiarde."

Cusard grunted. "I'll save the penny sheets for you."

"Just stay away from the warehouse or any of the other places I had to give them."

"No, I was going to walk around 'em with a sign on my back saying 'Arrest Me.'" Cusard sighed again. "That's like a son to me, all right, leaving me to fend for myself—"

"Your share is enough to buy a villa on the March—"

"High living will do you in every time," Cusard interrupted sententiously. Then he grinned. "Did the Count in, didn't it? High living and being too clever by half."

Nicholas tried to maintain a stony façade, but his lips twitched in a smile. "Yes, it did, didn't it?"

The shoremen came for the trunk then, grunting at its unexpected weight as they lifted it down from the wagon bed.

As Nicholas was signing the bill of lading, one of them, with the forthrightness characteristic of tradesmen in Ile-Rien, demanded, "What have you got in here, bricks?"

"Almost," Nicholas said, truthfully. *Small, highly valuable bricks.* He added, not so truthfully, "It's sculpture, actually—busts and small figures."

That was dull stuff for men who unloaded cargos from Parscia and Bukarin, and they showed no further interest in the trunk's contents.

"You'd better be going," Nicholas told Cusard. "It's a long drive back and you're so damnably old."

"You and your mouth," Cusard said, and cuffed him on the side of the head. "Tell her ladyship to take care of herself."

"I will," Nicholas said, as the old man climbed back aboard the wagon and lifted the reins. *At least I hope I'll have the opportunity.*

Once the trunk was loaded and the shoremen tipped, Nicholas could have boarded the ship and sought the comfort of the first-class cabin he had booked. Instead, he climbed the stairs to the upper level of the dock and sat down on one of the stone benches.

It was very late and in the chill night there were few people venturing to take the air. The bustle of last-minute loading and passengers arriving to board the ships was all taking place on the lower dock and this broad walk seemed very isolated. Hundreds of lamps still burned in the great hotels and the amusement pavilion at the opposite end, but that was far away.

He knew Madeline had gotten his message. He had gone to Coldcourt after escaping Brile's surgery to give Sarasate instructions to expect Arisilde and Isham. There had been a host of telegrams to send too, warnings and instructions to different parts of his organization. Sarasate had reported that

Madeline had been there earlier to pack a few of her things and had told him that Nicholas would be there soon with further instructions. She hadn't said where she was going.

Alone, he had watched the scene enacted in Montesq's library through Arisilde's enspelled copy of *The Scribe. So all the books are right,* he thought, *revenge is bitter.* Then he smiled to himself. *But I'll get over it.*

Seated on the bench, he waited long enough to get thoroughly chilled and very afraid when he saw a lone figure making its way down the promenade, moving into one of the pools of light from the wrought iron lamps.

Nicholas drew a deep breath in relief. He would recognize that walk anywhere.

It took her long enough to reach him that he had managed to school his features into a mild expression of welcome, instead of grinning at her like an idiot. Madeline sat down on the bench next to him, dropping a carpetbag near his feet. She was dressed in a conservative traveling costume under a new gray paletot. She looked at him a moment, her face bemused, then said, "I thought about making you wait and catching the pilot boat at the last minute tomorrow morning, but I couldn't be sure you wouldn't do something dramatic."

This time he couldn't help the grin. "Me? Do something dramatic?"

"Idiot," she said, and busied herself with adjusting her hat. "Now tell me how it was done. Where did you get the body?"

Nicholas let out his breath. "This afternoon, I sent Cusard to the city morgue to look for a fresh, unclaimed male corpse, of about the right age, with no obvious wounds. It didn't even have to resemble me. Fallier would take care of that when he made the golem and afterward, well, the Prefecture knows that Donatien is—was—a master of disguise."

"Couldn't Montesq claim that he shot Donatien in self-defense?"

"Oh, I'm sure he will. But before he arrived the golem placed a packet of letters in Montesq's desk. Some of them date back to the beginning of Donatien's rather checkered career and make it clear that Montesq planned most if not all of Donatien's activities."

"That must have been difficult."

She was right about that but the blow to his ego had been a sacrifice Nicholas was willing to make. "It did give me a twinge or two." He pulled off his black leather riding glove and shoved her the brown stains on his fingers. "I was more worried by what would happen if Ronsarde saw the stains from the tea I used to age the paper for the older letters. He would have known immediately I was up to something more than a simple murder. I'm lucky correct court attire demands gloves."

Madeline frowned. "That was terribly cruel to make poor Ronsarde think you were bent on shooting Montesq in some grand self-destructive gesture. He must have been very worried about you."

"It will teach him not to be overconfident." Nicholas continued, "My observations of Montesq through Arisilde's portrait made it possible to salt the letters with realistic and verifiable details. The later ones implicate the solicitor Batherat, who is a nervous sort and will probably break down under the first questioning session and volunteer information about Montesq's own indiscretions."

"Well, it turned out better than I hoped, I'll tell you that."

They sat in silence for a few moments, Nicholas watching the way the cold breeze off the ocean lifted the loose strands of hair that had escaped from her hat. "The theater rehearsal season will be just starting when we get to Adera. You can look for a part in something."

"A leading role, you mean," she said, in perfect Aderassi. "And what will you do?"

He shrugged. "There's the university in the capital. I could finish my medical degree. A letter from Dr. Uberque should help me gain admittance."

Madeline snorted. "That'll last a week."

"Probably," he said, smiling again. Sobering, he decided there was something else he needed to ask, and finally managed, "Do you blame me for Madele's death?"

Madeline shook her head slowly. "I did, at first. But it's more accurate, and more characteristic of me, to blame Madele for Madele's death. She knew what she was risking. And it probably maddens her, wherever she is, that she missed the whole fight against Macob. That's probably punishment enough." She gave him a sideways glance. "If you're going to get sentimental, let's get on the damn boat before I change my mind."

"Yes," he said, satisfied with that answer. "Let's go."

About the Author

MARTHA WELLS has written many fantasy novels, including the million-copy-selling *New York Times* and *USA Today* bestselling Murderbot Diaries series, which has won multiple Hugo, Nebula, Locus, and Alex Awards. Other titles include *Witch King, The Wizard Hunters, Wheel of the Infinite,* the Books of the Raksura series (beginning with *The Cloud Roads* and ending with *The Harbors of the Sun*), and the Nebula Award–nominated *The Death of the Necromancer,* as well as YA fantasy novels, short stories, and nonfiction.